THE RISE OF JONAS OLSEN

JOHANNES B. WIST

THE RISE OF
Jonas Olsen

A Norwegian Immigrant's Saga

TRANSLATED AND
WITH AN INTRODUCTION BY
Orm Øverland

FOREWORD BY
Todd W. Nichol

PUBLISHED IN COOPERATION WITH
THE NORWEGIAN-AMERICAN
HISTORICAL ASSOCIATION

UNIVERSITY OF MINNESOTA PRESS
MINNEAPOLIS   LONDON

PUBLISHED BY THE UNIVERSITY OF MINNESOTA PRESS
111 Third Avenue South, Suite 290
Minneapolis, Minnesota 55401-2520
http://www.upress.umn.edu

The University of Minnesota is an equal-opportunity educator and employer.

Library of Congress Cataloging-in-Publication Data

Wist, Johs. B. (Johannes Benjamin), 1864–1923.
   The rise of Jonas Olsen : a Norwegian immigrant's saga / Johannes B. Wist ; translated and with an introduction by Orm Øverland ; foreword by Todd W. Nichol.
      p.   cm.
   Translator's title.
   Includes bibliographical references.
   ISBN 0-8166-4750-X (hc/j : alk. paper)
      1. Norwegians—United States—Fiction. I. Øverland, Orm, 1935– II. Title.
   PT9150.W5R57 2005
   839.82'372—dc22
                                                         2005029093

Printed in the United States of America on acid-free paper

12   11   10   09   08   07   06   10   9   8   7   6   5   4   3   2   1

Contents

THE RISE OF JONAS OLSEN

Foreword

TODD W. NICHOL

The Norwegian-American Historical Association is pleased to collabo-
rate with the University of Minnesota Press in presenting Johannes
Benjaminsen Wist's widely read trilogy, here called *The Rise of Jonas
Olsen,* in a skillful English translation by Orm Øverland. These books
were meant by their author to be enjoyed foremost as novels, but Wist
also intended them to be read as portrayals of Norwegian-American life.
Professor Øverland's introduction and annotations enrich this volume
greatly and will help guide readers through these pages, whether they
are perused as literature, historical vignette, or both.

As Orm Øverland has noted, there is a certain irony about these
novels. Wist read the signs of his times and thought the strategies for
cultural preservation advocated by Waldemar Ager, O. E. Rølvaag, and
others were hopelessly romantic. Yet Wist wrote these books, three of
the finest Norwegian-American novels ever to appear, just as the community of readers for which they were written was about to abandon the
Norwegian language in favor of English as its daily language.

The irony, however, may be more apparent than real. Wist knew his
moment and considered fiction a legitimate, even essential, instrument
for the writing of history. He wrote his books to be read as literature,
but also to record and comment on a vanishing present. The question
of language, for example, was not for Wist merely about whether to use
Norwegian or English; he was also interested in how languages work in
changing contexts. He had an ear as good as Mark Twain's for dialect,
and our sense for the evolution of Norwegian-American speech would be
much the poorer were it not for these novels. A subtle raconteur, Wist also
gives us a rich sense of the humor of this community. As a satirist, Wist
probes deeply and ushers his readers into conflicts over mores and values

present in the Norwegian-American community portrayed in his books and present in the actual historical community that existed when the books were first published. When they appeared, these novels were thus, not surprisingly, controversial among Norwegian-Americans. They do not idealize or even flatter Norwegian-Americans—or their neighbors. Rural and urban, male and female, rich and poor, powerful and humble, Norwegian and Yankee, Wist's characters are all a part of the human and historical comedy as he saw it. His novels are the real thing. They are literature and they are history.

I am grateful to Orm Øverland for creating this fine English edition of Wist's trilogy and to the University of Minnesota Press for its partnership in bringing these novels to a new audience of readers. Pieter Martin and Douglas Armato of the University of Minnesota Press have been wise and capable partners in this work. Once again, I thank the board of directors of the Norwegian-American Historical Association for its unflagging support of the association's publishing program.

Saint Olaf College
Northfield, Minnesota
February 2005

Translator's Introduction

Johannes B. Wist (1864–1923)—journalist, editor, and novelist—was one among many. In the late-nineteenth and early-twentieth centuries there was a large and manifold American literature in the Norwegian language—large in relation to the size of the immigrant group by whom and for whom it was made, that is.[1] Books in a variety of genres—poetry, fiction, drama, memoirs, juveniles, history, travel, devotional texts, and theology—were written and read by first- and second-generation immigrants. This literary output was supported by a wide range of institutions such as publishers and printers, newspapers and journals, bookstores, libraries, and reading societies, all serving Americans who preferred to do at least some of their reading in the language they had brought with them to the United States.

Although the relative rate of emigration from Norway was second only to that of Ireland, the overall number of Norwegian immigrants residing in the United States was modest. At the time of the 1910 census, 403,858 Americans had been born in Norway, the highest number recorded. Their children numbered an additional 607,267. The second generation peaked in 1930 with 752,236. These are not impressive figures compared to those for immigrant groups from larger countries, but an important factor in the creation of an immigrant culture is geographical concentration: while the Norwegian-born Americans were only 3.49 percent of the total U.S. population in 1890, they composed 7 percent of the population of the Midwestern states. In 1910 more than 80 percent of Americans of Norwegian origin lived in the Upper Midwest.[2]

It would be a misunderstanding to think of the readers of Norwegian-American literature as inhabitants of a cultural ghetto, isolated from the cultural life of Americans who read English only or, indeed, isolated from Americans who read languages such as Yiddish, French, German,

[ix]

or Finnish. Most subscribers to Norwegian-language newspapers also subscribed to newspapers or journals in English, and even though many had some Norwegian-language books in their homes, those who had books probably had more that were in English. Most readers of Norwegian were in families that were evolving from being bilingual to being monolingual, speaking English only. The younger members of most immigrant families from Norway preferred to do their reading in English, even if they continued to speak Norwegian within the family and heard it every Sunday in church.

Consequently, an American literature in a language other than English was a transitional phenomenon. Some Norwegian-American writers believed their language could and would have a permanent status in the United States; most, however, had a view that time has proven more realistic: that English would soon become the language of the descendents of all immigrants. Johannes B. Wist, editor of the Norwegian-language newspaper *Decorah-Posten* and author of the trilogy here translated as *The Rise of Jonas Olsen,* was certain that immigrant cultures and languages in the United States were transitional. Responding to the question "Norwegian or English?" in a long article published January 27, 1905, in his newspaper, Wist insisted there could be no doubt about what language should be taught to the young: English must have first priority. Without a good knowledge of English, Wist believed, Norwegian Americans would not be able to make their voices heard. If possible, he wrote, it would be an advantage that the second generation also learned the language of their parents. This is a remarkable view to propagate in a publication dependent on subscribers who wanted a newspaper in Norwegian. But at this point in Wist's life—the time of the highest rate of immigration from Europe—he was convinced that immigrant cultures would not exist far beyond the first generation.

Later in 1905, in Minneapolis, Wist was the main speaker at a banquet for the second annual meeting of the small but culturally ambitious Norwegian Society. Here he presented an assimilationist view that was disturbing to many who had dedicated their lives to the development of a distinctly Norwegian-American culture, a culture that used the Norwegian language but that was firmly rooted in the American experience of immigrants and their descendents:

> In spite of individual expressions in our newspapers and other media about the possibility of a future Golden Age for Norwegian-American literature, apparently it may be taken for

granted that most of those who participate in our Norwegian
endeavors in this land—and for whom culture and feeling of
nationality is something more than the sounding of sonorous
chimes or tinkling bells—mainly agree that, in our period of
transition as Norwegian Americans, we lack several criteria to
be able to stand on our own feet—culturally speaking.

He characterized the immigrants as "nomads in transition from one
nation to another." While the immigrants might regard themselves as
Norwegian, this could not be true of their children, he said, "who do not
know any other country than America. For them, what especially dis-
tinguishes their parents as Norwegians . . . has become watered down,
while what draws our people and all other immigrant groups closer to
American ways has gained the upper hand." Indeed, this was as it should
be: "We did not come to this country as masters or conquerors; we came
as poor immigrants with the goal of making a better life. A large civilized
society stood ready and prepared to receive us—to assimilate us."[3]

Wist's optimistic view of Anglo-American readiness to receive and
assimilate immigrants was modified in the coming years in response
to increasingly negative attitudes toward immigrants and immigration
in the United States, attitudes that to some extent were a reaction to
the record number of European immigrants who entered the country in
the late nineteenth and early twentieth centuries. This reaction culmi-
nated first with the Americanization movement during the First World
War and later with the political agitation that resulted in the immigration acts passed by Congress in 1923 and 1924, the so-called quota acts,
which drastically limited further immigration.

Although Jonas Olsen, the protagonist of Wist's trilogy, would probably not have expressed himself as modestly as did his author and admit
that he had come as a poor immigrant, he was certainly set on making a better life for himself, and he also believed, at first, that Anglo-
Americans who belonged to the social class to which he himself aspired
"stood ready and prepared to receive" him. His experiences taught him
otherwise. The story of Jonas Olsen ends with the national and local
elections of 1912. The narrator's comments on the often contradictory expressions of the demands for Americanization and the prejudice against
immigrants, however, are responses to the political and social climate
that arose a few years later—during the period of the First World War
and its aftermath. We are told that, in the late 1880s and the early 1890s,
during Jonas Olsen's early years in the Red River Valley,

his main aim was to become an ideal American . . . But that was before he got to know the Americans. He had tried to get to know as many as possible so that he could all the faster become one himself. His first hope was that they would all want to be the first to wish him welcome into their circles, since he was so ready to accept all their ideals . . . Not a single door he knocked on was opened for him . . . Jonas had learned that, socially speaking, he could never become an American as he once had thought he could. The Newells, Brackens, and Sanborns were remarkably uninterested in getting to know the Olsens. You couldn't even get so close to them that you could learn the art of holding your fork in the American way . . . Through their ignorant prejudices of immigrants and foreigners and other countries, they unintentionally made him a stronger supporter of his own heritage.

There is much evidence that Wist himself had arrived at views similar to those of his narrator by the time he began his trilogy. In the December 7, 1920, *Decorah-Posten* he expressed his resentment of those Americans who,

like their relatives the English . . . have found it difficult to acknowledge other countries and any culture that has been developed outside of the Anglo-Saxon world . . . America's relationship with England has in a way been destined because England has been our "mother"—that is, New England was settled from England and New England has always been considered the birthplace of our American culture.

Although the authorized view was that Americans were Anglo-Saxons, Wist continued, this was in fact only true of about half the population. He insisted that the issue was not one of Americanism or anti-Americanism, but "about whether Anglicism should be accepted as Americanism with the exclusion of all of those cultural values that we as Americans have received from countries other than England and about whether we, who admit we belong to other civilized tribes than the Anglo-Saxon, are as good Americans as those who are of English origin." The occasion for his criticism was the chauvinistic excesses of the tricentennial of the landing at Plymouth Rock. While this was cause for celebration for all Americans, he insisted that the contributions of other ethnic groups (or "races," as he called them) should also be recognized and honored:

we who are immigrants from countries other than England and our descendents have much to learn from our Anglo-maniacs. In particular we should learn that if we wish to be strong and influential in our country then we must learn to honor our an-

TRANSLATOR'S INTRODUCTION

cestors more than we have done up to now. It may be fine to
honor the ancestors of others but we must above all learn to
respect ourselves and our own origin. Our youth must acquire
a more magnanimous view of our pioneers, who should have
a more prominent place in our minds than they now have. We
must place them on our mind's throne.

Wist had a greater confidence in the value of a unique Norwegian-
American tradition in the early 1920s than he had had two decades earlier. A contributing factor to this confidence may have been that he had a
greater confidence in his own gifts as a writer, in particular as a novelist,
than when he saw himself primarily as a journalist.

Wist and Decorah-Posten

Johannes Benjaminsen Wist was born in 1864 in Inderøy in North
Trøndelag, and he came to the United States in 1884, at about the same
time as his protagonist, Jonas Olsen. Wist had had some journalistic
experience before immigration and he became editor of several short-
lived weekly newspapers, first in a small town in Minnesota and then
in Minneapolis and in Madison. In 1889 he was appointed coeditor of
Nordvesten (the Northwest) in St. Paul and remained there until he
accepted a position with *Decorah-Posten* in 1900. The following year
he became editor in chief of that newspaper, a position he held until the
end of his life, December 1, 1923.[4]

Norwegian-language newspapers were published all over the Upper
Midwest and in other areas where there were concentrations of Norwegian immigrants. A microfilm series produced by Luther College
puts the number of such newspapers at 117, but this series only includes
newspapers from a private collection donated to Luther College. The index for Wist's 1914 history of the Norwegian-American press includes
406 periodical titles.[5] Most newspapers were weekly and most had a
local readership. Some were ephemeral publications initiated by an ambitious printer or editor (often the same person), local business interests,
or the local leadership of one of the two major political parties seeking
immigrant support in an election campaign. Immigrant newspapers
displayed a wide range of journalistic and literary quality, as well as a
wide range in size and circulation, but all served an important function
in the assimilation process, providing immigrants with news, commentary, features, and fiction that presented aspects of U.S. life in their

[xiii]

native language. "No other immigrant institution except the church," writes Odd Lovoll, "entered more intimately into all facets of the lives of Norwegian Americans."[6]

Three newspapers in particular achieved a national distribution: *Minneapolis Tidende* (Minneapolis Times, 1887–1935), *Skandinaven* (the Scandinavian, 1866–1941), and *Decorah-Posten* (1874–1972). The first two were in cities, Minneapolis and Chicago, while the third was in Decorah, a small town in northern Iowa. Decorah is home to Luther College, the oldest of the colleges founded by Norwegian immigrants, and it was also the administrative center for the Norwegian Synod, one of the three major Norwegian-American Lutheran church bodies. In addition to a weekly edition, *Minneapolis Tidende* also had a daily (1887–1932) and a Sunday edition. In its best years, *Skandinaven* had daily (1876–1930), Sunday (1889–1930), biweekly, and weekly editions, and for some time it also had a special "European" edition for subscribers in Norway and Denmark. *Minneapolis Tidende* and *Skandinaven* were thriving businesses but they never "fully attained the position of *Decorah-Posten*," as Lovoll has observed.[7] Increasing numbers of Norwegian immigrants in the early twentieth century settled in large cities such as Chicago and the Twin Cities and in smaller cities such as La Crosse and Eau Claire in Wisconsin, but the heartland of Norwegian America was the America of farms and small towns—and this is where the Norwegian language survived the longest. It was to this heartland that *Decorah-Posten* addressed itself and it was to this heartland that Wist's protagonist, who first made his appearance in November 1919 in the pages of *Decorah-Posten*, moved after he had failed to make his mark in Minneapolis.

After several unsuccessful attempts to establish periodical publications, Brynild Anundsen began a modest local newspaper, *Decorah-Posten*, in 1874. From the very beginning he eschewed party politics and other controversies, in particular ecclesiastical ones. In addition to giving domestic and international news, *Decorah-Posten* provided a variety of feature articles, fiction, and poetry. It soon attracted subscribers far beyond the confines of Decorah, and by 1885 it had a circulation of more than 20,000. A literary supplement, *Ved Arnen* (By the fireplace), appeared in 1882 and became a weekly feature in 1887. Every Tuesday, subscribers could read serialized novels by popular writers such as Dickens, Stevenson, Baroness Orczy, and Zane Grey in translation; Norwegian writers such as Jonas Lie, John Lie, and Johan Falkberget; and some Norwegian-American writers. For most of its ninety-eight years,

Decorah-Posten was a biweekly, appearing on Tuesdays and Fridays. Both the Friday edition and the Tuesday supplement featured serialized fiction.[8]

Wist and Kristian Prestgard, who became editor in chief of *Decorah-Posten* in January 1924, built up the subscription base, so that *Decorah-Posten* became the Norwegian-language newspaper with the largest circulation and the longest life. While *Skandinaven*'s biweekly circulation of 50,000 made it the largest American newspaper in Norwegian in 1910, *Decorah-Posten* had 45,000 subscribers in 1925, by which time *Skandinaven* had lost half its subscribers from fifteen years earlier. The kind of growth sustained by *Decorah-Posten*—especially in the face of anti-immigrant and anti–foreign-language agitation and the drop in immigration during the years of the First World War—required hard work and dedication from both the editor and his staff.

In between stints as the editor of short-lived newspapers in his first years after immigration, Wist had assisted an older journalist and amateur historian, David Schøyen, in compiling material for a history of Norwegian immigration. When Schøyen gave up his ambitious project in 1887, Wist took over and published two chapters of the projected work as a pamphlet in 1888: *Den norske indvandring til 1850* (Norwegian immigration before 1850). The American point of view signalled by the word *immigration* rather than the more commonly used *emigration,* is surprising in an immigrant only three years off the boat. In his later journalism and fiction Wist focused on the *American* experience of immigrants and their descendents: they were in his view Americans in the making rather than a Norwegian diaspora. As a writer of fiction he continued his early history project: his stories and novels present an insight into immigrant society not available in historical accounts.

His interest in Norwegian Americans as immigrants rather than emigrants does not mean that he was not interested in—even attached to—the country he had left. In 1905 he and Prestgard began publication of an ambitious but short-lived periodical, *Symra* (named for a flower of early spring, the anemone), addressed to "Norwegians on both sides of the ocean." It began as a 200-page annual publication, became a quarterly (256 pages in each issue) in 1909, and had six large issues in 1914, its last year of publication. The reading public that embraced the popular fare of *Decorah-Posten* could not support an ambitious publication such as *Symra.* As editor of *Decorah-Posten,* Wist eschewed what he thought of as "highbrow"—"God bless that word," he wrote to a friend and contributor.[9] But Wist was as sincerely involved and as much himself in the elitist *Symra* as in the popular *Decorah-Posten*.

Wist's Early Fiction

Wist was thirty-two when he published his first story in 1897. Even so there is a great distance in style and attitude between his later work and the heavy-handed sentimentality of "Paa Prairien" (On the prairie), a story of struggle and death on the prairie that concludes with the exclamation, "Terrible nature!"[10] His slow growth as a writer of fiction and his apparent lack of confidence in his own literary talent may be related to his lack of faith in an American literature in Norwegian. Tellingly, his later fiction in *Decorah-Posten* was presented anonymously, as the work of "Arnljot," and, moreover, it developed as a by-product of a humorous and satirical column in his newspaper. Two rather ambitious attempts, however, were published under his own name in *Symra* in 1912 and 1913.[11] Wist may have hoped that publication here would gain him the attention of critics in Norway, but, as he well knew, the journal never had a large circulation, neither in the United States nor in his former homeland. Norwegian intellectuals had never demonstrated much interest in the cultural life of emigrants. Indeed, they hardly recognized the existence of a culture among the poor and uneducated people who had—in their eyes—deserted their homeland. Wist's two stories in *Symra* address this situation in different ways.

The first, "Blade av en nybyggersaga" (Pages of a pioneer saga), takes the conventional literary theme of class-crossed lovers as its point of departure: Kari, daughter of a prosperous farmer, and Mons, a poor laborer, go to America to realize their love. Here, on the prairies of the Midwest, they succeed and prosper. Mons expands his property and after some years their home looks more like "a Norwegian manor than a farm in a relatively new settlement on the Dakota prairies" (27). But Kari, who had renounced prosperity for love, does not believe that happiness is found in material success. In spite of his prosperity, Mons—as so many characters in American literature who pursue the American Dream—is unable to transcend his spiritual and intellectual poverty, which becomes more evident with his material success: he is an embarrassment to his three college-educated children who depend on him for support. Ironically, the former farm laborer acquires the very social prejudices that had repressed him in the Old World: he refuses to give his daughter permission to marry her beloved, the hired hand.

Wist is a writer of satire and comedy rather than tragedy, and he provides his characters with a happy ending. But his satire is as critical of the Old World society, closed to the ambitious young without the advantage of class, as of the successful immigrant who loses his soul even though he has gained two sections of land and a mansion. Of the many immigrant fictions on this theme, the best known may be Abraham Cahan's *The Rise of David Levinsky* (1917). The most chilling is Ole E. Rølvaag's *Pure Gold* (1930).

In 1904, in a review of an anthology of Norwegian-American poetry, Wist had questioned the very notion of a Norwegian-American literature: "It all must depend on Norwegian influences and is only American in the sense that it is more or less by chance written while an author is residing in this country."[12] By 1913, when Wist published "Da Bjørnson kom til La Crosse" (When Bjørnson came to La Crosse), his second story in *Symra,* he seems to have changed his mind. In this he may have been influenced by the evident failure of his journal. The old homeland had no interest in being a nourishing center for a diasporic culture in the United States. Norwegian Americans would have to plant and find nourishment for whatever culture they had in the same soil on which they built their homes and in which they ran their ploughs.

From its opening paragraph it is clear that the 1913 story is addressed to an American rather than a Norwegian audience. Not only does it begin with observations on Norwegian-American newspapers in the early 1880s, which would be of little interest to readers in Norway, but it is written in a language that would seem vulgar to such readers. The dialogue presents the speech of uneducated immigrants through suggestions of a variety of dialects and a liberal dosage of such American-English words and idioms that were natural in an immigrant language. Code-switching, moreover, characterizes the style of the narrative itself.[13]

The story begins with the impact on an immigrant settlement of the news of the coming of the great Bjørnstjerne Bjørnson. Bjørnson, who had an international reputation at least the equal of that enjoyed by Henrik Ibsen in the late nineteenth century, toured the Midwest in the winter of 1881, lecturing and reading to immigrant audiences. Nils, the protagonist, is the only member of his Lutheran congregation who dares to defy the warnings of their pastor against this dangerous liberal. Nils not only goes to hear the great writer but even dares to go up to the front of the hall and thank him in person. Bjørnson, however, meets Nils with critical words about the materialism of immigrant farmers and their narrow religious views. On his way home, Nils begins to resent that "such a fine man from Norway came over here and pronounced judgment on poor immigrants without schooling and education because they had to struggle for their daily bread from early morning to late night. And what would such a bigwig himself have done had he been in their place?" (64) Wist could not have known to what extent Bjørnson had actually despised the common men and women who had come unwashed and intoxicated to his lectures.[14] Nevertheless, in the story, Bjørnson is a mouthpiece for views Wist knew were widespread among the Norwegian intelligentsia.

In different ways, the story of Mons, the successful immigrant with a stunted soul, and the story of the simple and somewhat naïve Nils, who is proud of his heritage but resentful of Old World class pretensions, point forward to similar themes in Wist's trilogy. The genesis of this work, one of the most entertaining fictional expressions of immigrant experience in the early twentieth century, may be traced in Wist's unpretentious satirical column "Mellemmad"—which may be translated as "snacks," something eaten between meals. This column appeared most Tuesdays during Wist's more than two decades as editor of *Decorah-Posten*. As Arnljot, Wist presented his observations of daily life among rural and small-town Norwegian Americans, the very kind of people who made up the majority of his readers. "Mellemmad" reported on the activities and views of characters in the fictive Iowa towns of Salt Grove and Lone Crossing, or gave space to correspondence from a fictitious farmer in Montana. Gradually these characters took on a life of their own, and the goings-on in Salt Grove and Lone Crossing became matter for sketches and stories.

As Wist began to take his writing more seriously, however, he also became more serious as Arnljot. The first volume of the story of Jonas Olsen was completed in the spring of 1920, and when the second volume began to run in fall that same year, it was no longer presented as "Mellemmad." From that time on there is often little difference in style and content between Wist's editorials and Arnljot's "Mellemmad." The change came rather suddenly September 14, 1920, with a "Mellemmad" series of six installments with the common title "Dyret i Mennesket" (The animal in man).[15] Here Arnljot reflects on the evil of war, on ethics, and on nationalism, beginning with a critical discussion of the

European nationalism that led to the First World War. The September 24 installment focuses on the failure of postwar international politics. On September 28 Wist writes about American nativism and the hysterical persecution of Americans of various origins who were perceived as foreigners. His editorials on this theme are critical of the ideology of the melting pot.[16] When Arnljot criticizes Americanization in the November 2, 1920, "Mellemmad" column, his style is indistinguishable from that of Wist's editorials. Wist had given himself the freedom to write humorously about human foibles as Arnljot. When Arnljot became a serious novelist, Wist's pseudonym gave him the freedom to write more personally about important issues that concerned him, without the constraints of being the editor of a publication with a long tradition of avoiding controversy.

The Trilogy, Decorah-Posten, and Reception

Inauspiciously, the first installment of *The Rise of Jonas Olsen* appeared November 4, 1919, as one of Arnljot's familiar "Mellemmad" columns, with the subtitle "Nykommerbilleder fra Otti'erne" (Newcomer sketches from the eighties). There is no indication that this is the first installment of a novel. Indeed, the mixture of English and Norwegian in the dialogue is very similar to the code-switching in a "Mellemmad" column that had appeared two weeks earlier.[17] Wist had probably completed the story of Jonas Olsen's adventures in Minneapolis before he began its serialization, but he seems not to have revealed his ambitious project of a trilogy to any of his colleagues. At this point he may not have had a clear idea of where the story of Jonas Olsen would take him. But fifteen years earlier he had entertained the idea of writing a series of novels about the tensions between the immigrants' need and desire to cherish and develop identities as Americans with languages and cultural traditions other than those of British origin, and their determination to be fully recognized members of the American nation.

On March 21, 1905, Wist wrote to an occasional contributor about his recent talk on "Our Cultural Stage," which had just been published in the newspaper. He admitted that he may have taken an extreme position, but he saw no other way of getting attention. "And, moreover, I will probably continue; I could write a *novel* in many volumes about this—not a *romance*." The distinction between the two genres was, he explained, that "the novel . . . is *realistic* while the romance is *idealistic*.

The former is concerned with our time and its realities; the other is often about the past but it may also be on a contemporary theme." He wrote about the differences at some length and used Howells as his example of an author of novels, while Scott, Hugo, and Dumas wrote romances. "Zola," he added, echoing the views of Frank Norris, "wrote what I would call a mixture of both—very realistically but with a nimbus of romanticism."[18]

Because of his long period of gestation as a novelist—in 1919 he was fifty-five, and he did not live to be sixty—Wist was a contemporary of the late-nineteenth-century writers rather than of the writers who began to appear after the First World War. He was a realist and a local colorist rather than a modernist. Wist, then, had thought of presenting his views on immigrants in American society in a multivolume work of fiction at least as early as 1905. So he may well have had ambitions that he kept to himself when he, in the summer of 1919, began to prepare a series of installments on the adventures of a brash, egotistic, ambitious, and naïve young male immigrant in a Minneapolis that Wist himself remembered from his own time there as a greenhorn in the 1880s.

As the installments kept appearing every Tuesday and as correspondence from subscribers brought evidence of their popularity, Wist's expanding work of fiction must have been a main topic of conversation among the editorial staff. They were not ready to let the apparent modesty of their editor in chief stand in the way of what might be a major factor in the continued success and growth of their newspaper. On December 19 a framed advertisement signed *"Decorah-Posten"* is the first recognition that the story of Jonas Olsen was something more than the common fare of "Mellemmad." Apparently Prestgard and other members of the editorial staff had ganged up on Wist and had insisted on an editorial notice:

> Our humorous column, "Mellemmad" by Arnljot, is without comparison the most entertaining "feature" in our press. The sketches that the humorous author here draws of the life that surrounds us and where he portrays us so accurately in all our ridiculousness and with all our weaknesses, is the result of his long and intimate relationship with the Norwegian people in the United States. There is more wisdom and common sense in "Mellemmad"—seasoned with wit and sharp irony—than in far more serious writing. He who does not laugh out loud on reading "Mellemmad" must be incorrigibly down in the mouth. Read the narrative of Jonas Olsen and his adventures

in Minneapolis. These are remarkable sketches of the life of a
newcomer in the Minneapolis of the 1880s.

The self-congratulatory notice uses the words "column," "sketches," and
"feature," but avoids the more prestigious words "book" and "novel."
The first indication that Wist had accepted that his story about Jonas
Olsen was to be a real book came April 20, 1920, when the installment
concluded with the announcement: "The story about Jonas will be published as a book in June. The price will be $1.00. Those who wish to have
the book should send their orders to *Decorah-Posten* right away so that
the size of the edition may be determined." The announcement is repeated in all remaining installments. In light of the December 19 notice,
we may assume that Wist's decision to go for book publication was on
the urging of his colleagues. His growing confidence in his project may
be signalled by his decision to have the installments of the second volume appear as one of *Decorah-Posten's* serialized novels rather than as
a Tuesday "Mellemmad" column: beginning October 1, 1920, "Hjemmet
paa Prærien" ran on Fridays and was printed in the book-page-sized columns used for serialized fiction rather than in the narrow newspaper
columns of the first volume. There could no longer be any doubt about it:
Arnljot was a novelist.

Wist must have been encouraged by the responses of his readers. A
prominent feature of immigrant newspapers is correspondence from subscribers, and it did not take long before letters with reference to the story
of Jonas Olsen began to appear. On December 12, 1919, a subscriber in
North Dakota writes about enjoying the story as well as the characters'
dialects, which reminded her of her own childhood. She concludes, "Poor
Jonas! I suppose he has become a pastor by now!" A week later another
subscriber makes clear that he appreciates Wist's satirical presenta-
tion of immigrant life: "Just lay it on, Mr. Arnljot, and don't hold back
any courses," he writes with reference to "Mellemmad." "We are tough
people here in the West and can digest quite a lot!" Among the many
who write appreciatively about "Mellemmad," there is one subscriber
who, on March 5, 1920, wonders how things will develop for Jonas and
Ragna. On April 30, another subscriber, who appears intrigued by the
romance aspect of the plot, exclaims, "I hope that Jonas will take Ragna
from the Swede." On April 2, a correspondent expects that Jonas Olsen
"will, in time, achieve both power and glory."

After the book's publication, on September 3, 1920, Wist wrote in
appreciation of the many reviews in Norwegian-American newspapers:

Let me thank those who have reviewed my "Scenes from the Life of a Newcomer" with such generosity. It is nice that one's own children win the approval of the world even though they in some respects may not always have behaved as well as they should. Personally, I had not realized I had made so good a book but when such men as Strømme, Mengshoel, Carl Hansen, L. H. Lund, J. G. L. in *Skandinaven,* and others say so, I will, in all modesty, accept their verdict.

Strømme thinks that Jonas has learned to speak Norwegian American a little too quickly, and he is probably right. But we must keep in mind that the hero of "Scenes from the Life of a Newcomer" is supposed to be a genius, and for a genius almost everything is possible. But I admit that Jonas started off a little too well. That may be the reason why his glory was so short-lived.[19]

But Wist is not modest about his command of his own language: he takes issue with the Wisconsin-born Peer Strømme's claims that he has made up some of his words and gives Strømme a brief lexicographical and etymological lesson.

There was no indication that the story would be continued. But Wist had evidently completed a second volume and his acknowledgment of his reviewers was part of *Decorah-Posten*'s preparation for the resumption of serialization on October 1, 1920. The previous Friday, one of several correspondents who missed "Mellemmad" assumes that "the reason is that the cook [i.e., Arnljot] went out to North Dakota to help Olsen with his harvest." On Tuesday, September 28, Kristian Prestgard has a laudatory review of "Scenes from the Life of a Newcomer." He has particular praise for how the novel evokes the late-nineteenth-century immigrant society in Minneapolis with its fine portraits of historical characters as well as its no-less-recognizable characters with fictive names, "all the way down, I regret to say, to the greatest writer in America and the most myopic man in the world, Arnoldus Bolivarius Lyvenfelt, who, *by the way,* here is adorned with a much grander name than he had when I last saw him in Wettergren's saloon on *Cider Ævnju.*"[20] Prestgard compares Wist's Jonas to Ibsen's eponymous Peer Gynt:

> Jonas Olsen too starts off with rather vague notions of what he is going to make of himself. But he knows it will be something great, perhaps a pastor or a millionaire. He has no particular calling, he is not blessed with any remarkable gifts, he is not weighted down by rigid dogmas of any kind, but he has a natural instinct that tells him what is profitable and what is not profitable for one who wants to succeed in the world.

"'Scenes from the Life of a Newcomer,'" he concludes, "is without comparison the funniest book I have read in a long time . . . I have realized that the story is so funny because it is so true."

Serialization of the second volume, "The Home on the Prairie," ran from the following Friday to May 13, 1921. Subscribers continued to write in appreciation of Wist's fiction. Quite often, correspondence suggested that the question of how things would turn out in the next installment was a topic of discussion in the many homes to which *Decorah-Posten* came twice a week. Ragna seems the most popular of the characters. On February 25, 1921, a reader claims that she knew the real names of all the characters in the first volume, suggesting that, to some, the novel had appeal as a *roman à clef.* On April 15, as the battle between Jonas Olsen and Elihu Ward for possession of the valuable section of land chosen for a railway depot is nearing its climax, a subscriber hopes that "Arnljot won't let the Yankee rascal con Jonas and Ragna into selling him their good Red River farm."

Apart from giving the author encouragement, however, comments on the installments of the novels had no influence on the composition: each volume was completed before serialization began. Thus on June 28, 1921, Arnljot responded to several subscribers who had wondered why there had been no "Mellemmad" column for several weeks on end:

> I can inform those who have asked why there has been no "Mellemmad" in recent weeks that I have been busy with other work. I have just completed a new novel that will begin serialization in October. Although it is a complete and independent story, it is also a continuation and conclusion of the two previous novels published in this newspaper: "Scenes from the Life of a Newcomer" and "The Home on the Prairie." So it will be the third and last part of the Jonas Olsen trilogy. Its title is "Jonasville."

But this does not mean that Wist relaxed in the months after he had completed his trilogy. "Jonasville" began serialization on Friday, October 7, and on the following Tuesday, under the familiar heading "Mellemmad," *Decorah-Posten* presented the first installment of yet another novel by Arnljot: the delightfully whimsical and comic *Reisen til Rochester* (The journey to Rochester), which in 1922 in Minneapolis became Wist's only novel to be published by an outside publisher, Augsburg Publishing House. No sooner was this serialization concluded January 10, 1922, than yet another mock journey epic, "Reisen til Montana" (The journey to Montana), ran from January 31 to March 14. The Jonas Olsen trilogy was concluded April 21 without any special notice of the event.

Two other serialized short novels were published in 1922: "House-cleaning," from May 28 to July 11, and "Aslak Farlaus: En fortælling fra Norge og nordlige Wisconsin" (Aslak fatherless: a novel of Norway and northern Wisconsin), from October 27 to December 22. In 1923 two more novels were serialized: "Hvorledes Lars Bakka blev akklimatiseret" (How Lars Bakka became assimilated) and "Sommerferie" (Summer vacation). But before the latter was completed in February 1924, Wist had passed away and Arnljot's vacation was made permanent. On Tuesday, December 4, 1923, Wist's successor, Kristian Prestgard, began his editorial with the words: "Johannes B. Wist, the editor in chief of *Decorah-Posten,* died in his home on East Main Street in this city last Saturday night."

Two years before his death, on October 4, 1921, Wist had used his "Mellemmad" column to reflect on the nature and purpose of his literary efforts. His point of departure was the observation that some Norwegian-American publishers advertised that their books were in "real Norwegian"; indeed, Wist had once seen an advertisement that claimed, "The language is entirely free of any error."

> There is a lesson to be gleaned from this. First, it reveals that somewhere there is someone who suspects that we Norwegian-American writers cannot write proper Norwegian and, second, it suggests that Norwegian-American books may actually have been published in a language that was not "entirely free of any error."[21] It is rather sad that we, in our old age, are making such insinuations about each other.

But the question of language must be taken seriously, he continues, and he explains that an immigrant culture cannot possibly remain in touch with the developing language in the home country.

> It is extremely difficult for a person who has not grown up in Norway or who has been abroad for years and lived under the influence of another country to be in full harmony with an organic sense of the Norwegian language. You cannot achieve this merely by reading Norwegian literature and even if you once have had a natural command of the language, you will easily lose it under foreign influence. This is particularly true of Norwegian Americans. The English language necessarily has an enormous power over us and ensnares us despite our efforts to keep our languages apart.

Such is the necessary condition for an immigrant literature. But, Wist argues, the alleged poor quality of the language is not germane to an evaluation of an immigrant literature. His appraisal of the conditions for an immigrant culture in 1921, a few days before the appearance of the first installment of his third volume, are similar to his views given in his talk in Minneapolis in 1905:

> An evaluation of Norwegian-American books must recognize that they are not primarily Norwegian but American litera-ture. They are in Norwegian—to the extent that Norwegian may be written outside of Norway—but they are nevertheless American. These are books designed for the needs of a migrant people, a people in transition from one nation to another.

Wist regarded his books as part of this process of transition—but not as products of its outcome. Such future books would have to be in English; Norwegian was a transitional language in the United States.

As any writer, Wist of course did not want his work to be forgotten and he regretted that there had been no concerted effort to ensure the archival preservation of "the best Norwegian-American literature . . . so that it may be available for future cultural studies."[22] But he was recon-ciled to the fact that American books in the Norwegian language would not be accessible to the American descendents of the immigrants, and it is doubtful that he entertained the thought that what he wrote would one day be available in English as the American literature he insisted it was.[23] All history, however, is about transition. The transition to which Wist's trilogy as well as his impressive journalistic writings bear witness, the transition of so many European immigrant groups from Europeans to Americans in the late nineteenth and early twentieth centuries, is an important chapter in the history of the United States. *The Rise of Jonas Olsen* is a valuable source for our understanding of this chapter. It is, however, in its own right a fascinating literary work that may continue to entertain readers long after the American transition of Jonas Olsen and his contemporaries has been completed.

Contexts

Minneapolis in the 1880s had a significant Scandinavian population. In spite of its large majority of first- and second-generation immigrants from many European countries, however, the city's political and cul-tural life was in the hands of an Anglo-American minority. Political power nevertheless depended on the votes of the immigrant majority. Consequently, minor public offices and many jobs on the city's payroll were given to immigrants. Near the bottom of this spoils system Jonas finds his cousin Lars Salomonsen, whose Americanized name is Lewis Salmon. When Jonas gets a job working on the city's expanding sewage system he enters a world dominated by Swedes. Norwegian immigrants could use their language in the administrative and public spheres of the city and could do most of their private business in establishments run by and for Norwegians. They could speak Norwegian in churches, saloons, stores of all kinds, banks, and insurance agencies. They might be answered in Swedish, but that would not be a practical problem, since the two languages are closer to each other than are the dialects of some other languages. Immigrants could take care of most of their needs in the language they had brought with them.

There is another Norwegian-American novel that demonstrates how the Norwegian immigrant society in Minneapolis of the 1880s was a self-sufficient community and how this community could be experienced as stifling by those who were not as ready to conform as Jonas Olsen: Drude Krog Janson's *A Saloonkeeper's Daughter*. This novel about a young immigrant woman who eventually becomes a Unitarian minister was originally published in Norwegian in 1889 in Minneapolis; it was published in an English translation by Gerald Thorson in 2002.[24]

The tendency for immigrants to establish their own ethnic enclaves in Minneapolis does not at all mean that the city was becoming "Scandinavianized," or that the immigrants were not assimilating: the Old World languages were used in New World contexts and in New World ways. Immigrant businesses were more like their counterparts run by English-speaking Americans than like those the immigrants knew from the old country. In immigrant churches, they would worship in much the same way as they had before immigration, but with the important difference that they—in American fashion—were themselves responsible for running the churches and for appointing their pastors.[25] At all kinds of gatherings—for social, cultural, or religious purposes—might indeed be considerable displays of nostalgia and Old World nationalism, but while immigrants might be separated by their memories of different regions or different lands, they were all united in their American patriotism.[26]

As Jonas begins his American education, his teachers are immigrants and his language of instruction is Norwegian. His first bewildering lesson is in local politics, as his cousin explains the vague party loyalties fostered by the spoils system. To begin with, however, Jonas is preoccupied with the politics of the country he has left and he is unwavering in his support of the Liberal Party, in his disdain for the Conservative Party, and in his intense distrust of Swedes—attitudes that only make sense in the context of late-nineteenth-century Norway, where the political struggle for democracy unavoidably became a nationalistic one, because the Norwegian monarch was Swedish and was also king of Sweden. Supporting the royal prerogatives, the Conservatives also supported the union with Sweden. The point here is not the relevance of Scandinavian politics for an appreciation of the trilogy, but that Jonas by the end of the first volume has become primarily interested in the politics of Minneapolis, Minnesota, and the United States; all that remains of his Old World political loyalties is a lip service to liberalism and a lingering distrust of Swedes.

The setting of the last two-thirds of the trilogy is the Red River Valley, a broad area of land with exceptionally fertile soil on both sides of the Red River that defines the border between North Dakota and Minnesota. The history of its Norwegian settlement began in 1869, when a Norwegian immigrant lawyer and journalist, Paul Hjelm-Hansen, traveled in the area by ox cart from Alexandria. He was impressed by the quality of the land and recognized its potential for the production of wheat. His series of articles praising the Red River Valley and recommending it for settlement was published in the Norwegian-American newspapers *Fædrelandet og Emigranten* (The fatherland and the emigrant) in Madison, and *Nordisk Folkeblad* (Nordic folk journal) in Minneapolis, and were reprinted by several newspapers in Norway. Homesteaders of many nations eventually found their way to this fertile area without the encouragement of Hjelm-Hansen's enthusiastic reports, but because of his articles, Norwegian Americans in the settled areas farther east, as well as new immigrants from Norway, got the advantage of an early start. The same year Hjelm-Hansen's articles began to appear, a sizeable group homesteaded there and laid the foundation for the ethnic dominance of Norwegians in the Red River Valley. There was little recognition of the rights of the people whose land this had been in Hjelm-Hansen's articles or in the letters the homesteaders sent to family and friends in Norway.

When Jonas and Ragna went west after Jonas's business failure, it is thus historically correct that they were surrounded by other Norwegians who had already established themselves on prosperous farms. The towns and settlements to which they came had a history going back fifteen or more years. The land Jonas had bought as an investment had been vacated by one of the many homesteaders who had given up. It is also historically correct that while the Norwegians were the largest ethnic group in the Red River Valley, the politically and culturally dominant group was a minority of Anglo-American settlers from the northeastern United States. Thus it is a Yankee, Elihu Ward, who is the political boss of the fictive Garfield County, and thus the conflict caused by Jonas Olsen's own unquenchable thirst for power must necessarily be an ethnic one. Jonas is an uneducated upstart while Elihu Ward is to the manner—if not the manor—born. This is how he is characterized in the opening sentence of chapter 11 of the second volume: "Elihu Ward was a man of good upbringing and excellent manners. He was an *Eastern Yankee* and beyond doubt the only person in the entire county who knew the name of his great-great-grandfather."

It may nevertheless not be evident why he should have such a solid grip on a county largely populated by Norwegian immigrants who, moreover, could have sought the support of a fair number of Swedes. The narrator explains:

> The prairie had no traditions for the pioneer and those of the country were not his; for in nine of ten instances he was an immigrant from another country and had his roots in another tradition and in another culture. This is what has given the *Yankien* his great advantage above the others in the shaping of the characteristics of the American West. This is what has made it possible for him and his kind to become a kind of upper class in the motley community of peoples that has sprung up in this part of the country. The *Yankien* brought the country's own tradition with him into the settlement.

Conflicts similar to that between Olsen and Ward were played out with different players in many American towns and cities with strong immigrant populations. They may not have been quite as dramatic as that in Garfield County, but the outcome—locally as well as nationally—was, as in Wist's novel, one of reconciliation and the mutual recognition of belonging to a common nation. While the historical backdrop to the story that enfolds in the second and third volumes is that of Populism and Progressivism in the West up to the election of 1912, the attitudes and views of the narrator are also formed by later events and politics: the antiforeign hysteria of the war years and the political campaigns to bring mass immigration to an end.

The Rise of Jonas Olsen provides unique insight into the politics of the period of the highest rate of European immigration: from the

1880s to the years after the First World War. Westerns, whether pulp fiction or Hollywood productions, are usually set in a West populated by English-speaking Americans (often confronting either Mexicans or Native Americans). Occasionally one of the farmers helped by the hero will speak in an accent that indicates he is a "Swede." In having an immigrant boss confront a Yankee boss in a struggle for power, Wist's novel of the West may be more in pact with historical reality than the better-known fictions that have made the immigrant populations of the West largely invisible.

As always, I have not been alone in the making of this book. Good friends read the manuscript and offered advice at various stages of completion: Øyvind T. Gulliksen, Todd W. Nichol, David Olson, and Werner Sollors. I would not have had access to many of my sources of information without the good help of Dina Tolfsby at the National Library of Norway, the staff of the Norwegian-American Historical Association, and the always friendly librarians of the interlibrary loan division of the University of Bergen Library. My good colleagues in the department of English at the University of Bergen have all contributed to the making of a supportive culture, and I appreciate the opportunities I have been given to pursue this project over several years. As I worked on this book, three new members of my immediate family have entered the world, giving me added incentive and joy. Without the support and encouragement of Inger, very little would have been possible, and I dedicate this translation to Maximillian Peder, Finn Christian, and Synne Johanne.

Aukra and Bergen, Norway
Portland, Oregon
October 2005

A Note on the Text
and Translation

Wist did not give his trilogy a title. The title used here, *The Rise of Jonas Olsen,* is the translator's but not the translator's invention. The first three words are part of the title of one of the classics of immigrant fiction, *The Rise of David Levinsky* by Abraham Cahan (1917). Cahan in his turn was deliberately echoing the title of William Dean Howells's best-known novel, *The Rise of Silas Lapham* (1885). The titles of both earlier novels are ironic: Lapham fails in business but wins a moral victory, while Levinsky succeeds in business but at the cost of his soul. Wist, as the reader will discover, gives Jonas Olsen a third way out.

The title is not the only liberty taken by the translator. The translation of the complete text has been cut from almost 241,000 to about 178,000 words. In particular, some satirical passages in the first volume of little interest to present-day readers have been removed. Two complete chapters have been omitted in Book I: the original chapter 7 (1,557 words) is a long letter Jonas writes to his sister, and the original chapter 18 (1,936 words) is about a failed attempt to create a Scandinavian literary society.[1] Care has been taken not to modify characterization, and all events of any importance in Jonas Olsen's career are included, with the exception of the failed literary society and his participation in the establishment of a short-lived newspaper in Minneapolis (1,514 words).

The translation, in particular of the first chapter of Book I, poses some problems, and practical answers had to be made. When people speak to Jonas during his first days in Minneapolis, he understands very little, whether the language is English or the peculiar mixture of English and Norwegian satirized by Wist. Lewis Salmon speaks in much the same way whether he thinks he is speaking English or he imagines he is speaking Norwegian. This is a confusion of languages that goes beyond code-switching: the speaker has forgotten much of his first language and has not yet learned much of a second one.

This is how the original text presents the first meeting between Jonas and his cousin Salmon:

> "Well sørri, in dis' her' Kontri'e er vi alle Læborers, ju 'no," svarte Fætteren. "No Læbor is simpelt in Amerika, og all Offic'holdera tek sin Tørn med at kline op." Men saa husket han pludselig, at Jonas naturligvis ikke skjønte Engelsk, og saa fortsatte han paa norsk: "Amerika er en demokratisk kontry, ju 'no! 'Onest arbe' er det, som kounter."

Since Jonas understands only a few words that seem familiar to his Norwegian ears, a translation of Salmon's speech into English would re-create neither the main character's bewilderment nor the speaker's inability to speak either language. On the other hand, Wist clearly assumed that his readers would have no problems in understanding Salmon's sentences or in appreciating the humor created by his linguistic bastardizations. The book was addressed to readers who were not only familiar with both English and Norwegian but who themselves on occasion confused the two languages. The reader was the target of Wist's linguistic satire. For readers of English only, however, the original text cannot have the complexity of meanings it had for the intended readership. So I have translated words that are standard Norwegian and left the bastard Norwegian-English or English-Norwegian as in the original text. This linguistic confusion is mainly limited to the opening pages, reflecting the main character's own problems in learning a new language. In Salmon's speech, however, there is hardly a phrase that is either correct English or correct Norwegian. So this is how the above passage appears in the translation:

> "*Well sørri, in dis' her' kontri'e er vi alle læborers, ju 'no,*" the cousin replied. "*No læbor is simpelt in Amerika, og all offic'holdera tek sin tørn med at kline op.*" But then he remembered that Jonas didn't know any English, and he continued in Norwegian: "*Amerika er en demokratisk kontry, ju 'no! 'Onest arbe' er det, som kounter.*"

The text that is identical with that of the original is in italics. What Lewis Salmon says to Jonas Olsen in "English" is: "Well, Sir, in this here country we are all laborers, you know. No labor is inferior [simple] in America and all the officeholders take their turn with cleaning up."

What he says in "Norwegian" is: "America is a democratic country, you know! Honest work is what counts."

This would be heavy going for the reader if it were kept up, but after a few pages, direct speech is mostly rendered in Wist's Norwegian with occasional code-switching, that is with occasional use of English words, often with a Norwegian phonetic spelling (e.g., *rønn* for "run") and a Norwegian grammatical inflexion (e.g., *rønne* for "to run").

For the sake of readability, italics have been used rather sparingly to indicate that words or phrases in the translation are as in the original. Wist wrote some of the dialogue by non-Norwegian speakers in English. The context will usually indicate this, and italics have not been used. The use of italics to indicate code-switching—in dialogue as well as in the narrative itself—in the original text has been limited to nonstandard language. Consequently, there is far more use of English in the original text than is apparent in the translation. Place names and addresses are thus only in italics if they appear in a non-standard form: Minneapolis/*Min'ap'lis*. Italics are also avoided for some English or Norwegian-English words that occur so often that it would be disruptive to always have them in italics. Even though such words may in the original have a "Norwegian-American spelling" (for instance, *ævnju* for "avenue") I have chosen to standardize the spelling of the most frequently used words rather than to italicize them. These are, in particular, words for institutions and policies for which there was no accurate Norwegian equivalent, such as congress, county, county board, county commissioners, courthouse, foreclose, land grant, lobby, Populism, school superintendent, township, etc.[2] Thus the words *bordinghuset* and *courthuset* in the original text are in the translation rendered as "the boardinghouse" and "the courthouse," without any indication of the code-switching in the original text.

Words in italics are often Wist's Norwegian transcriptions of Norwegian-American speech. The spelling thus reflects Norwegian pronunciation. This may make it difficult for readers of English to recognize *saasægmit* as sausage meat or *reit* as right. The use of Norwegian inflexions further complicates understanding. Thus *trit* is pronounced with a vowel that is the equivalent of the vowel in "treat," but the infinitive of this verb, "to treat," is *trite* and the imperfect, "treated," is *trita*, at least in the dialects of most characters. The noun "the crowd" as pronounced by characters in the novel is sometimes written *krauden*—the suffix -en having the same meaning as the definite article in English. Thus, *trita krauden* is an immigrant's way of saying "treat the crowd," or, pay for the drinks for all in a saloon. *Velsørri, nosørri,* and *jessørri*—immigrant versions of "well sir," "no sir," and "yes sir"—are transcriptions of popular idioms in much Norwegian-American speech and are used frequently by the characters, in the translation as in the original.[3]

Wist's transcriptions are further complicated by the fact that the characters are from different parts of Norway and thus have different grammatical inflexions as well as different pronunciations of words, also of the English words used in their Norwegian speech.[4] Some characters, such as Nyblom, speak Swedish, and their code-switching is given in a Swedish-like spelling. Much of the dialogue is given as reported rather than direct speech, and here too there is frequent code-switching, often with due attention to the dialect of the (reported) speaker. Most of this will not be appreciated by an English-only speaker, much in the same way that Wist's original text would not have made sense to his contemporaries in Norway, unfamiliar as they were with immigrant speech.

I have tried to retain enough code-switching in the translation to make the reader aware of how these characters are speaking. In most cases the meaning is fairly obvious, as in the sentence, "Moreover, Ole Dampen was a good *bisnesmand* and able to work out that if it became known that professors and preachers frequented Dampen's saloon, then this would *adverteise bisnessen* in a quite wonderful manner." Here the italicized words reflect immigrant pronunciation of "businessman," "advertise," and "the business." It may be less obvious that *loiert* is an immigrant version of lawyer, but the first time the word occurs, the person spoken to does not understand the word either, and it is immediately explained to him (and, consequently, to the reader as well). In instances where the meaning may not be easily understood, an explanatory endnote has been provided.

Another kind of code-switching that is difficult to appreciate for an English-only reader is where Norwegian idioms are used even though the words are English. Thus *"on American"* or even *"on United States"* reflects a Norwegian-American way of saying "in English." Much of such a bastardized text is necessarily lost in translation and there is little point in always making the reader aware of instances where, for example, Wist's Norwegian is so Americanized that it would not have been understood by Norwegians in Norway but only by those who had become Norwegian Americans. An example may be in the account of how the town Jonasville or Johnsville is laid out. Here we are told that one neighborhood is dominated by "professionals." This is my translation of Wist's word *profesjonelle* and is in keeping with his intended meaning (and probably his Norwegian-American way of speaking), even though the Norwegian word he used did not and does not have the meaning of the American English word, "professionals" (i.e., doctors, lawyers, etc.), but rather means people who do things in a professional manner or do it for pay. Similarly, *statsstyret* in the original text has been translated as "state government," his intended meaning, even though a Norwegian reader would take it to mean the national government. An attempt to have such linguistic irregularities and inconsistencies reflected in the translated text would have made it unreadable.

The full flavor of Wist's Norwegian-American language can only be had through his own text.[5] I hope that this translation lets enough of it come through to give the reader some awareness of how one writer tackled the problem of writing in an American language other than English.

THE RISE OF JONAS OLSEN

BOOK I

*Scenes from the Life
of a Newcomer:
Jonas Olsen's First Years
in America*

I.

Jonas Olsen came to America in the 1880s. He was twenty years old, had never learned to work, and wasn't much good at anything else either. So you may think that he lacked the necessary qualifications to be launched into an alien and indifferent world. But there is no need to worry. Jonas himself hadn't acquired much concern for tomorrow in the course of his short life and, moreover, he had a cousin in Minneapolis who was very highly placed and who was said to be almost a millionaire. He had more or less said so himself in his letters home, so there could be no reason to doubt it.

Everyone knows that the road to riches and respectability is easy in America. Jens Larsen, who had been a farm laborer in Norway, had written from the Red River Valley that he had seven farms covering an area as large as the entire township back home.[1] And Jensen, who had merely been a schoolteacher, had visited a theological seminary in the new country and was ordained after a brief examination. Now he had been called to a large and affluent congregation and lived in a magnificent parsonage, where he not only had cattle and sheep but countless horses as well. America was the land of the future, and Jonas, who had drifted here and there without much success at anything, wanted his share.

It had been difficult for him to decide whether he should go to *Dekora, Jova,* or to Minneapolis, Minnesota.[2] He had heard that there was a seminary in Decorah and that it was difficult to get enough pastors for all the Norwegian immigrants who now had become rich and religious. He decided on Minneapolis because of his cousin. In American fashion, Lars Salomonsen had become Lewis Salmon and Jonas had been told that Salmon's name was respected all over Minneapolis and even as far east as *Sankte Paul,* where his influence in state politics had caused

fear among the many Swedes there. He had written all about it in his letters. The conflict between Norwegians and Swedes was pretty much the
same in Minnesota as in the old country.[3] There was constant rivalry between them for the most rewarding offices. But thanks to Mister Salmon
the Norwegians were in full control.

His cousin had written that he was manager of public buildings in
Minneapolis and had his office in the town hall. Jonas's father had advised Jonas to write to Mister Salmon so that he would know when to
expect Jonas and could send a coach to the depot to pick him up. But
as usual, Jonas had put it off until it was too late and now he was at the
Depo'n and didn't know what to do. He had of course also forgotten his
cousin's home address. At last he succeeded in getting the Swedish immigration agent to understand that he was a cousin of Lewis Salmon and
that he, Salmon that is, had his office in the government building.[4] "You
probably mean the courthouse," the agent had said. He didn't know
Mister Salmon and to Jonas this was about as ignorant as you could
get. But finally he got someone to follow Jonas to the courthouse, which
wasn't so far from the depot.[5]

There Jonas entered an office and asked for Lewis Salmon—manager
of public buildings, he added in Norwegian. To him it seemed such a fine
phrase that he couldn't imagine that the Yankee wouldn't understand
him. The man he asked was well dressed but very ignorant. Not only
didn't he know what a *regjeringsbygningsforvalter*[6] was, but he hadn't
even heard of Lewis Salmon. Jonas concluded that Americans were
not a very enlightened people. However, he took the trouble of asking
another man.

"Lewis Salmon?" he repeated and thought about it for a while. "Lewis
Salmon? Let me see—. Oh yes, that's the fellow that's working with
the janitor. You'll find him upstairs—on the second floor." Jonas didn't
know what upstairs could be but he didn't want to stand there and gape
like an idiot, so he bowed, said *"yessør,"* and went back to the hall.

It should be noted that Jonas wasn't entirely without knowledge of
the English language. On his way across the Atlantic he had become
acquainted with a Norwegian who had sailed on Lake Michigan and
who taught him five English expressions, insisting that with them Jonas
could get along anywhere in America. They were *yessør* for yes, *nosør* for
no, *don'tno* when he was uncertain, never mind when he wanted to hide
his ignorance, *gudness* when he wished to express his wonder all right,
that could be used on all occasions, and one more that he could use when

he was angry but that the sailor had advised against using if a pastor was near. After arrival, Jonas had picked up a word here and there, and today he had learned another one, so he felt confident that he would soon be able to master the language.

In the hall he met a young man in a strange outfit and with golden braid around his cap. But Jonas was not to be deterred. He knew that you had to be bold in America, "bluff your way," as the sailor had said. And Jonas was determined to make it. So he placed himself right in front of the young man in uniform, showing no regard for his high rank, and said: "Lewis Salmon—upstairs?" He grimaced to make clear that he was speaking English.

The young man smiled and pointed up the stairs. "That's the second assistant janitor," he replied. "You'll find him on the second floor." Again he pointed up the stairs, and then he was gone. People seemed so busy in America, thought Jonas.

On the second floor Jonas saw a man with a broom. He was determined not to be daunted. He walked right up to him, poked him in the back to get his attention, and said: "Lewis Salmon—upstairs?" The man turned abruptly. He probably thought this was a rather strange way to be addressed.

"Lewis Salmon? That's me," he said. *"Hva' foro' you vant?"*

Jonas recognized his cousin. He was a little thinner than he used to be in the old country and Jonas hadn't expected to find him in work clothes with a broom in his hand, but there could be no doubt: this was Lewis Salmon. But Mister Salmon couldn't recognize Jonas. He had been four years in America, and back then Jonas had been considered a child. When Jonas explained who he was, Salmon was somewhat embarrassed. Not only was the visit unexpected but he had, in a way, been found out.

"Oh—is this the kind of work you do?" Jonas exclaimed. He hesitated and was obviously, to put it mildly, somewhat surprised.

"Well sørri, in dis' her' kontri'e er vi alle læborers, ju 'no," the cousin replied. *"No læbor is simpelt in Amerika, og all offic'holdera tek sin tørn med at kline op."*[7] But then he remembered that Jonas didn't know any English, and he continued in Norwegian: *"Amerika er en demokratisk kontry, ju 'no! 'Onest arbe' er det, som kounter."*[8]

Jonas still wasn't sure that he understood him, but he gathered that he was explaining something. Mister Salmon noticed that his cousin from Norway hadn't *græspa* his meaning: *"Jeg har getta saa jused te' aa speak English, at jeg forgetter mig right 'long naar jeg juser Norsk,"*[9] he said. "It takes time for a newcomer to get enough *hæng af languagen* to *kætche on te' de' most komment English,*[10] but it will come so *bey* and *bey.*"

Jonas understood about as much as he had before but he didn't want to appear unintelligent. So he thought he should let his cousin know that he too could speak some English and answered with a shrug: "Aa, never mind!"

"Well, you'll have to *exkjuse* me," Mister Salmon began again. *"Dis' her' office-læber* has to be done, *ju 'no,* so I can't *akkompagnere* you to *streetkarsen.*[11] But it's easy to find my house. You go one block to Washington Avenue and stop at the *korne' tu de' reit* or, if you're thirsty, you can walk two block south to a saloon called Stockholm-Olson[12] and stay there till Riverside *karsen* comes by. When you see it you wave to the conductor, and when he stops the *karsen* you *jomper* on. In fifteen minutes you'll be at the *korne'* of Riverside and Twenty-Second, and then you wave again to the conductor and say stop, and he stop, and *ju jomps* off. Then you take Twenty-Second to Ninth Street, and then you walk three block west and then you *tørne* and walk a half block straight north and then you have the house right in the *center'n* of the block on the left-hand side. There are only six houses on the block and mine is the fifth largest—a fine house with *lawn og porch paa fronten og tow'r i roffen.*[13] Easy to find! *Vell, gudbey*! See ju later. So long."

He continued his administrative duties and Jonas realized that this was his signal to leave and try to find his cousin's house as best he could. He had noted the names Twenty-Second, Riverside, Washington Avenue, and Stockholm-Olson, and he got out his notebook and wrote them down so he wouldn't forget them. But he had the names so mixed up that he thought he should take Riverside *karsen* on Twenty-Second and *jompe* off on Washington. It was quite a walk to Twenty-Second, according to his cousin, but he walked many blocks without finding it. Actually, he had walked half the distance to Lake Harriet. Jonas found it awkward that everyone he asked gave the impression of being terribly busy, so he had decided not to ask for directions. Just as he realized that he needed help, he saw a coal-black man coming in his direction. He didn't look very nice but he didn't seem to be in a hurry.

"Twenty-Second" he said to the black man. It was the middle of July and unbearably hot. The man stopped and smiled. He was very friendly and polite and in considerable detail he explained that Jonas had lost his bearing. "Twenty-Second," he said, was all of "twenty-three blocks south."

"All right," said Jonas and began to walk in the direction the man had indicated with his long index finger. But the black man wanted to give him better directions and called after him. He evidently had time on his hands; but Jonas had had enough of talk that he couldn't understand, so he just said never mind and walked on.

After he had accosted about twenty people, he eventually came to Twenty-Second and Riverside. And, just as he had been told, along came Riverside *karsen*. Jonas ran toward it and called stop, as he had been instructed, and the conductor stopped and took him aboard. With words and signs, Jonas explained that he wanted to get off on Washington Avenue, and then he sat down with a sense of relief. It had been a long walk. In a little while the conductor called out "Washington Avenue," and Jonas had to get off again. He wasn't sure what to do so he consulted his notebook. There he found the name Stockholm-Olson. Where, he wondered, would he find him? He asked and was told that the Swedish saloon was a mile farther north. Then Jonas said the word that the sailor had advised him not to use if a pastor was near, and walked on. It was five minutes past six when he staggered into Stockholm-Olson's well-known establishment, and he was into his second glass of beer when Cousin Salmon came in with his dinner pail, to quench his thirst before going home.

"Didn't you find my *hous'*?" asked the manager of public buildings. "I *explœna* it all for you."

"*Yessør,* I found it well enough," Jonas replied, "but I thought it was too early to go indoors and walked around to see how people live here."

Just how many glasses of beer they emptied that evening, I cannot say, but they must have celebrated quite a lot because when they finally got home, Mrs. Salmon was in an aggressive mood.

"Here the *supperen* has *veita* for three hours and is cold," she said. She looked at the cousin from Norway as if he had come right from the poorhouse.

"*Dis' her'* is Jonas Olsen, *kusinen min* from Norway," said Mister Salmon, "and this is the Mrs., my woman."

"I suppose he's as big a fool as you are," she said, and disappeared into the kitchen. Jonas looked around. The furniture was old and worn and not quite what he had expected of a civil servant. On the floor were two dirty-looking children. As was their custom, Mister Salmon got a pail of beer for their dinner from a saloon on Riverside and his wife, after many protests, helped empty it. She soon seemed almost polite to Jonas.

"And what have you planned to do in America?" she asked the newcomer.

"Oh, that depends," Jonas replied. "I'd prefer to become a capitalist or, as you say here, a millionaire. But this may be difficult to achieve in the first year or two, so I've been thinking of graduating from the seminary first."

"Yes, you have studied at the higher *commonskolen* in Norway,"[14] said Salmon, "and anyhow you don't need to know much Norwegian *fer te be prest in dis' her' kontry'e*.[15] It is mostly Greek they *driller* them in in *dis' her'* preacher schools."

"But don't they preach in Norwegian?" Jonas asked in surprise. In the letters from America it had appeared that the church was almost more Norwegian than in Norway.

"Yes *o'kors*," answered Mister Salmon, but seemed unsure. "Up to now they have been bound te preach Norwegian *ud af konsideration* for the newcomers. But in five or ten years Norwegian will be a dead language, and it will altogether be *spika* only English.[16] As for me now, for instance, if I'm to be edified by a sermon it must be on English."

"Oh, you fool," said his wife. "You've never *œttenda en meeten'* since you were confirmed."

"*Gudness!*" said Jonas.

2.

His first night in Minneapolis, Jonas had the strangest dream he had ever dreamed. He had been drafted for military service in Norway and was surrounded by officers who stared at him and inspected him as if he were a horse. "We may be at war with the Swedes any day," said one of them, "so we need men who can take a bullet or two." "*Gudness,*" thought Jonas, "are we going to have a war?" He had no appetite for war and had a powerful urge to run away. He wasn't a conservative.[17] Indeed he was quite radical in his views, and more than once he had said that if the Swedes wouldn't behave themselves we would simply have to march over the mountains and beat them up. But this was different; the war was for real and Jonas was a soldier.

As he speculated on how to get out of this tough spot the scene suddenly changed to America. He was in an enormous crowd of young men outside the biggest building he had ever seen. They were pushing and shoving to get in. Jonas didn't know why and the others didn't seem to know much more than he did. Finally he got through the door and entered a huge room. Over to the right, a lean clergyman was preaching to a group of five or six old women who all looked very worried. He went nearer. The minister's text was the parable of the rich man and Lazarus. He warned against striving for possessions. Jonas thought it a peculiar text for these old women, who surely had other problems than too much wealth.

The others didn't stop to listen. They had other things in mind. At the far end of the room a huge man sat at a table counting gold coins. That's where the crowd was heading, but when Jonas got to the table the man and his money had disappeared. Another well-nourished man stood behind a counter handing out drinks right and left. It was the same man he had seen at Stockholm-Olson's the night before.

There was a lively discussion in Norwegian and Swedish about the union between the two countries. An aggressive Norwegian spitefully asked what they thought would happen if the Swedish crown prince marched on Kristiania, as he so often boasted.[18] Another was sure that as usual there wouldn't be a Swede left to report on their defeat. And then a huge Swede suddenly appeared and a fight began. The blood almost made Jonas faint . . . But he woke up and discovered that it was a dream.

It must have been the loud voices in the next room that brought him out of his dream. A man and a woman were yelling at each other, accompanied by the sound of shoes kicked from one end of the room to the other and of dueling chairs and tables. Every now and then the screams of two children entered in strange and indescribable harmony with the terrible music of the two spouses. Jonas recognized the voice of Cousin Salmon and the shrill voice of his wife. He had returned to the real world.

"If he's staying in our house," said Mrs. Salmon, "he'll at least, *bey gosh, pey.*"

"Oh, be quiet and *sjøtt-op,*" said her husband. "He is my *relativen* and I am the man of my own *hous'.*"

"Oh, you can *sjøtt-op jurself!*" cried the woman. "You're not the man of your own *hous'* nor of any other." She threw a shoe at the wall.

"But dear me, Marja, how you work yourself up," complained Mister Salmon. "You must *juse kommen sens'.*"

"Use a little *kommen sens'* yourself, *humbugen!*" screamed his wife. "Here, take these kids and *dres' dem,* while I *tender* to the *brækfasten!*" She ran down the stairs, and to Jonas it seemed that the entire house was about to come down with her.

"Gudnes!" he said, and got out of bed. "Damn strange people," he mumbled to himself. It wasn't quite six o'clock and he wasn't used to being disturbed at this time of night. It was peculiar that such sounds should be heard at the start of day in the home of a civil servant. He had only a vague notion of what the spouses had been fighting about, but he had at least grasped that he was the subject of their dispute. But Jonas wasn't easily troubled by minor details. It couldn't be as bad as it sounded, he thought.

Soon Mister Salmon and the newcomer were at the breakfast table. The custodian of public buildings looked a little subdued and remained silent. His wife served them with a mean expression on her face and unkempt hair. The coffee impressed him; it was the worst he had ever tasted. The rest of the meal wasn't much to boast of either, even though Mrs. Salmon let him understand that it had cost more than usual be-cause they had a visitor.

"What do you call this?" asked Jonas as he, with considerable hesitation and some anxiety, was about to attack the meat dish.

"Dot's saasægmit," his cousin explained.

"Is it horse meat?"

"No, are you mad? We don't serve *hors'mit* in America! This is *greinda pigmit.*"

"Oh, I see," said Jonas. "You get up so terribly early in this country," he added after a little while. "In Norway working people are grateful if a civil servant makes his appearance before noon. Do you really have to be there at seven?"

"Yes, in Norway!" said Mister Salmon—he had his mouth full of something they called *pen'kek'*—"but *dis' her'* is America, and here they know how to *juse* the time *reit*. This is not as in Europe, *ju no'*, with big *pey* and *liddle vork* for *officeholdera*."[19]

"What does that mean in Norwegian?" Jonas asked.

"Oh, *exkjus' me*! I *forgetter reit 'long* that you don't understand English because I think *on American,* you see. What I was saying is that in Norway the *officeholdera* have much *pey* and nothing to do except to *æppira.*"

"What's *pey*?"

"That's what you are paid for your work on United States."

"And *æppira,* what does that mean?"

"*Æppira* is the same as to *æppira* in public."

"Oh," said Jonas, "is that what it means." He was no wiser, but he was determined to be Americanized as fast as possible and he had learned how to bluff in Norway.

"The *officeholdera* who are too *læzy* to take *kær'* are *defita* at the *'lektion.*"

"Oh, is that what they do?" Jonas said. "And *'lektion*—what's that?"

"Well, *'lektion,* you know, is the day when they *selekter* the men to *rønne officerne.*"

The newcomer wasn't quite sure what this *rønne officerne* was about, but never mind. He would likely understand everything in the fullness of time.

"And what kind of education is required of a civil servant here?" he asked.

"Do you mean if they are *edjukæta?*"

"That may be how you say it here."

"Well Sir, in English they have to be very well *posta.* They must *spik' fluentlig* as a *nætiv'* who is *bor'n* in America. *On de' hol'* it is difficult to move up in America."

"Oh!?" Jonas exclaimed. This was a new point of view. "I thought all did well here."

"*Vell,* yes—when you have *influens'* like me."

"And I suppose you have a huge salary?"

"Yes, Sir, quite big, almost eight *kroner* a day—more than twenty-three hundred a year."

"*Gudnes!*" exclaimed Jonas. That was a lot of money.

"But you need *pull'* to get such a job. You have to have *stænding* in *politiken.*"

"Of course. And how did you begin your political career?"

"*Vell,* Sir, I *vørka* for Warfield. He is sort of the *headbas* in *politik,* and when he realized that the Norwegians had to enter *citygovernmente',* I was the obvious choice."

"Of course. And do you have an elected office?"

"Do you mean if I am *elekta? Vell,* Sir, *'lektion* is not by *populær vot'* for all the best *offican'.* I for my part have been *selekta bey de' kustodian.*"

"Oh! And what kind of person is he?"

"Oh, he is sort of next to the *majoren* and the *guvernøren.*"

"And I suppose that you have many who work under you?"

"Yes, all on the *først' flor.*" But then his wife came with the *dinner-pailen,* and there was barely time for Mister Salmon to get to the court-house by seven.

"If ju calls at *mey offis'* at twelve I will *introduse* you to Carlstrøm and see if you can get a job with the city," he said as he went.

3.

Jonas took a walk to see the neighborhood. The street didn't look at all like the fine residential areas he had heard so much about. The houses were not well kept and the Norwegians in South Minneapolis didn't seem particularly well-off. A cow was tethered in front of a house. It wasn't like the huge cows in the letters from America. Nor was it well behaved. It simply looked at him, tossed its head, turned around, and grazed on. Jonas suddenly realized that this symbolized the reception a newcomer could expect. His initial enthusiasm had cooled off considerably after yesterday's adventures. It may not be as easy as he had thought to rise to a high place in society. But never mind: he would find a way.

He wandered from street to street, and at ten thirty he entered a saloon on Cedar Avenue. There were quite a few Norwegians there already. One of them seemed to be on good terms with the bartender and called him "Butch."[20] He was quite generous and *trita crowden* and entertained them with many stories. Jonas enjoyed himself so much that he almost forgot that he was supposed to be at the courthouse at twelve. He felt much more at ease with America; he could even speak English much more easily and was sure that he would like the *kontrye*.

Full of confidence, he boarded the Riverside *karsen* and felt he was just as good as the others who entered and left the streetcar. The conductor understood him when he said "courthouse." After a while the *mulene* stopped and he *jompa* off and went straight to the palace on Bridge Square where his cousin held such a high office.

Mister Salmon met him at the entrance. They had to hurry up, he said, to find Carlström before he went out to dinner. Carlström turned out to be a fine gentleman with a starched shirt and cuffs, a fine tie, golden chain, and new clothes. Jonas was struck by the contrast between Carlström and his cousin, and he was surprised that Mister Salmon was so meek and stood with his cap in his hand when he talked with a colleague and an equal, but he concluded that it must be the custom of the country.

The handsome Swede didn't waste many words on them. "Can't promise anything," he said, "but I'll see Sewal Olson. Probably he can take him in."

"And who is Sewal Olson?" Jonas asked when they were ⟨
again.

"*Aa, dot's de suerbas, ju no'*," Salmon answered, and sat down
box in the hall of the second floor and began to eat his dinner.

"*Suerbas?* What's that?"

"That's the man who *baser* those who *vorker* with the *suer'n*
you probably don't even know what a *suer* is! A *suer* is what they
sewer *on Norwegian*. They take all kinds of *refjus'* and shit out ⟨
houses and dig deep *ditcher* or ditches in which they lay *peips* or
as you would say, and then they *rønner* it through the *streeten* int
røveren, that's the river, the *Mississippien, ju no'*. The *vaterdepart*
supplies all houses with water. They have pipes for the water too.'

"And where does the water come from?"

"Oh, from *røver'n, o'kors*."

"From the same *røver'n* where they empty the stuff in the ⟨
pipes?"

"*O'kors*. The water is filtered and is just as good. Here in Am
they can do this sort of thing because they have such good machi

Jonas thought this was peculiar but said no more. It seemed to b
custom here to insist that everything was possible in America, an⟨
newcomer was determined to become a good American patriot.

When Mister Salmon came home that evening he brought good n
If Jonas turned up at the corner of First Street North and Plym
at seven the next morning, Sewal Olson would try him out. Jonas
proud that he too could "work for the city" and be a civil servant
would have one and a half dollars a day, not bad for a beginner.

The event was celebrated with a little party. Jonas, who still
some money left, *trita*, as his cousin had suggested. Salmon invit
fellow civil servant, Søren Torgersen, who was "something" in th⟨
fice of *countyauditoren*, and Ole Olson, who was bartender for Cap
Opheim in Normanna Hall—or perhaps it was for Wettergren at Vict
Hotel—Jonas wasn't sure he had it all straight.[21] It was a lively even

Olson and Torgersen were members of a Norwegian singing soc
and knew all the important Norwegians in the city. The greatest ma
America, said Olson, was a Norwegian who lived in Minneapolis.
name was John *Dobbelju*.[22]

"Isn't that a strange name for a Norwegian?" Jonas wondered.

"*Jes, o'kors*," Olson admitted, "but, you know, he's also called ⟨
tander and is a great *loiert*."

"*Loiert?* What's that?" asked Jonas.

"Oh, it's almost the same as a lawyer, only much more important. Well, John Dobbelju certainly *mæker* the rags fly," said Olson. "He has taken thousands of *kæses* in the *korten,* and he still has not *lusa* a single one."

"*Gudnes!*" Jonas exclaimed. If he didn't succeed with Sewal Olson, he could perhaps become a *loiert.* There may be more money in it than in preaching.

They had a lively discussion about who was the greatest Norwegian in Minneapolis. Olson's candidate was Arctander, but Mrs. Salmon claimed it must be Oftedal. Mister Salmon tried to be diplomatic. "Sverdrup and Falk Gjertsen aren't so bad either," he said. "They're all great in their own way."[23]

"Let's have a *skaal* for all of them," said Torgersen, who had no candidate and seemed more interested in the toddy than in the competition.

Jonas thought he learned a lot that evening. It was interesting that there were so many famous Norwegians. Perhaps he too would one day be a famous man in Minneapolis. It was past midnight when Torgersen and Olson left, and Jonas, who had to get up early, went to bed. He had learned that in America, civil servants had to take their duties seriously.

When Cousin Salmon woke him up at five thirty, the newcomer was dreaming that he met Arctander in the street and that the lawyer asked him to be his assistant. "A man with your gifts shouldn't go around wasting his time," he said.

The dream was so real that he was quite bewildered when he opened his eyes. "What happened to John Dobbelju?" Cousin Salmon smiled. "Are you sure you don't mean the bartender? You'll have to hurry up or you'll be too late for your *suerjobben.*"

"*Gudnes!* I had almost forgotten all about it," Jonas answered.

4.

I suppose you know all the great Norwegians in the city?" Jonas said to his cousin as they walked to Riverside for the *karsen* downtown.

"*Jessørri,* I do," answered Mister Salmon. "I am sort of one of them myself, *ju' no'.* Not so long ago I attended a bazaar, as they say, and met Ueland. He's a great *loiert* just like John Dobbelju, and the son of a man called Ole Gabriel, who was something in politics in the old country. Ueland has been a judge in Hennepin County. Lars Rand is another

great *loiert.* He has much *influens'* in *citygovernmente* and is *alderman,* but a friendly and nice man. You should hear him when he makes *syttendemai* speeches. He's *posta op* on history and knows all the great things done by the Scandinavians. He's what they call a Democrat."[24]

"But aren't all people in this country Democrats?" asked Jonas.

"Oh, no, far from it! Most people are Republicans, you know. The Republicans won the Civil War. The Democrats lived in the South and wanted to have slaves and when the Republicans didn't want them to have slaves they got mad and started the war. And they *mæka va'r* on each other for five years and the Democrats *lusa* and there were hardly any left when the war was over. But, you know, quite a few have come up again *aftervards.*"

"But why in the world would you elect public officials who want to have slaves?"

"*Aa, dot's diff'rent her in Minneapolis!* There's no *slaveri* issue here. The Democrats are for personal liberty and want the saloons to be open on Sunday so that *de' vorking* people can take a glass of beer and a schnapps. That's why Lars Rand is *reelekta* all the time. It's the same thing with *Major* Ames.[25] He believes that people should have the right to do what they want, so he is *elekta* every time he *rønner.*"

"So you're a Democrat?"

"*Sjur'* pop, in local politics for the time being, you know. But I'm a Republican too, when it's necessary to change the city government for *de' gud* of *de kommen* people. But now we have a Democratic city-government and then we *officeholdera* have to be *solidari,* you know. Otherwise it would be impossible to *meintæne* any authority, you know."

Jonas thought this was a strange view of public affairs but he didn't want to criticize the country's political institutions. Moreover, they were now on Riverside and there came the *karsen.* As the streetcar turned onto Cedar Avenue, Mister Salmon said, "There on the *korne'* is Scandia Bank. It's run by A. C. Haugan, who made a lot of money in the *grocery-bisness.* He's a very nice man. Kortgaard is another banker and they're both known for their Norwegian integrity. If you're ever able to *sæva* a shilling, you can *deposite'* it with Haugan or Kortgaard. They're as *sæf'* as the Bank of Norway. And the Riverside police station is in the same building. A Norwegian is in charge there too. He's a captain and his name is Louis Ness. Captain Ness is just about the most famous Norwegian in the city."[26]

"Are there many Norwegians in the police?" Jonas asked.

"On the *forcen,* you mean? No, just Captain Ness and Stavlo and Kvittum, and a few others.[27] It's the *Eirisa* who *rønner police forcen.*[28] But if there is a really great criminal or murderer to be *'restes* they have to send for Captain Ness. He's quite a guy!"

"And what about the *suerdepartementet?* Who *rønner* it?" Jonas took care to stress the word *"rønner"* since he wanted his cousin to know that he was learning English quickly.

"Oh, that is *de' Svid's.* Carlström is a *Svid,* too. It is a great *'onor* for a Norwegian to get in there."

"But what do the Norwegians do? There are so many of them."

"Oh, for the most part they *peile lomber* and some of them *vorker* in the sawmills and others in the flourmills. About two dozen are *klerker* in *storom* but they are in a sort of class by themselves—not much more than their collars and ties and clothes, you know, and walking sticks and shiny shoes and a brass front. There are many Norwegian *bartendera,* and they are pleasant and nice people. I know them all. But here is Nicollet and I'll have to *jompe* off! Remember that you must get off the *karsen* on Plymouth Avenue and then go to *de' reit* and then you'll get to the *suer'n* between First and Second Street North where you'll find Sewal Olson. *Gudbey!*"

And with that he *jompa* off.

Jonas was five minutes late when he arrived at the appointed corner. Sewal Olson was a huge, broad-shouldered Swede. Jonas was surprised to see the man who *rønna* the whole *bisnessen* in workman's clothes, but he was struck by the importance of the occasion as he approached the *basen.* He thought he was lucky to get a position with the city so fast.

"Ju' ban' the boy that Carlström was talking about?" Sewal asked without waiting for an introduction. "You're late," he grumbled. "Work begins at seven! Are you a Norwegian?"[29]

"Jessør," Jonas replied and straightened his back. He was certainly not ashamed of his heritage and he wanted the Swede to know this from the start. Sewal Olson looked at him in a manner that the newcomer disliked. Indeed, he had no liking for Swedes.

"Do you know how to work?" asked the *sewerbosen.* Jonas's hands were not those of a first-class workingman.

"O'kors," said Jonas. "I can do any kind of work."

"Ju' ban' worked on a *suer* before?"

"Ju bet—in Kongsvinger." Jonas realized that the *basen* knew he was lying, but never mind; here in America you had to make do as best you could.[30]

"*Vel, Sir, ju' skol hav'* a chance *fer te' prov' it,*" said the Swede, and he handed him a shovel and sent him down into the deep ditch where the others were hard at work. Sewal told another Swede he called Nels to make sure that the newcomer proved his worth, and then he left. Nels seemed friendly. He patiently explained what had to be done and appeared to be a kind of *underbas.* When Jonas had learned the rudiments, he started to work and Nels went off to check on another team over on First Street. Jonas had read that people worked much harder in America than in Norway. If you wanted to advance quickly you would have to get going. His workmates took it easy and laughed at him.

"How much do you get paid?" one asked him, and gestured to his neighbor.

"*Mæbbe* he's just working up an appetite," laughed another, and leaned on his shovel.

"Bet ye' he's just come fer to set a bad example," said a third.

"Bet ye', by gosh, that we can *getta* the starch *out'r 'im,*" exclaimed the first one. "We don't want a Norwegian to think he can teach free Swedish men a new way of life."

Jonas was no longer able to control himself. "Shut up, you scrap of a Swede," he said, and worked on. The Swede took a step toward him.

"So? The Norwegian gentleman is a little upset, hey?" he said. "Has he *mæbbe forgettat* that Norway is governed from Stockholm?" Now Jonas was in a rage.

"Norway governed itself before the Swedes were invented!" he cried. "And every time a Swede stuck his nose too far across the border he got his due." Suddenly Jonas found himself in a vice. Two arms strong as iron held him as he was showered with Swedish oaths and expressions the like of which he had never heard before.

Under ordinary circumstances Jonas wouldn't have dared to put himself in such a tough spot. But this had happened so fast that he hadn't had time to figure out a retreat. He was scared. Too late, he realized that he would probably be killed for having stood up for his fatherland. He shivered. Imagine coming all the way to America just to be beaten to death. The Swede shook him and insisted that if he didn't immediately and at once ask forgiveness for what he had said about the Swedes he would crush every bone in his sinful body. Jonas, who always had known how to keep out of danger, felt like a kitten in the Swede's powerful arms. Now he must come up with something—and fast. To ask forgiveness of a Swede was out of the question. Then he got the bright idea that if he didn't have the strength to beat up the Swede, he could at least use his mouth.

"A Norwegian has never begged forgiveness of a Swede!" he began.

"Is that so?" cried the Swede. "*Vel,* it will *hæpna* right now!" He held Jonas with one hand and was about to hit him with the other. But at that moment something happened. Nels had returned and witnessed the little play, and Jonas's assailant was given such a push that he rolled over like a sack. The others, who had been enjoying the fight, quickly took their shovels and returned to work. Even the aggressive one got up and joined them without a comment. Jonas did the same. Nels didn't say a word but they all felt his authority.

At the supper table Jonas told his Cousin Salmon that he had been attacked by a Swede because he had defended his land and his nation.

"And I suppose you were *licka*?" said Salmon.

"What was that you said?"

"You got a beating, eh?"

"A beating? Me?" Jonas exclaimed in surprise. "*Nosørri*! It was the Swede who got a beating—and he wasn't the first Swede I've had to take care of," he added with some dignity.

5.

When Jonas woke up the morning after his first day of work for the city, he was stiff in every joint. His muscles ached so much that it couldn't have been worse if the Swede had beat him up. So he concluded that working for the city wasn't the child's play he had imagined and he realized that it had been foolish to work so hard. He had to save his strength to survive. Now he understood that those who had learned the art of resting on the *jobben* were right. What was the point of killing himself in the service of the city? *Kille* himself—that's what they called it. Jonas had learned a lot of English his first day on the *suer'n.* As he dressed he wondered if it would be better to work in a private business. He didn't look forward to arguing and fighting with the Swedes—even though he loved his native land. But if he didn't turn up, the rascals would probably think they had scared him. Cousin Salmon encouraged him to persevere and he explained the many problems that could arise should he now try to find other work. He would get a better job with the city after he had learned the language.

So he decided to try. Nels had told the others to leave him alone, and for some reason took him under his protection. But when Jonas leaned on his shovel, as the others had done, he heard the voice of the *under-*

bossen: "Get to work, you devils!" If he wanted to be friends with Nels he would have to work—and right now he had no alternative. That evening Mrs. Salmon laughed when he limped in, pale and bent, and dropped his *dinnerpailen* on the floor before slumping into a chair. He realized he couldn't stand the woman and this became even more evident at the supper table: the bacon was spoiled, the bread stale, and the coffee beyond description. He had certainly arrived in America.

But he felt even worse in the morning. He was like a rheumatic eighty-year-old with one foot in the grave. *Gudnes!* Had he known that America was such a poor *kontry* he wouldn't have taken the trouble to come here. In Norway he had lived a good life and hadn't had to do very much. When he thought about it, he hated everything he had seen: the city, the country, the buildings, the streets, the *suer'n,* the Swedes, his cousin, and, especially, his *mississen* who couldn't even make a proper meal. But he had to get up. The woman was making fun of him again.

"This is different from hanging around in Norway," she said, "dancing all night and making trouble and then *slip'*[31] past dinnertime." And she laughed as if she had said something funny. "How haughty women are in America," thought Jonas, but he wisely kept his tongue. Cousin Salmon had told him that when the *mississen* had something on her mind it was common American politeness for others to remain quiet. A strange custom, thought the newcomer. He swallowed some breakfast as fast as he could and waited outside for Mister Salmon.

———•—•———

Jonas had worked four days, the longest and most difficult days of his life, and he still didn't know if he had done well enough to keep his job. But he wasn't so sure he wanted it. The truth is he felt rather sick. He couldn't even eat. People said this was because of the heat, and the heat was certainly awful, but the real reason he went hungry was that the food was so awful in America. It was unfit for a civilized human being. They had some sweet goo they called *ke'k* and something else they called *pei.* And then there was the *sommersaasasjen* and no one really knew what it was made of. The *beefstegen* was unchewable, and what they called *pen'kœks* was simply a mess. And if you got pork it was as old as Abraham. And they took the water from the *røveren* after they had emptied the *refjus'* from all the houses into it. Jonas hadn't had much experience with water; Nels had explained that beer was much better for your health, so that's what he mostly drank. But the beer wasn't good either.

They didn't seem to be able to brew beer the way they did in Norway. Nor did people seem to care much for each other. It was as if they only thought about themselves. If he only had money for the ticket home . . . But he didn't, so that was out of the question.

Jonas was in a bad mood when he sat down to breakfast the fifth morning. It was Saturday, and if he could survive till evening he would have $7.50 to keep himself alive though another week of misery.

Cousin Salmon was already devouring his *pen'kœks*. *Gudnes*! That people could eat such things and be satisfied with life! And the butter! *Gudnes*! It was so rancid that it smelled like a corpse even at a distance. Jonas shoved his plate away. He might as well show the woman that he was used to proper food.

"Can't ju' ita?" asked Mister Salmon, astonished. His mouth was full and huge drops of syrup were hanging from the ends of his mustache. The *mississen* just then came in from the kitchen with a new load, and Jonas started nervously when he saw her. His head was full of evil plans and his heart longed for revenge, but again he controlled his sinful nature and began to eat the cakes. The first thing he noticed was a hair in the syrup. He shivered and was ready to burst with all his accumulated anger. He shoved the plate away and again glanced up at the *mississen*. She looked vicious. He had better be careful.

"I'm not hungry," was all he said. The woman laughed spitefully. "Oh, I suppose it isn't good enough," she said. "We couldn't *expekte'* that what's good enough for us who have lived so long in America could be *satisfac'tri* for a fine gentleman from Norway."

Jonas's good intentions to be diplomatic and suffer in silence were whisked away. All he now felt was an uncontrollable rage. "I am not used to hair in my food," he hissed. "We had a clean home and my mother could cook."

Cousin Salmon was so shocked at Jonas's ill-advised speech that he dropped a big piece of *pen'kœk* in his coffee so that it spilled all over the not-too-clean tablecloth. He looked anxiously, first at his wife and then at the newcomer.

Since some of my readers are church members I will not give a detailed account of what followed. Simple justice, however, demands that I reveal that Mrs. Salmon denied all moral and physical responsibility for the hair in the syrup. It must have been from the *faktory'n* she said. But if he thought he was too good for her food, he was welcome to find himself another place to board. She was virtually born in America and wasn't going to accept bad language from a newcomer! He could leave the house as soon as he saw fit. Indeed, she would be happy to see him go. And she assumed that he had *plænty* of money so that he could *pey* for himself and didn't *nida* to *røn'* from the house like a gipsy!

Jonas did his best to get in a few words of his own here and there, but when the storm was over and he stood packed and ready on the porch, still filled with a terrible and indescribable rage, he had to admit that he had played a rather pathetic role in this thrilling drama, compared to Mrs. Salmon.

On their way in to the city Cousin Salmon tried to make Jonas understand how stupid he had been to fall into disgrace with his wife. These American ladies, he said, had to be *hændled* with the greatest care and respect. They were sensitive and easily offended, *ju' no'*.

"But aren't you the master of the house?" asked Jonas.

"*O'kors* I am the *bas, ju' no'*, but when you have *hitcha* up with a *married wife, ju' no'*, you have to be a *gentleman, ju' no'*, and *jus' kommen sens'* if you have it, *ju' no'*."

"Could you say that in Norwegian?"

"He who has common sense should use it, *ju' no'*."

"Oh, I see. *Jessør!* And as for me, I would use both force and sense when they get too crazy," Jonas declared. "If I had had such a stupid woman . . ."

"*Vat's dæt?*" Cousin Salmon exclaimed. "Is that an *insølt ægænst* my wife? The young people who now emigrate from Norway are *æbselut no gud'*," said Mister Salmon with great conviction as he *jompet* from *karsen* on Nicollet. "They have it all in their mouth and their rear legs."

6.

At last the wretched Saturday was over! Jonas was so upset after his humiliating battle with Mrs. Salmon that he had been touchy and aggressive all day. As the clock moved toward six he eased up a little but he still didn't know what his verdict would be when he got his *pey* for the week. What if they told him that they had no more use for him after he had almost *killet* himself. But when he had his $7.50 in his pocket and was told that he had worked well enough to continue through the next week, he finally noticed that the sun was still in its heaven, smiling down on the tired and sweating army of labor that streamed out of sewage plants, lumber yards, sawmills, and factories with their *dinnerpailene* to find a cool and nice place after a week of heat and hard work—in the nearest saloon or at home.

Nels had helped Jonas get a room in a nearby Scandinavian boarding-house where he lived himself. Nels insisted that the boardinghouse was really first class. Moreover, it was quite literally Scandinavian: the husband was Swedish and his wife Norwegian. And to top it off, a Danish girl served at the table. However, she spoke neither Swedish nor any other Scandinavian language because she was born in America and had lived among Americans.[32] But she was a very beautiful girl just the same.

The boarders, Nels had informed him, were mostly Norwegian, but there were a few Swedes, an Irishman, and two straw bosses from a sawmill who were always reminding the others that they were Yankees and making fun of their English. Before the day was over, Jonas had met them all, but he couldn't establish any relationship with the *Yankierne* since they were so ignorant of the Scandinavian languages. But they were looked up to by the others as authorities on most questions. Larry, the Irishman, was a friendly fellow who had grown up in a Scandinavian settlement and knew how to swear in Swedish. So he regarded the Scandinavians as family and even listened respectfully when Jonas tried out some of the English words he had learned. But the Americans merely shook their heads at Jonas. It irritated him that they obviously thought him a fool. But it troubled him more that he was unable to speak with the Danish girl, for there was no denying that she had impressed him.

But you shouldn't draw the conclusion that Jonas was a ladies' man. On the contrary, he boasted of not caring much about the other sex, and he had only been sort of engaged twice. This had all been due to circumstances. Circumstances were difficult to fathom. One can never foresee the unhappy complications into which they may lead an honor-able person! Jonas remembered it all too well. Inga and he were the same age. They both went to the pastor for confirmation classes and they usu-ally walked together to and from the parsonage. Later, when they were sixteen, they both liked to read novels. But it was difficult to find enough books, so they agreed to make their own little novel. No one knew about it until they were seventeen. Then Inga's mother became suspicious and sent her to a folk high school, and when Inga returned, she was so haughty that she hardly noticed him.[33] Jonas was about eighteen and was not inclined to beg for attention. Moreover, he had fallen in love with Anna Marie, who had been hired as help by his mother. She was such a sweet girl. But his mother had interfered and Anna Marie had been deeply hurt and had found a new position farther west in the valley.

Jonas had concluded that women only brought sorrow and embarrassment. At nineteen he pledged that it would never happen again; no, not even if he lived as long as . . . oh, what was his name . . . yes, as Methuselah. He had had enough heartache to last him the rest of his life! And Mrs. Salmon's cooking had strengthened his conviction that nothing could ever tempt him again, and certainly not these American women who were neither caring nor loving and who only expected a man to slave for them like a camel in the desert.

Such was his reasoning before Ragna Riis—that was the name of the Danish girl—entered his bachelor existence with a bright smile, and Jonas felt that circumstances were again taking over. She had smiled at him and he had smiled in return and she had asked him if he was "from Norway" and he had been almost overwhelmed with pride at being able to answer in English, *"Jessør."* And she had laughed and he had laughed and everything had developed by the book—except for the slight hitch that they didn't know each other's language. Jonas had never before felt so strong a need to know English. Imagine trying to propose to a girl who didn't know what he was saying! But there was no rush. For Jonas wasn't so mean a character that he wanted his wife to be a workhorse. American women were so used to comfort and were so sensitive. But he had met his fate and he wouldn't even try to struggle against it. Cousin Salmon had obviously been right when he explained that American women were of a more highly developed race than women in Norway. Come to think of it, Cousin Salmon had a fine natural instinct that commanded respect. His only problem was that he had drawn the wrong ticket in the lottery of marriage. If he had been given someone like Ragna, he may have moved on to higher things in life and . . .

After supper Jonas had gone downtown and met a hauler who had promised to take his homemade emigrant chest from the Salmons' to a store on Washington Avenue where he could buy a brand new American trunk. Jonas had so much respect for culture—especially now that he had met the Danish girl—that he realized that he couldn't have his things in an old Norwegian chest here in America. In two hours the splendid trunk was in his room. It may not have been as well made as his chest, but it was much more elegant. Instead of the large and rough fittings of iron, this one had fittings of brass that shone as bright as gold. Jonas had let the carter have the old chest for nothing—if he would help him get rid of it.

So now Jonas sat in his room and felt almost like a gentleman. The room wasn't large but it was nice to sit there and contemplate that Ragna would be taking care of his room, making sure that it was always clean and tidy . . .

When he was downtown he had gone to a bookstore on Washington Avenue and bought a copy of *100 Timer i Engelsk*, an English textbook for beginners, and he had worked out that if he used the evenings diligently, he should be able to learn enough English to invite Ragna to a dance and bazaar next Saturday at Harmonia Hall. He had seen the advertisement in *Budstikken*. Ladies had free entrance so it would only cost him a *daler*. The program had songs by John Dobbelju and a reading by Lars Rand of Ibsen's poem "Terje Viken." Jørgen Jensen, the editor, was to play the Hardanger fiddle. Jonas wasn't quite sure about the order of these items on the program but he knew that all the Norwegian celebrities would be there and he was sure that the evening held great promise.[34]

Some readers may have believed that Jonas no longer respected all things Norwegian just because he was beginning to feel American. They would have clearly been mistaken. As he strolled around downtown he thought of his coming marriage and that he should then be a member of a Norwegian congregation—preferably the Synod congregation where Vangsnes was pastor, since he didn't want to be in a Conference congregation along with the unpleasant Mrs. Salmon.[35] He had heard of a Scandinavian Workingmen's Society and he decided to join even though he wouldn't remain a laborer much longer. He was an ambitious man who wanted to get up and ahead in the world. He had given this much thought recently. He had decided not to be a pastor because Nels had told him that they hardly made any money. To become a *loiert* would take too much time now that he was about to place his feet under his own table. There were so many things a gifted man could make of himself in this country. But now it was almost midnight and he was so sleepy that he had better go to bed.

7.

It was Wednesday evening just after supper. There has never been a newcomer so serious about his English studies as Jonas was that week. He hadn't only studied till late at night but had even brought his textbook *100 Timer i Engelsk* to work and had used every minute left of the dinner break after he had eaten to immerse himself in the book. His Swedish colleagues had teased him and made all kinds of suggestions about his real motives.

"Bet je' he's goin' fer to get married," said one who preferred to speak in what he thought was English.

"*Mæbbe* it's the girl in the *bordinghuset*," said another.

"No, sir, she isn't planning to get married," said a third. "Women are smarter than *dey looks like* and I don't believe that he has a chance with the other sex on this side of the grave. I think he is getting ready to *rønna* for office."

"He'd *mæbbe mæk'* a good coroner," laughed the English speaker.

Jonas was determined not to pay them any attention but every now and then he couldn't help being a little irritated, and then he would blush, take courage, and bark back: "Oh keep your mouths shut, you idiots!"

He never went any further, partly because they were so many and he was so few, but also because they meant no harm. Moreover, Nels would have no fights and had threatened to fire anyone who started one. Jonas had great respect for his boss, and now that he was determined to become something in the world he had also decided that he had better stay on as friendly terms as possible with the Swedes, since they had so much influence in the city. There were far more Swedes than Norwegians with white shirts in the courthouse.

But he might as well be honest with himself: there was a woman behind the new and purposeful life that he so suddenly had embarked upon. In biographies of great men, he had read that they wouldn't have amounted to much without women to inspire them. He realized that he should be grateful that he—more or less in the last moment—had been so lucky as to find the woman who could support the ambitions that in so miraculous a manner had become part of his personality. What if he hadn't met her until it had been too late . . .

Jonas's current aim was to teach himself enough English to dare to ask Ragna to come with him to Harmonia Hall on Saturday. By Wednesday he had learned so much that he thought he could do it. He had written the words down several times and had learned them by heart, and he repeated them to himself all day long. And now he sat at the supper table as silent and as serious as at a funeral. He had suddenly realized that this wouldn't be as easy as he'd thought. The more he looked at Ragna as she waited on the table, the more problematic it seemed. Even though he had prepared himself so well, he worried so much that he lost his appetite. Just seeing her made him incredibly insecure. It was remarkable how such womanly affairs could become so complicated and take all energy and self-confidence from an adult person! Finally it had seemed so difficult that he even considered getting Nels to ask her on his behalf. But that too would have been rather awkward. So he had better just get it done with . . .

He was still wearing his work clothes, and the situation would no doubt be entirely different when he had changed to the new *sui'ten* he had bought for the event on the installment plan from John Øfstie on Hennepin Avenue, and the patent leather shoes that had cost him his last two-and-a-half dollars at the fire sale on First Street.[36] Clothes can have a remarkable impact on the great moments in a person's life. He took his time cleaning up and changing his clothes. At least she couldn't say that he came to her as a newcomer . . . For the last time, he studied the words and expressions he had put together for his great and final test, and he was quite confident when he finally entered the kitchen.

Ragna hadn't finished her work, and she nodded in his direction and smiled as usual. "Fine evening," she said to fill in the silence.

He couldn't have been more overwhelmed had she asked him to go to a hot place. As if by magic, what remained of his courage disappeared. He had never experienced anything like it—he who had twice been almost engaged! After a while he mustered the courage to say, *"Jessør,"* but then she laughed so merrily that he was again struck dumb by his own embarrassment.

So there he stood, a grown man, stupid as a donkey and with no idea of what to do. She smiled again, as sweet as ever. But now he felt that there was some spite in her smile. She was probably making a fool of him. That would be a pretty thing after all the trouble he had gone through for her sake. But that's the way it was with womenfolk! You could never rely on them. As soon as you thought you had them, they were off, and their fickleness was unmatched in all Christendom. But he couldn't stand here like a sheep much longer. After all, he was a man. He straightened himself to his full height and said slowly and with each word underlined three times: *"Ei vil taak to ju."*

He didn't dare look at her. She put down her dishcloth and smiled again, and this time she evidently felt some compassion for her helpless victim.

"Well," she said and looked inquiringly at him, "what did you want to say to me?" She didn't seem the least bit discomforted even though she was "just a girl"; so much for the logic of our existence! But he had to get his words out even if he had to pull them through his ribs.

"Ei vil to Harmonia Hall Saturday," he said bravely.

"Well," said Ragna, "Don't you know the way, perhaps?" Jonas didn't understand this. He assumed she was either teasing or taunting him, but there was nothing he could do about it. He had started and now he would have to show her that he wasn't a man to be fooled around with by any woman.

"*Ei vant ju to gaa,*" he said and looked right at her. "*Ei and ju gaa.*" He took a deep breath. Now he had said it! *Gudnes,* how tough it had been.

"You are probably afraid to go out alone after dark," the girl teased him. Jonas looked at her in dumb incomprehension. He was persistent.

"*Ei vant ju to gaa,*" he repeated.

"And s'pose I don't want to go, what'll you do then?" Ragna laughed. He had only the vaguest notion of what she was saying.

"*Ei vant ju to gaa,*" he repeated once more; now with more confidence in his voice.

"Well, can't you see, I'm thinking about it? What's your hurry, anyway?" she said somewhat impatiently. "It's for me to say whether I want to go, isn't it?" This too was far more than Jonas could construe, but he understood enough to realize that her arguments were getting weaker.

"*Nossør,*" he said quickly and took a step toward he. "*Ju sey jessør!*" His voice now had the ring of command. The girl laughed with open mouth.

"Yessir," she called out loudly. "If I can, I'll go; so there!" Whereupon she turned around and continued her work.

"Me very obliged," he said as he bowed and left.

The battle had been won. He felt strong and brave. It was almost as if all of America now lay at his feet. He had all along believed that he would be able to do it and the beginning was always the most difficult part. From now on things would be easy. And if he had Ragna at his side he would become a rich and famous man even though he would have to go through fire and water to achieve his aim! *Jessør, ju bet!* But the English language was a complicated contraption that could bring an honest man to dismay. *Gudnes,* why should the good Lord have made a world with so many languages . . .

8.

E ven though Ragna had more or less promised that she would go with him to Harmonia Hall, he nevertheless feared that something would bring all his plans to ruin. You could never know. You had to reckon with the uncontrollable circumstances. He had hoped that she would give him a firm answer Thursday night, but she had said nothing, and then all kinds of speculations began to circulate in his head. Perhaps nothing would come of it all! Fate might not care to bestow such happiness and blessing upon him! That would be just like . . .

It was Friday and she hadn't said anything. Even though she didn't look at all offended or anything, he was sure that she either wouldn't or couldn't go. Nothing was certain in this life and it would be difficult to find a world more fraught with insecurity! The only thing he knew for sure was that something terrible would happen just as he believed he was *sæf*. And he had prepared himself so well and taught himself English and everything and borrowed money for his new clothes and all that!

After supper he noticed that she was having fun with Nels. They laughed and joked and were in such good spirits that he found it indecent. Now he understood! They were making fun of him. She had been making a fool of him all along. As a newcomer he was evidently not good enough for someone who was born and bred in America and couldn't speak a word of anything but English! Oh, he understood them. She had known all along that Nels was taking her to the bazaar. But she had better not believe that he was going to interfere. He knew where to draw the line.

Saturday was gray and nasty and in the afternoon it began to rain. Indeed, for a while it was so bad that it was impossible to work. So Jonas had all the more time to contemplate his situation; his thoughts were in harmony with the weather. He had given up all hope and was both angry and frustrated. He was the victim of an obvious injustice, and Jonas had always been sensitive to injustice. He was sorely tempted to knock down one of the Swedes with his shovel when the Swede made a few remarks at Jonas's expense. It was the same scoundrel who had threatened to beat him up on his first day and he had been so insolent as to ask if he suffered from lovesickness since he was so silent and down in the mouth. Happily, Nels had just then been standing by, so Jonas contented himself with his heart's evil desires.

For the first time in America, Jonas felt an inexpressible longing for Norway. The glory of America that he had seen in Ragna was gone, and he realized that it had been an illusion. This was America! It could appear to be fine and bright and glorious on the surface but in reality it was but as a whited sepulcher filled with all manner of iniquity. No! Norway was different. It was a far better country and he would return to it as soon as he could.

When he entered the boardinghouse that evening he felt pretty much like an old, famished bull. But never mind, he wouldn't speak a word to a living soul. He would go right up to his room and change clothes—there was no reason why he shouldn't use his new *suit'n*. He was in debt anyway. And after supper he would go downtown and drown his sorrows and troubles at Stockholm-Olson's or perhaps even go to Butch's saloon down on Cedar. He wasn't particularly fond of liquor, and American whiskey was terrible, but it was just the thing for his present mood. He would fight evil with evil, as scripture advises.

Such were the thoughts that bounced around in his head as he dropped his *dinnerpailen* by the kitchen door before going upstairs. But no sooner had he done this than something happened. There is no saying what may happen when you stand in your own thoughts and expect absolutely nothing; and what now happened to Jonas was indeed quite a *sørpræs*! Would you believe that the door was suddenly opened and that a pretty and rosy little woman's face with two bright eyes appeared.

"Oh, there you are! When are we going?" she said. Had brooms begun to fall down from the sky or had the water in the Mississippi turned to Dutch geneva, Jonas could not have been more surprised. She was speaking Norwegian! She could obviously speak Norwegian and yet he couldn't quite believe his own ears.

"I . . . I . . . didn't know that you were Norwegian," he finally was able to stammer, "and . . . and . . . I thought you could only speak English."

The girl laughed. "I am neither the one nor the other," she said, "but my father was from Telemark in Norway and my mother from Lolland in Denmark."

"And you can speak Norwegian!" Jonas exclaimed. It seemed so impossible—too good to be true—that he feared that it would soon turn out to be a dream.

"As you can hear," said Ragna.

"And Nels said that you didn't know a word of any Scandinavian language! The liar!"

"Oh, Nels just wanted to have a little fun with you. Fun, that is. But now I decided that it was time to call it off."

So that's the way it was! The jester had convinced her not to say a single Norwegian word to him! His plan was to have them go to Harmonia Hall like two mummies so that Nels could make fun of him afterward and he would be the laughingstock of all the boarders. But thanks to Ragna the joke was over. She was a good girl to have on your side. He saw that clearly. To tell the truth, he was so happy that he could have embraced her in pure gratitude had it only been decent to do so. But it wasn't. So there wasn't more for him to do than set the time, eat his supper, and go up to his room and get dressed.

But there were some things that Jonas didn't know; for instance, that Nels had also invited Ragna to the bazaar in Harmonia Hall. She had answered that she didn't know if she would be free but that she would let him know later. After supper he entered the kitchen to hear what she had decided. Well, he actually wanted to know when she would be ready, because he was sure she was coming with him. They had after all been going out quite often, to the theater and to other events, and in his deep Swedish heart he had planned to use this occasion to let her know his true intentions. So you may imagine his dismay when Ragna regretted that she couldn't accept his invitation. She felt a little sorry for him because he was a good man, but she had made her decision. But Nels was unable to accept a simple no and wanted to know her reasons. But before he had time to ask he heard a merry song from Jonas's room. The tune was one he knew well from Sweden. Why Jonas happened to vent his feelings in a folk ballad from Sweden has never been told, but he did, and Nels's face turned gray as he listened to the well-known words:

> Oh the girl, oh yes, oh the girl, oh yes,
> Walking by on the country road, oh yes.
> Oh the girl, oh yes, oh the girl, oh yes,
> Walking by on the country road.
> She met me there on a clear morning,
> And the sun shone brightly in the sky,
> And she was as beautiful as the bright day.
> My heart—where did it go? . . .

Nels suddenly saw the light. He straightened up and looked Ragna in the face, but she avoided the lightning in his eyes. "I'll be damned," he said, and he left the kitchen.

9.

Ragna was at first rather quiet on their ride to Harmonia Hall. Jonas had no way of knowing about her meeting with Nels. Moreover, he was as happy and content as he could possibly be. He sat beside her with a sense of awe, knowing that he had invited her, would dance with her, and would pay for her when she took her chances at the wheel of fortune! Indeed, his thoughts were so pleasant that he couldn't free himself from a deep premonition that fate might nevertheless have some circumstances in store for him. Ragna became more talkative as Tom Lowry's rickety cart snailed its way into the city.[37] And God knows that the old and tired mules—that were, we may say, on their last legs and that would soon be superseded by modern streetcars—had served long enough to know how to take it easy.

When the two *jompet* off on Hennepin Avenue, the newcomer felt so at home in his new status that he couldn't have walked with firmer steps had he been a Yankee of the first rank on his way to church. He almost had to laugh at himself when he thought of how he had been ready to sacrifice his left hand to get back to Norway just a few hours ago. But this was a far better *kontry*. A new world had opened up for him—a new world of pleasure and promise.

First Ragna had to come with him to John Øfstie's store, where he paid five dollars on his new *suiten*. He wanted to demonstrate to the kind man from Trøndelag that he had done business with an honest man, and with a full sense of his own importance he opened a brand-new American wallet that he had swapped for a solid Old World but also old-fashioned one with one of his Swedish fellow laborers. An American wallet for American money! They were in no rush to get to Harmonia Hall. He bought her candy and chocolate and other good things. He didn't want to give her reason to complain that he was tightfisted on their first night out. There would be time enough for that after they were publicly engaged and had to plan a new home and a large family.

When they finally entered Harmonia Hall, Jonas felt as if he had known Ragna all his life. And now she had no problems in speaking to him in a language he could understand. He had never imagined that he would experience anything so wonderful and he let her know this quite often that evening. For Jonas was not a man to hide his light under a bushel and disguise his happiness. A handsome, middle-aged man was speaking as they entered the hall. Ragna told him it was Ames, the mayor of Minneapolis. There was a city election in the fall, she said, and Ames developed a great love for Scandinavians when elections drew near.

Jonas didn't understand much of what the great man said but he at least realized that the man was a great elocutionist: people were laughing and clapping throughout the speech. And afterward, Ragna gave him a rough idea of what he had said, at least as she remembered it. He had mainly spoken about the Scandinavians. They had a marvelous history, Ames told them. In the Viking Age they had just about conquered the whole world—England and Ireland and Brittany and Normandy and Frankland and Galicia, yes, even Jerusalem and Sicily. And when there was nothing left to conquer on their side of the goose pond, Leif Erikson had gone to America in a small boat, not much more than a washbasin, and discovered the United States. So this country was really theirs, and we others, he said, should be grateful for being permitted to live here.[38] The Scandinavians had settled and built the West and made Minneapolis the best city on the entire earth. It was nothing doing to govern such a city—you only had to let people have the liberty they wanted and then the rest would take care of itself. And you had to admire what the Scandinavians had done for church and Christendom. Nothing had pleased the speaker more than to witness this. In short, the Scandinavians were the salt and pepper of the country. Applause! "What's the matter with Ames?" "He-is-all-right!" And ovations without end.

Lars M. Rand was master of ceremonies and he added that when he thought about all the wonderful blood from Voss that circulated in his carcass, he was filled with awe. Among other gifts, he said, the Scandinavians had an intelligence whose "gigantic stupendity" was a living wonder for the entire world. Bravo! "He is too deep for me," Ragna remarked.

The affair at Harmonia Hall had been planned as a purely Democratic celebration, but John *Dobbelju* had heard rumors of this and turned up with no less a personage than A. J. Blethen, publisher of the *Minneapolis Tribune* and the worst enemy of the Democrats. And Arctander had of course made the necessary preparations: there were demands for a speech by Blethen from all parts of the hall. So Rand had to take the bitter with the sweet and invite him up on the platform. Ames and P. P. Swenson, the sheriff and the best-known Swede in Minneapolis politics at the time, left. It was said that Ames was to speak at a Catholic church auction later that evening, an event that also would be concluded with dancing and some kegs of beer. It was also important before an election that the Irish were told what great and marvelous people they were. Moreover, Ames probably didn't care too much about what Blethen had to say.

Of greater interest to Jonas was his meeting with the respected Carlström from the courthouse, who had introduced him to Minneapolis's great and only Ames. He had pressed Jonas's hand with a strength and a warmth that had gone right to the heart of the newcomer. The mayor assumed that a man from the free Norway was a Democrat, and Jonas answered, *"O'kors."* Now he understood American politics well enough to know that he would vote Ames for mayor; it would be hard to find another man as fine as he!

Blethen began by remarking that since he had arrived in Minneapolis he had felt a relationship with the Scandinavians. After many years of careful research he had concluded that they were actually related. He was of pure Scandinavian descent. He wasn't sure if he was related to the Swedes, the Danes, or the Norwegians, but he was inclined to believe that the relationship went back to the times when the Scandinavians were one nation.

Jonas was no less impressed by Blethen than by Ames, nor was Blethen less eager than Ames to say a few words to the newcomer and shake his hand. Jonas even got to meet members of his family. Indeed, he met several of the leading Scandinavians that evening and with a judicious use of his *"jessør"* and *"nossør"* and *"ju bet"* and the other phrases he had learned, he managed remarkably well. He regretted that Professor Oftedal, Pastor Vangsnes, and Pastor Falk Gjertsen didn't make an appearance. Ragna believed that they had stayed away because dance was included in the program.

American pastors weren't in favor of dance either. Ragna said that she liked to dance if the crowd was decent but that she hated drink: she would never marry someone who drank. Jonas argued that a glass of beer with your meal must be acceptable, but when she declared with great determination that this would never be permitted in her home, he thought it would be wise to agree with her. They danced and danced. Ragna was an extremely good dancer and Jonas wasn't so bad either, he thought.

The bazaar had all kinds of games and lotteries and other opportunities to waste your money. Jonas felt he had to play the gentleman with such a fine girl and his money flowed easily. As insurance, he placed a dime in his left vest-pocket to make sure that he had enough left for the *streetkarfær'*. They were not going to *kætche* him out of pocket when he was out with a lady after dark. He knew the ways of the world.

It was past one o'clock when they *jompet* off on Plymouth Avenue, but neither was in a hurry to get home. They strolled down the street, talking about everything and nothing—as is proper when fate has turned its smiling face on you. When they finally stood in the hall of the boardinghouse, he wanted to say something appropriate but the right words would not come to him. He wanted to come up with something dignified and poetic but all he could think of was the well-worn phrase: "Thank you for a wonderful evening."

"Thank you too," she said, "and goodnight."

Yes, it had been a wonderful evening.

10.

The first time Jonas met Professor Oftedal was in a store on Cedar Avenue. He had gone to Victoria Hotel to meet a friend from the old country who had just come from the West. His friend was out but had left a message that he would be back in an hour and Jonas had entered the store to pass the time. He had met one of the clerks, Monsen, over at Butch's saloon earlier that summer and he struck up a conversation with him. As they were talking, a broad-shouldered man with long hair, a quick step, and military posture came in. His sharp and fiery eyes under great bushy brows gave him an appearance of resoluteness. When Jonas heard the man speaking Norwegian to the storekeeper, he was sure that he was a prominent person, and the clerk told him the man was no other than Professor Oftedal.

Just why Jonas had imagined Professor Oftedal as a small, wizened, dogmatic-looking character is difficult to explain, but that's what he had thought. So when he had this giant of a man before his eyes, he couldn't help but exclaim: "*Gudnes*! Is that him! He has the bearing of a general."

"Oh, don't you worry," said the clerk. "He is a general in his way. He's a real general too—*mæbbe* the best one we have in this state. According to the Synod he would seem to be a general in the army of evil," he said, "but it *hæpner* that the parsons are *mistæken* too, so I wouldn't *empaseis* it. We've always had our share of theological squabbles in this country, you know."

Jonas had heard about such disputes but he was rather hazy about what it actually meant. "Aren't they all Lutherans?" he said.

"*O'kors*," answered the clerk, "and that's why they are always fighting among themselves. They stand together when it comes to other *dæmonitioner*,[39] but they are always at each other. This is the way in the best of families. The children fight and argue among themselves but as soon as they are among strangers they behave in an exemplary fashion."

"But why do they fight if they all agree?"

"Agree? Are you crazy? Of course they don't agree. They are only in agreement on the main issue—they disagree about everything else. Actually, there is one main issue that they disagree on as well."

"And what manner of main issue is that?"

"Oh, they can't agree on who is the biggest pebble on the beach." Jonas had a perplexed look. He had lost him completely. The clerk raised his index finger. "The greatest rooster in the barnyard, you kno' *on Norwegian,*" he whispered.

"Oh, is that what it's about?" said a surprised Jonas. "I thought that it was about doctrine."

"Certainly, it's about that as well. The thing is, you kno', that they can all prove—with reference to scripture—that the others have the wrong doctrine, and since a church must obviously be controlled by those who have the right doctrine, this is an issue of the highest importance."

Jonas began to suspect that the clerk wasn't all that serious and that he shouldn't pay too much attention to him. He didn't want to introduce Jonas to Professor Oftedal, but Jonas wouldn't let such a fated moment pass by without making use of it. Nor was he bashful and timid. So he went right up to the great man and introduced himself. In America he had more than once experienced that it was best to make oneself noticed. He thought it would be fitting to say something religious and he therefore remarked that he for some time had been thinking of joining a Lutheran congregation. He was sure that the professor would be pleased to hear this, but he didn't seem at all overwhelmed.

"Well, well, my young man," said Oftedal, "that is neither a very stupid nor a particularly original notion. I hope you will find yourself in good company."

Jonas was quick to add that he had been most attracted by the Conference.

"Oh, have you!" the Professor responded and fixed him with a look that almost frightened him. "And why do you believe that you find yourself most attracted to the Conference, my lad?" The question was so unexpected that the newcomer was quite perplexed. What in the world should he say? What did he know of the Conference or the other churches? Now he had brought himself into a pretty fix. But since he had been the man to get himself into such a spot, then he had better be the man who got himself out of it too.

"It has always seemed to me that the Conference is the church closest to the Norwegian mother church," he said resolutely. There he had him, so now let's see what he could do. But Oftedal merely laughed, and he laughed in a great, booming voice that could be heard all over the store. Jonas felt as if he had worms in his stomach.

"You're absolutely wrong, my lad," said the professor sharply. "The Conference is a free church with free congregations."

To Jonas it seemed that Oftedal had seen right through him and discovered that he was merely a hypocrite and quite insincere in his religious cant. And—if the truth need be spoken—his religious education had been rather superficial. He had only been to church once since he had been confirmed and that was while he was a farmhand at the parsonage. And if he hadn't been trying to flatter the dean's wife, he probably wouldn't have gone then either. But since everyone in America was so interested in church matters he had thought it best to pretend that he too was interested. Otherwise it might be difficult to get ahead. And now Oftedal was reading each and every secret thought in his heart! Now he was in a fine fix. But since he didn't want to surrender, he had to make up something. So—in a last attempt to rehabilitate himself—he said that he thought there was religious freedom in Norway too.

"Yes, for those who don't want to do or believe anything in particular there is all manner of freedom," Oftedal replied. "In the state church there is room for everyone and everything. It is much like a flexible ostrich stomach that can consume any rubbish you feed it. But that has nothing to do with a true Christian faith and a free church, my lad!" He clapped the newcomer on the shoulder, smiled, and advised him to go and listen to Pastor Falk Gjertsen. "Perhaps you will come to the conclusion," he said, "that you really belong in the Synod, for that is the spitting image of the Norwegian state church." And then he marched out of the store—like a general.

Such arrogance! thought Jonas. He hadn't been begging anyone to be admitted anywhere . . . Oh, no, the Conference could be without him for all he cared . . . He should probably join Pastor Vangsnes's congregation . . . He was a far better man than Oftedal, he had heard people say . . .

II.

When Jonas returned to Victoria Hotel, his friend Nikolai Skummebek was waiting in the saloon. He had already wetted his whistle in anticipation of their meeting, and now they could begin the more serious drinking necessary, in his view, for that bright and festive mood that was fitting and proper for a Norwegian from Norway when he met an old friend in another land after a long separation. In protest against social injustice, Nikolai had left the valley of his birth when he was eighteen. He had since wandered all over the globe, on land and on sea, and now came to Minneapolis from Wyoming.

To celebrate their meeting, Jonas drank to his health in a glass of beer, but the man from the West explained that this was against custom and tradition. Where he came from, people knew how to drink. Whiskey had proved its proof in the West, he said, and men had proved themselves as well. He swore to the pure stuff, or, as he called it, whiskey straight. When the innocent man behind the counter set before him a glass of water to chase it down, he took it as a personal affront and threw both glass and water in the face of the astonished *bartenderen*. Did he take him for a baby?

Jonas wasn't altogether comfortable with this introduction to their celebration. He remembered Ragna's words: never would she marry anyone who drank. But he couldn't insult an old friend. It wasn't easy to acquire friends in this world and you had better take care of those you had. They could be useful in situations it was impossible to foresee.

"That's dishwater," said Nikolai. "I never thought you would be such a suckling."

Well, then he had better take a shot of whiskey, but he would only have a tiny one, because he had drunk so little and so rarely recently that he feared that he wouldn't be able to stand very much. Nor did he like the taste of this American liquor.

"Taste?" his friend said in a spiteful tone. "Who do you think drinks whiskey for its taste? You must have become a regular church member since you came to this *kontrye*! Take a real drink, man, and show us that you've shed your milk teeth."

Jonas still had his doubts, but a shot or two couldn't do much harm. But he was determined to be careful and he poured about a quarter of an inch of whiskey in his glass. But his friend was on guard. No cheating! He saw that he couldn't trust Jonas . . . He had turned his back on the old gods and become a pietist. Nikolai realized that he had come just in time to save him.

"You can't place a tiny drop like that in front of a grown-up person," he said sharply. "It's as if you believe that I can't *pey* for a real drink. But there you are mistaken, because I have more than enough money." He pulled out a roll of bills so huge that Jonas was shocked.

"*Gudnes!*" he exclaimed, "you must have been very successful in America to have piled up that much money!"

"Well, I must admit that I have been quite a *sukces*," Nikolai responded as he straightened himself in his chair to give his words more weight. And with that he filled Jonas's glass to the brim. "In the West," he continued, "it would have been an *insølt at refjuse en fullgro'n normal seis whisky. Skaal,* man!"[40] Jonas took courage and emptied his glass. It tasted so awful that he had tears in his eyes. But his first reaction was soon followed by a pleasant sense of warmth, and life began to take on a different color.

"It's really good to see you again," he ensured his friend after yet another glass. He was beginning to feel rather sentimental about their meeting. And as the man from the West pulled out his roll of bills again to pay, there were two men farther down at the counter who glanced at him before they quietly left the room.

"If I were you I wouldn't expose my money in a *publik* place," the *bartenderen* warned Nikolai.

"Aa, you can *meinde* your *o'n bisnes*," answered Skummebek scornfully. "Or *mæbbe* you believe that I was born yesterday. Let me tell you that I have traveled all over the world and *rønna* up against all kinds of scheming devilry that man can devise. I have been on Sumatra and in Zululand and been a cowboy in Arabia and in Wyoming. And you think you have people smarter than me in this little one-horse town?" He pulled a gun out of his pocket and slammed it on the counter so that the glasses danced.

"You should let me place your money in the *sæfen*, anyhow," continued the *bartenderen*. "There is so much that *hæpner* after dark."

"So that's your little game," said Nikolai with a knowing smile. "So you think that I'm a real sucker, don't you—an easy mark, eh?" And he continued to talk about his travels and experiences that had taught him the lesson that if you couldn't trust yourself, you certainly couldn't trust anyone else.

Skummebek had had so many shocking experiences and gotten out of so many tight spots that he had lost count. He had led a mutiny on an English schooner; swum half a mile under water to escape from a pirate ship in the Aegean; leaped from a two-thousand-foot-high mountaintop somewhere on the coast of North Africa to save the crown princess of

Arabia from drowning, and turned down an offer of marriage; single-handedly arrested a dozen bandits in Wild Gulch and marched them with their hands in the air to the sheriff; won first prize for bronco busting in Wyoming; and had been in a whole lot of other adventures that had Jonas gaping with wonder. Nikolai was obviously quite a character. And yet he couldn't altogether rid himself of the thought that some of it sounded a little implausible. But as the many and frequent drinks found their way to his innermost being and kept his body warm and his mind bright, he was enthralled by their remarkable companionship. When he eventually had to leave for the last *streetkarsen* northward, it was difficult to tear himself away. When he had mustered enough strength to say goodnight to his friend, Ragna's image again appeared in his mind. His legs were not at all steady.

"*Gudnes!*" he exclaimed; "I think I've had too much."

"*Dot's nothing!*" declared the man from the West. "Have another drink and you'll be as sober as a hymnbook." And so they took another one. It helped. When Jonas entered the *karsen* he felt almost normal and he thought that if he straightened himself up a little in his seat, the two or three others who sat there would surely not see that there was anything wrong with him. He may have been right. The others had also almost missed the last *streetkarsen.*

———•———

After a little while the scene changed. Jonas no longer felt that he was observed by curious and suspicious eyes. He had entered a strange, dreamlike world where everything was quiet and beautiful. It seemed to him that he was in the castle of Soria Moria. It was difficult to climb the great staircase since his feet wouldn't do as they were told, but eventually he stood before the king himself who sat straight-backed and dressed up in silk, not on a throne, as one could have expected, but in a Norwegian *kubbe*-chair. And suddenly it was no longer the king but the queen sitting there, and she was even finer than the king. Jonas looked around in the great hall. Everything seemed so strange. And when he looked at the queen again, a beautiful princess had taken her place, and as soon as he recognized her she was a princess no longer but Ragna in her kitchen apron. She stood up and looked reproachfully at him, and when she turned and walked slowly away, Jonas could see that she had a troll's tail.[41]

"Hennepin *Ævnju*! Hennepin! Hennepin! Hennepin! Here, you fellow! Wake up! Get off!" It was the conductor who stood there yelling in his ear as he pulled his arm. Jonas woke up and looked astonished around him.

"Where am I," he asked in Norwegian. He had entirely forgotten any other language.

"You are on the *streetkarsen* just now," the conductor answered him in Swedish. "Tomorrow you will be in the hospital or *mœbbe* in purgatory. Hurry up now! Get off!"

Jonas got off, but not without difficulty. He often later speculated on how he had managed to get to the boardinghouse. But the fact is that he was in his own bed when he woke up at four thirty.

Jonas was unable to eat breakfast. Ragna regarded him with suspicion when she handed him his *dinnerpailen,* but she said not a word. Nor were words necessary. He knew what she was thinking. She had seen right through him just like Professor Oftedal and she had seen what a weak vessel he was. Now he had placed himself in a pretty fix. It seemed that he would never acquire sense. But he was going to change all that and become a decent human being. Next Sunday he would go to the Church of Our Savior and afterward he would have a private conversation with Pastor Vangsnes and apply for membership in his congregation . . .

12.

Nels hadn't been very friendly since the evening Jonas had taken Ragna to Harmonia Hall. Jonas hadn't understood what was the matter, but then something happened that gave him an answer. After having worked a while that morning, Jonas, who was tired, worn-out, and contrite, took a little rest, and suddenly Nels was there speaking to him in an unusually sharp and commanding manner. Jonas angered quickly. He had worked and suffered so much that he deserved to be left undisturbed. But before he had time to give expression to his feelings, Nels stepped closer and, speaking softly so that the others wouldn't hear him, he said, "You were out late last night and you weren't at all sober when you returned."

"What would you know about that?" Jonas responded spitefully. "Are you suggesting that my evenings are not my own do to with as I wish?"

"That's not what this is about," answered Nels. "You may go and drown yourself in the *røver'n* if you want, but if you do anything to bring harm to that girl, I'll personally kill you, just so that you're warned."

Now Jonas understood everything. Nels too was in love with Ragna. And he also understood that his motives for interfering went beyond jealousy. His troubled and sorrowful expression revealed him. The newcomer felt no more anger. A new sense of awe had taken its place. He felt that he stood before a sincere man and that they both shared something deep and true that was unknown to the rest of the world. Jonas was overcome by a sense of a holy obligation and was almost moved to tears when he responded:

"No evil shall *hæpne* to her if it's in my power to protect her—*nossør!*" And he understood that Nels had sensed what he was trying to say when he took his hand and pressed it so hard that it hurt. Then he turned around and went off without saying another word. The Swedes weren't so bad a nation, after all.

During their dinner break one of the workers had been off to get the morning edition of one of the newspapers. There they could read the following item:

A FOOL AND HIS MONEY
At four o'clock this morning, the Cedar Avenue police took into custody an apparently demented man on Cedar and 8th Street. He was taken to the Riverside Station where it was found that his condition was due to intoxication. Later, it transpired that during the night he had been robbed of three hundred and fifty dollars. Inquiries at a Cedar Avenue saloon divulged that the fellow, who gives his name as Nicholas Skummebek, had consumed substantial quantities of hard liquor, and left the saloon about midnight with a friend, a young man said to live in North Minneapolis. His companion is under suspicion.

The news had no particular interest for the men in the sewer. Such things happened every day. But the story made an overwhelming impression on Jonas. That Nikolai had been taken to the police station was one matter. That he, Jonas Olsen, was suspected of having stolen money from a friend was of an entirely different order. The more he thought about it, the more he saw the consequences of not being a virtuous and righteous church member and going sober to bed at a civil hour. Imagine . . . He had hardly tasted liquor since his first day in Minneapolis when he visited Butch and took a few shots just to be polite . . . and now this should *hæpne* just as he had made the best of resolutions . . .

You could never know the outcome of such a mess. Perhaps Nikolai had no recollection of how he had lost his money and perhaps he would even accuse him of having taken it! And for all his denials the court would probably find him guilty and send him to Stillwater . . .[42] *Gudness*, that he should land in such a mess now that he was on the road to success in America . . . He had probably made a bad misjudgment when he had come to this terrible *kontrye,* where there was so little justice that a man of moral standing couldn't enter a saloon and take an honest drink without getting into trouble with the law. The more he thought about it, the more desperate his situation seemed . . . What if Nikolai should die in the Riverside Station and not have time to tell the police that it wasn't Jonas but someone else who had taken his money! Then he would be sent into slavery for sure. He—an innocent man—would perhaps have to spend the rest of his life together with all kinds of criminal scum and perhaps his whole family would sicken and die of shame and sorrow because of his sinful life . . . This is what would happen to him . . . He felt it coming . . . A rigged case was probably being prepared against him right now. He had certainly chosen the right time to come to America. Should he confess to Nels and ask for the rest of the day off? No, Nels might tell Ragna. He would have to wait till evening . . . But so many things could happen before that time . . .

However humiliating and shameful, Jonas decided that the only solution was to pretend he was sick and tell Nels that he had to go home and to bed. He already knew that he had been drunk and the one was perhaps not much worse than the other. Nels let him go, but if he didn't turn up the next day at the right time he could expect trouble.

He was lucky: Ragna was out on some errand and Mrs. Johnson was taking her usual afternoon nap when he came home. He changed his clothes and about an hour later he was facing Captain Louis Ness at the Riverside Police Station. He was tall and slim with friendly eyes and a full beard. Jonas approached the representative of the law with respect and fear. With all the English words he could muster, along with the Norwegian that he needed in order to express himself, he explained that he had read the notice in the newspaper. The captain regarded him sternly, as may be expected of a uniformed policeman confronted with a suspicious person, but his expression soon became milder and he answered him in his good Trøndelag dialect.[43] Jonas had never been particularly fond of this dialect, but it now sounded like beautiful music in his ears. Hope returned.

First the captain made sure that Jonas had really been Nikolai's companion last night. Nikolai was not at the station just then but he wanted to send a *patrolmand* to North Minneapolis to bring in his drinking companion dead or alive. Jonas started. Did he really believe that he, Jonas Olsen, had robbed Skummebek? Yes, it certainly looked that way to Ness. All evidence pointed in that direction. *Gudnes,* thought the newcomer. He felt dizzy and he looked down at the floor in dismay. The captain fondled his beard. That would be twenty years in Stillwater, he said. But then he heard Jonas's deep sighs and continued:

"But you don't appear to be a criminal." Then he laughed, got up, clapped Jonas on his shoulder, and revealed that the two rascals who had robbed Nikolai had been caught three hours earlier at the railway station in South Minneapolis, just as they were about to leave the city. They had only spent $50 of the money and had the rest. Three hundred had been returned to Nikolai. And a little wiser and with a bottle of whiskey in his pocket to fortify himself on his journey home, he had taken the first train out of Minneapolis.

"So it's all right," said the captain, "but I would recommend that you *stirer klir* of such ne'er-do-wells as Skummebek if you wish to make it in this *kontrye*." Jonas solemnly promised he would and left the police station with a light heart.

Since he was in the right mood, he thought that he might as well pay a visit to Pastor Vangsnes and enter into his protection at once. He lived nearby and this was as good a time as any to become a member of his congregation.

A tall, handsome, and well-proportioned man with wise and knowing eyes met him at the door. He invited him into his office. Jonas told him that he felt that he needed the protection of the church because he had discovered that there were so many dangers on the road through life. The minister looked searchingly at him. He was surprised at the young man's candor. This was not the manner in which most came to him when they wished to apply for membership. What dangers in particular was he thinking of? Perhaps he could offer some guidance as far as one of them was concerned. No, Jonas didn't believe this would be necessary. His reasons for seeking membership were rather general. The minister had to smile. After giving the newcomer a few more questions, he promised to take care of his application.

"You have naturally considered that it isn't enough to be a mere member of a congregation," the minister concluded, "but a living member?" And, naturally, Jonas had considered this carefully! He was so sure about it that he had almost answered, *"Ju bet,"* but then he realized that this might not be fitting.

"Yes," he said solemnly, "I know."

That evening he was proud when he told Ragna that he had now entered the Synod congregation. He had expected her to be pleased, but at first she said nothing and her expression showed that something weighed on her.

"Don't you approve?" he asked.

"Oh, yes, there is nothing wrong in it, as long as you are a man," she said.

"What do you mean?" he asked.

"Oh, whatever," she said, and turned away.

13.

It took quite an effort for Jonas to rehabilitate himself after his adventure on Cedar Avenue. His greatest worry was that Ragna seemed to have lost faith in him. Ragna had become the only person that mattered to Jonas and he had really gone far out of his way to bring their relationship back to where they had been. He had not, of course, made a full confession. According to the books, this is what such a situation requires, and the newcomer had indeed almost accepted the necessity of such a solution. But as he listened more carefully to his inner voice, his natural inclination to avoid a confrontation became a decisive factor: he concluded that he would straighten things out as well as he could and with as few conflicts as possible. After all, he thought, they weren't really engaged yet. Although he chose "the line of least resistance"—or perhaps some would say, because he chose it—it was nevertheless necessary to make an effort to tidy things up. In this respect Jonas was much like most of us; instead of taking responsibility for his own actions he shied away from any kind of confrontation. Consequently, what could have been made up and done with in the course of a day now took weeks of worry and wasted effort.

He sought comfort in the church, which he regarded as an indisputable sign of his personal honesty and righteousness. He had joined the congregation of his own free will, and this was irrefutable proof that he walked the path of a Christian. Should anyone wish to know the truth, they could see with their own eyes where he went. They could see that he had made a decision and that he had the wisdom and the conscience to make the right one.

Jonas wanted to make it in this country. This had always been his intention. But the first condition for promotion was the possession of a good name and reputation, and here the church was so powerful that it was practical to wear its cloak of respectability. It would certainly do no harm during a business transaction to drop a reference to membership in the congregation of Our Savior. Vangsnes had made some remark about being a living member, and Jonas did not, in his own estimation, think this was unimportant. That too could be useful in many situations, both spiritual and material.

Strangely, Ragna was not, as we have seen, overly enthused by his church membership. She wasn't at all opposed to the church, but to her a scoundrel was a scoundrel, in or out of church.

Jonas had worked hard all week to get on the right side with the girl again. She had said very little and it seemed hopeless to regain her trust. One evening he was dismayed to see Nels and Ragna in conversation in the kitchen. You didn't have to tell him that this was significant. He was a man of the world and had so much experience of the female sex that he immediately realized what was going on. And he hadn't been mistaken; after a while Nels came down from his room in his best clothes, and a few minutes later he went off—publicly, openly, and for all in the boardinghouse to see—with Ragna to an evening's entertainment in the Norden Society's hall on Washington Avenue South. You may imagine that Jonas erupted, but that would be putting it mildly.

His first concern was to go where he could be alone, and up in his room he reflected on his situation . . . That she should go off and make a Swede of herself was taking things much too far. What had *he* done to deserve being thrown aside like useless scrap? Hadn't he treated her as a gentleman treats a lady and loved her with all his great Norwegian heart? And to see her run off with Nels as soon as the slightest misunderstanding came up between them—actually, it didn't even amount to a misunderstanding. American women were an unreliable lot. If everything wasn't right as rain, and they couldn't get a man to dance for them like a top, they would tell him *gudbey*. But if she believed that this would make him do something foolish, well then she was badly mistaken. She would see that he was a man.

Later that evening he met Karl Johan Arndt Lomwiig for the first time.[44] He had held some kind of public position in the old country without achieving the expected promotion and now he too had come to America. He had tried his hand at several professions: parish clerk in Chicago, bartender in Milwaukee, clerk for a *lumberkompani* in northern Minnesota, and *typesætter* for a Danish newspaper in Michigan. Strangely, he had not quite fit in anywhere. In his own eyes he was an undiscovered genius. One of his favorite sayings was: "The dumbest farmer gets the biggest potatoes." Norway was bad, but America was worse. Lomwiig had discovered that so-called democracy was really merely mob rule. America was a society without a nobility and without aristocratic minds.

The reader will have to guess how it happened that such a man sought a room in a boardinghouse for laborers in North Minneapolis. The fact is that at about eight that evening a bald, well-dressed man in his thirties had knocked on the door, and after a few minutes the necessary arrangements had been made. The only information Mrs. Johnson had was that he worked in a grocery store on Second Avenue. When Jonas shortly afterward came down from his room and became aware of the stranger, he wasn't inclined to seek his company. Lomwiig simply glanced at the newcomer with an unpleasant and supercilious smile and covered his nose with his handkerchief as if protecting himself from a bad smell. Neither said a word, and Jonas, who, as we know, had his own good reasons not to demonstrate politeness and friendliness, soon retreated to his room to continue his contemplation of the sorrows of the world.

At breakfast Mrs. Johnson's Scandinavian family had their first opportunity to scrutinize the new boarder. His presence created an abrupt change of atmosphere. Their usual relaxed joviality was gone. Lomwiig distinguished himself from his proletarian surroundings both by dress and demeanor. His white starched shirtfront and collar, short and correctly tied bow tie, and educated Norwegian were sufficient reason to regard him with a suspicion bordering on enmity.

"How did this fop get here?" asked Nels in a stage whisper. The question was for Jonas, but he had had a miserable night where his lovelorn thoughts had struggled with his misanthropy for ascendancy, and since he wanted to demonstrate to Nels that he was to be punished for interfering in his most personal and private affairs, he gave him no answer. It seemed to him that he and Lomwiig in a way were in the same boat, that they both had been placed in surroundings where they were misunderstood, unappreciated, and persecuted. And he would let Nels know where he stood as soon as they were alone.

It so happened that they left the boardinghouse together. Jonas hadn't wasted a word on Ragna all morning. She would see that he was a man. Nels was in a good mood and whistled a Swedish waltz melody as they walked down the stairs.

"Aren't we feeling fine today!" said Jonas when they were out on the street. "Had I had as little sense of honor as you evidently have, I would have been ashamed." It was good to get it out. But it didn't seem to make much of an impression on Nels, who just laughed. But then he stopped abruptly, gripped the newcomer firmly in his arm, and said:

"Do you know what you are?" This came as such a surprise that Jonas at first was nonplussed. He sensed that the Swede had robbed him of the offensive and he had no ready response. "Well, if you don't know," Nels continued, "then I do. You are the greatest Norwegian ass to ever cross the Atlantic."

This broadside immediately stimulated Jonas's slumbering intelligence. He felt that he could respond in kind and that he had the power of speech. "Then I must add," he said, "that it's a strange fate that I should travel 5,000 miles just to meet my master in the greatest Swedish ass ever to walk on two feet." Nels responded with a hearty laugh.

"You are not at all as stupid as you seem to be," he said.

14.

For several days Jonas had walked around in a bad mood without a word to either Nels or Ragna as he speculated on his situation. Regardless of how much he tried to convince himself that American womanhood was a worthless branch of mankind, he had to admit that there was nevertheless only one woman in the world for him and that the great question was how to get her back. For two reasons he didn't dare start a fight with Nels: in the first place, he would risk losing his job; in the second, the Swede was stronger than he. Nor was this the way Ragna would want him to rehabilitate himself; Ragna was such a sensitive person. Of course, if he went to her openly and honestly and admitted that he was ashamed of having been drunk and almost becoming involved in a public scandal, she and her good heart would forgive him. But it was exactly this kind of humility that was impossible for Jonas. He was a man and he couldn't let her get the upper hand before they were even publicly engaged.

He didn't speak to her again until Sunday. Once more he tried to make use of the church. Would she come with him to Our Savior? No, she said, she couldn't; she had to help Mrs. Johnson with the chores. So he went alone. At the dinner table he spoke at length of what a fine preacher Pastor Vangsnes was. The minister had greeted him and told him he was pleased to see him in church. Moreover, his application had been accepted without question.

Lomwiig listened with a sickly smile. "Church?" he said. "Well, I suppose one must put up a good appearance. For my own part I prefer walking my own way. I was once a member of the church for my daily bread, but that was the most bitter bread I have eaten."

Nels observed that the bitterness may have been mutual; it must have been a bitter pill for both minister and congregation to have Lomwiig as parish clerk. Lomwiig gave him a disdainful glance, but said nothing. After dinner he and Jonas sat in the parlor.

"Tell me, sir," asked Lomwiig, "what was the nature of your sin, that the good Lord should punish you with America?" The newcomer did not follow him at first and sat there like a question mark.

"You struck me as being of a somewhat civilized family. I have noticed that you can eat without swallowing your knife," continued the new boarder. He lighted a cigar. Then he asked, "Do you read books?"

"O'kors," Jonas replied.

"Listen, my man. You should stop using this awful language."

"Awful language?"

"Exactly! Awful language! This mixture of English and Norwegian is terrible. It makes an educated man want to puke."

"Oh, I see." Jonas remembered that he had heard distinguished people in Norway say the same thing about dialects, and he said so.[45]

"Yes, right you are," said Lomwiig. "It is an altogether suitable characterization; for among all the Mesopotamian languages, Norwegian dialects are the most awful."

"But they are the language of the people—the Norwegian people," Jonas objected. He didn't at all like the man's supercilious tone.

"Oh, the people!" said Lomwiig with a sarcastic smile. "I suppose you're a Liberal?"

"Ju bet!" Jonas replied. "And you, are you also a Liberal?"[46]

"May I request you not to make any slanderous remarks concerning the cultural standing of my family. I am of a respectable Conservative family and was born in Drammen."

Jonas was no expert in politics, but like most young people in Norway he had done his share of cheering at popular meetings. In those days, politics almost took the place of religion with rural youth. The new movement had implications beyond the grasp of Jonas for the future life and development of Norway. Nevertheless, his conviction that the events he had experienced were of the greatest import had become

ingrained in his character. The best-known actors in the political strug-
gles of his youth had, in his mind, achieved the status of popular saints,
whose names should be mentioned with veneration and respect. One
of the greatest moments in his life was when he had received a signed
photograph of the great Johan Sverdrup. Jonas still had it on the wall of
his room.

The newcomer had been brought up to believe that the Conservative
Party wanted to sell Norway to Sweden in order to continue the civil-
servant regime that had been such a burden on the farmer class. Nothing
of value could be expected from that side. He knew well the type he
had before him. He had seen it in many editions: paperbound, hard-
cover, and the finest gilded leather. And yet, strangely, he experienced
a certain pleasure in Lomwiig's company. It happens again and again:
to be brought together so far away from native shores creates a special
sense of brotherhood, in spite of political differences and mutual contempt. There was also another factor that influenced Jonas. Although
he despised all Conservatives, he nevertheless felt a certain respect for
members of the upper classes. Even though Lomwiig was a mere third
cousin of the aristocracy, he was still impressed. And he now had someone with whom to argue about Norwegian politics, and that in itself was
a pleasant pastime.

"Just wait! The time will come when you fine and mighty ones will
have to stoop to learn the language of the people!" This Conservative
snob would soon see that he knew how to defend himself . . .

"Well, should such times come about, I'm sure that all the better
people would prefer to immigrate to America."

"Oh, it shouldn't be necessary to go that far," Jonas responded. "You
could simply go east, over the border to Sweden, the country where you
really *belonger*."

"*Belonger?*" Lomwiig cleared his throat. "If you cannot speak, as
your gifts may permit, in simple Norwegian, then I hope you will understand that I won't be able to continue our conversation." Jonas didn't
like to be reminded that he mixed and now this snob was going to get
his due.

"We are in a free *kontry*," he said, "and we may *spike* whatever language we want." Lomwiig held his hands to his ears and grimaced as if
he had swallowed a mouthful of brine.

"*Donnerwetter!*" he said.[47]

"And this is the first time I have *notica* that you Conservatives are
so *ænxjøs* to preserve what is truly and purely Norwegian," Jonas

continued. "You who have fought to retain the Swedish symbol in our flag and have that and much more on your *consciencen!*"

"For all the glory of Jerusalem!" Lomwiig exclaimed. He pretended to wipe sweat off his brow.

"And who believe that it is plenty *good'n* for Norway to be *governa* from Stockholm," the newcomer persisted, "and who stand respectfully in your court stockings and bow every time the Swedish king makes a gesture, and who—"

But Lomwiig had had enough. He got up abruptly from his chair, scrutinized his hands as if to check if they had become soiled, and went quickly to the door. There he paused and said:

"I had thought of asking you whether you would be interested in taking part in starting a Norwegian literary society, but since you express yourself in the language of Eskimos I realize that that would be hopeless. I would enjoy continuing our conversation if it may be held in a polite manner and in one of the civilized tongues." Whereupon he left.

Nels entered shortly thereafter. He had bought new clothes and was as *slikk* as a new Swedish coin. Jonas had never seen the straw boss so nicely dressed. Something quite special must have happened and Jonas had no doubts about what it was. It was quite obvious. He had even shaved, had a new tie and polished shoes, and was humming merrily to himself.

In the meantime Lomwiig was visiting with Ragna in the kitchen. He had noticed her lively eyes and nice, red cheeks, and today he was so remarkably entertaining in his conversation that she laughed at his jokes. Jonas felt uncomfortable in the presence of Nels because of the implications of his new clothes and he left the parlor. Out in the hall he could hear Ragna's laughter and Lomwiig's voice from the kitchen. An uncontrollable rage of jealousy came over him. What business did this Conservative crow with all his reactionary views have courting the girl of an honest Liberal! And to imagine that Ragna could lower herself to laugh at his stupidities!

Jonas couldn't hear clearly what Lomwiig was saying, so he went closer to the door to listen, and now he could hear every word. And what he heard was this:

"You are much too sweet a girl to waste your time as a common servant." Jonas was a little vague about just what may have happened then, but when he heard Ragna scream he realized that the miserable creature had tried to kiss her. He rushed into the kitchen like a deranged man and filled with thoughts of revenge and other things the church has warned us against. Ragna was beating Lomwiig about the ears with a broom. The poor man was trying as best he could to protect himself, and as he retreated backwards toward the door he fell right into the arms of Jonas, who attacked him as a wolf may attack a defenseless lamb.

"You—you—miserable bastard!" he stammered as he took hold of the skinny and light representative of the Conservative Party and threw him up against the wall so that it echoed through the whole building. Ragna looked on with fear and was just about to beg him not to kill him when Nels came out into the hall to find out what was going on. Just then Jonas heaved Lomwiig through the kitchen door so that he landed in a heap at the feet of the Swede. Ignorant of the cause of it all, but with an instinctive understanding that the new boarder was guilty of something that made him deserve a beating, Nels picked him up and threw him out on the street. It all happened so naturally and with such precise and controlled action that it was much as if they were engaged in ridding the house of some impossible cat.

After Jonas had explained everything to Nels, they both returned to Ragna, from whom they expected praise and appreciation. But, on the contrary, she was angry.

"That was wicked," she said. "Two big, strong men like you beating up a poor and defenseless weakling! Shame on you!" and with that she turned her back on them and they slunk shamefully and uncomprehendingly off back to the parlor, where Jonas sat down with an album and Nels pretended to read a newspaper. Neither of them said a word for several minutes. Then Nels turned a page and said slowly, "Womanhood is a great mystery!"

"Yes, they sure are strange, *ju bet*," Jonas agreed as he put down the album.

15.

L ater that afternoon Jonas began to speculate on whether the Lomwiig affair could have unpleasant repercussions. When Lomwiig made no appearance at supper, his speculations turned to fear. Perhaps the unhappy circumstances that were always pursuing him were going to play tricks on him again. Wouldn't that be typical? What if he and Nels were brought to court and had to sit in *jailen* just because they had appeared as defenders of good Christian morality and decent behavior!

And Ragna would of course not move a finger to defend them. He now knew these contrary American women; if you took their side they would immediately cross over to the enemy and begin to *naakke* down their protectors . . . It was at least a good thing that there were two to share the burden . . .

After he had eaten, Jonas went out to disperse his dark speculations. On Washington Avenue he happened to meet Lanberg, a grocery clerk who had been quite friendly with him even though he was a lowly laborer. A man who had been here five years and had already advanced to a job in a store would usually not *mixe* with such plain folk. Lanberg's democratic behavior was all the more remarkable in that he also had literary interests and had contributed to *Budstikken*.[48] There were, however, bonds between them: Jonas had known the clerk's sister in Kongsvinger and, moreover, they were both Liberals.

As usual, Lanberg greeted him kindly. He was on his way to the Church of the Nazarene to listen to Kristofer Janson.[49] Would the newcomer like to join him? But Jonas excused himself, explaining that he was a Lutheran and shouldn't be going to a Unitarian church. He had heard so many things about this Janson. He was hardly a Christian, according to what people said, and he didn't want to be tempted away from the correct doctrine now that he had become a church member. Jonas had rather vague notions of just what this doctrine might be. Nor did he feel it was necessary for him to know much about it. Actually, he thought it sufficient that the ministers—who had religion as their *bisnes* and moreover were well paid for their trouble—should understand it. But Jonas didn't want to place himself in the position of an apostate. Moreover, should he go, Vangsnes would probably hear of it; people were ready to carry all sorts of tales. And, as we have noticed, the newcomer was an ambitious man who wished to advance in this world.

"Janson is an interesting lecturer," said Lanberg, "And a great writer."

"That may be," Jonas replied, "but his Christianity seems to be largely a product of his own imagination."

"For my part I don't care all that much for the religious aspects of his work," Lanberg remarked, "but there's much to learn from Janson. He's an expert in history as well as literature. And he's always entertaining. You should hear him knock down old gods. It's quite a picnic. I would rather listen to him than go to the Theatre Comique. And the way he makes fun of the other pastors," continued Lanberg. "That is a regular comedy!"

"*Gudnes!* Does he do that too?" Jonas exclaimed. He was now shocked by his own thoughts. He realized that Lanberg had been sent to him as an instrument of his temptation. So he said definitely no. He would not listen to Janson; not if he were given the whole world. He was content with his own church that was founded on the Bible, he said. Lanberg was accommodating and suggested that they could find other ways of spending their evening. They could, for instance, pay a visit to Arnoldus Bolivarius Lyvenfelt.[50] That too would be almost like a comedy, he said, only very different.

"Lyvenfelt—who is he?" Jonas asked.

"He is the famous writer of novels and plays. You must have heard of him."

"Oh, yes, of course, I had almost forgotten that he is in Minneapolis." The newcomer had never heard his name before, but he knew enough about literature never to admit ignorance of great authors. So, doing his best to pretend that he knew what he was talking about, he said, "Oh, yes, Lyvenfelt! He's almost as great here as Bjørnson is in Norway."[51]

"Yes, at least in his own imagination," Lanberg added with a good-natured smile. "And it cannot be denied that his books are very popular, whatever you may think of the man himself."

"And I hope he is progressive and popular," said Jonas. This was the most important yardstick against which all people should be measured.

"Well, yes, you might say extremely popular," said the clerk, and smiled again.

On their way to the Astoria Block, where the great author resided in an alcove in the rear of Franz Jeppesen's print shop, Lanberg informed Jonas about the literary history of Minneapolis. Knut Hamsun, who at that time was establishing a name for himself in Norway, had resided for some time in the mill town and had tried a variety of professions without much success. For a time he had been a secretary for Kristofer Janson. Then there was Arne Dybfest, who had been on the editorial staff of *Daglig Tidende,* which had been established by T. Guldbrandsen a few years earlier. He too was now in Norway. From Minneapolis he had gone to Chicago and mingled with the anarchists, and he was now said to have published something back home that had given him some attention.[52]

Finally they came to the Astoria Block. After fumbling through several dark hallways and staircases, Lanberg opened the door to

the Jeppesen print shop. There they found two typesetters sitting un-
employed, with an empty pail of beer before them on a box next to an old
lamp that sent off an evil-smelling smoke. To their right was the alcove
where they found Lyvenfelt himself behind another smoking lamp and
with his nose close to the paper he was writing on. Lanberg introduced
the newcomer. Lyvenfelt got up and offered him his hand and Jonas took
it with a sense of respect. To meet such masters in the world of the mind
was always a solemn occasion, he thought. When the visitors had found
two boxes to sit on (there were no chairs), the author folded his hands and
ensured them that their visit could not have been more convenient.

"And I assume you have a quarter for beer," he continued, speaking to
Lanberg, "so a dried-up carcass can have some nourishment."

"Of course," answered Lanberg, and he held up the desired coin.
Lyvenfelt called to the two typesetters, whom he introduced as "Life"
and the "Grave."

"Grave," he said, "here is a quarter for beer. Get going!" And off went
the Grave with the empty pail while Life, with a satisfied smile on his
face, turned an empty bucket upside down for a chair. Jonas found it
strange that the Grave rather than Life went out to get beer, but it wasn't
really his business. The Grave soon returned with the pail and placed it
on the table in front of Lyvenfelt. In these literary circles, glasses were
evidently not required. The author simply set the pail to his lips and
drank in long, deep gulps. He wiped the foam off his stringy beard and
passed the pail on to Lanberg, who carefully turned away and pretended
to drink without really touching the pail with his lips. Jonas realized that
the writer evidently couldn't see much of what was going on beyond his
immediate vicinity. So he followed his friend's example and passed on
the pail to the Grave who, with all the gravity suggested by his name,
emptied a large portion down his throat. Life was as thirsty as his companions, and when he was done there was nothing left. Without much
respect he set the pail upside down in front of the writer.

"I suppose you may have another quarter?" Lyvenfelt said after
a while to Lanberg, who again held up a quarter and placed it on the
table.

"Look, here, Life. Get going!" said the great man in the high seat.
Life grabbed the pail and coin and ran off.

When they had had another round, Lyvenfelt became quite con-
vivial and talkative. "Where do you live," he asked Jonas, and was
given the requested information.

"Then you may know a rascal by the name of Lomwiig?"

"*Jessør,*" answered Jonas.

"He is the hero of my new book," the author confessed. "You can read it yourself and find out who he really is. You can buy it here—seventy-five cents." From under the table he took a dusty paperback. *Fallen Nobility* was its title. Jonas paid and put it in his pocket. This was beginning to interest him.

"My next novel, *Shabby Prominence,* is based on real life here in Minneapolis," Lyvenfelt continued. "Great material; lots of dirt." And then he served up a long story about the "real" events. The author was obviously enjoying himself. He chuckled with pleasure every time he came to a scandalous climax in something he claimed to be the history of a well-known family. How much was fiction and how much was real, he couldn't say; but considering the fact that Lyvenfelt was a great novelist and that much of what he said seemed quite incredible, Jonas was skeptical about some of the "biographical facts."

"So, what do you think of him?" asked Lanberg when he and the newcomer finally were out on the street again.

"*Gudnes!*" Jonas replied.

———

Quite unexpectedly, Karl Johan Arndt Lomwiig was sitting at the breakfast table when Jonas came down the next morning. From the hall Jonas could see Ragna standing beside him, talking with him in a whisper. But when she saw Jonas she quickly returned to the kitchen as if ashamed. And for good reason, thought Jonas, considering how she had behaved. Strangely, Lomwiig gave him a friendly "good morning" as he entered the dining room. What insolence! Imagine that he could pretend that nothing had happened! The newcomer found it almost beneath his dignity to respond to his greeting, but he bowed slightly because he didn't want to be thought uncivil.

After breakfast Lomwiig took Jonas aside and surprised him even more by telling him that he had acquired a better position downtown and that he had recommended Jonas as his successor with Jenkins, the grocer on Second Avenue. He would advise him to go there himself during his dinner break and have a talk with Jenkins.

"I can't say I understand what this is all about," Jonas exclaimed. "But I must admit I want the job."

"Good. Then I'll see you later," said Lomwiig, disappearing out the door before the newcomer had time to ask any further questions.

At ten minutes to twelve Jonas introduced himself to Mister Jenkins and his Norwegian clerk, Lars Simonsen, and half an hour later he left the *grocerystoret* with assurances of a steady job and a good salary, with a raise when he learned to speak English and work more independently. And Jonas knew he was going to make it—no question!

On his way home that evening he had his first opportunity to tell Nels about what had happened. "Can you understand," he said, "how this character is put together? How could he have done this after what happened yesterday?" Nels spat dryly.

"Oh, that girl isn't so stupid," he said. "She has more than enough sense for both of you—which is a good thing considering that you have none of your own."

Jonas began to see a narrow strip of light in the dark.

16.

Jenkins had run his grocery business in North Minneapolis for as long as anyone could remember. He had made a fortune on the Scandinavians and there were rumors that all of it hadn't been made legally. Such rumors had increased after Johan Stunsrud opened his store on First Street and became an increasingly formidable competitor. In lively colors, Stunsrud would describe how "the old Yankee fox" frequently and systematically had cheated credulous Norwegian and Swedish workingmen's families. No wonder, he said, that they never got very far in life, since Jenkins gave them such poor quality at such high prices. And if they purchased on credit, as most people did, he also cheated them with his bookkeeping.

Lars Simonsen, who for years had been Jenkins's right hand and manager, had his boss's reputation for smartness. This had given him a good name in the Norwegian colony: he was evidence that a Norskie could be as smart as an American! The Norskies didn't have to take the *bæksi't* to anyone! Stunsrud referred to Simonsen as the "Bookkeeper on Second Avenue." He was the city's best expert in adding up debts, he said. Stunsrud's campaign damaged Simonsen's reputation, but many continued to do their business with Jenkins—some out of habit; others because they refused to believe ill of Simonsen, a respected compatriot; and yet others because they were always in arrears with the Jenkins *storet* and couldn't manage without the credit they could get there during the winter months when there was little work and no money.

This was the situation when Jonas began to work in the store as a deliveryman. He was free to go to public evening classes three nights a week to learn English and other useful subjects. Simonsen had explained that good beginnings were essential for success in *bisnes*.

On his first day in the Jenkins store Jonas learned some of the essentials of his profession. One was how to tell the difference between a fresh egg and a rotten one when buying, how not to be all that particular about this difference when selling, and then what to say when you were caught making the mistake of confusing the rotten with the fresh when selling to a customer who was poor or in arrears. On the whole, the art of not losing a customer who believed he had been cheated was an extremely important one, said Simonsen, and must be mastered. Another useful skill was to weigh in such a manner that the business would benefit, without giving the customer the impression that he'd been shortchanged. This was one of Simonsen's specialties. He had until recently been known all over Minneapolis for his liberality in weighing. He would let it appear that the customer got a little extra, but Stunsrud insisted that he actually gave too little. He had a way of throwing a package on the weight so that it went over the mark and then quickly taking it off before the weight had balanced, saying that a little extra meant nothing between friends.

Jonas learned quickly. Simonsen was proud of his new student, even though he didn't express his appreciation to Jonas. To teach him was almost like operating an automaton. As soon as he had his instructions he executed them with exemplary precision. Only once did Jonas come to Simonsen with a question on his first day. When Simonsen had explained how to sell a shipment of spoiled fruit by carefully blending it in small portions with fresh fruit, Jonas had wondered whether this, strictly speaking, could be said to be honest.

"At present the question of honesty is none of your business," said his boss. "We haven't hired you to pass judgment on our firm. We are responsible for our *bisnes* methods. You must simply do as you're told. When you start your own business you're welcome to hold on to all the rotten eggs and spoiled fruit you wish, should you come to the conclusion that that would be the more profitable method. But here you simply do as I say, see?"

"*Jessør*," Jonas said.

"At the moment this is also your road to a better life," Simonsen added.

"I understand," answered the newcomer, "but $40 per month is a somewhat small foundation for a better life."

"Oh, we should be able to find a solution to that problem," said his boss. "But, as you know, we are getting pretty tough competition from the jailbird on First Street. Your success will to a great degree be determined by how quickly we can get rid of him."

Jonas decided that as soon as he got the hang of things he would do his best to undermine the influence of Johan Stunsrud. He saw that this would be to his advantage, but there was another reason why he was eager to bring down their competitor. Some time ago Stunsrud had advertised for a clerk and Jonas had dropped in one evening to inquire, but Stunsrud had been overbearing and spoken contemptuously of a newcomer's qualifications for business. He could come back in five years or so, the storekeeper had told him. When he had learned the language and knew more about conditions here he might be able to get a job. The trouble with newcomers, he had added, was that they didn't know that they didn't know anything and they walked around with their heads filled with false perceptions of their own ability and worth. It was different in "the old days"—that is, ten years ago when Stunsrud himself was a newcomer and had been a clerk in Fargo. Then newcomers understood that they had to work patiently and that they couldn't expect to have their own business the first day. In short, Stunsrud had let his mouth run off with him and Jonas had left *storet* with his fist in his pocket. So Simonsen's seed fell on good ground.

Some days later Simonsen remarked that Jenkins was getting old and that perhaps he would retire from business in a year or two.

"And what will happen then," asked Jonas.

"That's difficult to know," answered Simonsen. "But it's at least one more reason to keep eyes and ears open. There are all kinds of possibilities in *bisnes*."

In Jonas's mind, Ragna loomed larger and larger in these possibilities. It had puzzled the newcomer that Lomwiig had recommended him of all people to Jenkins. Nels had suggested that the girl was somehow behind it. And gradually Jonas had realized that this must be the explanation. She had made use of Lomwiig's transgression to force him to get Jonas a job. Just how she had done it he couldn't fathom.

He would have to reestablish his relationship with Ragna as soon as possible. He could no longer regard Nels as a serious rival. She had wanted to give him some deserved punishment, but he had remained the man of her thoughts . . . These American women were indeed all right—as he had realized from the very beginning. When he again approached her, he did so with deliberate tact.

"I hope you aren't mad at me?" he asked. She laughed, and her laughter was spontaneous and natural. "You are a strange character," she said.

When Jonas learned that Simonsen was Lomwiig's uncle, he was sure of Ragna's role in getting him the position with Jenkins. So Simonsen must be Lyvenfelt's model for the character Kvastvik, the customs treasurer in *Fallen Nobility,* where two generations of his and Lomwiig's family had been described as a decayed and degenerate lot. The book had not increased Jonas's admiration for its author, but Lanberg had explained that much of his venom was obviously caused by the author's own disappointment and bitterness at the bad turns life had given him. Lomwiig was a snob, Lanberg added, but otherwise a kind and harmless fellow. Simonsen had his faults but was a good businessman of whom there had been no complaints until Stunsrud had established himself in North Minneapolis.

When Jonas began his work as deliveryman he was surprised to see a copy of *Fallen Nobility* in almost every home he entered, and the housewives often referred to the book. The newcomer also discovered that Lyvenfelt was a regular guest at Stunsrud's and that the latter boasted of him to his customers as the greatest Norwegian writer to have *krosset* the Atlantic. Jonas thought this was strange: he couldn't see that Lyvenfelt and Stunsrud had much in common. Stunsrud liked to boast of his genteel background while Lyvenfelt had struck our newcomer as a character somewhere between a proletarian and a bum. When Jonas heard that most of his customers had received *Fallen Nobility* in the mail last Christmas and that no one knew who their benefactor was, he added up his information. So one day he told Simonsen that he had the solution to the puzzle.

"Well what is it?" asked his boss.

"Stunsrud has used literature to *rønne* us out of *bisnes,*" Jonas replied.

"What do you mean?" asked Simonsen, impatient because he was wasting useful time on something in which he could see no profit.

"The Lyvenfelt book, you know," Jonas began again, "is in every Norwegian home in North Minneapolis."

"Well, what of it?" Simonsen exclaimed, yet more impatient.

"Simply that it has been written, printed, and distributed at Stunsrud's expense."

"Well, what do you know!" He scratched his head. "That was a nice piece of detective work," he added after a while. "We'll have to give this some thought."

A few days later—and Jonas had now been three months in the store—Jenkins told him that his salary had been raised to $50 a month.

17.

On his daily rounds, Jonas had become convinced that Lyvenfelt's book about Lomwiig and Simonsen had really hurt their business. Down on Fourth Avenue he had heard a woman call Simonsen a scoundrel and a cheat who would stoop to anything if he could turn a profit. He had asked her on what basis she made such unjust accusations and she had shown him her copy of *Fallen Nobility*. He should read it himself, she said, and see what kind of man he was working for. Wherever he went, similar comments were made to his face, and he realized that something had to be done to counteract this growing unflattering opinion among the *groceri*-purchasing public. Or else the business would suffer.

Simonsen had his own methods. He had been generous with Christmas presents to his customers and had made a great effort to demonstrate his interest in their welfare. He had also done what he could to make the wholesalers and banks reluctant to give his competitor credit. But none of this seemed to be of much help. Stunsrud continued his campaign, and as long as people believed that he had entered the business as their benefactor to save them from the greedy clutches of Jenkins and Simonsen, it had no effect that Simonsen now badmouthed Stunsrud as loudly and insistently as Stunsrud scandalized Simonsen. To make up for their loss of customers in North Minneapolis, Simonsen had acquired some new ones in a small Scandinavian area in South Minneapolis. In part this was thanks to Jonas, who had made advantage of his church membership and advertised among the members of Our Savior. Simonsen was impressed but Jonas realized that there was little real help in picking up a distant family here and there if they continued to lose customers in their own area. Even though Simonsen was sure that customers would return when they had grown tired of their gossip, this in no way satisfied Jonas. Far more than for Simonsen, his own future depended on the total defeat of Stunsrud. If they failed, his boss would at least be able to get other well-paid jobs or perhaps even retire and live well on his capital, but for Jonas everything depended on not letting go of what he now had achieved.

He had been eight months with Jenkins and had good reason to be satisfied with his achievement. He knew the business and was quickly learning the language. But in spite of his remarkable progress he knew that he had far to go before he became the rich and respected man of his dreams. The straightest road to wealth and respectability would be to hitch his wagon to the business where he had made such a creditable beginning. So if he could bring Stunsrud to ruin he would have laid the foundation for a solid business career. One day he got the idea to attack Stunsrud with his own weapons and take up the literary challenge of the scandalous book that the scoundrel had sponsored. The war would, in other words, be waged in the field of aesthetics. If Stunsrud had paid for a book in order to *rønne* Jenkins and Simonsen out of *bisnes,* then the psychologically logical and tactically correct move for Jenkins & Co. would be to publish a book and distribute it to the same public that was now reading and admiring Lyvenfelt's literary garbage.

Jonas worked this over many times in his mind and each time he considered it, it appeared more attractive. With his fine nose he had sniffed up aspects of Stunsrud's past that were amenable to literary treatment. This may not be recommendable from an ethical point of view, and he was fairly certain that Pastor Vangsnes would not have encouraged him if he had asked his advice. But, as Simonsen had so often and so emphatically said, *bisnes* is *bisnes*. Moreover, it couldn't be wrong to protect yourself from your aggressor. More importantly, who would ever be able to guess that he was the one behind it—he, a mere clerk and newcomer?

The essential question was: who should write the book? Jonas didn't want to mention his plan to Simonsen until he had all details in place. His problem was that there were not many he could consult. He had an instinctive sense that Ragna would not approve and that this was something he had better not discuss with women. Then he thought of Lanberg, and one evening he shared his plan with him. He even asked Lanberg to write the book since he had literary interests and had written in *Budstikken*. But Lanberg would not commit himself to such a major project. Neither did he wish to dip his pen in all the dirt that it would be necessary to dig up and give literary form in order to achieve a satisfactory product, he said. But he liked the idea and promised to help in its realization.

"There is," he said, "only one man I know who has the necessary qualifications and the robust conscience required for such a work."

"And who is this?" Jonas wished to know.

"Arnoldus Bolivarius Lyvenfelt."

"Are you crazy? He has written the other book."

"Yes and that is just why he's the man to do it," Lanberg replied.

"But don't you think he would refuse to do it on principle, since he is such a close friend of Stunsrud?"

"No, I don't. A hundred dollars can have a remarkable influence on a poor principle. Principles are primarily topics for conversation. They are not made for practical use."

Lanberg said that a thousand copies would, including an honorarium for the author, amount to about $300. Armed with this knowledge, Jonas approached Simonsen the next morning. He laid out his plan in all its details and his boss smiled with satisfaction when he began to realize the project's potential.

"So we are speaking of a sort of cops-and-robbers novel about Stunsrud?"

"Exactly, something that won't let people put down the book until they have come to the last page—something along the lines of *Fallen Nobility* but only far more powerful." Simonsen thought about it a while, smiled, and said, "Well, Sir, not that I believe that it will mean much as far as *bisnis* is concerned, but it's such a noble and beautiful idea that it would be a pity to let it go untried. So go ahead! Make as good a contract as possible with the hack and—mind you—keep me out of it."

"Of course," Jonas answered. This had been easier than he had hoped, and now he could organize everything as planned. That evening he arranged a meeting with Stunsrud's clerk, Nils Johansen.

"It's really none of my *bisnes*," said Jonas, "but it's a shame to hear how Lyvenfelt slanders your boss, considering all he had done for him."

"Is that what he's doing—the swine?" exclaimed Johansen.

"Yes, he has confided in several of my customers that Stunsrud hired him to write the awful book and that he afterward refused to pay him."

"The miserable liar."

"*Bisnes* good, I'spose?"

"Yes, excellent."

"By the way," said Jonas, as if in confidence, "our firm is gaining new ground in South Minneapolis. If this continues, we'll soon be in need of a new clerk or two. You should think about it. But remember that you've heard nothing from me, not about this nor about the other matter."

"Naturally," said the other. "I never misuse the confidence of a friend."

As Johansen rushed off to tell Stunsrud what he had heard about Lyvenfelt, Jonas continued down the street and dropped in at Sellefsen's shoemaker shop, knowing him to be one of Stunsrud's admirers.

"Isn't it terrible how Lyvenfelt goes around slandering Stunsrud," he said on closing the door. "I would have told him about it myself if it hadn't been for the squabble between him and Simonsen. But, as you know, it would have cost me my job and more. So don't use my name if you should mention it."

"*Ju bet,* I'll mention it but I won't say a word about you," Sellefsen assured him. "I've never been able to *stomœke* that scribbler."

Before Jonas returned to the boardinghouse, he had met a dozen people who had promised they would tell Stunsrud that Lyvenfelt was spreading lies about him. Most of them made it their business to visit the *storet* on First Street as early as possible the next morning so the storekeeper had overwhelming evidence of the truth of what Johansen had told him. Consequently, Stunsrud was ready to receive Lyvenfelt when he came on his daily visit just before noon. Their meeting was concluded with the following gallantries:

"I will not lower myself by any physical contact with your rotten cadaver," said the storekeeper. "I'll call a policeman if you don't get out of my store immediately."

"I'm sorry to see that you're the same miserable wretch you've always been," Lyvenfelt raged as he left.

Sunday morning Jonas went to church. He hadn't been there for some time and he feared that his absence would be noticed. He also had a vague notion that his recent activities may not have been fully in keeping with the orthodox observance of his religion. So he now wished to establish that he nevertheless stood on a good footing with the Synod. There was, it seemed to him, comfort to be found there. But it so happened that Vangsnes that very Sunday talked about the importance of being true to oneself and a steadfast Christian. What was needed, said the pastor, was not merely the mouth's confession, but the heart's conviction, that found expression every day of the year and every hour of the day in an active

Christian life. Had he been able to read Jonas's mind, he could not have found a more fitting theme. But there was little Jonas could do now. He had already gone too far with his preliminaries to give up his plan at this point. Moreover, who had ever interrupted a good *bisnes* and wondered what the pastor would think about it? *Bisnes* is *bisnes,* said Simonsen. But he went to the extraordinary step of dropping a whole quarter in the box, and after the service he took Vangsnes aside and gave him two dollars for the Zulu Mission. The pastor smiled and was quite friendly, and Jonas's conscience was redeemed.

Jonas and Lanberg had agreed to meet that afternoon to discuss their scheme. Lanberg's eagerness to help him had given Jonas the idea that he might be able to get his friend to arrange the matter so that he himself wouldn't be involved. He feared, he explained to Lanberg, that if he, personally, should approach Lyvenfelt, he would realize that Simonsen was behind it. This would ruin everything. Lanberg had no objections. To him it was all good fun. Jonas was greatly relieved. Vangsnes's sermon had made a powerful impression and left him with a sense of uneasiness about what he was doing. But now he could say, with some element of truth, that he had made no deal with the author. This, however, didn't keep him from retaining a lively interest in the negotiations, and he was more than willing to go with his friend when he suggested that they might as well set the machinery going at once.

Lyvenfelt was glad to see them, and when Jonas promptly went off for a pail of beer, this contributed to their festive mood, which, for the author, grew as the contents of the pail disappeared into his voluminous interior depositories. Their business with Lyvenfelt developed in an unexpectedly successful manner.

"Are you acquainted with the storekeeper Stunsrud?" Lyvenfelt after a while asked Jonas.

"I've heard of him, but don't know much about him," Jonas responded cautiously.

"He's the greatest scoundrel who has *krossa* the Atlantic!" the author insisted.

"*Gudnes*—that's saying quite a lot!" exclaimed Jonas.

"Not an iota too much. I'm just now writing a book about him." Jonas was visibly surprised. "It will be my best novel," Lyvenfelt confidently continued.

"Well, you do write marvellously well," said Jonas.

"Undoubtedly," Lanberg acknowledged. "And if your book about

Stunsrud is really hard-hitting, I am ready to give you my order for 600 copies right away."

"Are you drunk?" exclaimed the author. He had never come across such a mindless generosity in his entire literary career.

"I'm quite serious," insisted Lanberg, "but you will of course be paid on delivery. Nevertheless, you are a good man and have my complete confidence."

"This is kindly spoken of you, Lanberg." Lyvenfelt was visibly touched and there was a tremor in his voice when he cried, "Six hundred copies! A miracle! I had never expected to become so rich. Lanberg, you are wonderful!"

And when Jonas came back to his room that night he congratulated himself on being on the high road to success in America. He was so sure about it that he was ready to bet the $400 he had in the bank.

18.

Work had never been so hectic in Franz Jeppesen's print shop. Jeppesen had promised that the new book, which was expected to make history—not only for the author but also for the printer and publisher—would have priority to all other projects. The 600 copies had made a great impression on all, from the boss down to the printer's devil. The latter, who often tired of running back and forth with the pail and who protested if no extra coins were forthcoming, was the personification of kindness and courtesy in this period, well knowing the importance of the regular lubrication of talent—in the alcove as well as at the compositor's desk.

Lyvenfelt had a considerable number of manuscript pages ready after a few days and "Grave" and "Life" were in fierce competition to see who could set the more pages of this remarkable opus, which they believed would place Minneapolis on the literary map of the United States.

Lanberg supervised the literary process with painstaking care. His main concern was to make sure that the author didn't economize with his talent and hold back on his superlatives. Although there was little reason to have fear on this score, Lanberg was nevertheless conscientious in executing his duties and Lyvenfelt felt no compunction about exerting himself wherever his literary consultant found it desirable. It was best to remain on good terms with such a liberal fellow.

When a copy of *Whited Sepulchers* eventually was placed on the table, anyone with literary experience could see that it had been published by Jeppesen Publishing Co.: it had the same appearance as all the other works produced and distributed by the firm.[53] Even Jonas, who laid no claim to being a critic, thought it looked wretched. But the contents were excellent, and that was what counted.

Stunsrud appeared as Smutrud in the novel.[54] He was described as a totally corrupt character without any sense of shame and whose behavior was a disgrace and a warning to all. Contrary to common practice in Lyvenfelt's fiction, the main character's family was an honorable one, making his sinful ways all the more deplorable. Indeed, his upright and God-fearing father had taken his death of his scandalous behavior. When he, after all kinds of appalling escapades, finally slipped away to America to avoid the long arm of the law, he didn't arrive with empty hands but with sufficient ill-gained lucre to buy a business in the West, where he—partly through a series of fuzzy bankruptcies and questionable fires but mainly through regular extortion—eventually become one of the pillars of society and moved his business to the big city, where he could play the role of gentleman. But try as it may, a wolf cannot change its coat, and Smutrud eventually revealed his true character to his fine new acquaintances. The book went into considerable detail in its account of some of these revelations. In short, the book, as Jonas said to Simonsen, was a deep one.

"Yes, deep in shit," Simonsen remarked, and he rubbed his hands and smiled.

For good reason, Jonas had kept away from the Astoria Block during the period of production. Lanberg had his full confidence, especially because he had been promised a commission for his work as agent, which would considerably augment his meager salary. But Jonas suspected that he also had his own personal motives, and one evening this suspicion was confirmed by no less a character than Lomwiig.

This happened the very day that Lanberg had ceremoniously received his 600 copies of *Whited Sepulchers* and Jonas had given him $450 in cash in return for the books and his assistance, and had also organized the distribution of the book from Lanberg's room. Jonas and Lomwiig met each other at Dania Hall, where a well-known Danish actor gave a recital. Jonas had come with Ragna and did not really want to associate with Lomwiig. But it proved impossible to get rid of him. "If he sees you with a girl, he sticks to you like a fly in butter," Jonas whispered to Ragna as Lomwiig followed them out on the street. She, however, didn't appear to be bothered. She merely laughed and this made Jonas even more irritated. She could be rather frivolous at times.

Lomwiig was critical of the actor, who wasn't at all the artist he had been made out to be. Jonas naturally rose to his defense and thus the usual row between them began. Lomwiig was also critical of Lanberg, a shilly-shallier, he said. Until recently, for instance, he had been a friend of Stunsrud. But Lanberg had fallen in love with Stunsrud's niece and the scoundrel Stunsrud had interfered and badmouthed the clerk to his niece, who then declared that she no longer wished to see him. And then Lanberg simply gave it up. He had no backbone whatsoever. Had he been a man, he would have given Stunsrud a beating and insisted that the girl listen to his side of the story, but he was weak.

"And now," Lomwiig continued, "I hear that he has made an alliance with Jeppesen's scandal scribbler—whose miserable name I refuse to let pass my lips—and is about to produce some sort of filthy rubbish about Stunsrud."

Jonas was stunned. He had assumed that the new book was the deepest secret between himself, Lanberg, and Lyvenfelt. *"Gudnes!"* he exclaimed. "I can't believe it!"

"Believe it? It's all over town," Lomwiig declared.

"And Lanberg—does he know that everybody knows?"

"Lanberg is a fool," the other replied. "His only concern has been revenge on Stunsrud. That he too would be drawn into the muck has never entered his mind."

"But who can have told such a story?"

"Told? The scandal scribbler himself, of course. He has wagged his tongue to everyone and boasted of his respectable friends and admirers."

"Gudnes!" Jonas sighed again as he pulled Ragna with him toward the approaching *streetkarsen*. What was foremost in his mind was his luck in having such a good friend as Lanberg who had taken this great responsibility on his own shoulders. *Gudnes,* how close he had been to being placed in the stocks and then . . .

Actually, Jonas had had something entirely different in mind before they met Lomwiig. He had felt that it was high time he did something about his engagement plans. In a sense, considering what good friends he and Ragna had become over the last few months, you could say that they were sort of engaged already, but, still, something more in the way of a ceremony was required to make it all proper, and this hadn't yet taken place.

It may seem strange that a man who had become such a promising *bisnesmand* should show so little initiative in the affairs of love. In fact, he hadn't yet found the opportunity to say the words that custom and tradition require of a man in such a situation. He had certainly given it much thought, and every so often when they were together he had been struck by a sense of solemnity—something about halfway between religion and poetry—but then there was always some or other inconvenient circumstance that interfered at the decisive moment and silenced him. Of course he was aware that many became engaged without saying a word about it. This is how it often happened in novels from England. They just sort of read each other's thoughts and then it simply happened, even if they often themselves could be surprised that it had. But it would seem that Ragna didn't sympathize with this method. She had been brought up in the Hauge Synod, and he supposed that they held a dim view of becoming engaged in so frivolous a manner.[55]

You mustn't believe that Jonas didn't know the appropriate phrases. His bad luck, however, would have it that none of them turned out to be quite suitable for the occasion. More and more he had come to realize that for such a unique instance he would have to be original and not just stand there repeating what some lovelorn fool in England or on Tahiti had said a thousand times before. If he was to say anything at all, it had to be something he could remember for the rest of his life and that he could, so to speak, take out from his memory and contemplate like a lucky coin or an heirloom.

When they finally stood in the boardinghouse hall, he again had a sense of the solemnity of the occasion that had confused him so often before and he instinctively took her hand as if to say good night. Strangely, she made no attempt to withdraw it. Obviously she was waiting for him to get it said . . . And, considering that he was a man, this was not at all unreasonable. But to say it—no way could he do it! In the faint light from the smoking lamp in the hall he could make out her smile. This made him even more nervous; she was silently laughing at his own embarrassment! That's just the way with girls . . . Just fun and pranks . . . Easy enough for them, who were free from responsibility and expected the man to carry the whole burden . . . Easy for them just to stand there and look clever.

"I had a remarkable dream last night," he finally said with a sigh, so as to get started.

"And what did you dream?" she asked.

"I—I—dreamt—ahem—I dreamt that I was engaged to the best and most beautiful girl in *Min'ap'lis*." Ragna quickly withdrew her hand and preoccupied herself with a fold in her dress. He felt his blood rise to his head. It was so obviously stupid to begin as he had done. He could see that now.

"Do I know her?" she asked teasingly as she took a step toward the stairs as if ready to climb them. No matter what happened, he felt, he would have to speak out now.

"Yes," he said. "You are the one I dreamt I was engaged to." She laughed out loud.

"I don't believe in dreams," she said. And with that she quickly ran up the stairs. "Good night!" she called down to him.

In bed, Jonas lay awake for about a hour thinking of what he could have done differently and what an ass he was.

19.

Since he had started working for Jenkins, Jonas had been keenly aware of the social gap between himself and the Simonsen family. This wasn't at all because Simonsen was the least bit arrogant. On the contrary, Jonas had to admit that his boss had shown him confidence and been very generous and that he had found him a better friend than he had expected. But he could nevertheless not rid himself of the notion that the Simonsens thought they stood higher on the social ladder than people like him. With the country boy's respect for urban society and its representatives, he likely made more of this than the situation actually called for.

Mrs. Simonsen, an elegant lady of about forty, was the main reason why the newcomer had such a nagging suspicion that he was looked down upon by those who held the key to his acceptance in society. Simonsen had never invited him home and he had now worked for a year in the store. When Mrs. Simonsen came in, he always kept his distance. Her arrogance was evident and he could see that she looked down upon a workingman. The peacock feathers in her hat, her silk dress, and her proud appearance as she sailed into the store like a full-rigged brig made it obvious. She had evidently objected to having him, a mere clerk, in her home, even though Simonsen himself wasn't more than a clerk himself.

We wouldn't be fair in our assessment of Jonas if we believed that he didn't acknowledge some of the advantages of an urban culture.

One of the accomplishments of a city man is his ability to set up a fine appearance, and Jonas had seen so much of the world that he realized that this could be a great advantage. In particular he had seen that this could be important in business, where it is essential to be a friend of all. Consequently, he had done what he could to acquire an urban polish and he had made a special study of Simonsen, who, in Jonas's eyes, was a paradigm of how far a clever *bisnesmand* could advance in a vain and stupid world.

There was some truth in the claim that Mrs. Simonsen held a watchful eye on the family's social reputation. Regrettably, this had at times been necessary. Simonsen was admittedly more proper than most, but even the most perfect among us have a tendency to transgress, and Simonsen's one passion was pool. As may be expected, this was quite unacceptable to his wife. Had he played billiards or some other socially acceptable game it would have been a different matter; but to be addicted to pool, a game played by any farmhand or hobo, was almost scandalous! But Simonsen was not to be deterred. He played pool three nights a week and he cultivated his plebeian vice in saloons that were not always of the fashionable kind. Nor was he all that particular about who played with him. By nature as well as upbringing, he was a sober man, but on occasion it happened that one vice attracted another and he had a cup or two more than was good for him. On such occasions he could come home with some apocryphal character in tow to enjoy a nightcap. This was a custom that Mrs. Simonsen could not accept and eventually her husband had to give it up. It had been years since the last post-midnight performance in the Simonsen residence. But Simonsen still played pool—and was then said to be out "on necessary business."

Simonsen had assessed Jonas from a purely business point of view, and as time passed and he wasn't disappointed in his expectations he began to think of him as a factor in his own career. The newcomer had in short time learned the tricks of the trade that Simonsen believed were the essence of a complete business education, and he could perform them without compunction. In other words, he had turned out to be a success.

So when Simonsen one evening invited him home it was not at all as a social gesture but in order to talk business with him in private. To Jonas this made no difference. He was flattered. And Simonsen's wife, strange as it may seem, turned out to be more charming than he had dared to expect. Their daughter, Miss Dagny, who had just returned from a girls' school in the East, was even more charming. She was in her twenties, not as beautiful as Ragna, he thought, but more lively. It was amazing how she could hold up a conversation with a total stranger. He was almost ashamed of sitting there without being able to say much. But then the girl didn't give him much opportunity to do so.

You could hear right away that Dagny was cultured and *ædjukæta*: she talked about everything between heaven and earth except the *grocerybisnes*. Consequently, you may appreciate that it was no simple matter for Jonas to conceal his own ignorance. She played the pianoforte and gave a long lecture on the history of music, and she said that if she had been a man, Dr. Ames would never again achieve power and honor in Minneapolis, along with a lot of other things that seemed strange coming from the mouth of a young girl. To Jonas, Dagny was a revelation. She was obviously awfully talented the way she could talk about just anything, and there was no denying that she was both nice and pleasant . . . Occasionally he found himself comparing her with Ragna. Her hands, for instance. They were so small, elegant, and well manicured, and her nails were so carefully polished that they shone in competition with the four brilliant diamond rings on her fingers. Poor Ragna only had rough hands, since she didn't have a rich father to sweeten her life as had this fine lady.

Supper in the Simonsen family was quite different from what Jonas was used to. There was no end to the dishes served. He hadn't eaten so well since he had been in Norway, but he was nevertheless reluctant to help himself as much as he wanted because everything was so refined and proper. They even served wine but he didn't touch it. He excused himself, explaining that it always gave him such a headache. Dagny cleared her throat and hid behind her napkin, and Mrs. Simonsen winked slyly to her husband. He didn't really understand what was going on but he gathered that this wasn't the accepted way of saying that you didn't drink wine. He realized that he had much to learn. But apart from this, everything went smoothly. And their home was so elegant . . . This was just how he wanted his home when he was married. Well, perhaps he would have to manage with a little less to begin with. There was truth in the saying that money governed the world. He could see that clearly. If you have it, you may have everything you wish: a fine and splendid home and a beautiful and cultured wife and all the glory you could imagine . . . *Gudnes,* had he only had the money now. But it would come; it would have to come . . .

But, as already said, Simonsen had invited Jonas to talk business, and when they had eaten and Dagny had completed her several lectures and played the "Wedding March" from *Lohengrin* and something that she called *Sinfonia Eroica* by Beethoven, the two men retired to what Mrs. Simonsen referred to as her husband's studio—a funny name, thought Jonas, for a smoking parlor—and Simonsen eagerly took a pipe. Jonas didn't smoke, and when Dagny soon after came in with coffee-avec and discovered this, she remarked that she personally liked cigarettes imported from Turkey.

"So you don't mind smoking?" Jonas said, feeling that he should say something.

"On the contrary," she responded, "the more the better. Smoking is so masculine and charming." Then she probably wouldn't find him very masculine, he thought. He would have to take up smoking. He had tried it a few times and had been very sick. But you could get used to all sorts of things . . .

Simonsen poured some curaçao after she had left. "What's this?" asked Jonas.

"Oh, it's some mess the women call liqueur. It's really not much and I drink it out of politeness." Jonas had had liqueur in Norway and knew what it was.

"It's intoxicating," he said.

"Not that I know of," Simonsen answered. "I've been told it's supposed to contain 15 percent alcohol, but there are fourteen I haven't discovered. If it scares you, you can pour it in the spittoon." Jonas didn't touch his glass.

"And now for business," said Simonsen, after he had emptied his glass and tasted his coffee. "To make a long story short, the old man wants to sell!"

"Jenkins?"

"Yes, he wants to go to a milder climate. Minnesota weather is bad for his rheumatism. We can have it for seven thousand."

"*Gudnes,* that's quite a bargain!" Jonas exclaimed.

"Yes, it's my own estimate—the figure I have used in the annual accounts these past few years. The old man, you see, cannot do arithmetic."

"Can't he do arithmetic—an American!" Jonas hadn't seen much of Jenkins recently. His rheumatism kept him at home. He had never imagined that he didn't know arithmetic, because he had believed that

Americans were so learned. They were always talking about "the ignorant foreigner." He was only a newcomer, but he certainly knew his arithmetic!

"No, Jenkins has never understood anything about bookkeeping. He has left that entirely to me."

"Gudnes!" Jonas repeated. He thought about the expensive furniture, the fine carpets, and the brilliant rings on Miss Dagny's well-manicured fingers.

"He's worth a hundred thousand," Simonsen continued, "and I've run his business for him for twenty years, so he should give me a good price."

"And you have decided to buy?"

"Well—yes; but I need a partner. As you know, I have other interests—real estate and things like that—and I need a partner who will be able to take over the management of the business after a while." Jonas now understood why he had been invited for supper.

"Do you mean that I may have an opportunity here?" he asked with some hesitation.

"That's it! Just what I mean. You have a good head for business and we have worked well together. You can have one third of the store for $2,500."

Jonas had to admit that he only had $600 in the bank, but Simonsen suggested that he could get a loan from the Scandia Bank on the condition that an agreed-upon percentage of the profit on Jonas's share in the business was used to repay the loan.

Jonas felt as if he had awakened from an alluring dream and had discovered fortune standing by his bed offering him silver bowls with golden apples. He had achieved his first goal even earlier than he had expected.

"This is nice of you, Simonsen!" he said and took his boss's hand. "Thank you."

"Oh, there is no need to thank me, my boy," said Simonsen. "It's only *bisnes,* you know, and I've had my own interests in mind."

When they parted company, Simonsen presented Jonas to his wife and daughter as his partner. "Simonsen & Olson[56] will open business tomorrow," he said.

His wife took Jonas's hand and pressed it warmly, saying that she was incredibly happy this had happened. And now he would have to come to visit often. Jonas was ashamed to have thought so ill of her. Yes, you could easily misjudge other people . . .

And Dagny was so exquisitely friendly and said so many nice things that he didn't quite know which foot to stand on. "And if you won't come visiting real often, I'll be quite offended, you see," she said.

"Thank you so much, I'll be coming," he answered. He would have liked to have said something nice and suitable but this was all he could manage.

"Why, he's just a splendid-looking chap!" Dagny exclaimed as soon as he had closed the door behind him.

"Clever boy! Good head! He! He!" agreed Simonsen.

"That's certainly good for him," said his wife, "because his manners won't take him very far."

"Clever boy—he'll learn—good head," Simonsen repeated.

"That's what I say," Dagny agreed.

"Oh, dear," Mrs. Simonsen sighed.

———•◦•———

Ragna was in the parlor when Jonas returned to the boardinghouse. She looked up and smiled as he entered. This was the first time he vaguely felt that this smile might not after all be so important. But he quickly dismissed the thought. *O'kors,* he was fond of Ragna, and there was no one but Ragna in the whole wide world . . . And then he told her the great news.

"Imagine," he said, "I've been at the Simonsens. We are partners and are buying the Jenkins store. Tomorrow I'll have my own *bisnes.* Simonsen is certainly a good friend. And what a wonderful wife he has! And his daughter! Do you know Dagny Simonsen?"

"No," Ragna quietly replied. "I don't know her." She sat thoughtfully with her hands in her lap. Jonas could not but contemplate her hands. They were rough and red after an evening of washing dishes and cleaning the kitchen. And then he remembered those other hands, so nice, white, and manicured. It seemed to him that he could still feel the hand, soft as velvet, she had given him on parting.

He wasn't conscious of any reason for just then looking more closely at the parlor. Everything was plain and shabby compared to the other one. Take for instance the rickety, worn-down plush sofa with the stuffing showing here and there; in the corner he could see the ugly kitchen chairs; on one wall the framed and glazed Lord's Prayer; on the other the Ten Commandments and the yellowing portrait of old Kari Oppejord, Mrs. Johnson's mother, who had lived and died in a poor cotter's cottage in the old country; and above the door a faded "God bless our home." And as his eyes returned to the silent young woman at the table, they again fixed themelves on the rough, red working hands resting in her lap . . .

He suddenly pulled up his watch from his pocket. *"Gudnes!"* he said. "It's already late! I'll have to say good night." Whereupon he quickly left the room and ascended the stairs. Ragna gave a faint sigh as she watched him leave.

20.

There was no advertising to speak of among the Scandinavian businesses in Minneapolis. The larger and more centrally located stores advertised in the Norwegian, Swedish, and Danish newspapers, but on a small scale. Names such as N. H. Gjertsen, H. O. Peterson, John Øfstie, Knud Asleson, John A. Blickfeldt, the Vanstrums, Floan & Leveroos (in St. Paul), and a few others may have appeared in the advertising columns, but the only Scandinavian storekeeper who, in Jonas's view, understood the value of systematic advertising was S. E. Olson.[57] As everybody knew, he had the largest Scandinavian-owned store in America, so it would seem that his advertising had paid off. Jonas had suggested that Jenkins & Co. also should advertise, but even though Simonsen had a good business sense, he didn't appreciate advertising. When they had done so on occasion it had been a stingy affair, pretty much like giving alms to the mission. Simonsen didn't like experiments. Jonas had discovered that Simonsen was without a vision, that he didn't, you might say, see things in a broad perspective. He had gone along with the publication and distribution of the book about Stunsrud, which was a kind of indirect advertising, but not because he believed it was good *bisnes*. Jonas, however, had already been able to point proudly to some fruits of this project, which was, it may be admitted, a rather extraordinary undertaking for a grocery business. Some of the delinquent customers had begun to drop in at the store again, which meant that they once more were submitting to the good influence of Simonsen. But this negative advertising wasn't sufficient; there would have to be something of a positive nature . . .

Jonas's vision stood before him in greater clarity than ever before. Simonsen & Olson should and would become a truly great business— the greatest of its kind in Minneapolis—and in order to achieve this he would have to clear new paths. One of the first things he convinced

Simonsen they should do was to hire Stunsrud's best clerk, Johansen. Simonsen had protested at first, and when Jonas also suggested that they should hire Jens Vandland, who was largely responsible for the growth of Nicolaisen's store in South Minneapolis, making it one of the three to four largest in the grocery business, the senior partner observed, somewhat sarcastically, that it would perhaps be better to expand their sales first and then hire the necessary help. But Jonas was not to be budged and Simonsen finally had to give in.

Unlike Stunsrud, Simonsen had no imagination. Jonas believed this was the main reason why it had been possible for their rival on First Street to become such a dangerous competitor. Lanberg had once explained the importance of the imagination so well that Jonas had adopted it as an article of faith. A truly successful *bisnesmand,* Lanberg had said, was a combination of poet and philosopher. The only difference was that the poet dealt with the abstract and the businessman used his prophetic vision and imagination in the material world—with the inexorable logic of the philosopher. Jonas couldn't actually remember how it had been said, but it had been something along these lines, and he felt that he understood the point even though he couldn't explain it to others.

Nilsen, an architect, had been present when Lanberg had articulated his theory. He was always so critical and had complained that there was no craving for poetry in the American people, nor could Americans express spiritual values in their literature. But Lanberg had said that it wasn't necessary to express poetry through literature. An active people could express poetry through other means. Americans—including the Norwegians—had often expressed it in their great practical enterprises. We were poets of action rather than of words. A businessman could be a great poet in his way, as could a farmer, if they followed their calling. The businessmen and industrialists of America had composed the world's greatest poem.

"Well, then Stunsrud rather than Lyvenfelt would be our greatest poet," Nilsen responded, "and Jonas should be compared to a Shakespeare or a Goethe, considering how he has introduced fiction into the grocery *traden.* And to be honest, I'll have to admit that you probably must be a great poet to get the Norwegian wives of North Minneapolis to believe that the famous butter in the Jenkins store that Simonsen has been peddling these last twenty years was churned yesterday. You're right, Lanberg. I can see it clearly now. The city is packed with poets if you only have the ability to recognize them."

That was so typical of Nilsen. He was impossible! But he was really a kind and friendly man and you couldn't be angry with him. Jonas had no doubt that Lanberg was right. He could follow his reasoning and understood that a businessman could have great visions and exalted thoughts.

Simonsen had just bought a large consignment of Norwegian dried cod at a very favorable price from the estate of a bankrupt import firm in New York. His idea had been to sell the cod in portions to other groceries, but Jonas immediately recognized an excellent opportunity to realize his plans. His idea was to sell it direct to the customers at cost. The firm had more potatoes in storage than they could expect to sell at any reasonable price. The reason was that Simonsen had had a contract to deliver potatoes to a *grocerymand* on Second Avenue South, who later refused to take his part of the consignment, claiming that Simonsen was trying to cheat him. They were now fighting about the potatoes in court and they couldn't be stored much longer without rotting. So Jonas included the potatoes in his calculations. He decided to give them away—half a bushel to anyone who bought at least one dollar in cod; but on condition that they also purchased at least one dollar in other groceries. Cod and potatoes! That would look just right in the newspaper advertisements and on the posters he had planned to distribute to hundreds of Scandinavian households that had had no previous relationship with their firm. Simonsen thought this was rather lavish; they could, he said, just as well make $800 on the cod as to let it go at cost. Nor was he willing to let the potatoes go for nothing.

"There will be all this trouble," he insisted, "with the advertising and the extra help and all the rest, and when it's over it may have cost us an extra thousand—in addition to what we'll lose on the potatoes."

"If we won't *klirer* $2,000 on the whole business, I'll gladly give up my share in the store and go out West to homestead," Jonas firmly declared. Simonsen finally agreed to go ahead, but he was still in doubt about the whole thing.

A few days later no one spoke of anything but cod and potatoes in the Scandinavian homes in Minneapolis. Everywhere huge posters told how Simonsen & Olson through remarkable good luck had been able to secure a large consignment of prime quality Norwegian cod and gave a plausible story about the potatoes they had to give away in order to make room for this year's crop. The next day, the English newspapers carried conspicuous advertisements to the same effect, and *Daglig Tidende* devoted a whole page to Simonsen & Olson's cod and potatoes. Jonas had personally gone there with the advertisement and made use of the opportunity to meet the publisher, Thorvald Guldbrandsen, and the editor, Mr. Sartz.[58] It could be useful to be acquainted with such men.

As soon as the news of the remarkable bargain became known around town, people began to flock to the store in great numbers. Here they were ready with extra clerks in place. Business was splendid and Simonsen was so busy all day that he only had time to sit on the *counteren* a few times and exclaim: "A good head—clever boy—heh—heh!"

Jonas, Vandland, and Johansen were busy taking orders. Vandland focused on his old customers in South Minneapolis, Johansen took care of Stunsrud's traditional customers in North Minneapolis, and Jonas paid visits to former Jenkins customers who had recently switched to Stunsrud. Wherever he came, people talked about his despised competitor. Most had read *Whited Sepulchers* not only once but twice. They hadn't realized he was such a scoundrel; he had appeared to be such a fine man. There were even a few who could supplement Lyvenfelt's biographical account with similar stories of their own. Actually, they had never had any confidence in Stunsrud.

Jonas of course hadn't read the book and he doubted that he would ever care to do so. He was ready to believe that Stunsrud hadn't been a paragon of virtue, but we should remember that we too have our flaws. And there was an extenuating circumstance. He had been told that Stunsrud had been under a bad influence in his youth and been deprived of a Christian upbringing. His father hadn't been able to control him as a child and he had been sent to relatives out in the country who were Methodists or something. It was said that he had left his first wife, and he had to agree that that was a villanous thing to do—and he deplored the present increase in the corruption of marital relations—but he had also been told that the first Mrs. Stunsrud hadn't exactly been virtuous, so we should be understanding and try to see his actions in the best light possible. The worst thing, he had been told, was that he had abused her—actually beaten her; but he must have had his reasons!

At this point in the conversation he usually ran into trouble with the wives who without exception insisted that there could be no forgiveness for a man who behaved like a scoundrel to his wedded wife. And Jonas would then give in and agree that if it really was as bad as they said, then they were naturally quite right in their view. They had to remember that he hadn't read the book.

About then, Jonas would also discover little Mary clinging to her mother's skirts and he would begin to have fun and play with the child. Then after a while he would remember that he had a bag of candy just for Mary. He had thought of her so often since he had seen her play one day in the street. She was such a sweet girl! And should Johnny happen to come in to listen to their conversation then he too got a friendly word and some candy or licorice.

Well, this wasn't why he had come . . . but since he was in the neighborhood anyway, he wanted to make sure that they, who had been such good customers, would be able to make use of an excellent bargain. He was sure they would want their share of the cod? Of course, they all agreed. They had even checked Stunsrud's price and he was asking eight cents more for the pound, so it was obvious that Simonsen was all right, who sold it so cheaply and then gave away half a bushel of potatoes. And then they needed a little sugar too, and some cardamom, and a few other things; so it all added up to more than two dollars. Then Jonas would remember that they had just received such an excellent coffee. It cost three cents more for the pound than at Dillworth's and Arbuckle's but it was a rather special coffee! Well, then, they had better try the coffee too. By the way, he had almost forgotten to tell them that the hams he now had in the store were the best he had ever seen. Of course, if they wanted a taste they could just drop in at the store, but since he was here anyway he could spare them the trouble . . . Yes, thank you! Then it would all add up to $4.39. The cod at cost and the potatoes for free!

The cod was gone in four days. The whole consignment. The potatoes too. Every single one! Along with them, most of their stock, at rather stiff prices for the occasion, had also disappeared. Simonsen had never seen anything like it during his career in business.

When it was over, he played pool three nights in a row. Not until the fourth night, when he came home at a civilized hour, did he tell them what had happened.

"I could have told you!" Dagny enthusiastically exclaimed. And he winked understandingly at her and said, "A good head! Clever boy! Heh! Heh!"

But Mrs. Simonsen had three marked worry-creases in her forehead as she tried to understand her young daughter's intentions.

21.

The next morning Jonas was astonished to see Dagny Simonsen enter the store. This was the first time he had ever seen her there and he had to admit that she didn't quite fit in with the surroundings: the old Jenkins *storet* was far from a ballroom or even a drawing room. And there she came picking her way as fine and graceful as the Queen of Sheba, dressed in an elegant light-blue morning suit and a hat in the same color, and—in Jonas's judgment—slender as a young birch tree and sprightly in her movements. It so happened that he was just then busy in the rear of the store and she was received by Johansen. He bowed and scraped and made quite a figure of himself, but she didn't seem to pay him any attention, continuing in the direction where she had seen Jonas between all the crates, herring barrels, and butter kegs. Jonas was handling some smelly cheese, so he washed himself as quickly as he could on such short notice and he went to meet her: he would rather not have an inspection of the sanitary conditions in that section of the store.

"Hello, there!" she called in her usual direct manner. "I'm up an hour earlier than usual this morning to be the first to bring my congratulations!" She offered him her hand. He had a great desire to hold it more warmly and longer than he did, but he lacked the courage and realized that this could never be anything for him, so plain and simple a man. But it nevertheless gave him a special feeling to hold such a fine hand.

"Thank you! That was kind of you," he said, "but as far as I know I haven't done anything that deserves congratulations." Of course he understood very well what she was talking about, but he knew the world and he knew that modesty is a virtue.

"Oh, come off!" she replied. "I tell you, it's great! No one in all of Minneapolis could have done it! Father says it's the best business maneuver he has ever experienced."

"Oh—it's nothing," he said. "We must do as well as we can." He was flattered that she had come to compliment him on his achievement. And he was even more pleased at the thought that she wasn't here on business but because she was interested in him personally.

As she continued to talk about this and that and as she smiled and laughed and joked, he suddenly caught himself comparing her with Ragna again. Ragna hadn't spoken a word about his great coup, even though she knew all about it. All of North Minneapolis was talking about it and was predicting that Stunsrud would soon be out of *bisnes'n*.

The whole boardinghouse had been full of wonder. Nels had come to him and told him that he had always believed that he was a clever boy but that this had exceeded all his expectations; one day he would be a millionaire. Yesterday even Cousin Salmon and his wife, whom he had hardly seen since his first days in the city, had come to the store and tried to flatter him. And this morning he had met the *suer* boss himself, Sewal Olson, on his way to work, and he had also congratulated him on his success. But Ragna hadn't said a single word. A few times he had thought he should have some confidential words with her, but she had seemed so shy and reluctant that he had let her be . . . If that was all she cared for him he saw no reason to beg . . . But then he realized that his mind was wandering while Dagny Simonsen was talking to him. In his distraction he hadn't even heard all she had said; but he had a pleasant sense of her presence. Now he brought himself to attention and smiled obligingly.

"And do you know what I said to mother when father told us what you had done?" she asked. She looked at him with such intimacy and her eyes were so sparkling that he was almost afraid to look her in the face. And since it was quite impossible for him to guess what she had said to her mother, she told him. "I told her that you were my hero," she said. "Well, you understand that I may say whatever I wish now that you are my father's partner. But I'll have to go now. And you'll be coming to dinner tonight?" She must have mentioned this earlier even though he hadn't noticed.

"Yes, thank you!" he said in a hurry as she gave him her hand in farewell.

He stood looking as she walked to the door and he wondered what she would say if he asked her the little question that had just now come to his mind. And then he remembered the evening when he had been about to ask Ragna to marry him and how she had brushed him off saying that she didn't believe in dreams. Girls were strange animals. And Ragna hadn't said a single friendly or appreciative word to him since he had acquired his own business—so why should he offer her his hand again? She could at least have shown him common politeness as it was practiced among friends and near acquaintances . . .

His thoughts continued after he had returned to his work. Did he have reason to reproach himself in his relationship with Ragna? It was as if a tiny, faraway voice was saying that he was the one who had changed and that her shyness and reserve were an effect of his own behavior. If his attitude had been unchanged she would have been the first to meet him with an encouraging smile and a friendly word as he stood in the bright morning of his ambition and looked forward to a life rich in prizes for the strong and the brave . . . But what had he actually done to deserve her reserve? Had he with a single word suggested that he didn't care for her? Hadn't he time and again tried to find an occasion to tell her that he loved her and wanted to marry her? Hadn't he been sorry when she shrugged it off? Did she think that he, who now had his own *bisnes* and was a famous man in *Min'ap'lis,* should fall on his knee and beg her to be *exkjusa* for existing? Damned if he would . . .

After dinner that evening there was a little competition between Simonsen and his daughter for their guest's attention. Simonsen claimed that he had to discuss something with Jonas but Dagny observed that they had all day and all year for their conferences. She wanted to show him their paintings and that would be far more interesting than to discuss *bisnes* when he for once had taken time to go out for a little pleasure. And she had souvenirs from Europe, where she and her mother had traveled through all the countries and had seen absolutely everything a couple of years ago. Naturally, Simonsen surrendered.

They began with the paintings in the *parloren.* "This portrait of me is by Gausta. You should meet him. He's a bachelor and a very interesting man if you can get him to talk. But he regrettably thinks more than he speaks . . . has studied for many years in Europe and knows lots of languages, but very few are aware of it since he prefers to remain silent in them all. I fear he may have looked too deeply into my character . . . Don't you agree that he has given me a pair of coquettish eyes? And this one is by Kitty Kielland . . . met her when I went to Norway with mother two years ago . . . a great talent in the modern style . . . discusses politics and smokes tobacco like a man . . . but I forget that you're from Norway and will naturally know her better than I do . . . And this is Fritz Thaulow . . . we were together one evening at the Grand Café . . . brilliant . . . quite a citizen of the world, admired by all the young . . . is well known in Paris . . . imagine. And this is Ludwig Bøckman . . . one of our own. Imagine, we are developing a Norwegian-American art. Look at that bust over there . . . it's by the sculptor Fjelde. Isn't it great?"[59]

Jonas was no expert in the world of art, and confronted with all this expertise he was amiss for words to disguise his own ignorance. He felt that he had to say something so she wouldn't take him for an idiot, so eventually he threw out:

"Yes, we are getting along right well. If we could only get something going in literature as well . . ."

"There you said it!"

"But as far as I can see, Lyvenfelt seems to be the only one." She seemed puzzled.

"Lyvenfelt?" she said. "What kind of bird may that be?" They both laughed at her little joke. "I don't really know much about Norwegian-American literature but we do have Wilhelm Pettersen, who is a professor in the Conference. I think he writes beautifully. And then we have Askevold, a novelist and pastor in the Synod, and Falk Gjertsen and Oscar Gundersen and Buslett . . . and Kristofer Janson, of course. Do you know him?"[60]

"No, I'm Lutheran," Jonas said.

"*Gudnes,* yes, so are we, but I occasionally go to hear him lecture and recite fairy tales and that sort of thing. But where is this 'what-you-may-call-him' Lyver—"

"Lyvenfelt—he lives here in Minneapolis." But then he remembered the awful book he had written about her father. "But they say that he is not really respectable."

"Are you talking about the man or his books?" she asked. Jonas realized that she was really interested. But he also realized that he had brought up a touchy topic and that he had better move on with care. "Ahem—well—ahem," he said. "You know, I don't actually know the man personally . . . but people say that he writes rather scandalous tales."

"How interesting!"

"Do you think so?" Jonas was surprised.

"Yes," she openly admitted. "Be honest now. Don't you as well?"

"No." Jonas was firm. "I don't."

"So he uses real-life models then," she persisted.

"Well, at least that's what people say. Too real and too lively, they say. But I haven't actually read his books."

"What was his name again?"

"Lyvenfelt."

"Lyvenfelt—Lyvenfelt," she repeated as if she wanted to make sure that she wouldn't forget his name.

When they after a while returned to the living room, Dagny burst out, "Say, papa, we have had such an interesting time!"

"No doubt, no doubt! He! He!" Simonsen sighed and nodded to indicate that he understood perfectly well what they had been doing.

"And—by the way—who is that man Lyvenfelt?" she blurted out. Her father looked up. The question had obviously surprised him. Jonas felt his blood rising to his temples.

"Ly—Ly—what was the name again?" asked Simonsen, apparently unaware of what they were talking about.

"Lyvenfelt."

"Lyvenfelt?" Her father scratched his head and looked stupid.

"Why, yes, Lyvenfelt, the author, don't you know?"

"Never heard the name before," Simonsen lied.

"That's funny! You don't seem to know anything about our great literary men; and here Mr. Olson thinks he is the best-known writer of a generation."

"Oh, with Olson it's an entirely different matter," said Simonsen, getting up from his chair. "He is a literary man himself and has done great services for Norwegian-American literature." With this he indicated that the time had come to talk *bisnes*.

"Oh, dear," Dagny sighed. "Business! Business! I hate business!"

"Yes, poor girl! All this *bisnessen* has really given you a bad time," said Simonsen as he disappeared through the door to his studio. Jonas followed, convinced that he was in for a lecture. His senior partner grabbed his pipe and closed the door. Then he examined some cigar boxes he had on his table but apparently without finding what he was looking for. Then he turned his back on Jonas and began to rummage in a drawer of an old smoking cabinet in the corner. When he turned to face Jonas he was holding a couple of black cigars in his hand.

"I didn't intend to mention him," Jonas began. He didn't know how he was going to get out of this blunder. Simonsen seemed surprised. "Intend?—Who?" he asked.

"Lyvenfelt, you know."

"Oh, the scribbler? Never mind about him! She is always like this, Dagny, you know. Just a little emancipated, you know. Great girl, by the way, if her father may say so. He! He!" Jonas breathed more freely. A burden had been lifted from his heart.

"Would you like a cigar?" offered Simonsen. He proffered him the two black objects.

"I would like to try one; but aren't these terribly strong?"

"Oh, never mind; have one! These are the mildest cigars available . . . only domestic, you know . . . not a trace of nicotine in them . . . a child could smoke them."

After Dagny had told him that smoking was so masculine, Jonas had now and then tried to smoke a cigar. It wouldn't do to take part in fine society without being able to do the things expected of such people. He had only taken a few puffs each time, and it hadn't been so bad: after half an hour he felt just as good as before. He understood that the point was to keep at it a little at a time through the whole evening, and since this one was so mild, he was sure he would be able to manage at least a little piece. He was after all an adult! He lighted it carefully. Simonsen was already smoking at full steam. He sat with a satisfied smile in the heavy leather couch and stretched his legs on the floor. Jonas wondered what he was smiling at and assumed that it must be his awkward way of lighting his cigar.

He took some long puffs and didn't feel at all upset so it probably was really mild. And since he didn't want to give Simonsen more reason to laugh, he took a few more. He was still okay. Simonsen was talking about the cod business. They had netted $4,000, he said. But Jonas was unable to make much of what followed because now the cigar was beginning to take effect—deep effect. Simonsen's voice came from far away. Now and then he caught a word of what he was saying. It was something about the mess at the Scandia Bank but he couldn't make heads or tails of it . . . He straightened himself and got rid of his cigar and then he sank back into the deep leather chair. The objects in the room as well as Simonsen himself were dancing a polka before his eyes . . . He hadn't felt so sick since the day he had celebrated with Skummebek at Butch's saloon.

Simonsen had been contemplating him with increasing interest and satisfaction and now his face was one big smile. Finally he got up, stood in front of Jonas, and laughed as he said, "So you aren't so much of a man, after all?" But Jonas just looked at him in quiet desperation and didn't understand anything. The only thing in the world that he knew with any certainty was that he was now about to die.

Happily, there was a door out to the yard from the studio, and when Simonsen had made enough fun of his miserable partner, he helped him out and placed him on a bench in the backyard. Then he returned to his studio and continued to enjoy his cigar. "Clever boy! Good head! He'll soon mend! Heh! Heh!" He laughed to himself.

Dagny soon came in and looked around. Where was Mr. Olson? Had he already left?

"Yes, Dr. Skaro has been here and said that Lomwiig was sick, so I let Jonas go to see if he could be of any assistance. He asked your forgiveness for leaving without saying good night."

"I'm sorry," said Dagny as she returned to the living room.

Simonsen filled a new pipe.

22.

Jonas was a regular guest at the Simonsens. He came to dinner at least twice a week, and one evening he mustered the courage to invite Dagny to the theater. He was beginning to feel more secure and was no longer embarrassed by her fashionable surroundings. Dagny was an inspiration and his confidence was strengthened by the trust and interest demonstrated by her father. After his humiliation in the studio, they had been better friends than ever. Jonas had told the story to Lomwiig, who explained that this merely meant that Simonsen now considered him worthy of his company and friendship. The first thing he did when he made a friend, said Lomwiig, was to take him home and either ply him with an excess of drink or poison him with one of his Mexican cigars. If they tolerated this treatment without making too much fuss afterward, then there was no limit to all the good he would do for them. And this was Jonas's experience too. The first thing to happen was that Simonsen had suggested that he could use a thousand dollars of their profits on the cod deal to pay down his loan with Haugan.

"You'll put in your third," he had said, "and I'll contribute the rest, and you'll manage the remaining $1,500 by the end of the year." Jonas had thanked him and insisted that he was far too kind, but the senior partner had ensured him that it was only *bisnes*.

Simonsen was an enigma. He seemed not at all concerned that he and Dagny were so much alone. Jonas was less at ease with Mrs. Simonsen. Not that she wasn't polite. But he couldn't free himself from the notion that she would really have preferred to be rid of him.

In the meantime Ragna Riis reflected in quiet on her own problems. We come upon her one Thursday evening in late August. It was past ten o'clock and the Johnsons had retired for the night. The boarders were out enjoying the beautiful evening. Jonas had come home early to change clothes and had gone out for supper. She thought she knew where he was.

Ragna was crocheting, but this was not the reason she hadn't gone to bed. One by one the boarders returned home, stopped for a moment in the hall, and looked at her through the open door. Then they went upstairs without saying anything. Most of them were young men who had been in love with her in turn, and as she heard their footsteps on the stairs, incidents in their relationships came to her mind. They had all confided in her and she knew their stories.

There was Little Tollefsen, scion of a merchant family in Kristiania. Only the gods knew why this innocent and simpleminded young fellow had been sent out into a cruel and ungodly world so far from the care of his mother. Tollefsen couldn't hurt a fly. He didn't drink; he didn't fight; and he wasn't good at much else either. He called himself a literary man, and his literary activity at the moment was the translation of a sewing-machine pamphlet into Norwegian for Swan Turnblad, publisher of *Svenska Amerikanska Posten*. Nels had helped him get this job through his Swedish connections. Tollefsen had been similarly engaged in a work on Dr. Peters's "Kuriko" and had been a translator for a company that fitted people with electric belts. He was known to have written a profound article for *Feltraabet* in South Minneapolis, but Halvard Askeland, the editor, had told him that it was more suitable for *Minneapolis Tidende*. But there they never seemed to be able to find the necessary space: the daily news had priority in their columns. He had told all this to Ragna. He seemed to be able to manage one way or another, whether he had work or not, and when he came to her one day as she was dusting the *parloren* and said that he had decided that it would be best for them to marry, he explained that he wouldn't be a financial burden on her because his family sent him $25 a month for his subsistence.[61]

Pontoppidan Kingo Johnson from Finnmark was a music teacher without students and he therefore had to find other ways of making a living. At the moment he was a member of Nels's *suerkru*.[62] Pontoppidan was a member of a choral society and occasionally gave private recitals in the boardinghouse for an unappreciative audience. He had once given a reading of "Terje Vigen" for Mrs. Johnson's subjects and had the humiliating experience of discovering that they had all disappeared by the time he had come to the nineteenth stanza. On another occasion he had sung a ballad about courting for Ragna, and had been so moved by his own rendition that he had fallen on his knees and proposed to her on completing the last stanza . . . She laughed at the memory even though she wasn't exactly in a merry mood this evening.[63]

And Ludvig Napoleon Stomhoff—also known as "The Weekly News"—who had clerked in a wine business in Kristiania and was a pretentious gentleman in his forties. His present profession was the exchange of gossip among the prominent Norwegians of the city. He visited his "customers" regularly once a week, gave them an account of his business, and requested a "loan" of one dollar. If his request was turned down, his more reliable customers could expect an extra delicious morsel on his next round—along with a request for two dollars instead of the usual one. Napoleon had quite a reputation in the colony. He drank free of charge in the saloons, and should it so happen that you wanted to smirch the reputation of a brother or a sister in your flock, he would always be able to provide the necessary goods at a reasonable price. Our story is silent on what motives Stomhoff may have had for contemplating matrimony. But recently he had kept a watchful eye on Jonas and Dagny Simonsen, and when Jonas happened to be absent from the boardinghouse, he tended to have something interesting to tell about them. He had seen them together in various places and, he claimed, it was more or less decided that Jonas was to become Simonsen's son-in-law, even though he had heard that Mrs. Simonsen wasn't very happy about the arrangement. Ragna knew Napoleon, but his stories had nevertheless made her uneasy since they agreed all too well with her own observations. However, she was totally unprepared when "The Weekly News" suddenly began to bare his heart for her and place it at her feet . . . She had left him immediately, having no words for such behavior.

And John Quincy Adams, one of the two Americans . . . He was in his fifties and people said that he had laid aside a comfortable nest egg. She hadn't been able to keep from laughing and he had been terribly insulted and asked her if she took him for a joke? She should know that he was a Yankee and born in Connecticut, don't you know?

And, of course, Larry—the Irishman. It was now two years since he first had confided in her. Her excuse had been that she was much too young to think about such things. Well, Larry concluded, then we'll wait till you're older. Three months later he was there again. Was she old enough now? No, not yet. All right, then we'll wait, *begorry,* some more, but he was getting impatient so she would have to hurry up. After she had begun to go out now and then with Nels, Larry came to her for the third time. He had noticed, he said, that she was getting older and more mature day by day. How about it? But she had just shook her head and said that she never seemed to get old enough for what he was interested in. And then Jonas had suddenly appeared in her life. She was out more often now and the invincible Larry decided that it was time for a final decision. Now he *begorry* wanted a firm answer . . . Such a persevering suitor may have deserved a better fate, and he wasn't at all a bad sort, but luckily Larry didn't take his death of her refusal.

Nels had been the most difficult to dismiss. He was quiet and reserved and their relationship had developed without so much being said. He had never said that he loved her but his whole being and behavior spoke more clearly than words. She knew that he one day would have let the words fall—had she only given him occasion to do so. Before Jonas turned up, she was sure it would be Nels. She had such complete trust in him and she felt so confident in his company. And recently she had often asked herself whether she perhaps may have made a mistake—done both him and herself a wrong—when she had let another man take his place in her life. But the answer was always the same: she loved Jonas. As soon as she had seen the handsome, half-fumbling, half-decisive newcomer, she had known that he was the one who would decide her fate. And today she would have done it all over again.

She had seen that he was unreliable in many things and she had tried to support him as well as she could so that he would recognize the valuable aspects of his character and lay aside what was mere affectation and false ambition. And she had been happy in her belief that he to some extent was living up to her expectations. Her reason for not supporting him in his attempts to express his feelings was that she believed that this too would contribute to the development of his character and help prepare him for life . . . This may have been an error.

Ragna's life had been a life of work. Her father had died early, and while she was still a girl her mother too had succumbed to the heavy burden of providing for them both. Since then, she had been on her own. She knew all too well that she didn't have her mother's solemn outlook on life. She wasn't attracted to prayer meetings like her mother, but her example and her admonitions had nevertheless helped her to find meaning, even in her modest life, and to walk through it with a straight back and lifted head.

People had said she was beautiful. But recently she had realized that all the cooking and scouring, washing and dusting had worn on her beauty, and that even though she still was a young woman, she was beginning to fade. Instinctively she studied her fingers as they nervously followed the crotcheting needle. Frequently she missed a loop. Her fingers had become so chubby and red and stiff, and the cream she applied every night didn't make much difference. But she didn't care any longer . . . No one really cared about her looks . . . A little tear found its way down her cheek; then another, and another . . . And then the door was opened and someone walked into the hall . . . She dried her tears with her handkerchief, put away her crocheting, and stood up. There were some journals on the table and she began to look them over . . . It had better not appear that she had been waiting for someone.

It was Nels—the last person she wanted to see this evening. She would have liked to hide her eyes from him because she knew they were red, but she couldn't just turn away. He gave her a worried look as he came into the living room and began to pace without saying a word. Finally he stopped in front of her. Evidently, he had something on his mind, and it wasn't without some suspense that she sat there waiting to hear what he would say. She instinctively felt that it would concern her.

"You're up late, Miss Ragna," he began.

"Yes," she answered, staring at the floor.

"Hmm. It's a beautiful evening." Nels often began in this manner when he had something important on his mind. But nothing followed. He just turned away and paced back and forth again. She got to her feet. "I had better get to bed," she said. At the door she turned and said good night. When she was at the top of the stairs she heard him express a powerful Swedish oath between clenched teeth. Before she had reached her room she heard the entrance door open and close again. She stopped automatically and held her hands to her heart. She knew the latecomer must be Jonas.

He had been with the Simonsens as usual and as he was walking home he had thought of how fine everything was there compared to the little boardinghouse with all these Swedes and other plain people. He had more or less decided to move to a more suitable apartment. Simonsen had remarked that a man who had advanced to have his own *bisnes* shouldn't *mixe* too much with the proletariat. And Dagny had been so charming . . . But he didn't like the presence of another guest, a Lieutenant Booker from Fort Snelling. Ragna obviously had to pay him some attention for politeness' sake. The lieutenant had even sat next to her at the table, and during the entire meal she had had to talk to him and listen to his nonsense . . . He supposed it was the way things were done in higher circles . . . But he didn't really like this Booker. He was arrogant and a few times he had corrected Jonas when he in all modesty had opened his mouth. And he had the haughty smile so typical of his kind of people . . . He could see that Simonsen wasn't too happy with him either.

Such were the thoughts weighing on his mind when he entered the boardinghouse and found himself face to face with Nels. He stood right in his path with an expression that left Jonas with no doubt that he was about to confront some unpleasantness.

"You're late," muttered the Swede. Jonas felt anger welling up in him.

"That's none of your business," he answered abruptly and tried to get around Nels, but without success. The *suerbasen* placed his hand solidly on his shoulder. With a lowered voice he said, "Can you remember what you promised me one year ago in the *suer'n*? You had made yourself drunk the night before."

"Yes, I remember it well," he said. His voice was now more subdued.

"And can you remember what I promised in return?" Jonas had no difficulty in remembering that Nels had said he would kill him if anything ever should happen to Ragna.

"Yes, I can remember that too," he said, "but nothing has happened to her."

"Well that remains to be seen," Nels replied. "I just want you to know I'm man of my word, and you damn better believe it!" He let go of Jonas's shoulder and went quickly up the stairs. Ragna hastily closed the door to her room when she heard him come.

23.

His meeting with Nels was not without effect on Jonas. He knew the Swede and was aware that he wasn't one to fool around with. Even if he may not have been entirely serious about killing him, he would at least give him a sound beating and that too would be bad in lots of ways. The worst was that it would without doubt create a public scandal. No way could such a story, involving a man with his own *bisnes* and who had, so to speak, become a prominent man in the city, be kept quiet. It would be trumpeted all over Minneapolis and would be a feature in all the newspapers, and all the wives would jabber about it, and his *bisnesen* would *luse* because of it, and more . . . And he would probably become an invalid for life and would have to give up his plans of becoming famous in *bisnes* and happy in marriage . . . He couldn't *expekte* a young, wealthy girl—nor a poor one for that matter—to walk up to the altar for a man who no longer had command of his limbs . . . He may even not be able to *mæka levinga* and would die in the poorhouse. *Gudnes!* Why should it be so difficult to get through life in a reasonable manner? Had he only had enough sense to remain in Norway . . . Swedes could be a nuisance there too, but you were free to say what you wanted about them since they were safely on the other side of the border. But here you kept bumping into them all the time. But don't think that Jonas would let himself be bullied or scared off . . . If he decided to have Dagny Simonsen he would damn well stand up to the consequences.

But rumination and speculation open up the mind to all kinds of strange thoughts. The more Jonas reflected, the more insecure he found his position. He realized that he hadn't really kept the promise he had given Nels in the *suer'n* . . . But he hadn't actually promised Ragna anything, and no jury and no judge could say that there had been anything definite between them. Still, when he thought about it he saw that there nevertheless had been quite a lot between them. They had been sort of engaged anyhow, even if there had been no contractual agreement, and he couldn't deny that he had a certain responsibility.

But surely a man owed it to himself to think of his own future. A poor and ambitious man couldn't simply throw away the opportunity to become Simonsen's son-in-law. This would give him entry to the higher social circles and he would become as well known and respected a man as Dr. Hoegh and Professor Breda and Oftedal and A. C. Haugan and Søren Listoe and Hans Mattson and Professor Stub and all the swells who were always written up in the newspapers . . . And then there was the important factor that Dagny Simonsen was a lady with culture and *æddykætion*. Such a wife would lend luster to the name of Olson.[64]

It was very late when sleep interrupted Jonas's many and conflicting thoughts. In the morning he discovered that he had decided to be as polite and kind to Ragna as he could. He saw no reason to hurt her. Consequently, he said good morning to her in a friendly voice when she came in to serve at the breakfast table. "Good morning!" she answered quietly and lowered her eyes . . . Damn! She was a nice and brave girl . . . it would be a shame to say anything else. And then he remembered the lieutenant . . . The squirt!

———◆———

But love could only be of importance for a brief moment in an active man's life—Lanberg had explained this and Lanberg should know—and there were soon so many other things that demanded Jonas's attention that he had little time for either self-examination or self-justification, except what could be done within the four walls of the boardinghouse. He had decided to tolerate the plain company in Mrs. Johnson's unattractive pension a little while longer for the simple reason that to leave would create the appearance of an open breach and it would seem that he was attempting to get away from Nels and Ragna.

Stunsrud's store burned down a few days later. One morning all that remained was a heap of ashes. Nothing was saved. The old wooden structure had burned down in minutes. The fire had started in the cellar and found its way to some cans of oil. An explosion and a bonfire and that was it! People said that Stunsrud had good insurance but he himself claimed that he suffered great loss. There were all kinds of rumors about how the fire had started. One insisted that Stunsrud had been observed in the neighborhood just before it was discovered, while others could witness in all conscience that he had been sound asleep in his bed at the time. His version was that the fire had been instigated by his enemies and competitors and that they would be prosecuted. For the next few weeks the fire was the most popular topic of conversation in North Minneapolis. Simonsen was sure that the arsonist was no other than Stunsrud himself. It wasn't the first time, he said. And Stunsrud had his own good reasons for doing it just now: his time was past; that was evident from the recent increase in their own business. This year they would have the best annual profit since Simonsen had come to Jenkins twenty-two years ago. Most people tended to agree with Simonsen. And if Stunsrud hadn't done it, he at least could have done it: the book about him had revealed that he had done this sort of thing out West. And all knew that the book was entirely reliable.

The case was never brought to court and Stunsrud left the city about three months later with his insurance money. Later, it was discovered that he had gone to the gold fields in Alaska. There, all tracks disappeared, for him as for many other adventurers who went out there in the 1880s and 1890s.

In this period there were two other events of some importance for Jonas. The first was that he had Simonsen's approval to withdraw $1,500 from the business as down payment on his loan with the Scandia Bank. Simonsen had agreed because it gave him far freer hands with the rest of the firm's capital, which up to now had been entrusted to three different banks, but that he now wished to place in the Soria Moria Bank, of which he had recently become president. Jonas had at first questioned whether this was a really *sæf* way of doing *bisnes*.

The second event was that Olaf Searlie talked Jonas into buying a quarter section in the Red River Valley.[65] Jonas didn't think much of the deal and believed that the land would never have any value. But he had $1,200—his accumulated salary—in the bank, and he had discovered that all *bisnesmænd* seemed to have land property they could brag about, so he thought he might as well buy it now that he could pay in cash. He also decided to purchase a city lot or two. His bachelor days would soon be over and he looked forward to moving into his own house and home . . . And should Dagny Simonsen become his bride, he would need a fine house, so he should probably have held on to the $1,200. A family could grow faster than imagined . . . But—it had been done.

Jonas's ambition got a new boost when Simonsen became bank president. To be bank president was a sign of power and respect. And why shouldn't he too achieve such a position in society? He increasingly sensed that he was becoming a man to be reckoned with when something was to be done in the colony.

24.

It was Saturday night. Jonas came home late to the boardinghouse. It had been an unusually busy day in the store. He was tired. For the first time since he had begun to work in the store he had admitted to himself that to be a *bisnesmand* was a tough life. There was never a moment to yourself and you could grow tired of the constant demands on your attention.

He looked around in the rooms downstairs. They were empty except for Ludvig Napoleon Stomhoff, who sat there speculating on something or other; and Stomhoff held no interest for Jonas. He had never liked him and seldom had a word with him if he could avoid it. It was dark in the parlor. He looked into the kitchen. It was dark there too. "The Weekly News" followed his movements with interest and an ambiguous smile when Jonas had his back to him, but took on a solemn expression every time the young man turned and looked in his direction. Turning unexpectedly, Jonas saw his smile. So the scoundrel was smiling at his expense. And for that matter, what was he himself doing here, sniffing and snooping like a bloodhound. There had been times when someone else used to sit waiting for him where Napoleon now sat. Had he hoped to find her there tonight? Far from it . . . He was simply tired. There was really no home for him here. Jonas suddenly became aware that he missed a home. That was it. This boardinghouse was no home. It was filled with Swedes and poverty and discomfort and the meat of old cows. There wasn't even a good chair for a tired man to sit in . . . and now this unpleasant fellow . . . You shouldn't have to mix with his kind. He would be damned if he would stand it any longer. He had to move. He could get a nice room with Mrs. Bakstrøm on Fourth Avenue. They made Norwegian food and he could consort with Lanberg, Nilsen, and Lomwiig and other prominent people of his own class and position in society. And yet—did he really want to move just now? It wouldn't be a real home with Mrs. Bakstrøm either. And those fellows were a boring . . .

"We're having nice weather," Napoleon remarked in a soft and ingratiating voice.

Uff, that awful man! Jonas thought. Was he speaking to him? *Gudnes,* would he have to be polite to such a scandal monger . . . "Oh, I suppose the weather is good enough." He was surly and began to move toward the door. He may as well go *streit* to bed; he saw no reason to stay here any longer . . .

"You seem a little distracted tonight," Stomhoff said. "Were you looking for Nels?" he carefully added. Jonas turned around, straightened his back, and stared at him. What was that slime daring to suggest?

"Nels? Why in the wide world would I want to look for Nels?"

"Oh, there could always be a reason," replied the other. "You are such good old friends, and with friends you may share both happiness and sorrows. And Nels certainly seems to have good reason to feel happy, doesn't he?"

"Just what are you talking about?" asked Jonas rather crossly. But he had become interested and he tried to appear as condescending as he could to keep this from Napoleon.

"Oh, well, we may all envy Nels," continued "The Weekly News" as he got up from his chair. "We can't all have such luck with the ladies . . ."

"Luck with the ladies? What nonsense is this?" Jonas automatically came closer.

"Well, you see," said Stomhoff as he lowered his voice almost to a whisper. "They have *mæka op* again."

"*Mæka op?* Who has *mæka op?*"

"Oh, I think you know," Stomhoff answered and squinted mysteriously with his small greenish yellow eyes. "I know what I'm talking about and tonight I saw them go out together. They are still out. So we'll have to be happy with the happy even though we ourselves may be both disappointed and dejected."

Jonas found it difficult to hide his surprise. "I don't know what you're talking about," he said, "but if anyone *mæker op* then let them *mæke op* for all I *kærer*. This has been a busy day and I'm tired." He took another step toward the door.

"Yes, I suppose you can get tired of such a big *bisnes*," Napoleon remarked. "You have expanded quite a bit since you got rid of Stunsrud."

"Stunsrud got rid of himself," Jonas replied. "You have to do *'onest bisnes* to *sukside*."

"Naturally, naturally," he still whispered. "And do you know what? It was a true masterstroke on your part to get Lyvenfelt to write that book! What an excellent demonstration of the truth in the old saying that the pen is more powerful than the sword."

Jonas stared at him in astonishment. What was the rascal daring to accuse him of having done? Everybody knew that he hadn't had anything to do with that wretched book. "Have you gone mad, man?" he cried with his fist in the air. "If you dare say that again I'll damn . . ."

"Take it easy, take it easy, my dear Olson!" parried Stomhoff, holding up a cautionary finger. "I have it from a very reliable source—from Lyvenfelt himself, if you please!"

"Never in my life have I ever had any *bisnes* with Lyvenfelt, so he is evidently lying."

"I even know the exact sum you paid him, you see! Moreover, anyone can see that someone has been pulling strings: Lanberg never had that kind of money."

"And Lyvenfelt told you all this? The fat sow! But it's a lie. You may have my word of honor . . ."

"Oh, honor is such a relative term nowadays," Napoleon interrupted him with a cold laugh. "But," he continued, again in a whisper, "I can well understand that it would be rather inconvenient if this became common knowledge. A man in your position . . . and with such a fine *bisnes* . . . and as a suitor at the Simonsens I suppose you must be even more careful . . ."

"Damn! You had better . . ."

"Today I heard," continued his evil spirit undisturbed, "that this lieutenant from Fort Snelling is there all the time. And one evening I actually saw them at the theater . . . I thought it might interest you . . . By the way, you wouldn't have a dollar that you could do without for a week or two? Just as a loan, mind you. I'll have to pay for my board tomorrow . . . And, as I may have mentioned, should anything come about that I know will interest you, you may be certain that I'll always be at your service."

Jonas had an almost uncontrollable urge to knock him down—to kill the beast. But he mastered his inclination. He couldn't deny that Napoleon's news had interested him . . . If he only hadn't known about the book. And now the swine would *œdverteise* it all over *Min'ap'lis* if he didn't give him a "loan." But his information might prove useful . . . He had become suspicious of that soldier. He was a nasty character and, to be honest, Dagny had been giving him more attention than was proper for a girl with a Christian upbringing. Not that he really cared. But it would be nice to know what they were doing when they were on their own. And then there was this other matter. Napoleon's gossip had made him uneasy and it would indeed be interesting to have him keep a close eye on Nels as well . . .

But suddenly he felt a powerful disgust with Napoleon . . . He just couldn't place his fate in the hands of such a man. That would be almost like selling himself to the devil . . . "I'm sorry, but I have no money about me," he lied. "I'll see you in the morning. Good night!"

"Good night, Mister Olson!" said Stomhoff, bowing respectfully. After Jonas had ascended the stairs Stomhoff slipped quietly out of the house. Nels and Ragna could be expected home from the dance at Normanna Hall at about this time, and when two confide in each other after a dance there may be something to pick up.

Jonas lit his lamp with a sense of loathing. That miserable carcass . . . He and his words stank. But it was strange that Nels and Ragna were going steady again. He hadn't really expected that of either of them. But as far as he was concerned, he couldn't care less . . . They could *mœke op* all they wanted for him . . . And, come to think of it, it suited him well! It gave him an opportunity to get away from the boardinghouse. If Nels wanted her himself, he wouldn't beat him up for making her available. He should rather be grateful that he didn't interfere. But he didn't like it. It was in a way like being pushed aside at a dance. He had, after all, been sort of engaged to her. And then there was that slimy lieutenant . . . *Gudnes,* a Christian could no longer have a girl undisturbed by these chicken thieves . . .

He couldn't sleep. He tried to read but couldn't do that either. He just lay there speculating on what would come of it all. He didn't really have time to waste on such things either, but he couldn't leave them be.

He hadn't been so often to the Simonsens recently, even though he had what Dagny called a "standing invitation." But whenever he came, that slimy Booker was there too, as, for instance, when he had dropped in one evening a couple of weeks ago. The lieutenant was sitting there fingering and stroking the eleven hairs on his overlip that he evidently imagined was a mustache. And he laughed and sniggered and behaved like a *dæmful* whenever anyone said a sensible word. And then he had taken a box of cigarettes from his pocket and asked Dagny if she would permit him to smoke. As if smoking meant anything! And she had answered that it would be *"sich'en plæsjure,"* or some such polite nonsense. And after he had sucked on the paper nipples a while, he had offered one to Jonas, even though he knew that he didn't smoke, so it must have been to insult him. And when he had said, "No thank you," the lieutenant had remarked in a sarcastic manner, *"Aa, jæs,* that's true, Mister Olson can't stand tobacco! I forgot!" And then he had winked slyly to Dagny as if to make her aware what a *smartælek* he could be. And poor girl, she had to laugh and be polite and pretend that she appreciated all he did, because that is the way with these fine families . . . it was all hypocrisy and farce. He couldn't really understand why they let him come all the time. He was only a poor lieutenant who hardly could pay his own way and who certainly couldn't support a wife and *ræse* a family.

And Booker was such an arrogant fellow. He was always making remarks about being a Southerner. As if that was anything to boast about! The last time at Simonsen's he had talked about his distinguished family in Tennessee. Once upon a time his family may have amounted to something but it seemed pretty obvious that this must have been a long time ago. He said that they once had had an estate there with a mansion and all. But then came the Civil War and his folks were of course rebels who owned Negroes and had never done a day's honest work themselves. They just lolled around and had these black people to slave for them. And when Lincoln had come along and said there had to be an end to this Negro *bisnessen* and that all people should do something useful for *e' living,* the first thing they did was to secede from the Republic and rebel against authority. And the father of this little shit began to call himself a general and marched against the North with a regiment of rebels. And the North wanted to *sæve* the Union and stop these Turks from trading in human meat—even if it was black. And of course almost the entire regiment was cut down. Booker had given quite a vivid account. And Mrs. Simonsen had been thrilled by their unparalleled bravery. And the general? Jonas had asked; had he too been cut down with the rest? Hm—no, not quite. The general came home in the end, but he didn't weigh many pounds and was in a miserable condition. He was wounded, naturally? And Mrs. Simonsen had been quick to say: "Why, *o'kors, jœs,* that goes without saying—he was a general." And Dagny had looked sort of strangely at Jonas and said *o'kors* too. And the lieutenant had started work on his eleven hairs and nodded and said, *"Uh-hu,"* or something like it. But worst of all, he had said, his family had *lusa* everything they had and the children had to learn to work for a living. And that had been a great sacrifice.

And Mrs. Simonsen had said some nonsense about the Bookers being an old family down South and the lieutenant had agreed. They had lived there for 250 years. Jonas didn't think this was anything to boast about. He should visit Norway and there he would see some really old families. Some had been there more than 2,000 years. And then the fop had grimaced and said: *"Gudnes,* Norway, it's hardly a country—it belongs to Sweden and is a spot on the map on the outskirts of civilization." But, strangely, not even Mrs. Simonsen laughed at that witticism. And Jonas had been so mad that he had said good night and left.

Eventually he fell asleep. And he slept so deeply that he didn't even hear Nels and Ragna come home around two o'clock. He was later given the time by Napoleon, who had just happened to be there when they came home arm-in-arm . . .

"Arm-in-arm!" Jonas exclaimed. It slipped out of him.

"Ju bet, and as far as I can understand, the temperature between them is quite a few degrees above average," said Napoleon.

Jonas thought that if he was going to subscribe to "The Weekly News" anyway, he may as well pay decently. That would perhaps put an end to the wicked rumors about his connection with the book. He gave Napoleon a five-dollar bill. The colporteur of news looked eagerly at the bill. "I'm sorry, but I don't have any change," he said.

"Aa, never'ju mein'. A little loan is not worth mentioning," Jonas said grandly.

"Just as I have always said," exclaimed "The Weekly News" fervently. "Grocer Jonas Olson is, I insist, the finest and most liberal Norwegian *bisnesmand* in *Min'ap'lis."*

He offered his hand in gratitude. Jonas accepted it, but quickly let it go. It was as slimy as a fish's tale, he thought. Agh! . . .

25.

It was a month later that Jonas heard about the big party at the Simonsens. Napoleon was of course the bringer of news and knew all the details. Jonas hadn't been told a word about it. Simonsen himself had said nothing and it was evident that it had been kept a secret. But Napoleon wouldn't have been called "The Weekly News" if he had not had information about such an important social event.

He had noticed that Jonas was at home that evening, he said, and had thought it a little strange, he being such a close friend of the family and all. The lieutenant had been in full dress uniform. Mrs. Simonsen had planned the party as an engagement celebration. She had done everything she could to attract Lieutenant Booker and make a couple of him and her daughter. Simonsen didn't approve of her designs. With all his faults—and Napoleon had a full catalogue—he was straightforward and democratic and didn't like such fawning. Simonsen had his own plans for his daughter, said Stomhoff with a confiding smile, which implied that Jonas knew what he was talking about. Indeed, it was commonly known in high society in the Norwegian colony that Simonsen had taken Jonas to heart and thought highly of his business acumen and of his future prospects.

Jonas listened to all this with mixed feelings. He knew that it wasn't simply a fabrication since it roughly corresponded with his own understanding of the situation. But even though he was deeply hurt by not having been found worthy of an invitation to the grand party, he had made up his mind not to get worked up about it. He would at least not have Napoleon running around saying that he was the least bit concerned about what the Simonsens did or didn't do. As far as he was concerned, they could have the lieutenant. So he said, "People will talk. But there has of course never been any kind of understanding between Miss Simonsen and myself. *Gudnes,* there are girls everywhere!"

"Naturally! Naturally!" Napoleon nodded. "And for a man as yourself, with your position and your prospects . . ."

"Oh, that doesn't seem to matter much for a lady like Mrs. Simonsen." It slipped out of him, and no sooner had the words been said than he realized he would have to correct the impression he had made. "But then she has always been very kind to me," he added.

"You are referring to the daughter?"

"The mother," Jonas corrected him.

"I see." Napoleon stood for a moment as in deep thought. Jonas noticed that he had suddenly adopted a humble, almost pious posture. He wondered what would follow. "But appearances may often be misinterpreted," Stomhoff observed after a while. He fingered the edge of his vest as if he found it difficult to continue. Then, finally, the words came to him. He hoped Mister Olson would not be upset with him for telling the truth. He only wanted to give him a helping hand—the hand of a friend, he might add. He had always been reluctant to pry into people's private affairs, but for a good friend . . . And, by the way, would he happen to have a dollar or two in his pocket that he could do without for a week or so . . . just to help him over an unexpected embarrassment . . . a short-term loan?

Jonas thought he had some cash. He was, of course, only a poor man himself, but such a trifling sum between friends . . . it was a duty. He pulled out a five and the sight of the bill had an effect on Napoleon similar to that of sixteen ounces of whiskey. When he, as usual, said that he had no change and Jonas, as usual, said it was *aalreit* and that he could keep the bill, Stomhoff eagerly continued his story.

To make his long story short, Mrs. Simonsen had from the start objected to admitting Jonas to their home. Simonsen, however, had insisted when he discovered his business talent. Their daughter, who was curious to find out what sort of man was the occasion of their quarrel, sided with her father, and when she discovered that Jonas was a fine young man and that he had a great future in *bisnes*, she fell in love with him. The mother had declared that Jonas was a mere greenhorn, an uncivilized farmer's boy, and that for the life of her she couldn't understand that even a man with so little taste and polish as Simonsen could imagine imposing such a clod on a respectable family. To begin with, Lieutenant Booker had been a frequent visitor of the recently widowed Mrs. Oppesen, who was then said to be on the market, and Mrs. Næppesen had conspired with Mrs. Simonsen to introduce Dagny to the recently commisioned officer. In many ways she was a remarkable girl and was as little concerned with conventions as her father. But she had a tendency to be a little loose. He wouldn't say that she actually did anything improper, even though there had been some rumors a couple of years ago about her and a younger brother of Stunsrud . . .

"Stunsrud?" Jonas couldn't hide his surprise.

Yes, that was beyond doubt, said Napoleon. It had almost been a scandal. The young Stunsrud was hardly worth the water he had been baptized in—a useless creature, a rake of the worst sort. But nothing her parents said made the least impression on her. Eventually they eloped in the dark of night and planned to take the train to Fargo to get married. The older Stunsrud was an accomplice and even followed them to the *depo'n*. But Simonsen had smelled a rat and came upon them unawares, attended by a police officer. After a dispute more violent than edifying, the girl had to follow her father home since she was not yet of age. That was when the mother had taken her to Europe, and afterward she had been sent East to a school for young women. But her behavior there had not been above reproach either, he had heard people say. Napoleon didn't have the details, but Mrs. Næppesen had dropped some words that could only be interpreted one way. The girl, he was sorry to say, had, to the best of his knowledge, been thrown out of school. But for all that, Dagny was a strapping girl. No one could deny that. Still, there was her deplorably fickle nature. She had supposedly become engaged in Europe and had then done her best to attract Jonas; but as soon as the lieutenant appeared on the stage, she was wildly in love again.

The enmity between Stunsrud and Simonsen had its origin in the affair with Stunsrud's brother. That's when it all began, Stomhoff explained.

"And how did the engagement party develop?" Jonas asked.

"It really wasn't an engagement party," said Napoleon. "Dagny had second thoughts and threatened her mother with a scandal if she made the engagement public." According to Mrs. Næppesen, the whole affair had been more like a funeral.

"I can't make heads or tails of this," Jonas remarked. "It makes no sense from any point of view."

"That may be," Napoleon replied, "but then neither does Dagny Simonsen. By the way, and since we are on the subject, I may as well let you know Dagny's reason for her last-minute change of mind. Her mother refused to invite—you."

"Me?"

"Exactly! She wanted to play fair with you, you see, but her mother wouldn't let her."

"But the engagement, then? Has that also come to an end?"

"Well, you see, it's difficult really to know too much about that—not until the wedding, and perhaps not even then. But the lieutenant is still a frequent visitor, I've heard, so it will probably all work out in the end."

They had this conversation just after dinner and Jonas realized that it had taken up more time than he had to spare. He indicated that he had to return to the store, but Napoleon held his arm as he got up from his chair. "One more thing," he whispered. "Nels and Ragna are going to Pastor Skogsberg's church this evening.[66] I was at the door to the kitchen this morning. He is evidently preparing her for a Swedish future. *Gudbey,* Mister Olson!"

Jonas stopped and took long breaths of fresh air as soon as he got out of the room. It was as if he had just left a morgue. Standing there, he saw Ragna pumping water in the backyard. As on impulse, he went quickly toward her. She had *køttet*[67] out Nels before. She could damn well do it again! Could he have a few words with her? It was very important . . .

She looked up at him with a worried expression on her face. "I didn't think you had any more to say to me," she quietly said.

"Why?" he boldly asked. "I'm going to the theater tonight. Would you like to join me?"

"No," she replied, "I can't."

"Perhaps you're going out with someone else?"

"Yes." She turned away.

"With Nels?" He could scarcely control his voice.

"Yes, and you had better go out with the one you are used to consorting with."

"Me? And who would that be?"

"You should know."

"So you won't go with me?"

"No."

"But if I should ask you—to—to marry me, what would you then answer?" Well, he had said it! And he thought he had done it quite nicely too.

"There is no answer to such a frivolous question," she said in a low voice.

"I'll be damned . . ."

"Time will show that I'm right." She took the pail but he took it from her and carried it into the house. "Will you promise to wait until you have seen if you are right?" he asked.

"I'm not promising anything—not now."

"So the story about Nels is true?"

"You can never tell the truth anymore," she answered as she opened the door for him. He left like a whipped dog.

Napoleon's words had smarted. In particular the part about him not being good enough for Dagny and their fine party. Well, he wasn't going to run their door down. He wasn't really surprised either. Nor had he ever harbored any affection for Dagny Simonsen. At least not in the way you feel for the person you are thinking of marrying . . . No, that was a different kind of love. And Ragna was the one person he had loved all the while. He felt it so clearly now. The more he thought about how Nels had taken her from him in such a vile manner, the more angry he became. Those damn Swedes! They were always after us Norwegians . . .

He had come to the *storet*—the damn grocery that he was so tired of with its smell of rancid herring and rotten eggs and old butter and spoilt cheese and all kinds of corruption . . . He could have been a free man wandering off on his own in the wilds of the old country . . . Spruce and fir and juniper—they certainly smelled nicer than this miserable thing called *bisnes*. But wasn't that a buggy standing outside the *storet,* and with a lady in it . . . And that was surely Simonsen's brown *timet* . . . The lady was getting down . . . It was Dagny . . . Well, he certainly wouldn't notice her . . .

But there she was, coming toward him, offering him her hand as free and easy as ever. "I'm married," she said. "Won't you congratulate me?" There was no shame in her. Imagine speaking just as if she were talking to someone not at all involved . . .

"Married? Are you married?" He exclaimed. "But what in the world . . ."

"Is that so remarkable? Do you find me too old?" She laughed.

"No, but . . ." And he realized he was blushing . . . Well, he had better congratulate her, wish her good luck. He had to say something. And when he examined her more closely he could see that she wasn't as attractive as he had imagined.

"And now I'm going to live in Washington," she said. "Isn't that great?"

"Is—is—it that—that Booker?" Jonas asked. He couldn't help envying the lieutenant.

"Do you mean Lieutenant Booker?" she laughed. "Why no! What makes you think I'd have anything like that? No, my name is McCarthy—Mrs. McCarthy. My husband has been in the foreign service in Europe and he now has a position in the State Department in Washington. We met each other in Copenhagen two years ago and one day he turned up here and we got married. That's all!" But she had to go, she said, because the train East was leaving in half an hour. She had wanted to say good-bye first, and she would always remember the good times they had had together. With that, she smiled and was off.

Jonas stood a long time following the buggy with his eyes . . . *Gudnes,* what strange creatures these girls were . . . And then he wondered whether Napoleon's stories had been worth the ten dollars.

26.

Few words were exchanged between Jonas and Ragna the next few weeks. He tried to get her attention when they were alone but it was evident that she had hardened her heart against him. She avoided him with the cunning he had found typical of the feminine sex, so he realized that he had no further hope. Then circumstances were again on his side. It had always been like that for Jonas: just as he was about to give up and didn't know what to do, something would *hæpna.* It happened quite naturally. He came from his room in a great rush to get back to the store after dinner and she came running up the stairs. They almost collided, and when they suddenly became aware of each other and came to a stop in the dimly lighted hall, there was only a step between them. Sometimes this is all that is required to lose your senses. It was naturally Ragna who first regained control of herself. Jonas had often wondered that a woman who may become hysterical on seeing a mouse may be so incredibly cold-blooded in situations where he felt stupid and embarrassed. This was but one of life's many enigmas that neither the learned nor the lay could explain. The hall was so narrow that it was difficult for two to pass, and there he stood, big and broad, in her way.

"Let me get past," she said when she became aware of the situation. He was about to do as she said, when he had the lucky idea that this might be his last chance to let her know what was on his mind. So he made himself even broader and blocked her passage.

"Tell me," he said, "tell me—" And he paused, the better to achieve control of his voice, which didn't seem to be functioning as it should.

"I've nothing to tell you," she cut him off. "Let me get past you, you hear! I'm in a hurry." But this angered him. He wasn't just an old stick she could throw around.

"You'd better tell me if this thing between you and Nels has been *fixa op for ki'ps.*"

"Well, s'pose it is—what are you going to do about it?" She was mocking him—she was actually standing there and making fun of him because she had made him unhappy! He would make a last attempt to appeal to her good heart—if it hadn't been turned to stone under

Swedish influence . . . She should at least feel sorry for him; he was after all a human being, and they had had some good times before misery set in . . .

"If I only knew that there was the slightest hope then I would gladly
wait, even for a full year," he ensured her. "But this is more than a poor
creature can survive."

"Yes, it would be too sad if the wedding you had planned should
veinde up in a funeral," she said. And then she added, "Perhaps you had
better pay a visit to Washington since I hear that the *Mississen* there isn't
so happy either. Perhaps you could get together again." She was ruthless.
And then she turned around and went quickly down the stairs.

And he stood there, no wiser than before, or, rather, now he knew. It
was probably *fixa op for ki'ps* between her and Nels. So much was clear.
And now they were getting married . . . Actually, he hadn't been much
in doubt about it. And this thing about Dagny . . . he was sure it was
something Napoleon had said, so it could have no basis in fact.

Jonas hardly ever spoke with Nels anymore. After his despicable behavior, the least he could do was to show him his contempt. Strangely,
the Swede didn't seem to pay much notice. At times he joked in the most
unbecoming manner.

Jonas had become a lonely man. People had changed and he no longer
found pleasure in their company. He was tired of them even though
many were polite and spoke of how well he had done in *Ammerekka*
and all that, but without sincerity . . . And Nels and Ragna weren't even
polite. Well, Nels wasn't a Swede for nothing . . .

One evening after some business in South Minneapolis he had the
impulse to visit Cousin Salmon, since he hadn't set foot inside their door
after his first week in the city. It would be poor entertainment, he knew,
but he had to see people. They were just about to have supper and the wife
wouldn't let him go without a meal. And since Mister Salmon had only
stopped for a few minutes at Stockholm-Olson's, something he seldom
did since he no longer had credit there, he was already home. But then he
had to go over to Riverside and buy some meat, and his wife, who didn't
know that Jonas had become such a temperance man, also gave him a
quarter for some beer. But at Butch's there happened to be someone who
trita because of some *'lektion,* and Salmon, who was a *pu'blik* man, had
to be polite and have three or four glasses. So supper was rather late.

They were both extremely nice to Jonas and Mrs. Salmon insisted
that she had always said that he would become a great man. And his

cousin said he had written home to Norway and given them the details of the success of this young man in *Ammerekka* and said that Jonas Olson was already as famous in *Min'ap'lis* as S. E. Olson. And he had talked with Carlström about running him for alderman in North Minneapolis and he had answered that it was a *greit idi* that he would keep *in mein'*.

Jonas listened to all this with an uncomfortable feeling. Not so long ago he would have been flattered to have so much attention. Now it all seemed strangely irrelevant.

"And I suppose you have *investa* in stock and everything there is since you have *mæka* so much money?" said the cousin. Jonas answered that he had placed almost all his money in the business in order to become an equal partner with Simonsen. He didn't say much beyond that. But Cousin Salmon took deep draughts of his *lagerbeer* and talked with emotion of his pride in having a relative who had been such a great success. Yes, there was good reason to be proud of Jonas who would soon *indlektes i City Konsiln* and perhaps one day would even have a seat as a representative in *Kapitoliet* in *Sankte Paal, perhæps, ho'no's?* become governor of all of Minnesota . . . Imagination ran deep in that family.

Jonas realized that there was little point in trying to speak with them about what weighed on his mind. There was no reason to tell them the truth, that prosperity and respect had not brought him the expected happiness and that he had become a different man . . .

He gave more of himself to his business than ever before, but it no longer gave him much pleasure. Sometimes he would relieve the delivery clerks and pay visits to customers himself for a change. And then, as he was visiting with Mrs. Jensen or Mother Hansen, he might happen to see their promising young daughters and he would try to imagine what his life would be like if he should find someone other than Ragna. But he was never able to produce a tempting vision. These other girls had little to recommend them . . . they were so conceited and had no *bræns* in their head; nor were they much to look at.

Simonsen soon became aware that his partner was not the same cheerful boy he had been. He was of course still thinking of Dagny. And he would have liked to comfort him since he felt that he wasn't without blame. So one day be began to talk with Jonas about overworking himself and vacations and things like that. But the young man wouldn't listen.

"I hope you haven't been hurt because of what Dagny did?" He finally let it out.

"What has Dagny done?" Jonas was surprised.

"Nothing much except that she got married, you know."

"Yes, and she is of course happy?"

"As far as we know! But you may perhaps have expected a different turn of events . . . I must admit that I had other expectations too . . ."

Only now did Jonas understand what he was aiming at. He didn't really know what to say. If he said he was in mourning because of Dagny, it would be awkward, and if he said that he couldn't care less, it would be even worse. But, happily, his worries hadn't deprived him of his natural gift for compromise. So he answered: "If she's happy and content then it's not for me to think one way or the other about it."

Simonsen was reassured and Jonas was happy to contribute to his peace of mind. Simonsen had recently had quite a lot of pressure. The bank was giving him more and more work and responsibility and there had been board meetings every night this past week so that he had even had to relinquish his beloved pool.

But to reassure Simonsen was one thing; to reassure himself was far more difficult. Eventually he again began to go to church. He hadn't been there for a long time and in his present state of mind it seemed the right place for him to be. Perhaps Vangsnes would say something from his pulpit that would give consolation and new strength to a foresaken soul who had lost his girlfriend. He was welcomed. The congregation knew of his success and many felt it was a good thing to have such important members. Moreover, they felt they had some part in his success. But you mustn't imagine that all were so generous. To speak the truth, some sat in their pews and envied Jonas and criticized the Lord for having let such a newcomer have so much success while they, who had deserved it, had received so little.

Jonas enjoyed being in church and thought that the pastor had given a good sermon, but it couldn't cure a bleeding heart with an all-too-worldly desire for a woman.

27.

It was a miserable, bitterly cold fall afternoon. People went in and out of the store and they all complained about the weather. All day Jonas had listened to the same monotonous comments. He was in bad spirits himself and all he saw and all he heard—the dark, threatening clouds, the shivering people, their unhappy faces and complaining words—had hour by hour darkened the vale of tears that was his mind.

It had truly been a day to try men's souls. It had started right after breakfast when Napoleon had confronted him on the porch and told him that the date for Nels and Ragna's wedding had been set. Nels had been seen in the courthouse yesterday. And what other business could he have there than to arrange for his marriage license? And he had more evidence. Reliable people had seen him leave the county-*clerkens* office with a document in his hand, and when they had asked him about it he had simply been confused and left them. So the circumstantial evidence was as strong as you could wish. Napoleon had succeeded in lowering his spirits quite a few degrees, and they hadn't been so high to begin with.

For weeks Simonsen had spent most of his time calculating figures—or whatever kept them so busy at his bank. And when he once in a while entered the store, he was so bad-tempered and cross that he wasn't much comfort. Yesterday he had suddenly become sick, and today Mrs. Simonsen had sent the message that he had to stay in bed. This was particularly inconvenient because it was the first in the month, the day they wrote out checks to the wholesalers for the goods purchased within the last thirty days. Simonsen usually took care of the monthly settlements and Jonas had no desire to intrude on his senior partner's special field. But there was no avoiding it today because Simonsen & Olson had always prided themselves on paying in full and on time and it wouldn't do to have it said that they had changed their policy.

As Jonas was sitting with the bills and checking them against their own accounts, a well-dressed and closely shaved man entered the store. He was exceptionally polite and said some nice things about how efficient and well-organized he had found the store and the good taste of its appointments. Everything confirmed the view they already had of such sound and respected businessmen as Simonsen & Olson, he said. Jonas recognized him as Mr. Kennedy of the wholesale company of Kennedy, Ramsey & Co., and they bought about one-third of their goods through this firm. Jonas wasn't so naïve that he imagined that Kennedy had come to pay his compliments. This was the first time he had honored them with his presence and Jonas realized there must be a special reason for so distinguished a visitor. It didn't take long before the reason was revealed. Kennedy had made so free as to come personally for their settlement. This might be seen as somewhat extraordinary since he knew that they would receive their check the following day, and he hoped that Jonas wouldn't be inconvenienced. But special circumstances demanded that he would have to request payment today, and he hoped that Jonas would not take it amiss. But Jonas did. Simonsen & Olson had never begged credit of anyone and they always paid promptly, so this was a very peculiar request, almost an insult, he thought. Someone must have been spreading lies again. But he saw no reason to get involved in a dispute. Resolutely, he picked up pen and checkbook. Kennedy would see that Simonsen & Olson could pay at any time. No problem there! But even before he had started writing, Kennedy placed his hand quickly but carefully on his arm.

"We prefer as much cash as you have on hand, if you please," he said. Jonas looked up in surprise. What could he possibly mean? He had almost said something that shouldn't be said when doing *bisnes* with such a closely shaved and diplomatic Yankee, but he stopped in time. He regretted, he said, that they had no cash. They had placed all they had in the bank when it had opened that morning. The fine gentleman eventually accepted the check but didn't look very pleased about it, and Jonas could no longer hide his irritation.

"You needn't fear that we haven't got the money," he remarked in an offended voice. He wanted the polished American to know what he felt about his behavior.

"Of course," the wholesaler politely answered, "I have unlimited confidence in your firm, but, to tell the truth, I'm not so dead sure about the bank. That's why I'm here."

"You don't mean to tell me that Soria Moria Bank . . ." Jonas stared, astonished. This was beyond anything he could have imagined. The very thought made him dizzy.

"The failure of the United Mills Company, which was announced this morning, involves your bank to the extent of probably a hundred thousand dollars," Mr. Kennedy informed him. "I doubt if it'll survive the day. I'm sorry, Mr. Olson." And with that he gave a bow and left the store.

Jonas's first thought was to go right to Simonsen and talk it over with him. But he was interrupted by a representative of one of the other wholesalers, and the Kennedy story was repeated all over again. Just as Jonas was about to leave, Lanberg made his appearance. He not only confirmed that Soria Moria Bank was deeply involved in the failure of United Mills but he could also tell that there had been a run on the bank just before closing time by several hundred depositors, mostly Scandinavians of humble means. The main group of depositors had been Scandinavian laborers and businessmen. They had been convinced that the bank was solid since it was based on Norwegian integrity. And Norwegian integrity stood in high regard in Minneapolis. It was virtually the first article in the national catechism and was often cited by those who were after Norwegian votes, money, or trade. Nilsen, the architect, was the only man in the city who had dared to suggest that Norwegian integrity was no more than a fairy tale. But no one took Nilsen seriously since he was regarded as a mere jester and a pessimist.

Some of the depositors had been furious when the bank door was closed in their faces, said Lanberg. But most had just gone their way in silent desperation. On his way to Simonsen, Jonas read in the evening newspaper that the bank wouldn't open tomorrow. Wild speculation, bad loans, and unrestrained management were some of the reasons for the bank's plight. On arriving at Simonsen's door, he was met by a servant girl who told him that his partner was so ill that the doctor had given strict orders not to let anyone enter.

The situation was still not fully clear to Jonas. He had reason to fear that Simonsen had been ruined and that quite a lot of the firm's money had been lost, but he had been unable to work out a full picture of the consequences of the bank failure. So he had a new surprise when he an hour later returned to the store and found it closed on the demand of the wholesale houses who had struck while the iron was hot to make sure that the stock didn't disappear. The clerks were on the sidewalk waiting for him and people who had come to do their shopping stood around in groups talking in low voices about what had happened.

"You're a fine fellow, aren't you, getting me to leave Nicolaisen," Vandland hissed angrily as he turned on Jonas.

"And I had a good position with Stunsrud," sputtered Johansen. "And here I am with a wife and children and the approaching winter. If it hadn't been for your rascality, Stunsrud would still have been in business and he was a more honest man than you and Simonsen, even though we all know he was no angel."

"But dear friends," Jonas responded, "you must understand that this is not my doing." This statement was met with a cold laughter.

"Would you imagine that he is trying to *jøstefeie* himself too," Vanland derided him. "The next thing he will *mæka* us *beleiv'* that he is as innocent as Eva in paradise."

"Well, he is probably about as innocent as the serpent in paradise," Johansen seconded him.

"I stand to lose all I have," answered Jonas. He found their accusations so unjust that he could barely control himself.

"You can try that on those who are naïve enough to believe you," Vandland scoffed him again. "We won't swallow anything as hairy as that. With the little circulation I have up here I can at least understand that you are in with the other thieves who have *bøsta* the bank and I can only hope that a righteous providence will see you all in Stillwater."

"It's useless to reason with people who won't use their senses," said Jonas impatiently.

"So you will *insølte* us as well, will you?" asked Vandland.

"I haven't *insølta* anyone."

"Didn't you just tell us we were *kræsi*?"

"I said you didn't use your senses."

"Well, you might as well have said we were *kræsi,*" Johansen insisted.

"Oh, the pox take you all! Be as *kræsi* as you wish!" cried Jonas. He stood looking at them for a while. "And I suppose we owe you a whole lot of money?" he asked.

They looked at each other. They had both taken an advance on their salary.

"No, we can't exactly say that you owe us anything," said Vandland. "I must admit that I've received more than we've agreed on."

"*Aalreit!* Then we have no more to talk about. *Gudbey!*" With that, Jonas turned quickly and walked off.

Only after he had walked a good distance down the street did the full implications of the day's events begin to overwhelm him. He was almost crushed. He walked with lowered head and heavy, dragging feet. Where he went didn't matter anymore. This had come like lightning from a bright sky. Yes, like lightning . . . and it had to hit him. This was just the way it had always been . . . Just as he was on his way to success—and a catastrophe knocked him down. *Gudnes,* it hurt . . .

He felt an urge to do something desperate, like going to the nearest saloon and drinking himself into a stupor and making a public scandal; or throwing himself into the *riveren* and never coming up again; or wandering out into the wilderness where there were no human beings, to be alone with his misery. But he just walked slowly on down the street. People who recognized him turned and stared at him. Some shook their heads and mumbled to each other that it was a pity it should happen to him, such a smart fellow. Others sniggered and said that he had it coming, the smartass of a newcomer who had blown himself up like a windbag as if he believed that he owned all of *Min'ap'lis*. And if a few felt an obligation to say hello, they did so in a remarkable hurry. Without being aware of where he went, he happened to pass by Mrs. Bakstrøm's, and, too late to avoid them, he saw Torgersen and Larsen as they were leaving the house to go downtown after supper.

"Too bad, too bad," Torgersen said hypocritically as he stopped to say hello. And Larsen, who always had a quotation on his tongue, sighed as he offered him his hand, "Yes, it is as the Book says, How the mighty are fallen! Too bad indeed! But you'll have to take it like a man. At least you have the sympathy and understanding of your friends."

Sure, Jonas had heard that one before! The understanding of friends usually meant to be laid out on the table for dissection. And when they were through, you could be glad if you had as much as a skeleton left for those who wished to be present at the funeral.

"I have feared the wind would blow in that direction," Torgersen comforted him, implying that had he only been asked in time, then everything would have been different. "I'm a conservative man," he added. "You've been taking too many chances."

"Yes, the common view is that you've been too impatient," agreed Larsen. "A foundation needs time to settle."

"And Simonsen has always been a *plunger*," commented Torgersen, "and it was to be expected that you, a mere newcomer . . ."

"*Aa, never mein,*" Jonas interrupted him as he turned on his heels and left them. At the corner he attempted to avoid Nicolaisen, who was getting out of a buggy in front of one of the wholesale houses. He had never been on very good terms with Nicolaisen after he had lured away Vandland and many of his customers. But Nicolaisen had seen him and stopped.

"Oh, how are you! How are you!" he greeted him almost merrily. "I'm happy to hear that you finally drove into the ditch. It had to happen, my boy! Our—our—nemesis awaits us all. But if you want a good position at fifty a month, then just drop in. Always glad to help a compatriot, you know!" And he went off without waiting for an answer.

Jonas walked on to the boardinghouse where he met Nels at the door. He was dressed for traveling and had a carpetbag in his hand. Jonas pretended he hadn't seen him, but the Swede took his hand and pressed it so that it hurt.

"You have all my sympathy," he said. "And I don't want to see you give up now!"

"Are you leaving?" asked Jonas, staring at his carpetbag. Yes, he was going to Duluth, where he had a sister, and come spring he would be taking over the city's sewer works. He would have left earlier, but he had to wait for his citizen papers, and they hadn't arrived until yesterday. So that was why he had been in the courthouse, thought Jonas.

"And Ragna? Is she going with you to Duluth?" he asked. He feared the answer.

"Well, you'll soon find out," Nels answered. Jonas thought his face had a sad expression. "You have all my best wishes," he quickly added and left.

Jonas didn't understand any of this. His world had become an enigma. When he came into the hall he saw that the *parloren* was empty, and since he couldn't imagine eating and feared meeting anyone, he entered. With a little sigh he sat down on the old plush sofa that stood there like a faithful witness to poverty and need with its stuffing in full view. They suited each other today, the old sofa and he; this was just how he felt—like an old well-used piece of furniture. If there still was a place for him in this world it would be one like this, a dark corner where he wouldn't be noticed since he was no longer in fashion.

How long he sat in his dark, deep thoughts he didn't know. And who cared? It made no difference where he sat—a failure . . . He felt and knew that he would never again *kutte a figger* in *Min'ap'lis* . . . Suddenly he felt so tired . . . He had better go upstairs. But before he was able to realize his intention he fell asleep on the sofa and began to dream feverishly about the day's happenings . . . Mr. Kennedy and a police officer were throwing him out of his store and outside his two clerks were waiting to fall upon him with their sharpened knives while Nicolaisen, Stunsrud, and Lyvenfelt stood by laughing.

<hr />

The door was opened quietly. A figure appeared in the opening. Silently it observed the sleeper in the sofa. Now Jonas threw out his arms and cried loudly, "Use your senses!" and then, "*Gudnes,* are you going to kill me too?" The figure moved toward him but stopped as if undecided. Then another step, and yet another. Then it stood beside him. Jonas awoke and felt something pass gently through his hair. He started. *Gudnes,* what was this? Confused, he looked up. And there Ragna stood smiling at him! And it was even the same smile he could remember from their first meeting. But he knew he was dreaming. Ragna couldn't really be standing there smiling. It was just fate playing another trick on him, as if he hadn't had enough misery for one day . . . He closed his eyes so that his dream would go away. No more lies . . . Then she stroked him gently on his forehead and he looked up again.

"Are you here?" he exclaimed in surprise, staring at her.

"I have just come to tell you that you were right," she said quietly. *Gudnes,* she was beautiful!

"But you know I've lost everything," he objected. "I'm no bargain anymore." He hid his face in his hands.

"When you lose something, you often win something as well," she answered. "And when all comes to all, what you've lost probably had no value."

He looked queryingly at her.

"And you have that quarter section in the Red River Valley!" she said.

The quarter—he had forgotten all about it! He got up.

"And I'll go there with you . . . if you want me?"

What a question!

So that's how it came about that Jonas, who just a short while ago was utterly crushed, a poor and persecuted human being, suddenly felt he was richer than the richest man in the world. For the first time he embraced his greatest wealth. And she did the same, for that matter. And their wealth was considerable—they both had their arms full.

Would he dare kiss her now?

He certainly would.

BOOK II

*The Home on the Prairie:
Jonas Olsen's First Year
in the Settlement*

I.

The settlement was called O'Brien's Grove at the time Jonas and Ragna Olsen arrived. It was named for Jim O'Brien, the first settler. That part was simple and straightforward. Since there wasn't a real tree, let alone a grove, in a circumference of many miles, the "Grove" part may have been difficult to understand for those who don't realize that names are as much about wishes as about realities.

It was a typical prairie landscape—a never-ending plain providing no rest for the eye. The monotony of the prairie could be oppressive. Even though the soil was good and could yield in abundance as soon as you began to work it, there was little in the landscape itself to console settlers in their transition from their old to their new lives. There was so much they missed in their new surroundings and many a new settlement was named for what they missed the most. Just as the people in western Norway, where there is such a plenitude of rock and sea and skerries but so little arable land, have added the word "land" to the name of almost every spot that isn't washed by the sea, so the prairie settlers have created place names that have little relation with the actual natural conditions. In this as in so much else, memory and imagination have had to fill in the spaces in the settlers' existence.

A forsaken little willow that languished by a dry creek bed was the closest thing to a tree on the quarter section that Jim O'Brien had homesteaded a few years earlier. Jim had arrived from the South, where he had been used to forest, so he planted a few elm saplings close to the willow and called the place the Grove. Among the Norwegian settlers, whose numbers were steadily increasing, it was usually called *O'Brien-Groven*—*Groven* for short—in spite of the fact that a grove had never materialized: the saplings had withered and died and the willow was as solitary as ever.[1]

So much of what Jim O'Brien had attempted in his life had gone the way of the elm saplings. Neither he nor his projects had been very successful and he was now a man in his fifties. Although he had a good head on his shoulders, he was an exceptionally poor farmer. His Norwegian neighbors made good-natured fun of his husbandry, but almost all of them were his good friends, and for good reason. Both Jim and his wife were very friendly people whose doors were always open and who always generously shared what they had. You could say that this wasn't very much, but whatever their hospitality may have lacked in the way of a lavish table and a tidy home was more than made up for by an unqualified generosity that wasn't so unusual in the pioneer period in most western settlements.

Many of those who had arrived after the O'Briens had been received with open arms and had been welcomed to use their house as long as they wished. Ole Trulsen, a carpenter from Trondheim, had come five years ago and stayed with the O'Briens until he had built a home for his family. The Trulsens were among the few who had a little cash when they settled on the prairie and their house was the still the largest in the settlement. Nevertheless, it had been quite a struggle to get the O'Briens to accept a decent compensation. The Flasmo family from Stjørdal had also been helped.[2] They had first gone to Iowa, where he had farmed rented land for two to three years and she had worked as a midwife. Lars Jorshaug and his wife and their two little boys, who for three years had suffered a miserable existence in Chicago, had also found temporary shelter at the O'Briens'. And there were others. They had all been on the best of terms with the friendly couple. Even Mrs. Flasmo, who was said to have such a sharp tongue, excused Mrs. O'Brien's housekeeping, although she was quick to find fault with anyone else. Nothing was fancy at the O'Briens'; you had to take things as they were.

The only one who hadn't come to terms with Jim O'Brien was Torfin Glombekken, and, according to what people said, this wasn't Jim's fault. Bickering and wrangling was Torfin's nature and he was extremely difficult to get along with. When he was determined to convince O'Brien that the Pope was Antichrist and St. Patrick an old cheat and a con man, even the amiable Irishman finally lost his patience.

———◆———

So it was natural that Jonas and Ragna too were taken in by the O'Briens. Searlie in St. Paul had written to Jim and asked him to meet them in Normanville, the closest town, about twenty miles from *Groven*.[3] He was there with his team and lumber wagon when they got off the train, and they couldn't have wished for a more heartwarming welcome.

It was April. The last snow had just melted and it had rained that night and morning. Roads and streets were muddy, and more rain threatened. Jonas and Ragna agreed that the weather was miserable. As they left the train Jonas had even remarked that his usual bad luck seemed to have met them here too and that it was a bad omen that they should arrive on such a terrible day. So they were somewhat surprised when O'Brien's first words after his greeting was his assurance that the weather was wonderful. It was always like this, he said, a truly superior climate.

"Faith, and I niver seen the like iv it, havin' been over a good deal iv the wurruld, including Ireland." This was his introduction to a lecture on the unequaled fertility and salubrity of the region. Cattle and sheep and potatoes and grain and children all grew and flourished like wild mustard in a field of wheat. To Jonas it sounded as when a land agent got his claws into a naïve city dweller, thinking he could make him believe that the cows on the prairie milked swiss cheese. But Jim O'Brien was no land agent. He was merely an optimist.

Jonas couldn't understand how they were going to get through on the muddy roads but for Jim this was no problem. On the contrary, the good roads were one of the most important advantages of the region. They had planned that Ragna should stay in Normanville until Jonas had built a house, but Jim wouldn't hear of it. That would be an entirely unnecessary expense, he insisted. They had space to spare and enough food for all. But before they started on their journey he wanted them to enjoy the wonders and pleasures of the town. It was quite a town, he told them, with many businesses, a great location, and everything well kept. As a market it had no competition within a circumference of fifty miles. His description did not correspond to Jonas's impression as they walked down the muddy street, and Ragna, whose galoshes were safely in her suitcase, which they hadn't yet collected, was no more enthused than he, since her feet were wet. As far as they could see, the town consisted of a single street, with a few homes spread out here and there on the prairie without any order. Jim admitted that the population was only six hundred, but it would at least be doubled by next year.

On the main street—as O'Brien, somewhat pretentiously, called it—there were two banks: Ward's and Torgersen's. The banks were always the first to come, he explained. Then came the lawyers, the politicians, and the *chinchbuggen*.[4] A little distance from the main street, by a sidetrack of the railroad, was a *kornelevator* managed by Roxberg, a

Norwegian. And Jim said that Roxberg was known to *docke* the farmers on their wheat and that you should keep your eyes open when doing business with him. In other respects he was a good and righteous man and a pillar of support for Pastor Vellesen and the Lutheran church. The town had a Scandinavian Hotel, owned by Nicolai Johnson. Rivesand and Morlund had substantial general stores and a Swede named Settergren had a hardware and furniture store. Sam Lindermann, another Swede, had a land office, and there were two lawyers, the Norwegian Hans Floen, and Bert Newell, who was a politician and held a seat in the legislature. The town had two churches, one Catholic, the other Lutheran; a lumberyard; and four saloons: Ole Dampen's, Larry O'Connor's, Swan Nelson's, and the one in the Scandinavian Hotel.[5]

Jonas wanted to get started with his building, so they went to the lumber *officen* to look at prices and see what building material was available. O'Brien promised that he would do the hauling, but explained that they should negotiate with Trulsen about the construction. There was no better carpenter west of the Twin Cities, said Jim. And Lars Jorshaug had worked for the largest bricklayer company in Chicago. Indeed, everyone and everything in *Groven* was first class. Jonas bought some carpentry tools at Settergren's *hardwarestoret* while O'Brien made some household purchases. Then they had what Ragna called an unspeakable dinner in the hotel and they were ready for their long journey. She was eager to get started: she had had enough of Normanville.

But then Jim suddenly recollected that there was something he simply had to talk to Larry O'Connor about. He had almost forgotten all about it, but it was an important church matter that couldn't be put off. It would only take him a few minutes, and if Jonas, who had traveled so far, would like a beer or a whiskey, he was of course welcome to join him. His wife could just sit and wait at the *tavernet* until they returned. Jonas, however, preferred to keep her company. They waited two hours. When Jim finally turned up, he was obviously intoxicated but so polite and friendly that they soon forgot the long wait. The church matters had taken more time than planned. He himself was a Catholic and his wife, a Southern Yankee, was a Presbyterian, but they got along very well for all that.[6]

They returned to the wagon in a hurry and Ragna was helped up on the back seat. She had never been on a lumber wagon before and was unused to being perched so high up from the ground. She also wondered whether the driver would be able to hold on to his seat in his present condition. Jonas had climbed up beside her when two well-dressed gentlemen stopped to have a word with Jim. They were introduced to Jonas and Ragna as Elihu Ward, a bank director, and Newell, a lawyer. Jim said that they were from Minneapolis and had come to settle in *Groven*. This gave Newell the bright idea that they should drink to the newcomers' health and good luck.

The saloon sign on the corner with huge gilded letters glittered temptingly in the bright sun, which just then came from behind a cloud and reminded them that it was already late in the afternoon. Jonas thanked them but said that he didn't drink so they would have to excuse him. A live man who didn't take a glass was evidently an unprecedented phenomenon in Normanville; Ward and Newell exchanged looks and smiled. If Jonas had been aware, he would also have noticed that the bank manager looked him over as if wanting to know what kind of man he was. From Jonas, his eyes turned to Ragna, whom he evidently found even more interesting. Then he too asked to be excused and suddenly saw a man on the other side of the street that he had to talk to. With renewed assurances that he would be back in a moment—at most five minutes—Jim went off with Newell and disappeared for the second time through the door of the saloon.

After ten minutes Ragna insisted on getting down from the wagon seat. "I can't be expected to be on display all afternoon," she said. They spent a boring afternoon till supper time at the hotel. Every now and then Jonas would get up to stretch and look out on the street for O'Brien. *"Gudnes,"* he sighed, "This *farmerkontriet* isn't what it is *krœkket* up to be."

When Jim came reeling out of the saloon around half past six it was of course too late to set out on their long journey, so they had to settle for beds in Nicolai Johnson's Scandinavian Hotel.

"Faith, and I can't stand the darn stuff like I used to," Jim said in a half whisper to Jonas; "Reckon it's old I'm getting."

2.

Jonas used to boast that he had seen the world and that he knew a thing or two about poor hotels. He had been to Hamar and Gjøvik as well as to Kristiania, so he had some experience.[7] And he had stayed at emigrant hotels in Glasgow, New York, and Chicago. Moreover, as a deliveryman in Minneapolis, he had ample opportunity to study the cooking and other mysteries in Scandinavian hotels and boardinghouses in that city. So he thought that he had earned himself the right to an opinion. But after they had spent a night in Nicolai Johnson's Scandinavian Hotel he admitted that to live is to learn. Ragna agreed that in her wildest fantasies she hadn't been able to imagine anything quite as remarkable as the special atmosphere of this inn. Supper had reminded Jonas of Mrs. Salmon's cooking in South Minneapolis, but that turned out to be a minor matter compared to what had followed.

Their host, a squinty-eyed and round-bellied saloonkeeper, assured them that the building was in all respects "modern" and "first class," considering that this was a new *kontry*. They were given a narrow, dismal room, from which wafted an indescribable odor of months' old stuffy air. There was a single small window facing an alley, and Jonas immediately did what he could to open it, but without success. Finally he had the desperate idea to use his new tools. But they proved of little use. The only result of his exertions was a broken window and the innkeeper, who had been alerted by the unholy din, came running up the stairs and wanted to know if he was tearing down the house. They now had some air, but soon discovered that it wasn't as fresh as they had hoped. There was an enormous heap of manure right outside the window, and to protect themselves from the stink they agreed to plug the hole with Jonas's coat.

The furniture consisted of an old bed and chair and something they gathered was supposed to be a bureau. On it was a miserable lamp that the innkeeper had lighted when he showed them to their room. Ragna complained bitterly of the smoke but Jonas observed that it might make them less aware of the many other smells. Ragna fearfully began to inspect the bed. She spent some time trying to figure out what the suspicious-looking bedclothes were made of. There was no telling how many species of the animal kingdom were hiding in these inscrutable blankets. Her worst shock was when she saw that there were no sheets. She couldn't possibly undress and lie down in such a bed. Even though it was still early spring, the bedbugs, which they were acquainted with from boardinghouses in Minneapolis, had begun their season and were so busy that there wouldn't be a moment's peace for Jonas, who had the courage to lie down. Ragna decided to sit on the only chair. And then they discovered that their room was just above the saloon, and the remorseless din the whole night long made sleep impossible.

In the morning Jonas went on an expedition to find something to wash in and dry themselves with, and when he eventually returned with some water and a towel and many impious thoughts in his heart for Johnson and his "modern, first-class tavern," Ragna refused to use the towel, which did indeed look a little darkish. Her husband was by now in such a mood that he felt a strong desire to use some powerful language, but since he had promised himself that he would guard his tongue in his wife's company, all he said was, "*Gudnes*. This *biter* everything I have *rønna op ægænst* even in America!"[8]

She evidently agreed, for she sank down on the edge of the bed and drew a long, deep sigh. That was when he got the sudden notion that they had had such a bad start that the best they could do was to get away as fast as possible, so he said with conviction, "Darned if we aren't going *streit* back to *Min'ap'lis* again!" But Ragna simply smiled as she got up and made herself ready for breakfast and the journey ahead. "No," she answered him quietly but with determination, "that wouldn't make sense. And everything will be much better when we get to the O'Briens', where there is a large house and good housekeeping."

An hour later they were on their way to their Canaan.[9] Jim complained of a headache. The reason, he said, was that he hadn't slept a wink all night. These taverns weren't for people. This was the first cloud they had noticed on the bright horizon of O'Brien's spirit.

Jim's health gradually improved and as the day progressed he became more and more expansive. He told them about the "pioneer days"—the time when he had moved out on the prairie. Conditions then were very different and things could be a little awkward at times, but considering the excellence of the country, they were only trifles. But now everything was so much better. Civilization had indeed made great progress!

Most settlers in *Groven* were quite well-off, Jim informed them, compared to how they initially had been. There had been one year with a poor harvest and some who had just started were forced to leave their farms because they had mortgaged them to Elihu Ward and other fleecers. Ward in particular was a hard man to do business with. There were still farmers that were entirely in his pocket. Jim too had been forced to take a loan from Elihu, but this year's crop promised to be so good that he would manage his debt and much more. Indeed, for O'Brien the future seemed to be the best medicine for all ills. His only regret was that it no longer seemed that their settlement would get the railroad for which they had been waiting so long. The Northern Pacific and the H. & B. companies had planned a branch from Normanville to Stockdale through O'Brien's Grove. But there now seemed to be some complications and

Ward and Newell had explained that the project had been abandoned. But Jonas didn't set much stock in these railroad rumors. Searlie had also talked about a railroad; all new settlements could boast of such rumors: there was always a railroad in the future.

As they talked, the horses progressed slowly on the muddy roads. But the weather was bright and sunny. Even Jonas had to admit it. Nor did Jim let him harbor any thoughts to the contrary, exclaiming every now and then, "Faith, and this is a great day!"

This was repeated so many times that Ragna tried to change the subject. In an attempt to be funny she said, "But your roads, Mr. O'Brien? I thought you said you had the best roads in the world!"

"Faith, and we have, Madam," Jim answered, "for a new country." And thus she was reminded that in this world, things are relative.

In the afternoon they eventually arrived at the O'Briens'. "Well, here we are," said Jim when the horses stopped in front of a small shanty that proved to be the farm's stable. While Jim was unharnessing the horses, Jonas and Ragna studied their surroundings. They wondered what things were like in this place where they had come with such expectations. A few rods[10] from the stable they saw another miserable shanty, and wondered what it could be.

"But where is their home?" Ragna finally exclaimed.

"Just wait, and you'll see that they live in that there *chickenkupen*," said Jonas. Ragna laughed. She found the idea ridiculous.

Jim had taken care of his horses and came up to them. They were welcome to come in. He walked ahead of them to the other shanty and Ragna realized that the poorly built log cabin was the "main building." When they entered they discovered that the spacious dwelling Jim had led them to expect consisted of a single room and a kitchen. Along the whole length of one of the end walls in the *livingrummet* a bed stood quite unashamedly in full view. At the other end another bed was partly hidden behind a curtain of *kaliko*. The wall opposite the entrance was entirely covered by an oaken bookshelf filled with books. The many books made a strange impression in these surroundings. Out on the floor was a small table with a plain lamp, and along the wall on either side of the entrance were four kitchen chairs. This was the furniture. Through the open door to the kitchen Ragna could see a small stove and a table covered with an oil cloth that had at one time been white. Now the color could not be determined. Ragna needed only three minutes to decide that whatever other qualities Mrs. O'Brien might have, she was not a model housewife. The bed wasn't made, the floor had, to put it kindly, not been scrubbed recently, and dust covered tables and chairs.

Mrs. O'Brien was about fifty years of age, tall, and with a pleasant face that no doubt had been beautiful in her younger days. She struck Ragna as a lighthearted and easygoing woman, and she was quite shapely except for some unnecessary fat. Her natural and friendly welcome warmed Ragna to the heart. She felt sure of her welcome.

They were then introduced to the O'Briens' daughter, Mrs. Nyblom, who in outward appearance seemed a fair copy of her mother, and equally friendly and obliging. The name Nyblom reminded Jonas and Ragna of a young Swede they had known in Minneapolis. The very same who had threatened to beat up Jonas the first week he worked in the *seweren*. Not much later, he had moved out of Johnson's boardinghouse and left town. Unknown to Jonas, he had been among the many who had opened their hearts to Ragna and who then became miserable upon discovering that she didn't reciprocate their feelings. Ragna was greatly surprised and Jonas had almost spoken words that wouldn't have suited the occasion when the O'Briens' son-in-law just then entered the cabin. He was indeed the Nyblom they had known in Minneapolis. The young man himself was no less surprised. The Swede ensured them that he was happy to see both of them again. Jonas, however, found their meeting unpleasant and began to speculate on a possible hidden significance.

Ragna's main concern was how they all would be able to find a place to sleep in a single room. "We'll probably have to stand up against the walls and sleep there," she said when she and Jonas happened to have a moment to themselves outside the house.

"*Uff!* If there only had been an unused wall," Jonas sighed.

But a solution was found. The women had the house to themselves and the men slept in the hay, in the shanty they referred to as the barn. Ragna thought it very kind of Nyblom and O'Brien to leave their home for her sake. When the men crawled out of the hay the next morning, Jim said to Jonas, who had not been thrilled by the atmosphere in their lodgings, "Well, sorr, and what do ye think iv it! Grand country, isn't it?"

"Of course," Jonas lied, "there is nothing like the country, especially when you fall in with such good people."

"Well, sorr," O'Brien answered him, "with some people, begorrah, you're apt to fall out rather than in."

3.

Jonas and Ragna had a powerful sense of the solemnity of the occasion when Jim that morning drove them over to their own land. It was in the same section as the O'Brien farm, which made up the northeastern quarter while Jonas had the southwestern one. The two other quarter sections belonged to Iver Flasmo in the north and to Lars Jorshaug in the south. The road to Normanville followed the southern section line. It was a beautiful piece of land, one of the best quarter sections in the entire settlement, Jim said. A stone's throw or so from the road there was a little elevation of the ground and this is where Jim stopped.

They stood there quite a while looking at their property, which lay there in virginal opulence waiting for the touch of a human hand to yield of its abundant fertility. A couple of years had passed since Jonas had bought it. Little did he then suspect that it would have any significance for his future. It had been fashionable for businesspeople in the city to possess land and he didn't wish to be behind the others. If he could make a few dollars on it, he wouldn't mind it a bit, and at worst he assumed he would be able to get his money back. He certainly hadn't suspected that his bad luck would make him a farmer.

For the first time in his life he stood on his own land and property and this gave him a sense of awe. This was his land! This was where he and Ragna would build and live, not for a day or a year, but for life. Indeed, they would not only build and develop their land for themselves but for future generations of Olsens who would have him as their progenitor. He felt a certain greatness in thus founding a future home for his lineage in this new land, and in his mind's eye he could see how generation after generation of his descendants, as they progressed in prosperity and renown, would bless him because he had had the wisdom and the initiative to come here and carry the burden of a pioneer's life. He would work hard and create something of lasting value. And Ragna would have a good life here; his work would be mainly for her . . . and for their children. They would come in time . . . and they would live in plenty. And when they were old enough he would send them to schools and make some of them ministers and professors and others would be bank managers and lawyers and businessmen and politicians. His children would be the best in all of America.

As Jonas contemplated his vision, Ragna was also preoccupied with the future and its possibilities, and she even had a slight premonition that the beginning of those generations with which he in his imagination was peopling the prairie was closer than he realized. She hadn't said a word about it yet, since she wanted to be quite sure before she mentioned it to him. She too felt happy at the thought that this was all theirs, and she vowed that she would do her best to create a home that was a real home.

They were interrupted in their reflections by Jim, who had been looking to the horses. O'Brien assured them that this was God's own country and said they should build here where the view was so magnificent. They had their own thoughts about this, since the elevation was so insignificant that it was hardly noticeable; but all in all the place was as good a site as any and when they continued on their way to negotiate with Ole Trulsen about the building of a farmhouse and a barn, they agreed that this was indeed where they would build.

They had spent much time discussing their new home. Jonas had found it unacceptable to let Ragna begin her new life as the wife of a poor man, and in order to afford a reasonably decent house and still have enough left over for the first year, he had borrowed a thousand dollars from Davidsen's Bank in Minneapolis against a six-month mortgage on their land. The bank had assured him that renewal would be a formality. They had asked a carpenter for advice and he had told them that a house with four small rooms including a kitchen could be built for $500, and that a barn would cost them $100 or $150 at the very most. When they came to Trulsen, he found their plans within reason and he promised to do the work, suggesting that they begin digging the cellar immediately. O'Brien offered to help them when he had time off from the spring work on his farm. They were well received by the Trulsens and had an excellent dinner. Mrs. Trulsen was both friendly and competent, thought Ragna.

When they returned to the O'Briens', Jonas helped Jim unharness the horses. Nyblom happened to pass by and said some words to the effect that horses and harnesses might not be quite the thing for someone more used to the big city. He probably meant no harm, but Jonas was piqued. So the Swede wanted to make himself important at his expense. It was just as he had expected and just like a Swede. He had an urge to say something in return, but he couldn't start a fight after all the friendliness demonstrated by the O'Briens. But he decided to avoid more contact with Nyblom than was absolutely necessary. He was obviously the same villainous character he had been in Minneapolis. On the first occasion he and Ragna were by themselves, he advised her to keep him at a distance.

Strangely, she didn't agree. On the contrary, she liked Nyblom. But then he lost his temper and said that the Swede was a base and insolent character who had threatened to beat him up when they worked together in *seweren.*

"But you didn't let him do it!" she exclaimed.

"Damned no, I didn't," Jonas replied; "he was the one to beg for fair weather. But he's a vindictive lout and now his only thought is to try to get back at me."

"Well, let's wait and see," she said. "You can't judge him simply on the basis of being Swedish. We have known nice Swedes, both you and I." She was thinking of Nels. Jonas did the same, but he nevertheless disliked her tendency to always *leine op* with the Swedes. It was peculiar that wherever he went he could not be in peace from this so-called "brother nation"! Ragna stopped their dispute by throwing her arms around his neck.

"Let's not waste our time with such nonsense," she said. "Let's think about ourselves and our new home." And as he held her closely, felt her warm breath on his forehead, and read the expression in her beautiful eyes, he had to admit that she was right. With such a woman at his side he had no need to let a minor incident with a Swede bring him out of balance.

One morning a few days later a full crew was at work on their site. Trulsen and Iver Flasmo were digging the cellar. Jorshaug was working on the foundation. O'Brien, Erik Nesteved, and Peder Tarvesen brought bricks from the Næperud settlement, thirteen miles farther south, and lumber from Normanville. This was the way they did things in *Groven.* When a new family moved in, those who had come earlier helped them as best they could.

Torfin Glombekken, their nearest neighbor to the south, hadn't been asked. Jonas's arrival had on the whole been inconvenient. A cousin had bought this quarter section but it had reverted to the land company three years ago and since then Glombekken had simply used the ten acres that his cousin had cultivated. Torfin's only consolation when he heard that the new owner was going to settle on his land was that at least he hadn't plowed the land last fall. But this didn't keep him away from the site, pretending that he was offended at not having been asked to help. Perhaps it was just as well, he suggested, since he wasn't a certified carpenter, bricklayer, or midwife . . . Jonas had never bothered to mention his free use of his land. Torfin was a sly character that it would be best to keep at a distance.

———•——

While the men were at work, Ragna had good opportunity to get to know Mrs. O'Brien and her daughter. She was increasingly impressed by the older woman. She was unselfish, understanding, intelligent, and interesting. She had read widely, and from their conversation Ragna gathered that she had been a teacher somewhere down South. But she was certainly not a good housekeeper. There was no system in anything. Even her books—of which several were in languages that Ragna couldn't even recognize—were just strewn around wherever they had been dropped. It was a strange fate, she thought, that had led this woman into this kind of existence with a man like Jim O'Brien, with whom she only seemed to have one thing in common: a bright outlook on life. How it had happened would have to be an unsolved mystery for the time being, but Ragna often returned to it in her thoughts.

Mrs. Nyblom shared her mother's friendly and carefree attitude as well as her lack of interest in housekeeping. The consequences were obvious. Emma—for that was her name—had only been married for a few months to Gust Nyblom, who had been her father's hired hand. In spite of their status as newlyweds it was obvious that their feelings for each other had already cooled. The living room was never presentable. In the kitchen, unwashed plates and bowls stood everywhere except on the shelf, and most meals were terrible. Ragna shuddered at the thought of how much good food was spoiled in the cooking.

One evening Ragna offered to make a bread pudding, and at the supper table Nyblom ate it with such relish that it was noticed, since he usually sat in low spirits during meals. Afterward he went to her and said in Swedish, "I'll bet you are responsible for the pudding!" His face shone with satisfaction. Ragna made no answer. Jonas heard what he said and observed his wide smile. The whole thing irritated him.

4.

As time passed it happened more or less of itself that Ragna took over the cooking at the O'Briens'. It had been natural for her to take her share of the women's work, and gradually the house had become clean and tidy—insofar as this was possible under the circumstances. Clean paper appeared on the shelves, and pepper, salt, cardamom, and other things that are necessary in cooking were for the first time given their defined places. The stove was brightly polished, and kitchen utensils were scrubbed every day and hung shining bright from hooks or nails that had been hammered into the wall. Floors, tables, and chairs were clean, the beds made, and the house aired.

Mrs. O'Brien had such complete confidence in Ragna's housekeeping skills that she gladly let her do as she pleased. Now she could sit with her books or, if she so wished, sit with her hands in her lap and lecture for the two younger women on history or literature. Strangely, her daughter didn't appreciate her learned expositions. Emma had little education and said that she didn't care for the learned stuff that interested her mother. Ragna found it strange that Mrs. O'Brien had allowed her daughter to grow up in virtual ignorance.

Ragna had regretted that she hadn't been able to acquire a better education. She had been an intelligent child, and was at the top of her class when she had to leave school at her mother's death, when she was fourteen, and begin to support herself. Thanks to her mother's influence she had to some extent acquired the ability to grapple with some of the problems of life. She saw her relationship with Jonas against this background. She had a strong desire to imbue it with something beyond what she had seen in most marriages: a more profound view of life than the one expressed in the common story of a man and a woman who are attracted to each other, marry, make a home, raise children, and tolerate each other because they have no other alternative. She had from the very beginning been aware of their contrasting personalities. His strong interest in the material aspects of life had at times frightened her. Her mother had so often spoken of what she called a serious life, and she wished to share this sense of responsibility with her husband. This had become a central purpose of her love.

In Mrs. O'Brien she found an understanding of what had preoccupied her mind in quiet moments. Mrs. Nyblom was a more superficial person, but she was kind and Ragna couldn't but pity her for lacking the qualities that a woman must have in order to be important in a man's life. There was little wonder that Nyblom was dissatisfied. Had it been up to her, Ragna would have helped Emma regain his respect. The only thing she could do was to demonstrate by example how a house should be kept, but Emma didn't seem to notice any difference. Nyblom, on the other hand, soon realized that their home was undergoing a change. One day, when he came in and sat down at the table, he expressed his satisfaction in Swedish: "*Golli!* This is the way to live!"

Ragna blushed at his praise, which she both appreciated and disliked. She was of course pleased that Nyblom had noticed that there had been a change in the housekeeping, but she could see that Jonas reacted to Nyblom's praise as to salt in sore eyes. Nor had the episode gone unnoticed by Emma. She had pricked up her ears and demanded to know what Nyblom had said. Why couldn't he speak the language they all understood? Nyblom merely laughed at her curiosity.

"That's the only privilege we from Europe have over you Americans," he answered. "We know at least two languages, and can use whichever one we like."

"Which may not always be strictly proper, though," said Ragna as she began to clear the table.

"I should say not," Mrs. Nyblom agreed. "Mother is a linguist . . ."

"Oh, that's another story," her husband interrupted her, "and besides, I've heard that before."

"The point is," Emma continued, "she never speaks Latin in the presence of people who don't understand it."

"Yes, but these people understand Swedish," he answered, as he took his cap and left. Jonas followed him after a while. Emma and Ragna began to do the dishes in silence.

Ragna was glad that Mr. and Mrs. O'Brien were not witness to this episode. They had gone to Normanville that morning on an important errand. The county superintendent of schools had resigned to take another position and some businessmen wanted to nominate Mrs. O'Brien for the vacant office. Hans Floen had visited them a few days ago to discuss the situation with her. Her strongest support was among the Norwegians. Ward and some other Americans preferred another candidate, Ward's brother-in-law, Andrews, who was headmaster of the school in Normanville. But the Norwegians thought they would be able to secure the job for Mrs. O'Brien because she herself wasn't a Norwegian. Even though she hadn't been active in education for some time, the settlers in *Groven,* with the exception of Glombekken, were convinced that she had the best qualifications for the office. Indeed, most of them had reason to be grateful to her and her husband for what they had done for them. Mrs. O'Brien was pleased with this demonstration of confidence, and Floen's visit had brought slumbering ambitions back to life. All day yesterday Ragna had helped her make one of her old dresses presentable, and she had gladly let Ragna fix her up before she left.

Mr. and Mrs. O'Brien hadn't yet returned from Normanville at dinnertime the next day.[11] Emma had been in a bad temper since the unpleasantness at the supper table. Ragna had tried to comfort her, insisting that Nyblom had said nothing of importance, but she didn't dare repeat what he had said, since that would have confirmed Emma's suspicion that it concerned her. The atmosphere was strained as the four sat down to dinner and no one said anything until Nyblom, who had helped himself to a plate full of Ragna's meatballs, held them up to his wife and sarcastically advised her to learn how to cook while she had the opportunity. Her face turned white as chalk. Deeply hurt, she left the table and walked out.

After the men had left, Ragna had to use all her persuasive gifts to get Emma to sit down and eat her dinner, and they spent a miserable afternoon together. Nothing Ragna did to ease the situation was of any help. She who had married a gentleman had nothing to complain about, said Emma; but Emma had to tolerate a lout who was never satisfied with what she did.

Ragna decided to do what she could to reconcile the two. Nyblom was working in the fields and came home for meals before Jonas, who was still either helping Trulsen raise the house or working with Flasmo on the ten acres the neighbors had helped him to plough. She met Nyblom outside the shanty as he came home for supper. She had to talk with him, she said. She was brief and to the point. Since he had married Emma, he owed her the respect due to his wife, she said. Her fear that her presence had revived his old feelings for her was confirmed by his response.

"I have loved one woman," he said in Swedish, "and to this day I would go to the end of the world with her . . ."

"I don't want to hear another word of that!" she interrupted him at once. "Your one obligation is to find happiness with Emma!"

"That is no longer possible," he answered her. "You should never have come here. After you've left you shouldn't be surprised if you hear that I've left this misery."

"You must for God's sake never think such thoughts!" she said. Then she saw Jonas coming quickly across the prairie. He was only a stone's throw away and she was sure that he had seen them.

"Remember what I've told you!" she said as she quickly left him and entered the house. When she came in, the look Emma sent her was evidence that she too had seen them.

Nothing could have upset Jonas more than to see Ragna and Nyblom together. His bad feelings for the Swede had grown, and Nyblom was no less inclined to pretend friendship. Jonas had begun working on his house with a will. It might not be a castle but it would be his and Ragna's first home and his hopes and longings had gone into every log and every plank. But he was no longer able to find pleasure in his work. Today he had decided to bring the Swede's attentions to Ragna to an end; you could never know what that sort of thing could lead to. Such were his thoughts when he saw them talking intimately together. The result was that four sullen and hostile individuals sat down to supper that evening. Ragna and Jonas had already decided to take a walk on their land after supper so she could see how far the building had progressed. The roof had been raised and Trulsen had started the inside work. They had walked quite a piece without saying a word and finally Ragna began to laugh. "We are walking as if to our own funeral," she said. "What is the matter with us?"

Well, he had to admit that it was Nyblom. He was careful, since he knew that the subject was a touchy one. What had they been talking about? The look she gave him made him reconsider. He had seen it before. It was the same defiant countenance as in the period after his affair with Dagny Simonsen. He supposed it meant that it was none of his *bisnes*. But he was her husband and she had promised at the altar to be submissive and obey him as her master . . .

"You should be very careful about such things," he said after a while. "He is after all a married man and a bad man to boot."

She had planned to tell him all about it—that she had merely tried to straighten out the relationship between Nyblom and Emma—but because of the way he reacted, she decided not to explain anything. "Oh, I like Nyblom," she said. This came rather suddenly. He hadn't expected her to make a confession all at once.

"And he's a Swede," he exclaimed sarcastically, "so I suppose it's much like meeting an old sweetheart." He regretted his words as soon as they were said, but a man had to stand by his words. When they came to the site he tried to improve the situation by explaining everything in detail. She listened without speaking a word. When they stepped outside, it had become colder and she wrapped her scarf over her shoulders.

"Imagine," he said, "how nice it'll be when we're in our own home."

"*Uff*, it's so cold!" she responded. "Let's hurry."
He gave a start. They hurried.

5.

It wasn't long after this that Ragna got to know Mrs. O'Brien's life story. She admired the older woman, who in many respects was quite unique in these surroundings. Her husband was a character in whom there was no deceit. No situation was so difficult that he couldn't see some reason for optimism. The sun always shone on O'Brien. But he lacked initiative and he hadn't succeeded in any of his enterprises. They were as poor now as when they came eight years ago. Elihu Ward's mortgage on the farm was for a loan after the crop failure three years ago, and they had only been able to pay the interest. He could take their farm should anything go wrong with this year's harvest. It was with these prospects that they had gone to town to negotiate with those who were in opposition to Ward and who wished to have Mrs. O'Brien appointed school superintendent.

It hadn't entered Ward's mind that he wouldn't be able to convince Mrs. O'Brien to turn down the nomination. After all, he had a mortgage that he could foreclose, and he didn't recognize the existence of any human being who could neither be bought nor be threatened by economic pressure. So he was greatly surprised to discover that the O'Briens didn't behave according to his expectations. He explained that they had a choice between having their farm brought to auction and withdrawing Mrs. O'Brien's candidature. If she withdrew, they could continue to pay the interest on the mortgage.

O'Brien left the decision to his wife. He was sure he would have a good crop and that they would be able to redeem the mortgage bond. At first she didn't know how to respond. She had no confidence in Jim's expected bumper crop. His calculations had almost always proved wrong and she knew that Ward would show no mercy. On the other hand, the wish to have her appointed had taken on the character of a popular demand. Nor could she deny her own interest in the new position. Moreover, she was better qualified for the job than Andrews, who didn't have much education. Her long-dormant fighting spirit had been revived by Ward's attempt to push her aside. He couldn't touch their farm before spring. If she succeeded in winning the fall election, she should be able to get someone else to take over the mortgage. But neither the election nor a new mortgage were guaranteed. Such were her thoughts when she told the banker that she had no intention of withdrawing her candidature. His only response was that he had done his duty and given them due warning. Afterward she and Jim went to see Hans Floen, and he was so sure that she would get the appointment that Jim became enthusiastic and decided to celebrate at O'Connor's. And this was why their errand took all of two days.

Meanwhile, signatures were collected on a petition for Mrs. O'Brien's appointment. Most Scandinavians on the farms signed. Among the other nationalities and the town population, opinions were divided depending on people's personal or financial relationship with Elihu Ward. The petition was the idea of Floen and Torgersen. They were interested in giving Ward and Newell a black eye and they knew that the county board, who had the final decision in the matter, would bow to the wishes of the majority.

Ward withdrew his candidate when he realized that his influence wouldn't help him in the face of such an overwhelming majority. He recognized that he had lost the battle but he also knew that the O'Brien farm would soon be his. Moreover, he was also sure to beat Mrs. O'Brien in the Republican county convention and thus hinder her reelection in November.

As the time for Mrs. O'Brien to take over her position in the courthouse approached, Jim suggested that they should both move to town and let Nyblom and Emma take over the farm. He was sure he could get something to do there, he said. She was aware that it wouldn't make much difference so far as the farming itself was concerned. Nyblom was after all a better worker than his father-in-law. But she got O'Brien to drop the idea because she knew the dangers such an arrangement would create for him.

Ragna looked forward to Mrs. O'Brien's departure with sadness. She said she would be home some of the time, especially Sundays, but the younger woman felt that she would be lonely when she no longer could see her and talk with her regularly. Ragna was actually beginning to feel depressed by her surroundings. It was so different from what she had been used to, and the unpleasantness with Jonas and Nyblom made it worse.

Mrs. O'Brien had noticed that Ragna was no longer the lively and happy woman she had been when they arrived, and this became the occasion of an intimate talk between the two women one day when Emma had gone to town with her father. She recognized the situation, said Mrs. O'Brien. Most people, and women in particular, could be oppressed by the loneliness. The prairie could cause an overwhelming sense of despair. Luckily, a healthy individual would usually survive. To begin with she had suffered from depression, but life had gradually improved. And then she told about herself and about why they had moved west.

Mrs. O'Brien—or Elizabeth Langdon, as her name then was—was the daughter of a Kentucky clergyman. Her childhood had been happy and carefree, with the wilderness as playground and with dreams of a glittering world beyond the mountains. When she attended college in Louisville, one of her wealthy friends introduced her to circles where she met visiting artists and where social conventions counted for little. Eventually she fell passionately in love with a young musician. They had planned to marry as soon as she was through college, but before her graduation the young man disappeared and it was rumored that he had a wife somewhere in the East. She was shamed and humiliated, but even after she had been so badly deceived, her heart still spoke in another language than her intellect. Her struggle to regain control of her soul was waged in the region of her birth, where she returned after graduation as a teacher. There in the foothills she hoped she would be able to forget the bright and fascinating world of her dreams.

Many years later Jim O'Brien entered her life. The student of eighteen had become a woman of twenty-eight. One by one her friends had disappeared into more or less attractive marriages. She alone was left single, she, the pastor's daughter with the better education and the finer manners, all factors that served to keep the young men at a distance. These young men tended to be both ignorant and primitive. They belonged to an old Yankee race that had lived among the mountains for a long time and they had no awareness that they had become part of a nation where a more developed civilization had taken root. There were yet no public schools in this region and only very few could afford to give their children private tuition. Ragna was surprised. She had thought that only the immigrants—Norwegians, Swedes, Italians, Bohemians, and the like—were ignorant in this country. This was what she had been told by the Americans themselves. And now a genuine American was telling her that there were areas inhabited by the most blue-blooded Yankees who had no schools for their children!

Jim O'Brien had recently arrived from his green island and had been employed by one after the other in the little Kentucky village where the lonely preacher's daughter had hidden herself from the world. He was a jack-of-all-trades and could figure out most things if he only tried. He was glib and entertaining and even though he was past thirty, there were girls younger than Elizabeth Langdon who found him lively and interesting and who would gladly have followed him up to the altar. One reason why this became her fate was that there really wasn't much choice. Although they were different in most respects, she thought they should be able to get along with each other. What she missed most was the company of people who had a brighter outlook on life than she herself was able to muster—and Jim was a happy-go-lucky kind of man. He had no book learning and his grammar was unspeakable. She loved her books above all else; but she could also at times fear them since they led her further and further away from life. This was the reason why she decided to break with her life of seclusion and accept Jim.

Her father tried to convince her of the absurdity of such a marriage, but she had made her decision. She had no fear of their financial situation because Jim had a hundred or so shares in a gold mine in Nevada that would soon yield enough to pay for all they needed. But when the shares hadn't given any earnings after two years, he sold them to a saloonkeeper for five cents a share, and for the saloonkeeper this was the beginning of a large fortune. But Mrs. O'Brien hadn't had her heart set on wealth. Rich people were hardly ever satisfied, and what was the point with wealth if it didn't bring happiness? She and Jim had got along without a great income and without the great moments that are the foundation of a romantic marriage; but they were fond of each other and had tolerance for each other's weaknesses.

She had talked him into going West to homestead in order to get him away from his drinking companions and his old life. For two years they were virtually alone here with their child. Their nearest neighbor was an old and unfriendly Swedish bachelor. Passing by his homestead one fall day, Jim found him hanging from a rope inside his cabin. That was a fate shared by many. She had survived the loneliness thanks to Jim's merry disposition and her blessed books. Since life here had seemed so pointless, she had tried to set meaningful goals for herself. But she had neglected other and, she now realized, more important things. She had neglected her home and her child—and, well, she now felt that she had neglected Jim too, she said. But Jim was always satisfied if she was content. If she had some food ready when he came home, then that was fine, and if she had forgotten the food because she had been immersed in her books, then they were as good friends as ever. He was proud of his learned wife.

Mrs. O'Brien now had a request. Ragna knew so well how to take care of a home and could make such good food. Couldn't she take Emma under her tutelage, teach her the basics of housekeeping and try to bring about reconciliation between her and Nyblom?

Ragna was touched by her appeal. She recognized that the older woman's life had been one of resignation and that her books had been as a sheet anchor in a sea of despair. Ragna was all the more willing to do her best since she on her own initiative had already made a beginning with Nyblom. But she realized that it would be no easy matter to educate Emma in housewifery and reconcile her with her husband. Emma hardly spoke to Ragna any more. Her own appraisal of the situation was that this strange woman had come from the big city and taken her place in her husband's affection.

The misunderstanding between Jonas and Ragna had also been allowed to develop freely. To begin with, he had felt badly about his thoughtless remark the evening they had gone to look at their future home. A few times he had even tried to tell her that he hadn't really meant what he had seemed to say, but this had in no way placated Ragna. Had he only been reasonable, then she would have explained everything, but when he actually suspected her of such despicable behavior, then he should indeed be made to suffer. Consequently he had found her discouraging and reserved.

The festering relationship between Jonas and Nyblom was also a source of constant vexation for both. They were careful never to mention the underlying issue. Jonas hated all scandal; and he didn't want to admit to the Swede that Ragna could possibly harbor feelings for him. But there was a sufficient supply of other irritants. One evening Jonas had carelessly left a hay fork lying outside the barn, and in the dusk Nyblom had tripped on it and hurt his leg. When he came in, he gave vent to his anger. Didn't Jonas have any brains? To leave a hay fork lying around like that? He had better remember that he was on a farm and not in Minneapolis.

Another evening Jonas had to help milk the cows and Nyblom had let him milk Bridget without telling him that this particular cow had a mean streak and would sometimes play a trick on whoever milked her. And when Jonas was milking, Bridget became impatient and kicked so violently that both Jonas and the milk pail rolled on the grass. Nyblom bent over with laughter, and afterward he entertained the others with his account. But they all sided with Jonas. Emma said that such underhanded behavior was typical of Nyblom, and Ragna sat down beside Jonas after supper and began to ask him about the furnishing of their home.

6.

A church service had been announced the first Sunday in June in O'Brien's Grove. It was almost two months since Pastor Vellesen had been there, so they all looked forward to his arrival. These services were held at the Trulsens, who had the largest house. Even their house, however, was not large enough for the many who used to come during the summer season, when all, from the youngest to the oldest, came together and filled not only the house but the yard as well. Pastor Vellesen wasn't the only reason they came. Distances between neighbors were great and people didn't see much of each other. Church services were popular gatherings where people spent the whole day together, listened to the word of God, and afterward had a good time with their lunch baskets and coffee kettles.

The Trulsens also housed the minister, who belonged to the Conference, as did they.[12] Moreover, Trulsen was sexton and taught the confirmation class. Three were now ready for confirmation: the two sons of Lars Jorshaug and a daughter of Mr. and Mrs. Nesteved. There were also two babies to be baptized. No wonder people longed for Vellesen's arrival and prayed devoutly for nice weather.

Jonas and Ragna had also looked forward to the first church service that summer. When the much-longed-for Sunday finally came with a clear and sunny sky, O'Brien, with his usual generosity, offered them his horses so that they could drive the five miles to the Trulsen farm. At the last minute Nyblom also decided to come along. The few Swedes in the settlement usually attended the Norwegian services since there was no ministry in their own language. Nyblom had demonstrated little interest in religion and had, as far as anyone knew, not yet attended a meeting, so they all thought it a little strange that he suddenly had such an urge to listen to Pastor Vellesen. Nyblom announced his decision at breakfast, and Ragna immediately responded, "That'll be fine!"

But Jonas couldn't see what a Swede had to do with a Norwegian church service and his resentment of Ragna's positive reaction could be read in the two ominous furrows that appeared upon his brow. Nor was Emma enthusiastic about Nyblom's decision to go to church. But the next thing that happened caught her with such surprise that she almost fell off her chair. Ragna said, "And Emma, she'll go along too. Won't you, Emma?"

Emma acknowledged, after ensuring that she had interpreted her correctly, that she would indeed like to join them. "But you'll not understand a darn thing of it," Nyblom objected. It was obvious that he didn't like this unforeseen turn of events.

"Now, that isn't so," said Ragna; "you understand Norwegian quite well, don't you, Emma?" She winked to Mrs. Nyblom, who was even more surprised at the way things were developing.

"Her mother will be here soon from town," Nyblom continued his opposition, "and I suppose she'd rather stay home and visit with her."

"Mr. and Mrs. O'Brien can follow us later," Ragna replied. "That is, if she does not come before we go." As she left the table she said to Emma, "Now, let's hurry to get the lunch and ourselves ready." Emma stared at her with big, moist eyes. It was difficult to understand that Ragna, whom she had blamed for her recent unhappiness, now was taking her side. "Thank you, thank you," the words just dropped from her mouth. Then she dried away a couple of tears and they laughed together as they began to prepare the food, while the men went out to get ready for the journey.

Nyblom obviously disliked the change in the program and looked upset and angry. Jonas tried to put two and two together in an attempt to make sense of it. When they were outside he suddenly turned to Nyblom and asked, "Do you know what you are?" The situation suddenly appeared ludicrous to the Swede. He began to laugh. "I'm a man from Småland, *Gudnaa's*," he replied.[13]

"Yes, and you're a fool of a Smålending too," said Jonas. "Had there been any worse heathens than the Swedes, I would have taken you for a Turk."

"Is that supposed to be an *insølt*?" Nyblom clenched a fist that looked like a large sailor's knot. But then he put his fist in his pocket and walked quickly to the stable.

At nine thirty the lumber wagon was ready. Nyblom was already up on the seat holding the reins. He was in a reflective mood and was humming a Swedish song. Jonas came with the lunch basket, and after him followed the two women, both in high spirits. They took the rear seat so

Jonas had to sit up front with Nyblom. This sure looked promising . . . And to think that he had been waiting for this Sunday almost a whole month and even had sentimental feelings about hearing a Norwegian pastor again . . . *Gudnes* . . .

Just how it had come about was a mystery for both Jonas and Nyblom, but there could no longer be the slightest doubt that Ragna and Emma had again become the best of friends. It was a marvel to hear how they talked and laughed and joked. But silence reigned on the front seat. They had driven a couple of miles when Ragna said with a mischievous smile to Emma, "My, such noisy and sociable husbands we have." Emma burst out laughing. "The seriousness of the occasion don't seem to bother them at all," she said.

"No, it's just awful how they're cutting up." Neither Jonas nor Nyblom appreciated being the butt of this kind of attention. They sat there as if determined not to say anything as the wagon rolled on and the women's conversation turned to other things. After a while Jonas suddenly turned to his neighbor:

"It sure is a fine day," he said. This wasn't a very controversial statement. It was a bright summer day with a dry and firm road under the wheels and a blue sky above. But Nyblom turned as if stung by a wasp at Jonas's remark. It was so totally unexpected that he had been able to say anything at all, that Nyblom had to look at him more than once to make sure he hadn't heard wrong. "It certainly is a lovely day, you bet," he finally conceded.

"There they go again," cried Ragna. "They're surely having lots of fun," Emma laughed.

"The prairie isn't as bad as it's said to be," continued Nyblom, as if he hadn't noticed the fun the women were having at their expense.

"No, it's not at all bad," Jonas agreed.

"Much better than the big cities."

"Oh, the cities are *alreit*," Jonas replied. He wasn't quite sure what the Swede had in mind. At this point they were interrupted by Ragna who reminded them that it wasn't polite to speak a language that everyone present didn't understand.

"Especially since I'm sure you're talking about something very interesting," said Emma.

"We'll teach them better manners," Ragna continued. Both Jonas and Nyblom admitted that they may not have been polite to the women.

"Well, the sooner you mend your ways, the sooner we'll quit," Ragna responded. By now Jonas and Nyblom had thawed out so much that they laughed along with the women.

After they had arrived at the Trulsens', Jonas and Ragna had a moment to themselves and Jonas remarked that perhaps Mrs. Nyblom wasn't as silly as she looked. But she was so poorly dressed compared to her husband who was always so proper. He was trying to get her to reveal what had been going on between herself and Emma, and she replied with an impatient gesture, "Poor Emma! She gets no money for clothes. If I had had such a husband I'd have taught him another dance."

My, oh my, thought Jonas. Is that how it is now? He stood there staring at her. These women were certainly a mystery all to themselves. No more than an hour ago he was sure that she would have insisted that Nyblom was a gallant and honorable gentleman and that Emma was a careless and lazy woman. Indeed, she had virtually said so before. And now the two women had become so fond of each other that he had never seen anything like it. *Gudnes,* the way this other *sexen* was made, anyhow . . . "This is ridiculous," was all he said.

"Ridiculous? What's so funny here?"

"I find it hilarious."

"Well, anyhow, Emma is a wonderful person—so kind and loving and . . ."

"Since when?"

"Oh, you men are hopelessly stupid. You simply don't understand anything!"

"Well, you may be right, there," Jonas replied, "and I suppose that's why the Lord has given us such clever women."

And they both laughed—the first real laughter they had shared in many weeks. But there came Trulsen and the minister and they had to be serious, as became good Christians.

7.

Pastor Vellesen was a middle-aged and fragile little man with a disproportionately large head, a small mouth, and a friendly face, where he had a pair of smiling, friendly eyes that looked straight at whomever he was talking with. When he heard that Jonas and Ragna were from Minneapolis and that Jonas had been a member of a Norwegian congregation there, the pastor pricked up his ears. So Jonas had been a member of the Conference. Did he know Oftedal? Well, Jonas had met Oftedal, but he had belonged to Vangsnes's congregation.

"Oh, the Synod! Well, that's very interesting. Good people there, had they only been able to rid themselves of their centralized church government and their Calvinism![14] Well, well," the pastor continued with a warm smile, "we'll come to an agreement if we settle it in the light of the word of God. So you have lived in Minneapolis? Well, that, I must say, is very interesting! And where did you live in Minneapolis, my good friend?"

Jonas told him. The pastor seemed to have a special knack of asking questions and Jonas decided not to allow himself to be fished out more than would be in his own interest.

"Well, well, and what did you do there?"

Jonas didn't think this was Vellesen's *bisnes* but thought it would be best to excuse his curiosity since he was a man of the cloth. "I *rønna* a large store," he said.

"Well, well, so then you have experience in big business. I have heard that several merchants down there were involved in a big bank failure last winter."

Jonas had no intention of discussing his bankruptcy with anyone. Should it become common knowledge there would be no end to it.

"Well, it couldn't have been nice for those who were involved," the minister suggested.

"Of course, not." Jonas speculated for a moment on what the next question would be. Vellesen stood as if thinking deeply about something. After a while he asked:

"You said that you lived in North Minneapolis?"

"*Jessør!*"

"And that you *rønna* a grocery store?"

"*Jessør!*"

"Well, then you may have known a *grocerymand* called Lars Simonsen?" This question came as a total surprise. The impudent fellow was out to unearth a scandal.

"Ahem—yes, I knew him," he answered evasively. But what interest could Vellesen possibly have in his relations with Simonsen? Jonas's private affairs were none of his business. Was he now bound to confess his entire life's doings just because he had *rønna 'krost* such an impudent prairie pastor? No, he would be damned . . .

"Well, well," the pastor persevered. "Simonsen was such a nice man. I met him when I was a student at Augsburg. And he is well, I presume?"

"Ahem—so far as I know."

"And you are quite a young man to have already had his own business—or didn't I hear you say that you had had your own business?"

"*Jessør!*" *Gudnes,* there seemed to be no end to these questions.

"And how old may you be?"

"Twenty-four." To Jonas's relief, there was no more mention of Simonsen and the bankruptcies. Vellesen turned to Ragna, who had hardly been able to restrain her laughter while Jonas was being cross-examined. Still addressing himself to Jonas, the pastor continued, "And your wife— how old is she?"

Ragna could no longer keep quiet, nor could she deny herself some fun at the minister's expense. "Who, me?" she quickly asked. "I suppose I am already getting so old that I would like to keep it a secret, even from the pastor." Vellesen laughed.

"Well, well," he said. He looked at her more carefully. She had obviously awakened his interest and Jonas was not at all sure that it was in place for a man of the cloth to stand there and stare so openly at another man's wife.

"You're not as old as your husband," the pastor persisted. "My guess is that you're twenty-two."

"You are not so bad at guessing," Ragna replied. "I'll be twenty-three on my next birthday. I was born in 713½ Cedar Avenue September 23rd 1867."

"And baptized and confirmed in the Lutheran church?"

"Of course! I was baptized October 17, 1867, and confirmed the fourth Sunday after Easter 1882." At first she was almost ashamed at having blurted out with all this, but there seemed to be no reason to have any fear of Pastor Vellesen.

"Well, well, this is very interesting! And I assume Pastor Vangsnes . . ."

"No, Pastor Eisteinsen. Mother belonged to the Hauge Synod."[15]

"Well, well, she could have done far worse than that. And perhaps Pastor Eisteinsen performed the wedding?"

"No, Pastor Vangsnes. We were married on a Friday. Actually, it was Friday the thirteenth of March. And we had quite a wedding."

"Well, well! And you—you are from Norway?" He now addressed himself to Jonas again.

"*Jessør,* from Kongsvinger."

Trulsen, who had been busy making preparations for the church service, now came to consult the pastor concerning the hymns and other things that had to be decided.

"We'll soon meet again," the pastor gave a friendly nod as he turned away to follow Trulsen. Then his eyes fastened yet again on Ragna and he turned once more to Jonas and said as he clapped him on the shoulder, "You have a beautiful and intelligent wife, my man." Thereupon he walked off with Trulsen toward the house.

Meanwhile, Jonas had spotted Iver Flasmo and Lars Jorshaug and walked over to say hello. And Ragna became aware that Mr. and Mrs. O'Brien had just arrived and went over to meet them. Just then Nyblom happened to leave the group of men he had been talking with and walked over to join another group standing near the road. His path crossed Ragna's.

"How are you, Ragna?" he asked as he came to a stop. Rather than reply to his greeting she decided to tell him a word or two about his relationship with Emma. But she knew that she would have to be quick to avoid creating a stir . . .

"You should rather inquire about your wife," she admonished him. "She is the poorest dressed of everyone here. You should be ashamed! No one can fill her place in life without being appreciated by the person she loves."

"*Such'e präkare*[16] you have gotten to be, Ragna," he exclaimed with a bitter smile.

"Yes, and I hope my sermon has not been in vain," she said as she turned away, and they both continued on their separate ways.

A little distance from where they had stopped, Torfin Glombekken sat gossiping with a few others. Torfin's critical eyes wandered from one group of people to the other and he had something to say about them all. "There is the fine lady from *Min'ap'lis*," he quipped spitefully to his friends, when Nyblom and Ragna met each other.

"Yes, and it's that there Swede she is talking with too," added one of the others.

"And you may *bette* a trouser button that it isn't the first time either," continued Torfin. "She probably has *svitharter*[17] all over the place."

Jonas had also kept an eye on Nyblom and Ragna. He was sure there was some secret between them. In the meantime Ragna had hurried over to Mrs. O'Brien to tell her about her new friendship with Emma. She also told her that she had had a word with Nyblom about their relationship and she hoped that everything would improve by and by.

"God bless you, my child," said the elder woman, and kissed her.

They were joined by Emma and Jonas and they all wanted to know more about Mrs. O'Brien's new work in town. She was enthusiastic about her job but had little good to say about the town. But some of the townspeople had been very friendly. Even Elihu Ward had paid her a visit and said that she shouldn't worry about the mortgage. If all went well there would surely be a way to have the note renewed. In passing he had mentioned that there was a man from Illinois who wanted to buy a farm in O'Brien's Grove, and Ward had thought of the Olsen farm. He would bring it up with Jonas as soon as he had the opportunity, but if she were to see him she could let him and his wife know that this was an excellent opportunity to make a good deal. Considering his defeat in the superintendent matter, observed the innocent Mrs. O'Brien, you had to admit that Ward was nice and friendly. The possible transaction gave Jonas something to ponder on. This might be a way of making a lot of money . . .

But the service was about to begin. It was eleven o'clock. Many had a long ride, and getting off early wasn't easy for those who had both cattle and horses to take care of, lunch baskets to prepare, and children and themselves to get ready for such an important occasion as the summer's first church service.

"What did Nyblom want?" Jonas whispered to Ragna as they walked a couple of paces behind the others toward the house. He didn't like to ask but he couldn't leave it be.

She looked at him with an expression that he knew well. It dismissed him. "You are just like a spoiled child who cries when he can't hang on to his mother's skirt," she said.

And that was all they had time for. Vellesen was at the door waiting for the people to find their places so he could begin. But Jonas had much to think about through most of the sermon. *Gudnes* how arrogant Ragna could be . . .

The examination of the confirmation class went on and on. And in Jonas's view the sermon was far too long. But finally they came to the baptism, and when the service closed with the singing of the hymn "God's Word Is Our Inheritance," the time was half past one.

"That was quite a portion," Jonas exclaimed to Lars Jorshaug as they got up.

8.

Everyone was hungry after the long service, and people assembled in groups outside the house to enjoy their meals. For the hosts, the pastor, Jonas and Ragna, Mr. and Mrs. O'Brien, and Mr. and Mrs. Nyblom, a table was set in one of the living rooms. In the other, the Flasmos, the Jorshaugs, and a few others were invited to eat at a smaller table. As Jonas and Trulsen waited while Mrs. Trulsen, Ragna, and Emma were laying the table, obviously enjoying themselves, Trulsen asked him how he liked Vellesen.

"Oh, he isn't at all bad," Jonas replied, "but he can't hold a *kand'l* to Vangsnes."

"For my part I have little patience with the popes in the Synod," Trulsen bit him off.

"*Velsør*, in ecclesiastical matters I have found it *sæfest* to *joine* those who have the purest doctrine," Jonas declared. Trulsen smiled.

"Yes, I agree," he said, "but I haven't found pure doctrine with the Missourians."[18]

At that moment Jonas would have given five dollars to know what the Synod doctrine was. He suddenly realized that if he was going to command any respect out here on the prairie, where people seemed to be so engaged in church issues, he would have to learn more about theology. He had gathered that the anti-Missourians and the others on that side didn't want to leave the question of salvation to Our Lord alone, while the Synod insisted that good works wouldn't help you the least bit. But he thought there might be a few other points they differed on. He regretted that he didn't know more, but in Minneapolis they argued about quite other issues, and when he occasionally had been in Synod company and there had been occasion to talk of church matters, there was little information to be had since all were in agreement. He realized that he had actually never known just what he had agreed with. This should not lead you to assume that Jonas wasn't firm in his Synodal faith. On the contrary, the one thing in his life he was sure of was that he was an orthodox member of the Synod and that he would never join the other camp. Whatever happened, he was determined to defend Synod doctrine.

Mrs. Trulsen came in with the pastor and invited them all to sit down. He sat next to Vellesen and he interpreted this as a token of respect for his background as a Minneapolis *bisnesmand*. "I hope that my friends from the big city have been edified by my sermon," said the pastor.

"*O'kors,*" Jonas replied. "It's always a blessing to hear a good sermon."

"Well, well, to be quite honest, I think I was quite successful today myself." Vellesen had a satisfied smile as he began to help himself to the many courses.

"Yes, it was an excellent interpretation of the text," said Jonas. At that Ragna gave him a look that to him took on the meaning: "*Gudnes,* what a hypocrite you are, Jonas Olsen!" He almost blushed. That was Ragna's way . . . almost too *streit* for everyday use . . .

Not much was said during the meal since they all were hungry. Meanwhile, Jonas preoccupied himself with the two topics that to him seemed the most pressing: Nyblom, and his prospects for making a good profit on the sale of his farm to Ward. In a way, the two were connected . . . It would be a falsehood to say that Jonas was happy about his situation in *Groven.* Everything there was so primitive and life was boring. He had always wanted to have a store or something like that, and if he could get a good price for the land he would be able to establish himself in a little *bisnes* in one of the many small towns where a man with his talents surely would succeed in making his mark . . . But Ward was probably a fox. If he saw his *chans'* he would most likely *chita* whoever came along. But Jonas had been in tough weather before. So if the Yankee scoundrel wasn't up and around too early in the morning, he wouldn't be able to scratch out the eyes of a good Norwegian.

After the meal he asked Ragna what she though about selling the farm. She answered that she didn't think it made any sense now that their house was almost finished.

"Oh, a house isn't much to speak of if you can make a good deal," he objected.

"Oh, I don't know," she mused. "A home can be sold too cheaply at any price." Moreover, she pointed out, they had crops of all kinds that seemed to be getting on very well—potatoes and a kitchen garden—and the wheat on the ten acres also seemed very promising. It would be a pity to leave it all behind . . .

"Well, yes, but that would *perhœps* mean that much more to fill up Glombekken's bins," he said. "That rascal has used those ten acres illegally for two summers after that *relativen* of his had to leave it three years ago. Actually we should *prosekjute* him for theft."

"*Gudnes,* no!" Ragna replied. "We would have nothing but trouble in return. The ten acres certainly haven't made him any richer and we have all reason to be happy that his relative *brækket*[19] the ten acres so it was done before we came."

There was no opportunity to continue their discussion; the young people were about to have some fun out in the yard and they wanted to join them.

———◆———

There was much to do at a church gathering on the prairie. The afternoon passed all too quickly, especially for the women, who for the most part hadn't seen each other in a long time. Their only opportunity for socializing was the Ladies Aid and the six annual church services—and the Ladies Aid didn't meet during the winter season. Mrs. Trulsen had taken the initiative to get it started. She was good at organizing things and some suspected her of looking for opportunities to show off her large house. The Trulsens, they claimed, thought they were a little better than others. Mrs. Flasmo, in particular, had dropped some words now and then to that effect. And after Flasmo and Trulsen had quarreled about predestination, it may be that Mrs. Flasmo had harped on Mrs. Trulsen's grand airs more than was strictly speaking necessary.

Mrs. Tarvesen had expressed the view that when a man like Trulsen was supposed to be both church warden and master builder and was, moreover, in the pastor's pocket, it was quite natural that they also had to have a better house than most people. The Trulsens had four large rooms downstairs, but—and this was the worst part—they even had two small bedrooms upstairs, and Mrs. Trulsen insisted on calling one of them "the guest room" because that was where the pastor slept when he was visiting. Just as if the room was made any better by Vellesen lying there snoring and smoking tobacco and dirtying the *kørtena'n*.[20]

"I think it's nice that there is someone with a large house and a good heart to take in the pastor," said Mrs. Sven Ericksen. She thought they were going a little too far in their criticism of Mrs. Trulsen.

It was mostly Mrs. Flasmo and Mrs. Tarvesen who seemed called on to stand in judgment of the other women. Thus Mrs. Tarvesen had discovered that Ragna was wearing a fine dress, used a corset, and did her hair in a manner that she didn't approve of. This was tantamount to interfering with God's creation, which had already been completed. So typical, that Mrs. Trulsen should be attracted to such an affected and conceited woman.

"I suppose she'll get the fine lady from *Min'ap'lis* to *æssiste* her to *rønne* the Ladies Aid now," ventured Mrs. Glombekken. "She is supposed not to have had any real parents, so you can hardly *expekte* much."

"To me she appears to be a real nice and comfortable person," said Mrs. Sven Ericksen. "And she has a nice husband too."

"Nice! Do you call him nice?" Mrs. Tarvesen exclaimed. "*Sech* a conceited turd?" But just then Ragna came along. Mrs. Tarvesen turned to her and asked if she liked life in the settlement. "Yes, indeed!" Ragna replied. "It's been much nicer than I had expected."

"Oh, I can imagine that you had hardly *expektet* to find civilized people here on the prairie," said Mrs. Tarvesen. Ragna blushed. She would have to think twice before speaking.

"You may *mæbe'* not have been to a *mitin'* before either?" asked Mrs. Tarvesen.

"Certainly!" She looked around as if for an opportunity to get away.

"So you are baptized and confirmed?"

"Of course, I was brought up in the Hauge Synod."

"Oh, dear, are you in Hauge's?" exclaimed Mrs. Nesteved. "I have a brother-in-law who has a cousin who is a Hauge pastor."

"Oh, well, I suppose it may be better than nothing at all," said Mrs. Tarvesen. "But I've heard that they are supposed to be *lus*[21] in their *konfession'*."

Ragna was embarrassed by this examination and she was relieved when Trulsen came and invited her to come in. *Supperen* was ready.

"*O'kors,* naturally, there is a *differens* between people!" said Mrs. Tarvesen as Ragna left them and followed Trulsen.

———·+·———

Jonas hadn't had a good day. After he had eaten, he had run across Torfin Glombekken and that was in itself enough to make him upset. To get away, he had told him that he had better try to find his wife, and then Torfin had remarked that there was no need to be worried about her. She was doing all right. He had seen her having a good time with Nyblom. Weren't they old friends from Minneapolis? Jonas realized that people were already talking about the Swede and Ragna. He had been sure that it would end in a scandal . . . He had walked away from Glombekken without saying a word. On the way home, Nyblom in vain tried to get a friendly word out of him but finally gave it up. Ragna was more lively than ever and was so loud that Jonas was bothered . . . Yes, he could see that he would have to sell the farm. Otherwise he would go bankrupt in his marriage as he had in his *bisnes*. If he only had had the brains not to come to this miserable *kontrye'* . . .

9.

It had taken longer than Jonas had planned to complete their new house: Trulsen had his own chores to attend to, and O'Brien, who was eager to help, couldn't leave everything at home to Nyblom. Jonas had done as much as he could, but he was no carpenter, and the indoor work had to be done in style and couldn't be left to an amateur. They were already into the second week of June and Trulsen had said that he would need yet another week. And then Peder Tarvesen could begin to paint, so it would be at least a couple of weeks before they could move in.

Ragna longed for the day when they would begin housekeeping on their own. Mrs. O'Brien's move to Normanville had, as Ragna had expected, led to a deep-felt sense of loss. Although she did all she could to be happy and content, there were times when she had to admit failure. But she never swerved from her plan to assist Emma, and it pleased her to see how Emma was taking charge of the household and that she seemed to have realized that cleanliness and order are a housewife's two most desirable virtues.

In her last weeks with the O'Briens, Ragna more than ever endeavored to have everything done as well as the circumstances allowed, and to have the meals ready and the food appetizing when the men came home from work. On a few occasions Emma exclaimed that she would never be able to be so careful, but Ragna insisted that there was simply no other way to keep these men satisfied. A man, she explained, was born a materialist. If his surroundings were nice and tidy, if he was filled up with good food, and if you allowed him the illusion that he was master of the home, then you could do whatever you wished with him. Her precepts were infallible:

"Feed the brute," she said, "or he will, sooner or later, turn into a cannibal." And then she would tell strange stories about her many suitors and male acquaintances at Mrs. Johnson's boardinghouse, and she and Emma would end up laughing. But she had succeeded in gaining Emma's attention. Emma had begun to think and she was soon picking up some secrets of the culinary arts from Ragna. Gradually it fell upon Emma to make some of the courses that they had agreed on. One evening she made the pudding that had been the occasion for the outburst that had set off the difficulties with Nyblom. Ragna hadn't ventured to serve that pudding again, but now she set it on the table after they had completed the rest of the meal with the words, "And now for Emma's pudding! It's delicious!"

Nyblom stared at the pudding. "Did you really make this?" he asked, turning to his wife after he had tasted a spoonful.

"Of course, she did," Ragna replied on her behalf.

"Well I'll be damned . . . excuse my Latin . . . it's good!" he said.

"That's what I told you," said Ragna, "far better than I could make it."

Jonas insisted that it was just about the best pudding he had tasted since he had left Norway. Not really understanding what was going on, he nevertheless felt that the occasion called for a compliment. Emma was quite touched.

———•———

The next week, Trulsen was finally through with the carpentry and Tarvesen had begun to paint indoors. In a few days they could move in. But Jonas was still speculating on the wisdom of selling their land. They would probably have to move soon anyway and now that they had such a good opportunity to make money on the land he would rather sell it before they bought furniture for the house and moved in. Jorshaug had been in town a few days ago and Ward had again talked about the man from Illinois who was so eager to buy a farm in *Groven*. But if Jonas wanted to sell he would have to make up his mind soon or the man would look around for another farm. But Ragna didn't want to sell. The fact that they finally were about to have their own home meant so much to her that she couldn't resign herself to the thought of moving again. She was so insistent that Jonas thought she took on greater authority than she by rights had. After all, he was the man . . . But she had become so stubborn and *kontrari* that he hadn't dared to argue with her.

The very next day, Elihu Ward unexpectedly turned up with a stranger he said was the man from Illinois who wanted to look at the land and discuss the deal. After they had left, O'Brien declared that the stranger looked just like a railroad bum he had seen in a saloon in Normanville seven years ago. It was the same year that Ole Dampen had had to sell a half section he owned down in Norman County in order to cover the cost of a lawsuit. At the time, Ole had run a roadhouse about thirty miles west on the prairie where three lumberjacks, who had been on their way from Fargo to Minneapolis, had been robbed of their entire winter earnings. The man now said to be from Illinois had witnessed for Dampen, who with good help from his lawyer, Newell, had been found not guilty. But it had been necessary to buy quite a few witnesses, so the affair had cost a nice sum of money. Nevertheless, Ole had one way or another established himself in the *saloonbisnes* in Normanville, and in a few years become both well-off and respectable. And now the very same bum had apparently made himself a fortune in Illinois.

"Sure, and this is a great country," Jim said. "All ye need is to get next to a lawyer or a banker, and, begorrah, he'll turn ye into a capitalist, a patriot, or a politician overnight, while you ought to be in the penitentiary."

Ward and his companion hadn't only inspected Jonas's land carefully but had also visited the two neighboring farms: Jorshaug's and Flasmo's. The man from Illinois had seemed particularly interested in the Flasmo farm and gave Jonas the impression that he didn't care so much about which farm he bought so long as he got himself a good piece of land in *Groven*. No price had been mentioned. The stranger had said that he would leave that to Ward, and Jonas promised that he would come and talk it over with the banker when he had another errand in town a few days later. Jorshaug had made up his mind not to sell, and Flasmo said that it would depend on what they were ready to pay.

So this was the situation when Jonas one evening came home and told Ragna that Tarvesen had completed the painting and that they would have to decide either to do business with Ward or to buy furniture and move in. They agreed to go to town the next day and hear what Ward was willing to pay. Jonas had bought a team from Erik Nesteved and a new lumber wagon, so they could travel whenever they wished.

As they drove to Normanville, Jonas and Ragna avoided the topic that was uppermost in their minds. Although they were aware that things would not be as they should between them until they talked through their relationship, neither was eager to take the initiative.

What they did talk about was the farm deal. The farm had cost them almost $2,800, including the buildings. Jonas decided that the land was now worth about $700 more than when he bought it, so they should be able to sell it for $4,000. But Ragna saw things in a different light and was determined to do her best to block the transaction. Nor did she like Jonas's idea of going into *bisnes* again. But she said nothing about this now. Her present plan was to insist on such a high price that it would preclude any deal. So she argued that a profit of $500 on the farm was far too little. They would have to take their moving expenses from Minneapolis into account, as well as their future expenses in moving to a new homestead, wherever that might be. Nor should they forget that they owed the O'Briens for three months' room and board, and that neither of them had earned anything during this period. And then they had the note in Minneapolis. What was the point in coming here if they were to leave it as poor as they had been on arrival? If that Illinois man was so eager to buy, then he should at least pay a decent price. She thought they should let it go for $5,000. Jonas, who had looked into the current value of land in *Groven,* knew that no land was bought there at such a price. But Ragna was stubborn. If they couldn't make a decent profit on the deal, why not keep what they had? And she mentioned one item after the other that she insisted they had to consider. Jonas was surprised at the businesslike manner in which she defended claims that were quite preposterous, according to his way of thinking. He hadn't known that she was so interested in *bisnes.* He had actually had the impression that she couldn't care less about it, and here she sat arguing and reasoning like some *loiert* . . .[22]

Their first visit in Normanville was of course with Mrs. O'Brien. They had never seen her so bristling with energy. After Jonas had left them to meet Ward, the older woman confessed to Ragna that her only concern now was for Emma and Jim. It was lonely for him on the farm, she said, and it might well be that she would have to take the risk involved in letting him move to town. As for Emma, she was comforted by what Ragna could tell her about her marriage. Things were shaping up, she said, and she was sure that all would be well.

Ward received Jonas with great courtesy. But to begin with he said nothing about the farm deal and Jonas began to fear that he might not be so eager to buy the farm after all. The banker seemed primarily interested in the year's harvest and the nation's finances. The harvest wouldn't be as good as expected, he said, and it would be difficult to raise the money that people would need. The capitalists in the East were no longer so eager to invest in the Northwest. One reason was their suspicion of the Populist movement that had grown out of the *Farmeralliancen.* They feared that it would lead to socialism and financial ruin.[23]

Ward mentioned that he had heard that Jonas had been in *bisnes* in Minneapolis so he surely knew what was involved in doing business in such uncertain times. He was glad that Jonas had settled in the county since it was so important that men who were used to larger circumstances—indeed, if Jonas would permit, people with a solid business education and a broader perspective on life—would settle among their compatriots out here and take financial as well as spiritual leadership. But such a man should not be a farmer. His real calling would be as a businessman. Only then would his fine qualities be fully appreciated. And he would of course be pleased to be of help . . .

Jonas was an ambitious man who appreciated that people thought well of him. But in business relations he was also gifted with a level head and it didn't take him long to see through Ward's carefully disguised flattery. He might not, he thought, look particularly intelligent, but at least he wasn't so naïve that he could be ensnared by this kind of sales pitch . . . "Well," he finally said, "I'm here to see about that deal."

"Oh, yes, I had almost forgotten that," the other replied. "And what is your price, Mr. Olsen?"

"Six thousand dollars." His voice was clear and firm. The banker jumped up from his chair, visibly surprised.

"Six thousand dollars for land in O'Brien's Grove?" he exclaimed. "I can appreciate a joke, but I admit I wasn't prepared for anything quite that strong."

"Well, that's what I want for the farm," Jonas replied.

"You'll never get it, my dear man. It's an absurd price."

"Well, sir, it's my price and my land."

"True, but my client would never consider it."

"That's his business," Jonas said as he got to his feet. Ward stood looking at him. It wasn't every day that he came across people he couldn't move with either cunning or reason.

"However, I'll write to him and inform him of your terms," he said as he gave him his hand in farewell. "And be sure to call on me when you are in town, Mr. Olsen."

And on this they parted.

When Jonas joined Ragna and told her what had happened between him and the banker, she exclaimed enthusiastically, "I knew you would be able to fix him!"

"Oh, I have been out on a cold day before," he said and straightened his back. He was really quite proud of his wife . . . She had a remarkably good head on her shoulders . . .

10.

A s Jonas and Ragna left Mrs. O'Brien's office on their way to Setter-gren to buy furnishings for their new home, they noticed a man coming out from O'Connor's saloon. They thought they recognized him, but assured themselves that they must have been wrong, and they continued on their way. The man, however, had also noticed them and stood looking after them. Then he smiled, quickly crossed the street, and caught up with them. When he tipped his hat, there could be no doubt. He was no other than their friend from Mrs. Johnson's boardinghouse, Ludvig Napoleon Stomhoff, a.k.a. "The Weekly News." Neither Jonas nor Ragna were particularly thrilled at meeting him again; nor had they expected to come across him here.

"*Gudnes!*" exclaimed Jonas, "how in the world have you come here?"

"Oh, I had the call, and felt that I had to respond by coming."

"The call?" Jonas stood there with his mouth wide open.

"Yes, I have been called to serve the church."

"Serve the church?" Now I have heard everything, thought Jonas. Ragna also stared at him. She could sense a powerful stench of whiskey from their old acquaintance.

"Serve the church?" she repeated. "What's the joke?"

"It's no joke," Napoleon replied without a smile. "One does not make fun of serious matters. In the midst of my sinful ways, God's grace allowed me to see the light."

Ragna turned away in disgust and Jonas laughed. But Stomhoff was not a man to stumble so easily in his act. It had come about, he explained, when he one day happened to be leafing through one of the many church journals and had come across an advertisement for a teaching position in O'Brien's Grove. The settlers there, it said, wanted an experienced and pious man to teach their children. They also, the advertisement added, wanted him to lead devotional meetings until a congregation had been organized. The call had come upon Stomhoff then and there and it was as if he had been filled with a new life. Ragna's disgust grew as he talked. She turned to Jonas and said that she had better hurry on to Settergren and that he could follow when he was ready. On this she left them.

"So, you see, now I'm here," Napoleon continued, with greater confidence now that she was gone.

"To teach school and preach?" It was difficult for Jonas to grasp something so utterly strange.

"*Yessør,* for board and $25 a month. As far as I know, the school will be ambulatory.[24] My first lodgings will be with a farmer named Torfin Glombekken."

"I know him," said Jonas. "We're neighbors. And how are things in *Min'ap'lis?*"

"Oh, mostly crappy, thank you!" His voice began to sound more worldly and a careful smile appeared on Stomhoff's countenance. "There has been little activity since you left us. The Simonsens have moved to their daughter in Washington. They say that she and her husband are like cat and dog and that the old man has money in spite of the bankruptcy. Lomvig has some sort of employment with the H. & B.'s main office in St. Paul. Little Tollefsen has returned to Norway. Pontoppidan Johnson plays the organ in a church in Fargo. Nicolaisen is bankrupt, and yesterday, as I was about to leave town, I read in the *Journal* that Davidsen's Bank was wiped out."

"Has Davidsen's Bank failed?" Jonas exclaimed in surprise. He couldn't but think of his mortgage. Perhaps he had been a fool not to have sold the farm after all . . .

"What else could one expect?" Stomhoff continued. "Careless loans with questionable security and all that sort of thing." He looked longingly at Dampen's saloon. "This journey has been very tiring," he said. "It would indeed be good to have something bracing. Regrettably, I spent every penny getting here. You wouldn't happen to . . ."

"You hardly ever see ready money out here," Jonas parried.

"But a settler surely has credit?"

"I am unknown in these saloons. I don't drink, you know."

"No, of course not. Neither do I. I only imbibe on rare occasions as a God's gift for my poor nerves. By the way, I forgot to bring you greetings from your old friend Lyvenfelt. He has published a new book, *Servants of the Word.* It's about the clergy and is an altogether miserable literary product. I *visita* him recently and he told me again about the details concerning the scandalous lies you had him write about Stunsrud. That was the best deal he had made in his life, he said. And he added that when such an upright member of the church as Jonas Olsen could be involved in such an affair, then there was no reason why he should have anything on his *konsjiensen.*"

"By the way"—and Napoleon now stepped up close to Jonas and his little yellowish green eyes lit up with a strange brightness—"by the way, what manner of Lutheran trickery are you involved in out here?"

Jonas was furious. Damn that this specimen of lowlife now turned up with the old story of that worthless book, which he believed had been dead and buried long ago. As by instinct, he put his hand in his pocket and pulled out a dollar, which Napoleon accepted with expressions of gratitude. "But don't mention money to me again!" said Jonas with emphasis.

Then he walked with determined steps and a bad temper across the street to Settergren. Napoleon stood looking at him. Then, with a nod of his head, he resolutely went to Ole Dampen's saloon, where the saloonkeeper stood ready to receive his new guest.

"You *ban* a stranger in *dis' hare contry, I gass?*" said Dampen. Napoleon gave him his card, on which the saloonkeeper read in elegant print: "Ludvig Napoleon Stomhoff, Professor." Dampen bowed respectfully. This was the first time he had had such a distinguished visitor. "*Mœbe'* you are one of these preacher teachers?" he asked.

"Ahem—no; I am a pedagogue."

Ole was not at all sure what that might be, but he realized that it must be something fine and mighty and that he might just as well *trite* sooner than later.

"*Hev'* one on me. *Vot'yu* drinks?"

"I mostly hold with the pure and strong," Stomhoff replied. "Some Kentucky rye, please!" And this increased the saloon owner's respect. You could see that he was some *proffesor*—a man who had been around in the world and knew the value of good liquor!

"*Hare's ho,* and welcome to town"! You'll *perhœps starte'n* college or something?"

No, Napoleon had no such plans, at least not for the time being. He had promised the people in *Groven* that he would organize an elementary school and preach now and then.

"Preach?" Dampen exclaimed. "Do you preach too?"

"I preach when I have the call."

"*Hev'nodder,*" Ole insisted. This was turning out to be very strange indeed. "Are you a follower of Schmidt or Missouri?"[25]

"Strictly speaking I am neither. I am an opportunist."

"What was that, you called it?"

"Opportunist."

"Oh, so that was it!" Dampen had heard about something they called "Calvinist" and something they called "synergist." Just what these words implied, he didn't know, but there had been much debate about them recently in his saloon. Torfin Glombekken and Iver Flasmo had, with the assistance of two or three innocent shots, almost come to blows about these very terms. But "opportunist" was a new one for the saloonkeeper. At least he realized that he had a learned man in his establishment, and since this was the first *proffesor* who had done him the honor of dropping in for an exchange of pleasantries, his good heart led him to the decision that the visit should at least not cost him anything. Moreover, Ole was a good *bisnesmand* and able to work out that if it became known that professors and preachers frequented Dampen's saloon, then this would *adverteise bisnessen* in a quite wonderful manner. So when they had emptied their second rye, Ole shoved the bottle over to Napoleon and said, "It was real nice to meet you, *proffesor. Hev'nodder!*"

Before Napoleon left the saloon, the two had become the best of friends. When Ole heard that he was going to board with Torfin Glombekken, he even sent with him a quart of something he insisted was prime quality and that they could use to enliven the evening. And he wrapped it with great care so that no one would be able to guess the contents since, as Ole put it, one could always *rønne op agænst* some member of the congregation with a fine nose, and preachers had to be a little careful of their good name and reputation.

Jonas was so irritated with Napoleon's appearance that he hadn't offered him a ride to *Groven,* but Stomhoff was not to be daunted. When they were ready to go home, he was suddenly there and said that he was certainly lucky to have met them since he now would have a ride all the way to Glombekken.

It was a sad ride home—not because Napoleon was drunk and unpleasant; he was almost never really drunk. Neither Jonas nor Ragna felt comfortable in his company. When they finally reached the road to the Glombekken farm they had listened to all the scandals that had happened and that could have happened in Minneapolis since they had left the city. They were glad to get rid of him.

The Glombekkens gave the new teacher a warm welcome. It was unexpected to be selected to house such a learned man. The minister always lodged with the Trulsens. But it had been decided that the teacher should stay with them and suddenly they had become almost as prominent as the Trulsens. Stomhoff was an interesting and affable man who had a lot to tell them about faraway lands and people. And he was such a likable fellow. When Glombekken went to the stable, Napoleon joined him, and between them they emptied the pint of rye that Napoleon had bought for sixty cents of the dollar that Jonas had given him.

When Torfin heard that Stomhoff had ridden with Jonas and Ragna and that he had even known them in Minneapolis, it became a new link in their growing friendship.

"I suppose they were rich and prominent people down there?" Glombekken asked cautiously.

"Oh, yes! He was in *bisnes,* you know."

"It *biter* me," said Mrs. Glombekken, "that he could leave behind a good *bisnes* and come out on the prairie and farm."

"Oh, you know, strange things can happen," opined Torfin. "And city life isn't healthy."

"And *farmerkontryet* has its attractions too," Stomhoff remarked diplomatically.

"And his wife is of a good and well-known family?" Glombekken kept on.

"I've heard that she served table at those *bordinghusa,*" said his wife.

"Ahem—yes, that's what she did," Napoleon acquiesced.

"And that she is supposed to have been brought up kind of without any real parents?"

"Her parents died when she was young," he responded. "They seem to have been rather poor, so she had to find work."

"Oh, is that it? No worse than that!" Glombekken laughed. No more was said about this just then. It was best to move with caution.

On their way home, Ragna's ruminations on Stomhoff were from quite another point of view than those of her husband. She had done nothing that she didn't want the whole world to know about. So she had no reason to fear Napoleon. It didn't enter her mind that Jonas didn't have as clear a conscience as herself. She was upset that such a man was to be teacher for the children of the settlement. "You cannot possibly let it happen," she said when they were alone.

"Well—what can I do? The minister has appointed him and no one will appreciate the person who makes any trouble. We are lucky that we don't have any children ourselves."

"What if we had?"

"Well, that would be another matter."

"Not that I can see," she answered. There was always this weakness in Jonas—his discouraging vacillation and his business ethics that entered into every kind of relation . . .

II.

Elihu Ward was a man of good upbringing and excellent manners. He was an Eastern Yankee and beyond doubt the only person in the entire county who knew the name of his great-great-grandfather. The prairie had no traditions for the pioneer and those of the country were not his; for in nine of ten instances he was an immigrant from another country and had his roots in another tradition and in another culture. This is what has given the *Yankien* his great advantage above the others in the shaping of the characteristics of the American West. This is what has made it possible for him and his kind to become a kind of upper class in the motley community of peoples that has sprung up in this part of the country. The *Yankien* brought the country's own tradition with him into the settlement.

Ward was proud of his family and of the New England tradition. In his youth, people in the East had regarded the West as a newly discovered hunting field where they could send their sons when the crib was empty. With exotic notions both of the vast area west of the Ohio and of their own English heritage and their own importance, these young men found the wilderness quite literally full of game: immigrants from Europe who had just barely had time to make the land inhabitable for the more civilized American.

The American often forgot both his fine heritage and his cultural mission in his eagerness to make himself the lord of creation. But some took their mission seriously and tried to raise the pillars of puritanism under western skies, convinced that they were preordained to rule here as their fathers had done in Maine, Rhode Island, and Connecticut. In neither instance did they find it difficult to reconcile their traditional values with their opportunity to bring home their share of the bounty of the battle for survival.

Elihu Ward had had a greater understanding of this opportunity than most. He was the first to arrive on the spot where Normanville was established. He hadn't come with the same intentions as those who had come before and after him as pioneers and homesteaders. He had come as capitalist and entrepreneur. He had not come to sow but to harvest. He was backed by a powerful banking syndicate in the East, and by the time the railroad arrived he owned all land in a circumference of three miles from the little depot that was the nucleus of the town. The town soon became the center of a settlement—now about twelve years old—of Norwegians and Swedes, with a few Irish and Germans here and there among them. Before Normanville, these settlers had had from thirty to forty miles to the nearest market, so for them the establishment of the town had been an event of the utmost importance.

In about the time it takes to describe it, the little town grew up on the prairie, fully equipped for its commercial mission among the farmers. One business after the other was set up in a hurriedly assembled wooden shanty where people could buy all they needed to satisfy their physical needs, from calico to Kuriko, and get rid of their own products at the lowest market price. Even though Normanville in the early 1890s hadn't grown to more than an oversized prairie village, Ward had already acquired a relatively large capital that he, with the shrewdness and quick eye for profit of the Yankee, had increased year by year. Not only did he have full control of all town property, but he had provided the merchants with loans at interest rates he found reasonable and with all they owned as security.

Nothing of importance happened in Normanville without Ward's consent. The rule was rather that nothing happened except at his initiative. That he was more feared than loved, and that people planned to reduce his power, was only to be expected. But such plans had come to nothing. The nearest anyone had come to defying him was the appointment of Mrs. O'Brien as superintendent; but this was due to the farmers' influence. To be sure, Ward also had a good grip on quite a few of the farmers, but they were on the whole more independent of him than the people in town. This appointment had irritated Ward more than he pretended, and when Mrs. O'Brien's friends found comfort in the thought that he had given in and that she would be nominated without much opposition by the county Republican convention, this was merely an illustration of how little they yet knew of Elihu Ward.

But now he had other affairs on his mind and had decided to let the fate of Mrs. O'Brien depend on her usefulness. One day last June he had made an unexpected appearance in Ole Dampen's saloon, where he had never been in all the years Ole had been there. Ward was on the whole not so fond of Norwegians. Some of them had turned out to be rather stubborn and not easy to *hændle*. Moreover, there were too many of them. They took the best land and usually managed it quite well, so that relatively few had to borrow money from him, and when they were successful they had begun to place their money with his competitor, Torgersen.

To begin with, everybody in town had to go to Ward for a loan. But then Torgersen had arrived—thanks to the endeavors of Hans Floen. If Ward had known what was going on, he would have taken his precautions and stopped the establishment of a new bank. But when Floen bought the lot next to Settergren, he had said it was for himself, and he had even given Ward his word that he wouldn't sell it, or, should he build on it, rent out the building, if Elihu should want to have it for himself. This was while the two still were friends and when Ward still thought that he had an ally in the Norwegian lawyer. When Floen immediately had sold to Torgersen without asking Ward's permission, their friendship was over. They hadn't spoken to each other since the new bank opened a year later. Ward had decided that the Norwegians were an ungrateful lot. But they were remarkably forward, considering that they were, according to Ward's New England view of the world, a backward race.

But although Ward thought he had good reason to resent the Norwegians, he was usually polite and obliging with them. He was a cultured man who fully understood the importance of appearances and he had a remarkable ability to control himself regardless of his personal feelings. Even when he "found himself forced" to foreclose a farm, he would come with the most sincere assurances of his warmest sympathy with the victims. Floen used to tell the story of how Ward once, after having taken the farm from an Irish widow, cried with her and gave one of her children a dime for candy to lessen the pain. But outside of his business affairs with common people, Ward had no relations with them. Socially speaking, he and his family were high above all others in Normanville, except for Newell and Brackens, the judge, who were in his pay and who were Yankees like himself.

So it was no wonder that the regulars at Dampen's saloon made big eyes the day the distinguished American made his appearance among them and then without hesitation introduced his visit by declaring he would treat the crowd. However polite Ward always appeared to be, no one had thought that he was such a fine fellow. The conversation soon concentrated on conditions in O'Brien's Grove and the people there. Dampen talked and Ward mostly listened and *trita krauden,* which was the best way to Ole's heart. He hadn't been much out in the Grove lately, Ward explained, and he was very interested in learning about the changes that Dampen could tell him about. Many of the settlers were his customers and it pleased him to see that they did well and that they were such hardworking and reliable people. The news that the much-needed railroad wouldn't be realized in a good many years had saddened him. Dampen had also heard the bad news.

The saloonkeeper paid special attention to the most recent arrivals in *Groven*. He knew them all. Yes, he could even tell about the man from Minneapolis who had such fine airs that he hadn't yet dropped in. And it wasn't because he didn't drink. He had heard that he used to get quite drunk while he was in Minneapolis. It had finally become such a scandal that his wife had had to interfere. Ole hadn't actually met Jonas in person, but according to Torfin Glombekken and other reliable men in the settlement, he must be rather stupid; even though he had only lived here for a few months, he had already rubbed against everyone out there. Dampen had a friend who knew Jonas from Minneapolis, a professor called Napoleon who recently had moved to *Groven*. He had visited his saloon and Dampen now had a little *indseid'track* on this Olsen.

"They may judge him a little too quick," Ward remarked apologetically. "I've met him, and he looks to me a rather intelligent young man." This remark, followed by Ward again "setting them up," gave Dampen an excuse to retell the little he had heard about Jonas, with the addition of his own interpretation of every episode. Ward could, by the way, talk with the professor himself. He knew Jonas very well and he was a pedagogue, a minister, and a preacher, so he was a man to trust! Ward laughed. "Have another, boys," he offered.

As he was saying goodbye a little later, he remarked as in passing, "I'd like to meet that preacher—what's his name—Napoleon? Naturally, I'm interested in making the acquaintance of everybody moving into the county."

"Sure, Mike! Me the *sam'*," replied Ole confidently. "I'll fetch him over when he comes to town."

12.

Since neither of them had confided in her, Ragna didn't know the details of what had happened between Nyblom and Emma. But that there had been some changes in their matrimonial relationship was evident. Mrs. Nyblom was happier, at times even light-headed, and her husband gave her much more attention than earlier.

Even Jonas noticed this and speculated on what the meaning could be. He had thought of asking Ragna, but he was reluctant to discuss Nyblom with his wife. Moreover, in their last days at the O'Briens' there had been few opportunities for them to talk with each other, and when

Ragna was working in the garden or getting things ready on their own farm, Emma was always helping her. It had irritated him that it was never possible to have a private conversation with his own wife. But now things would be different when they moved into their own home. Even though he suffered under their present relationship and wished of a full heart that it had been different, he nevertheless feared, more than anything else, the storm it now probably would be necessary to go through in order to find calmer waters.

Jonas admitted that he had never actually suspected Ragna of doing anything wrong. When he reflected on their relationship, he had to acknowledge that he had been more vacillating than she. Yet he couldn't rid himself of the notion that she had somehow wronged him by being friendly and obliging with other men. Why didn't she speak to him? It didn't enter his mind that he had any responsibility for the present lack of openness between them. She was the one to blame and he had been hurt.

In this state of mind, Jonas stopped in at Jorshaugs' on his way to the O'Briens' from his farm, and he met Napoleon, who was waiting for him down by the road between Jonas's and Glombekken's farms. Torfin was just then leading his horses to pasture a little way off. It was nice, he said, to be among so many old friends. And he thought it must be particularly interesting for Ragna to get together again with Nyblom since they had been so close in the past. No more was needed to pour oil on the fire of suspicion that raged in Jonas. "What do you mean by saying that they have been close?" he asked sharply.

"Oh, you should know that just as well as I," Napoleon responded with a suppressed smile. "All the lodgers in the boardinghouse knew all about it."

"Knew about what?" Jonas felt that his voice trembled and that his heart had a quicker beat.

"But my dear Mr. Olsen! It was no secret that Gust Nyblom was courting Ragna!" Jonas suddenly saw the light. So that was at the bottom of it all! They had been lovers!

"Oh, is that all?" he said, pretending indifference. "Ragna has had many suitors."

"Yes, so it is only natural that you'll come across some of them later in life. By the way, would you do me a little service for old friendship's sake? You know, on occasion a man in my position will have to appear in a black coat . . . Would you be so kind as to . . ."

"No, damned if I will!" Jonas was quite determined. These subsidies of Stomhoff would have to come to an end. They had never led to anything but trouble.

"All right," said Napoleon. "I'll remember your helpfulness when the time comes." Then Jonas realized that he should perhaps not have denied Napoleon this service. But at this point they were joined by Glombekken. "It's a damnd fine *levinghus* you have built," he said to Jonas.

"It will do," he answered. "It cost us a pretty sum."

"Oh, it costs to be fine and mighty!" said Torfin with a sly look at Napoleon. Jonas couldn't be bothered to respond to Glombekken. He couldn't stand his insinuating and spiteful character. With a cutting smile he turned away from them and continued on his way.

———

Ragna had experienced one of her lonely days. Just like Jonas, Ragna had imagined that all would be better now that they were to have their own home. Now, however, she was beginning to fear that it would be even lonelier than it was now. They hardly ever had visitors, and company would probably be even scarcer when they were on their own. When she was overwhelmed by such feelings she would sometimes leave the house as if driven by a vague need to air her troubled mind under God's heaven. Again and again she went down to the lonely willow by the dry creek bed. It had become a friend in her contemplations. She could sit here for long periods of time when the weather was warm, and stare out across the endless prairie. But regardless of where she looked there wasn't a single fresh impression that came to her from without. The *gopheren* was just about the only living creature she ever saw—*gopheren* and *blackbirden*—yes, and of course the cows and an occasional flock of grazing sheep.[26] The coyote had taken a couple of lambs from the O'Briens the other night. She had heard its howls but not yet seen it. She had come to appreciate the cows. They were so calm and content. On the forsaken prairie the animals could be dear friends.

There had been times when she had been tempted to give in to Jonas's wish to sell the farm, but on contemplating the alternatives she had always dismissed the idea. It had been a long time since Ragna had had anything she could call a home and now she had committed herself to this place. She feared that she wouldn't be able to do it all over again. But, she thought, Jonas couldn't understand such things. To him this was simply a house and a piece of land that could be exchanged for any other house and piece of land.

On the whole Ragna thought she had understood Jonas's more or less evident weaknesses from the very beginning. There had been many things that she had decided she would have to do something about. Take for instance his *bisnes*-is-*bisnes* ethics and his tendency to resort to hypocrisy when he thought it would be to his advantage. She had thought that she would be able to heal him with her love and the little wisdom that the Lord had given her. So far, all she had accomplished was to find yet another natural weakness in him: the nasty, unhealthy, and egoistic notion that he was not the only man for her and that a woman is unreliable. This had strengthened her in her conviction that men had to be educated in matrimonial life. There was a flaw in their view of woman. She had no existence for them as an independent being, only for their pleasure and ambitions. And Jonas's unreasonable jealousy was an expression of this attitude. His autocratic nature and his censuring mind had surfaced every time she tried to come to some understanding with him concerning this nonsense about Nyblom. Instead of showing her his confidence, he had hurt her deeply. She had done nothing she could be reproached for and nothing for which she could ask his forgiveness. He had been avoiding the issue. As usual he was prepared to let their relationship adjust itself to the situation so that they could get along, rather than to face her in a more manly manner. But when they moved into their own home it would have to come to a crisis between them. She couldn't accept a marriage of half measures.

———

When Jonas hadn't come home by six o'clock, Ragna went out to milk the cows. Nyblom had promised her and Emma to take them out for a ride in the evening. He wanted to make a tour of the settlement to see how the crops were getting on and he also wanted to meet a young Swede from his own village who had just arrived and was staying with Axel Nykvist on the West Prairie. He was sure he brought greetings from his family. So they had better get done with the chores and get off before it got too late. So when Ragna had come out on the *pasturet,* Nyblom, who had just completed his work out in the fields, came to help her. He also wanted to have a few words with her, he said, on joining her. She paused, believing she knew what he wanted. "Things are much better now, aren't they?" she said.

"Much better," he replied. "You have been wonderful, Ragna! Thank you so much!" He gave her his hand and held hers in his firm grip.

Just then Jonas happened to enter the farmyard. He immediately saw them as they stood holding hands, and in uncontrollable rage he came pacing toward the *pasturet* only a few rods' distance from the yard. When he had closed the gate behind him, Nyblom and Ragna had already started milking. They hadn't seen him, and Ragna had her back to him. Nyblom looked up when he heard someone approaching and became aware of Jonas as he came to a stop beside him, obviously upset.

"You'll have to *exkjuse* that I interrupt and *kutter komedien* short!" he said.

"The comedy—what do you mean?" Nyblom asked, staring at him in surprise. Now Ragna had also turned around.

"Yes, the comedy of love with you in main role!" Nyblom got up and set his pail to the side.

"Have you lost your mind?" he asked, as he prepared himself for an attack.

"No worse than I am able to *spotte* an old lover and a chicken thief when I see him," hissed Jonas. The Swede stood looking at him a while. Then he said:

"You are a damn fool!" Whereupon he again took his pail, sat down, and continued his milking as if nothing had happened. With his hand raised for a blow, Jonas took a step toward him but was stopped by Ragna, who was on her feet and had quickly moved between them. "Jonas!" she cried, as in shock.

"Oh, I know all about it!" he said hoarsely. "I know why you want to *protekte* him." He let his hand fall down to his side.

"But can't you see that you're all wrong?"

"That isn't so easy to grasp for one who can see with his own eyes," he replied. "But you may keep the swine since you prefer him!"

Ragna's only response was a hurt and angry look. Jonas walked quickly back to the house. She sat down and began to cry.

13.

A great Fourth of July celebration had been planned in Normanville. According to the first announcement in the town's newspaper, *Garfield County Gazette*, something quite extraordinary was to be expected. As usual, the initiative lay with Ward and Newell, but to pacify the Scandinavians they had made the wheat merchant, Roxberg, committee president.

The featured main speakers were the state governor and Knute Nelson from Alexandria.[27] The local speaker, as yet unnamed, was later announced to be Sefanias Thompson from Arrowtown—better known as Seff. He was Ward's candidate as state representative at the county convention, and Hans Floen explained that this was to present him to the people. Seff would speak in "Scandinavian," a welcome decision to the many inhabitants of O'Brien's Grove who had come to the country so recently that they didn't know much English. Most knew Sefanias by name, but few had seen or met him since they rarely came to Arrowtown, which was about twenty-five miles away in the northwest corner of the county—that is a few miles farther from *Groven* than Normanville, the county seat, in the southwestern part of the county.

Seff had been one of the first Scandinavians to settle in the area between Normanville and Arrowtown, where he homesteaded in the late 1870s. Some years later he moved to the new town that was just taking shape and established himself in the hotel and saloon business. In the course of a few years he acquired a good deal of the most fertile land in the area. This was done by hiring people to *jompe* the claims of unsuspecting homestead takers or by having them use his tools and implements to *prove op* a claim and then "buy" the land from them.[28] But as the years went by, the lucrative deals that had once been highly regarded and that had made Seff a wealthy man were no longer respectable, and one day he decided that he could afford a change in style. So he sold his hotel and his saloon, raised the largest and finest building in town, and opened a real-estate and money-lending business.

No one could deny that Sefanias was versatile, but it nevertheless caused surprise that he aspired to a seat in the legislature and to a career as public speaker. Most could list at least a dozen acquaintances who were better suited as lawmakers than him. But whatever people thought and at times said—when only two or three were present—had no influence on his position. With his wealth and with his ability to maneuver in tight spots, he was the town's first citizen and a leader who went first where others followed.

Until recently Ward had had his doubts about allying himself with Thompson. Regardless of his achievements, it couldn't be denied that he had a "past," and his rugged manner and personality didn't attract the more polished Yankee. But after Ward had seen again and again—

and at times with regret—how the man from Arrowtown could manipulate politicians and, when called upon, get out the Scandinavian vote on short notice, the banker realized the value of a better understanding between them. The price of this understanding had been Thompson's billing as Fourth of July speaker and the promise of his nomination.

———◦———

Ward's alliance with Seff Thompson was not only of a political nature. He had recently been preoccupied with a planned fifty-mile branch line from Stockdale south to Normanville. The H. & B. Railroad needed the branch for direct access to the trunk line of the Northern Pacific. Moreover, within a few years the company could expect increased traffic on the branch because the land between the two towns was of the best in this part of the state and was rapidly being developed. Other engagements, however, had required more capital than foreseen and made it necessary for the management to adopt a more conservative policy.

As the reader will have guessed, Ward had confident information that the company had planned a depot in or near *Groven,* halfway between Normanville and Stockdale. This meant that a new town would grow up here virtually overnight and would be a dangerous rival for his own town. Indeed, it might even threaten his financial and political power. So Ward had decided that he had better be in control of the new town as well.

He had kept himself informed through a reliable source. Two alternatives gave a reasonably straight route between Stockdale and Normanville: one through the East Prairie, that is through O'Brien's Grove, and the other over the West Prairie, a few miles to the west of *Groven* and closer to Arrowtown. A survey had been made two years ago and since then nothing had been done. But last fall, Ward had been informed that the decision had finally been made to lay the railroad through the West Prairie settlement. The land selected for a depot—if the necessary rights could be had on reasonable conditions—was the northwestern quarter of section 13, adjacent to the Nykvist farm. This section, owned by the bank syndicate represented by Ward, was situated between six and seven miles from the Olsen and O'Brien farms on the East Prairie. The banker had immediately acquired this land for himself—covering up the transaction by using an intermediary—and he congratulated himself with having secured a gold mine and a source of invaluable future power.

He had already begun negotions for purchase of the Nykvist farm and other land in the neighborhood, when, early the next spring, his source sent him the unexpected information that the West Prairie route had been discarded. The branch would go through the East Prairie. This, Ward's correspondent had written him, was the final decision; Mr. Lyman, the company manager, had decided that the depot should be built on the southwest quarter of section 18. A look at the map told Ward that this quarter was the Jonas Olsen farm. The northeastern one was O'Brien's. The two other quarters belonged to Flasmo and Jorshaug.

These changes in the company's plans had at first angered the banker. But since he had paid very little for section 13 on the West Prairie, he couldn't really speak of any loss. Moreover, he would have many opportunities to sell it again. In the meantime he had to have his hands on the Olsen and O'Brien farms—and, if possible, the Flasmo and Jorshaug farms as well. He already had a mortgage in the O'Brien farm, so if the good Lord didn't give Jim his bumper crop he would be able to foreclose on it in the spring. But it was most important to have Jonas's farm and he immediately set out to get it at the lowest possible price before the news about the railroad route became known.

Ward had had agents who kept him informed about the railroad company's plans. But he didn't have access to the company board itself, and he had tried to develop a friendship with the vice president, Mr. Miller. Last summer he had gone to St. Paul with the intention of discussing his plans with him. His hopes to establish a relationship with Mr. Miller were based on his long-standing friendship with a Mr. Warren, a trusted servant of the company. Ward had suggested that if he could be fully informed of the Stockdale-Normanville project in all its details and as it developed, he would return the favor by assisting the company in acquiring the necessary right-of-way.

Mr. Miller had replied that the matter was entirely in the hands of Mr. Lyman. He had referred Ward to this gentleman, who turned out to be the same Lyman who Ward knew from the time when he had been *divisionssuperintendent* with the Northern Pacific some years earlier. This was an unpleasant surprise for the banker. The railroad executive had an excellent memory. He had done business with Ward at the time they had planned to build a side track to the elevator in Normanville and he had to buy a narrow strip of land from him at about six times its real value. They had departed as enemies and had not seen each other since.

Without the faintest reference to their earlier acquaintance, Mr. Lyman had politely declined to accept Ward's proposed arrangement and explained that when the company was ready to go ahead with the branch, it would make a public announcement. A private arrangement was entirely out of the question. But Ward wasn't ready to give up. He had discovered that his friend Mr. Warren was a personal secretary for Mr. Lyman and, moreover, that he didn't have a great love for his superior. Ward realized that this was a man he could use, and after they had talked it over in a private room in Donnely's saloon on Wabasha Street that evening, everything seemed to have come about even better than Ward had hoped. Warren was more than willing to inform him about anything in his interest from Lyman's office, especially after he had been promised that he would receive ready payment from the start and that he was to have a good rake-off when the money began to roll in.

This was the situation when Ward told Mrs. O'Brien that he represented a man from Illinois who wanted to buy the Olsen farm. He had come to know Jonas as a stubborn young man who wouldn't sell except at an exorbitant price—the impudent newcomer! However, he didn't doubt that he would get what he wanted. There were many ways to force a poor man to trade. He had condescended to make a friend of Ole Dampen and had taken the initiative to strike an acquaintance with Torfin Glombekken and Napoleon Stomhoff and now he had even swallowed the bitter pill of an alliance with Seff Thompson—all this to ensure his future influence with the Norwegians in the county in general and in *Groven* in particular. He had often noticed that while the Norwegians stubbornly refused to accept the leadership of their natural superiors, they could be talked into doing almost anything if directed by one of their own . . . Oh, yes, Elihu had no doubt that he would succeed . . .

In the meantime Ward had sold section 13 on the West Prairie to the Swede, Sam Lindermann. This is how it came about:

A well-dressed and apparently well-to-do stranger in his forties, who gave his name as McCarthy, entered Sam's office one day after the arrival of the morning train and requested information about land in the county on behalf of a group of prospective settlers in Ohio. They wished to buy several sections. Lindermann laid out the county map and described both land that he had and land he knew could be bought. The man was particularly interested in the West Prairie. Did Sam have any land there—in particular, section 13? Sure! Sam could sell anything. If they came to an agreement, he would buy the section from Ward. It would be fun for once to have the better of Elihu. So Sam took the man from Ohio out on the West Prairie. McCarthy liked it. And the price? Well, it couldn't be less than $25 per acre! The man did some sums and said that this was rather more than he was prepared to pay, but he should be able to make $20. Lindermann, who by now was convinced that the stranger had little experience in the real-estate business, insisted that he could not possibly go below $25. But they finally agreed on $20. McCarthy would return in a couple of days, as soon as he had done some business in Fargo. In token of his serious intentions, he paid Sam $50 in cash. On this they parted, and no sooner had the man from Ohio got on the train the next morning than Lindermann hurried over to Ward's office to buy section 13.

Ward wasn't eager to sell. That particular section had such excellent soil. Moreover, the railroad would probably come through the settlement and then the land would easily be worth twice as much. Lindermann brushed aside the talk of a railroad. That wouldn't be in their lifetime, he said. He made an offer of $15 per acre. Ward demanded $20, and they compromised. Lindermann bought the land at $17 per acre.

Had Sam known that Ward and McCarthy had met in the Arrow-town hotel the previous evening, he may not have been quite so eager to acquire section 13. Ward enjoyed winning his little game with the Swede. The banker had paid a little more than twelve dollars per acre for the land so his profit was $3,000. The $250 he had paid "the man from Ohio" and the $50 he had given him for advance payment had been a good investment.

After having waited to hear from McCarthy in vain for more than a week, Lindermann began to suspect that the Yankee had been behind it all. He was now in a tough spot. He had borrowed $3,000 from Torgersen to pay the $4,000 that Ward insisted on having in cash. For the rest he had given him a mortgage on section 13.

14.

After the episode in the *pasturet,* if Jonas and Ragna had had the opportunity, the powerful pressure of their emotional turmoil would probably have been released in an open fight. But there was no such opportunity in their present situation, since neither of them wished to reveal their miserable relationship to Emma and O'Brien.

In his present state of agitation Jonas felt an irrepressible urge to get away—far away. At least he didn't want to see more of the Swede nor of Ragna that night. Emma found it strange when he looked in at the door and told her that he had to do some work over on his farm and that he wouldn't be back that night. It was stranger still that he didn't want to have his supper before he left. But she asked no questions and didn't think more about what reasons he may have had. And Ragna didn't seem surprised when she was told about it. She didn't really want to go out on the drive with them that evening, but she feared that if she stayed home they would understand that something was wrong.

The first notion that entered Jonas's mind was to sell the farm to Ward and *skippe kontryet*. But as he cooled off he began to realize some of the problems involved. In the first place, he couldn't just go off and sell the farm on his own. For a legal transaction he would need Ragna's signature on the deed. And then he began thinking about the son she said they could expect in December—the boy who was to be a minister or a *loiert* or something else high and mighty. He couldn't run off from a woman in such a condition. That would be a terrible scandal. Perhaps they would even send the police after him and his whole future would be ruined. No, he saw no other alternative than to suffer and endure . . . The worst thing about it was that the paint was almost dry and they were going to move into their new home in a day or two. Yes, that was certainly something to look forward to . . .

When he came to the house, his temper has subsided to a considerable degree and he was reminded that he was a hungry and starving man. Perhaps he shouldn't have left without his supper . . . And then he remembered the chickens that he had bought from Mrs. Tarvesen. They had already been here two days and he had collected five large eggs this morning. Now he ate them all raw. It alleviated his hunger, but the rough and indelicate meal in such a lonely situation made him reflect on the miserable existence of the many men who sat alone on their homesteads without anyone to keep house for them. *Gudnes* . . .

And then his thoughts came back to himself and the O'Briens' *pasturet*. What was it she had said before they parted? That he should have been able to see that he was wrong—those were her words. Had she really meant it or was it just some *bønk* and *tamfuleri*?[29] Could it be that he hadn't *seisa op* the situation correctly? Could that Swedish dromedary possibly have had some acceptable *bisnes* fondling her hand? Jonas wanted to believe the best. It wasn't natural for him to be suspicious! In this ambivalent state of mind he began to set up a kind of status account of what had been done on their property.

Everything was ready for them. The area around the buildings had been cleared of all rubbish. A little kitchen garden was growing nicely and there were also a couple of flower beds. Jonas had dug up the garden himself early that spring and Ragna, helped by Emma, had planted, watered, weeded, and kept it tidy. Behind the barn he had set up a chicken fence, and the six Plymouth Rocks were parading there, clucking and enjoying themselves, with the proud and swaggering rooster among them.[30] And over there, beyond the farmyard, their cow was grazing along with the beautiful shiny horses he had bought from Nesteved. Their new house had a nice and comfortable feel to it. They had even been able to afford a porch, which he thought gave it a town-house appearance. The barn wasn't much to speak of. Jonas would have liked to have a huge one, since great barns had always made such a powerful impression on him. They were such glorious witnesses to *prospœrity*. But there was a lot of space for two horses, two cows, hay, and wagons.

Jonas would have liked to have a white picket fence around the yard; back in Norway, anyone with social pretensions had one. But everything had cost more than they had thought it would, and although he had got the horses and the cow as well as some of the furniture on credit, he only had $150 left of the $1,000 he had borrowed from Davidsen's Bank. And that was money they would need even if they had a reasonably good harvest on the ten acres he had planted. He suddenly realized that he hadn't settled with O'Brien yet . . . He had also had to control his desire to own a buggy. But the brand new red and green lumber wagon from the T. G. Mandt factory in Stoughton was quite a sight too.[31]

The furniture was in place. It wasn't luxurious but it was new and comfortable. Ragna and Emma had been there that morning and he had helped them lay the carpets. They were cheap carpets, but as they now were laid out you would hardly notice it; and just to have them was a luxury that no one but Trulsen in O'Brien's Grove had been able to afford. The parlors were rather small, Jonas thought, but there would be enough space until the family got a good deal larger. Out in the kitchen was the new cooking range, and the new crockery and tinware shone from the shelves and walls. He had to admit that it wasn't really a distinguished and stately home—certainly nothing that could be compared to Simonsen's home in Minneapolis. But in its modest way it was both decent and beautiful. Few settlers had so much to show for themselves or could move into as good a house as this.

So there was good reason for him and Ragna to be happily content. Both had looked forward to their moving day as a festive event in their relationship. As we have seen, however, there was now a fissure in their feelings for each other. To Jonas, the reason was that she had changed. He was, as he had always been, a sincere man who wanted to get ahead in the world. Hadn't he done quite well by himself down there in *Min'ap'lis* until that damned bankruptcy came along? Hadn't he been a church member and hadn't he demonstrated to the whole world that he was reliable in business? And that he could *supporte* a family? Nothing had been so much in his mind as his ambition that Ragna should be content and happy! What more could these women-folk have *expektet* of a decent man?

When he looked out on the beautiful field where everything seemed so promising and he remembered with what pride he had dug in his very own soil; when he looked at the house and everything and considered with what happiness he had seen it take shape—the cellar dug out, the foundation raised, the framework going up—until it was ready for human habitation; when he now again looked at it and remembered what hopes he had attached to each and every item as well as to the whole, then he had to admit that he was a disappointed man. He had had such great expectations and now he looked forward to this great occasion in their life as something sinister. And all this just because Ragna had changed! He supposed this was the way with women. You couldn't so to speak *bænke* on them!

———◆———

Jonas returned to O'Briens' early the next morning. He couldn't remember having been so hungry before. When Ragna saw him in the yard she hurried into the kitchen and made waffles for breakfast, and he took this as evidence that she wasn't so angry with him after all; she knew this was his favorite breakfast food. But she had better not think that he came as the prodigal son, asking for nice weather! So he ate in silence. "We *mover* this afternoon!" he said to Ragna as he was about to leave. "Have everything ready by one o'clock."

"But that's impossible," she objected. "I can't be ready until tomorrow."

"We *mover* today!" he answered in a determined voice. "I'll be here with *teamet* at one." And with that he left.

At one o'clock sharp he drove into the yard. O'Brien helped him with the suitcases, which were all ready and packed. Emma had insisted that they should bring with them a good supply of provisions so that they would have something to begin with. These were all packed in a box that they also placed in the wagon. With all the many packages it was a full wagon. Ragna called to him that she was almost ready. She just had to say goodbye to Emma.

When the two women finally came out on the doorstep they were both crying. You could almost believe that Ragna was going to Australia or somewhere far off among the heathens to stay there for the rest of her life, thought Jonas, and not that she was only going to *kros raaden*.[32] And they had to keep on kissing each other several times! *Gudnes* ...

O'Brien also was visibly moved when he said goodbye to Ragna, but at least he didn't kiss her. "Sure, and we'll be lonely when ye're gone," said Jim as he gave her his hand. "May the holy Mither bless you! And it's happy ye should be in ye'r new home!"

Jonas was thinking that the Swede had enough shame to stay away, when he saw him come out from the barn. Jonas almost boiled over when Nyblom came and gave Ragna his hairy paw. She took his hand and squeezed it warmly. Jonas also noticed that she said something to the Swede that it seemed that no one else was supposed to hear, and that Nyblom responded with a furtive nod. He was so sweet and charming that he almost ran like syrup. Ragna was finally helped up to the wagon seat. Jonas thanked O'Brien for everything, without paying attention to the Swede, and said that he would have to come over soon so that they could pay him what they owed for his hospitality. And then he cracked the reins.

They didn't say much. When they came to a stop in front of their new house, Ragna jumped swiftly down and went right in while he unharnessed the horses. If he had been able to observe her as she quickly moved from room to room, he wouldn't have doubted that she found everything to be better than expected. She danced around like a happy child. She had to touch and feel everything: the furniture, the doors, the carpets, the range, the bed—she had to fondle it all and say hello. God! She would make this a good home ...

But when she heard him enter, her face took on a solemn expression, and he found her sitting motionless in a chair like a stranger. Her thoughts seemed a thousand miles away . . .

15.

When Jonas came in and found Ragna sitting silent and thoughtful, every line in his face spoke of his bitter disappointment. She didn't move. Not a word passed her lips at their first meeting in their new home. He suffered and she could see it and feel it, and suddenly she was overwhelmed by a strange compassion. She was about to stand up and throw herself into his arms and sing out her joy in having their own home where happiness would be their daily guest for the rest of their lives! But she controlled herself and remained seated. She would punish him severely while she was at it. He had wronged her and it was his duty to speak first. Jonas took off his cap and walked through some of the rooms. She got up and went into the kitchen and began to put things in order. He stood contemplating for a while and then he came after her. "Have you seen everything?" he asked.

"I was here yesterday with Emma!" she answered, without raising her eyes.

"Yes, but today is the day we sort of are supposed to move in!" he said.

"I know!" She continued to look down.

"But it may not be good enough for you?" he asked after a while.

"*Gudnes,* yes, it's more than good enough." To Jonas her words seemed cold and indifferent. She didn't seem at all happy . . . He had never believed that things would be quite as bad as this. He didn't care much for the demonstration of emotion, so that wasn't what he missed, but he had at least expected some sense of contentment from his own wife on such a day. And then he thought that it might be an American custom that the husband kissed his wife on such occasions. Perhaps that was what she was waiting for! And since they had been under constant observation at the O'Briens', it had been some time since they . . . But his heart wasn't in the kiss. The miracle had yet to manifest itself. Nor could Jonas know that Ragna had to draw upon all her willpower in order not to succumb body and soul when he, cautiously and somewhat reservedly, embraced her. When he released her he said, "There seems to be no way for me to make you happy! You should have accepted Nels. Then you could have lived in Duluth and been somebody!"

At these words Ragna restrained herself even more. Now she was less ready than ever before to take the first step. His remark about Nels was yet another expression of his suspicious and egotistical nature. And he who hadn't committed himself until she had accepted him was now deriding her because she had behaved decently to a noble man like Nels! There was no answer to such an affront! She silently went about making coffee. Actually she could hardly wait to begin to use her new kitchen utensils and the stove too—it was all so new and lovely. They drank their coffee in depressing silence.

As he got up Jonas said, "I can't understand you, Ragna! You have become so different from the way you used to be."

"It is not I who have changed," she cut him off. "But I do know one who has become different." She got to her feet and began to clear the table.

"And who may that be?"

"The Honorable Jonas Olsen."

This was pure malicious evil, thought Jonas. He couldn't make sense of the way she had begun to behave. What had he done to deserve it? Nothing except for . . . But the way they could make ado about nothing . . . *Gudnes* . . . "Be careful! This is beginning to go a little too far! It's strange how you womenfolk don't know how to *ris'ne*."

"No, I suppose it's only you men who know how to *ris'ne*. And sometimes not even you are too good at it."

"And just what may I have done?"

"You who can *ris'ne* should know that yourself."

"Gudnes!"

"And what is it you imagine that I have done?" She stood there in front of him holding a teaspoon and with an offended look.

"You should know that yourself."

"Oh, I do?"

"You damned well do!"

"Well, I haven't done anything wrong, not the slightest, if you want to know."

"No, perhaps not—yet," he said slowly. "But it's clear that you no longer care about me." He looked so miserable that she couldn't but feel sorry for him. What if she . . . ? But, no, he needed a radical cure and it would be best to have it done now that they had started. "So that's what you have discovered, is it?" she replied. "But I don't see why that should bother you since you don't care for me."

The things he had to listen to! As if she wasn't the most important thing in the world for him—all his life and future and all! "And what do you know about my caring for you?"

"Are you aware that you have been sulking for several weeks and hardly spoken a word to me all this time?"

"And I suppose you know why?"

"Why not let me know what you really think—for once."

The three ominous wrinkles on Jonas's brow became even more marked as he spoke. So it had come so far that she could stand there and insinuate that he was a brute and a liar! He took a step toward her as he felt his blood rising to his head. She had never seen such brightness in his eyes. "You—you—are thinking of another man!" he cried hoarsely.

She was almost afraid of him. He had once told her that his grandfather had been insane. Was his jealousy madness? Didn't doctors say that mental illness could appear in the same family after several generations? She shivered at the thought. "I have no thoughts of any other!" Her voice had become milder. "And let's not talk more of this now. Some other time . . ." She smiled wistfully as she looked at him. Then she walked into the kitchen. From there she heard him leave the house.

Jonas went toward the O'Briens'. He didn't feel at all well as he set out and decided to walk rather than take the horses, since he felt a need to rid himself of his present state of mind. He had to get out. There could be no pleasure in his home with such a beginning and he might as well settle accounts with Jim right away.

But Jim wouldn't allow him to pay much. It wouldn't do to keep close reckoning between friends and neighbors. He wouldn't hear of taking anything for the work he had done on Jonas's house, and the help they had from Ragna was more than enough in return for their lodging. And they had enjoyed having them there. If Jonas insisted on paying something for the food, then that was all they could accept. Jonas had feared that this would be the outcome. He had offered Jim money a couple of times but he had answered that there was no hurry and that they could talk about it after they had moved out. No wonder the O'Briens had difficulties in managing their economy with such business methods. They had been with the O'Briens for more than two and a half months—eleven weeks in all—and Jim thought that two dollars a week would be more than enough for their board. Jonas finally insisted on giving him fifty dollars and Jim had to give in even though he protested and complained that getting so well paid for a little neighborly help sort of spoiled the pleasure.

Jonas didn't have much else to say and O'Brien noticed that something was on his mind. This wasn't the first time he had felt that his young friend wasn't as happy as could be expected of one who had just been married and could begin life here under such favorable auspices. "Sure, and it's a fine home ye have," Jim said to remind him that he should be happy and thankful. "And niver stood the crops better, *begorrah*! Faith, and this is a glorious country. Bless ye, I wouldn't trade my lot for a kingdom. It's happy we should be!"

He was interrupted by Emma. She came out with a basket with some needlework and other things that Ragna had left behind. On top were some issues of *Minneapolis Tidende*.[33] Jonas took the basket, thanked them for their kindness, and started on his way home. Ragna was probably wondering where he had gone, he thought. But she deserved a little worry . . .

On the main road, Torfin Glombekken came driving. He had been in Normanville and, as usual when he came from town, he wasn't quite sober. Jonas could see a gallon jug in the wagon box and guessed it contained liquor. Torfin offered him a ride, and although Jonas would have preferred to walk, he didn't want to insult Torfin, even though he didn't much like him. He sat beside Glombekken on the wagon seat and placed Ragna's basket behind him. Torfin pulled out a smaller bottle from his pocket. He wanted to *trite* a drink, he said. He had bought some extra fine whisky from Ole Dampen and he was welcome to a taste.

"Just go ahead," said Jonas. "I don't want any."

"Don't want any!" Torfin exclaimed. "Are you too high and mighty to go have a drink with a neighbor?"

"That's not it at all. I just don't drink."

"What kind of contrariness is this? Surely you can take a shot?" Glombekken uncorked his bottle.

"I suppose I could; but, as I said, I don't drink!"

"I can't believe it! A grown-up man like you. Here!" Torfin tried to give him the bottle but Jonas was resolute. Glombekken then took a swallow of the whisky himself before he again urged Jonas to have some.

"I have my own reasons not to drink," he said.

"There's only one reason not to take a sip that I know of," Torfin insinuated with a smirk. "Just a nice neighborly drop now?" Jonas pushed the bottle away and a considerable portion of its contents spilled over on his coat sleeve. The stench was powerful and as Jonas, who had become quite irritated, rubbed his sleeve with his handkerchief, he didn't notice that Torfin stuck the bottle under the newspapers in Ragna's basket behind the seat. "All right," Glombekken continued, "if you can't *stæn'* an honest drink, then it's probably *sæfest* to let be. But I hadn't thought that a man so young in years could be so weak and decrepit!"

"I'm no more decrepit than you are," Jonas replied, "but that's no reason to want your swill!" He was now so angry that he could have boxed Torfin. Luckily, they just now came to the driveway up to Jonas's farm and Torfin stopped so that Jonas could get off. Jonas walked quickly home with his basket while Glombekken had a good laugh.

<hr />

Ragna had paced restlessly for almost two hours wondering what had happened to Jonas. She began to regret that she hadn't done more to clear away their misunderstandings. This nonsense could have serious consequences. It wasn't at all like him to go off like this without letting her know where he was going. She was on the porch when Glombekken stopped his wagon and Jonas got down. She was relieved when she saw him approach the house and when she noticed the basket she remembered she had left it at the O'Briens' and realized where he had been. She was resolved to take up their problems with him. She was partly at fault herself. She had been stubborn and uncompromising . . . But now all would be well . . .

He was still quite far away when she smiled and waved in welcome. Jonas was somewhat puzzled. It was probably some new quirk, a characteristic of the female *sexen*. But he waved back. He was certainly not going to demonstrate unwillingness to compromise if she had decided to *ris'ne* and behave like an adult . . .

"I just went over to O'Brien and *settlet* things between us," he began when he came nearer. He was almost overjoyed to see her smile again. He was soon at her side and gave her the basket. But her smile disappeared in the same moment and, instead, her lips formed the same sorrowful expression he knew so well from their difficult times in Minneapolis. "Jonas!" was all she said.

At first he understood nothing, but then he remembered that his sleeve smelled of liquor. "You have misunderstood," he answered her eagerly. "It all happened because . . ." But in the meantime she had peeked under the newspapers in the basket and seen the half-empty bottle of whisky! She began to cry! So that was why he had become so difficult lately . . . he had begun to drink!

"It's all because of Glombekken," he said, somewhat perplexed.

"Is he the reason you've been drinking?"

"I haven't been drinking! Damned if I have!" But she was no longer listening. She disappeared behind the door. He stood looking at it. And then he mumbled to himself, "*Gudnes,* the way these ladies are difficult to get along with!" And with that he ambled over to the barn.

When he came in again, Ragna thought it was strange that he seemed quite sober. Had she been mistaken as he said? She relented a little, but neither of them made the necessary step toward an understanding. She was determined to wait and see what happened next.

16.

The news that Seff Thompson was scheduled as a speaker at the Fourth of July celebration had been received with considerable interest. People wondered what he had to say and how he would say it.

The people of O'Brien's Grove had long since begun to prepare for the celebration. All had decided to go to Normanville on the Fourth. Even the two Democrats in the settlement, Erik Nesteved and Axel Nykvist, were set on taking part. Jonas and Ragna too had decided to go. O'Brien had had an accident with one of his horses and Jonas had promised him a ride to Normanville on the Fourth. Emma had come to Ragna the day before the festivities and expressed her regret that she and Nyblom would have to stay home since they had no transportation. Ragna invited them to drive with her and Jonas. But afterward she began to realize that Jonas would probably not appreciate her guests. When she aired the matter that evening at supper, his expression immediately revealed how he would respond.

"How could you promise something like that without asking me?" he exclaimed. Ragna sensed the approach of a violent storm. But she was not at all inclined to give in. And it would be impossible to tell Emma that she had changed her mind without explaining the entire sad and stupid situation to her.

"Do you alone decide and rule over the little we have?" she asked quietly. "Am I not supposed to be a partner?"

"It *œppirer* that you are more or less a partner with this Nyblom!" he responded stubbornly. "You show little interest in what I may want."

She sat a while in thought. Then she challenged him with a smile, "Should I tell them that they can't drive with us because you're jealous of Nyblom?" He glared at her.

"Who has said that I'm jealous of Nyblom?" he asked bluntly.

"You've more or less said so yourself."

"Me? Have I? This is damned more . . ."

"So you're not jealous of Nyblom, then?"

"Jealous? Me? Of such a rascal! *Gudnes,* no! Do you think that I don't grant you common *kommensens?*"

"At times I've almost feared that that is exactly how you think of me," she replied.

"*Velsørri,* you are *mistœken!* What I have *œgœnst* Nyblom is that he has *insølta* me—that he actually tried to *kille* me in the *suern.*"

"But he didn't succeed."

"Damned, no!" He looked at her sharply. "Perhaps you had preferred that he had?"

"Jonas!"

"Yes, because you can never be sure what kind of *eidier* that *developer* inside the skull of a woman!"

"I see! But then they may drive with us then—for Emma's sake? And since you aren't jealous, then . . ." He scratched his head. There really wasn't anymore to be said. She had succeeded in getting her way again.

———

When they got to Normanville they heard that the governor couldn't come and that Knute Nelson had also canceled his engagement. Floen ventured that neither Nelson nor the governor had probably ever promised to speak and that their names had just been used to get people to come. But there was no harm done; they had Sefanias Thompson. And Scott, a lawyer from Crookston,[34] was a stand-in for Nelson. He didn't make an overwhelming impression. He reminded the Scandinavians that they had come from a poor undemocratic country and should be grateful for living such good lives in the wealthy America.

"What is he saying?" Iver Flasmo asked Jonas. This part of the celebration was held in Ward's pasture, which Ward himself referred to as "the park," and the two neighbors from *Groven* happened to be standing side by side. Iver wasn't all that comfortable with English, so he had the impression that he had missed something important. "Is he saying anything about us Norwegians?"

"Yes, he says that it must be a wonderful experience for us who haven't eaten anything but salt herring and oatmeal porridge to have *emigræta* to such a *kontry* and happened upon all this *prespærity'n!*" Jonas answered.

"Is the man crazy?" As they discussed this possibility, Scott concluded his speech, and Roxberg introduced Seff Thompson as one of the pioneers and most prominent citizens of Garfield County, a pride to his nationality, and so on, as the genre required. For those who saw him for the first time, he revealed himself as an impressive figure of about 270 pounds. His speech was short and to the point and was held in a Norwegian-American language that was characteristic of the time and place.

Jonas noticed that he began to address the crowd in Swedish as he called out in a powerful voice, "Ladies and gentlemen!" Roxberg had announced that all speeches would be apolitical, but Seff did not seem to bother much with such promises. There was hardly anything more important than politics, he said. What the church was for our spiritual needs, politics was for our earthly existence. It was always in order to speak politics because even though the Democrats weren't in power now, they could well be so in the future. They *kjita* themselves to the *lekjen*[35] in 1884, and this could happen again. And we all knew what kind of times we would have in this country if Cleveland was in the saddle.[36] And now we even had another and almost more dangerous threat hanging over us. He referred to the Farmers' Alliance and to Populism, which had begun to spread like an epidemic.

Seff Thompson had only one rule of conduct in politics: he was a Republican and all others, not only Democrats and Populists, but prohibitionists and all and anything that ended in "crats" or "ists" were an abomination and led to the dissolution of society. Salvation lay in voting a *"streit* ticket." To vote for other than Republican candidates was to embrace alien deities, and to recognize anything good in a Democrat was the same as to openly engage in idolatry. It would lead to the de-Christianizing of the country and to moral degeneration.

"We have plenty of *evidens* in history," said Seff, "for they have been the same rascals up through the ages and hadn't we had so many splendid men with the right political faith, then we would have been governed by a czar like in Russia. You recall Washington—the man who *organeisa* the Republic and established the Fourth of July—well, Washington, he was a Republican. It was he who lay the foundation for the party when he had *rounda op* all the horse thieves and Democrats and *chœsa* all the Englishmen out of the *kontrye'*. And he told the king that there would be no more milking the American people like a cow, he said. Now he could go *streit* home to England and milk himself, he said, and then he would find out how well he liked it!" Thompson also brought another great Republican to their attention; one he called Jefferson . . . But at this point he was interrupted by Hans Floen.

"I think Jefferson was a Democrat," said Hans. "They even call him 'the father of American democracy,' if I'm not mistaken."

"Order! Order!" Roxberg called out. "The speaker must not be disturbed."

"I'm not disturbing the speaker," answered Floen, "just correcting his history."

"Well, we can't waste our time with all kinds of corrections and historical interruptions," Roxberg explained. "We must go *'head* with *programmen*." The speaker, however, was not in the least affected by the interruption. "Jefferson was a Democrat in name only," he replied. "In spirit he was as good a Republican as I am myself."

"Yes, let's hope so," Floen laughed, whereupon Seff continued and developed further his concept of Republicanism. He mentioned Lincoln and the Civil War. Then the Democrats had really demonstrated what they were made of. But we were able to do them in. However, they were such liars and had so little respect for anything that they got to the feeding trough as quickly as they could and began to steal and plunder. And then this *slavedriveren* Cleveland succeeded to *hœnde* the people a gold brick again. And they sure had to *søfre* for it. But now, thank God, we once more had the right kind of government in the *kontryet* . . .

There weren't many Democrats in the county and only a handful had come to hear Thompson. So his attack on the Democratic Party for the most part fell in good soil. But he wasn't quite so successful with his remarks on the Farmers' Alliance and the Populists, who had quite a few supporters in the audience. Seff expressed his surprise that *Norskera* could be Populists. He used history to demonstrate what a fine people they had always been. That a race that had the intelligence to discover America before Columbus should be so stupid in politics that they went against their own interests, was more than a rational person could understand. He admitted that he was running for a seat in the legislature, and he told them what he was set on doing when he came there. There were a few things, in spite of the excellent government we had, that weren't exactly as they should be, and one of the first things he would see to was that the farmers were fairly treated in the grading of their grain.

At this point the speaker was interrupted by a drunk who had been sleeping under a tree at some distance from the speakers' platform and who now had been awoken by the speaker's loud voice. "What's the matter with Populism?" he cried out. When no one answered, he got up, waived his arms around, and screamed, "Why, Populism is all right!" Then he turned to Seff: "And what's the matter with Seff Thompson?"

"Why, Seff's all right!" was heard from several in the audience.

"You said it, by heck. Seff's all right," the drunk bellowed, and then added in a slightly lower voice, "for Seff." With this he navigated out of the *pasturet* and in the direction of O'Connor's saloon. The intermezzo caused much amusement and it took some time before Sefanias got going again.

Roxberg introduced Jonas to Sefanias after his speech. He was very friendly and said he had heard that Jonas had been in *bisnes* in Minneapolis. He had, perhaps, thought of setting up a business out here? There was good space for another store in Arrowtown and he had a vacant building that he would let him have at half price if he wanted to establish himself there. Thompson's description of the town and its prospects seemed quite attractive to Jonas. He liked the man as well. He said he would think about it.

Later that afternoon, liquid goods began to float around quite freely and openly. Several of the men from *Groven* were visibly touched by the festivities, and Flasmo and Glombekken had several rounds of Kentucky Rye and theology in Ole Dampen's saloon.

Before they had left home that morning, Jonas had arranged to have their cow milked by the hired man at Jorshaug's so that they could stay overnight in Normanville should they wish to do so, but Ragna insisted on returning home. Only in the direst need would she renew her acquaintance with Nicolai Johnson's Scandinavian Hotel.

17.

To say that the women of the settlement were curious to find out how things were at Jonas and Ragna's would hardly be to put it too strongly. At the Ladies Aid meeting at the Trulsens' in late July they had talked about how grand everything was on the Jonas farm. Mrs. Flasmo and Mrs. Tarvesen had dropped in one day and could report on how well they lived. New furniture and carpets and everything you could think of. And that the house was larger and grander than any other except Trulsen's could be seen by anyone from the road. Two other women had visited the Olsens, Mrs. Trulsen and Mrs. Jorshaug. Ragna and Mrs. Trulsen were of course as thick as thieves, Mrs. Tarvesen said. And as for Mrs. Jorshaug, it was a well-known fact that she fawned for that Minneapolis woman.

It would have added to their interest had they known that when the Trulsens and the Jorshaugs had paid a visit to Jonas and Ragna, Jonas and Trulsen had become enemies. There were, as said before, plans to establish a Lutheran congregation, and Jonas insisted, along with Flasmo, that the congregation should be organized in the Norwegian Synod, while Trulsen was of the unyielding conviction that they had to join the recently established United Church.[37] There had lately been much ecclesiastical agitation and the people of the settlement were divided in two camps. In addition to Flasmo, Jonas, and Jorshaug, who were uncompromising supporters of the Missouri side, Peder Tarvesen and Erik Nesteved had joined the opposition against Vellesen and Trulsen.

Mrs. Tarvesen suggested that they should organize a *sørpreisparti* for the Olsens. When decent people move in among decent people, she said, it was no more than their simple duty to give them some token of their appreciation. Everybody agreed. This would give them an opportunity to see how Jonas and Ragna lived and, moreover, it was always nice to have an occasion to get together. Mrs. Jorshaug was quite enthusiastic. She had suffered from the isolation and the unfamiliar ways of prairie life and she had felt attracted to Ragna on their first meeting and they had since become good friends. Jorshaug and Jonas had also struck up a friendship since they had discovered that they were in agreement about all kinds of things, in politics as well as in church matters.

The only argument made against trying to *sørpreise* the Olsens was that they were so uppity that it would perhaps be difficult to do something that would satisfy them. But Mrs. Glombekken immediately rose to Ragna's defense and explained that they had to excuse her for having a better taste than most since she had been a servant girl at boardinghouses in Minneapolis. And as for being fine and mighty, this was certainly not anyone else's *bisnes*. They must have bought what they had with their own money, and they obviously had money, since Jonas had been in *bisnes* and had gone bankrupt.

"Has he gone bankrupt?" asked Mrs. Tarvesen, surprised. Others also pricked up their ears.

"*Jessørri,* and in the grand manner too," Mrs. Glombekken replied. "But that shouldn't make the slightest *differens* for anyone else; and they are both nice people!"

While some discussed the many possibilities offered by this piece of news, others continued to talk about the practical details of the planned party. They decided to assign to Glombekken, who was going to town one of these days anyway, the task of buying a present, and the date was set Sunday after next. At eleven sharp all would come to the Jonas farm with food-filled baskets. Mrs. Tarvesen volunteered to take responsibility for the coffee, and Mrs. Jorshaug, who had no sense of economy, offered to bring the cream. To keep Mr. Jorshaug, who was known to be a little tightfisted, from protesting, Mrs. Flasmo suggested that he should be asked to make a speech and present their gift. The problem was that Trulsen expected to shine on all occasions and it wouldn't do to pass him by. But Mrs. Nesteved untied the knot. It would only be proper to give two presents, one for the husband and one for the wife, and then Trulsen could present one gift and Jorshaug the other. All agreed.

The only thing left to decide was the nature of the presents. At this point Mrs. Trulsen arrived. She fully agreed to their plans, and added that they had to buy gifts that wouldn't shame them. She always had to show off, Mrs. Trulsen! They finally agreed on a rocking chair for Jonas, a real *isi* one. It was more difficult to think of something for Ragna. Mrs. Jorshaug had a bright idea. She had been watching Mrs. Olsen closely, she said, and knew that an important event was soon expected in the family. And she was certain that they hadn't yet bought a cradle. Mrs. Flasmo liked this idea, but Mrs. Trulsen said that it was indelicate to disclose that they knew something of such a private nature. Mrs. Tarvesen actually agreed with Mrs. Trulsen, but she could in no way publicly acknowledge that she supported her. So she said, "*Gudnes græsius,* such things *hæpner* every day, don't they?"

"*Vel, I gess* so," said Mrs. Flasmo. But Mrs. Trulsen insisted, and when it appeared that a majority agreed with her, they decided to buy a set of real nice coffee cups for Ragna.

——◦——

The sun shone brightly on the day of the *sørpreispartiet.* Unfortunately, Ragna woke up with a bad headache. That evening she and Jonas had discussed the business opportunity that Sefanias Thompson had laid out for him. He had brought it up almost every day after the Fourth of July celebration, but without convincing her that it was much more attractive to be a *bisnesmand* than a farmer. Last evening they had both become rather irritated, and this had in turn contributed to renewed reflections on the old misunderstanding between them. It had been temporarily resolved and no longer disrupted their day-to-day relationship; but the stinger was still lodged in their flesh since neither of them would take responsibility for pulling it out. What had served, more than anything else, to soothe the situation was their little secret that they still believed was theirs alone. They had agreed that it would be a boy and had begun to plan his upbringing. Jonas had more or less determined that he should become a *bisnesmand,* but Ragna didn't like this perpetual *bisnes* talk. At times she caught herself wishing that it would be a girl.

With yesterday's conversation about a merchant's life in Arrowtown fresh on her mind, Ragna sat on the edge of her bed wondering about the cause of her frequent headaches. One thought followed the other and—as a thousand times before—she wished that Jonas would reconcile himself with their situation and be content with a farmer's life. He could be so impatient when all didn't go just the way he had planned. And now he was messing up everything in the chest of drawers just because he could never remember that his shirts were in the bottom drawer . . . *Uff,* had she only been able to get some sense of order into him . . .

At this moment, Jonas—who was about to express his dissatisfaction that nothing ever was in its right place—suddenly came across a little box containing some tiny clothes. They were so small that he couldn't comprehend that anything could be small enough to get into them. But he certainly knew what they were and he was struck with an image of her sitting there in her lonely hours sewing these things for their son. He stood there for a long time with the box in his hand. It was all so nicely done and with fringes and fancy sewing of the kind that only Ragna could do. Then he put it carefully back in place, went to her, took her in his arms, and kissed her.

To Ragna, who hadn't seen what he had been inspecting with his back turned to her, this was so unmotivated that she was almost confused. But the bitterness that had been with her only a moment earlier was blown away. And when she a little later was making their breakfast her headache seemed to have disappeared.

A few days ago Mrs. Trulsen had said that she and Trulsen would come over for a picnic dinner with them on Sunday. Mrs. Trulsen had insisted that Ragna shouldn't do anything extra and that she would bring everything except coffee. So Ragna had made her parlors and kitchen spic and span; she knew Mrs. Trulsen was a persnickety woman. That morning, Ragna dusted the furniture once more to be sure that there wasn't a speck of dust anywhere.

A little before eleven the Trulsens drove into their yard, and they had hardly come indoors before one *teamet* after the other stopped outside and the yard was filled with people. Jonas and Ragna, in particular the latter, were happily *sørpreised* by it all, and the intention was for that matter achieved. Jonas had heard that people in America sometimes turned up unexpectedly at their friends' and neighbors' in this fashion, but he hadn't before fully realized that a *sørpreisparti* was one of the country's great social institutions.

The event was not significantly different from other parties of the kind. They ate and drank coffee and enjoyed themselves—that is, the men enjoyed themselves since they had nothing else to do. The women were busier than ever. After dinner, Lars Jorshaug stood up and held a memorable speech for Jonas and said that the people of O'Brien's Grove were lucky to have such a fine fellow in their midst, one who had influence in government as well as in church matters. With these and other words and with great ceremony he presented him with the rocking chair and placed the guest of honor in it.

"*Gudnes!* It won't be easy to live up to all this!" Jonas sighed as he fell into his new chair with a sense of his new responsibilities.

The speech Trulsen made for Ragna didn't take second place to the one held by Jorshaug. She was a truly remarkable person. No one had ever heard Trulsen so eloquent. She had evidently made a great impression on him, said Mrs. Glombekken.

Jonas, on whom Jorshaug had bestowed such remarkable gifts, of course had to respond for himself and for his wife. And he did so with considerable success. It had always, he said, been his great dream to acquire a farm and live amongst people of his own nationality. He had traveled widely and had seen and experienced much, but nowhere in the entire world had he found such fine folks as in *Groven*. Three cheers for the future of O'Brien's Grove. The last speaker was Mrs. O'Brien—the only woman who without censure could stand up and perform in public. She spoke with insight about pioneer life on the prairie, with the approval of all except Torfin Glombekken, who thought that it was a dubious experiment to let a Presbyterian, who was married to a Catholic, speak at a Lutheran gathering.

The house was carefully inspected. Mrs. Tarvesen expressed the opinion that they could have made do with less, but she supposed Jonas had made quite a fortune of his bankruptcy.

They couldn't have a party entirely without liquor. Glombekken had paid a visit to Ole Dampen, who had sent a gallon jar as his contribution to the feast. Neither Jonas nor Ragna appreciated the presence of the alcoholic punch, but they realized it couldn't be avoided. Glombekken was rather tipsy quite early in the afternoon and he tried to get Jonas to drink. When Jonas refused, he was teased with being afraid of his wife. Ragna heard it all and was happy when she heard Jonas, with more emphasis than elegance, threaten to "bleed" Torfin if he didn't shut up. Glombekken was angry but didn't dare challenge the younger Jonas. But he held out the glass to Lars Jorshaug's fourteen-year-old son, saying, "Have a drink, Sivert, now that you're grown-up!" But in the same moment, Jonas hit his hand with such strength that the glass tumbled across the grass. He held his hand. It burned.

"You're going to pay for this, you damned arsonist!" he screamed as Jonas was about to leave. When he heard Torfin's words, he was un- pleasantly reminded that he recently had slighted Ludvig Napoleon Stomhoff.

18.

Ward visited Mrs. O'Brien some weeks after she had taken office as superintendent. He wanted to talk with her in person about the convention, he said. He assumed that she would be a candidate. Yes, she replied, she had given it some thought since her friends had said that they wanted her to remain in the position. But she had little understanding of politics and had left the matter to them.

"Well, I'm not disposed to deal with your associates," he answered. "It's my habit to do business with headquarters; that's why I'm here."

At first, Mrs. O'Brien didn't fully understand his implications. But she suspected that he was planning to push her aside in the convention in favor of Andrews, his brother-in-law. Floen, who had volunteered to take care of her interests, had mentioned such a possibility. But why had Ward now come to her? What could she do if he really would block her nomination. She was soon to see it all in a clearer light.

The banker was quite blunt about it; she couldn't get the nomination without his help. And this was what he had come to talk to her about, he said. In the brief period she had been superintendent, she had, he understood, done as good a job as could be expected. As far as that was concerned there was no reason why she couldn't be nominated and elected. But politics was politics and if she wanted to hold on to her office she would have to ally herself with the existing political forces. Even though his organization was fully prepared to support her interests, she must understand that if he were to enter into any kind of agreement, whether in business or in politics, then this meant cooperation and mutual understanding. This was why he had come for a confidential talk with her, and since it was in her own interest he was sure that all that was said between them would remain between them.

Mrs. O'Brien answered that she didn't run around reporting on private conversations. Thus assured, Ward explained that his price for her nomination was that they came to an understanding that would also be in his interest. He wasn't in charity. He knew he could talk with her about this, he said, because they both were Americans. The foreigners who now came from all corners of the world didn't always appreciate what he with one word would call American solidarity. Their only thought was for their own interests and they had little concern for the commonweal. It was now necessary for the country's own children to stand together. It had pained him that Mrs. O'Brien had sought support from Scandinavian newcomers, who really shouldn't have had the right to vote. There was absolutely no reason why she couldn't just as easily ally herself with him and his organization.

"Do you propose to have me turn my back on my good old friends?" asked Mrs. O'Brien. His speech had upset her.

"Not at all," Ward replied; "many of them—I dare say most of them—are my own friends. They are capable, thrifty, and good people. They are fine workers. In hiring servants, I've always preferred the Scandinavians. Of course, we want their support; and we'll give them all they're entitled to in lieu of it. But I'm not willing to let them run me out of the country."

Mrs. O'Brien couldn't quite free herself from the thought that it might have been good for many if Elihu Ward had been run out of the country, but she kept this to herself. She did ask him what he had thought of asking from her in return for the help he offered.

He replied that she could be of great use to him among the Scandinavians. They knew her and trusted her. So now was the logical moment for her to strengthen her position by becoming part of his political and financial ring. Those who now conspired to destroy him would later, if they were in power, have no more mercy for her than they had for him, and they would throw her overboard and elect a Norwegian as super-intendent in her stead. But they would never be in power. It was not his intention to be shamed by Hans Floen and Torgersen and their set. They would find no mercy in his hands. She had better not believe that it was for love of her that they had been so eager to place her in office. They had only used her to weaken him. For appearance sake they found it useful to have an American. On the other hand it would be in his and her inter-est to retain the confidence of the Norwegian settlers. With her contacts among the Scandinavians, she would be able to do much to have them realize the importance of standing together with the commonweal as our only guiding principle. So he didn't really expect her to help him much with actual political work but with this far more important task. He was not, of course, working against her friends. It was only that these new citizens had to be led on the right path . . .

As she listened, Mrs O'Brien gradually realized that all his talk of her influence, the commonweal, and American solidarity was only a cover-up for a cunning plan he had hatched out to profit from his neigh-bors' losses, a cover for the dirty cards he was dealing . . .

"Now, Mr. Ward," she eventually said, "this may all be very well so far as you are concerned. As for myself, I'm not built for propaganda of any sort. In other words, what you are talking about has no application with regard to my humble person, and you know it. May I ask, what is your real errand here?" The banker smiled.

"I'll put it a bit straighter," he said. "As I've told you, I control that convention."

"Yes."

"And you want that nomination?"

"Yes."

"And you can have it only if I wish you to have it."

"Well, suppose this to be the case."

"Would you under these circumstances go a little out of your way to get it?"

"I should refuse to do anything not strictly honorable."

"I assure you, I'd be the last person in Christendom to conceive of such an outrageous idea as to propose anything dishonorable."

"Possibly," was her only response.

He sat for a while as in thought. He knew her situation. He had a mortgage in the O'Brien farm and could let it go on auction next spring. O'Brien was an impossible provider. It was a question of survival for her to hold on to either the superintendent office or the farm. It was in her interest to hold on to both. He could take both away from her. Elihu Ward had stood face to face with many people in similar circumstances, holding the sword of power over them, and he had never failed to get what he wanted. He didn't recognize any other factor in life than money—financial security. All else was but rhetoric. An idealist with empty stomach and pockets was no longer a hero. A hundred-dollar note in front of his eyes could make him poison his own grandmother. It never failed. Money talks every time . . .

Did she remember that he had a client in Illinois who wanted to buy Jonas Olsen's farm? he asked when he again began to speak. Yes, she remembered it, but Mrs. Olsen was against selling. Ward said that was his understanding of the situation too. But now his client wanted to buy two farms in *Groven*—320 acres—and they would have to be near each other since he wanted to use them as one farm. Ward had thought of the O'Brien farm. He assumed that they wouldn't be against selling if they got a good price, especially if she could continue as superintendent. Mrs. O'Brien didn't care much for the farm. Her experience as a farmer's wife was not much to boast of, nor was the living they made of the farm. But then she wondered why Ward had gone on at such length if he merely wanted to buy their farm?

"You mean then," she said, "that if we are willing to sell you the farm, you will guarantee me the nomination?"

"Well—er—yes—that is, if you'll assist me in making a deal with the Olsen people also. As I told you, my client doesn't want your farm alone. He'll buy it only in connection with the other farm."

In her weeks as superintendent, Mrs. O'Brien had come to love her work. This was the first time in many, many years that she had been able to work at something that she liked to do and at the same time be helping others by doing it. She would be very disappointed if she couldn't continue. And if he took their farm they would stand with empty hands in their declining years . . . And what about Emma and Nyblom . . . If they had to begin all over again there was no way of knowing how it would work out. She was quite sure that if she and Jim really tried, they would be able to get Ragna and Jonas to sell—at a price. Would it be dishonest of her to do it? It would certainly not be illegal; but what about the openness and trust expected between friends? Nor could she free herself from her suspicion that Ward had his own secret plans with this farm business and that it was really something quite different that he was trying to achieve, other than what he had told her. The more she thought about it, the less she was attracted by the notion of giving in to Ward in any way. Ward, however, had seen that she found a decision difficult.

"You may think about it for a day or two," he said, "and talk it over with Jim."

But that was exactly what she wanted to avoid. Jim was kind and good and well-meaning but he had little firmness of character, and one could never know what a cunning man like Ward could convince him to do if the decision should be delayed.

"Mr. Ward," she finally said, "I've already thought the matter over, and have made up my mind. I'm sorry, but I shall have to decline to be of any service to you whatever."

The look he gave her at this unexpected reply was full of surprise and anger. For once, Elihu Ward forgot his obligations to a noble tradition.

"You're a silly, sentimental old woman, Mrs. O'Brien," he exclaimed. He got up from his chair and was about to leave. "And you know what'll happen," he added.

"You may ruin me, if you like," she replied. She stood up and opened the door for him. "But I wish to remind you that I'm an American and a Presbyterian."

"So am I, by gosh," he hissed in a voice that shook of exasperation, as he hurried past her and disappeared down the corridor.

19.

For Jonas and Ragna it remained a mystery that Napoleon Stomhoff got along as well as he did as teacher in O'Brien's Grove. To be sure, all were not satisfied with him and some had criticized his private life, but all in all, the settlers thought that their teacher was a very learned man. In Stomhoff, Glombekken had found a faithful confederate and both he and his wife did what they could to strengthen his good standing in the settlement. Stomhoff had particular benefit from his friendship with Mrs. Glombekken. Few liked Torfin, and if it hadn't been for his fierce support of the majority position in the question of church affilia-tion, he would have had very little influence. But his wife was popular with the other women; she had an uncommonly good knowledge of the personal history of the settlement and knew how to let others have part in her knowledge in a sociable and delicate manner.

The teaching of parochial school was fraught with difficulties. The Glombekkens had two rooms and a kitchen, and since the rooms were small there wasn't much space for the twelve to fifteen children who regularly attended the school. To begin with, the children had shown great respect for their new schoolmaster. They flinched at his slightest movement and were saddened by his reproaches. But they soon discovered that he wasn't dangerous. He was evidently just a human being who drank whisky and chewed tobacco like their own fathers.

One event that contributed to the teacher's difficulties took place after the school had moved from the Glombekkens' to the Flasmos'. Sivert Jorshaug, who had learned his catechism partly from his father and partly from Trulsen, one day caught Stomhoff giving a wrong explanation to a question about the catechism. As he was holding forth on the work of the Holy Spirit, he happened to confuse the terms "sanctification" and "justification" in a manner that Sivert found questionable.[38] When Sivert told about this at home, his father would at first not believe him. So learned a man could not possibly make such a stupid mistake. Sivert must have gotten it wrong. But Sivert knew what he was talking about, and after he had explained it all carefully from first to last, it was clear that he had it right. Jorshaug thought that the teacher had looked too deeply into his bottle, but since he didn't want to damage the school's reputation he excused Napoleon as well as he could and said that even the best man could sometimes be in error and that the incorrect explanation was of course due to carelessness rather than ignorance. Sivert, however, couldn't care less what the real reason may have been; to him it was simply a fact that he enjoyed sharing with the other children. And for some time, Napoleon's slip provided his students with considerable entertainment and served to undermine their confidence in the teacher from Minneapolis who was supposed to be so clever and learned. Of course it also meant an end to what was left of discipline in the school.

Iver Flasmo couldn't prove that Stomhoff had actually taught wrong doctrine at any specified time, but he knew he was of the same ilk as the pastor and Trulsen, and that was all the evidence he needed. He had known Koren and Professor Larsen and he had even heard Preus, the old Synod president, speak at a conference in Decorah, and he knew he couldn't be fooled in such matters. There was always something underhanded about the anti-Missourians, he said. They moved in secret ways and they tricked people into accepting synergism and unionism drop by drop as a slow-working poison, so that it took an expert to disclose what they were doing.[39] Now they were at work in *Groven*. Little by little they had confused one after the other, so that now only a handful were left standing on the foundation of truth. Iver, Jorshaug, and Jonas had held a little conference on the matter during the *surpreispartiet* on the Jonas farm and they considered what they should do in the fall when the meeting to organize a congregation was held. Jorshaug thought that the few Missourians wouldn't be able to keep the congregation from joining the new United Church but they were all agreed that they had to protest as loudly and clearly as possible. They weren't so sure about what they would do after the decision had been made, however. They were too few to have their own congregation. Flasmo was adamant in his refusal to belong to a church that wasn't built on the unfailing foundation of the Formula of Concord.[40] Jonas agreed in principle but was doubtful about standing apart. He had begun to sense that it could be an uncomfortable situation to be among an excluded minority. It might have a negative influence on his future . . .

Stomhoff had never been in doubt. He was a born supporter of the majority. This gift was a considerable boost to his reputation. It had been evident at his first prayer meeting. The minister had decided that Stomhoff should hold an evening meeting with the settlers every other week, and the first was held at the Glombekkens'. It may be that many were motivated as much by their curiosity as by their desire for edification, but the large turnout was regardless a vote of confidence for the teacher. For Jonas it was obvious that he and Ragna would have to attend the meeting, but she immediately made her objections known. "Do you really think that I would demean myself by taking part in such fraud?" she said.

"Well, one must avoid gossip, you know."

"Gossip? What is there to talk about?"

"People will talk about anything."

"So let them blather! I won't go to anything so cheap as a sermon by Napoleon."

Jonas didn't like her attitude. She was beginning to be opinionated. Of course he had no desire to listen to Stomhoff—far from it—but he had worked out that it wouldn't be worthwhile for him to turn his back on him. Nor did he want to give people the impression that he kept away because he didn't agree with them. He was, of course, a man of principle, but it was just as important to know how to deal with your fellow human beings. And he was certainly man enough to go where he wanted without asking his wife's permission! "Well, if you won't come with me, I'll go alone!" he declared.

She was irritated by his attitude and behavior. It was so undignified; he despised Napoleon as much as she did. And she was alone day after day, week after week, but it was more important for him to make an impression on Stomhoff and Glombekken than to please her by staying at home . . . "You should show them that you're man enough to stay away from such deception!" she said. "It's a sacrilege to take part in such things."

This made an already bad situation worse. Had she only spoken with reason, he thought, he could perhaps have stayed at home, which is what he would have preferred anyway, but he wouldn't be ordered about. Damned if he would! "There you are with your unreasonableness again!" he said. "It's strange how you women can't think logically."

"But dear, how could you expect it? We who are so poorly endowed? We have been told that only men have the ability to understand."

"Well, it's we who have had to *rønne* the world up till now."

"And it couldn't have been *rønnet* in a more stupid way."

Oh, so that's the way it is, Jonas thought, and said, "Well, *gudbey,*" on his way out.

Her first reaction was that he was so unreasonable. Then she began to cry. She was so lonely and unhappy . . . But then an idea suddenly came to her. When he could afford to be so damned independent, why couldn't she be the same? When he went where he wished without considering her feelings, why couldn't she do the same? Moreover, she had promised Emma that she would soon drop in on her.

An hour later she was at the O'Briens'. It was a beautiful and cool evening so the short walk across the prairie had been comfortable. She was glad that she had come. It was good to see how the relationship between Nyblom and Emma had changed. He had become as nice and considerate a husband as could be wished. The two women had so much to talk about now that they had discovered that the expected important events in their lives would take place at almost exactly the same time. They wondered how Mrs. Flasmo would manage if it should happen on the same day.

It was late when Ragna finally had to say goodbye. Emma and Nyblom wouldn't allow her to go home alone, and when she refused their offer to take her in the buggy, they insisted that she at least would let Nyblom walk with her.

Walking across the prairie, Nyblom made use of the opportunity to thank her for what she had done for Emma. She was an entirely different wife! The food was better and the home more pleasant. "But you are unhappy," he said.

"Oh, happiness will always come to those who wait and believe in it," she replied.

"And it may go away as we wait. Jonas Olsen isn't the man you deserve."

"That's enough!" she said sharply. "I will not discuss my husband with anyone!" He asked her forgiveness and they continued their walk in silence.

———————

Jonas found the house empty when he returned. He was in a bad temper. Stomhoff had made a better performance than he had expected and most had been quite satisfied with his sermon, which had been delivered in typical lay-preacher fashion with an abundance of pious clichés. Afterward even Mrs. Flasmo said that he was a better preacher than a schoolmaster. He was even sober! Jonas would have been more satisfied if Napoleon had made a scandal. As things now stood, he had to admit that the prayer meeting had strengthened the teacher's standing and they might not be able to get rid of him so easily.

His mind was busy with such thoughts as he entered the house, and after looking for Ragna in the parlor and the kitchen and after making sure that she hadn't gone to bed, he became anxious. Something must have happened to her! Worried, he ran out to the barn, but there was no sign of her there either. Then back into the house. He couldn't help but think about the little quarrel they had had before he left. *Gudnes!* He may have done something he would regret. Why couldn't he control his temper, especially now—in her condition. He vowed that if he found her well and sound, he would never again say a cross word to her. He would carry her in his arms the rest of his life no matter the cost . . .

A little later Ragna and Nyblom came to the house. She saw a light in the parlor and asked if he would come in. Jonas was startled when they opened the door. He had been pacing back and forth, contemplating his alternatives. When they entered, he was so shocked that he had to grasp the edge of the table in order to keep his balance. He could hardly believe his own eyes. This was the most scandalous thing he had seen in his entire life . . .

20.

"G ood evening, Mr. Olsen!" Nyblom greeted him, as he and Ragna entered the room. "I have the honor to *fetcha* your wife home in good shape."

Ragna offered him a chair and sat down as well. Jonas remained standing, speechless with indignation. The Swede immediately understood the situation.

"I hear that you have been to meeting," he continued unruffled, "and I *bettar* you have had a good time."

Ragna could not help smiling at these words, and Jonas, who was staring at her, noticed it. So they came to scorn and mock him to his face in his own house . . . His first impulse was to throw Nyblom out, but he controlled himself . . . "I don't seem to be the only one to have had a good time," he replied. The Swede laughed pleasantly.

"That I would believe," he said. "You would hardly be the only one to be edified by the occasion."

"No, and I can also see that there are other ways to be entertained. Some seek comfort in the word of God while others find pleasure in breaking His commandments." Jonas himself sensed that this sounded somewhat artificial and solemn, but he only thought of it as an introduction to what he wanted to say to them.

"The word of God?" the Swede exclaimed. "I thought Napoleon was a bootlegger from Minneapolis."

"Any human instrument of God has his faults," Jonas continued in the same high-flown style. "We are all sinners."

"Surely not all of us? I didn't think that you . . ."

Jonas suddenly took a step toward Nyblom. He felt that the cup was now full.

"What does this mean?" he asked. His voice shook with anger. Ragna looked at him in alarm. He was flexing his large and powerful hands.

"Nothing wrong has happened," she exclaimed. "Please don't!" The Swede got up.

"The only thing that has *häpnad*," he cried out in anger, "is that an ass of a man has created a hell for a faithful and honest woman."

"Say that again and I'll throw you out!" Jonas screamed.

"Well, then I'll say it again!" Nyblom thundered; "go ahead. Let's see if you dare!" They stared at each other like two crazed roosters about to go at each other. Ragna got up and stood between them.

"Have you both lost your wits?" she exclaimed. "Two grown men, and such behavior! Shame on you! Sit down and settle this nonsense. I'll go out and make some coffee." Nyblom calmed down and found his chair. But Jonas was not to be stopped so easily. "I will not take an *insølt* from nobody in my own house!" he cried.

"*Vot's dot?*" the Swede exclaimed. "Do you dare call me nobody?" He got up again.

"Yes, I damned well do . . ."

"Here now, quit that, and be two good little boys," Ragna admonished them. Nyblom suddenly began to laugh. He saw that the situation was ridiculous. He sat down again. Ragna pushed Jonas into the chair she had been using. He was still fuming with rage but he didn't resist her. And then she walked through the kitchen door, which she left ajar behind her.

"Well, what do you say?" asked the Swede.

"I say as I've always said that the Swedes are the same damned rabble they have always been through all history!" Jonas replied with emphasis.

"And I say that the Norwegians could have been a decent people if they hadn't been spoiled by Tartars like yourself. You are a shame for all Scandinavians!"

"I'm no Scandinavian," Jonas answered, stressing the last word with contempt.

"Well, that's just what I'm saying. You're a savage!"

"This Scandinavian nonsense is just something you Swedes have used to subdue the Norwegians, but now we are damned well through with you and you can go there by yourselves and suck on the empty teat you call your great history."

Ragna could hear every word in the kitchen. Now that they had begun to quarrel about the Union she knew that the worst was over. Her experience as well as her instincts told her that if they had to thresh it out between them they would realize that they really had no reason to be enemies. They didn't want to admit that their anger was leaving them, so their nationalist bickering served as a convenient transitional phase during which they could take time to regain their composure while they were still showing their teeth.

"Oh, a great history shouldn't be scorned," Nyblom replied. Ragna could hear that there was no longer any fight in his voice.

"Especially when there isn't much else to brag about," Jonas remarked. He was still sarcastic but his voice was lower. After a few seconds of silence Nyblom looked around in the parlor and said, "It's a nice home you have here!" This was unexpected. But the Swede's words came as a relief. He had just been thinking that he had behaved rather stupidly. Ragna had of course gone to visit Emma and then they wouldn't let her go home alone in the dark.

"Yes, it's not so bad," he admitted, "to be out here on the prairie."

"And the prairie isn't so bad either," Nyblom added. "The soil is excellent."

"Had it only not been so dry! We won't have much of a crop this year."

"Yes, the *kroppen* won't be so plenty many places, but you shouldn't *grumla*. The wheat looks good here." Ragna came in with the coffee.

"Our crop is just as it should be," she said with a smile. "They say that the dumbest farmers get the biggest potatoes." Jonas thought this was rather irresponsible of Ragna, considering who she was talking about and to whom. But he had had enough fighting for one night, so he took it as a joke and said, "All comes easy when you have such an excellent wife, *ju'no'*!" The ice was broken. They laughed as they sat down at the coffee table.

"It's as I've always said," said Nyblom, "This is a *bully kontry* for farming."

"Yes, if we had only had some hills and forest," Jonas replied.

"Yes, and lakes and birds and song in the air," the Swede said, "as in Sweden."

"Yes, and in Norway!"

"Yes, in Norway—*dot's right*—Norway must be a wonderful *kontry*."

"*Ju bet!*"

"If only there hadn't been so much stone," Ragna said, "in the soil as in the people."

"I've never been to Norway," Nyblom admitted, "but I've heard much about Kristiania from my mother. For her it was the only city in the world." Jonas looked at him in surprise. "*Gudnes,* you're half Norwegian!" he exclaimed. "Why haven't you said so?"

"I feared that you wouldn't recognize our common nationality," laughed the Swede. "And father was after all Swedish."

"We should try to forgive you for that," said Ragna, "especially since you probably didn't have any say in the matter of your paternity!" It all ended in friendly banter and Nyblom had to have another cup of coffee before he left. By then it was midnight.

"You'll have to look in on us again," Jonas said as he followed him out. "And take Emma with you. You know, she and Emma are such fine friends!"

"Yes, I know," the Swede replied, "and you and I have gone around like two idiots." He gave his hand to Jonas in farewell.

After Jonas had come in, he and Ragna stood for a long time looking at each other. Then she broke into a merry laughter. "Well," she said, "what do you have to say?"

"We may have been wrong about Nyblom," he said, slightly embarrassed. "He's actually quite a nice man." Ragna admitted that he had improved. And then she told him everything; how she had talked to Nyblom for Emma's sake and that she had been over there tonight and found them reconciled and happy. "And now what?" she insisted.

"Oh," Jonas replied, "when a man sees that he has *mæka* a fool of himself it may be best that he keeps his mouth shut."

She had won the battle.

21.

Iver Flasmo and Lars Jorshaug came to Jonas one Monday evening in early August. He was in the barn, and Ragna invited them in. Visitors were so rare, especially two at the same time, that she sensed something was up. She ran out and asked Jonas to come at once.

It turned out that they had come on an ecclesiastical errand. Church service had been announced for next Sunday and Vellesen had asked Trulsen to let people know that there would be a meeting Saturday night to discuss the forming of a congregation. His two neighbors were sure that the congregation wouldn't be in the Synod, but the Synod people should nevertheless be present and express their disapproval. Perhaps they could even get the new congregation to be independent of the synods. Since Jonas had both the right doctrine and the ability to express himself, it would be best if he would lead the opposition.

When he and Ragna talked it over after Flasmo and Jorshaug had left, she remarked that it was perhaps just as well to keep out of it. Their relationship with the Trulsens was already difficult because of these church squabbles and she didn't think it would be right to close the door on them. The minister had been quite nice, she thought, and they couldn't really afford to be at war with so many of their neighbors either.

In spite of his earlier doubts, Jonas was now attracted to the notion of becoming a leader in church matters and he countered by reminding her that she had always insisted on being true to oneself. Now that he wanted to take a firm stand, she shouldn't hold him back. "You should remember," he said, "that the people who agree with me are without leadership and that this is an opportunity for me to work for a cause that is in the true interest of our people." She said no more about it. He would have to do as he saw best, and she promised herself that she would support him as best she could.

Even though most of settlers were working late and early at this time of year, almost every man in the settlement came to the meeting at the Trulsens' on Saturday night.[41] Their parlors were packed.

Vellesen explained why they had been asked to come. There had long been a desire among the pioneers in the settlement, he said, to have their own congregation. Twenty miles farther west on the prairie the settlers had just established the Salt Grove congregation, and they could now agree to share the same pastor. Vellesen said he would recommend the organization of a congregation and he asked if there were any proposals.

Trulsen got up and proposed the organization of O'Brien's Grove Norwegian-Lutheran congregation. He was seconded. Jonas, Iver Flasmo, and Lars Jorshaug sat together at the far end of the parlor. Iver whispered something in Jonas's ear just as Napoleon entered, humble but dignified in his long coat. Sven Ericksen, who happened to be seated next to the minister, got up and let the schoolmaster have his chair. Peder Tarvesen suggested they should constitute themselves before they went any further in their proceedings. Trulsen agreed and proposed that Napoleon be appointed secretary.

"*Gudnes!*" Jonas said in a stage whisper in Iver Flasmo's ear. Then he got up. "Shouldn't we first elect a chairman?" he asked.

"The pastor is of course chairman by custom," Trulsen replied.

"Certainly. Had we been organized as a congregation, all tradition and custom would have him in that position," Jonas replied, "but we haven't come that far yet."

"Well, the pastor is the natural chairman anyhow," Torfin Glombekken argued. "Anyone who has attended a church *miting* knows that much." There was hate and spite in the look he gave Jonas. Vellesen didn't look too kindly at him either.

"No one is obvious as chairman," Jonas insisted. "We may elect the pastor but we may also elect someone else. I move that we now elect a chairman for the meeting."

"Yes, we can do no harm in electing him," said Sven Ericksen. "It'll have to be the pastor anyhow. There isn't anyone else here who is qualified." Vellesen, who had been standing since he had explained the reason for the meeting, now sat down.

"It seems that I'm superfluous here," he sulked. Trulsen then proposed that Vellesen be elected chair. Flasmo proposed Jonas. The minister was elected with an overwhelming majority. Jonas only had two votes—Flasmo's and Jorshaug's.

"I cannot deny that this seems to be a strange procedure," said the pastor as he again got up, "but if this is the way you insist on doing it . . . Who should be our secretary?"

"I propose Mr. Stomhoff," cried Glombekken.

"I propose Jonas Olsen!" said Flasmo. Napoleon was elected by a narrow majority.

"It's a scandal!" Jonas whispered to Flasmo. Lars Jorshaug got up and said that as far as he was concerned it would be perfectly in order to organize a congregation, but before they voted on the proposal it would be best to know a little about what kind of congregation it was going to be. Jonas added that as far as he had heard, the Salt Grove congregation had decided to join the United Church, and if they were going to share the same minister, he supposed the intention was for them to also join the new church body. It would be interesting to know what the meeting thought about this before proceeding any further.

"It could be interesting," he concluded, "to find out if the intention is to do this on the sly or if we are to have everything out in the open." He certainly got people's attention. The minister looked severely at Jonas, and the others looked at each other. Peder Tarvesen laughed contentedly and turned to Erik Nesteved: "Now we're going to have some fun!" Others also revived noticeably at the prospect of some change in their drab monotony.

Iver Flasmo stood up and said that he fully agreed that they would have to know what they were doing. He had heard that in earlier pioneering days, preachers had come to the settlements and gotten people to organize congregations and they had then discovered that they had become Mormons and had agreed to practice polygamy . . .

Vellesen called him to order.[42] This was blasphemy, he said. They all knew that they were Lutherans and that this would be a Lutheran congregation. It was wicked to insinuate that he, a Lutheran minister who had served them for some time, had plans to deceive them. He had come on their request and he had assumed that he had their confidence.

"Well, I think it's best to inquire," said Flasmo. "I would rather be cautious than find myself trapped."

"Yes, and there are as many kinds of Lutherans as there are days in a month," said Jonas. "It's only reasonable that we find out whether this is to be a congregation that trusts in God alone or one that believes in the efficacy of their own works."

Vellesen wasn't used to being interrupted at church meetings. "I would like to answer the young man who we have the pleasure of seeing amongst us for the first time," he said. "Before a congregation can make any decision about what church body it should enter, it must first be organized as a congregation. There cannot be a quorum before there is a congregation."

Jonas got up again. He had been thinking about what the minister had said about his youth and he couldn't let that pass by without a response. "As far as my youth is concerned," he said, "it will have to be up to the meeting to decide whether I'm too young to vote and speak." Lars and Iver nodded to each other. "But I'm of age and an owner of property, so if I have the minister's permission . . ."

"You are mistaken . . ." Vellesen interrupted him.

"But perhaps those who have left the Synod are only interested in old people?"

"You are mistaken, Mr.—what was your name?" the minister said.

"Olsen," Trulsen said in a low voice.

"Well, our friend—ahem—Olsen is mistaken. I am convinced that all will wish him welcome in our congregation. But I also assume that you won't simply leave all decisions in congregational matters to Mr.—ahem—Olsen."

"What I wanted to find out," said Jonas, "was whether it's the pastor or the members who decide. After Pastor—ahem—Vellesen has assured us, we now know that it is the congregation, but we still don't know how much of the congregation the minister is—whether he, for instance, is a third or perhaps two-thirds." Napoleon was solemn as he stood up. "I call the young man to order!" he said, whereupon he sat down again.

"Since I am involved, I must leave the decision to the meeting," said Vellesen. "All who find that Mr. Olsen is out of order may say yea."

Trulsen and Glombekken said yea. The others remained silent. "I assume that the meeting finds Mr. Olsen out of order?"

"There is no reason to assume anything like it," said Iver Flasmo. "It seems that this is a view held only by Trulsen and Stomhoff and Glombekken."

"Very well," fumed the minister. "Will those who find him in order please say yea." Three yea's. Vellesen was confused. Jonas was quick to get on his feet, and said, "I think it's rather irrelevant whether I am in order or not. There is no order here anyhow. Should we conduct our *bisnes* in this manner, we wouldn't get anything done."

"I suppose we would be bankrupt, then," Glombekken said, "like some shopkeepers in *Min'ap'lis* who think they can *rønna* the church and everything even though they can't *rønne* a simple grocery store." Jonas bit his lip. There was no point is saying anything.

"It would be best to have this decided once and for all," said Sven Ericksen. "I move that we organize a congregation and apply for membership in the United Norwegian Lutheran Church in America."

"Well, if that is what the meeting wants . . ."

"That remains to be seen," said Flasmo. "I move that we join the Synod since we all know that they have the correct faith." Jonas seconded the motion. The minister then put Ericksen's motion to the vote, but Jonas protested. Flasmo's motion was a subsidiary motion and according to parliamentary rules of order it had to be put to the vote first.

"Mr. Olsen is wrong again," the minister said. "We will of course vote on the motions in the order they were presented."

"And I insist that this is illegal!" Jonas responded eagerly. Flasmo whispered to him, "Are you sure that you're right?"

"Absolutely!"

"Then go 'head!" Iver was so pleased that he giggled.

"You are evidently quite a contentious young man!" the minister rebuked Jonas. "All who are for organizing a congregation and entering the United Church . . ."

"Listen . . ." Jonas interrupted him. Vellesen ignored him. "All who are for the motion please say yea." There was a chorus of yea's. "If anyone is against it you may say nay."

Jonas got up. "If this had been a legal vote I would have said nay," he said, "but since the procedure is illegal I will simply protest against the entire proceedings."

"*Dot's* it!" Tarvesen seconded him.

"Yes, *dot's* it!" said Flasmo.

Vellesen was evidently not interested in pursuing the matter any further. "I hereby declare that the motion to organize a new congregation and enter the United Church has been passed," he said. "And two weeks from today we will have our first congregational meeting here at the Trulsens'."

Jonas and the five or six who wouldn't compromise left under protest.

22.

Recently, Torfin Glombekken and Napoleon had been in Normanville every Saturday. Few people in *Groven* paid any attention to these frequent visits. Jonas hadn't been in town for a long time. He had plenty of work on the farm, and Mrs. O'Brien came with their mail every Sunday. Everything stood very nicely on the ten acres they had cultivated, so he enjoyed working on his own land, especially since his relationship with Ragna had again become as it should be. There could no longer be any doubt that they would have a good crop. The wheat could be taken at any time. Flasmo and Jorshaug, who had already cut a lot of theirs, had promised to help him next week. Jonas had built a small granary. Trulsen had come to show him how to go about it, but there was no longer any friendship between them. Church controversies threatened friendships between all who couldn't see eye to eye, and people found it more and more difficult to meet without getting into arguments.

After the first church service in June, Jonas had subscribed to the Synod's monthly, *Kirketidende,* and had bought five earlier volumes.[43] So now he had a better understanding of what the doctrinal controversy was all about. The more he read, the more he was assured that he had chosen the right position. Ragna too had become somewhat more interested in church matters, but she had not acquired the uncompromising views that Jonas propounded whenever he had an occasion, especially after the founding of the congregation. At times she would get tired of listening to his interminable explanations, and she had to think of ways to stop his ever-increasing torrent of words and try to divert his mind to brighter and more optimistic themes. She wouldn't say that she actually disagreed with him, but she would have liked him to admit that also those who saw things differently should also be accepted as good Christians.

At times he was angry when Ragna ever so carefully tried to suggest that, for instance, the Trulsens were good and righteous people—in spite of the weakness of their theological views. But he said it was sinful—indeed unionism, synergism, and more—to think or say such things in favor of those who wouldn't accept correct doctrine. Ragna was unhappy that they now were isolated from the congregation and from much else. But the way Jonas felt he had been treated at the meeting, he insisted that they had no choice.

He was so engaged in the controversy that Ragna was relieved when people who talked about other things came to visit. When Mrs. O'Brien came over on Sunday afternoons with the mail from Normanville, she seemed to bring a new world with her into their home. She could talk about things of interest that had happened in town and about her work to improve the schools. This summer she had traveled around in the county and established personal relations with those who ran the schools in the districts. Most rural schools were in bad shape. The settlers would have to be taught to understand that their children's education was more important than any other function of their society. She knew it wasn't all that popular to spread that kind of message, she said, since better schools would cost more money, but she didn't care. She had to do as she thought right, regardless of whether people liked it or not. Moreover, she didn't have any prospects of holding on to the job as superintendent next year anyway.

Both Jonas and Ragna were saddened at the thought that Mrs. O'Brien might have to leave her post. They tried to comfort her, saying that things could go differently, but she just shook her head. Ward was too powerful in the county, she said, not mentioning her conference with the banker. But she did tell them that Ward had recently been seen several times in the company of Glombekken and Napoleon at Ole Dampen's. She had no explanation of what this might mean, but Jonas was suddenly struck by the implications of this new friendship between the banker and his two neighbors from *Groven*.

For in the mail that Mrs. O'Brien had brought him there was a letter from Ward, who informed him that he had purchased the note and the mortgage Jonas had with Davidsen's bank. The note had fallen due and Jonas would have to come in to settle it. When he had first read the letter he was sure that the note could be renewed, but now he wasn't so sure any longer. At least he realized that he would have to see to this business immediately.

A Republican caucus had been scheduled the next day, to elect delegates to the county convention, and Jonas wanted to be present and do what he could to see that those who represented the town were in favor of Mrs. O'Brien's nomination. But the letter from Ward gave him no peace. You could never know what that sly fox was up to.

That evening he went over to Jorshaug, who thought that there was surely not a man in the entire town who was against the nomination of Mrs. O'Brien. Even Glombekken had said that it would be senseless to nominate another candidate for superintendent. Jonas was assured by this information and he prepared himself for a visit to town early next morning. If all went well he should be able to return in time for the caucus.

Ward was polite as usual when Jonas entered his bank. He was sorry, he said, that he had to inconvenience him, but he knew that Jonas too would want to have the matter closed. "I suppose you're prepared to pay up the note?" he asked as he showed him into his private office.

"I'd prefer to have it extended," Jonas replied. "You know the security is first class."

Yes, but Ward would nevertheless not renew it. He had to insist on having it paid immediately, but if he didn't have the money there was still the offer to buy the farm on behalf of the man from Illinois. Jonas replied that he and his wife had agreed to hold on to the farm. He realized that he might be forced to let it go, but he would at least see to it that Ward would have to pay for it. It was obvious that he was set on having it . . . If Elihu could *bluffe* than he could *bluffe* too.

"That note is a small matter," he said in a tone of voice that suggested indifference. "If you don't want to carry it, I'll get someone else to do it." Ward immediately thought of Torgersen. Should Torgersen get his hands on the note, Ward would never get it back. He felt it was time to play his trump cards. "I don't see how a man with your past can afford to be so doggedly independent," he said.

"My past?" Jonas exclaimed. "What's the matter with my past?"

"Oh, come off! You know very well . . ."

With that he began to go through a long list of Jonas's sins. Did he remember a man named Nikolai Skummebek who was once robbed of $300 by a drinking companion in Minneapolis? Did he perhaps remember a grocer named Stunsrud, about whom ill-minded competitors had a scandalous book published and then had his store burned down so he had to leave town a ruined man? If he thought it over, he might remember another grocer in Minneapolis who scandalized the entire grocery trade by getting his innocent customers to buy a large consignment of rotten cod? Could he confirm the story that the same man had filled his own pockets when a bank failed, a bank where one of the directors was his own partner? Or if he had forgotten all this, he might still remember that this same man for some time had made weekly payments to a certain Napoleon in return for his silence?

Jonas listened in surprise. Of course, most of it was untrue. But the question was how he would be able to defend himself should these rumors be made public. He put up the most defiant face he could under the circumstances and insisted with much indignation that all that had been said about him was the *pureste* lie, but Ward merely smiled and answered, "If you're to follow up the rumors and disprove them, you'll be the busiest man in the county, once they're common property." Jonas realized the truth in this but he admitted nothing.

"Now be sensible," the banker continued. "What is your present price for the farm? You'll either sell it to me or to someone else. It's for your best interest to sell it to me; I'll pay you more for it than anybody else, and your reputation will be quite secure with me."

Jonas had been so unprepared for this that he was almost discouraged. He sat for a while before he collected his wits sufficiently to say that if he were to sell he would at least demand $6,000. But Ward shouldn't believe he would do it because of these lies.

No, of course not, Ward agreed. There was no reason to bring that into their discussion at all. Business was business. Their motives were their own concern. Instead of calling it $6,000, he said, he would give him $4,000 cash, sign the note from Minneapolis as paid in full, and let him have this year's crop. And they could live on the farm till spring if they wished. Jonas realized that this would amount to about $6,000, perhaps even more, and that he in this manner would have netted about $3,000 on the farm if nothing disastrous happened to his crop before it was harvested. He would speak with his wife about it, he said. It wasn't unlikely that they might sell after all.

"Well, my offer holds good for three days and no longer," said Ward. "I'm not going to waste anymore time on the blamed deal." Jonas realized that this was another bluff, but he had no need to respond in kind just now. He and Ragna would come for the county convention on Thursday, he said, and would then drop in to close the deal.

23.

Jonas was in a hurry to get out of town, so he got his other errands done in no time. All that remained was to confer with Hans Floen about the meeting. He was sure that the meeting had broken the rules in its decision to form a congregation and that what they had done therefore was illegal. Both Flasmo and Jorshaug had said that if they could create an obstacle for the majority, they should go ahead and do it. He explained everything to Floen, and the lawyer answered that the legality of the proceedings could perhaps be questioned but what could they gain by a suit? Wouldn't the majority simply make the same decision with due attention to rules of order and wouldn't the minority then be as powerless as before? Jonas hadn't thought it over so carefully and he had to admit that this is what would happen . . .

"Better forget it!" warned the lawyer. "This would be like beating the ocean. This is how it's been with so many of the battles fought by our church leaders. As a result, our strength has been wasted so that we can no longer unite for our common good."

Jonas disagreed. The church controversy was necessary, he thought. You couldn't let false teachers do as they wished within the church. But his arguments had no effect on the lawyer, and Jonas didn't have the time to go into the matter as deeply as he could have wished since he had to get home.

He was halfway to *Groven* when dark and threatening clouds appeared in the southwest. It had been uncommonly hot and humid, the kind of day that so often ended with bad weather. But if it didn't come too soon, he might still get home in time. A little rain wouldn't hurt him or the horses. He drove on, but the horses were hot and lazy and didn't want to run. And then the rain came down in torrents. He had never seen it come so suddenly. He would have to take shelter at the first farm, just a little farther ahead. When he entered the farmyard he was already soaked. The farmer came to the door and shouted that he could drive the horses to the north side of the barn where they could stand in lee, and then come in.

It turned out to be an Irish family, Donavan. They were nice people, welcomed him, and let him borrow some clothes so he could get his own clothes dried. After a while there was a short break in the rain and Jonas thought it would be best to get on his way. But Donavan didn't like the look of the sky, and advised against it. The worst was sure to come and it would be best to stable the horses. No sooner had they done it than the storm was over them again. The house shook in the wind. Jonas thought of Ragna, who was alone and unused to such weather, and wondered if the weather there was as bad as here. It lasted a couple of hours. Then, after a brief spell, the rain poured down again; but by now the wind had dropped.

Jonas was increasingly restless now that he realized the roads couldn't be traveled that night. The caucus would have to manage without him. Ragna sitting alone on the wide prairie was another matter. Donavan comforted him as best he could. Usually all went well when the worst was expected, he said. The main danger was not in the calamity itself. We always found a way of surviving an adversity. It was our fear of danger, very often a nonexistent danger, that caused our anxiety. To protect ourselves against these troubles of the mind we needed faith, and our fear, more than anything else, brought us nearer the object of our faith, Providence, God, whose strength we felt in our own fear and lack of strength . . .

Donavan, who proved to be an Irish Protestant, was quite a religious philosopher. True, the centerpiece of his Christian philosophy was nothing new. Jonas had heard all this before. Nor could he see that his views were entirely orthodox. He was right about faith—the faith that can move a mountain—but one must first have the correct doctrine. Donavan was eager to discuss these matters. For him it was all a question of understanding the core in the teaching of Christ, and this great core of Christianity was to love God above all else and to love your neighbor as yourself. That was the ultimate goal of life. He recognized that man couldn't achieve perfectibility, but it was God's will that we should strive for it. Jonas asked if he thought that the conduct of your life had any influence on the salvation of your soul, and Donavan couldn't deny that this was how he saw it. It was the working of Christ's spirit in man's heart as it found expression in our lives that was our last hope, not a specific dogma.

Jonas felt that Donavan at least had something that was of value in his own life. He was in the possession of an equanimity of mind that Jonas right now envied. They spoke of the weather and of their crops. Some were still not cut and some stood in shock. Jonas was worried that most of these crops would now be damaged by the storm. His loss would amount to three or four hundred dollars. Such prospects didn't seem to worry the Irishman in the least. Had he himself been responsible for squandering God's gifts, he said, then he would have reason to be worried: "It's God who giveth, and God who taketh," he said, "and sure, it's not for me to worry over what He does. If he wants to take back what He has given, good and well, it's His, and that's all there's to it. It's faith we must have."

Jonas admitted that this may be right in its way but he couldn't get himself to accept that this man, an evident heretic, had a stronger faith and perhaps even a deeper understanding than he who was in possession of the correct doctrine. That wouldn't make sense and, moreover, it would be counter to the teaching of the church.

Religion was an occasional topic in his conversations with Ragna. She was certainly not a theologian and she admitted that she had little understanding of doctrine, but she held firmly on to her faith and always insisted that a doctrine that wasn't a force in your life was of little value. To live in one way and to teach in another was mere hypocrisy. He had objected that you after all had to do *bisnes* and use common sense and all. You couldn't let the sons of this world cheat and swindle and use you as they wished. She agreed, but she insisted that it was a greater sin for one who regarded himself a good Christian to swindle a son of this world than for one of these to swindle a Christian. Ragna was not pious. She enjoyed fun and had a bright view of life, but she was serious when it came to her principles. She might be right when she said that he was preoccupied with worldly matters. But surely the Lord would approve that he did his best to husband the gifts he had been blessed with . . . But Donavan's talk had disturbed his balance of mind. He didn't feel as safe and self-confident as usual. Perhaps there was something lacking in his faith after all . . . And what if God should deprive him of both his crop and Ragna as punishment for not living as he taught?

Toward evening, the rain stopped and Jonas and the Irishman went out to inspect the damage. The uncut wheat had been beaten flat to the ground in many places but things looked better than they had feared. Donavan thought that a few days of good sunshine would set it all right. He wouldn't let Jonas set off for home that night. He could get stuck on the soaked roads, and they couldn't be sure there wouldn't be more rain either. Things were probably all right in *Groven* since it didn't look too bad here. God had surely held his hand over his wife as well as his crop. Although Jonas still doubted this, he found comfort in seeing that this area had survived the storm relatively well. He knew he would have a miserable night but he would have to put his trust in God . . .

24.

Meanwhile quite a few things had happened in *Groven* in Jonas's absence:

After he had left, Ragna had done her chores and milked the cow. Then she had sat down to her sewing. She still had a few things to make for the new expected member of the family and she enjoyed doing it while she was alone. Nothing could so distract her from feelings of loneliness as when she sent her thoughts off into the fantasy world she had created for her coming child. It was fascinating to sit here and build castles in the air for their son! They probably disagreed about his future. Jonas would want him to become a *bisnesmand.* How she had tired of that word. *Gudnes, bisnesmand . . .* Mrs. Jorshaug had talked about sending her son Sivert to Luther College in the fall. She so wanted him to become a minister. Indeed, the ambition of many a Norwegian family was to have a son become a minister . . . That could be nice, but pastors had a great responsibility, and she had arrived at the conviction that it wasn't for every man to live up to such a calling. And then she happened to think about the church controversy and all the hatred and evil that followed in its wake . . . No, her son was not going to be a minister. But what if it wasn't a boy . . .

She suddenly laid down her sewing, got up, and looked at the clock. It was half past nine. In her window she saw O'Brien and Nyblom with their horses and the *reaperen* cutting the wheat out on their large field. They would have it done in a day or two and, God be praised, it looked as if they would have a fine harvest . . . If only Jonas now could come to an arrangement with Ward. He would probably be late . . . And then she thought that she might as well walk over to see Emma, since she was alone anyway, and no sooner had she had the thought than she started to dress, and fifteen minutes later she was on her way across the prairie. She had to take it easy because of the stifling humidity.

When Nyblom and O'Brien came home for dinner they too complained about the heat, and O'Brien was sure it would end in a storm. After they had eaten, he went out to see what it looked like and he discovered a funnel-like cloud in the southwest. That was a bad sign. No sooner had he come in again than it got quite dark. Nyblom had in the meantime told the women that it would be safest to be in the cellar, and they were climbing down when Jim returned. There was just barely room for four people in the little, dark hole under the house. It was not at all a pleasant place to be and Ragna felt as if she were choking from lack of air. But her fear gave her no time to reflect on her immediate circumstances. Nor was she primarily concerned with her own safety, but for Jonas's. Was he safe in town? Had he only not started on his way home? He was always so careless . . .

"Is weather like this really—I mean—er—really dangerous?" she asked. She knew it was a stupid question. Of course it was dangerous; she understood that much. Still, she hoped that the answer would give her a little comfort. Jim was always so optimistic . . .

"It's grateful we should be, if it doesn't hit us," O'Brien replied. This was the only comfort he could give her. She made no further questions but sat close to Emma. They sat like that for about ten more minutes. They could occasionally hear the wind screaming through the air like people in extreme danger. Then all suddenly became silent, and then a pouring rain.

"Sure and the lord has spared us," said O'Brien. "Blessed be the Holy Mither." He began to climb up. The others followed. Ragna realized that the danger had passed but her heart beat violently.

The men ran out in the rain. Ragna and Emma stood at the window. The rain was still pouring down and they couldn't see much, but they did glimpse the outline of the barn and knew that it was still there. Then Ragna began to think about her own property, and the more she thought about it, the more she became reconciled to the possibility that it had been hit. But she was prepared to accept it. Her fear for Jonas was another matter.

Her premonition was soon to be confirmed. O'Brien and Nyblom returned in an hour and told her as gently as they could about what had happened. The tornado had come from the southwest. It had touched down on the northwest corner of the Glombekken farm and then gone straight to the center of Jonas and Ragna's farm, whereupon it had continued in a northwesterly direction over the southern corner of the Flasmo farm and then on to the northwestern part of the O'Brien farm before it finally spent its last force on the next quarter section that was still unsettled and uncultivated. The damage done to the O'Brien farm was not inconsiderable. Much of their wheat that had been in shock on the field where the tornado had passed by had disappeared without a trace. But this wouldn't hurt them so much, Jim thought, since they had much left elsewhere. On the Flasmo farm, the tornado had cleared off a nice field of wheat where they had just begun cutting, but the damage was limited and shouldn't cause any serious problems. On the Olsen farm, however, just about everything of value had been destroyed. The house was gone, the barn was gone, and there were only two thin stripes of wheat left on either side of the passage of the storm. Boards and planks and broken furniture were spread all over, and some of it had settled on the Flasmo and O'Brien farms. Nyblom and O'Brien still didn't have a full overview of the damage, but they had seen enough to know that Jonas and Ragna in reality had lost all they owned except the land itself. And O'Brien was now trying to explain this to her. He found her calm remarkable.

"If I only knew that Jonas was safe, I wouldn't give a ding about the rest," she assured them.

"Sure, and he is safe," Jim comforted her. These local twisters were serious where they hit, he said, but they only destroyed limited spots. Emma added that she could trust her father in this since he had lived in all parts of the world and experienced all kinds of weather.

When the rain stopped soon after, they all went to have a look at the damage. It was a sad sight and even though she had promised herself that she would remain calm, Ragna was overwhelmed and sat down and cried on the ruins of their destroyed home. There had, after all, been so many happy hopes, so many a dear dream that she had carried in her heart and had taken out to comfort herself with in difficult times, which now, in this hour of evil, had been taken from her—perhaps forever. It seemed to her that what she had now lost was what connected her with the coming years—the bridge to an unknown future. But then she again remembered Jonas . . .

When she got up, she saw an object wedged in the ruins of the foundation of the barn. When she looked more closely she discovered that it was one of her drawers, and to her surprise she saw that its contents were untouched, even though they were soaked by the rain. It came to her that even nature when it is at its angriest may still feel sympathy and compassion, for this was the drawer where she had kept the baby clothes. The little cardboard box lay there just as she had left it when she went to see Emma that morning . . .

The afternoon and evening were filled with restlessness and anxiety. In spite of O'Brien's assurance that all was well with Jonas, she was unable to suppress her fear that something had happened to him. When he failed to turn up at bedtime, she was sure that he had had an accident. Nyblom had offered to drive out to meet him, but O'Brien was convinced that there had been even more rain out on the prairie and that this was the obvious reason why Jonas hadn't come home. He was surely still in Normanville, and Nyblom merely ran the risk of getting stuck somewhere on the soaked roads, said his father-in-law.

"Sure, and he'll show up in the morning," Emma said to Ragna.

She had no answer to this. It was a long and miserable night, the longest and most terrible night she had experienced. Emma couldn't get her to go to bed. She couldn't sleep anyway. She prayed, and she could have sobbed, but she had to control herself so she wouldn't wake up the others. Emma had insisted on sitting up with her, but Ragna had begged her to go to bed, and Emma had fallen asleep at once.

Finally it was morning and a day of sunshine and peace on the prairie. O'Brien repeated his words of comfort at the breakfast table: "Sure, and he'll show up before long." But when he saw Ragna's tear-reddened eyes he realized that she no longer believed him. So they decided that Nyblom should drive out to meet Jonas.

"I'll fetch him safe and sound," were his last words to her as he got up on the wagon seat and drove off.

She spent the morning at the window or out on the porch with her eyes constantly trained on the road. Around eleven she saw two teams on the road just where it turned to the south at the east end of Jorshaugs'. That gave her hope. Shortly after she saw them turn in on the road to the O'Brien farm. And now she saw Jonas. Her prayers had been heard . . .

"Thank God that we have each other!" she exclaimed as she threw herself around his neck when he got down from the wagon.

Nyblom had told him everything. Jonas had felt it as a heavy blow. Now he might as well sell the land to Ward. But he had Ragna . . . What if the Lord had taken her as well? He embraced her . . .

———

Jorshaug could later report that few were at the caucus. The roads were bad after the rain and some had suffered damage from the *tornadoen*. He had come late. By that time Glombekken and Ericksen had already been elected delegates. He had tried to have them instructed to vote for Mrs. O'Brien, but the objection had been that it was quite unnecessary. Trulsen had said that as far as he knew, no one had imagined the possibility that the delegates from *Groven* would vote for anyone but her at the convention. But just to make sure, he would ask what Glombekken wanted to say. His answer was that so long as there was a possibility to have Mrs. O'Brien nominated, both he and Ericksen would of course give her their support, but should it appear that she was without chances, then they would have to have full freedom to support another candidate. That was good political sense, he said. And that was it. Jorshaug had heard that the day before the caucus Ward had given Vellesen $500 for the building fund for the new congregation. Flasmo remarked, "Well, it certainly all adds up! Ward and Vellesen and the new congregation, yes, and then Glombekken as delegate! I'm not exactly a mathematician but I can at least add two and two and this should make exactly four, if it doesn't actually add up to five."

"*Gudnes, jes!*" Jonas sighed. "Bad luck seldom comes to visit alone."

25.

After the destruction of their farm, Jonas and Ragna again sought shelter at the O'Briens'. It was like beginning all over again. Jonas was especially affected by the destruction of their property. This was the way things always were with him . . . Getting started was no problem. Mostly things went better than he had expected. It had been like that in Minneapolis, and this is the way it was here. It could seem that he was lucky in all he did. But then something *hæpna* . . . And something always had to *hæpne* the moment he felt he had solid ground under his feet. *Gudnes,* to be born with such a fate . . . He almost lost his will to start over again when he thought about it. It didn't help him much to have the pure doctrine . . . Imagine! Even Glombekken had gone *skotfri*. He couldn't understand it . . .

Ragna appeared to be less touched by the calamity. She too felt the blow, but at least she didn't complain. And with Jonas so depressed, she realized the importance of not giving in to worry and anxiety. Now, as when misfortune had struck him in Minneapolis, he needed her support. They at least had the farm and that was after all the essential thing. And when all came to all, it wasn't so sure that what had happened had been such a calamity. It could be that it turned out to be for the best. Jonas merely laughed and said it was so like a woman to reason in this manner.

———

The day before the county convention, Jonas and Ragna went to Normanville to make some purchases and to decide on the farm deal. Now no power in the world could convince Jonas that it didn't make good sense to sell. Ragna was still in doubt. She didn't like the idea of drifting before the first and best wind. And here they had all their memories of their first home. But for Jonas these memories were bitter. He wanted to get away, especially when they could sell at such a good price . . . Finally she gave in when he convinced her that there was no one who would take their mortgage. This was actually a dodge he thought of to bring her objections to an end, since he was sure Torgersen would lend him the money he needed to pay Ward. He sensed that he wasn't entirely open with her, but he comforted himself, as he used to, that *bisnes* is *bisnes* and that women—in spite of their many advantages—did not have the ability to *risne streit* in such matters.

As usual when they were in town, the first thing Ragna did was to visit Mrs. O'Brien. In the meantime, Jonas would discuss the deal with Ward, and then she could look over the papers and sign them in the afternoon if she found them to be in order. In their conversation, Ragna and Mrs. O'Brien also touched upon the next day's convention, and Mrs. O'Brien said there was little hope for her nomination. Ward was against her, and she had heard that he and his men were in full control of the caucuses. Ragna thought it would be terribly unfair if Mrs. O'Brien was denied the nomination. But Ward also had the mortgage on the O'Brien farm and he might not stop at taking her job from her. Mrs. O'Brien, however, seemed to take it rather philosophically. She admitted that she didn't like to be pushed aside, but if there was nothing to be done about it, then she would have to accept it.

At dinnertime, Jonas and Ragna met Floen at the hotel and he told them that the *tornadoen* in *Groven* and the heavy rain in other places had taken away the last hope of getting Mrs. O'Brien nominated. There had been awful weather all over the county but Ward's men had defied both the rain and the bad roads. There could no longer be any doubt that Ward's son-in-law, Andrews, would get the nomination, the lawyer said.

Jonas had met with Ward and he told Ragna that all seemed to be in order. The banker hadn't changed his offer because of the *tornadoen*. Jonas had signed the documents and she could do it in the afternoon while he met with Sam Lindermann, who had offered to sell him two quarters of section 13 on the West Prairie if he wanted to buy land again. Jonas didn't think it likely that he would make a deal, but it couldn't do any harm to find out what price Lindermann was asking. Ragna, who still had her doubts about moving to a town and starting a business, encouraged him to buy.

"Well, you know that we'll never farm it ourselves," he said, "but if the price isn't too high we could perhaps hold on to it until the price of land rises."

In the meantime Ragna had thought of something else. For some reason Ward was set on buying their farm. Why not set yet another condition for the sale? She was thinking of Mrs. O'Brien's nomination. Jonas didn't think this was a smart idea at all. To mix these two things together at this point would spoil the entire deal, he said. But she was stubborn.

"Well," he said finally, "I won't have anything to do with it. *O'kors,* if you absolutely want to squander it all away now that the deal is almost concluded, I suppose I can't keep you from doing it." With that they parted. He went over to Lindermann's office and she headed for Ward's bank.

At the bank she was shown the way to Elihu's private office, where she was met with studied politeness by the banker and offered a seat in one of the two magnificent leather armchairs. It was the finest office she had seen. Ward looked at her with interest. She noticed it and remembered that some of the women in *Groven* had told her that Elihu couldn't be relied on in his relations with women. Indeed, rumor had it that he was so appreciative of the Scandinavian maids in his own home that they were seldom there long.

"I take it you've come to sign that deed," he began.

"That's why I'm here, Mr. Ward," she replied. "But there is one more condition I must insist on before I sign it." This answer surprised him.

"And what is your condition, Mrs. Olsen?" he asked. His voice was almost soft as his eager gray eyes feasted on her well-formed figure and her nice and regular features. She sat before him, well-built, healthy-colored, and beautiful and she answered him in a calm but firm voice. She had been told, she said, that Mrs. O'Brien's nomination depended on him.

"And what, may I ask, has that to do with the matter in hand?" he asked with a pleasant smile.

"Only this," she replied, "that unless you agree to have her nominated, I'll not sign the deed." There was a touch of command in her voice that surprised Ward. Under normal circumstances he wouldn't have dreamed of taking such a condition seriously. He wasn't used to doing business with women. The West was a male domain. That may also have been a reason why its business ethics were of a rather robust nature. The few times he had *bisnes* transactions with women, he had his way. They were not so used to practical affairs, and with a little diplomatic finesse it was an easy matter to convince them. But the impression he already had of this young farmer's wife had convinced him that she, at least in some respects, was different from other women he had met in business. She appeared to be so damned independent. It was quite irritating! But he was fascinated by her appearance. If it hadn't been for this interest, he would have dismissed it with a joke. And he had to have that farm!

"But my dear Mrs. Olsen," he said after he had thought about it for a while. "This is business and that other affair is politics."

"It so happens that Mrs. O'Brien's interest is part of my business in this matter," she replied, unruffled.

"But you surely can see . . ."

"In this I can see only a single point, Mr. Ward. That's the reputation of women, anyhow." The smile that accompanied these words could have restrained a man less given to the pursuit of women than Ward, from pursuing the matter further. "Of course, if you don't want the land . . . ," she added, and collected her things.

"Oh, yes, I want the land," he hurried to say. "But supposing the matter could be discussed at all, how do you know I could grant your wish?"

"That's up to you, Mr. Ward." He got up and paced the floor as if in deep thought. Then he stopped in front of her. "This request of yours, being entirely outside the deal, nobody would consider, of course, for one minute, without some sort of extra compensation," he said carefully.

"Then I won't sign."

"You are an insistent young lady, Mrs. Olsen."

"One has to be when dealing with men, and knowing them like I do." Ward sat down again. "I hear the O'Briens have lost some of their crop too, in the tornado," he remarked after a while. "Of course, I'm sorry for them."

"I'm not appealing to your sympathies, Mr. Ward."

"Why not?"

"You have a reputation of having none." Ragna smiled again as she said this. She sensed that she may have gone a little too far and a smile would hopefully sugar her sting.

"You're a clever woman, Mrs. Olsen," he said, "and, I dare say, an attractive one. I should love to grant any wish that you may have . . ." As he spoke, he had gotten up from his chair and stood before her again. Again she felt his desire, and to disarm him she looked him straight in his face. "Now, you understand . . . ," he continued, as he lay his hand on her arm. She shook it off impatiently and rose quickly. At that he laid his arm around her waist. She freed herself with a vigorous move. "You pig," she cried, "how dare you?"

With a sudden expression of wounded dignity he stepped back. "You're spoiling your own case, my dear lady," he said.

"I'll soon show you whose case has been spoiled," she exclaimed angrily.

"Well, how are you going about it?" he asked derisively.

"Don't I have a husband?"

"Oh, yes, what about your husband?"

"He'll naturally soon know of your disgraceful conduct."

"And then?"

"There'll be a funeral."

"Oh, I see!" Still in a derisive voice.

"And what'll happen to your husband after the funeral?" This with a forced smile.

"Nothing much, only that your savage reputation and my testimony will clear him, and the population of Garfield County will thank him for ridding it of such a dog as you are." He sat a while in thought. Then he suddenly said:

"I'll see to it that Mrs. O'Brien is nominated, and—I—beg your pardon—I forgot myself. You promise not to mention this matter to a living soul, and sign the deed, and tomorow your friend will be made the nominee for superintendent. Is that a fair bargain?" He laid the deed on the tale and held out a pen.

"I'll sign the deed when she has been nominated," Ragna replied. "As to the other condition, I don't know if I'll promise anything." She remained standing, thinking about it. It seemed to her that it wouldn't be right of her not to say anything to Jonas about Ward's shameful behavior. On the other hand, she feared that if she told him about it, he would do just as she had said. Jonas would at least seek revenge. And she wasn't so sure that it would be so easy not to have him prosecuted. Ward was of a wealthy and influential family . . .

"You are far from deserving any consideration at all," she finally answered him. "However, I shall not tell." She was at the door. "When Mrs. O'Brien has been nominated tomorrow, I'll be here to sign the deed."

He stood in thought, looking after her as she disappeared through the door. "Some woman," he mumbled. "Some woman, by God!"

26.

"Well," said Jonas when he returned to the hotel and found Ragna already there. "So you signed the deed?"

"No," she replied, "I won't sign until he has fulfilled his part of the agreement."

"What agreement?"

"Oh, the one about Mrs. O'Brien's nomination, you know."

"*Gudnes,* did you really set that as a condition?"

"Of course, why not?"

"But he'll never accept it! You should know that."

"He has promised!"

"Promised?"

"Yes."

"And how in the world did you get him to promise such a thing?"

"I merely refused to sign if he wouldn't do it, and then he finally gave in and promised. Don't you see that he won't let that land slip out of his hands?"

"I can see that well enough, but I still don't understand . . ."

"Oh, you men aren't all that *smarte* as you like to believe! I simply threatened not to sign. That's all."

"But he'll never keep his promise. You can be sure of that!"

"Well, we'll see! I told him that we would stay in town till after the convention tomorrow and that we would come to the bank after the nominations. But let's not say a word to Mrs. O'Brien or anyone else about this. I don't want her to believe that she owes her nomination to us."

"But my dear, why not?" Jonas looked at her in surprise. What kind of a notion was this? If it at all would be possible—and he still had his doubts—why shouldn't she take the *krediten* for it? That would have been his first thought. Why do other people a good turn and then let them believe that they owed it all to others?

"The O'Briens have done so much for others," she replied, "for us as well, and you have never heard them go around boasting about it. And I'm anxious to hear how people will try to explain that Ward in the last minute threw his influence behind Mrs. O'Brien."

"So it's for curiosity's sake that you want to keep it secret then?"

"Yes, you may put it that way if you wish."

"*Gudnes!*"

⎯⎯◆⎯⎯

The next day, the weather was beautiful. Jonas and Ragna were up early after yet another sleepless night at Nicolai Johnson's Scandinavian Hotel. The bedbugs appeared to be well fed and more active than when they first had met them and they appeared to be so numerous that resistance was hopeless. In the saloon below, the disturbance was of another nature: a group of migratory harvest laborers sent out by an employment office in Minneapolis, and a lively crowd of delegates to the county convention who had arrived on the last train and had to make use of their opportunity to enjoy urban life while they were in town. Their opportunity to do so was greatly enhanced by the free drinks provided by the breweries and the candidates for office. Garfield County had been placed on the political map. Why be a convention delegate if one didn't accept what was offered?

As Jonas and Ragna were taking a morning walk down the main street they met Sefanias Thompson and his political followers from Arrowtown. They had evidently had a sleepless night and looked tired even though they came from Ole Dampen's saloon, where they no doubt had taken in some refreshments. As becomes a political leader, Seff seemed more awake and intelligent than the others. Jonas stopped and asked him what he thought would happen at the convention. He replied that he was convinced things would go well for him, but aside from that he had no information. It all depended on the delegates. One could never foresee what they would decide to do in a Democratic *kontry*. And what did he think of Mrs. O'Brien's prospects? Well, sir, the way the matter now stood, he thought she would be nominated. When he left home he had seen no hope for her, but when he came to town last night he had been told that Andrews had withdrawn, so if there was no other candidate at the last moment he was almost sure that she would win the nomination. But, as he had said, in a Democratic *kontry* you could never say for sure until it was over.

"There you are!" said Ragna as they continued on their way.

"It beats me," said Jonas. He was still unable to see how this could make sense. "And the way I have *seisa* up this Ward fellow, I'm sure he will have you fooled in the end."

"You'll see," was all she said.

And he did see. When the delegates returned to the hotel around one o'clock, after a long and tiring session, they reported that Mrs. O'Brien had been unanimously nominated. After they had their dinner they walked over to the courthouse and congratulated her. She was of course happy with the results, since a nomination in reality meant that she was elected, but she couldn't understand how it had happened. Strangely, Ward had not opposed her. Indeed, it actually seemed that her nomination was due to his support. Who could explain such a turnabout? Jonas and Ragna agreed that it seemed strange, but the convention had only done what it should have done, so there was no reason to complain.

A half hour later, when Jonas and Ragna had placed themselves in the massive leather chairs in Ward's office, the banker asked, turning to Ragna with a smile, "Well, Mrs. Olsen, have I delivered the goods?"

"You have, Mr. Ward, and I'm here to sign that deed," she replied coldly.

After the deed had been signed and they had gone into the bank lobby, they met Jim O'Brien waiting for his turn to enter Ward's office. He had had a drink or two, perhaps even three, by Jonas's judgment, and he seemed pleased with himself and the world. "I've come to pay that mortgage, begorrah," he said to Ward, who couldn't disguise his surprise.

"You always were a capital joker, Jim," he laughed.

"Faith, and there is no joke about it," Jim replied, as he pulled out a roll of bills from his pocket. "It's paying that mortgage I'm doing, and the sooner you dig up the darned thing, the sooner you'll get your money, begorrah."

Later that day, Jonas and Ragna found out that Torgersen had taken over the loan on the O'Brien farm. He had been all the more willing to do so now that Mrs. O'Brien had been nominated. If possible, this was an even harder blow for Ward than being forced to give the nomination to Mrs. O'Brien. But he could still congratulate himself on being the owner of the Jonas Olsen farm, which he, for his own reasons, had worked on for so long.

Jonas and Ragna walked around with a strange feeling as they did their errands. Now that they had sold their farm they were quieter and more pensive than usual. Even Jonas had at one time had quite a few proud expectations of this piece of land that they had thought of as their future home. And now they no longer had a home in O'Brien's Grove, or any other place for that matter. They had no immediate plans. Jonas was of course set on using their money to establish himself in business in one of the small towns in the region and he had just mentioned it to Ragna again. But she was no more enthusiastic about this now than she had been, and she tried to convince him that since they at least had a wagon and a team of horses, it would be better to get themselves a new piece of land. So in order to please her, rather than for any other reason, he had asked Lindermann about his price for land in section 13. But Lindermann had demanded an impossible $25 per acre. Jonas had more or less promised to drop in again in the afternoon, but he now saw no reason why he should have pointless discussions with this Swede about something that would never lead to anything anyhow. Ragna, however, said one could never know. Perhaps Lindermann would let his land go at a lower price. It would be grand to have a really big farm, she said. So, the result was that they decided to visit the Swede's office. It couldn't do any harm . . .

Jonas started off in his own way. They had decided not to buy land again, he told Lindermann. There were so many other things they could do, he said. Thanks, but no, there was no reason for them to sit. There was no purpose in staying, and it was already late in the afternoon and they would have to get home. It made no sense to farm if you had to pay so much for land that was so far from the market, especially considering the current prices for wheat. They had just dropped in to let him know.

"Had the price only been somewhat reasonable," said Ragna.

"Twenty-five is dirt cheap," Lindermann replied, "but we can always agree on a price if you want to do business."

"No, we can't possibly do it now," said Jonas. "I have *deseidet* to enter into *bisnes* so I'll need the money I have."

"*Ho'* much would you say is a *fär* price if you were to buy?" asked the Swede.

"Fifteen dollars. Not a cent more."

"You must be *kræsi*."

"Not that I know of," Jonas replied. The Swede thought it over. After a while he said, "If you'll take the whole section, I'll *mäka* it twenty-three."

In fact, Lindermann had great difficulties in holding on to this land since he had used all his ready money to acquire it, and in addition he had to borrow some from Torgersen at a high interest. Moreover, his first installment on a loan from Ward was due in four months. Business had been slow lately and he feared that he might have to return the section to Ward.

Jonas replied that in no way could he get involved in so big a deal.

"And certainly not at that price," Ragna added in a low voice. She was afraid of interfering since she knew that Jonas didn't like it, but she also feared that the negotiations might run aground.

Finally the Swede was able to get them to sit down. He would rather sell the entire section, he said, and he would let it go at $20 an acre but not a penny less. Well, then they would just have to let it be, said Jonas.

He could pay $15 or perhaps $16 at the very most, but not a cent more. Now the negotiations really got started, and the more they kept at it, the more Jonas tried to convince Lindermann that $20 was an unconscionable price. The Swede wanted to know whether he had sold his own land for less, but Jonas wouldn't say anything about that. That had been an extraordinary deal, he said, and there were other items involved than the land itself. A good portion of it had been broken, and it was far better land. Every acre of the land he had sold to Ward could be cultivated, but on section 13 about one-fourth couldn't be used for anything but pasture, and not very good pasture at that.

As Ragna sat there listening to all these arguments going back and forth, she had to laugh to herself. To her, Jonas had said that section 13 was excellent land. But when he had an occasion to talk *bisnes* he was in his right element and there was no end to the things he might say. Ragna witnessed his transformation with concern, but it also pleased her to see how smart he was and that he could hold his own against one of the shrewdest landsharks in the area, for that's what people said about Lindermann. Finally Jonas got up. "But we've been sitting here and wasting a *bisi* man's time to no purpose. I wouldn't buy that section for more than $16 an acre, and even then I would think twice about it."

"You are impossible, Mr. Olsen!" said the Swede. "Would you consider a deal if I set the price at nineteen and gave you a ten-day option?"

Jonas looked at Ragna. "A ten-day option?" she said. "Let me see— that would mean that we may buy it or leave it be within ten days?"

"Exactly," the Swede replied.

"*Mæk'it en* option for eighteen," said Jonas. "You won't get a tenth of a penny more from me and I doubt that I would make use of an option at that price." Lindermann had to reconsider. A few months ago he had bought section 13 from Ward for $17 per acre. If he now sold it for $18 he would have a slim profit after he had paid interest on his loan, but at least he wouldn't have lost on the deal. He worked out that he would have about $400 in the end. Not much, but more than nothing . . .

"It's not much of a price," he finally said, "but since you'll be taking the entire section . . ."

Jonas reached down into his pocket. How much did he want in cash for the option? The Swede said that $50 would do it. After the money had been paid and the papers done and signed, they took his farewell and left. Then to the post office and then home.

27.

Now Jonas and Ragna felt more at home with the O'Briens than when they first took in with them. Everything had become so different after their relations with the Nybloms had been settled, and all four did their best to cultivate their friendship. For the two women it was a source of much pleasure that their husbands had become so intimate. After their visit to town, Jonas could think of little else but his option on section 13. The question was discussed back and forth every evening.

O'Brien completed his threshing in two days. This year the farmers in *Groven* did their threshing earlier than usual. Axel Nykvist, who owned the threshing *riggen,* had come early, and since the harvesting was done in *Groven* he had decided to start here. Neither Jonas nor Ragna had seen a threshing crew in operation before. There was much more stir and bustle than usual the two days it lasted, and this made for a refreshing contrast with the uninterrupted stillness of everyday life on the prairie. The settlers joined forces and all the neighbors, with the exception of Glombekken, came to take part in the O'Brien threshing. It was hard work and it had to be done quickly. By compensation, their meals were regular feasts. The very best the house had to offer wasn't too good for the threshers, and Ragna and Emma and Mrs. Flasmo, who had come over to help them, were on their feet from early morning till late at night as long as it lasted. But then all were agreed that this year the food at O'Brien's surpassed that of all the other farms with the exception of Flasmo's, where Mrs. Flasmo had the reputation of being a great cook and a provider of wonderful food.

After he had done with his harvesting, O'Brien had taken his team and a wagonload of wheat to Normanville, and said that they shouldn't expect him back for a few days. Before leaving he had advised Jonas to buy section 13. The soil was excellent and the price was low. Indeed, he said, the only way to live an independent life was to be a farmer. Nyblom agreed. The price of land on the West Prairie would go up in the near future and it would be strange if this much-talked-about railroad didn't eventually turn up. Jonas didn't believe there would ever be a railroad and he regarded both O'Brien and Nyblom as incurable optimists. He was more inclined to set himself up with a little store somewhere.

Ragna wanted to buy the land but didn't want to force the issue now that all was so nice between them. He must do as he saw best. He certainly knew how to look after himself, so she could safely leave it in his hands. But it was already Thursday evening and the option expired at noon on Saturday. So it was time to make a decision. What had most been on Jonas's mind these last days were the *bisnes* opportunities in Arrowtown that Seff Thompson had held out for him. He wanted to take a closer look at the situation, and he and Nyblom decided to go to Arrowtown the next morning. The Swede had a wagonload of wheat he wanted to sell and he had also promised to pay a visit to an old friend, Lars Lindström, who was a builder in Arrowtown and who he hadn't seen in a long while. Jonas agreed with Ragna that if he decided to make use of his option on the land he would take the train from Arrowtown to Normanville in the afternoon and complete the deal. In that case he wouldn't be home until Saturday evening.

In Arrowtown they went to see Lindström, who was setting up a house on one of the side streets. Nyblom then had to go to the *elevatoren* with his wheat and later to have dinner with his Swedish friend. Jonas couldn't join them since he didn't know what plans Thompson might have. Nyblom was going to stable the horses at the hotel and they agreed to meet there at one thirty. Lindström informed them that the local train to Normanville left at two thirty. He wasn't too pleased when he heard that Jonas had business with Seff but he said nothing until Jonas had left. To Nyblom he said that he hoped nothing would come of it. Thompson was not a man to get involved with more than absolutely necessary.

On his way to Seff's office Jonas tried to assess the town he was visiting for the first time. He was struck by the anomaly of four two-story brick buildings on the main street in between the poorly built wooden houses. Their city-like appearance contrasted with everything else that he could see. He was told that they had been built and were owned by Thompson. To Jonas this was a sign of the man's character. He was evidently solid and conservative and yet a forward-looking businessman who did not only build for the moment. Minutes later he stood face to face with the 270-pound imposing figure as Thompson got up and held out a hand that had the appearance of a good-sized ham. Seff remembered their meeting. Had he come to talk about *bisnes* prospects in Arrowtown?

"Well," Thompson said, "Arrowtown is the place for the man who wants to *mæke* money *fæst*. It's the liveliest town west of Crookston." What had Jonas thought of starting out with?

"Oh, that depends on the *circumstancerne*," the young man replied. "*Som'* kind of paying *bisnes*."

"Yes, *o'kors!* How would he like to start up a saloon?" Jonas looked at him in surprise. What did he take him for, anyhow? Jonas Olsen, who had run a large grocery *bisnes* with Lars Simonsen in Minneapolis and had some of the best church people as his customers and had himself been a member of pastor Vangsnes's congregation, start a saloon?

"Nosørri!" he exclaimed. "I don't want anything to do with that kind of *bisnes*. Drink is an abomination and I have been a *totalist* for several years.[44] And I'm a church member."

"O'kors, so am I!" said Thompson. "And I'm of just the same *mein'* about drinking. Theoretically and morally, *saa tu* speak. But we'll always have saloons as long as there are people who will drink, and someone will have to *rønne* them. And those who are set to *rønne* a town know that it can't be done without saloons. If people won't get anything to drink here they will take their wheat to a town where they have saloons and that's where they'll do their other business too. And then it's *gudbey* to our town, sir. See the point?"

"Yes, *o'kors*. I understand all that. *Bisnes* is *bisnes, o'kors!* But to stand behind a saloon bar—no . . ."

"Certainly not, certainly not," Seff seconded him. "I'm of the same mind exactly."

They talked about other possibilities in Arrowtown. Jonas was interested in groceries or clothing but Thompson said there were already so many with that kind of *bisnes*. What about a drugstore? They had a druggist but he was no good. He wouldn't take in a proper range of merchandise. The problem was that you couldn't get a decent drink in the saloons. Moreover, there were many who would not be caught dead in one. A drugstore, however, was a place that everyone could enter with a clean conscience and that meant that you could get the upper and respectable part of the *traden*. But, of course, one would have to have the very best brands of whisky. Jonas couldn't understand what Seff was talking about.

"Whisky?" Jonas exclaimed. "Do they sell whisky in the *drøgstora?*"

"Ahem—yes! All they need is a government *lisence, ju'no!*"

Jonas couldn't see the difference between this and running a saloon, but Thompson explained that you were called *blein'pig*[45] if you ran a drugstore and that the best people in town *pætronæsa* the drugstore so there could be no danger. All you had to do was to make sure you had good relations with the *polisen*. He himself had *æppointa* Olander, the marshal. These business opportunities didn't seem so tempting to Jonas.

The major problem, however, was that Thompson seemed to control everything. The rent in his buildings was unreasonably high. Most businessmen had at some time or other had to borrow money from him in order to keep up their credit with the wholesale houses in bad years, and once he had them in his power he dealt with them as he wished. At least that's how Jonas saw it. And under these circumstances he saw no possibility to become the leading man in this town. But he didn't share these thoughts with Thompson.

After Thompson had introduced him to some businessmen and showed him a couple of his buildings, he invited Jonas home for dinner. As they ate, Thompson received a telegram that seemed to be of great interest. They agreed to meet again in the hotel at about one thirty, and then Seff retired for his usual midday nap while Jonas walked into town alone.

28.

When Jonas and Nyblom went to Arrowtown that morning, Glombekken took off for Normanville with a wagon of wheat. When he came to town at about ten, he met Bert Newell at the driveway up to the *elevatoren*. He had just come from Roxberg's office and stopped for a chat. Torfin could report that some of the farmers in *Groven* took their wheat to the *elevatoren* in Arrowtown. The two towns were in competition and Glombekken found pleasure in revealing that Nyblom and Jonas were taking their trade to Arrowtown. Newell didn't have much to say to this and soon went on his way as Roxberg came out to receive Torfin's wheat. Roxberg was also told that the two men had gone to Arrowtown.

"Too bad about the destruction on the Jonas Olsen farm!" said the wheat merchant. "Strange that the *tornadoen* should take everything they owned."

"Yes, pride goes before a fall, as it is written," Glombekken said. "But he was still lucky who got to sell. It sure *biter* me how a so *smarte* man as Ward could go off and buy that miserable farm. I hear that he got an unusually good price for it too."

"Oh, you don't need to feel sorry for the Ward fellow," Roxberg replied. "I suppose he knows what he's doing." They looked at each other and smiled. After he had been paid for his wheat, Glombekken shambled over to Ole Dampen's saloon.

When Ward came to his bank a few minutes earlier, he discovered a private letter from St. Paul in his mail and went into his office to read it. Hardly two minutes had passed before Walton, the treasurer, and the bookkeeper heard him rage around in there as if there had been a serious accident. When he came rushing out of his office like a madman, the two younger men stood bent over their books and pretended to be hard at work. He ran past them and out into the street without looking right or left as he thundered, "That confounded scoundrel." But no sooner had he placed his foot on the sidewalk than he was transformed into his public self, and when he some minutes later entered Lindermann's office, no one could have imagined that moments earlier he had been in an uncontrollable rage.

The Swede, however, immediately realized that something was up, since Ward was even more polite than usual, was in no hurry, and talked about everything but *bisnes*. He even demonstrated a remarkable interest in Sam's family. Then, as he was at the door and about to leave, he suddenly happened to remember that he had just had a query from a banker in Wisconsin about the possibilities for the purchase of land. Sam might still have section 13 on the West Prairie?

Yes, Sam still had the land, he admitted, but Jonas Olsen in *Groven* had an option on it, and even though he assumed that he wouldn't make use of it since he still hadn't come to him, he could do nothing about it until Saturday noon when the option expired. Lindermann, who now realized he had an opportunity to get even with Elihu, regretted that he had entered an agreement with Jonas, but there was little he could do about that for the time being. Ward was even more upset to learn that Jonas had an option on the land but he did his best not to show it. There was that newcomer again . . . always in his way.

Sam offered him an option from Saturday at twelve if Jonas didn't turn up. He would have to have $25 per acre, said the Swede. Ward immediately objected to such an unreasonable price. Did he think he was born yesterday? Well, Sam suggested, he could do as he wished, but the land now stood at $25. This was Jonas Olsen's price and others were willing to pay it too. Elihu made a rough estimate. This would give Lindermann a profit of $4,000 since he had bought it from him for only $17 per acre. That was a bitter pill to swallow and it didn't help much that he knew he was lying when he said that others were willing to pay the price. But he had no choice. He had to have that land regardless of price.

"You're a hog," he exclaimed, "and most likely I'd lose out on it, should I get the land, but I'll accept your terms." And how much should he pay for the option? Lindermann demanded $200. He would have to make hay when he could, he thought. Elihu protested again. This was unheard of. It was, after all, no better than a lottery ticket since Jonas would probably not let his option expire unused. But Sam wouldn't give in. That was his price, he said, but if Ward found it was too high, he could let it be. They lived in a free *kontry*.

Ward left Lindermann's office some minutes later with the limited option in his pocket. His next visit was to Newell. Ward always sought him up when he had a serious problem. He had often had the experience that it was useful to have a legal yardstick at hand when doing *bisnes* to avoid coming too close to the law. After half an hour with Newell, who shared Torfin Glombekken's report that Nyblom and Jonas were in Arrowtown, Ward rushed over to the railroad station, where he sent off a telegram and gave the operator a five-dollar bill before he left. On his way back to his office he dropped in at Ole Dampen's, where he met Torfin and *trita paa crowden*. He placed two dollars on the bar and said to Ole that he could keep the change. With that, he left as quickly as he had entered. But a few minutes later Glombekken came to the bank and met with Ward in his private office. When he came out, he was in a hurry, and a short time later he was seen driving in the direction of *Groven*. With him was Hans Nerlivika, who worked for Ole Dampen.

<hr />

After he had dinner, Jonas went back to the hotel, where he expected to find Nyblom since it was already a little past one o'clock. On his way he reflected that it would perhaps not be all that bad to get started in some kind of *bisnes* in Arrowtown. He didn't much like the blind-pig thing but he could see that a drugstore could be a profitable business.

He was just about to walk up the stairs to the hotel when he stopped to look closer at a man coming out the door. He looked just like Johan Arndt Lomwiig, but he must be wrong . . . They stood looking at each other like two question marks.

"Good gracious!" Jonas finally exclaimed as he held out his hand.

"If it isn't Jonas Olsen from Kongsvinger, the one-time store-keeper and capitalist and resident boarder at Mrs. Johnson's in North Minneapolis. Well! Well! What a *sørpreis*."

"I am pleased to hear that you have been Americanized and that you have begun to *mixe languagen*!" Jonas laughed.

"Well, if you can't beat them, join them," the other replied.

"Well, anyhow, it's damned good to see you!" said Jonas. "Napoleon tells me that you work for the *H. & B. Roaden*."

"Yes, I do have a position with them, but where have you *rønna krost'* Napoleon?"

"Oh, Napoleon is my neighbor out on the prairie and is at present a Lutheran schoolmaster and preacher. But what are you actually doing out here?"

Lomwiig said that he wasn't really supposed to talk about it, not even mention it, but since they now had met each other in the middle of this dark continent he may as well reveal that he was here as a benefactor. It so happened that his company was now going to go ahead with their planned branch between Stockdale and Normanville. It would be laid over the West Prairie and it had been decided to build a station on section 13.

The impression this made on Jonas may be more easily imagined than described.

"Is this true?" he asked. He grasped the other's arm nervously.

"True? Of course it's true," Lomwiig replied. "Work will begin in early spring. There will be a town in section 13, one of these two-by-four contraptions like the other places you call towns out here. And tomorrow I'll be going to Normanville to negotiate with the owner of the land, a certain Lindermann. We'll have to have acceptable arrangements for the station and the yards and such things, you see. You have a farm around here, don't you?"

"I've sold the farm," Jonas replied, "but I may buy another one." Lomwiig's wagon was waiting. He promised he would visit Jonas and Ragna at the O'Briens' if he could, and he walked down the stairs to the *livery-teamet* and drove off on the road to *Groven*.

29.

Nyblom returned to the hotel just after Lomwiig had left, and Jonas told him what he knew about the railroad and section 13. Nyblom wouldn't believe him.

"Have you been drinking?" he asked, laughing.

"Not that I know of. If I'm drunk then it must be of fresh air."

They finally agreed that Nyblom should leave for home immediately and that Jonas should go to Normanville and make good on his option.

But Seff turned up a few minutes later and invited them to come to his farm just a few miles out of town. People came from afar to see the farm, he said, and since they were here anyway they would probably find it worth their while to inspect it. Jonas and Nyblom had both heard of Thompson's model farm as one of the county's greatest sights. Nyblom, who recently had become more interested in agriculture, said that he would be pleased to accept the invitation even if it meant that he would be a little later getting home. Jonas didn't really mind going along either, but he had some important business matters to tend to in Normanville the next morning, he said, so he would have to take the afternoon train and couldn't possibly accept the invitation. But Seff told him that he would be in Normanville in plenty of time for all kinds of *bisnes* the next morning even if he took the evening *trænet*. That would give them time to talk more about business opportunities in Arrowtown.

"Well, I have *konsidera* the matter pretty closely since I left you," Jonas replied, "and it's quite possible that I'll settle here, but I can't *deceide* until have talked it over with this man in Normanville. And I'll also have to confer with my wife."

"Yes, *o'kors*," Thompson agreed. But there was still no reason not to come to the farm. It wouldn't take them more than a couple of hours, three at the most, and the evening train didn't go until ten o'clock. So in the end Jonas decided to go. But first Thompson wanted to show them more of the town. They looked at a few more of Seff's business buildings and met a Norwegian doctor, Dr. Hornemann, who Seff had thought could possibly be persuaded to join them.

"He is good *kompani*," he had assured them. And he turned out to be right. The doctor, whom they knew by name, was a friendly and jovial man in his early forties. He had emigrated from Solør as a boy, and since Jonas was from Kongsvinger they were virtually neighbors from Norway.[46] But the doctor was unable to join them. He had half a dozen patients waiting. Thompson wanted to take them to visit Söderberg as well so that Jonas could have a look at the building, which would serve just as well for a store as for a saloon. But it was already three thirty, so they would have to meet Söderberg after they had returned.

One hour later they drove to the farm. It was one of the most handsome agricultural properties that Jonas and Nyblom had seen. Their host showed them everything. They were most impressed by the cow barn and dairy but they also admired the horses and other animals. It was very interesting but both Jonas and Nyblom began to feel that it was getting late. Finally Thompson invited them to the large farmhouse for supper. Before eating, they must have something for their dry throats, Seff said, and he fetched them a large pitcher of beer that was brewed on the farm. Nyblom was happy to accept a glass but when Jonas excused himself, it was quite obvious that their host didn't like it. Nyblom became quite talkative after his first glass and after he had had a few more, Jonas could see that he had problems keeping his balance as they went into the dining room. Happily, the Swede had an excellent appetite and when he got up from the table he seemed to be doing well.

It was almost nine thirty when they got back to Arrowtown. Thompson stopped outside the depot and got off, saying that he would check to see if the train was delayed. A moment later he was back and told them that it wouldn't be in until twenty minutes past ten. That gave them almost an hour and they would have plenty of time to drop in at Söderberg's and have a look at the building. Nyblom parted company with them outside the hotel since he had to get on his way home. It would take him most of the night to drive to *Groven* and his conscience was beginning to trouble him. The women would be anxious . . .

But at the hotel Lindström was waiting to see him. There was something he had to tell him. He had happened to notice the town marshal, Olander, in a conversation with a town brawler named Wladimir Syversen, who, when he wasn't in jail, trawled the saloons looking for fights and drinking what people would buy him. It was strange to see Olander talking with Syversen for any other reason than to arrest him. Lindström hadn't heard what they said but later he had seen Syversen show off by placing a whole dollar on the bar in Söderberg's saloon. Since the man never did any respectable work, this was alone a sign that he was into something shady. It had also caught his attention that Söderberg and Syversen were whispering together and that the name Jonas Olsen was mentioned. Lindström was convinced that something underhanded was being planned. This was what he had wanted to tell Nyblom, who at first couldn't understand what reason there could be for a conspiracy against Jonas. But when he had told about the day's happenings, what Jonas had learned from Lomwiig and his option on section 13, Lindström pointed out the obvious connection.

"I *bettar* that someone is planning to *deteina* Mr. Olsen so that he won't be able to *jusa* his option," he said. Now Nyblom realized why Seff had been so eager to have Jonas spend so much time on his farm. The only thing he couldn't understand was why Seff had brought them back to town before the time for the train departure. Lindström could explain that too. Seff was making it appear that he was uninvolved. But now they would have to think of something and fast. Lindström suggested that Nyblom go over to Söderberg at once and try to get Jonas out of there before the train came. In case this failed, Lindström would hurry home and harness his two yearlings to his light *buggyen* and tie them up down by the *elevatoren*. Jonas's heavy workhorses and the huge lumber wagon wouldn't be of much use in an emergency. But with his light *teamet* they should be able to get out of town fast and *bita dem tu' it*.

"On the right-hand side of the *elevatoren*," Lindström whispered as they parted outside the hotel. "And in a little while I'll join you at Söderberg's if you haven't already *skippat* from there."

After he had introduced him to Söderberg, Thompson showed Jonas the saloon and explained how excellent a building it was for all kinds of *bisnes*. Then they had to have something to drink. Thompson had a good shot of whisky for himself and Jonas, who smoked as little as he drank, pocketed a cigar. There were three other men in the saloon. Thompson hadn't introduced him to any of them, so he couldn't know that the powerful fellow who was playing pool was Olander, the marshal, and that he was playing with a man named Arvid Anderson, who worked as a bartender at whichever of the town's four saloons needed him. At the far end of the bar was a shabby-looking fellow that Jonas heard was Norwegian when he spoke to Söderberg.

No sooner had Thompson had his drink than he suddenly remembered that he had an errand at the *drugstoret* and had to get there before they closed. He would be back in a moment and Jonas could wait for him here. Jonas didn't like this at all. The whole saloon idea had become disgusting to him. But he had no choice. If he left, Thompson would think him a real crank. So to be friendly, Jonas ordered a glass of soda water.

"*Vot's dat?*" asked the saloonkeeper. He didn't know if he had heard right.

"Pop," Jonas repeated. Söderberg stared at him, apparently offended.

"Pop!" he exclaimed. "Do you think I *rønnar* a pop factory or a Ladies Aid business?"

The shabby person from the other end of the bar suddenly appeared at Jonas's side. It was Syversen. "If the gen'l'man'll set'm up I would apprec'ate a whisky dram," he said. Jonas looked at him. "And what's the gen'l'man taking?" the shabby one persisted.

"I don't drink," said Jonas, irritated, "and I don't set them up either."

"Oh, you don't, don't ya?" Syversen sneered. "Where does this gen'l'man come from since he believes he's too good to have an honest drink with a countryman?"

"None of your business," Jonas replied with emphasis. The other one took a step closer and was visibly offended. "So all you have to serve up when you meet a Norwegian brother is an insult!" Syversen said.

Söderberg blinked to Olander and Anderson. "*Tak'* one on the house, boys," he said. The two others smiled as they leaned themselves against the bar. The saloonkeeper placed a bottle and glasses before them. Jonas said he was not having any and turned away.

"I'll drink his as well," said Syversen after he had emptied his glass. Söderberg laughed and let him fill it again. He drank and smacked his lips. Then he straightened up, put his hand on Jonas's arm, and said mockingly, "You are *mæbby* a minister?" Jonas brushed his arm away. "Don't touch me, you swine!" Jonas's voice was sharp and commanding.

"What is it you *dærer* to call me?" Syversen exclaimed, waving his fist at Jonas. Jonas was angry and pushed him so that he fell against the bar, where he hit his head and received a few nasty cuts in his face. Jonas was fed up. He was getting out of this place where a decent man couldn't be left in peace. But as he was on his way to the door, Olander took him by the collar.

"You are *'restad* for brawling and attacking an innocent man!" he announced as he opened his coat and showed the star he wore on his chest. At the same moment the whistle of the train approaching the station could be heard. Jonas was horrified when he realized that the train was coming in before it was ten and he tried to pull himself loose.

"*Hare, hare,* don't be *fony*," the marshall warned him and took a better grip on him. Again the whistle was heard. It was close to the depot now. *Gudnes,* thought Jonas, now you've made a mess of it again . . . With a powerful jerk he made Olander let him go and then he tripped him so that he rolled over on the floor. Again he headed for the door but this time he was stopped by Arvid Anderson, whose strong arms held him as in an iron claw. By now Söderberg had come out from behind the bar. Again the train whistle was heard. Jonas was sure he would never get to the depot in time. He still couldn't understand what had happened, but he did sense that his option on section 13 was slipping out of his hands.

As Jonas unsuccessfully kept trying to get out of Arvid's hold and saw the marshal come at him again, the door suddenly opened and Nyblom blew in like a hurricane. Never in his entire life had Jonas been so happy to see anyone as when the Swede came barging in. He knew what Nyblom could do in a situation like this. The Swede immediately surveyed the room and joined the fight without a word. With a powerful blow, he first got Olander on the floor again. Then he attacked Arvid from behind so that both he and Jonas fell down. Jonas got up again, and while Nyblom held on to Arvid, Jonas again ran for the door. But now Syversen was on his feet again and was in his way. But he had had too much to drink and Jonas had no difficulty in pushing him into a corner, where he remained. Now Söderberg had placed his broad back against the door to block Jonas, but he hadn't foreseen that his more prominent than muscular frontal dimensions presented an inviting target, which Jonas boxed with one hand as he protected himself with the other until the corpulent gentleman had to ask for a cease-fire and then got out of the way. As Jonas opened the door he ran right into Lindström, who had come to help them. Nyblom joined them as they heard the departing train whistle as it left the depot.

A few minutes later the dark prairie night enveloped two young men in a buggy pulled by two lively yearlings, which galloped at full speed down the flat and dusty road.

30.

Wisely, Seff Thompson had kept out of the brawl at Söderberg's and was calmly waiting for his henchmen's report. The battle had been carefully planned and it didn't occur to him to doubt the outcome. He was so sure that Jonas was in the town jail that he congratulated himself for having done so well in the first important test of his alliance with Elihu Ward.

But the two men from *Groven* had disappeared into thin air. Olander was sure that they were still in town. Their horses were in the livery stable and he asked Arvid to stand guard there. It wasn't easy for the town marshal to report to Thompson on his total failure. Seff raged. That a marshal with the help of three others couldn't manage to *'reste* a boy, *saa tu* speak, from the prairie was too much. Thompson was sure that they were already far away. It was stupid to assume that Jonas had no other means of conveyance than his team and lumber wagon. Nyblom was a good friend of Lindström and Lindström had of course been involved. This wasn't the first time he had interfered in Seff's business. They were probably on their way to Normanville. He would send a telegram immediately so that the police could meet them there. Olander and Arvid had to go to *Groven* as fast as they could in case they had gone that way. And fifteen minutes later the marshal was on his way, with an order for the arrest of Jonas Olsen in his pocket.

In the meantime Jonas and Nyblom had acquired a considerable lead. They had decided to go direct to *Groven.* The women would have no way of knowing what had happened to them if neither of them came home that night. Moreover, those who were after them would most likely assume that they had gone straight to Normanville. Few words were exchanged between them. Nyblom exclaimed, "This *bitar* everything I have ever *rønnat akros!"*

Jonas was bleeding from a nasty cut on his face from Arvid Anderson's fist, and he had to apply his handkerchief to it all the time. His only comment was, "*Gudnes,* what rascals."

It was two in the morning when they came to *Groven.* They had agreed to stop at Jorshaug's first and borrow his team for their continued journey to Normanville as soon as they had seen to their wives. Lindström's yearlings had had a tough trial and needed rest. When they finally got Jorshaug's attention, he was eager to let them have his *teamet.* It turned out, however, that the horses had been let out of the *pasturet* during the night. They were quite certain who had done it, but they had no time to lose and would have to manage with the horses they had.

Ragna and Emma had been up worrying about what might have happened. When Ragna saw Jonas's bloody face she became even more worried. But Nyblom explained the situation in as few words as possible and said that Jonas had to leave at once. But Ragna would hear nothing of it and immediately began to wash the blood off Jonas's face and clean his wound. She didn't care about the option, she said. Life and health came first. Jonas finally succeeded in getting her to understand that they had a fortune within their reach and that they just couldn't let it slip away. The police in Arrowtown were probably at their heels and if they were caught they would be brought back to Arrrowtown and all would be lost. He wasn't sure when he could get to Normanville even if he left right away. Lindström's horses just couldn't be made to run anymore. But the women insisted that Nyblom should go with him. With this, the two ran out to continue their interrupted flight.

The men who had let Jorshaug's horses out of the *pasturet* had apparently taken off with Lindström's team. The horses were nowhere to be seen. Jonas looked in the direction of Glombekken's and thought dark thoughts of Torfin and Napoleon. As they stood reflecting on their situation, they saw a faint light a good piece down the road. It seemed to be a lantern, and it didn't take them long to conclude that it had to be the men from Arrowtown who had caught up with them. They didn't really know what to do but they decided to hide in the stable and see what came up. They couldn't get anywhere without horses.

After a while Ragna and Emma heard someone knock on the door. When Ragna opened the door she was greeted by Olander, and Arvid was right behind him. They were strangers on their way to Normanville, said the marshal, and they weren't sure of the way. They had seen a light and had come to ask for advice, and since they had been on the road all night they would be grateful for a cup of coffee and some food. Then he excused himself and said that she might not understand Swedish. That was no problem, said Ragna, but she did find it strange that they would come to people at this time of night and expect to be entertained. They could come in, but they were alone on the farm, she said. The men had gone to Arrowtown yesterday and hadn't come home yet. She couldn't understand what had kept them.

Olander and Anderson were now sure that Jonas and Nyblom had gone straight to Normanville. There they would be met by others, so they could now take it easy. Ragna's coffee was good and strong and her sandwiches were delicious. The women were nice and it was much more comfortable indoors than out in the chilly fall night.

Meanwhile Jonas and Nyblom had discovered Olander's team outside the stable, and without exchanging many words they jumped up on the *buggyen* and the next moment the frothing horses were galloping on the road to the Flasmo farm. Their plan was to borrow his *teamet* and use Olander's buggy to get to Normanville. Without bothering to wake him up, they rushed into his *pasturet*. There were no horses there either and Jonas's thoughts again went to Glombekken and Napoleon. They evidently had prominent roles in this drama.

At least they had the Arrowtown horses. How far they could go was another matter, but they would have to take things as they came. It would take some time before Seff's henchmen got their hands on another team and could take after them. But as they were about to turn onto the main road, Jonas suddenly thought of how irresponsible it would be of them to leave Ragna and Emma alone with the two nasty men. You could never know what such people could do. So he decided to go off alone while Nyblom returned home to make sure that nothing happened to the two women.

Meanwhile in Normanville, three men were playing poker in O'Connor's saloon. They had come at eleven the night before and they were still at it at five in the morning. Ward didn't often spend the night in a saloon. But extraordinary situations demand extraordinary precautions. After a hectic day, Ward had received the telegram from Thompson informing him that the bird had flown and that Olander was on his way to *Groven*. Ward and Newell had been prepared for this eventuality and Ward had told Tuttle, the sheriff, to be prepared to meet Jonas and Nyblom on the road from Arrowtown, should they come that way. To be on the safe side, the sheriff and two assistants took the Arrowtown road while Duffy, the deputy sheriff, and another assistant took off for *Groven*.

After these precautions the banker was sure that all roads to Normanville were blocked. Early last night he had thought of the possibility that Lindermann might discover what this was about and see an opportunity in it for himself in helping Jonas in some way so that the deal could be concluded before their contract expired. So Ward had kept a close eye on the Swede, and since poker was one of his weaknesses it hadn't been difficult for Newell to persuade Lindermann to join him and Ward for a game of poker at O'Connors that evening. And the banker had been losing money all night to keep Lindermann happy . . .

31.

O lander and Arvid had enjoyed the coffee and sandwiches. The two women had been nice and obliging and hadn't made the slightest objection when they took up their pocket flasks. Neither Ragna nor Emma would taste the whisky themselves, but when Olander said that they must soon be on their way, Ragna assured them that there was no need to rush as far as they were concerned. Men who traveled at night on unfamiliar roads certainly deserved a good rest. So they remained seated, and since Olander had packed a quart in the bag he had left in the *buggyen,* there was no reason not to enjoy life and take it easy. To begin with, Olander had been on his best behavior, but under the influence of the contents of his flask he began to make remarks that were so obscene that the women realized that their comedy might turn into something less innocent than they had foreseen.

Meanwhile, Nyblom had returned to the farm. He stopped out in the yard to consider the situation and then noticed the clothesline that was stretched from the corner of the farmhouse to a post at the far end of the yard. In a moment he had his pocketknife and was cutting the rope, when he heard the front door open. It was Arvid, who had been told by Olander to feed and water the horses before they returned to Arrowtown. They had been so comfortable that they had entirely forgotten their *teamet.*

When Arvid came out he discovered that the horses were nowhere to be seen. He was so drunk that his mind worked slowly as he speculated on what may have happened. He looked this way and that and couldn't make sense of it. Over on the road he could see someone driving south at full speed, but he had no way of determining who it might be. Nyblom observed him from behind the corner. It was almost five o'clock and quite light.

After a while Arvid turned toward the house. He had decided that he had better report to Olander. But before he had made many steps he felt a noose around his neck, and then a pull on the rope laid him on his back. He saw stars, and then all went dark. When he came to, he discovered that he was trussed up and could hardly move a finger. He was about to call for help when a commanding voice silenced him: "Get up! Be quick now, fool! Get up!"

Arvid was slow in getting on his feet since he didn't have any arms to help him. When Nyblom repeated his order, he accompanied it with a few kicks, which made lying there so unpleasant that Arvid found it best to do as he had been told. He got up and Nyblom led him to the stable, warning him: "You'll be dead if you so much as say a single word . . ."

Arvid seemed to have lost his courage. He let himself be led like a sheep to the stable door and Nyblom pushed him in so he fell on the earth floor. Nyblom then tied his feet as well, locked the door, and left him.

Olander had become more and more obnoxious after Arvid had gone out. He had suggested that Ragna give him a kiss and she had run to the door, trying to get out of his reach. He was just about to follow her when Nyblom suddenly entered the parlor. Without waiting for an explanation he rushed over to the drunk marshal.

"Miserable cur!" he cried as he threw the marshal to the floor. "I'll *fixa* you, just wait!" Whereupon he began to work over him with his hands as well as his boots until Ragna and Emma had to ask him to spare the poor man. They were afraid he would kill him.

"Well, the swine doesn't *deservar* to live," Nyblom declared.

Nyblom had thrown the rest of the clothesline on a chair by the bookshelf and he now turned away from the marshal to complete what he had set out to do. As he passed by Ragna, who stood by the chair with the rope, frightened and anxious about what would now happen, he said, "*Golli,* and this is supposed to be the authorities . . ."

But before he was able to complete the sentence he was interrupted by a sound of something falling to the floor behind him, followed by a scream of pain as his wife came running to him.

Emma had been sitting at the table, worn out and tired after the night's adventures, and from the moment her husband had turned away from Olander to get the rope she had given the uninvited guest on the floor all her attention. When Nyblom had his back to him, she noticed that the marshal quickly moved his hand behind his back, and she grabbed the whisky bottle he had left on the table. When Olander's hand appeared again and she saw he was holding a gun, she resolutely flung the bottle with all her strength at the marshal and hit his arm. Paralyzed, the arm fell to his side and the gun slid out of his hand and down on the floor.

Again Nyblom attacked his countryman and again the women had to beg him to spare his life. Complaining that he hadn't been allowed to complete what he had set out to do some moments earlier, Nyblom took the marshal's gun and looked through his pockets. The only thing he found of interest was the order for the arrest of Jonas Olsen, which he confiscated. Then he calmly began to tie the marshal's hands behind his back without much concern for the law officer's comfort, and Olander finally begged him to loosen the rope a little.

"You'll have to share a room in our hotel with Arvid," Nyblom informed him. Accompanied by Nyblom's scorn and derision, he had no choice but to go along to the "hotel," where the young man completed his project by tying up the marshal's feet as he had with Arvid. "This may not be so fine a *kommedation,*" he said as he was about to leave them, "but it's the best you can expect out here in *farmerkontriet.* Good morning, gentlemen!" Whereupon he locked the door to the stable and went into the house to the two women.

"I'm hungry," he said as he again entered the house, but Emma had already started to cook breakfast. It had been a tough night for them all so they needed a proper meal. But Ragna was unable to eat much. She was nervous and restless, thinking of what might happen to Jonas. Nyblom, however, had planned a rescue operation and when he had told her what he would do and when she heard the strong and resolute and also self-confident young man promise to "see the whole darned business through," she felt reassured. Gust Nyblom was made for situations like this.

One hour later, Nyblom, Flasmo, Jorshaug, Jorshaug's hired man, and the fourteen-year-old Sivert, who had insisted on coming with them, were all in Jorshaug's lumber wagon on their way south to assist Jonas. At dawn, Jorshaug had gone out to look for his horses and had eventually found them far out on the prairie. When Nyblom and Flasmo turned up at six thirty, he had already harnessed his *teamet* to go over to the O'Briens' to find out more about the night's adventures. Mrs. Jorshaug, who had been ready to come with him, was more than happy to cross the prairie on foot with their thirteen-year-old, Lars, who had been persuaded to stay behind and stand guard over the two prisoners in the O'Brien stable. The men had no time to lose because they would just barely be able to get to town before noon.

They weren't very well armed for such an expedition. Flasmo had taken a dung fork, which he had found to be the most suitable weapon to *hønte skonk*[47] with, and he hoped that he would see it planted in Napoleon's behind, or in Glombekken's for that matter, or, even better, in the ass of Mr. Elihu Ward himself, so that he could draw Yankee blood. Nyblom had Olander's gun and Sivert had an axe. Each sat with his own thoughts. The only one to break the silence now and then was Jorshaug, who made remarks that were more striking than they were aesthetically satisfying.

They had been driving south about an hour and Nyblom had just remarked that Jonas was probably safe and sound when the horses gave a sudden start and Jorshaug had to pull in the reins to keep the wagon on the road. Sivert discovered a white cloth on a thistle on the border of a stand of tall weeds along the edge of the road. They stopped and he leaped out to see what it could be. It turned out to be a handkerchief that had scared the horses. Sivert turned it over to Nyblom. It was rather dirty but they could make out the three letters stiched in one of the corners.

"L. N. S.? What in thunder is that supposed to mean?" Nyblom exclaimed.

"I know what it means," said Sivert.

"Oh, sure," said his father.

"The letters *stæn* for Ludvig Napoleon Stomhoff," Sivert continued, trying his best to appear grown-up. Nyblom took an interested look at the handkerchief. "What a head on that boy!" he exclaimed. He got down from the wagon, followed by the others. Flasmo was the first to begin examining the place where the handkerchief had been found. Some of the weeds had been trampled on and broken but it seemed as if attempts had been made to make them stand again. He elbowed his way through the thicket but was stopped by a fence. North along the fence, however, he could see that either people or animals had gone before them. Sivert rushed by him along the path. By now he was entirely caught up in the adventure, and some of the more exciting episodes in the novels by James Fenimore Cooper that his uncle in Chicago had sent him last Christmas were very much present in his mind.[48] Eight or nine yards farther ahead he came upon a ditch dug to lead water away from the road, which here passed through low-lying land. The fall had been unusually dry so there was no indication of water. Instead, Sivert could see that the bottom was covered with weeds that had been pulled up and thrown into the ditch. This had obviously been the work of human hands. His heart was beating from excitement when he suddenly heard a low grunt from the ditch and it seemed to him as if something was moving like a snake or a gopher among the weeds. He shivered.

"Father! Father!" he called out to Jorshaug, who was coming with the others toward the ditch. "There is something alive in the *ditchen!*"

Nyblom was the first to arrive. He pushed aside the weeds that covered the bottom of the ditch and disclosed the figure of a man tied hand and foot and with a bag over his head. In a moment, he had released him and helped him up. It was Jonas, as he had suspected. His mouth was covered by a red kerchief, which explained the inarticulate grunts that Sivert had heard from the ditch.

Jonas told them that he had been stopped and attacked a couple of hours earlier. First a man had run up to the horses and held them. Two others had leaped into the wagon and tied and gagged him almost before he realized what was happening. Since they had immediately pulled the bag over his head, he couldn't be sure who had been the perpetrators. They hadn't hurt him; he was without a scratch. When they showed him the handkerchief, he said that it was just as he had thought. They would have to hurry . . .

32.

When Mr. Walton, the treasurer of Ward's bank, came into his boss's private office that morning, he discovered what had caused Elihu's rage the day before. One of the drawers in Ward's desk was always locked and this was where he kept his private correspondence. But the lock hadn't been a problem for Walton, who was fully informed about the drawer's contents. He had started his career as an apprentice in a mechanical workshop and he could easily pick an old-fashioned lock. As he had expected, the explanation of yesterday's explosion was in the most recent letter from Warren.

Ward's friend and co-conspirator wrote that the railroad project had developed in rather unpleasant ways. Lyman, the director of the company, had proved to be a lot cleverer than they had thought. He had from the very beginning been aware of their conspiracy and had kept them in the dark in order to get his revenge on Ward for some unknown reason. Warren didn't know what had happened between the two, but Walton knew it was all because of that land deal in Normanville several years ago when Lyman had been so thoroughly swindled. When the final decision on the branch was to be made, Warren wrote, it turned out that the projected line across the East Prairie had never been an alternative. At his first meeting with the engineers, Lyman had decided that the branch should go across the West Prairie, with a depot on section 13. When Lyman had told Warren that they had changed their minds and that the branch line would go through O'Brien's Grove, this had been done to misinform Ward. The writer hadn't known about any of this until the day before when his boss had taken him aside and told him that he had been watched carefully and that they had no further need of his services. He saw no way of supporting his large family through the winter but hoped that Ward would prove generous and help him since he was the one who had encouraged him along a road that had ended in misery. He would soon be to Normanville. "And then," his letter concluded, "your reputation in your locality will largely depend on how you agree to settle the matter." The letter had a post scriptum with the information that a man from the office had been sent that day to begin negotiations with the current owner of section 13 about the rights sought by the company and that within a few hours the company's plans would no doubt be known by all the inhabitants of Garfield County.

Walton had no difficulty in understanding why such a letter had infuriated Ward. And he began to wonder whether he himself would now be sacked and Warren made the new treasurer of the bank. From their correspondence, Walton had concluded that the two had worked together on more than one questionable deal that Elihu didn't wish to be made public. It would be just like Ward, he thought, to turn away a man who had served him faithfully for ten years and who had had to advance through the ranks from stable hand and errand boy to become his right-hand man. This was Ward's way of recruiting his assistants. They had to slave for him for years before they *graduerte* to the bank and were paid a miserable salary. Afterward he boasted of having supported them.

Meanwhile, as Walton was busy reflecting on his life, Ward and Newell were at the hotel eating breakfast. They had had to do without Lindermann's company at breakfast, since he had a wife who was distinguished by two characteristic traits: she loved money and she insisted on knowing where her husband spent his nights. So since Sam had been at O'Connor's all night playing cards, it was absolutely necessary for him to go home and pacify her by sharing his winnings with her.

As the two men got up from their table, Napoleon entered the dining room. He, Glombekken, and Hans Nerlivika had also been up all night. Stomhoff and Hans had come to town half an hour earlier. It had been a tough night so, on arrival, Napoleon had put need before pride and followed Hans through the front door of Dampen's saloon. He had now had four shots of whisky to regain his balance and was famished. He and Ward spoke together in a whisper as Newell continued into the hotel parlor.

"Everything all right?" Ward asked.

"He's out of commission, all right," Stomhoff replied, and then gave a brief report on his part in the events of the night.

"And Torfin? Where's Torfin?"

"He thought he might be needed, so he went back to look for Olander."

"Good, good!" Ward rubbed his hands and his eyes shone with satisfaction. "And, as I said before, I'll do the right thing by you," he added. "You may depend on that, Mr.—er—Napoleon!" Napoleon made a short bow as the banker left him to join Newell.

Glombekken had indeed thought he might be of more use out in *Groven*. The simple fact that Jonas had come driving toward Normanville with a livery team from Arrowtown, after Torfin and Napoleon in the course of the night had taken Lindström's from O'Brien's farmyard, was suspicious in itself. Glombekken didn't know that Olander and Arvid had come in pursuit of Jonas from Arrowtown, but he understood the situation when he found a carpetbag with Olander's name tag in the *livery-buggyen* containing a whisky bottle, some handcuffs, and a box of sandwiches. So he returned to *Groven* with the *livery-teamet* while Napoleon and Hans went on with Lindström's horses to Normanville.

Not long after Mrs. Jorshaug and thirteen-year-old Lars had come to the O'Brien farm, the boy said that he would have to see to the prisoners he had been appointed to guard. His mother wanted him to stay indoors but he was able to sneak out unnoticed while the three women were talking together. At the very least he wanted to have a look through the window at the two rascals, who were trussed and bound on the earthen stable floor.

But when he, full of excitement, looked in through the little window of the barn, he couldn't see a living soul. The prisoners must have escaped . . . Indeed, he soon discovered that the stable door was ajar. Should he dare open it and enter? Nyblom had appointed him guard and it was his duty to carry out his work as conscientiously as possible . . . But he didn't like the idea of entering a dark barn where there may be murderers and robbers. His mother wasn't far away, so he had better go to her. Mrs. Jorshaug and Ragna immediately followed him to the stable. None of them could explain how it had happened, but Olander and Arvid were gone, just as Lars had said.

The truth of the matter was that the law officer from Arrowtown and his assistant were already on their way down the road toward the place where Jonas had been left a few hours earlier. The marshal couldn't thank Glombekken enough for having saved them in the eleventh hour and he now perceived a way of restoring his professional honor. It would be an easy matter for him and Arvid to arrest Jonas since he was already both bound and gagged. Olander would have liked to demonstrate his gratitude with more than mere words by offering him a drink, but neither his bottle nor his carpetbag were in the *buggyen*. They must have fallen into the hands of the enemy . . .

"Yes, they certainly have a *tæst* for liquor," Glombekken remarked. And the man with the star swore that they would get a *tæst* of something quite different before he was through with them. Torfin went with him to the main road. Then he trudged slowly homeward as he smiled to himself. He had passed his home on his way to *Groven,* had left the whisky bottle there, and then had thrown the carpetbag behind O'Brien's chicken coop.

But when Olander came to pick up Jonas at the place described by Glombekken, there was no Jonas to be seen. It hadn't entered his or Torfin's mind that while he and Arvid were being liberated, Nyblom's rescue force was on its way south to Normanville.

When Ward joined him after his conversation with Napoleon, Newell expressed surprise at seeing Stomhoff in town so early in the morning and the banker decided to let him know about the exploits of Torfin, Stomhoff, and Nerlivika. Newell listened, first in surprise, and then turned suddenly serious.

"That's to go pretty far," he said. "If your connection with this should become known it would constitute a charge against you for criminal conspiracy to defraud the man of a legally acquired option; and your own option would be valueless."

The lawyer's admonitions were an awkward reminder. In his eagerness to acquire section 13 he hadn't paid much attention to the criminal aspects of his procedure. Nor was he overmuch worried about them now. The man who had the judge in his pocket and a good lawyer had little to fear. It was another matter entirely that he might not be able to hold on to section 13 if his complicity in the detention of Jonas Olsen became known. There were limits to how far even the friendliest of courthouses could stretch the law . . . But it had been done and he would have to accept the consequences. To retreat now was unthinkable.

Meanwhile Jonas and his companions had continued on their way to Normanville at full speed. Only by driving as fast as they could did they have any hope of getting there before noon. After they had been on the road for an hour or so, they were stopped by the deputy sheriff, Duffy, who wanted to arrest Jonas and Nyblom for battery, assault, and disorderly conduct in Arrowtown.

"Well, where's your warrant?" cried Nyblom. He knew that the only existing arrest order was in his own pocket. Duffy said grandly that they would see it in due time; he had his papers in full order. But he seemed in no hurry to produce them nor did he make any move to take the two by force. Indeed, he was warned not to try anything by Flasmo, who called out as he picked up his dung fork, "If you make a single *mov'* to *'reste* the boys, there will be a slaughter here that will be renowned in seven kingdoms. You won't get them alive."

"What's the man bellering about?" asked Duffy, who didn't understand much of Flasmo's dialect since he, as an Englishman, wasn't much of a linguist. Jorshaug translated for him and added that he and the others were in complete agreement. With this, he slapped the horses with his reins and they continued at their former speed. Duffy followed at a safe distance.

"You can't tell what these Norwegian Indians might do," he said to his companion. "They're a wild and lawless people."

It was twenty minutes past eleven when Jorshaug's lumber wagon stopped outside Floen's office in Normanville. The deputy sheriff drove over to the other side of the street and kept an eye on the *Groven* men from there. Jorshaug gave the reins to Nyblom and entered the office. In a few minutes he came out followed by the lawyer, who greeted them with a bow. Without further conversation they continued to Lindermann's office farther up the street, still followed by Duffy and his assistant some steps behind.

Ward had gone to Lindermann a few minutes earlier to make sure it was clear sailing. He didn't for a moment suspect that Jonas would turn up to make use of his option. He just wanted to detain the Swede with talk until noon, and then conclude the deal.

Ward, however, had barely closed the door behind him when a buggy stopped outside the building and a stranger dressed in city clothes entered. After the stranger had made sure which of the two men was Lindermann, he gave Lindermann his card, on which the Swede read the name Johan Arndt Lomwiig. He had come to talk with him about section 13 on the West Prairie, he said, but perhaps he should rather wait. He looked at Ward. He was sorry that he didn't have much time since he had to take the afternoon train east . . .

"Section 13? What about section 13?" Ward and Lindermann exclaimed at once.

"Oh, nothing much," Lomwiig replied; "only that it'll be the principal townsite on the Stockdale-Normanville Railroad, and undoubtedly is destined to become the capital city of the county in a few years. I represent the H. & B."

The looks exchanged between Ward and Lindermann at this moment may be more easily imagined than explained. A smile that spoke of pride and victory spread over the face of the banker while Lindermann gave expressions to his feelings by saying something in his mother tongue that Elihu couldn't understand but that brought forth laughter from Lomwiig.

"I haven't heard that expression since I was in Gothenburg when I was eighteen," he said. "In my experience no language can compete with Swedish in the power and musical cadences of its expletives."

"Had every word been a tongue of fire and the flame been lined with dynamite this would still not have *expressa* the anger I feel in this moment!" Lindermann ensured him with an expression so sad that Lomwiig contemplated him in silence. He understood nothing.

And then the door opened and in came Floen, followed by Jorshaug, Flasmo, Jonas, Nyblom, and Sivert. At their heels followed Duffy and his assistant, and, as by coincidence, Newell. Ward couldn't have been more surprised had the ceiling fallen down. He sat a moment as if paralyzed by what he was seeing with his own eyes. Then he got up, his face all white, and said, turning to Duffy, "Why—that man is under arrest. How did he get here?"

"Yes, he is under arrest, and I'll take him now," Duffy replied, and made a move toward Jonas.

"Give me the gun!" said Flasmo as he turned to Nyblom. Nyblom, however, pretended not to have heard him. Floen spoke. If anyone so much as touched Jonas Olsen, he said, he would immediately request an order for the arrest of Ward and he would be prosecuted for the meanest criminal act that had ever been committed in Garfield County. "You may take your choice, gentlemen!" he threatened.

Duffy looked at Ward, Ward looked at Newell, and Newell looked back and forth between Lindermann and Floen.

"This looks to become a real *sørpreisparti!*" said Flasmo in his colorful dialect.

"This is a frame-up," Ward declared. His voice quivered with his anger. "Floen's charges are, of course, absolutely false." Newell seconded Elihu by saying that he knew nothing of what all this was about but that he was at all times prepared to give his word that Ward was an honorable man. Floen related the main facts of the matter to his colleague and observed that since Mr. Olsen had come in time to make use of his option, there was no power in existance that could keep him from becoming the owner of section 13.

"Well, what of it?" Newell smiled ironically. "I'm sure Mr. Ward will be the last man to begrudge him his good luck. I assure you, gentlemen, this foolishness is due entirely to some misunderstanding. I never heard Mr. Ward even mention section 13." The lawyer looked straight at Ward as he spoke and the banker answered with an expression that was only understood between them. It was clear to everyone present that Ward had regained his usual composure. He was his superior and calm self when he took a step toward Jonas.

"Young man," he said as he gave him his hand with a smile, "Mr. Newell has told the truth. I'm glad you've made such a splendid deal. I congratulate you, Mr. Olsen! And—we'll meet again!"

"You're darn right we will!" Jonas replied. Whereupon Ward left the room, straight-backed and dignified, as Jonas was congratulated by Newell.

Lomwiig, who had witnessed with increasing amazement what he assumed was the concluding act in the drama of section 13, waited until Jonas had been congratulated by Floen and his neighbors in *Groven* before he went up to him, shook his hand warmly, and said, "You have done well in America, my good friend! That section is a goldmine. Let's have dinner together at Hotel—ahem—Delmonico.[49] There we'll discuss how you plan to deal with the privileges that my company needs in order to lay the foundation for your fortune. I'm sorry that I'll have to leave this afternoon, but I'll be back in the spring to place the crown on your head when you move into your new kingdom."

"You better *sæt 'em op*," said Flasmo. "I'm thirsty!"

And that's what Jonas had to do, even though it really was against his moral principles. At O'Connor's they met Jim O'Brien, who now heard about the strange happenings at *Groven* during his absence.

"Faith, and you're a lucky boy," he said as he took Jonas by the hand. "Sure, and I've felt it in me bones something like it would happen. Something's bound to come to him that's got a good wife, begorrah; and your's a peach. Rimember, Jim O'Brien told ye so."

33.

It won't take long to relate the other things that happened to Jonas and Ragna during their first year on the prairie. The foundation of their new home on section 13 was laid by Jorshaug and his hired man that fall. It was going to be a grand house, one that could fully compete with Ward's in Normanville and Seff Thompson's in Arrowtown. Torgersen had promised Jonas unlimited credit, and with the railroad work scheduled to begin in the spring, there was no one who had the slightest doubt concerning the unique potential of his land.

Jonas and Ragna had agreed to offer Lomwiig a free right-of-way for the railroad across the section, and a lot for the depot free of charge as well. They had thought that this could help him with his company, and since they had been so lucky themselves, this was the least they could do for an old friend. They were not mistaken in their assumption. This more than anything else made Lyman, the company director, aware of the qualities of the well-behaved Johan Arndt, who had originally been appointed for some political reason and who had been thought useful in negotiations with Scandinavians. He was transferred from the land office to Lyman's office, and not long after he became the director's right-hand man.

People in Minneapolis speculated on how Lomwiig had been able to advance so quickly. But it was not until February that tongues really got busy. That was when it was first rumored that Dagny Simonsen had been divorced from her husband and married to Lomwiig in Chicago. Among those who were surprised were Jonas and Ragna, who read about the wedding in *Minneapolis Tidende*. A few days later Jonas received a letter from Johan Arndt telling him about the event:

> When we unexpectedly met each other in a party at Doctor Anders Daae's and I was told that she had been in Chicago the last four months and had just been given her freedom, it came to me as a revelation that it is not good for man to live alone. She was brilliant, beautiful, and happy. And I thought: why not? Yes, indeed, why not? We were after all second cousins, so we certainly knew each other. In short, we had a brief talk about it and at dessert the inimitable Daae announced our engagement and gave a wonderfully entertaining speech for us. As could be expected, Mrs. Simonsen insisted on a church wedding. Pastor Juul objected at first but it is now all done and we have taken temporary quarters at the Merchant's Hotel here in St. Paul, where we live in joy and harmony like a pair of doves.[50]
>
> Had we only not had all these politicians who are hanging around here while the *Legislatur* is in session. They come in all kinds of versions and my mission is to secure their friendship and loyalty. Our company has a few minor interests to take care of to the tune of about twenty million dollars. By the way, this fellow Seff Thompson is quite an original and not so honest that we can't do business with him. Indeed, he is a man who may turn out to be very useful—*unter uns gesagt,* naturally.[51]

His letter concluded with the information that Dagny had decided to accompany him when he came out to them in the spring on business. When Jonas had read the letter he gave it to Ragna. "What news!" he said, laughing. But Ragna didn't appear to see anything particularly funny in the letter. Two things puzzled her: that Dagny wanted to visit them, and this thing about securing the loyalty of the members of the *Legislatur* and that Seff could be "useful."

"What does he mean?" she asked. "Could it be possible that these companies spend money to get those who sit in the *Legislaturen* to pass the laws they want passed?"

"*Tu-be-sure*," Jonas replied. "They have significant interests to take care of. That's *bisnes!*"

"Then it's dirty *bisnes*," she reflected.

"Well, *bisnes* is *bisnes, ju' no!*"

"And how in the world are we going to receive this fine Dagny—Mrs. Lomwiig?" she added after a while. It was obvious that she didn't relish the prospects of such a visit.

"Oh, that won't be difficult at all," Jonas replied. "She is both charming and . . ."

"Oh, so she is, is she!"

He laughed. "You're not jealous, are you?"

"Jealous? Of course I'm not jealous."

—————

Before the arrival of winter, Jonas had had surveyors lay out lots in the forty acres of the projected town center. From all over, he had queries from people who were interested in establishing businesses there. Indeed, there seemed to be a clamor for lots. The situation of the projected town right in the center of the county suggested that it would not only become a serious competitor with Normanville and Arrowtown in attracting business but that it would be a strong candidate should the question of moving the county seat ever come up.

Hans Floen, who had helped Jonas with all legal matters, had secured a town lot in the center of the business district, where he had decided to set up a brick building and establish a law office. Jonas wanted a store for himself. The foundation was built late in the fall but he had already contracted Trulsen to set up a large shanty as soon as work could begin in March. He would begin business there until the more solid brick building was ready. He wanted to be the first to open a business in his own town, benefitting from all the advantages that would give him. He had thought it all over very carefully. Right now he wasn't all that eager to sell downtown lots, so he kept the prices very high. He was so preoccupied with his many plans that he thought and talked about little else.

Ragna wasn't sure whether she was happy or sorry that all this had happened. In a way it was good that he had achieved his goal, but she was worried when she saw how absorbed he was by all these *bisnes* affairs. She hadn't the slightest doubt that he would be what is called a *sukces* as a businessman. What gave her cause for concern was the thought that he might become more of a *sukces* than would be good for him. But come what will, his wishes had been fulfilled and fate had given him an opportunity to realize his potential. So it was all in the hands of Our Lord . . .

It was late in the morning of December tenth. There was hardly any snow and the weather had been exceptionally clement. So Jonas had found something to keep himself busy on section 13 almost every day. He had gone out there that day as well since there was nothing that morning to indicate that anything special was about to happen. Ragna had slept soundly and she had not even woken up when he got out of bed. He had stood there for a long time looking at her before he left. He thought she was even more beautiful than before . . . and she must have been in the middle of a pleasant dream since she had such a wonderful smile . . .

O'Brien and Nyblom had added to the house that fall. Jonas and Ragna now had their own little comfortable room. Much else had been changed and things were far better organized than earlier. O'Brien had planned it all since he now felt that they could afford it. It was only as it should be, he thought, that the young should have more comfort than the older generation had experienced. Times had changed since he had come here in pioneer days.

It was, as already said, late in the morning. Nyblom had just gone out to the stable and Ragna and Emma had sat down for a rest after their morning chores when Ragna suddenly had a spasm and had to lie down in her bed. In a few minutes Nyblom was on his way to get Mrs. Flasmo, and Iver drove her over to O'Brien's at once while Nyblom continued west to get Jonas. When they finally got home, all was over. They found Mrs. Flasmo sitting with the baby in her lap.

"Is it a boy?" Jonas asked, eager for the answer, but in a low voice.

"Ahem—well—you may get that too in time," Mrs. Flasmo replied, "but what I'm holding here is a little girl."

"Oh, shucks!" he whispered. He had been so sure it would be a boy. He was disappointed but it was too late to do anything about it now. He would have to accept what couldn't be changed. And she was such a nice little thing. He was quite solemn when he carefully took her in his arms. *Gudnes* how tiny and how light she was . . . She was so vulnerable and so delicate that he hardly dared touch her . . .

"She takes after her mother!" said Mrs. Flasmo. Yes, thank God, he thought. Well, he couldn't see this himself but Mrs. Flasmo should know . . . Since it was a girl it was, after all, best that she looked like her mother . . . If she would only become like her in other respects as well . . . Had it been a boy . . .

Ragna was pale and weak, but she smiled at him. He had to go to her and kiss her on her forehead and her lips. She seemed transfigured . . . Yes, he was a very lucky man to have such a wife! This was more than he deserved . . . He was very much aware of this now . . .

"Aren't you disappointed?" she whispered.

"Me—disappointed? Why should I be disappointed?"

"Well, it was, after all, a girl." He kissed her again. Then he held her hand ever so gently. Her skin was as soft and as beautiful as the finest silk . . . It was like being in a church . . .

"Yes, and that has made me so happy," he said. "And it was, of course, what God had decided," he added. But Mrs. Flasmo now decided that this had been going on too long. He had to leave. And he did, with a clear sense of his new responsibility as a father.

Mrs. Flasmo stayed with them for more than three weeks, for five days later Mrs. Nyblom had a big and lively boy. Jonas thought that Nyblom was unnecessarily proud of being the father of a boy. He himself had always been of the opinion that girls were ever so much nicer to have around the house than these boys who were so difficult to control . . .

Both babies were christened the same day—on Boxing Day. Vellesen had made known that there would be a Christmas service the second day of Christmas, and even though he wasn't reliable in doctrine, Jonas had arrived at the conclusion that this wouldn't do much harm to Signe Marie. The Nybloms were not church people, so as far as David Rytterskjold was concerned, it couldn't matter less . . .[52]

Congregational relations had been rather strained that fall. Jonas, Flasmo, Jorshaug, and Tarvesen had kept away from the October service in protest against the majority decision to enter the United Church. Jonas had said that he would build a church for the Synod in his town as soon as possible. This had made both Vellesen and Trulsen reflect on their situation. The congregation was small enough as it was and its members were hardly affluent. To begin with, the minister as well as the deacon had taken a hard line against the breakaway faction of the congregation, and the majority was far from inclined to show mercy to the "apostates." Nor did the minority, for that matter, demonstrate much charity or a conciliatory spirit toward the majority.

Although Vellesen himself may not have been aware of it, the dramatic change in Jonas's fortune seemed to have a soothing effect on the pastor. He did his best not to be provocative and he ceased to address Jonas with the authority and superior manner that had been so characteristic of his earlier relations with the younger man. Both Vellesen and Trulsen realized that it wouldn't benefit the congregation to turn away people who would soon be playing a leading role in the community. Consequently, they paid attention to both Jonas and Ragna at the Christmas service when their child was baptized, and they were given the distinction of being the only parishioners who were invited to dinner with the minister at the Trulsens' after the service.

But, as became apparent in the spring, this turned out to have little effect, since Jonas nevertheless took the first step in realizing his threat to build a Synod church by setting aside a lot for this purpose. It was one of the largest and nicest lots in the center of the projected city. A sign proclaimed in large letters: "This property is reserved for the use of the Synod congregation." This created quite a stir. Most people took it seriously and realized that he was set on erecting a competing altar. Others took it as a joke and said, "Well, there are four of them so they will need a big church." Jonas was aware of all that was said, but he couldn't care less. The church would be built even if he paid every penny himself. He was already corresponding with Pastor Vangsnes about who he should call as pastor when the church was ready.

Because of Glombekken's and Napoleon's involvement in the conspiracy to deprive Jonas of his option on section 13, Jonas now had a nasty hold on the anti-Missourians. The summer school was over in September but the plan had been for Napoleon to hold prayer meetings through the fall and winter. But they couldn't let a scoundrel like Napoleon preach after his escapades had become known. Moreover, Jonas threatened to have him prosecuted if he didn't leave the settlement, and Stomhoff had to seek the protection of Ward, who succeeded in placing him with Seff Thompson in Arrowtown. Thompson soon discovered that Napoleon was quite useful, especially now that he himself had to spend several months in the legislature.

To begin with, Jonas was inclined to use the law against Glombekken and Napoleon. And he wouldn't mind if this also meant that Ward
was brought to justice. He deserved it. But Ragna interfered and insisted
that he forget it all. Nothing was gained by taking revenge, she said.
They should forgive their enemies, and they could certainly afford to do
so since Ward's machinations had not hurt him in the least. Jorshaug
agreed. Acting on Ward's behalf, Newell had been exceptionally friendly
whenever he met Jonas in town and he had even asked his advice on a
problematic collection of delinquent accounts in Minneapolis . . . This
was the usual Yankee way of ingratiating themselves with immigrants,
Jonas observed when he mentioned it to Ragna. They assumed in advance that we were at least 50 percent more stupid than they were themselves. But he agreed to drop all charges.

Jonas didn't see Ward all winter. People said that he didn't seem to
have been much affected by the loss of his wife when she gave birth to
their second child at Christmastime. Their first had been a daughter,
who was now about eighteen. Ward too had longed for a son. Now he
had one, but he had lost his wife.

Spring came exceptionally early. The winter had been mild and
beautiful, and there was hardly any frost in the ground in late March
when construction work began on section 13. The railroad people also
began to stir, and soon movement and commotion were everywhere.
Trulsen began work on the large *shantyet* that was to serve Jonas as
the temporary premises for his new store, and Lindström came from
Arrowtown to build the new home for Jonas and Ragna, which was to be
ready by July first. In April, Jonas sold one of the corner lots just opposite
the depot to a hotel owner from Grand Forks at a price that even he found
fabulously high. Some other downtown lots were also sold at good prices.
But he still held on to some of the best lots. He was convinced that he was
sitting on a virtual gold mine, and he had made up his mind to work it for
all it was worth. In all this he benefitted from Floen's expert advice, and
a friendship developed between the two that was to last for life, in spite
of their ecclesiastical differences. Floen was not a member of any church.

Lomwiig came in the middle of April and visited Jonas and Ragna
at O'Brien's. Dagny had changed her mind at the last minute. Ragna
was pleased, but Lomwiig assured them that he would soon be back and
that Dagny would then certainly come along too. One of Jonas's main
concerns while Lomwiig was with them was a name for the new town.
The company had planned to name the depot Olsenville, after the owner

of the land, but Johan Arndt didn't approve. He thought it sounded so common.

"I'll tell you what we'll do," said Ragna, who had been listening to their deliberations. "Let's call the town Johnsville for Jonas."

"Why not Jonasville?" Lomwiig asked.

"It won't look good in English," she said. "And Americans have problems with names of more than two syllables."

The discussion went on yet a while, but it turned out that they couldn't make up anything that was better. So they finally decided that the town should be called Johnsville.

"So long as the name is reasonably decent," Jonas said, "it *mæker* no great *differens'* what we call it. The main thing is that we make it a town where you can make a good *bisnes.*"

July had almost come to an end before the house was finished. In the final phase, Lindström had set all the people he had to work on it day and night, but it was a large house and there had been all kinds of problems and difficulties. Now it stood ready. Ragna had inspected it four or five times during the summer to make sure that the plans laid by her and Jonas were followed in all details. She had also gone to Normanville and bought the furnishing. But apart from that she hadn't been out much, since the little Signe Marie hadn't been entirely well and attending her had taken all of Ragna's time.

For a while it seemed that the baby was seriously ill, at which time both parents had been beyond consolation. Jonas was the one who was most concerned. This had given Ragna much food for thought. It was in a way strange, she thought, that a man who was so engrossed with the material world at times could be so sensitive and emotional. She had wondered whether he could be sincere, but now she felt that she understood it better . . . This was the way he was made, this husband of hers: a man for all seasons . . . a blend of extremes . . . egotistic, ruthless, and brutal, and yet at his best he was sensitive and understanding . . . all at once pathetically naïve and penetratingly shrewd . . . incredibly dense when it came to many of the most simple aspects of life, and an unscrupulous fox in *bisnes* . . . pious and orthodox in his own eyes, yet in fact he was . . . Oh, well, when all came to all he was probably neither much worse nor much better than most people . . .

Ragna had made these reflections as she sat on the edge of her bed the morning of the day they were moving to section 13. There was so much to hope for and to be fearful of in this new life that was about to begin for them. Respect, wealth, and power beckoned. She had reason to believe that her future would offer her more of such things than she had ever dared dream of. And yet she sighed with a worried heart when she thought about it. She was afraid! She prayed to God to remove this fear from her heart . . . She may have nothing to fear. But she still did.

"My, how happy you must be!" Emma exclaimed when the two of them were left alone after breakfast. "To think that you are moving into such a great, big, nice house, and with such prospects. My!"

"I suppose I ought to be glad and grateful," Ragna replied seriously. "In a way I am too. Yet, life is a curious thing. The delights of the sunny morning may mean only that you'll get drenched before night." Mrs. Nyblom stared at her in wonder. This was something she couldn't fully understand.

———

Carrying Signe Marie in his arms, Jonas, followed by Ragna, went up the steps to their new home with a sense of pride that surpassed anything he had to that time experienced. He stopped on the wide porch and looked out on his kingdom. He expected her to say something but she was silent and full of thought. He opened the door and they entered. Everything was in perfect order. Everything spoke of their new prosperity . . . the decorated walls, the nice new furniture, the beautiful carpets, the engravings that hung in silver wires from light-blue lists that ran below the ceiling. They went from room to room. Mrs. Jorshaug had been there the day before and had made sure that all was in order. Not until they entered the kitchen did Ragna utter a word.

"My, this is fine!" she said. Then she again became silent, and she suddenly sat down on a chair and began to cry. Meanwhile, Jonas had placed Signe Marie on the floor. He was almost shocked. Wasn't she satisfied now? His self-esteem received a sudden blow.

"*Gudnes!*" he said. "Aren't you feeling well?" She got slowly up as if she were struggling to shake off her mood. Then she resolutely dried her tears and said, "No, no, I'm fine . . . Can't you understand . . . I'm just so happy, so happy . . ."

At that moment Jonas felt like a powerful and a happy man.

"*Vel-sørri,* we haven't done all that badly in America!" he declared as he sat down and pulled her onto his lap.

At that moment Signe Marie began to cry. *Gudnes,* how that child could cry . . .

BOOK III

Jonasville

I.

A sunny winter morning on the prairies the Christmas of 1909. The roads are covered with yesterday's snowfall. From the east the sun is looking down on the wide plain, but the cold is more powerful. Blue-gray columns of smoke rise up from the farmhouses. People on the roads peek out from their fur coats and other packaging, looking to one side, then to the other, and cannot help shivering a little at the thought of the warm fireplace that is the source of the smoke. Then they look straight ahead and drive a little faster to shorten their journey.

At first the winter had been unusually mild. There had been a little snow in October but it was gone after a few days, and there hadn't been snow for sleighing until two days before Christmas. Today many had made use of the opportunity to venture out with their cutters and harness bells.[1] Most were heading to Johnsville. This was the town's official name, but only Americans used it. Norwegians and Swedes in the settlement had from its founding called it Jonasville. New times had announced their arrival and a younger generation was taking the place of the old. The first automobile had come a few years ago and with it telephones on the farms.

It was the third day of Christmas and the new pastor in Jonasville was to give his inaugural sermon. This must have been the reason why so many people had come the seven or eight miles from O'Brien's Grove to hear Pastor Sivert Jorshaug, who had grown up in *Groven*. Indeed, his parents Lars and Else Jorshaug still lived on their old homestead.

After Sivert had begun his studies at Luther College in Decorah, Iowa, he had hardly been in the settlement. Summers he had mostly worked on farms in Winneshiek County.[2] His father had ruined his health by working too hard at an early age, and since he had to have a hired man on the farm all year round, he didn't have much money left for the education of his sons. With time, the Jorshaugs, like so many others, had become prosperous, but when Sivert attended Luther College and the younger Lars was at the school in Willmar, there had been less than $100 for each.[3] So they both had to work during vacation periods.

After ten long years Sivert had become a pastor, and Lars, who had pursued an academic career, was a professor at a college in the East. Sivert had come home for Christmas his first year in Decorah and then twice while he studied theology at the seminary in Hamline.[4] One New Year's Day, while still at the seminary, he had preached in the church in Jonasville, to which he had now been called. In between he had served in the inner mission on the Pacific Coast and in Texas, and for three years he had been pastor in Minneapolis.

Pastor Jorshaug was thirty-three and unmarried. His single status made moving less complicated. Some days ago, six large boxes had arrived with his library. He himself had come yesterday with the evening train, with one large and two small suitcases that contained his other possessions. Jonas Olsen, the founder and leading citizen of the town, had met him at the depot. He had taken him to his home and said that he would have to live there for the time being. They had just redecorated and painted the parsonage, Jonas explained, to make it fit for human habitation after all the tobacco smoking of his predecessor, Pastor Leidahl, who had left a few weeks earlier. Leidahl was a theological candidate from Norway who had immigrated in the 1870s. In his study he was sometimes almost invisible because of the smoke, and the entire parsonage smelled of tobacco. For this and other reasons the atmosphere there hadn't been to Jonas's liking. Another was that Leidahl was a man of authority who insisted on full control of his congregation. Jorshaug had been informed about some of this in the letters from his mother. Jonas had not only founded the city but had also to a great extent made it what it now was. He had organized the congregation and he had built the church, and it was well known that for years he had paid most church expenses out of his own pocket. Nor was he a modest man who made little of his merits. Mrs. Jorshaug had written that Jonas's tendency to dominate had increased with the years. If things didn't go his way there was bound to be trouble.

Leidahl had only been four years in Jonasville. Before him there had been a young man by the name of Romsby, who had used English for services and confirmation classes to such a degree that it offended Jonas. Jonas finally got rid of Romsby by having the Synod find him another calling. Romsby had no great desire to move just then and he submitted a conditional resignation to the congregation, hoping the people would ask him to stay in spite of his conflicts with Jonas. His resignation was accepted against one vote—that of Abrahamsen, the saddler.

When Leidahl accepted the call, Jonas had looked forward to having an experienced man with a Norwegian degree who was so comfortable with the Norwegian language that he wouldn't exaggerate the introduction of English. But with Leidahl language also became a problem. The young members of the congregation insisted on an occasional English sermon. The minister, however, had never properly learned the country's official language and he made himself look ridiculous with his attempts to satisfy these demands. But Leidahl was a grave and venerable man, and no one dared to defy him openly—no one except Jonas. Even Jonas hesitated, but when he eventually had a word with the minister, things were said so clearly that it marked the end of their friendship.

When Jorshaug wrote to his mother that he had decided to accept the call to Jonasville, she had replied that he must be prepared for quite a lot. She had remained the best of friends with Ragna Olsen. They had shared sorrows and happiness. This might to some degree make her son's work less difficult. She feared though that her friendship might be endangered if Sivert should fail to satisfy Jonas. But Sivert couldn't see why he shouldn't have a good relationship with Jonas Olsen, whom he had gotten to know so well when he was a boy. And now he was here.

In *Groven* only a few families belonged to the Jonasville congregation: the Jorshaugs, Flasmos, Tarvesens, and a few others. Nyblom too had become a member, partly because of the close friendship between him and Jonas and between Ragna and Emma, and partly because the Swedish church was quite a few miles away.

As usual, Vellesen had held service in his church on Christmas Day, so there was no good reason why any of his flock should set out on a journey of several miles in the cold in order to hear yet another Christmas sermon, in particular by a man who was misled in his doctrine. Nevertheless,

[273]

quite a few had set out for Jonasville today. Their reasons were obvious. They were curious to find out whether this boy who had grown up amongst them was any good as a preacher. Some may have had their doubts about going to town to listen to Pastor Jorshaug, but they were so well versed in correct doctrine that by all human reckoning they ran little risk.

Even Mrs. O'Brien and her daughter Mrs. Nyblom, who didn't understand Norwegian, had come to pay their respects to pastor Jorshaug. Mrs. O'Brien had retired three years ago from her position as superintendent. She was respected all over the state for her work. Since her husband Jim's death the previous winter, she lived with her daughter and Nyblom, who had become quite prosperous. She now lived a quiet life with her many books out on the old *claimen,* now one of the most beautiful farms in the county.

It was about ten. Jonas Olsen was dressed for church and was reading his newspaper in a large leather chair in the parlor. As the minutes passed by he looked up impatiently every now and then through the wide opening to the hall and the great oaken staircase.

It was soon time for church and the women would probably not be ready in time. And the new pastor was still in his room. What a fine thing it would be if the congregation had to wait for the new pastor . . . *Gudnes.* Why couldn't these pastors ever learn to be *bisnes*-like. He took his watch out of his pocket—it was a gold watch that friends had given him on his fortieth birthday. It was precisely ten o'clock. The service began at ten thirty . . .

Jonas looked older than his age. His thick head of hair had been such a handsome ornament when he began his work on section 13, eighteen years ago. Now Jonasville had become a lively prairie town and his hair was both thin and gray. His face was wrinkled and gave him a grave appearance when he—as now—was worried. The lines on his forehead and at his mouth were witness to a life of hard work, and his tight lips and prominent chin betrayed a man who wouldn't hesitate to crush those who stood in his way. It had been a struggle, and even though he had come out on top, it required constant vigilance to hold on to the little he had.

But there was the pastor, tall and slender—a handsome man. The blond, well-groomed hair and the friendly but serious face; the blue, dreamy eyes and the mild set of his lips—the index of a harmonious mind, but not so much of strength or stamina. Jonas smiled in welcome. His look still had much of the brightness the pastor remembered from the past.

The pastor took in the room. Its pretentious oaken solidity gave it a somewhat somber and rigid appearance. An enormous leather davenport, a no less ponderous sofa, and a table and chairs in the same style; the large bookcase with books in brilliant bindings; the gilded picture frames on the fresco-covered walls; the enormous bronze electric chandelier; the impressive upright Fischer piano, on which a marble bust of Johan Sverdrup seemed unconcerned with his surroundings[5]—it all had an impressive aura of indestructibility but it lacked the legitimacy of tradition.

But even if the furniture was ponderous and out of scale for a room of this size, a visitor could see that there had been attempts to diminish the disharmony—small, gentle signs of a desire for symmetry, discretion, and taste—softer hands that had interfered to give it a touch of mildness and impermanence . . . a Japanese vase here, a knickknack there, a watercolor landscape between the family portraits, and two or three quite decent reproductions. And there were roses on the piano and carnations on the music cabinet . . .

Jonas got up.

"Well, we had perhaps better get moving, pastor!" he said. "The women will never get ready in time!" Jorshaug looked at his watch.

"Oh, we have lots of time," he said calmly. "And, please, let's not be so terribly formal," the pastor continued. "If you insist, you may use my family name if my father isn't around, but I would prefer that you call me Sivert." The other stared at him somewhat surprised. Was this a minister? "In return I'll call you Jonas, as I did when I was a boy in *Groven*," Jorshaug added with a smile.

"Certainly—certainly—I've always been proud of my Norwegian name!"

"As you should. We all could not have been more proud than we are of our Norwegian names, as well as of other things that are part of our heritage." After a pause he said, "Tell me, whatever happened to Napoleon? I'll never forget the expedition to Normanville. It's probably the only time I've played the role of a real hero." Jonas explained that Napoleon Stomhoff had settled in Arrowtown, where he was still employed by Seff Thompson.

"I've never been able to forgive myself," he said, "for not sending the whole lot of scoundrels where they belong—Ward, Napoleon, Glombekken, and the rest."

"You did the right thing by being forgiving," said the pastor. "That is our duty as Christians."

"At the cost of truth and justice?"

"No, no, of course not. But on the other hand it isn't always so easy to tell whether what we call truth and justice is always deserving of such names." Jonas again gave him a look of surprise. What kind of talk was this? But they heard the sound of feet running down the stairs and now Signe Marie rushed into the room like a tornado.

"Dad, dad!" she called. They both turned toward her. Jorshaug assumed something had happened.

"It's such a shame," she continued, "that we always have to freeze almost to death on a holy Christmas day. Don't we have both firewood and coal in the basement?" Her voice was half-joking, half-reproachful. Jonas was evidently a little embarrassed. He had quite forgotten about the *furnacen*; he excused himself and left the room. In a little while they heard him down in the basement. Signe Marie laughed.

"I don't find it the least cold," the pastor remarked.

"No, you're right," she admitted, "but the point is that every time we are going anywhere, father is ready an hour before there is any need to leave the house, and then he's always upset and makes an awful din about how late we are. So this little drama about the *furnacen* is my own little method of protecting myself against his bad temper, you see."

"I do see. Look here, shouldn't we be on first names?[6] I was a godfather when a certain little girl was baptized. That's how old I am."

"All right, that's fine by me!" She gave him her hand. It was soft as velvet but had a strong grip.

Signe Marie could only remember meeting Pastor Jorshaug twice: when he gave a sermon in their church nine years ago, and last summer when she and her mother had visited him in Minneapolis. He was almost a stranger and now they were on first names and she talked with him as with an old friend. The pastor looked at her: a well-developed, almost plump girl of about eighteen years, with short hair, lively brown eyes, a well nigh perfectly formed and naturally colored face, lips like a newly sprung rose but perhaps too full to complete the otherwise harmonious countenance. It was as if a secret voice whispered in his ear that life was standing before him and that he must be careful, for life was always young and challenging. He had heard this voice before, once in Texas and once in Minneapolis. And each time it had warned him to be careful and said that life was full of danger.

She brought him out of his meditation with a new infectious laugh. He realized he was blushing. She noticed his reaction and stopped laughing. "Well, there you can see how irresponsible and flighty I can be," she said. "I entirely forgot that you must be reflecting on your sermon. Mercy me, how I would have been bored if I were in your place and had to make up such a sad and serious sermon every week." She surprised him. This wasn't the way young girls talked with their pastor. She turned to go into an adjoining room.

"So you wouldn't have liked being a pastor?" he said. She turned and faced him.

"Mercy me, I would have made a fine pastor!" she laughed. What a natural and unconstrained laughter she had! Then her father came up from the basement and sent her an admiring look. Signe Marie was some girl . . . So like her mother when she was younger and yet so different. Her mother entered the parlor as well, and she pointed a well-manicured, admonishing hand at her daughter and smiled as she said, "Now, now, Signe Marie, don't scare Pastor Jorshaug out of his wits the first day he's with us!"

Ragna had become a little rounder but had preserved her youthful appearance remarkably well. She was still an unusually handsome woman. Her features were perhaps a little more marked but this merely served to give her face even more character and to emphasize her intelligence. Sivert Jorshaug could remember how he as a fourteen-year-old had been quite in love with Ragna when she came to O'Brien's Grove as a young bride. Now he saw her as a representative of that nobility of soul who lived a deliberate life. And how did he see Signe Marie? As life itself—life from which he tried to protect himself. Should the day come for him too when he no longer protected himself from life? He hurried out after Jonas. Church service could not wait.

Walking to church, the pastor and Signe Marie were first and Ragna and Jonas a few steps behind them. "Mercy me, winter is so beautiful!" she suddenly said.

"Yes, there is beauty everywhere for those who have been given eyes to see with," the pastor replied. She wondered at his words. Her mother sometimes spoke words like that but she wasn't always sure that she understood them. But she was sure that she was in his thoughts as he walked beside her. That was why he was philosophical. Nor was he the first one who had spoken philosophically to Signe Marie . . . mercy, no!

They parted ways at the entrance. He hurried in and walked with determined steps toward the sacristy. Signe Marie and her mother stopped outside. "Mother," she whispered, "how old is Pastor Jorshaug?" Ragna studied her.

"Why do you ask?"

"Oh, because!"

"He's fifteen years older than you are, so you should be able to work it out yourself." Signe Marie whistled. But then she saw Jim Nyblom. God knows why they called him Jim when his name was David Rytterskjold, but that's the way it was. Of course she had to say hello to Jim. She had once eavesdropped behind a half-open door and heard the two mothers speak of how it must have been the good Lord's intention that the two would make a couple. This was just before he had been sent to Gustavus Adolphus College, and now he had come home for Christmas.[7] She was fond of Jim, of course. He was a good dancer and he always blushed when she looked at him. But it had taken him so long to properly grow up. Recently she had decided that she would wait and see what he would amount to. Her father had said he didn't think Jim would go far. He had offered him a position in his store, but like an idiot he would rather go to college than begin in *bisnes.* The two only had time to exchange a few words before the bell rang.

Half an hour later Signe Marie was still thinking about how red Jim's face had been when she called out "Good morning!" to him. And Jorshaug, who was fifteen years older than she and Jim, had also blushed when she teased him a little before they left home. Men were like that.

But now Pastor Jorshaug had begun his sermon.

2.

Pastor Jorshaug's inaugural sermon made an unexpectedly good impression on his listeners. Whether they belonged to the Synod or were members of Vellesen's congregation they all agreed that Sivert had grown up to become quite a man. He spoke well and made an impressive figure in the pulpit. After the service, Mrs. Trulsen congratulated both him and his parents. Since the troubled beginnings of the *Groven* congregation, relations between the Jorshaugs and the Trulsens had been strained, so Else Jorshaug was quite moved.

Mrs. Trulsen had never felt comfortable with this conflict between churches and it had pained her to have to stop seeing old friends and neighbors. Things had become better with the years. The fury that had characterized relations was no longer quite so spirited, but there was still a residual of bad feelings. It had been so different when they had all been poor and had come together under one roof (which quite often was heaven itself) to listen to the word of God. Mrs. Trulsen had particularly missed the friendship of Else Jorshaug and Ragna Olsen. The conflict had grown like a cancer and had entered the most intimate relations. Trulsen was a man of few words, but he was tough and persevering once he had made up his mind. Nor could she really reproach him for his obstinacy since Jonas had been so unrelenting himself. He had done all he could to make things difficult for pastor Vellesen and his congregation. He had ploughed ahead, built his own church, and called a pastor, all at his own expense.

Recently, relations between Mrs. Trulsen and Ragna had improved, especially after Trulsen had been granted a loan in Jonas's bank. Trulsen had first approached Elihu Ward but was told that he didn't have sufficient security. Since Trulsen didn't know the banker who had succeeded Torgersen, he had no other option than to go begging to Jonas. He needed the money to save his property in Montana, which he hoped would be a good investment. But it was only after Mrs. Trulsen had approached Ragna about their difficulties that Jonas had relented and let him have the money. Mrs. Trulsen had shed tears over their broken friendship, and all had ended in reconciliation. Ragna had disliked the conflict as much as had Mrs. Trulsen. But they still stood in their separate camps, and God alone knew whether it would ever be any different. Ragna had invited the Trulsens to dinner, along with the new pastor, his parents, the Nybloms, Mrs. O'Brien, and a few others. This would be their first social relations in eighteen years and Mrs. Trulsen looked forward to it in childish anticipation.

She had found nothing to criticize in Pastor Jorshaug's sermon. It could just as well have been given by a minister in the United Church. It had moved her with such power that she had almost cried and she said right out to Mrs. Flasmo that the time had come for them all to be reconciled. And Mrs. Flasmo agreed.

The sermon had also made a powerful impression on Ragna. She hadn't thought much about Jorshaug's mastery of Norwegian, nor of his eloquence. She had been taken by his calm and earnest composure and his candid approach to the text for the day. He spoke about God as the source of all love and about Christ as the only road to the glory that is without end. We made ourselves a Christianity according to our own needs and desires. One of the greatest Christian faults was that of hypocrisy, our inclination to put on a social display of faith to please others. We lied to ourselves and we lied to God. We dressed up in our religion like a suit of clothes for fine occasions. But the Lord wasn't fooled. Not even the world. We only succeeded in fooling ourselves. This was no news to Ragna, who had often heard it all said before. And yet, because he addressed himself so directly to each and every individual, his words had a strong appeal.

Life had given Ragna so much that she was grateful for. Things had gone well for them and, having grown up in poverty, she had appreciated the comforts that were the fruits of their prosperity. Her husband was the leading man in their small community. She had a small circle of friends she was devoted to and who were devoted to her, and she enjoyed the prestige that comes with being the wife of a leading citizen. At times, however, her awareness of having become a slave of bodily comfort and pleasure made her miserable, and she reproached herself for being on the road to accepting the ethical half-measures that she had so deplored in others.

She comforted herself that there had been no storm clouds in the sky of their married life. They had shared one great sorrow—the new life that had been kindled only to be snuffed—and their grief had perhaps been as valuable to them as many of the things that were considered life's blessings. Signe Marie had given them much happiness but also some worry, and it seemed that there would be much more to worry about. It had become more and more difficult for her lively nature to adjust to the straitjacket of an American prairie town. She wanted out. So last year they sent her to the Ladies Seminary in Red Wing, but she had refused to return to school for a second term.[8] Then, after a few months at home, she had again started talking of going away. Such was youth . . . Ragna was unable to control her daughter, and her father spoiled her.

Jonas could be unreasonably lenient but also unnecessarily strict. He was still the same split personality—for good and bad—that Ragna knew from their days of courtship: often far too indulgent and accommodating at home, at times stubborn and uncooperative abroad. He could be harsh and insensitive toward those whom an unkind fate had denied the ability to take part in that race with death, called "free enterprise" by modern society and the "survival of the fittest" by the theory of evolution. So far as she knew, he hadn't been unfair in his dealings with anyone. She had to admit that this could hardly be said of some who he had confronted. Their ways had often been crooked. For years he had been at war with Ward, a war that was now about to enter its perhaps most violent phase: the last battle in the war for the county seat. Many times she had tried to have him give up the struggle. They had enough. Why make their lives miserable for no purpose? But her remonstrations had been fruitless. Nothing could make him swerve from his ambitious plans.

She had found much in Jorshaug's sermon that also applied to Jonas, so she was anxious to learn how he had liked it. She was fully informed on their way home from church.

"That was quite a sermon Sivert gave us," he said.

"Yes, it was a good sermon," she replied.

"Indeed, straight and uncompromising Synod doctrine. I have always said that our own deeds are mere illusions and of no importance for our salvation, as these people in the United Church would have us believe." So that's how he had understood the sermon . . .

"I have invited the Trulsens for dinner," she suddenly said. He shrugged.

"Trulsens? Why the Trulsens? I suppose I should be able to stand her, but Ole is the same fox he's always been. And we haven't had contact with them for a long time."

"You'll have to stand them both today. I've invited them," she said. He noticed an unusual firmness in her voice.

"People will be saying that we are holding out our hand to the United Church."

"I couldn't care less." He made no answer to this.

———

Flasmo brought up the question of church unity after dinner. Flasmo had matured in these eighteen years. He had become almost quiet and gentle. He had just read an article by Professor Kildahl in *Lutheraneren* that suggested an agreement was not far away.[9]

"Are you saying that we should all become United?" Jonas was irritated. The pastor answered for Iver. "If we all agree, then no church will have to be swallowed by another," he said. "I too think that we are now closer to church unity than we have ever been before." Jonas stared at him. What kind of talk was this from a Synod pastor?[10]

"Oh, so do I!" Mrs. Trulsen exclaimed. "May it happen soon!"

The pastor suddenly turned to Signe Marie, who had been talking with David Rytterskjold over at the piano. "I suppose you don't believe much in union either?"

"Oh, certainly," she responded quickly. But then she hesitated. "That may, of course, depend on just what kind of union you are talking about." Jorshaug noted the slyness in her voice. "Ecclesiastical, of course!" he said.

"All unions are ecclesiastical in this town," she laughed. "Old Mr. Hoff, the master shoemaker who is our justice of the peace, says that we haven't had a civil marriage these last five years." The pastor smiled. "You seem full of mischief today," he said. "We were talking about the possible union of our different synods."

"Bother! That is certainly something I know nothing about! The only one around here who talks about such things is Jørgine in the South Flats."[11]

"Jørgine—who in the world is Jørgine?"

"She is the most interesting character in Jonasville, " she said, as she now abandoned the young man at the piano and sat down beside the pastor and began to tell him about Jørgine, Hoff, and other remarkable citizens of the town. When Jim Nyblom realized that she no longer recognized his existence, he got up, said to his father that he had an appointment with Karsten Floen, and left.

3.

From the Early History of Jonasville

When Jonas Olsen acquired section 13 on the West Prairie in spite of Elihu Ward's machinations, luck had been on his side, and he had for the most part continued to have good luck for the past eighteen years. This doesn't mean that there hadn't been ups and downs. On the contrary, he had often had to struggle to hold on to his position of power. Moreover, his unquenchable desire to secure and improve his position had constantly led him into new conflicts. On a small scale he had become an undisputed master, but he had to pay a price, perhaps a higher price than he himself realized.

The first and entirely unexpected obstacle was a *determineret* attempt to deprive him of his title to section 13. Someone had discovered that certain sections in the area through which the H. & B. built their new railroad between Normanville and Stockdale had been included in an earlier land grant to the D. & T. Railroad. There had been some irregularity with the grant—some formality that had been neglected when it was passed in the legislature—and when an attempt was made to correct the error there was so much opposition that it was decided to let it rest until a new legislature had been elected. Then the D. & T. Railroad was bought by the C. & M. Company, who in the summer of 1892, just as the first buildings were going up in Jonasville, achieved a temporary court order to stop all further traffic on the disputed sections until the question of ownership had been determined. Consequently, the H. & B. decided to approach the new legislature when it met in January.

Opinion was divided as to what the legislature would do about the land grant, but the C. & M. had long arms, politically as well as financially, and many agreed that the company had a good case since the original intention had without doubt been to include these sections in the grant. In the meantime things came to a standstill in Jonasville. Jonas and those who had bought downtown lots from him and begun building had put up makeshift roofs on their half-finished buildings and had started to do business on a small scale. No one dared run the risk of a major investment until the question of property rights had been decided. Consequently, there was far less hustle and bustle than Jonas and many others had envisaged.

The interested parties had come to the session with their best artillery, and an expensive lobby was active in St. Paul. The C. & M. were represented by their best legal advisors, and the H. & B., Jonas, and other property owners had joined forces and secured the assistance of two of the best-known lawyers at that time, Bill Ervin and Cy Wellington.

All details of the history of the land grant were reconsidered. The C. & M. Company stressed the circumstances under which the list of those areas of Garfield and adjoining counties included in the grant had been "left out" of the clean copy of the act, and that this hadn't been discovered until after the governor had signed it. It was explained that failure to have the error corrected was due to the tireless opposition of one man, the gifted and quick-witted, but rather erratic, Irish politician and writer Ignatius Donnelly.[12] He had argued against the grant from the very beginning and he had used his not inconsiderable eloquence to argue against a new round in the legislature. The railroad company hadn't dared let the question come to a vote and risk having it decided against them then and there. And now that the question was to be determined once and for all, Donnelly was again active.

The railroad representatives claimed that corrupt means had been used to deprive the D. & T. of their rights. Indeed, a St. Paul newspaper edited by Joseph Wheelock,[13] Donnelly's most unrelenting adversary and the best journalist in the entire Northwest, hinted that the copyist had been bribed to change the original text. Questions were asked about Donnelly's motives. It was said that the president of the D. & T. had stood in the way of the crafty politician's ambitions when he some years earlier had sought election as U.S. senator.

According to the newspaper recapitulation of the first round in the legislature, the copyist had explained that the clause concerning the disputed sections had been deleted when he had received it from the senate. The secretary of the senate, however, had testified that it hadn't been deleted when he had given the document to the clerk who brought it to the copyist, and the clerk had insisted that no one else had touched the document while he had it in his possession. It had never been disclosed who wasn't telling the truth. Indeed, rumor would have it that no one had been very interested in finding it out.

Donnelly was still opposed to granting the land to the railroad company, but he hadn't yet said anything. Now that the legislature was about to resolve the issue, however, he took the floor. Wheelock's newspaper had once again attacked him that morning. The general public as well as the members of the legislature had expected that he would have his say, and since there was more entertainment in one of his speeches than in any circus, both the gallery and the corridors were packed in anticipation of his response to Wheelock. The latter was an English immigrant, born in Nova Scotia, who had come to the Northwest as a young man. He had achieved considerable influence as editor of the major conservative newspaper in St. Paul. The clashes between him and Donnelly had been many and spectacular. Now he again had his say, and the next item on the agenda was Donnelly's revenge.

When the man from Nininger—Donnelly's hometown—stood up to speak, he had Wheelock's newspaper in his hand. It had paid him a memorable tribute under the title "The Great Cryptogram," a nickname that had stuck to Donnelly after he published a book with that title, on the origin of Shakespeare's plays.[14] He held the newspaper so that all could see it. Accompanied by laughter and applause from the audience, and interrupted by whistling and cat-calls from a small minority who to little effect demonstrated against the speaker, he opened with some jokes about English stupidity and their lacking sense of humor. When the laughter ceased, he placed the newspaper on his desk and began to speak with a solemn mien and ditto voice about the American nobility who, like the salt of the earth, permeated American history with their high aspirations and their selfless deeds. America's nobility were its pioneers, the pioneers who today were misrepresented by a bigoted press that even had the affront to decorate themselves with their honored and beloved name. The pioneers were the incarnation of national self-sacrifice and devotion. In powerful colors he portrayed the generosity, the nobility of heart, and the true patriotism of those who gave all for others—for the family, the country, and the future—who created a civilization in the wilderness, and who founded new states for the nation, all in order to make it a paradise on earth for future generations. The American pioneers—in the forests, on the prairies, in the shops, mills, and factories, and in the mines—wherever honest and true work was done—had had to suffer many trials and tribulations in order to tame the land. But the struggle with nature was only part of it. They also had to perform their labors with girded loins and to defend themselves and their families and the fruits of their labors against Indians, railroad companies, and capitalists, so that the country, the people, and the generations to come could live in freedom. And in the darkest hour of need, when the trumpets of war were heard throughout the land, then too the patriotic pioneers followed the holy commandment of duty and devotion. They left their homes and their loved ones, their property and possessions, to do battle for the safety and honor of the republic. They went forth with the fear of God in their hearts, strength in their arms, and courage in their breasts . . . And what do you think, my ladies and gentlemen, what do you think happened at home while the patriotic fathers were away fighting and suffering and sacrificing their blood for land and liberty?

He made a slight pause. All held their breath. They knew that the climax was at hand. They felt that the incomparable Donnelly was again about to outdo himself. In ten minutes the entire city would only have one topic: the words he was about to utter.

I repeat, the speaker called out, what do you think happened in the settlements as the patriotic fathers fought for their country and their homes on the battlefields of honor in the days of peril and disaster? Well, God have mercy on us, my ladies and gentlemen, what else do you think happened than that a band of robbers from Nova Scotia came sneaking into the settlements in the dead of the night and did violence to the women of the absent protectors of our country and stole their chickens?

Pause. Endless cheering. Applause. Whistles. From the speaker's desk: "Order! Order!" which no one heard.

And eventually, when the patriots—those who had survived—returned home, Donnelly continued, they were angered when they discovered what had happened. The moral waste from Nova Scotia were soundly whipped and sent off into the wilderness with the promise that they would be sent to a warmer place if they ever returned. They didn't. Not to the settlements. But when the pioneers looked more closely at the modest property they had left behind, they discovered to their dismay that the chicken thieves from Nova Scotia had taken possession of their land by promising to build, at some convenient time in the future, a piece of railroad some place or other out on the periphery of civilization.

One hour later, the proposal to legalize the land grant was turned down with a majority of three votes. Jonasville was saved. Jonas, who was present and had listened to Donnelly with great pleasure, forged his way to the great man's desk, followed by Floen, and thanked him. There was not quite as much warmth in the handshake he gave the representative for Garfield County, Seff Thompson.

At first Thompson had avoided taking a stand on the issue. As time for a decision came near, it was rumored that he had said that he found the railroad company unreasonable in their demands. Even when the proposal was debated in the committee of the whole, he remained uncommitted, and his place was empty when a vote was taken. He had now cast his vote for the railroad and against the settlers—voted to take their property and give it to the C. & M. Both Jonas and Floen were sure they knew the meaning of these maneuvers, and they promised each other that Seff would be repaid for his betrayal.

While Jonasville hadn't grown into much of a town the first year because of this awkward affair, it exploded with activity after the decision had been made. Large numbers of people moved in and the resulting sale of lots and the growth in all kinds of business related to building brought joy to Jonas's heart. By fall the town had 500 inhabitants. More than half had arrived during spring and summer.

4.

All small towns have their characteristic traits. But you don't get to know them until you have lived in one for some time yourself. The superficial impression is that one small town is like another. They are all made according to the same pattern. They have the same streets, the same stores. The streets often have the same names. People look much alike, they move at the same speed, and they think the same thoughts.

Jonasville in 1909 was a town that made an impression. Not all small towns make an impression. It was well constructed, and many small towns are not well constructed. The buildings were solid, durable. It had come into existence in more recent times and hadn't, like so many other prairie towns, had to suffer through difficult pioneer conditions. In a manner of speaking, it was a model town from a material point of view. This may to some extent be because it was the work of a single man. To create it had been his life's ambition and he had created it after his own mind and heart. He didn't want it to be a patchwork. The business district had four quite impressive brick buildings.

Jonasville was a lively place of business. The streets were clean and well maintained. The stores were similar to those in Grand Forks and Crookston, although perhaps not as large. Everything was in proper order and the business streets had sidewalks of cement. Drummers were well received, fussed over in the Commercial Club, and sent back to the outside world to boast of the marvels of Jonasville and the achievements of Jonas Olsen.

The town may conveniently be divided into three sections. There was the business district with the main street, Lincoln Street, and two side streets—one of them with the unavoidable name, Main Street. As usual, Main Street didn't live up to its name. Except for Johnson's smithy, Jens Mastad's *barbersjap,* the shoemaker Konstad, who lived above his shop, and Nils Benvold's livery stable, there wasn't much to note about Main Street apart from its name. Lincoln Street was a longish street of five to six blocks with four saloons, six so-called department stores, two butchers, Hoff's shoe store, and two drugstores, one of which was run by Lorentz Essendrop Berge, who also turned an extra two bits with illegal sale of whiskey. Further, there was Ole Fundeland's jewelry and watchmaker business, two banks (Jonas's and Moland's), and two hotels, one of which, the Scandinavie, was run by a former sloop skipper from northern Norway named Captain Elisæus Hermansen. There you would also find Iver Jacobsen's machinery agency, Mrs. Hans Tømmerland's millinery shop, and Einar Movik's tailor shop.

The *Johnsville Enterprize* and the building that housed it were both owned by Jonas. Half the building was now let to a soda fountain and cigar store. The town actually had two newspapers. The *Garfield County*

Herald was also owned by Jonas and was edited by a Dane, Søren Jepsen. There was an obvious advantage in having two newspapers. People had all kinds of opinions, and some had none. Consequently, the *Herald* was independent while the *Enterprize* was a voice of the Liberal Populist Party. Joe Lamm had his literary business in the same building as the *Herald*; that is, in addition to soda pop, lemonade, and candy, he sold newspapers, magazines, tobacco, and the latest dime novels. Lew Sharp, a Civil War veteran with a wooden leg, ran a land office.[15] Moreover, there were two pool halls, a movie theater, a telephone exchange, and, at the very end, an electric power station.

The parsonage was to the side of Main Street, a fine building on a high foundation, and beyond the power station Jonas had set off a whole block that he planned to give to the county for the building of a new courthouse when the decision was made to move the county seat to Jonasville. Down by the railroad there were two huge grain elevators, one belonging to a farmers' cooperative. Axel Nykvist, who had sold his farm, had a hardware store, and Nicolai Nelsen had another. Severin Hansen and Johan Utgard were prominent businessmen, as was, of course, Jonas himself, who in addition to his bank had the largest department store. Nicolai Nelsen and Severin Hansen had both been assistants in Jonas's store, as had Henry Siversen, who had been promoted to the position of cashier at the bank. If we include Ole Abrahamsen's saddler shop and the post office, the major attractions of Lincoln Street have been accounted for.

One of the side streets to the north was called V. Koren Street, and here was found the Norwegian church on a large and well-kept lot.[16] The town's public school was across the street. There were three doctors, Dr. Ludvig Hornemann, who had moved from Arrowtown when Jonasville was founded; Dr. McClosky; and a homeopath who had no patients. Of the four lawyers, Floen had been there the longest and had the largest business. One of the two dentists, Dr. Lenstad, had just arrived from Wisconsin.

The second part of town—the residential district—consisted of five streets that ran parallel with Lincoln on the north side: Kongsvinger, Sverdrup, George Washington, Summit, and Fifth Avenue. This was where the town's businessmen and professionals lived, in other words its more affluent citizens. Jonas and Ragna's home was on a nice corner on Kongsvinger Street, surrounded by a large lawn and a solid railing. The Floens lived on Summit, and the Hornemanns on George Washington.

Trees had begun to come up everywhere in the residential district. The homes had a prosperous look and the surroundings bore witness to the pride the leading citizens of Jonasville took in their city.

Johnsville Park, to the south of the business district, had a music pavilion and benches that were painted green. Here too the trees had become large enough to provide shade from the hot prairie sun. Southwest of the park there was a narrow strip of open prairie that Jonas planned to lay out as residential lots, but for the time being the lots were used for haying and for pasturing his cows and horses. Farther west was the Lutheran cemetery. Few had been laid to rest there. The Jonasville congregation had enjoyed good health. One monument was remarkable for its size. It was a family stone—a marble obelisk—on a lot Jonas had reserved for himself. In one corner of the lot was a small mound. The grave of Ole Sivert. It was covered by a little slab of marble.

Southeast of the cemetery and separated from the rest of the town were three modest streets with one-story homes and unkempt yards. This was the third section, known as the South Flats even though it was no less hilly than the rest of the town. Workers on the railroad and others of humble means lived here, where the ceilings were low and the rooms small. Among the better-known inhabitants of the South Flats were Jørgine, Dorte on the Porch, and Lars in the Bend. Jørgine was janitor in Jonas's bank. She was married for the second time and her present husband was Hans Andreas, also called the "Dome." When he had a glass or two, he often complained that Jonas and other bigwigs were unable to appreciate the situation of a workingman because they were dimwitted and needed more light under their dome. It was for the most part Jørgine who had to provide for the family and to work hard to feed both him and her many children from her first marriage. Life had been tough for Jørgine. That was probably why she was so bitter and had a habit of dwelling on the weaknesses of others. For many years, Lars in the Bend had insisted that she had herself to blame for her misery. She could have been much better off. But that is another story.

The origin of Lars in the Bend's nickname was unknown. He did odd jobs around town, lived alone in a small cabin, and kept chickens and a cow that helped him turn a shilling for milk and eggs. He was known for his skill in hitting on apt characterizations of prominent citizens, who seemed to have forgotten that they themselves not so long ago had fed on crumbs from the tables of others.

Lars in the Bend was not alone in thinking that some of the town's second rank made too much of themselves. Take for instance this Nicolai Nelsen, who just a few years earlier had sold *kaliko* in the Jonas *storet* and who had suddenly become so *svæll* that he no longer greeted fellow citizens on the *streeten*. Jonas felt that he had received little gratitude for giving Nicolai employment when he had come to Jonasville with empty pockets. Nelsen had seemed to have a good sense of business, and since he tended to agree with Jonas, he also struck him as intelligent. Everything had gone so well to begin with. Nicolai went to church regularly, taught Sunday school, and was zealous in his support of the Synod. So the few times it seemed that something had stuck to his fingers, Jonas wouldn't accept his own suspicions even though Nicolai's bank account was growing faster than could be reasonably explained. Nelsen had said that he had sold his land on the coast and was thinking about investing in a business of his own. Jonas was relieved when Nicolai asked him to rent or buy the soon vacant business building next to the hotel. And Nicolai had succeeded in the *hardwaretraden*. But—as Jonas was alone in knowing—after Axel Nykvist had begun his competing business, things no longer went so well for Nelsen. He had been a little too eager to display his affluence. He had even built himself a house on Fifth Avenue that was larger and finer than Jonas's. Everyone, Jonas included, thought that was taking it a little too far. It was also known that Nelsen made frequent visits to Minneapolis, where he stayed at the best hotels and acted the aristocrat. For these and other reasons he was short of cash now that his lease with Jonas was up for renewal for a new three-year period. He had again had to eat humble pie. Jonas had relented and accepted his promissory note, with his inventory as security, and Nicolai had begged him not to register the note since that would hurt his already damaged credit. Again Jonas was generous, even though he really didn't like Nicolai anymore.

But Nicolai was a man of many accomplishments and Jonas knew only of a few. He didn't know, for instance, that he had for some time been looking for a partner with capital and that he had had confidential negotiations with Napoleon Stomhoff. Nor did Jonas, for that matter, know that Napoleon had laid aside some money. Napoleon had done well taking care of Thompson's land office but he had been disappointed in his ambitions to become treasurer of his bank and a partner in his business, something he felt he deserved after having served the interests of both Seff and Ward so long and so well. Nevertheless, he had managed to make good use of his many opportunities to secure his own future. He was an expert bookkeeper, an art that remained a mystery to Seff, and in more than one land transaction, a hundred or two had disappeared without Seff's knowledge. So in spite of his modest salary, Napoleon was not a poor man. He had $3,000 in the Stockdale bank.

Recently he had thought much about having a home. Stomhoff had never had one and he was now a man of forty-six years. And Nicolai's daughter, Nellie, who seemed to be available, would do as well as any other, even though she was no Venus. But Nicolai was a good *bisnesmand* and was thought to be quite well-off. With time, all this would be Nellie's, and then Napoleon would be a worthy competitor of Jonas Olsen. He had it all worked out. Napoleon was a welcome guest at the Nelsens', so everything seemed to be on track, and when Nicolai happened to let fall a word about expanding his business and his plan to get a younger man into it as partner, Stomhoff was no longer in doubt.

While Nicolai had proved himself unreliable in the congregation, there were others who could be counted on. One of these was master shoemaker Hoff.[17] Hoff no longer practiced his trade. He had done so in Kristiania, which is why he was honored with his title even though all he did was sell shoes. Hoff was an amenable man. He hadn't become very Americanized and showed little interest in public affairs. Dr. Hornemann claimed that this was the reason why Jonas had him elected alderman and introduced him to his social circle. Jonas also enjoyed the full support of Hans Tømmerland and Einar Movik, and Iver Jacobsen always seconded his proposals at meetings of the congregation.

The pharmacist, Lorentz Essendrop Berge, was indispensable from a social point of view. He had a keen eye for appearances, but little interest in church matters. Dr. Hornemann had imported him from Chicago and owned the drugstore himself. Mr. Berge ran the liquor business on his own account. One thing that Jonas found irritating with Berge was his tendency to speak disdainfully of small towns. Nor did Jonas like to be constantly reminded that Berge had studied at the university in Norway and that America was all dirt, money, and barbarism. Berge expected an inheritance from a rich uncle in Norway, who never seemed quite ready to die. Lately this uncle had been doing poorly, however, and Berge frequently found occasion to talk about his future wealth.

Severin Hansen was in the same business as Jonas, specializing in yard goods and ready-made clothes. Jonas initially had a monopoly on clothes but then people began to say he was becoming too powerful and that he wouldn't allow others to make a living. Severin had been clerk in his store from the beginning and had for several years been engaged to Kristine Hoff. They naturally wanted to marry, but Severin thought this wasn't possible on his small income. Eventually, the question of marriage became acute when Berge began to invite Kristine to dances at Olsen Hall. Jonas had early on discovered good qualities in Severin and he now decided to set him up in *bisnes*. Jonas would provide the working capital and own two-thirds of the store, but officially no one was to know he was connected with it in any way.

This was how Severin Hansen could open his magnificent store. Everybody knew that he didn't have money, and there was much speculation about who stood behind him. Especially when he and Kristine married soon after and their apartment above the store was furnished in a grand manner. Some were sure that he had helped himself while he worked for Jonas. Others thought they were spending Hoff's money. But this was found unlikely since all knew that Hoff was miserly, and moreover Hoff wasn't all that happy about the marriage and thought Severin a fop. So some said that Jonas may have signed for his loan. But this theory too had to be abandoned when it was reported that Severin had stood behind his counter and used the vilest words about his former employer.

Soon the two competitors were speaking ill of each other in their advertisements in the *Enterprize*. Neither minced his words. This caught people's attention, and many who hadn't done their shopping in Jonasville before now came to see what manner of men were involved in such a commotion. And those who found their way from afar to either Jonas or Severin were given special attention and lower prices and they soon became regular customers. Severin Hansen & Company turned a nice profit its first year. Thus Jonas was again praised for his liberality: all knew that it had been up to him to allow Hansen to establish himself in business. And Jonas gradually changed his mind about the free competition that he had feared so much in the past: his own business had increased in volume after he began to compete with himself through Severin. Over the years others established themselves in the same business, but none were able to threaten the dominant position the first two had achieved for themselves.

Their only serious competitor in the clothing business was Johan Utgard, who had come to Jonasville five or six years ago with a modest sum of money. A bachelor of about forty-five, Johan was reserved and taciturn—not at all the kind of personality usually associated with a successful *bisnesmand*. He joined the congregation but otherwise kept to himself. After a while, however, people began to visit his store, in particular those from the farms. They had heard that he was a fool and thought it would be fun to see for themselves. And then they discovered that they could buy things at a lower price from Utgard than from Jonas or Severin. And he attracted a growing number of customers. One day he got a message from Jonas. He wished to see him. Would he drop in at the bank? Utgard responded that Jonas knew where to find him if he wanted to see him. This was a new experience for Jonas. When he asked people to come, they came. What kind of impudence was this? Later that afternoon he went to Utgard's store. How was the *bisnessen* going? Oh, Johan couldn't complain.

"I've heard that you've been selling at ridiculously low prices," said Jonas.

"Not at all," the other replied. "My profit is reasonable." Well, they had to hold to roughly the same prices, argued Jonas. Otherwise they would all be hurt.

"I'll set my own prices for my own goods!" Utgard declared. Jonas stared at the man who behaved in so incomprehensible a manner.

"Do you understand that we can drive you out of *bisnes* if we want to?" he asked.

"No, but you can try!" With this he turned away and busied himself with something in the rear of the store. After this, relations hadn't been very friendly between the two.

Ragna didn't like the covert partnership between Jonas and Severin. When they were partners, she said, it wasn't fair to give people the impression that they were competitors.

"Well, *bisnes* is *bisnes, ju'no*!" Jonas replied.

"Yes, I suppose so," she said with a little sigh.

He was used to Ragna's disapproval of his business methods and he told himself that it was natural that a woman couldn't understand the complicated affairs of a modern *bisnes*.

The saloons had caused the greatest disagreement between them. Jonas too had at first thought it would be best not to have saloons in town. But gradually he realized that there was a *bisnes* aspect to it. And then one day the tempter arrived in the shape of Arne Stevens from Fargo. He paid a good price for one of Jonas's brick buildings and when Stevens's application for a saloon license came to the town council, Jonas, who was mayor, didn't have to vote since there was a solid majority in favor. Hoff,

Jacobsen, and Tømmerland had long been aware that Jonasville lost a lot of good *bisnes* because people couldn't get a drink there. And it was a widely shared opinion that the whisky sold in Berge's drugstore was diluted. Moreover, it was awkward to run into avowed prohibitionists in the shabby back room of the *drugstoret*.

Jonas had spoken with regret of the town council's decision to Ragna. There was no way he could block it, he said. But hadn't he sold a building to Stevens? Yes, but that was a simple *bisnes* transaction. He saw nothing wrong in doing legitimate *bisnes*. And he himself had been a teetotaler all his life, he said. She suggested that he had responsibilities beyond himself, but just then he had neither time nor inclination to discuss this any further. In two years the town had three *salooner* and now Ole Dampen was coming from Normanville, where he had been denied a renewal of his license because of some disagreement with Ward.

5.

As a consequence of the conflict concerning the ownership of section 13, Jonas and Floen had begun to cooperate in county politics. In St. Paul, the night after the question about the land grant had finally been decided, they had agreed to get rid of Seff at the next election. But their war was not so much with Thompson as with Elihu Ward, the powerful county boss. He still controlled the strongest coalition in the county and it was considered dangerous to oppose him. He had done what he could to thwart them. It was obvious that he had used his influence in the legislature on behalf of C. & M. and against H. & B. and the landowners.

They first made a desperate attempt to control the Republican nomination in 1894. Floen wanted a seat in the legislature himself, and he and Jonas made sure that the county wasn't ignorant of Thompson's activities in St. Paul. This, however, had no effect on the nomination. Seff was the candidate, as Ward had wished. So they had to get rid of Thompson in the election itself, where he was defeated by an unexpectedly large majority. To a man, Jonasville was on the side of the other candidate. Politically they were far apart—he was a Populist—but the main thing was to get at Elihu. It was a good start.

Jonas had no ambition for any office outside of his town. Floen, however, was convinced that he was the right man to represent the district in Washington DC, and for years he awaited an opportunity to begin his rise to prominence. For Jonas it was an honor to have a man with such ambitions in his town and, moreover, to be his good friend and councilor. But the driving force behind his political activities was a burning desire to get at Ward. County politics was an opportunity to keep the war between them going. And if a final victory was in the distant future, then he could in the meantime at least become a boss himself and gain more power as he waited for the right moment to knock the old Yankee cock off his perch.

It hadn't been easy for Floen to convince Jonas that a relatively new immigrant could take on the role of political boss. Jonas had thought that Floen, who was an experienced lawyer, was the obvious choice for leader, but Floen already had his sights set on Washington. A man with political aspirations rides into Washington on the crest of a wave of popular demand and he cannot sit there himself in public and create this popular demand. But Jonas wasn't so naïve that he didn't see he didn't have all the qualifications needed for such a position. But power tempted him. He practiced in the town council and the school commission and studied the affairs of the county carefully. He was no public speaker but he fully mastered the art of more personal persuasion and, moreover, he had no lack of self-confidence. He knew that his pronunciation of the English language wasn't quite as it should be, so one day he surprised Ragna with the proposal that they should use English only for a while at home. And she was to correct him whenever he mispronounced a word. She was sure that it was all about some *bisnes* deal, and she agreed. Jonas held his maiden speech in the town council when he spoke for his own motion concerning the beautification of Jonasville. The idea was to appoint a street cleaner with the rather pretentious title of street commissioner. He stressed the importance of having not only streets and alleys but also private property nice and tidy and he pointed to Normanville as a negative example. The *Johnsville Enterprize,* edited by Peter Markussen, praised his speech. Maliciously minded people said that he had begun to praise himself in his own newspaper, but Jonas was confirmed in his conviction that Floen was right in his faith in him as a political leader.

It soon became clear, however, that the defeat of Thompson was not a reliable measuring stick for Ward's political power. In 1896 Floen was a candidate for the legislature nomination but it turned out that Ward was still dominant. One of his relatives, a young man named Bradish, who had just passed his bar examination, was nominated. Floen ran as an independent. Everyone said that Bradish was without experience and that Floen would win with a wide margin. But it was Bradish who won with a wide margin. No one could understand how it had happened, but so finely had the old master managed his manipulations that there wasn't a single electoral district in the entire county outside of Jonasville and O'Brien's Grove that had given Floen more than a handful of votes. Many were sure that all had not been strictly aboveboard, but they had no evidence.

But Jonas was no more disheartened by Floen's defeat than Ward had been by Thompson's two years earlier. He was, on the contrary, even more convinced that he must continue his war for the good of the county. He almost believed that Providence had made him a tool in the battle of Progress against Reaction. And this conviction was strengthened as Ward continued to interfere with his business. Elihu had become increasingly active after Jonas had opened his own bank in Jonasville. He had even tried to hurt his relations with financial institutions in Minneapolis, saying that it would be unsafe to place large sums for loans at his disposal, with farm mortgages as security. Another dirty trick of his had been to increase the interest on deposits in his bank to 4 percent and to let the farmers borrow money at 10 percent with an additional 5 percent commission, while the usual rate was 12 percent interest and 8 percent in commission. Naturally, Jonas had to follow suit. But it was impossible to run a proper *bisnes* without a decent profit . . . And you could be sure that Ward had his own methods to *skinne* people . . .

The county commissioners had long delayed a referendum on a special county tax for a new courthouse. Their reasons were many and sound. Harvests hadn't been good. Prices on farm products were low and money was tight. People were dissatisfied. The political parties had done their best to encourage the popular belief that while God surely provided sunshine, rain, and growth for the crop, the politicians did the rest. When the price of wheat had been low and the economy sluggish in 1885 to 1888, this was, they explained, because the Democrats had control of Washington. It was always like this when the Democrats were in. Their principles were all wrong. Things would quickly improve when the Republicans took over in 1889. True, President Cleveland lost his bid for reelection in 1888 and Benjamin Harrison was duly placed in the White House, to get the country out of the Democratic mire. But nothing changed and people were in a bad mood. They had been cheated again, they said. So in pure desperation they went to the polls in 1892 and brought back Cleveland. But now things got really bad. The Democratic

Party had again proved to be a power for evil and had to be defeated. People were reminded that they had again been fooled by the old party of slavery. The country would be run to ruin if the Democrats weren't turned out of power. It would spell the end of all prosperity, all progress, and all democracy in America.

Meanwhile many had begun to distrust both parties and said that from a practical point of view it made little difference which of them was in control, especially for the farmers. The price of wheat was low and the interest rate was high regardless of whether the president was called Cleveland or Harrison and whether Congress was Democratic or Republican. It was pretty much the same with state government, they said. This view found expression in the political movement known as Populism, which surged among the rural populace of the Northwest and other areas. At times it was called by other names but it was much the same everywhere. The farmers wanted the downfall of grafters, and in the view of the disaffected masses they were all grafters—the railroads, the grain elevator companies, the politicians, the bankers, the land companies, the press, the speculators, and virtually everyone who ran any kind of business in towns small or large and who owned a white shirt.

Hand in hand with this movement went the propaganda for the patent medicine for all ills: the free coinage of silver. To many this was the miracle medicine that would cure all social evils. This theory swept the prairies, and many intelligent people were convinced that the call for sixteen-to-one was the only natural and permanent cure for the ills of the times.[18]

Although Jonas benefited to some degree from this political turmoil, neither he nor Floen shared the views of the Populists or the free-silver men. On the contrary, their interests were with the other side. But they realized that only by leaning toward the reform element among the farming populace could they nourish any hope of gaining significant support for their main goal. Populism had zealous spokesmen in the county. They had the support of many former Republicans, and the few Democrats, tired of always being on the sidelines, had also joined them. But the Republicans had a comfortable majority and the opposition would have to capture a significant number of their supporters in order to win.

Ward controlled two-thirds of the Republican Party and was opposed to all political heresy. Anything that smelled, however faintly, of Populism was an abomination. But Ward fully understood the popularity of these new ideas and knew that a heavier tax burden could easily generate disaffection and radicalism. This was why he had agreed for so long to put off asking people to pay for a new and modern courthouse. But there were other factors to be considered. Of equal importance to Ward was that Jonasville had had such an alarming growth. No one had yet suggested that the county seat should be moved from Normanville, but he never doubted that Jonasville would demand to be the county seat as soon as it had achieved the size and importance to do so without shame. So it was essential that Normanville build its new courthouse before the new town became too powerful. He could relax once he had the courthouse. People wouldn't be inclined to waste a new courthouse. Once it was there it would mean that Normanville would remain the capital of Garfield County—at least during his lifetime.

Jonas and his followers were of course as opposed to the building of a new courthouse as Ward was for it. Jonasville as county seat was a major monument in Jonas's dream of the future. But his vision would never be realized if a new courthouse was built. So a new courthouse must not be built. Not at any price could he allow a new courthouse.

The proposition to have it built was first presented in 1900 and created quite a commotion. Loads of promotional literature for and against was spread all over the county. On the one hand, people were educated in the view that it was essential that a new building be put in place of the old shanty because the irreplaceable county archives could be lost in a fire or otherwise be destroyed. It was a shame for the proud Garfield County—one of the wealthiest and most progressive counties in the entire state—to have to make do with such a miserable shack. On the other hand, people were no less forcefully explained that this notion of a new courthouse was merely another ploy by Elihu Ward and his political gang, who from the beginning had run the county as they wished until they had now become so aristocratic that they were no longer satisfied with a decent though simple building for their offices. They had become an oligarchy, and now wanted the people—the impoverished, persecuted, and suffering people—to build them a palace they could loll around in.

Floen was again an independent candidate for the legislature. Bradish was the Republican candidate and Newell was candidate for the Senate. Floen used to say of the latter that he was the slyest fox outside of Stillwater.[19] The Populists had their own candidate. The situation seemed quite unpredictable and Jonas feared for the outcome. So he forced Floen to withdraw his candidature in favor of the Populist. For a while this made for a sore spot in their friendship, but in return it made all the Populists outside of Normanville and its immediate environment firm opponents of the building proposition and it was rejected with a solid majority. The Populist was elected representative and Newell was elected senator. Each of the three groupings had gained something and no one had suffered a total defeat. Jonas was, for his part, happy about the result, which was more than could be said for Floen, whose Washington aspirations seemed to be further and further off in the blue.

There was another reason for Jonas to feel proud and happy that fall: his son Ole Sivert was born in November. That came about a few days after the election. It had been a difficult year for Ragna. All the strife and conflict had touched her more deeply than it had him. To her it all seemed so unnecessary. How could it lead to any good? Politics and business occupied more and more of Jonas's time. His days were too short and she was alone with Signe Marie in their large home most evenings. It happened that Jonas found her in tears when he came home late at night. Then his heart softened and he promised that things would be better from now on. She realized that this was merely the sentiment of the moment and that things would remain pretty much the same. She was right. But the son they had awaited for so long brought happiness to her as well as to him.

But Ole Sivert was not as strong and robust a child as Signe Marie had always been. He had delicate and sickly eyes, and their light went out three years later.

6.

Four years later the proposition to build a new courthouse was again put before the electorate. Jonasville had become a town of about 1,500 inhabitants. Jonas was older and wiser and as fearless as ever. Floen had finally been elected state representative two years earlier. This had further weakened Ward's dominance in the county and had strengthened the position of Jonasville and of Jonas as political boss. His hopes of becoming a public orator had not been fulfilled. Nor did he want any political office for himself. So he had all the more time and opportunity to direct the political battle and to this he devoted himself fully. He had all the strings in his hand. Nothing of importance was beyond his ken, and his sleuths were everywhere. He was resolute and self-confident and had succeeded far beyond his expectations in allying himself with the Populist farmers, who in later years had been more and more inclined to ask his advice. Floen's election was made possible by his earlier withdrawal in favor of a Populist candidate.

Jonas had succeeded in getting the Populists to accept his organization rather than their own when the two groups joined forces. They both had pretty much the same aims, he said. So why stand divided? Why not have a common front against their archenemy—and crush him? Gust Nyblom and Lars Jorshaug had been close to Jonas in this process and they were of great help in his efforts. In spite of their ecclesiastical differences, the people of *Groven* had full confidence in Jorshaug in public affairs. He was an informed, thoughtful, and reliable man, politically astute and with a clear view of the interests of the farmer. Nyblom had been active in the Populist movement from the very start and he enjoyed considerable respect as a leader. When the two opposition groups merged as the Liberal Populists, Nyblom became county chairman. Some had talked of placing Jonas in this position of honor but others had been skeptical. He was after all a banker and there was some talk of instances when he hadn't been all that lenient with people who had borrowed money from him. But Jonas had no desire to be county chairman. His aim was to be the power behind the throne. Ward had never sought election to any office, but should anyone aspire to office his view would be decisive. That was the kind of position Jonas wanted for himself. He had never sympathized with Populism. It was an unhealthy movement that could prove dangerous for the legitimate interests of *bisnes*. Some of the farmers' demands were just, but they went too far. So he thought it was for the best that he had forged a union between the opposition groups and brought about a moderation of the demands for reform. There was still a plank or two in the party platform that he disliked, but there would be time for that later. He and Floen had born witness to their good intentions by having Floen sponsor an act passed by the legislature that created some sort of state control over the elevator companies to protect the farmer. Just how this would work in practice no one knew for sure, but at least it looked promising.

But it was above all the political consolidation of the county that was a victory over Ward, and this was the reason why the courthouse proposition was once again voted down in a new referendum, even though the old building by now was so unfit for the needs of county government that the county commissioners had to rent offices in one of Ward's business buildings in order to conduct the affairs of government in a reasonable manner. And then in 1907 came the extra referendum about moving the county seat to Jonasville. It had proved difficult to get the necessary number of signatures required for a proposition, but in the last moment many who belonged to Ward's regular Republican organization had added their names to the petition. Their motives became obvious later.

In July of that year, Nathaniel Buchanan Lewis arrived in Jonasville. He was editor and printer by profession and he came at the right moment. Peter Markussen had resigned the day before as editor of the *Enterprize* because of some disagreement with Jonas. Markussen had originally come to Jonasville as a lightning-conductor agent and had been very successful, since all the new buildings needed lightning rods. Jonas had been impressed by the man's business talent and as the *Enterprize* then was without an editor, Jonas offered Markussen the job along with half a promise of employment in one of his other businesses that required more brains than editing a small-town rag. Now he was glad that it had remained half a promise, because Peter had proved to be an uncooperative fellow who was unable to take an order.

And then there was Lewis, on the spot just as if he had come in with the north wind for the occasion. But Jonas didn't know that Lewis had been in Normanville and had a conference with Ward, who had provided him with a couple hundred dollars for bed and board just so he could be available for Jonas when the occasion, as now, arose. Elihu, who had a nose for everything, had discovered that a conflict was brewing between Jonas and Markussen and he saw that here was an excellent opportunity to have an editor in the enemy camp. So it was as a wolf in sheep's clothing that Lewis one morning entered the bank and began to talk *bisnes* with Jonas. He would prefer to buy a newspaper, but he would also consider taking a position as editor, depending on the conditions offered. He had excellent references, but Jonas wasn't overly interested. He didn't know any of the signatures. But he immediately perceived that Nathaniel Buchanan Lewis was a clever fellow, and Jonas had a weakness for clever fellows.

However, had Jonas known anything about Lewis, he would have watched his step. The glib journalist had edited newspapers a couple of places in southern Minnesota. In both instances he had gained confidence by taking on a battle with a set of politicians who controlled the courthouse and county politics in conspiracy with some allegedly corrupt banker or other forces of evil that specialized in cheating farmers. At first he beat up a lot of dust. People thought him a new Moses who had come to lead them out of slavery. What happened, though, was that Lewis sold out to the enemy when the conflict approached a climax. When the political bosses were tired of his scolding, they got together and decided to get rid of him. They may have preferred a more direct and—for Lewis—painful method but they realized it would be cheaper and more convenient to throw him a few coins and have him change his political views, and then watch him flee the revenge of the proletariat.

Jonas quickly realized that Lewis was an extremely talented man and he was confirmed in this conviction when he found that they saw eye to eye on how a newspaper friendly to reform should be managed. They both agreed that Ward must be stripped of all power and influence. So the two were in beautiful harmony and Lewis began bombarding the old pillars of society. One may have thought that the editor would have showed some moderation at first since he had accepted remuneration from Ward. But such was not the manner of Lewis. On the contrary, he started off as usual with a full-scale attack on the political machine. The *Garfield County Gazette,* Elihu's main organ, responded to the attack with a very personal diatribe against Jonas and a few remarks on Floen. Lewis answered in kind and announced that in a week or two the *Enter-prize* would begin a series of articles presenting the life story of a certain well-known banker, if it proved possible to come to an arrangement with the person who had the manuscript as well as the documentation. This was primarily a question of money, the editor shamelessly explained. The person in question had had major expenses in connection with his research on the history of a certain New England family. So it would naturally be necessary to protect him from loss. But with a sufficient number of new subscriptions, the county could look forward to its greatest sensation. As Lewis thus kept warning Ward of what he could expect, he would daily discuss his great plans with Jonas, who lent him $500 so that he could bring his family to Jonasville. His agents were all over the county, mainly farmers who, for the sake of the good cause, worked for free or for a free copy of the newspaper. Hundreds of new subscribers signed up. The dollars kept rolling in and old subscribers lined up outside the newspaper office to renew their subscription before the sensational series of articles began to appear. No one wanted to miss a single installment. Jonas became more and more convinced that Nathaniel Buchanan was one of the world's seven wonders. An extra edition of the newspaper would be ready a couple of days before the election.

Not until the petition for a referendum had acquired the necessary signatures did Ward begin to play his trumps in the Normanville newspapers. Then it became clear why so many regular Republicans had signed: Elihu had actually wanted to have the referendum that year. His newspapers harped on the theme that all could now see why Jonas so stubbornly had opposed the building of a new courthouse. He wanted to make his own town the county seat. Self-interest governed all his actions and now his true nature was obvious to all. He had let the pig out of the poke. He and his people couldn't care less about the welfare of the farmer, and now they were set to skin him properly. First an expensive move from Normanville to Johnsville and then the building of a new courthouse.

But time flew by and the well-known businessman's sensational life story announced by Lewis had yet to appear in his newspaper. He made all kinds of excuses and ensured his readers that what he had in store for them was worth waiting for. The entire life story would be published in the extra edition of the newspaper. He was sorry for the delay but would make sure that it was even more sensational than he first had planned.

The referendum was set for September 15. It was now the thirteenth. The extra edition was off the press, and Jonas had already read some of the articles and they were very much to his liking. It was ready for distribution that night. The next day every voter in the county would study Ward's long and sad list of sins. Finally he would get what he deserved. Jonas was visibly proud and went for a little walk around in town to show off his power and dignity.

But alas, the much-advertised extra edition of the *Enterprize* never got out to the public: not a single copy was read outside of Jonasville. The next afternoon Lars Jorshaug drove into town and told Jonas that the mailman hadn't brought the newspaper to the subscribers in *Groven*. Jonas rushed to the newspaper office, where he only found the compositor, Push Clark, who was given to drink and who wasn't capable of much for the moment. He hadn't seen Lewis, he said, since Lewis had given him a ten-dollar bill around six and had told him to go and get something to drink; he had spent most of the night in Stevens's saloon. Jonas couldn't see a trace of the extra edition. The safe was empty. In the bank, Siversen told him that Lewis had made no deposit the last two weeks and that he moreover had withdrawn several hundred dollars from the newspaper account in order to buy new type. Further inquiry brought to light that Lewis had sent three large crates with the evening train to Normanville and that he himself had left town by horse and carriage right after the train had left. Benvold, the *liverymand,* from whom he had rented the horses, said that a boy had just brought them back from Stockdale with the message that Lewis had to go Minneapolis that morning on urgent business.

Jonas had been through many frustrating experiences but none that could be compared to this one. But it was merely a prelude to an even greater disappointment. When the results of the referendum were made public, it turned out that Ward had won again.

The next evening the citizens of Normanville celebrated their victory by drinking fifty barrels of beer in Ward's Park. The party ended with a public burning of the entire extra edition of the *Enterprize.* A year later Lewis turned up in the southern part of North Dakota, again engaged in battle against a corrupt political machine and—when the time was ripe—he again ran off with money belonging to the farmers, the machine, and the newspaper.

———

One evening in the late fall of 1909, Pastor Jorshaug was visiting with the Olsens. In the course of their conversation Jonas related episodes of the many battles he had been in, among them the story of Nathaniel Buchanan Lewis—now so much part of the distant past that even Jonas could laugh at it. But he still insisted that Lewis was one of the best minds he had come across—a genius, he added. He had only met one man who was smarter than Lewis, and that was Elihu himself. Jorshaug, who heard most of this for the first time, found this confession strange.

That Signe Marie had had a brother was another chapter in the family's history that Jorshaug had heard very little about. Nor did Jonas or the other members of the family ever talk much about him. Ole Sivert was a topic to be avoided. He had been their great joy and had become their great sorrow. By pure accident, the minister happened to get a glimpse of the grief that this little tragedy had brought upon the family. When the child was two years old they had a small portrait in oils made of him. It stood on the piano in a golden frame, but discretely placed behind a vase, like something that is deeply appreciated and always present, yet hidden from the profane stares of frivolous eyes.

After Jonas had concluded his narrative, Ragna retired to the kitchen and Jorshaug got up to look at a watercolor that he hadn't noticed earlier on the wall above the piano. Then he saw the little portrait behind the vase and he picked it up. Jonas, who had followed his movements, was also on his feet, and when the minister was about to ask him a question, he suddenly went into the adjoining room. Jorshaug and Signe Marie were left alone.

"It's my little brother," she said quietly. "Ole Sivert." Jorshaug too had turned solemn.

"And he died as a small child?" he said.

"Yes. Four years old. He was very sickly and went blind when he was three. And then God took him home. I cannot forget it. It's the only time I've seen tears in my father's eyes. He became so ill that he had to go to bed, and he wasn't out of the house for days. We all loved Ole Sivert so. Then he went blind—and then he died. Mother believes it was our fate because we hadn't been as we were meant to be. Father cannot stand to be reminded that his highest desire had once been that the boy should be a rich and powerful man, far richer and more powerful than himself."

Jorshaug saw that she was struggling against her own tears and he didn't say more about it. He thought he had discovered something. Signe Marie hadn't said much, but it had been enough for him to decide that he had seen an aspect of her character and emotional life that he hadn't known existed. It was so unlike her to sit here and talk about God and be sad. This lively and merry young girl could evidently also be solemn. On his more and more frequent visits to the Olsens he had come to fear that Signe Marie was without her mother's seriousness. His discovery made him happy. And he continued to think about this new Signe Marie long after he had gone to bed that night.

7.

Three years after the founding of Jonasville, the Norse Society was established, and every other year Jonas was duly elected president. The society met in the hall over his store, and dances were often on the program. Both meetings and dances were open to all Norwegians. The society was democratically organized and no social privileges were recognized. Democracy was one of Jonas's great fundamental principles. He knew that all people in America—even in Jonasville—weren't exactly equal, but in the *hall'n*, inequality was not tolerated. No one should find reason to say that Jonas was promoting grand airs and conservatism.

For a more select group of young people Signe Marie and Sigrid Floen had organized a dance club that gave them weekly enjoyment in a smaller hall above the bank. Among the members of this band were Else Abrahamsen, Nellie Nelsen, Augusta Jacobsen, Amanda Hermansen, and Lovise Tømmerland. Male members were Karsten Floen, Ove Mastad, Louis Fundeland, Dr. Lenstad, the dentist, and a few others, among them Berge, who like Nellie Nelsen was really too old, but who maintained his membership due to his status as the town's only authority in matters of etiquette. It was a lively set who were the cause of much shaking of heads and worry among people who did not themselves have children.

For married women there was the Ladies Aid, and for such who had other interests there was a Friday Club, at which English was spoken and discussions were on matters related to American literature, as when Mrs. Tom Percy presented her annual paper on Abyssinia and Bolivia, based on the 1870 edition of *Chambers Encyclopedia,* or when Mrs. Sharp lectured on the art of cooking for foreigners. The club had once passed a resolution on the right of women to vote, but its main concern was the town's reputation for health and cleanliness.

The men had their Commercial Club. Moreover, a few gentlemen of the town had a Whist Club, where Dr. Hornemann was both the best player and the main source of entertainment. The doctor had a large practice and he was respected as well as popular. He was the only one of Jonas's friends who could joke freely with him. Jonas had forged a friendship with him during extremely trying times in his life and he accepted most of what he said. But he didn't like it when Dr. Hornemann went too far in his remarks on his relations to the church, as when he had commented on the news that Pastor Lampe was going to leave town: "If I were you I would simply have myself ordained. Then we would all be sure that we would be kept in line concerning correct doctrine. Why have a pastor when you rule over him like a pope anyway?" Jonas thought this was going too far, even for the doctor. In church matters even Hornemann should respect his position.

Toddy was served at the Whist Club, and Martin Bollemo, a bookkeeper in Jonas's bank, regularly began to forget his partner's lead at the second glass. The club was gathered at the Olsens' the second week of November in the year Pastor Jorshaug had come to the town. Bollemo's partner was Hoff, who was proud of his game and who showed no mercy for those who slipped up. Hoff led in clubs and Bollemo followed in diamonds, the doctor's lead.

"What are you doing!" thundered Hoff. "Are you so drunk already that you believe you're the doctor's partner? Can't you see the difference between clubs and diamonds?"

And then there was a telephone call for Dr. Hornemann, and he got up to take the call. Could he and Jonas come to the parsonage immediately? Signe Marie had had a bad accident. It seemed that she had broken a leg. It was Pastor Jorshaug who called and he seemed very nervous.

"A leg?" the doctor raised his voice. "What leg?" The pastor suggested that it was the left one.

"Above or below the knee?" No reply. The connection was broken. Hornemann excused himself and left without offering an explanation or saying anything to Jonas.

This is what had happened:

Jorshaug had been out for his regular evening walk. It was around nine o'clock and he was just passing by Floen's house on Summit Avenue when Signe Marie came out the door. They met, and she explained that she had been to see Sigrid but that she hadn't been home.

"Do you dare go out alone when the nights are so dark?" he asked.

"Yes, what's there to be afraid of?"

"No, of course, probably nothing. But drunks sometimes roam the streets."

"I have no trouble with drunks. Where are you going?"

"I'm just out walking—an old habit. Now I'm on my way home." They stood there facing each other. There had been a little wet snow earlier that afternoon. It was now icy and the weather was cold. Her neck and shoulders were covered by a large boa over her warm coat of sealskin; her head and the upper part of her face were covered by a wide-brimmed hat. In the weak light of the electric lamp at the corner he could just barely make out her mouth and her nose in all the winter wrapping. He was used to wearing only a light coat on his promenades so that he would be encouraged to walk fast, and now he studied her solid costume.

"I'll walk you home," he said, and turned north toward Kongsvinger Street. She didn't move.

"You know, I haven't been in the parsonage since the arrival of your new housekeeper—I can't remember her name."

"Miss Mikaelsen."

"Yes, that's it. Miss Mikaelsen. I should really be jealous of this Miss Mikaelsen." She took his arm. "I'll walk with you to the parsonage so that you may introduce me to her." Reluctantly he gave in and let her lead him in the direction of Lincoln Street. A strange girl, he thought, and her notion to go with him at this time of day to the parsonage was no less strange. He was worried. They would surely meet people on their way.

"Miss Mikaelsen is shy and a good person," he said. Well, he had to say something. Her arm felt warm and firm against his. He found it pleasing. What would people say? But why should he always be concerned with appearances? What if they had been engaged? A pastor had the same right to be engaged as did others. They turned onto Lincoln Street.

"Would you mind introducing me to Miss Mikaelsen?" she suddenly asked. He hesitated before he said that it would be a pleasure. What else could he say? He couldn't insult Signe Marie Olsen. And then he suddenly realized that this was just about the time when people would be coming out of the Majestic Theater after the movie, and he tried to walk a little faster. But she resisted. It was such a lovely evening, she said. Why hurry? And he was right. They were soon in the crowd coming out of the Majestic. The pastor looked aside to avoid the many inquisitive eyes. Signe Marie smiled and nodded to right and left with undisguised pleasure and noticed that Mrs. Abrahamsen and Mrs. Nelsen whispered knowingly to each other as they passed them.

As they continued their walk she talked to him as to an old friend. She remembered her year at the school in Red Wing and told him how the girls had played jokes on the teachers. Occasionally she regretted that she hadn't returned to Red Wing or gone to a university or a music school. The problem was, she said, that since she had had so much private tutoring, she didn't really fit in anywhere. In some subjects she was quite advanced while in others she was far behind those who had been to a high school. But she would try something next year. She was so tired of always seeing the same people. He listened to her words and now and then murmured agreement, and she felt that he understood her. She had often wondered how she could speak with so much more freedom to him about herself than to friends her own age. And he was so patient and understanding. He was mature, even a man of the world, compared to the young men she was acquainted with. And he appreciated her longings and needs even though she was a frivolous young girl and he was a solemn and profound clergyman. She knew that he was fond of her and she was rather flattered by the attention given her by this tall, reticent, and reserved man.

But now they were at the parsonage. He opened the gate to the large yard and then they were at the stairs up to the entrance. They were slippery, he said, so they should be careful. She quickly freed her arm from his.

"Careful! Careful!" she exclaimed. "I didn't think you would be one of all the timid people we have in this town! If you merely take a breath, someone is sure to cry out: 'Oh, God! Be a little more careful!'" Then she laughed and moved as if trying to take all the steps in one leap. Halfway up, she slipped, fell, and was lying like a heap of clothes at his feet.

"Oh, my dear, have you broken anything?" he asked. She tried to get up but couldn't.

"Mercy, my leg! My leg! Something is wrong with my leg!" He shivered. She had broken her leg. This would be a pretty story! He looked desperately around in the dark. He had to get her into the house. He bent over and reached out his arms to her.

"I'll carry you in," he said.

"That will be quite a burden," she ensured him. He couldn't make up his mind about how he was going to deal with this, but eventually he got the courage to take her in his arms, whereupon she resolutely threw hers around him—so that he would be better able to hold on to her, she explained. If only he didn't fall himself, he thought. He had never experienced anything like it. She was in his arms, warm and soft, and her arms were around his neck. He hardly dared think about it . . . this strange, lively girl. What if anyone should see them?

But he finally got her placed on the sofa in the living room. And just then Miss Mikaelsen came in. It was unavoidable. My goodness! What has happened? The pastor explained everything as objectively as he could, but his housekeeper's disapproving and distrustful face made it clear that she didn't find it at all proper, to put it mildly. And then they called the doctor, and Hornemann was there in ten minutes.

"Have you been fighting?" he asked. "That's not quite the way engagements are usually announced!" Jorshaug was silent. Signe Marie tried to explain what had happened, but the doctor wouldn't listen to her. "Oh, don't try any fibs on me," he said. It turned out to be a complicated fracture in her ankle. "You two have certainly made a mess of it," he continued. "This is going to take a long time to heal and she cannot be moved."

"Can't she be moved?" Jorshaug involuntarily cried out. Hornemann laughed. Then he went to the telephone. They heard him ask Jonas to come and get her. Thank God! thought the pastor. So she can be moved after all. In fifteen minutes she was in her father's carriage.

"Good night, pastor!" the doctor called to him as he left the house. "Better luck next time."

8.

At the Norse Society they had had quite a few lecturers over the years. After 1905 there had been an increasing number of meetings and festivities.[20] A couple of great musicians and quite a few lesser ones had visited the town to stimulate national nostalgia. But no visiting artist had made as deep and lasting an impression as Abelsen, a poet from Norway, according to a newspaper. He had written and read verses about how he imagined that the Norwegians in America spent their days sighing and longing and wishing they were back in Norway.[21] But this is not what he was remembered for in Jonasville.

Abelsen had been Jonas's guest for two weeks and would have liked to stay longer if it hadn't been for the unfortunate circumstance that he had begun to write Signe Marie, who was then sixteen, into the manifold adventure of his life. The rapture wasn't mutual and one evening after he had read some of his verse to her, he tried to make use of the poetic mood to steal a kiss. The result of the girl's powerful reaction and the commotion that followed was that Ragna sent him with little ceremony out of her home. So he spent his last night in town with the captain at the Scandinavie. Jonas had objected that this would be noticed in town and would not only hurt Abelsen and the poetic profession but that it would also harm the cause that he in a wider sense represented, the Norwegian nation. But Ragna wouldn't listen to reason. To avoid speculation, Jonas had mentioned to several that the poet had to take the four o'clock southbound train that morning and that he didn't want to disturb the family at that early hour. This seemed reasonable. The hitch was that Abelsen didn't depart on the four o'clock train but stayed at the hotel till the next evening. The captain tried several times to get him to reveal why he had so suddenly left the Olsen residence, but the young man was apparently wiser than he looked and had avoided the topic.

However, there was no danger that the town would be kept from enjoying the pleasure that such a tiny scandal can give the self-indulgent public of a place with so little entertainment. The servant girl had heard Signe Marie's scream and seen Ragna run into the parlor and she had placed herself at the door where she could hear all. She had, by the way, had some premonition of what would happen, because Abelsen had tried the same trick on her a few days earlier. To her there seemed no difference between the two happenings. And then she told the Nelsens' maid, and she told Nellie, and Nellie told Else Abrahamsen. Consequently, the town was entertained by the story for almost half a year.

The Abelsen episode would probably have taken on a new and more racy character had something else not captured the attention of the town. Every now and then something happened in Jonasville. This time it was a death. Jørgine's first husband passed away. This may not in itself have been so much to go on about, since people are constantly passing away. But when you pass away as did Alexander Wilhelmsen, it's different. Alexander took his own life. And this was the first time such a thing had happened in the history of Jonasville. Even though it was commonly known that Jørgine was a hard-working woman with a houseful of children and with a husband who wasn't capable of doing much, there was whispering that she had spoken rather harshly to Alexander. It was a difficult time for Jørgine, but she survived. And after a year or so she married Hans Andreas, a new arrival and the town's worst drunk. Dorte on the Porch, who was at war with Jørgine because they both had chickens and children who wandered across each other's boundary lines, had recently seen Jørgine leaving Utgard's *storet* with three dollars in her hand. There were even some who had seen that Utgard gave her the money. And Dorte suggested that he had done so for a reason. One could never know about a quiet and shy man like Utgard, she said. There must be something more there. Moreover, Jørgine had recently been to church in new shoes . . . And, stranger still, Utgard and Hans Andreas had been seen whispering between themselves, so they were probably agreed about it . . .

But—to return to our story—Jonas had by no means only had trouble because of the hospitality he showed to people of more or less apocryphal prominence who visited his town. Some had given him considerable pleasure and some had even been to his advantage. Take, for instance, Sakkarias Videnstrup, candidate of philology, who had turned up unexpectedly one day about a year after Abelsen's visit. From other itinerant pliers of the confidence trade, he had heard that Jonas was quite the guardian angel for all gifted Norwegians who resided in America. He came on his own two feet. Nor was this the first walking tour in his life. After he had been thrown out of a Norwegian newspaper in Chicago, he had walked all the way to San Francisco, and had returned via Seattle and St. Paul.

In Chicago, Videnstrup had been called the "Ship," a nickname that stuck with him. He survived by begging and extortion, and his victims were prominent Scandinavians. With time he became quite an expert. He could speak many Norwegian dialects, two Danish ones, and Swedish. Moreover, he had a fabulous store of information of a personal nature that he made use of in the proper place and at the proper time. He presented himself as Norwegian, Swedish, or Danish as the occasion demanded. And if he saw no other way to get out of financial straits, there was always a friendly Scandinavian saloonkeeper willing to let him have some food and an occasional drink for a few days.

As the years went by and the Ship began to return to places where he was known, his earlier sponsors tended to protest against his extortion. So he avoided large cities and became a scholar, collecting material for a large dissertation. His topic was "The Norwegian Nationality's Influence on the New Ethnographical Formation in the United States of North America." With this project he came to Garfield County, with the intention of staying there for a while. For the occasion he had taken a Turkish bath and had bought a new suit in Crookston.

"I've known your name for years," he insisted when he introduced himself with a bow to Jonas in the bank one cold November day, and he explained his reasons for coming to Jonasville. Jonas was flattered that he was so well known and Videnstrup was of course invited to be his guest. That first evening Videnstrup was quite drunk and he talked about so many interesting and strange things in the outside world that he had Signe Marie laughing almost all the time and even Ragna was of the impression that they had made a find. Jonas had a great idea. What if they could get this young man to teach Norwegian to Signe Marie so that she could study it as it was studied in Norway. He was certainly learned enough to do so. Jonas had always insisted that his daughter should have a Norwegian education and they had occasionally had a private tutor for her, so she was already quite advanced.

The Ship had some misgivings. He wasn't really a pedagogue and his research consumed most of his time. The truth is that Videnstrup had only done one week of honest work since arriving in the United States. This was in the Chicago newspaper, and the editor had concluded that he was worthless and moreover extremely lazy and altogether impossible. But Jonas was in an expansive mood and said he could set his own salary—what about a hundred dollars per month and room and board?

Well, the Ship had to admit that this was generous, but he was quick to add that money was of course of little importance to a scholar, but it would help him to get his work published. He wasn't thrilled at the prospect of having to do useful work, but he comforted himself that he wouldn't have to take his duties all that religiously. And the girl was lively and nice of appearance so he couldn't really turn his back on such an opportunity. Moreover, the winter was cold. So he agreed.

Videnstrup was in Jonasville for all of six months. At first there wasn't much to be said for his teaching. He didn't do much and his student didn't seem to mind. But gradually the Ship made a strange discovery. He had fallen in love with his student. At this point, classes became frequent. He actually found pleasure in his work—a new sensation in his mottled experience. Jonas and Ragna were more than pleased. A couple of times Jonas had persuaded him to perform in the Norse Society. He could tell stories that made people laugh so much they almost cried. The main problem for the Ship was to stay away from intoxicating beverages because he soon realized that this was an absolute condition for his employment. Temperance was a cornerstone in the Olsen family tradition. So he manfully abstained and limited himself to two shots of whisky in all secrecy in his own room before going to bed. In short, he lived the good life; he had an income, was respected by the family, had started to attend church, and had begun to get a taste for the respectability that he only knew by name and had till now looked down upon.

But then something happened again in Jonasville.

The outcome of the referendum had convinced Jonas that a Norwegian newspaper was needed in Garfield County. He was sure that the enterprise would make a profit, but he was willing to try it even at a loss. He knew that the next referendum on the county seat in four years would be the final and decisive battle. Most now agreed that they couldn't get along with the old courthouse. They would either have to build a new one in Normanville or move the county seat to Jonasville and set up a new building there. His last skirmish with Ward had been about the legitimacy of renting a private building for temporary county purposes, since the courthouse was no longer sufficient for the county's growing needs. But he realized that he couldn't keep this battle going much longer without hurting his own interests. For some time he had been corresponding with Little Tollefsen, who had returned to the States several years ago. Tollefsen had recently been attached to a newspaper in Fargo and had agreed to come and edit the newspaper, but he would first have to visit the town and acquaint himself with the situation. And

Jonas thought it would be a good idea to have a look at Tollefsen as well. After his experience with Videnstrup, he had almost regretted that he had already negotiated with Tollefsen, for he was convinced that the tutor would make a fine editor. But he wouldn't turn down Tollefsen—at least not without good cause. For quite different reasons, the new newspaper, *Nordlys,* didn't get started until the fall of 1910.[22] But Tollefsen's visit to Jonasville in May two years earlier to have a look at the situation, marked the beginning of the end for the Ship.

It happened that the two were acquainted. Tollefsen knew everything about Videnstrup's life and family in Norway, and a few years ago they had met in St. Paul. The Ship had run into difficulties and seemed destined for the penitentiary, but Tollefsen had struck a deal whereby he was set free on condition that he immediately left town.

It was purely by chance that Videnstrup discovered that Tollefsen was in town. He was out on an errand when he saw him walk from the depot to the hotel. With heavy heart and broken ambitions he stood looking at him. Then he resolutely went to the bank and asked to have the pay he was due. He had received a telegram from Chicago that his brother was on his deathbed. If possible, he would return in two weeks. He expressed his gratitude. A few minutes later he took farewell with Ragna and Signe Marie. They noticed that he had tears in his eyes when he rushed out. "Poor man! He truly loves his brother!" they said.

And then he was off by horse and carriage across the prairie. In Normanville he took the train to St. Paul. It had been many years since he last traveled by train. He was unhappy and defeated and yet he felt quite the gentleman. He had clean and decent clothes and money in his pocket. But he wasn't long in this state of glory. In St. Paul he happened upon some old acquaintances and their reunion was such a joyous occasion that Videnstrup's savings were consumed by the next break of dawn. Again he wandered on foot through a cold and disconsolate world. And Signe Marie never found out that she owed her excellent Norwegian education to the unrequited love of a poor drifter.

9.

Signe Marie was in bed for weeks because of her accident on the stairs of the parsonage. It had been an extremely unfortunate affair, happening at the time of year when people of all ages were busy entertaining themselves. There had been the firemen's masquerade ball and the

Commercial Club's annual ball in Hotel Scandinavie, and all the private parties given by her many friends. The dancing club had met four times without her, and they had had such great fun. Sigrid Floen had told her all about it. And she had to lie there with her leg and die of boredom and depression. Mercy me, to be young and have a leg that couldn't even manage the stairs to a parsonage . . .

Signe Marie was glad she had learned Norwegian because there were so many good books in Norwegian. When a book arrived from Norway or when something by a Norwegian-American writer was published, she and her mother both wanted to read it first. They also fought about the English books, except those that Mrs. O'Brien sometimes came with. They were beyond her grasp. She had tried to read some but it was as if the words disappeared in a fog, and if she tried to reread one, she was no wiser. Often she had seen her mother sit and ponder on one of them till late at night. It didn't seem easy reading for her either. What was the point in writing books that were so difficult to understand?

Her father didn't read much except newspapers. And the first thing he looked at was the financial news. He seemed to find the stock market a grand entertainment. Mercy me, how could anyone have interest in something so boring? But she supposed it was necessary for a *bisnesmand* who wanted to *mæke* money. Well, she supposed it was good that someone was interested in making money. How else would they be able to buy all they needed? Goodness, yes, money could be put to all kinds of use—dresses and shoes and hats and pearls and the thousand other things a body needed for a civilized life . . .

She shifted her position, impatiently pushed the books away, and felt that her leg still hurt. Mercy me, what if she should get limp or something! And this led her thoughts to Jim Nyblom. When he was home on vacation last summer he had been so terribly jealous just because she had paid a little attention to Pastor Jorshaug. She had, after all, merely tried to be polite. And Karsten Floen had recently been behaving with such solemnity that he obviously had something in mind. Mercy me, how stupid and awkward men could be . . .

When she reflected on the times she had been with Jim last summer she remembered things that she then hadn't thought were important. She had often noticed a certain male arrogance. A woman didn't count for much. When she had talked of going to school again to learn more, he had said that she had plenty education for a woman. Only men were of any importance. Mercy me, how important they were in their own eyes . . . She could no longer see any future with Jim. There had been a time when she only had eyes for him, but that was when they were children. And she had learned that men could be had for the asking . . .

For instance, Jorshaug. He said so little, and he probably thought that she was unaware of his intentions. But his intentions were pretty obvious. She often found it irritating that he tried to hide his thoughts and feelings. But she supposed that he had to consider his congregation and pretend that women didn't exist. Some members, like Mrs. Abrahamsen, had daughters themselves. For a month or two, Mrs. Abrahamsen had spoken highly of their new minister and he was a frequent guest at the saddler's. He was such a nice man. But Jorshaug did nothing rashly. Every move required reflection. And he was also often at the Olsens' even though Mrs. Abrahamsen couldn't see what business he had there. To make things worse he had also gone riding a few times with Signe Marie. And then came the unpleasantness on the stairs of the parsonage. It was a scandal for the congregation! Sigrid had kept Signe Marie informed about the talk of the town and, in her seclusion, she had been entertained by her friend's stories. Mercy me, Jonasville certainly had a lively imagination.

While Signe Marie was fully aware of her narrow-minded opposition, she was no less cognizant of her friends and supporters. Sigrid had reported that Dr. Hornemann in particular had spoken harshly of those who had such dirty minds that they assumed impure motives in any event that was a little out of the ordinary. Johan Utgard had expressed himself pretty much like Dr. Hornemann. What was wrong about an unmarried minister going for a walk with a young woman? he had asked. Wasn't the man human? And what was indecent about falling on the icy stairs of a parsonage and breaking an ankle? The taciturn and reserved Utgard had almost waxed eloquent. But Utgard must be up to something and Mrs. Abrahamsen guessed that he was trying to ingratiate himself with the Olsens.

Strangely, the last time Jørgine had cleaned house for Mrs. Abrahamsen she had declared that she wouldn't believe Signe Marie had done anything wrong, even had she broken both legs on the parsonage stoop. But Mrs. Abrahamsen explained that Jørgine was clearly influenced by her goings-on with Utgard . . .

Pastor Jorshaug knew nothing about the gossip. Nor did Ragna, until her suspicion was raised when Mrs. Hornemann's tongue slipped one day. Her friend had to explain herself and the result was a lively scene in the family. Jonas was rash and said things he immediately regretted, and Signe Marie, whose first reaction had been laughter, broke off all further discussion by bursting into tears and saying that she would take revenge on all of Jonasville.

Meanwhile Pastor Jorshaug had been preoccupied with worries of his own. Ole Dampen had recently moved into town and opened a saloon in one of Jonas's buildings on Lincoln Street. How could Jonas have helped such a notorious person establish himself, especially after he had warned him against it! Nor was Ole Dampen his only problem. There had been quite a few rumors about Jonas's political methods. Abrahamsen had just told him that Jonas had bought votes at the last election—actually bought them for cash, said Abrahamsen. And he could prove it. He had it from Hans Andreas, also known as the "Dome," who was one of those who had taken money from Jonas. Abrahamsen had mocked Jonas's interest in reform and had said that he was no more for reform than Ward. That the town had a conservative and a liberal newspaper was a sham. Jonas owned them both. There was no honesty in politics any longer, he said. It was one big confidence game and the greatest con man of them all was Jonas. People were also talking of the secret partnership between Jonas and Severin Hansen. Indeed, after the rumors about Signe Marie and the pastor, there was more talk than ever before. Jorshaug had himself heard Jonas speak ill of Johan Utgard, an upright and kind man who was always generous to those who came to him for help.

The more Jorshaug heard and the more he reflected on it, the more he felt it was his duty to speak to Jonas as his pastor about all rumors that were about. Many a time he had been on his way to the bank and then changed his mind. His pastoral duty was one thing, that Jonas was the town's first citizen and the congregation's mainstay quite another. And thoughts of Signe Marie also entered into his calculations.

One evening he had visited the Olsens with the intention of speaking openly with Jonas. But it had come to nothing. He had just listened to Signe Marie's laughter and talk about her ankle, which now was so much better that she could receive him in the parlor. The next day he had been invited to speak at a church convention in Grand Forks. Some people from the Hauge Synod had taken the initiative.[23] What should he do? Jonas was opposed to all this talk of a union between the synods . . .

IO.

A mong Jonas's ambitious plans to promote the cause of Norwegian culture was to have an annual grand celebration of the Seventeenth of May in Jonasville—not just for Jonasville but for all of northwestern Minnesota.[24] They would have well-known speakers and all that was proper for the celebration of Norway's freedom. He had many motives and it is difficult to determine which of them was foremost. Jonas was probably not conscious of his motives. His pride in all that was Norwegian was authentic and sincere but without sentimentality. When he had come to the United States as a twenty-year-old youth, his mind had been full to the brim with liberal politics and contempt for Swedes. His conflicts with Swedes and the few conservative Norwegians he had met as a newcomer in Minneapolis had strengthened him in his political convictions and had made him more conscious of his nationality.

But it was above all in his few relations with Americans that Jonas had been confirmed in his conviction that if the Norwegians were to amount to anything they must remain Norwegian. His American acquaintances may not have been sufficiently numerous, or intimate, to serve as an objective basis for universally valid conclusions about the relationship between the two peoples, but for Jonas it had been more than sufficient. The few Americans he had known—with the exception of Mrs. O'Brien—had made it all too obvious that they held themselves above immigrants and their American-born children. He had often seen how immigrants proudly claimed to be American. But those who in their own and others' eyes were the real and original Americans were not at all proud to accept immigrants and their descendants as fellow Americans.

If you asked young people of Norwegian descent what nationality they were, they would immediately answer—not without some indignation at being asked—that they naturally were Americans.[25] What else could they be? But if you asked a Yankee what kind of people these children of immigrants were, they would invariably answer without hesitation that they were foreigners or Norwegians. It was not uncommon to hear more or less cultivated Americans use expressions such as "half-civilized foreigners" or "dirty Norwegians" when speaking about the native-born American descendants of Norwegian immigrants of the second or third generation.

But at the same time, Americans strongly insisted on the duty of all—including the immigrants—to identify themselves as Americans. Indeed, it was almost a criminal act to live in America and have a non-American identity. Consequently, while it was your duty to be an American, you were not permitted to be one. To be American was a duty but not a right. The young people regarded themselves as American while the Americans regarded them as foreigners. Among the immigrants, only those from England were allowed to count as what Americans said it was the duty of all to be. Contrary to all statistics, such immigrants were immediately accepted as Americans, and in the second generation it was considered an honor to be able to claim even the lowliest English descent.

As a young man Jonas had great faith in American ideals and he had been among the first to applaud them at Fourth of July celebrations and other patriotic events. He may not always have had a precise sense of these ideals but he had never doubted their greatness. He couldn't really help being Norwegian. It wasn't possible to be born a second time and choose parents of another nationality. But he nevertheless wanted to be an American. He would gladly sing "America, the Beautiful." Here he had found all his heart desired, and he hoped that here his descendants would find yet greater treasures. Norway was a land of memory, a dear and lovely country—a land of tradition and history. America was the land of real values. Here all had space to move around, and if you had a little *bisnes* sense you could go far in America. It was the land where great opportunities could be realized. He had invested in these opportunities expecting a great harvest—and he had not been disappointed. And he said to himself that just as his country had been good to him, so would he be a good and loyal citizen and in all his work would keep the commonweal in mind.

In short, Jonas was proud to be an American. He was no less sincere in his pride in being Norwegian even though his Norwegian-ness to a great extent existed in a world beyond the realities of everyday life. His appreciation of his heritage had grown with his years. He was the only Norwegian in this part of the state to keep a Norwegian private tutor. His home had been open for well-known and lesser-known Norwegian men and women who had visited Jonasville. Many of the speakers and entertainers in the Norse Society had been paid out of his own pocket.

He hadn't been so interested in things Norwegian in the early years of Jonasville. There was so much else that preoccupied his mind, and this was also the period when his main aim was to become an ideal American according to the design for the Americanization of foreigners laid down by a few well-intentioned ladies in Boston.[26] But that was before he got to know the Americans. He had tried to get to know as many as possible so that he could all the faster become one himself. His first hope was that they would all want to be the first to wish him welcome into their circles, since he was so ready to accept all their ideals. Moreover, he was a rising sun in the world of business and any fool could see that he would cast a bright light on the firmament in a few years. To top it off, he surely had a cleverer wife than any of them and she was born in Minneapolis. For a year or two he had patiently knocked on the social doors of Stockdale and Normanville. But they remained closed. Not a single door he knocked on was opened for him. On the contrary, it turned out that most who were active in opposing his interests were Americans. This may have been fortuitous or perhaps a consequence of his battle with Ward, but Jonas had learned that, socially speaking, he could never become an American as he once had thought he could. The Newells, Brackens, and Sanborns were remarkably uninterested in getting to know the Olsens. You couldn't even get so close to them that you could learn the art of holding your fork in the American way. Meanwhile, he got to know more and more Americans through *bisnes* and politics, and the more he got to know them, the more Norwegian he became. Through their ignorant prejudices of immigrants and foreigners and other countries, they unintentionally made him a stronger supporter of his own heritage. Take for instance the Norwegian school.

At first the people of Jonasville had been content to have a month of instruction in Norwegian in the parochial summer school.[27] Jonas had spent quite a lot of money on his congregation, and one month of parochial school would suffice. His daughter was after all in good hands with Miss Molly Wessendrop as her private tutor in Norwegian and music. Signe Marie was to have a Norwegian as well as an American education. The others wouldn't mind. It was the same for them whether they learned much or little Norwegian. Such was his attitude in those days.

But then Romsby became their pastor. Without asking Jonas's advice he decided that the English catechism should have the same status as the Norwegian one, in the school as well as in confirmation classes. Indeed, he had said that for his part he would rather see that the children used the English text. At that time the question of power may have been as important in determining how Jonas reacted as the question of language. But be that as it may; Romsby's English program was soon considerably modified, and when the minister took another calling, Jonas had the summer school expanded from one to two months. He himself paid the teacher's board and salary for the extra month.

But what really got him going and made him a staunch supporter of all things Norwegian was a bill presented by an Americanized Norwegian in the state legislature to limit the freedom of private and parochial schools.[28] The bill never became law but was much discussed in the press. This had made him so angry that he had gone right to the parsonage where he and Leidahl had agreed that the only sensible response to such nonsense would be to have three rather than two months of Norwegian religion school. And he didn't stop there. As chair of the school commission he saw to the appointment of a Norwegian teacher in the town's two-year high school. There was some opposition. Lew Sharp, a member of the commission, said this was taking it too far. It amounted to internationalism, he said, and internationalism led to socialism and socialism led to the end of the world.[29] But Dr. Hornemann expressed the view that if the world should come to an end there would no doubt be other contributing factors at work than a Norwegian teacher in Jonasville, and that it would be all the more important that the children learned enough Norwegian to say the Lord's Prayer.

The first large Seventeenth of May celebration was organized in 1911 and was a great success. For Jonas this was particularly important because the final decision concerning the county seat would be made the next year. A well-known professor from Minneapolis gave the main oration. He was a clever fellow and he gave a clever speech, and Jonas was proud when he heard Signe Marie talk with him in excellent Norwegian about Ibsen and Bjørnson and *Peer Gynt* and Grieg and other matters that he himself knew little about and therefore said nothing.[30] She is a remarkably well-informed and intelligent young girl, the professor told the father. She should be sent to school so that she could develop her talents.

Floen gave quite a good speech at a dinner for the professor. He too had recently become more Norwegian. A good thing, thought Jonas, for his hoped-for election to Congress the next summer. *Nordlys*, started by Tollefsen a few months earlier, had a long account of the events, with portraits of the main speaker and of Jonas. Jonas put this issue of the newspaper in his desk drawer where he kept newspaper cuttings that concerned himself and Jonasville. He kept them there for his descendants. They would read them with pride a hundred years later . . .[31]

II.

E arly next summer the Jonasville newspapers reported that Jonas Olsen had bought a lot from Lindström in Arrowtown. The lot was in the business district and the newspapers reported that Jonas would probably set up a building there in the near future. Seff Thompson, Napoleon, and others speculated on what Jonas was up to.

The immediate cause of the business transaction between Jonas and Lindström was as follows: Sven Ericksen in *Groven* had decided to move to Canada. He had an excellent farm of 320 acres and Jonas, who owned the adjoining 320 acres, was eager to purchase it. Jonas's bank had a mortgage on Ericksen's farm and when he asked Jonas what he would pay for the farm, Jonas had asked what Ericksen thought it was worth. Well, he wanted $60 an acre. Many were interested, he said, but he would give Jonas the opportunity to make the first bid. Jonas thought the price too high but he said he would think about it.

And then one day Torfin Glombekken entered the Arrowtown bank and reported that Sven Ericksen was about to move. Someone would be getting a very good farm, he said. Jonas Olsen, who owned the adjoining land, was very eager to buy, said Torfin. Seff Thompson sent Napoleon out to have a look at the farm. If it was as good as they said it wouldn't make much sense to let Jonas have it. He already had more than enough land in O'Brien Township and was getting far too powerful.

The next day Napoleon came to Sven Ericksen and said he was here in a private capacity but that for a reasonable compensation he might be able to get Thompson to make a bid very much to Ericksen's advantage. Ericksen told him the price he had suggested to Jonas and insisted that he couldn't let it go for less.

"That's dirt cheap," said Napoleon. "Here's what we can do. Set the price at $65 an acre. That will be $1,600 more. But then I must have a modest fee." Sven wanted to know how much Napoleon wanted, and Stomhoff said he would be happy with a thousand dollars.

"You can keep the $600 and I'll take the rest," he said. "That will give you a total of about $20,000. But naturally, nothing must be said to a living soul." Sven assured him that he wouldn't talk, and he thought he was on his way to making a pretty good deal.

And then Napoleon drove on to see Glombekken.

"There will be $200 in your pocket if this works," he said. "When Seff comes to look at Ericksen's farm tomorrow, you will just happen by, and when they seem to be getting on in their negotiations you will take Sven aside and offer him $64 an acre." Torfin nodded in agreement and the two smiled at each other when they parted.

Back in Arrowtown, Napoleon praised the farm to Thompson. The soil was superb and the buildings were in good shape. But he had to hurry up because Jonas had been there almost daily and had offered to buy at $63 an acre and would surely go higher if necessary.

"If it's worth that much to him, it is surely worth that much to me," said Seff.

"But it's a large transaction," said Napoleon. "Too large for me to take on alone. You should go there tomorrow and have a look at the land yourself." All right, said Thompson. He'd do it.

The next afternoon Seff and Sven sat on the front steps and talked it over. Thompson had inspected the farm and had a close look at the buildings. Napoleon had been right in his judgment. But he thought $65 was too much. He had bid $60 and now he had offered $63. Not a cent more, Seff had insisted. Well, then there was nothing more to discuss, said Sven. He wanted $65 and not a penny less. Thompson got up as if to conclude their negotiations. Just then Glombekken came driving by. He parked his Ford down by the fence and came walking up to them. He nodded with respect to Seff.

"I see that we have people visiting from afar in *Groven* today," he said, and indicated that he would like to have a word in private with Sven. They went off a piece and Thompson sat down again.

"I'm not here on my own behalf," Torfin began. "I have a buyer for your farm. He'll give you $64 an acre in cash—every cent in cash."

"And who are you speaking for?" asked Ericksen.

"You have probably guessed it, but I'm not permitted to mention a name."

"Oh! I see!" Sven waved to Seff, "Torfin offers me $64 an acre on someone else's behalf," he called.

"Who else?" Thompson asked.

"That's for you to find out," laughed Torfin. "I can say no more!" Then he turned to Sven and added, "So call me tomorrow morning and let me know." With this he gave a nod to both, and he left them. When Seff left the farm an hour later they had agreed on $65 an acre.

Two days later Sven Ericksen came to Jonas's bank to redeem his mortgage.

"I've been thinking of our little conversation about your farm," said Jonas. "If you'll accept $56 an acre I'll buy it."

"You're a little late," Sven answered. "I've sold it to Seff Thompson for $65." He looked superciliously at the banker as if to let him know that this was of his own making.

"Seff Thompson—sixty-five . . ." Jonas was speechless.

"Yes, and here's your money for the mortgage, including interest and all that is necessary," said Sven as he gave him a check for $3,300. "You can't buy farmland in *Groven* for nothing any longer," he observed, as he turned around and left the bank.

"I'll be hanged!" Jonas exclaimed.

A few days later he bought the town lot from Lindström.

There were other causes for worry. Eventually, versions of the gossip about Signe Marie's alleged escapades with the pastor reached her father's ears. There were also stories of a scandal in the dance club. A drummer from Minneapolis had been invited to one of their evenings, and not only had she danced with this stranger, she had even smoked cigarettes, shocking Else Abrahamsen and Nellie Nelson, who had seen it with their own eyes.

Hoff had carefully broached the subject one day when he came to talk with Jonas about some church matters. He began by telling about the devious schemes of the United Church congregation. A few in their own congregation often went to Vellesen's services in his country church and through them, Hoff had heard that a lay preacher was going to hold a meeting at Abrahamsen's. But that was far from all. Vellesen had been trying to rent a hall in town so that he could hold regular services in competition with the Synod. He had actually asked the school board about the use of the school's assembly hall. But Jonas scoffed at this, even though he didn't trust either Johan Utgard or Leiv Sharp, who had become members of the board at the last election. The others were, after all, Jacobsen, Hornemann, and Lawrence. He assumed Nicolai Nelsen was behind these irregularities, and if so, he would certainly foreclose the mortgage he had on his inventory if Nicolai didn't have the necessary cash when it fell due. But Hoff had explained that Nelsen seemed to have had a change of mind and had told him that while he couldn't keep his wife from running around, he himself desired to live and die in the Synod. Jonas was pleased. Nicolai turned out to be a better man than he had suspected. And Abrahamsen and a few women couldn't possibly be much to worry about. Well, that may be so, said Hoff, but there was quite a lot of discontent. Some thought that Jonas had become too much of a pope and they had resented that he wouldn't allow any dissenting views when they appointed their new pastor. And now it appeared that Jorshaug was frivolous. Hoff didn't like to be the one who said this, but Jonas had better know the truth. Mrs. Abrahamsen had said, without mincing her words, that righteous people couldn't belong to a congregation where the pastor was involved in affairs with wild girls.

"*Gudnes!*" Jonas exclaimed. "So this is what they are saying!" He scratched his head.

Hoff continued that last Sunday Mrs. Nelsen and her daughter had been in *Groven* to have dinner at the Vellesens', and Napoleon had been among the guests. It was said that he and Nellie were quite close. And the Trulsens were there? No, said Hoff. Their relationship with Vellesen was not what it used to be and they were no longer at his beck and call.

The last issue of *Nordlys* was in the mail that Jonas received after Hoff had left. As usual, Jonas first looked over the local news and the advertisements. And then he read the personal notes. Mrs. Jacobsen had been in Minneapolis; Tømmerland had bought a Buick; Movik had four pastor's vestments on order; the captain at the Scandinavie had celebrated his sixty-fourth birthday last Saturday; Leiv Sharp had sold a quarter section in Johnson Township to Gust Nyblom; and Flasmo had been in town to see the doctor on Wednesday. Two notices in particular attracted Jonas's attention. One said that Pastor Jorshaug had returned the day before from the church convention in Grand Forks. He had said to the editor that it had been a good and a well-organized meeting conducted in a Christian spirit of conciliation. A merger of the synods now seemed to have much support among the laity. Jonas of course knew that the pastor had gone to the meeting and he also knew that he had returned. It was bad enough that he had been there against his expressed desires, but that he now appeared in his own newspaper in support of church unity was going too far. Sivert had turned out to be a more independent-minded young man than he had thought possible. He now realized that he should have interfered at an earlier stage and grabbed him by the neck when the first symptoms had appeared, as he had done with the other pastors who had tried to *rønne* the congregation as soon as they had settled in.

As he sat reflecting, his eyes moved from one news item or advertisement to another. Then he read Tollefsen's two editorials. One was on Norwegian politics, which now seemed so different from what went on when Jonas was in Norway that he didn't understand much of it. He assumed the article was sound. The other was on the lack of justice in America. The editor claimed that the authorities were too slack in enforcing the law. There was hardly any police. You could see this even in small towns like Jonasville, and it was all because of corruption in society. Honest politics, for instance, were rarely found in the United States.

Jonas read this with increasing amazement. What had the puny little Tollefsen imagined he had the freedom to do? It might be acceptable to criticize American society in general and in a more abstract manner. Everything wasn't as it should be and this large and powerful country would most likely not be harmed in any way by whatever the little Tollefsen put into his Norwegian newspaper. But now the sneak was actually criticizing Jonasville! He would have to find another editor.

He turned the page and looked at the local news again. And now he was truly surprised when he saw a little notice right under Jorshaug's announcement of coming services: "Pastor Vellesen will give a sermon at 7:30 P.M. on Thursday in the School Assembly Hall." Jonas said the word that his traveling companion across the Atlantic had warned him against using when a pastor was present. So it had gone this far! *Gudnes*! What brazenness he was surrounded by! And who had dared to let Vellesen use the school hall? And then even advertise the service in his own newspaper . . . In five minutes he was in the *Nordlys* office and Tollefsen could see that something serious had happened before he had opened his mouth. Who had come with this advertisement? Tollefsen reminded him that he was new in town and said he couldn't remember.

"And even so you have criticized and denigrated the town in your stupid editorial!" Jonas exclaimed. But his main concern was Vellesen's notice. Tollefsen was humble and asked if it wasn't all right.

"How can you stand there like a sheep and ask such a stupid question!" Jonas shouted at him.

"I quite honestly don't understand what this is about." Tollefsen was obviously confused. He had really done his best to make this issue of the newspaper as good and as interesting as possible. He felt so small and so humble in the presence of this great man. He still couldn't understand why it wasn't a good thing to place a church notice in the newspaper. Especially since Vellesen was a Lutheran just like Jonas. He tried to explain this, but this didn't improve the situation in the least.

"Lutheran!" said Jonas in an even angrier voice. "Any idiot should know that there are a hundred different kinds of Lutherans; but they are all synergists except for a small minority who have the correct doctrine.[32] And in this town we belong to that minority. Is that understood?"

Of course, if that's the way it was, then Tollefsen would try to understand it as best he could. And no more nonsense in the newspaper about Jonasville not being okay and prime number one! Tollefsen agreed but pointed out that he had been especially proud of precisely that article, and that the pharmacist Berge had congratulated him on it. And Berge was an educated man—educated in Norway!

"It's better to have intelligence than to have an education!" said Jonas. "Berge is a fool." Tollefsen sighed. He was, he repeated, not yet well acquainted with the town.

The next to be visited by Jonas was Iver Jacobsen. On his way, Jonas regretted that he had taken Ragna's advice and not become a member of the school board. This was what you had to expect when you didn't keep a hand on everything. It was obviously Utgard who was behind this *monkeybisnes*. Jacobsen could tell him that the decision to let Vellesen use the school hall had been made last night. But Utgard had voted and spoken against it.

"Did Utgard vote against it?" Yes, he had. And he had said that this could cause offence and that it wasn't wise to cause offense.

"Did Utgard say that?" Yes, that's what he had said. It was Lew Sharp who had made the proposal to let the hall once a month to Vellesen, and he and Lawrence had voted for it—and Dr. Hornemann. He had also voted for the proposal.

"Dr. Hornemann!"

"Yes, Dr. Hornemann."

"And what did Hornemann have to say—did he say anything?"

"He said that it would be a good thing for Jonasville to have a little more variety in its Lutheranism."

So that's the way it was. Utgard had spoken and voted against. Hornemann had voted for. *Gudnes*! How could this be explained . . .

12.

Pastor Jorshaug met Seff Thompson from Arrowtown for the first time in twenty years at the church convention in Grand Forks. He had been introduced to him by a Pastor Thuesen as one of the most prominent laymen in northwestern Minnesota. And Thompson had made a good impression on Jorshaug. He was not at all the man he had imagined after all he had heard of him and of what he could remember of Jonas's first battle with him twenty years ago. Seff was an elderly, distinguished, and well-dressed man who intelligently and mildly spoke for a union of the synods. Thuesen had said that he was far more wise and forgiving than Jonas Olsen. Jorshaug had wanted to know how he could pass such judgment on Jonas, who had done so much for both his congregation and his synod. And Thuesen had repeated what he had heard concerning Jonas's questionable methods in *bisnes* and politics, including the rumors that he had made use of money at elections and that he had spread lies about his political opponents as well as his business competitors.

Jorshaug felt more and more uncomfortable with these rumors. He knew that some of them were untrue or at least exaggerated. He had, for instance, found out that Abrahamsen's story of Jonas trying to bribe Hans Andreas was nonsense: a few days before the last election Jonas had persuaded the town's street commissioner to give Hans Andreas some work and then he had scolded him for being drunk when he was supposed to be on the job. He had even failed to exercise his duties as a citizen on Election Day. The "Dome" had interpreted this in his own way and had said that Jonas had given him the job in return for his vote for the Liberal Populist ticket. But he wasn't for sale, he said, and had fooled him. Indeed, it was an easy matter to fool the high and mighty since they had no light under their dome.

But the pastor couldn't quite free himself from his suspicion that there was some truth in what people said about Jonas. After he returned from the convention in Grand Forks, such thoughts troubled him more and more, and the next day he decided to do something about it. That very evening he would go to Jonas and make him aware of the many rumors that threatened to undermine his good name in the county. But would he dare to talk openly about these matters with the man he soon hoped to call his father-in-law? Yes, he said to himself, he would do it. And his relationship with Jonas's daughter made it all the more necessary to do it right away. He had to be open and honest with her father. Their relationship could not be based on a lie. Such were his intentions when he left the parsonage around seven that evening.

Jonas was irritated after his talks with Hoff and Jacobsen and his conflict with little Tollefsen. What had upset him the most was his belief that he couldn't rely on Jorshaug. Jonas realized that he had to intervene and keep the pastor from making even more of a fool of himself. Yes, he would go to the parsonage this very evening and read him book and verse. At supper he told Ragna and Signe Marie about his collision with Tollefsen and that Vellesen had rented the school hall. Ragna said he had been too hard on Tollefsen. He was a good man, she insisted, and Jonas couldn't really expect him to know about these church matters. And for that matter, why not let Vellesen preach? Ragna was being difficult tonight.

"I think I'll go to hear him preach myself!" she said defiantly. "I'm getting tired of all this disagreement." Jonas had never heard her so contrary.

"I'll go too!" said Signe Marie. "We need some change. We're always wading around in the same little pool!" Jonas looked from one to the other. What was going on with these women? He was confident that they weren't serious about going to listen to Vellesen; they were only trying to aggravate him yet more. So he merely said: "I am not willing to believe that any member of my own family would think of selling the Synod." After that they ate in silence.

On his way to the parsonage a half hour later he met Jorshaug outside Berge's drugstore. They looked at each other and were more guarded in their greetings than usual.

"It's a good thing that I met you," said Jonas. "I have a few things I need to talk with you about and I was on my way to the parsonage."

"And I was on my way to you," said the parson.

"All right," said Jonas. "Then I may as well turn around." They didn't speak much as they walked.

Signe Marie met them in the front parlor. She welcomed Jorshaug and criticized him for having stayed away for more than a week. And then she took his hat and shoved him with a laugh into the parlor. Her day hadn't been the least fun either. The night before, she had received a letter from Jim Nyblom. He was in his third year at college. When he graduated from Gustavus Adolphus he intended to go on to Yale or Harvard to learn more, but first he wanted to tell her that he loved her, as she certainly knew, and ask about her feelings. She had pondered his letter all night. The letter had come at an awkward time. In the morning she had talked with her mother about it. She would write and tell him it was too late, she said.

"Too late? Why is it too late?" Ragna asked.

"Oh, because!"

"Because—there is someone else?"

"Yes."

"Has he said anything?"

"No, but . . ."

"I don't think he'll ever say anything. I think he is procrastinating. And how do you think you would do as a parson's wife?"

"Oh, I suppose it wouldn't hurt if all parson's wives were not cut of the same cloth."

"God! How frivolous you can be! But what if he doesn't say anything?"

She had spent the whole day thinking about it. She still hadn't written to Jim. She felt sorry for him in a way, and also for her mother and for Mrs. Nyblom, who had always thought the two would make such a great couple. But she was quite certain that it couldn't be Jim. Not now. She said to herself that if Jorshaug had proposed to her when he had come here two years ago she would probably have kept him on a string for a while and then sent him off as she had all those others. But now she had become a grown-up woman—twenty years—she was an adult . . . And although the tall and somber man with the dreaming eyes could have been her father . . . Well, anyhow, there was something so solid and real about him. He was one she could look up to and lean against. She didn't care if he was a pastor.

So this was her mood when she welcomed him and when her father suggested that they had some church matters to discuss she protested. They always had matters and affairs. Mercy me, why not forget about all that stuff and be plain nice for once? And Jonas gave in, as he usually did when faced with his daughter's wishes. He sat there for a while and then he suddenly realized that he had to speak with Floen tonight. And when Ragna heard this, she remembered that she had forgotten to stop at Mrs. Hornemann's on her way home from the Ladies Aid and tell her that she had been elected member of the visiting committee. If Jorshaug would please excuse them! They would soon be back . . .

The pastor didn't say much that evening. He thought of what he had come to say to Jonas and of how difficult it was for him to say it. And now his feelings for the woman he loved interfered with his thoughts: she was so full of life and talked as if unconcerned about anything at all. "Mercy me, how serious you are!" she said when they were alone. "Is something the matter?" Jorshaug had got up when Ragna and Jonas left and now he sat on the sofa with Signe Marie.

"I actually came to talk with your father," he said. This piece of information didn't appear to thrill her. She turned away, but only for a second, and then she smiled and said, "Yes, but now you have no one to talk with here but poor little me; so that's just what you'll have to do!"

He studied her. He had never seen her so beautiful as just now, in her light and trim summer dress. She had become more full-bodied in these two years. A little taller too. He looked away. She was life and life was dangerous. And now she was twenty. He suddenly realized that he had to make his decision. If he turned life away now, it would be for ever. Someone would come to take the place that should have been his. He had waited for two years and had at times given her advice and guidance so that she would become more mature, more serious, and develop as becoming his future wife. Had he misinterpreted her when he had hoped that she loved him a little bit? What if the free friendliness with which she had met him from the very beginning had only been a superficial fancy. She may not have meant anything special at all. As these thoughts raced through his mind he had a strange vision: he saw her in the arms of another man. She had moved out of his life. She was sailing on the blue seas in a golden boat toward a silvery, sunny coast, as another's bride. He felt his heart beat with a strange fear in which there was also an immense jealousy of someone unknown. He sat up with a jolt. He had to control himself.

"Yes," he said quietly; "nothing can be more dear to me than to talk with you—alone. And this is actually one of the reasons I came tonight." She laughed.

"So that's one of your reasons?"

"Yes!" Now his voice was more firm.

"You make me curious. Have I perhaps done something wrong again?"

"No, but at times I fear that I myself may be doing something wrong—something stupid. I am not exactly a youth—and that's why I had thought—hm—that—that I should—talk with your father . . ." He no longer knew what he was saying. This was all pure nonsense. He looked down as he met her partly challenging and partly ironic eyes. And she, for her part, didn't know whether to laugh or to cry at his awkwardness. Talk with her father! Mercy me, what did her father have to do with any of this? These pastors certainly had little experience in love affairs! Imagine, here was an adult man trying to propose to her and then talking confusedly about asking her father! And she suddenly had an urge to tease him a little. He deserved it.

"It may be best that you talk about it with father at the bank tomorrow," she said coldly. "I assume it's about some business matter that doesn't concern me. Indeed, I know nothing about business." His eyes pleaded with her.

"You misunderstand me completely," he stammered. "I only meant that ..."

"Yes, you only meant that you wanted to protect yourself against doing something wrong—something you would regret. I understand you." Her voice was hard.

"Oh, show me some compassion!" he exclaimed as he took her hand. "You know very well what I want. With your intelligence you have surely seen into my poor heart many a time." She smiled up at him and did not remove her hand. Then he suddenly acquired the courage to embrace her and to kiss her again and again. Finally, she withdrew from his embrace, got up, and said, "Now that was not a nice thing for an old and respected pastor to do!"

And then they both laughed together. They thought themselves so happy. When Jonas and Ragna came home a little later, Jorshaug had quite forgotten his original errand. And when Jonas understood the situation, he said to himself, "Well, I'll have to tell him about his pastoral duties some other time."

13.

Jonas had never forgiven Seff Thompson for his acquisition of Sven Ericksen's farm. Later that summer he was offered a cultivated section by the Minnesota Land and Colonization Company in Minneapolis, and if he had had the Ericksen farm in addition to his own half section, there he could have made an excellent deal. But the Ericksen farm had been sold to the Midland Farm Development Company in St. Paul, leading to new losses and more irritation for Jonas.

"We'll buy that farm at any price if we can only get it," was the message he gave Siversen in his bank when he got the letter from the Minneapolis company. And Siversen wrote asking their price. It had now risen to $70 an acre. But in a few weeks the company would be sending one of their men—Mr. Tomlinson—to Garfield County to survey all their land there, and then Jonas could negotiate with him in person.

Mr. Tomlinson was a partner and could close a deal on behalf of the company.

A week later Tomlinson was there. He was of medium height, fat and broad shouldered, and about forty years old. He was impeccably dressed and gave the impression of unimpassioned solidity. Siversen took to him immediately. But Tomlinson regretted that he was unable to linger; he had to take the southbound train at noon and it was already eleven. He had just had a telegram that he was needed at the main office for a major transaction. They could have the Ericksen farm for $67 an acre if they could close the deal now. He also had a bid at that price from Mr. Ward in Normanville and he was so kind as to let Siversen read the letter from Ward. To Siversen this seemed good news, but since Jonas was away there could be no sale if Tomlinson was unable to wait till Jonas returned from Stockdale, where he had gone to do some business with Mr. Winthrop, the president of the Stockdale National Bank. But Tomlinson was expected in St. Paul in the morning and had to stop in Normanville, where he had important business with Lindermann. So he was indeed sorry that he couldn't meet Jonas, whom he knew so well by name. Siversen knew that Jonas would have done almost anything to keep Ward from getting the Ericksen farm. So he telephoned Jonas and explained the situation. Tomlinson had offered him an option for $1,000. Should he close the deal? Yes, of course, said Jonas, and Siversen did. He signed the contract on behalf of Jonas, and Tomlinson signed for the Midland Company and then left with a cashier's check for $1,000 in his pocket.

Meanwhile, in Stockdale, Jonas told Winthrop what he had just done, and their conversation naturally moved on to Seff Thompson. Winthrop said that he had never really understood the situation of Napoleon Stomhoff, who had an account of more than $3,000 in Winthrop's bank. Now he had emptied it, and what puzzled Winthrop wasn't the transaction in itself so much as why he hadn't used Thompson's bank when he worked for Thompson? They both agreed that there must be some reason for it.

On his way home Jonas continued to speculate on what he had been told. That Napoleon had laid aside some money was one thing, and it wasn't difficult to understand that there could be good reasons why he didn't want his boss to know just how much money he had. But the really interesting question was what Napoleon had done with the money he withdrew from the bank. He had surely bought land! Then he remembered what he had been told about Napoleon's engagement with Nellie Nelsen and the thought struck him that the $3,000 may have contributed to making the engagement possible. If Nellie married Napoleon it would certainly not be for love. And the more he thought about it, the more sense it made, and he was pretty pleased with himself. And then he thought about the note and the mortgage that Nicolai had given him and that they had been renewed for another year. As far as he could remember the loan was due on August 23. Actually, he hadn't thought too much about it after he had heard that Nelsen didn't want to disrupt the congregation. But Jonas didn't like this business with Napoleon, and should it turn out that he had placed his money in Nelsen's *bisness,* then the note would have to be paid on the date it expired. There was a limit to how flexible he could be. *Bisness* was after all *bisness.*

When he entered the bank the next morning he was still thinking of Nicolai and his note. But first he must look at the option they had bought on the Ericksen farm and hear what else Siversen had to tell him about what had happened while he was away. After satisfying himself that all was in full order, he entered his private office, and the first thing he did was to open a small safe where he kept bonds and contracts and other papers concerning his more private transactions. He wanted to see the date on Nicolai's note, but it wasn't in the drawer where he had placed it. Nervously, he searched through the contents of the whole safe without finding the paper he was looking for. Siversen had of course never seen the document. In a drawer in his desk Jonas had found a piece of paper that confirmed the date. It was indeed the twenty-third and today was the twentieth. In the meantime he searched everywhere for the missing papers, even though he realized they were lost for all time. Who could have entered his private office and walked away with those papers? Nothing was missing but Nicolai's note and mortgage. He lay awake at night thinking about it. Ragna realized that something was wrong but Jonas wouldn't say a word about it. He was unreasonable and didn't say a word at the table. On the morning of the twenty-third he entered Nelsen's store. He hadn't been there in a long time, and the first thing he noticed was that there was so little on the shelves. He had the impression that nothing had been bought recently and that Nicolai was trying to sell out the little he had left. Nelsen greeted him pleasantly but Jonas hardly answered him.

"I have come for the money on your note," he said abruptly. Nicolai looked at him as if surprised.

"Note? What note?" he asked.

"Oh, you know very well what note I am talking about! The note for the mortgage that was renewed last fall. You surely remember that I even have a mortgage on your inventory for the full sum?" No, Nicolai couldn't remember anything about it.

"I have never given you a note with a mortgage on my inventory!" he said. "What are you thinking of?"

"You—you are the greatest rascal on earth." Jonas had his fist up under his nose.

"But my dear Jonas," Nicolai was smiling, "if there really is such a note and such a mortgage then all you have to do is to let me see them." Jonas was so angry that he could have knocked him down, but he was able to control himself. Instead he let his right fist fall heavily on the counter.

"You—you miserable candidate for the penitentiary! I'll have you yet!" he cried so that it could be heard all over the store. Then he marched resolutely out with Nicolai's laughter following him out the door.

But now it was time to close the land deal. The next day Jonas was going to St. Paul to make some purchases and he would take the opportunity to finalize his agreement with the Midland Company about the Ericksen farm. He hadn't yet had a letter from the company confirming his option or acknowledging receipt of the thousand dollars but he didn't give this much attention since Tomlinson after all was a partner in the firm. The next morning at about nine o'clock, as Jonas was busy in his store making a list of what he needed to get in St. Paul, a tall and powerful-looking man entered the bank and gave his visiting card to Siversen, adding that he wished to see Jonas Olsen. Siversen looked at his card. "Charles W. Tomlinson, representing Midland Farm Development Company, St. Paul, Minn.," it said. Siversen stared at the huge man in front of him.

"Tomlinson—Tomlinson?" he said hoarsely. The man gave him a friendly smile. Yes, he was Tomlinson. Siversen whispered something in the ear of the bookkeeper, Bollemo, who got up quickly and left. A few minutes later he faced his boss in the store. A new Tomlinson had just arrived, he informed him. He was in the bank right now.

"Another Tomlinson?" Jonas roared. "Another Tomlinson? What is it you are saying, man. Are you seeing things?"

But when he a moment later came into the bank himself, he saw that all was as Bollemo had said. Another Tomlinson had suddenly made his appearance. Moreover, this Tomlinson had papers to prove he was Tomlinson. The first one, who had been given $1,000, was a con man who had no relations with the Midland Company. When Jonas realized that he had been conned, he said no more about the first Tomlinson. He did not like being conned but there was nothing he could do about it now. He still wanted to have that Ericksen farm and he signed an agreement before the company representative left town. The only snag was that the price, as the company had informed him, was $70 for the acre and not $67, as the first Tomlinson had offered. But there was nothing he could do about that either. He would finalize the deal in St. Paul tomorrow.

But after Tomlinson had left, Jonas had his say. Siversen had never seen him so mad. Attempts were made to cancel the check but it was too late: it had already been accepted by a small bank in Hopkins, Minnesota. Later that afternoon Jonas suddenly saw the light.

"Tell me," he said to Siversen, "did that rascal ever set his foot in my office?" Siversen had been dreading that question. He had dreaded it since the day he had heard that Nicolai Nelsen's note had disappeared. He had known it would come.

"Yes," he admitted. "This is where the option contract was signed. I thought it would be best to close such a deal in private."

"Sure! *O'kors,* Siversen! And tell me, Siversen, was he ever alone in here?" Siversen was quite confused.

"Yes—no—yes—when I think about it he may have been alone a few minutes while I took care of some elevator checks for Torfin Glombekken. There was more business in the bank than Bollemo could take care of alone and Torfin was in such a hurry."

"That's just as I thought, Siversen! You are still an ass, Siversen!"

Bollemo listened to this with his nose in the ledger and he thought: "Well I would have gotten worse, had he only known . . ." And Bollemo had good reason for his fears, because one evening in Stevens's saloon he had happened to boast to Arvid Anderson about Mr. Tomlinson's expected arrival and Jonas's plans to acquire the Sven Ericksen farm. It had happened at his seventh whisky.

14.

In late summer, Pastor Vellesen preached every third Wednesday evening in Jonasville—to the great indignation primarily of Jonas, but also of many others who didn't like this incursion into their ecclesiastical territory. Quite a few, such as Tømmerland, Jacobsen, the captain at the Scandinavie, Hoff, Movik, and Konstad, who otherwise were inclined to unification, had become angry at this attempt to fish in troubled waters, so Jonas gradually acquired a little army of eager supporters. The one advantage Jonas saw in Vellesen's monthly visit was that it so clearly demonstrated who was with him and who was against him. Moreover, it helped clarify his relationship with Jorshaug. Jonas hadn't failed to make Jorshaug aware of the underhanded methods of the United Church. Jorshaug thought it was wrong to lay the behavior of a few individuals at the door of an entire church. Surely this was a local affair that had no bearing on the work for unification. Jonas agreed, but insisted that they could at least no longer cooperate with Vellesen and that Jorshaug should not be so prominent in the work for unification. The pastor responded that he neither would nor could change his views but that he appreciated the points made by Jonas and he agreed that the situation demanded caution. Jonas was sure that he now had the pastor under his thumb.

And then Jorshaug quite unexpectedly brought up another matter he had been thinking about for a long time. It had caused him pain and he wouldn't have peace with himself until he talked with Jonas about it. He was certain that it would make Jonas angry, but to his surprise it seemed not to bother Jonas in the least. After the pastor as tactfully as possible had made him aware of the nasty rumors that were circulating, Jonas began to laugh.

"These are all lies and nonsense!" he ensured him. "It's been going on for more than twenty years. All I have done is to defend myself as well as I could. And I hope that is permitted!"

"Yes, with proper means," Jorshaug answered.

"*Velsør*," said Jonas, "when one has to do battle with cannibals and wild animals he must use the weapons at hand."

Jorshaug was not entirely happy but felt disarmed.

After a confrontation with Jonas one morning in the bank, Jørgine had been inclined to join those who went to listen to Vellesen. She had asked Jonas for an advance of five dollars and he had been in a bad mood and had told her that it was unworthy of capable people like herself and her husband to go begging. Did she perhaps think that he was made of money and could throw dollar bills at whim to the wind? Jørgine hadn't minced words with him. If he wasn't made of money, then she didn't know what he might be made of, except that she hadn't seen that he had much fear of God, mercy, or any other of the qualities required of us in the Bible. And she had concluded that he need not bother; she knew where she could find someone who would lend her a five-dollar bill. Jørgine had evidently been in no better mood than Jonas that day, and Jonas's mood certainly didn't improve with her onslaught. So he blurted:

"Yes, I suppose you do. Johan Utgard will no doubt give you one!" He regretted his words as soon as they were uttered, because this was after Jacobsen had told him about the school board meeting and he had already begun to think that he had misjudged Utgard. Indeed, he had to admit to himself that other things also spoke in Utgard's favor. The problem with Utgard was that he was so contrary in *bisnes*. Even today, two farmers had been in Jonas's store asking about prices on clothes and said that they could get them much cheaper at Utgard's. This was unfair. And for that matter—there may even have been something behind those rumors about him and Jørgine . . . But anyhow he shouldn't have let fall those words about Utgard . . .

He realized that fully when he saw how Jørgine reacted. No sooner had the fatal words left his lips then she sat right down on a chair and began to cry. And this was the first time he had ever seen her in tears; she never complained, even though she had many reasons to do so. He had stood there for a while like an idiot. Then he found a five-dollar bill and tried to give it to her, but she refused it, something he yet couldn't understand. Jørgine went to Vellesen's meeting the next Wednesday.

This was how matters stood when she one day met Pastor Jorshaug in the street. He wanted to be friendly, and stopped to have a few words with her. How was she? Oh, things could have been worse. She supposed he came from the Ladies Aid? Yes, she was right, but he hadn't seen her there. Had she stopped attending? She didn't know quite what to say about that. It wasn't so easy for a poor workingwoman like her and who had such a good-for-nothing husband. And the Ladies Aid was all silk, airs, and grand manners, so she didn't quite fit in anyhow. She had been to Vellesen's meetings a few times and things there were much simpler and more comfortable. At least they took notice of a poor woman who didn't live in a palace. And how was the pastor doing? She supposed he had more than enough to do between wooing Signe Marie and taking care of the competition. To be the son-in-law of Jonas Olsen was more than most could handle, *I'bet'ju*. The pastor wasn't sure whether he should laugh at this or be angry.

"What do you mean?" he asked.

And then he was told the story about the five-dollar bill—everything except the mention of Utgard. Jonas had said, she told the pastor, that there was no reason to pity them since Hans Andreas spent all his time in the saloons and did no honest work, and that they had a houseful of kids and should be ashamed of themselves. As if it was her fault that the house was full of children. And whose fault was it that there were so many saloons? Had she established saloons? Wasn't it Jonas who had opened his town to these saloons that were a gateway to Satan for the weak and the poor. Who ran the city council and all the other affairs people were involved in, such as the *kommersklubben* and the congregation and the free masons and all that, even down to the Norse Society? Didn't he *rønn* it all himself? And if he would just return to her one quarter of all the money Hans Andreas had left behind in the saloons, then you would see that they too could compete with others in finery.

"You are talking against your better judgment, Jørgine! The church certainly has its faults but . . ."

"As the Lord well knows. The pastors are no better than others in following the bidding of the rich."

"There is much less difference between people in the church and those outside the church," the pastor said seriously. "You can enter the church at any time and sit down next to Mrs. Jonas Olsen and with the same right as her and feel that you are as important in the eyes of the Lord as she is."

"I've heard that before," said Jørgine, "but I've never felt anything like it nor has anyone else. Don't try to tell me or anyone else that Mrs. Jonas Olsen and I have the same rights—in or out of church. I'm not blaming the Lord, of course. Men govern the church as they do everything else, and Mrs. Olsen is Mrs. Olsen while I am, well, I'm Jørgine—whether in or outside the church."

"Is this the church's fault?"

And Jørgine said yes, the church didn't do enough to correct the wrongs of the world. But the church was of another world, said the pastor. Jørgine agreed but added that it had its mission among people. It didn't make sense to respond to the injustice of the world with, "Excuse me, but I am of another world!"

Jørgine was unusually eloquent and Jorshaug gave up the argument. And there was truth in what she said. The church hadn't always lived up to its responsibility.

As he left her he remembered a few things that friendly souls had told him about her alleged relationship with Utgard. He hadn't put much faith in this. But it now seemed to him that it was most important to clear the name of Jørgine. He would have to have a word with Utgard about this. He felt sorry for Jørgine. Life wasn't easy for her, and she was right about what she said about society being without mercy.

A few days later, Arvid Anderson found a dead body in the alley behind Stevens's saloon. It was Hans Andreas. He had been drunk for several weeks. Some said, "Jørgine will be better off without him." And others said, "Poor Hans Andreas . . . a good man . . . had he only not gotten mixed up in that marriage . . ."

All were surprised when Johan Utgard took care of the body and paid for the funeral, even though some said he had his reasons. And at the funeral, only one person felled tears, and that was also Johan Utgard. People found that strange, and some even then added that he probably had his reasons. He must have realized that there would be a day of reckoning . . .

15.

Jonas had it out with Dr. Hornemann concerning his vote on Vellesen's use of the school hall. Even though he himself had little use for the church, he should at least have a little respect for the feelings of others, he said. Weren't they supposed to be friends? The doctor responded that it was a question of principle and had nothing to do with friendship. The great and basic principles of ethics and ideas were above all personal considerations.

"Basic principles?" said Jonas. "What nonsense is that?" It was so irritating to hear such frivolous talk from Hornemann.

"This is not nonsense, my friend, but the most important question we have had to decide on in our town," the doctor answered. "It is about whether we are to have freedom of religion or not in Jonasville. Your idea is to tell people what they may believe and what preacher they may listen to. You want to bring us back to the Middle Ages. No, my friend. That won't work. We are living in the twentieth century!"

Jonas and the doctor could never see eye to eye on this question and they didn't talk about it anymore. But it didn't interfere with their friendship. Hornemann was unique. You couldn't deal with him as you could with the others.

Another issue they disagreed about was the promotion of Norwegian culture in the United States. The doctor would tease Jonas and say that some of the musicians he got to play in Jonasville were of doubtful value as inspirers of national sentiment. This had been a longstanding topic of discussion in the Whist Club, and at times it got to the point where the druggist began to speak in Latin. Hornemann would then switch to another topic or begin to play cards again. He was able to take many kinds of torture, he said, but Berge's Latin was unbearable. This winter there was no shortage of entertaining topics. The conflict in the congregation always served the doctor well, but he could also bring up the approaching final battle about the county seat, Floen's dreams of becoming a congressman, and other topics.

One whist evening in February someone brought up Madame Mansini's (née Monsen) recital last week in the Norse Society. Hornemann pronounced it a scandal and claimed she had a voice somewhat like that of a night owl. Signe Marie joined in and agreed with the doctor: it had been terrible.

"Let's play cards," said Jonas. He thought they had made enough of this now. But Hornemann continued. They should take Norwegian music and culture seriously, he said. It was too important a matter to be left to cheats and quacks.

"Well, anyhow, we had better not turn our backs on anything Norwegian," said Jonas.

———◦———

Right now Jonas was busy organizing the annual celebration of the Norse Society, and Signe Marie was looking forward to the event. The fall and winter had been quieter than usual—a consequence of her engagement with Jorshaug. At times it struck her that something was missing in this engagement. There was never any talk of marrying. Nevertheless, she had many opportunities to realize there wasn't much fun in being the one who was to marry the pastor. While he hadn't tried to interfere with her comings and goings, her mother certainly had. She had to stop attending the Dance Club and she had not been allowed to go to the fire brigade's masquerade. She had cried, and her father had said, "Oh, let her go!" But Ragna had remained firm. Signe Marie found her mother unreasonable. She was all the more grateful to Mrs. O'Brien, who a few days ago had taken Ragna with her to Minneapolis, where she was going to attend something at the university and where Ragna planned to visit some old friends. That very day Signe Marie had a letter from her mother. She would be away longer than she had intended, she wrote. "But remember what I have said to you about the Norse Society!" she added.

By tradition, the meetings of the Norse Society concluded with dancing, even though nothing was ever said about it. So Jorshaug was ignorant of this part of the program when he promised Jonas that he would be the main speaker. But two days before the festivities Jonas suddenly thought it might be best to let the pastor know about the dancing. And so he told him. But there was no need to be the least worried about it. If he didn't like to see people dance, then he could simply leave after he had given his speech. But the pastor had objected. He could in no way countenance dance, and if he was part of the program, he would share responsibility for the dance that followed. Why couldn't they cancel the dance? No, that was impossible. People wouldn't come if they couldn't take a few steps on the floor afterward, and then what about their work for Norwegian culture? They had a long discussion. Jorshaug was stubborn. But they had to have a speaker and there was no one else to turn to. Finally, the pastor gave in, but he wanted it known that he had protested against the dance.

"Yes, *o'kors*, naturally—you may protest as much you want," said Jonas. Afterward the pastor regretted his decision, but then it was too late.

<hr />

No one but Berge had any objection to Jorshaug's oration. It was a good and conservative lecture on Norwegian culture and loyalty to America—a little of both—as was fitting for a Norwegian-American audience.

Jorshaug made himself ready to leave after his talk, as Signe Marie had expected. She disagreed strongly with the view that dictated that the pastor had to leave a party as soon as people began to have a little fun. He came over to her when he had put on his coat.

"It's a pity you have to leave," she said. He looked inquiringly at her.

"And you—do you plan to stay?"

"Goodness, yes, naturally."

"But—it would be better if you left. People will believe . . ."

"Oh, let them believe what they want," she said impatiently. He studied her closely a while longer and then turned to leave.

"Good night," he said, "I must go." And with that he disappeared, as if he felt a need to remove himself from a place he could no longer tolerate.

That evening Signe Marie danced every dance and was so merry that even those who thought well of her made remarks about her behavior. To her this was her last encounter with life and youth—a future pastor's wife's farewell to what she left behind. She needed this night. And then she would burn her bridges . . .

16.

S igne Marie's behavior was not without consequences. Ragna came home from Minneapolis just in time for an afternoon coffee at Mrs. Hoff's. She sensed that something was in the air and noticed that Mrs. Abrahamsen and Mrs. Nelsen, who both had come early, looked meaningfully at each other when she came in. This didn't surprise her in the least the way things had been recently. But then she noticed that both Mrs. Fundeland and Mrs. Tømmerland were looking oddly at her. When asked, Mrs. Fundeland answered that her children were well and that she was glad they were still so small that she could have pleasure in them. Because it was getting difficult to bring up children to become decent people. There were so many temptations everywhere . . . But then Mrs. Fundeland suddenly remembered that she had left her crocheting in the front parlor, and Ragna sat alone until Mrs. Hornemann and Mrs. Floen came over to hear what she had to tell them about Minneapolis.

Mrs. Floen told Ragna about what had happened at the Norse Society and that their daughters again were the talk of the town. Both Signe Marie and Sigrid had a lively night, said Mrs. Floen. Neither had behaved indecently. She had been there, and they had been wilder than she had ever seen them, so they had decided to send Sigrid to Northwestern University, where she could put her vitality to better use. But Ragna found little comfort in Sigrid being no better than Signe Marie; Signe Marie was to be the pastor's wife. On her way home she went into the bank to talk it over with Jonas. Why hadn't he stopped her from dancing and behaving like a wild girl? Didn't he have responsibility for his own daughter?

Jonas scratched his head. But what could he have done? Could he be everywhere and even take a mother's place? In his view this was Ragna's fault, he said. She hadn't been strict enough in her upbringing methods. Mothers were always too soft and too forgiving. It would have been far different if she—just as he was right now—had been more consistent and strict and not always let her go when and where she wanted . . . That's how he went on.

Ragna had heard it all before and didn't even answer him. She just sighed and left. Farther down the street she saw a woman who was tired and bent after a long day of work and who walked in the direction of the South Flats. She stopped and looked after her as the woman turned into the park and sat down to rest her weary limbs. Ragna quickly crossed the street and entered the grocery store, where she gave them a long list of food and other things to be sent home to Jørgine. But Jørgine was not to know who had done it.

That evening, she had it out with Signe Marie and insisted that Jonas be present. She had known all along, she said, that Signe Marie was unfit to be a pastor's wife. That was why she hadn't encouraged her engagement. But now that it had been done, her daughter had better take the consequences. Jonas added that he fully agreed. That's how it had to be. Not that he saw anything wrong with dancing and having fun or that he cared the least about what people said, but, still . . . what her mother said was right . . .

"Oh, I'm so tired of it all!" Signe Marie sighed. "I'm going away in the fall."

"Going away?" said her mother. "Where are you going?"

"I don't know. It doesn't really matter. I'm just going away!" And then she threw herself down on the sofa and began to cry, as she often did under such circumstances. She had thought it over. She would go away for a year. If she went to the music conservatory in Chicago she would at least be able to see Sigrid now and then. And Jorshaug could wait. That would be his punishment for being so boorish. But her more immediate need was to silence her parents. So she continued to cry.

"It won't help you at all to put on such a show!" said her mother. "You can't get out of the situation you have made yourself by lying down and crying!" Jonas was still in agreement and he added that she would have to take it like a man.

"And you're not going anywhere!" Ragna continued. "You'll stay here and go through with the mess you have made for yourself. Your father and I have talked it over and we'll hold your wedding in the fall. That's all there is about it."

"Yes," said Jonas, in a not entirely successful attempt to make himself as firm and as determined as his wife. "That's all there is about it! Business is business!"

And to put an end to all further discussion, Ragna left the room. But that was a signal for Signe Marie to cry even harder, and it finally became more than Jonas's heart could take. He went to her and clapped her shoulder and stroked her hair and said that she mustn't be so upset. There would always be a way. And with that she leaped up and embraced him and kissed him as she so often had done when something was not going quite in the direction she had planned. And she told him that he was the kindest and greatest father in the entire world. And Jonas was so moved that he almost cried himself. No one could quite measure up to Signe Marie . . . and then, they had only her . . .

Mother and daughter didn't exchange so many words in the following days. Ragna was not to be budged. Relations between Signe Marie and Jorshaug weren't so good either. The recent happenings had increased his feelings of doubt—doubt of himself and doubt of her. He rarely came to the house, and when he came he said little. Signe Marie convinced herself that her own lack of words for him and her lack of pleasure in his company had been caused by his reticence. But they both felt that they couldn't keep on like this. They would either have to make up or break up. But the last thing Jorshaug wanted was to break the engagement. He was scared of the thought. That was why he said so little. He didn't dare run the risk of saying the wrong thing. So he kept his thoughts to himself.

Meanwhile, preparations were being made for the year's main event— the battle for the county seat and, indeed, for the control of county politics. The Jonasville side had begun their campaign in early spring. Jepsen wrote with warmth and conviction in the *Herald* about the tremendous growth and future of the town and he made vicious attacks on Ward. Before Jepsen came to Jonasville, he had a small newspaper in Normanville. To get started, he had had to borrow some money from Elihu, but things went well and his position was secure. But then Floen became a candidate for the legislature for the first time, and Jepsen, who knew him, wrote that Floen was a good man and should be elected. That was the beginning of the end for him and his newspaper. Six months later he had to leave Normanville. In Jepsen, Jonas found a loyal supporter. There was a good head on the shoulders of this excellent Dane . . .

But Jonas hadn't been so lucky with Tollefsen in *Nordlyset*. There wasn't enough power in his writing, as Jonas had often pointed out. It was especially important that the Norwegian newspaper lash out at Ward. With his present political control Jonas was pretty sure about the county seat if only the Norwegians would stand united. But he knew from experience that some Norwegians were envious of those who had been successful, and that others were quite fanatical about religion. And Jonas didn't like fanatics. For his part, he claimed that he had always been a solid supporter of the Synod but that he had never been a fanatic. But now he needed the votes of all—even the fanatics. Tollefsen had promised to do his best but he hadn't been able to satisfy Jonas. Now he had to respond to some innuendoes in the Normanville newspapers.

"Write something powerful," Jonas told him, "something that will tear up their guts. Attack their morals. Say that they all would have been in the penitentiary had it not been for my nobility. Don't mince your words. You have nothing to fear."

"All right," Tollefsen replied, "I'll do my best."

Just to make sure, he was to show his article to Jonas before he printed it, but Jonas was very busy, and when Sophus Jensen, the typographer, had the proof sheet ready for Tollefsen, Jonas was out of town again. He felt let down when he saw the newspaper. It was the same lemonade as always. He never called anything by name. It was all so abstract. So he had a new talk with the editor. Did he think that their opponents were a Ladies Aid? Didn't he know that Ward and his henchmen were criminals and that dynamite was needed? Jonas became more agitated as he talked. Didn't he have any brains? Was he no better than a cow?

Finally the patient Tollefsen had had enough. He tried to write as a gentleman, he said. He couldn't throw off all civilization just because it had been his fate to be among the savages in Jonasville. And he also reminded Jonas that he was of a good Norwegian family.

"I couldn't care less about good Norwegian families," said Jonas. "I've heard enough of this nonsense and *tommyrot* about fine Norwegian manners. I've never seen that it has given any results in politics. In this town we do *bisnes*, my boy, and if you don't want a part in it then *gudbey* to you."

"I suppose that means that I have been dismissed," said Tollefsen.

"*Velsør*, we are not playing in a comedy! This is the real world."

"All right," said Tollefsen, "I'll leave. I've had enough of your ways."

When Jonas came home for dinner he told Ragna about what had happened between him and the editor. Sofus Jensen would have to take care of the newspaper for the time being, he said. Jonas was quite agitated and paced the floor. Ragna followed him with troubled eyes. He was no longer the inspired fighter, but the bitter and angry avenger. This fight was consuming him. How often she had hoped and prayed that his unbendable strength would find some other challenge than politics! And now poor little Tollefsen was out on the street . . . a well-meaning and conscientious man . . . And his old mother still lived in Kristiansand . . .[33]

"You shouldn't have fired him, Jonas!" she said.

"Fired him? Have I fired him? The idiot said he would go himself. You surely don't mean that I should then follow him and beg him to return?"

"Why not, if you have been unfair to him?"

"Unfair? Have I been unfair?"

"You may have been too hard on him."

"Shucks! I only gave him a little *commonsens*! No one can make use of a man who doesn't have common horse sense. He has been unfair. But the way you see things I suppose no one has ever been unfair to me! I'm always the one who is unfair to others! That's the way you see it."

"No, that's not the way I see it at all," she answered. "I know that many have been unfair to you; and for that very reason you must be very careful that you don't behave the same way to others. Is it not written that when someone hits you, you should turn the other cheek . . ." Jonas had a bitter laugh.

"Yes, that would have made a fine *bisnes*!" he said. And Ragna had to smile too.

When Jonas came home that night he was in a friendlier mood.

"I thought some more about what you said," he confessed, "and I found Tollefsen and told him that it would perhaps be best that he returned to the newspaper." He could almost see the gratitude in her eyes.

"That was kind of you," she said.

"That may be, but it was at least plumb stupid. Do you know what the idiot replied?"

"No. How could I?"

"He said that I could go to a certain place where it's hotter than late summer in the Red River Valley. I probably supposed, he said, that I was a great man and that I had the power to take the bread out of his mouth. But I was wrong, he said, because I hadn't fired him; he had left *Nordlyset* on his own accord and he had made up his mind to do it some time ago, so he would have quit soon anyway. So now I could have my little rag and Sofus Jensen all to myself, he said."

"But what is he thinking?"

"Thinking? Do you believe that little Tollefsen can think? *Gudnes,* no! Ward has approached him some time ago and now he's moving to Normanville to start a Norwegian newspaper there, with money from

the courthouse ring. He told me so himself. The print shop and everything is waiting for him, he said."

"*Gudnes!*" Now it was Ragnas turn to say it. "And what did you tell
him?"

"Hm! I don't like to swear in my own home," Jonas responded. He
went upstairs to change his clothes because they were going to have
a reception for Lyman, the president of the railroad company, at the
Commercial Club.

17.

Pastor Jorshaug hadn't been able to establish a good relationship
with Dr. Hornemann. He regretted this but he had accepted it as
one of the many unavoidable accidents in life. They were different; they
belonged to different worlds. The doctor wasn't at all interested in the
church. Not that he opposed it in any way; nor did he ever speak nega-
tively of religion. But he had no patience with the clergy. At any opportunity he would make fun of them, something Jorshaug had personally
experienced more than once.

The doctor gave his jocular inclinations free rein among his acquaintances and his favorite target was Jorshaug. Ragna had noticed
how this hurt the pastor and she had mentioned it to Mrs. Hornemann.
But Mrs. Hornemann had replied that if her husband was told of his
success, he would eat Jorshaug alive. But he didn't really want to harm
him. It's just the way he is. And so it happened that Jorshaug bore an
increasing grudge against the doctor. He was particularly upset by all
the merriment Hornemann had at the expense of pastors who weren't
as good in Norwegian as they should have been. Hornemann continued to make fun of Pastor Romsby's Norwegian sermons, and Pastor
Leidahl's English ones fared no better.

Jorshaug was particularly bothered by the doctor's remarks on
what had happened to Signe Marie on the parsonage stairs. He kept
at it every time they met. He assumed the pastor had begun early with
his theological indoctrination and had given her a practical lesson in
the subordinate position of women. Once, at a party at the Floens's,
Hornemann had even asked Jorshaug point-blank if he was always so
awkward when he tried to kiss a lady. Jorshaug had often been angered
by these remarks, and he had even turned down dinner invitations just
because he knew that Hornemann would be there.

For his part, Dr. Hornemann continued to collect new material so he could avoid repeating himself too much. An event during one of the walks of the pastor and Signe Marie had provided him with variation in his program. It was a beautiful day and they had gone quite far out of town. On their way back they had both been in their own thoughts and the little conversation they had was, as usual, of little importance. Then Jorshaug suddenly said that they couldn't be engaged forever and asked if she didn't think they should have their wedding in the fall. Perhaps, she replied, and continued to hum as she walked. At the dirt road that crossed Jonas's hayfield and connected the South Flats with the town, she stopped. She was tired, she said, and wanted to rest a little. In the middle of the field—perhaps twenty or thirty rods[34] from where they were—was a haystack. She walked toward it. She wanted to smell fresh hay, she explained. He followed her.

She was no stranger to his thoughts on marriage. This was the first time he had actually said anything about a wedding. But she too had accepted it as a possible outcome, and for quite some time she had, she thought, been as proper and old-fashioned as her pastor could possibly expect of her. Her mother had made her notion of giving him a year of punishment quite impossible, so she had no other alternative than to put on her best manners. But her future didn't seem as rosy as she had hoped. Soon she would be spending all her time in a lonely parsonage . . . No dancing, no card games, no loud laughter or funny stories, and no confessions to others about how much fun she had when she was young . . . And she would probably have to be dressed in black, a color that didn't become her at all.

She sat down in the grass behind the haystack. Before he sat down he placed a white handkerchief nicely beside her and asked her to sit on it. She appreciated his many small tokens of respect. The hay smelled so nice. He remembered the smell from his childhood on the prairie. Although he couldn't see anyone, he remained standing facing her. It seemed more proper. She rested on her elbow and her cheeks blossomed after their long walk.

"Don't you really find it pretty boring to be a pastor?" she asked after a while. The question was so unexpected that he just looked at her.

"No, my dear, how could you imagine such a thing?" he said finally.

"Oh, because!" She returned his look and smiled. He was a fine man, but so serious, she thought—too much the preacher. Suddenly she got up and stepped up to him.

"So you think it is boring to be a pastor?" he said. "But it isn't. It's a wonderful calling." She didn't answer him. Instead she began to play with the folds of his coat. And then the event happened that gave Hornemann so much material for continued teasing. Jorshaug took her in his arms and kissed her. Neither thought of the possibility that they might be observed. But even the smallest town has a thousand eyes. It was only a second or two. Then they let go of each other at the sound of a woman's voice.

"Goodness gracious if it isn't the pastor and Signe Marie!" the voice said. "Oh, dear me! Why did I have to come just now? Well, love has its ways and is a lot more hot than many wish to believe, as the good book says!"

It was Jørgine. She had tied her cow in the field on the other side of the haystack, she said. And then she had heard voices and thought she should see who it was. She hoped they would forgive her; she had certainly not thought of interrupting anything. Jorshaug blushed. Signe Marie laughed.

"I hope you are aware that we are engaged," he said after a while. He thought he should at least say something.

"Oh, we all know that," said Jørgine. "And had anyone been in doubt whether what you were doing was proper, then they would have known it when they saw it was the pastor. And after all, such an innocent . . ." But now she was interrupted by Signe Marie.

"Never mind, Jørgine," she said. "How are the children?" Oh, a little up and down as usual. And now that Hans Andreas had left her and she was alone, she wanted them to know that it wasn't always so easy . . . But Signe Marie interrupted her again, took two silver dollars from her handbag, and gave them to Jørgine. She had planned to drop in on her on her way home, she said, but she had other things on her mind . . .

"*Jæs, o'kors*, naturally," Jørgine agreed. "When you . . ."

"So here they are. They may be of some help for the children," Signe Marie added. Jørgine thanked her and began to walk away, but after a few steps she turned and said: "I won't say a word about this, you know."

"Yes, we know that, Jørgine," said Signe Marie. "You are as good as gold, Jørgine."

"Well, I suppose . . ." She left them. But then they saw the doctor's car down the road and that he had stopped to have a few words with Jørgine. That was all. The next time he and Jorshaug met—it was in the Scandinavie—the doctor said: "I happened to see you behind a haystack the other day, pastor."

That's how he was. No one had told the pastor that he and Signe Marie had no more faithful defender against all scandal mongers than the doctor. But that's how he was too.

———◆———

Some days later Jorshaug's father was suddenly taken ill out on one of his fields. It was his old hernia problem. This time it was pretty bad, and Mrs. Jorshaug had to telephone her son and ask him to bring the doctor as fast as possible. After a few words to the patients in his waiting room, Hornemann came running. He was serious in a way the pastor had never seen him before. They drove in the doctor's Ford and it was the fastest automobile ride Jorshaug had ever had. He was scared all the way and sure that they would run off the road. They arrived none too soon. The doctor had to operate right away. As Hornemann and Mrs. Jorshaug made the necessary preparations, the son fell on his knees at his father's bed and prayed. The old woman wiped her eyes with her apron as she followed the doctor's bidding.

"How do you think he will manage?" the pastor asked when everything was ready.

"You can never tell with old cases like this," Hornemann replied. "This should have been done forty-five years ago."

But all went well and old Jorshaug survived. When the doctor returned to town three hours later, he said that there was nothing to fear at the moment and that he would be better. Both mother and son had been impressed by Hornemann's dedication and loving care. After he left they sat for a long time and talked about him.

"You could almost believe he has several different personalities," the mother said.

"It only appears that way," her son answered. "The fact of the matter is that it often takes a crisis to get to know some people."

18.

J onas was in full control of banking in Jonasville. True, there was the Moland bank, but it had been established in about the same way as Severin Hansen's clothing and dry-goods store. Elias Moland had come to town in the late 1890s with $2,000 and a few ideas. He was pretty brash and threatened Jonas with opening a competing bank. And then they began to negotiate. Moland claimed he had influential people with disposable capital behind him. Jonas didn't take this seriously, but he realized that sooner or later there would be competition, and Moland was a man with guts and drive and it might be profitable to invest in him. Moreover, there were the occasional transactions that Jonas didn't want to be personally involved in because of church or politics. So Elias might be useful for several reasons. Consequently, the Moland Land and Banking Company was established. Apart from Jonas and Elias, investors included Jacobsen, Hornemann, Floen, and a few men in St. Paul. Outside of this little circle, no one knew that Jonas owned 60 percent and thus had full control. Officially, he only had a few shares, in order to support a local business.

In Arrowtown, which now was far behind Jonasville in population as well as in business volume, Seff Thompson was still the only banker, and he was far more afraid of any kind of competition than even Jonas had ever been. So it shouldn't come as a surprise that he was quite upset when he read a short notice in the *Enterprize* about the town lot that Jonas had bought from Lindström. Jonas would begin building on it early next year, and he was planning to establish a business there. Seff worried about this for a week or so, and then *Nordlys* brought the news that Jonas had decided to open a bank in Arrowtown the next summer. That's what the new building was for. This might be the beginning, the newspaper wrote, of the realization of Jonas's plan to establish a chain of banks in this part of the state and in North Dakota. This was shocking news for Thompson.

Seff had recently had quite a few setbacks and he didn't take things as lightly as he had in his younger days. Take for instance his problems with Napoleon Stomhoff. It had started with a careless remark by Mrs. Sven Ericksen when she had come into his office the year before to sign the documents for the sale of their farm to Thompson.

"You got a good price for that farm," Seff had said.

"I don't think so," she had replied. "We didn't even get $20,000, and surely the farm was worth at least that."

Thompson was immediately on the alert. Less than $20,000? What was she talking about? He had paid almost $21,000. And then she remembered something about a *kommission* that she had promised not to mention to anyone. So she tried to cover up and said that of course it had been almost $21,000. She was always so forgetful. But Seff could see that she was worried. After Mrs. Ericksen had left, he called Arvid Anderson in Jonasville and asked how much Jonas had bid on the Ericksen farm. Well Arvid went to Bollemo and Bollemo found out from Siversen that Jonas had stopped at $56 an acre, but that that had been after the farm had been sold to Thompson. Arvid was sure that Jonas would never have made a deal through Torfin Glombekken. So on who's behalf had Torfin acted? Thompson thought of Ward, but Elihu hadn't been interested in that farm. And then Seff remembered that it was Torfin who had first made him aware that the Ericksen farm was for sale. So he thought about it for a day or two and then called on Napoleon.

"I understand that you made quite a lot of money on the sale of the Ericksen farm," he said, and looked at him in a way that was open to interpretation. "It is easy *aa mæke* money *paa den maner'n*," he added.

But Napoleon was not easily perturbed. Anything, even the most inconceivable, could happen at any time. This was something life had taught him to expect. So without the least sign of any discomfort he said with a smile: "You have developed quite a sense of humor with age my good Seff! Was there anything else you wanted?"

The one thing that Sefanias Thompson couldn't stand was that people believed he was getting old. Any reference to his age irritated him. He was only sixty-seven and every bit as good as when he had been thirty-seven. And those who thought different didn't know him well enough. Nor was Napoleon ignorant of his sore spot.

"I'm no older than I can still observe what is going on around me," Seff replied in his Norwegian-American style of speech. He was obviously offended. *"Vot's becom' af dem tusen dollars, mor'or'less, som disapira*[35] between Sven and me in that farm deal?" All his 270 pounds were shaking in anger.

"If anything has disappeared, then that is surely something between the two of you," said Napoleon. "How should I know? You dealt with Sven yourself and wrote him a check for the amount. What are you carrying on about?" Stomhoff played the injured party and had all the appearance of being angered. But the old man wasn't fooled so easily. This wasn't the first time he had reason to distrust Napoleon, but Stomhoff was adamant.

"Let's have the evidence! Where is the evidence!" he cried, and banged his fist on the table. "And may God protect you if you don't have any evidence! This is going to cost you dearly." Thompson was beginning to waver. The scoundrel may have it in him to sue him!

"Oh, I've got plenty of proof," he ensured him. "That's not a problem." He regretted that he didn't have time to take care of him today because he was about to leave town. But as soon as he was back again . . .

And Thompson really did leave town. Before he left the office he called Sheriff Duffy and asked him to meet him at three on the Normanville road just beyond the Ericksen farm. Then he drove off. Soon after, Stomhoff took the road to Stockdale. That was the day he withdrew his money from the First National Bank. Later that day he was observed by Dorte on the Porch, who cleaned house at the Nelsens', arriving with Nikolai Nelsen for supper.

Sven Ericksen's auction was the next day, and he was busy making things ready when Thompson and the sheriff arrived. No, he had certainly not had any kind of transaction with Napoleon, he said. Well, they would find out about that, said Duffy, because he had come to arrest him and put him in *jailen*.

"And then both you and Napoleon will be heading for the penitentiary," said Seff, and added that he had never thought that a good man like Sven would end his days there. But there was nothing he could do about it since they lived in a civilized and free *kontry*.

Sven wasn't so well versed in the law that he knew exactly what they could and couldn't do with him, but he did realize that his affairs with Napoleon may not have been according to the books. So rather than run any further risk, he told them everything. And then his wife came running and begged them not to throw Sven in *jailen*. Duffy thought it over for a while. He took Seff aside, and after a few minutes they told Ericksen they would let him go on condition that he signed a document admitting everything.

With Ericksen's confession, written by Thompson and signed with the sheriff as witness, Seff turned up the next day at the land office, and Napoleon—after they both had quite a lot to say about it—finally gave in. He never really confessed to anything. He was a poor man, he said, and had served him faithfully for many years. In fact, he had sacrificed himself for Thompson and his *bisnes*. He would nevertheless rather give him this $1,000 than bring their relationship to an end, he said, and he hoped that Seff would give him a little time to raise the money. But Seff wasn't ready to let him go so easily. He had broken the law and had to go to jail. He thought he had better scare him properly now that he had him. But then Stomhoff got mad and began to beat his fist on the table, and behaved as if he, and not Seff, was master of the house. If that was the way the rent was to be paid, he said, and this is what he was getting in return for years of faithful and loyal service then . . . In brief, he too had a tune they could dance to. You could go to jail for more than one thing. And then he began his long list: Do you remember this, and do you remember that, and perhaps you may also have a memory of this? Napoleon was no simpleton. He had a good sense of history. And when he was through, Seff merely smiled and said:

"*O'kors*—naturally—the jail was *mærli' a'* joke! I only said it to *tise* you."

"Yes, you have always been a great joker!" said Napoleon. He had to smile too. "By the way, do you know what I've been thinking of?" No, said Thompson, how could he know what Napoleon was thinking.

"I've been thinking that you should be a candidate for state senator. You've always been such a great politician. It would be a great loss for the state if you don't put your gifts to the service of the public."

This would have been music in Seff's ears had it come from anyone but Stomhoff. And even now he was flattered. Ever since his first unsuccessful bid for office as a representative in the 1890s, his greatest regret had been that he hadn't been able to fulfill his political ambitions. His greatest desire was to become a state senator before he died.

"Oh, no, that won't ever happen!" he said with a sigh. "Ward isn't the man he was. He has forgotten those whose help he once needed."

"He's never been in greater need of help from Arrowtown," Stomhoff declared. "But you shouldn't think anymore of Ward. Others are becoming more powerful than him."

"Jonas Olsen?"

"Yes, and why not?" Thompson thought it over. Napoleon continued: "If I can get you into the senate, you'll return the thousand dollars! Is that a bargain?"

"Hm—yes. But you can't do it."

"You'll see! Jonasville gets the courthouse and you'll be senator." Seff laughed conceitedly.

It took Napoleon three months to pay the thousand dollars to Thompson. He had borrowed the money from a friend in Minneapolis, he said—someone he had done a small service when they both were young. A few days later Seff learned that the Ericksen farm had been sold to Jonas Olsen, and he began to regret that he hadn't held on to it himself. There was no reason why his competitor should be acquiring so much property . . . He was a mere youngster. And then he thought about what Napoleon had said about the coming election. He had heard no more about it and was convinced that nothing would come of it. He had occasionally thought of meeting with Jonas but with all their old conflicts he realized that there would be little point in it. And he wasn't all that eager to join forces with Olsen either.

And then—many months later—he saw the news about the planned new bank in Arrowtown. He would certainly not want to have anything to do with such a man. But Napoleon remained calm.

"I've got plans of my own," he said. "There won't be a new bank in Arrowtown."

At about this time—the end of May—Johan Utgard surprised Jonas by entering his private office in the bank for the first time. Things had remained the same between the two. Jonas hadn't found it worth his while to make amends. Even though he had to admit that Utgard had behaved quite decently in many ways, he still felt that he was interfering with his own business. Last spring Utgard had a two-week sale that took the wind out of the sails of all the other merchants in the county. His prices were spoiling the customers . . .

But there he was in front of Jonas's desk. He greeted him briefly and without ceremony, as was his wont, and he had a slight smile as he looked around. It was a nice office with a good carpet and solid, handsome furniture, and Utgard was not one for finery and comfort. His store wasn't exactly a showpiece and he himself lived in a simply furnished bachelor's apartment that no one had ever seen—with the exception of Jørgine, who cleaned for him once a week. And Jørgine, who could have lots to say about others, never had a word to say about Utgard and his apartment. And people knew what that meant.

Jonas invited him to sit. He sensed that Utgard had something important in mind.

"Are you perhaps interested in Nicolai Nelsen?" asked Johan.

"Nicolai Nelsen?"

"Yes, I thought there was a certain mortgage . . ."

"Hm—yes—that is . . ." What was Utgard's concern with the mortgage, he thought. What was he after?

"I have such a mortgage," Johan continued. "And Nicolai is bankrupt."

This was not news to Jonas. He had observed that Nelsen for some time had been preparing to leave business, and it was no secret that his colleagues all had more or less worthless notes for large and small loans given to Nicolai over the past year or so. A few days ago he had left town saying that he had to go to Minneapolis on business and yesterday a representative of the wholesale houses had come to foreclose on his debts to them. This meant that Nicolai was history as far as Jonasville was concerned. He had put his home and all its furnishing in his wife's name, so the creditors wouldn't find much there. Jonas was sure that Nelsen had set aside some capital, but he was glad to be rid of him. But why did Utgard come to tell him this? In a not quite successful attempt to be friendly, he answered: "Yes, I know that Nelsen is through here. But I was unaware that you were in the same boat as we others."

"Yes, for once we're in the same boat, you and I," Utgard smiled. "My mortgage was better than yours, but now they have exactly the same value, even though your loss is of course much greater than mine, since you also paid this Tomlinson man a thousand dollars."

"What do you know about that?" Jonas asked sharply.

"Oh, I keep my eyes open," said Johan. "You may know a man by the name of Napoleon."

"Regrettably!"

"And that he was supposed to marry Nicolai's daughter?"

"*Yessør,* I've heard that too."

"But nothing will come of it. It's all over."

"Now, that's news to me."

"Yes, because Napoleon is also in the same boat, even though on somewhat different terms." Utgard took a letter from his pocket and gave it to Jonas. "There is quite a lot here that doesn't get into the newspapers," he said. Jonas took the letter and read it with obvious interest. Then he gave it back to Utgard.

"*Gudnes!*" he said and shook his head. Utgard held the letter for a moment and then he gave it back to Jonas and said he could keep it. It might turn out to be of use. And then he got up as if to leave. "That's all I came for."

"And where did you get the letter?" Jonas was also on his feet.

"I helped Mr. Watson, the representative of the wholesale houses, a little in Nelsen's office last night . . . He's an old friend of mine . . ."

"And you found this?"

"Yes, and quite by chance; Nicolai had thrown it in the wastepaper basket. It made me think of you."

"And I'm grateful, Utgard!" said Jonas, and took his colleague's hand and grasped it warmly. "This is more than I had deserved from you."

"Oh, I don't know about that," said Johan. "Let's not think too much about the past."

"No, I suppose not," said Jonas, "considering that we both belong to the Synod."

"And to the human race!" said Utgard, and left.

19.

The three great events of that summer were approaching. First, the primary, then the new referendum on the county seat on September 1—for which the lists with the necessary petition were ready for submission—and, finally, the election in November. The campaign for the county seat overshadowed all else, and as late as May nothing had been heard about the coming primary. About the only thing people knew was that Floen had the support of a majority of the leaders in the district for his congressional aspirations and that Newell again would be the candidate of the Republican Party leadership for state senator.

One day Jonas, to his great surprise, received an invitation from Napoleon to come to Stockdale. Jonas couldn't imagine that his old enemy had anything of interest to discuss with him. So he simply turned down the offer. Three days later, after he had had time to think it over and had begun to see some potential in a meeting with Napoleon, he called him and said he would meet him in room number seventeen at the Stockdale Hotel the next afternoon. He had already made a reservation, he said.

Napoleon turned up, but found it in his interest to play the offended part since Jonas had turned down his initial invitation. Jonas pretended not to notice.

"And how are things in Arrowtown?" he asked. "I suppose you are all hoping that Normanville will remain the county seat?"

"No," said Napoleon. "We are neutral. Why should we bother when there's nothing in it for us?" Jonas looked at him. Napoleon was no longer a young man. He was bald and his red beard was mostly white—much like the bristle on an old pig, thought Jonas.

"It's been some time since we last talked together," he said. And Stomhoff agreed. "I've thought of the good old days in Minneapolis. But tell me, what is it you want?"

"And what do you want?" Napoleon was still offended. "You invited me. I suppose you had a reason."

"Well, I thought you would appreciate an open hand. But if there isn't anything you want, I would like to be told right away. I'm a *bisi* man." Jonas stood up.

"Oh, there's no need to play so important," said Stomhoff. "You can't get the county seat without help."

"Is that so? Is that what you wanted to tell me?"

"Yes, if Ward and Seff stick together there won't be any change." Jonas laughed. "Your only possibility lies in an understanding with Seff," Napoleon continued.

"I see! But I don't want any understanding with Seff. On the contrary, I'm just beginning to fight him for real. I've decided to cook his fat to the last drop. You may know that I am building a bank in Arrowtown."

"And then you'll lose your last *chans'* to get the county seat. Arrowtown holds the balance of power. I've come to you as an old friend to offer you a deal with Seff: The Liberal Populists will sponsor Seff as candidate for the state senate and give him full support in the fall election, and Arrowtown will stand behind you in your bid for the county seat."

Jonas sat down again.

"And you are offering me all this out of generosity and love?" he asked.

"There is no need for spite. Personally, my only interest in this affair is to make a little money—you may call it a loan—about a thousand dollars . . ."

"You must take me for a sucker."

"Ward has offered the Republican nomination to Seff. What about that?" Jonas laughed again.

"So you are still in your old profession," he said. "If there had been any truth in that, I would have answered that then we'll sink Seff in November."

"And then you'll go under with him, Jonas Olsen."

They sat like two inveterate horse traders, looking at each other and weighing every word to make sure that nothing would come out that could give the opponent the least advantage. Jonas knew that Napoleon was lying when he said that Ward had promised to support Seff, but he also knew that Jonasville would benefit greatly from Arrowtown's support. He couldn't be sure of the election, and if he turned down this offer he would open a possible alliance between Seff and Elihu. He had worked out in the smallest detail what steps should be taken to further the interests of Jonasville in the county seat campaign. Among them was a mass meeting just before the referendum. He had planned it as a real stunner, something quite unique in this part of the state. In his mind's eye he could already see Seff and Napoleon standing up on the tribune and ensuring the huge crowd that Jonasville was fighting a just battle and that the future happiness of the county depended on the outcome of the referendum. That would be some show and it would give him many votes. He mentioned the meeting to Napoleon.

"Not that I need Thompson's help," he said, "but if I should agree to make a deal with you then both must promise to appear at the meeting." Napoleon was sure this could be done. Then Jonas took a piece of paper from his pocket and wrote some lines on it before giving it to Stomhoff. Would he sign? Napoleon read it and shook his head. No, he would have to think about that, he said. Well, said Jonas as he got up from his chair, then there didn't seem to be anymore to talk about. Without his signature there could be no agreement.

"But you'll have to give me time to think about it," said Stomhoff. Jonas took his hat.

"It's all the same for me," he said. "And I didn't like the taste of this deal, anyhow! I don't want anything more to do with it." He was at the door. Napoleon got on his feet.

"Wait, wait!" he said. "For your own sake . . . for the future of Jonasville . . . Have you lost your wits?" Jonas interrupted him with more laughter.

"And just what is your interest in the future of Jonasville? No, I'm leaving!"

"But if I sign . . ." Stomhoff had his hand on Jonas's arm. His hand was slimy and bloodless, like a dead man's hand dipped in oil. Jonas shook it off as if it had been a snake.

"But I'll sign, man, I'll sign! Can't you hear me?" Napoleon's voice was a hoarse whisper. His thoughts were on the thousand dollars he had had to give Thompson and that he would get back if he made a deal with Jonas. He also thought of the other thousand he wanted to "borrow," and of Nicolai, the rascal, who had cheated him out of his savings, and of Nellie, who had led him on . . . What an evil world, full of dishonesty and betrayal . . . Jonas had begun to pace the floor as if in deep thought. Suddenly he faced Stomhoff.

"*Velsør*," he said. "I had never thought that I would sink so low as to make any kind of deal with you or Seff, but since it means doing you a favor, and because my responsibility to the public is of more importance than my personal inclinations, I'll go along with your proposal." Napoleon's face showed signs of relief.

"So: No bank in Arrowtown, Thompson as senator, and Thompson's full support for Jonasville as county seat! That's the bargain."

"All right, let her go!"

"And a thousand dollars after the referendum."

"What are you thinking of? Of course I don't have any money for you. Remember that I'm a poor man who couldn't possibly afford such a sum." Now it was Napoleon who laughed, even though he felt more like crying.

"Yes, I'm sure poverty is crushing you down," he said. "According to Bradstreet you are only worth $200,000. Do you really think I would come here and set up a deal between you and Seff and leave myself out of it?"

"No, that wouldn't be at all like you."

And then they argued back and forth about the thousand dollars for half an hour or so before Jonas finally gave in. Then Napoleon signed what Jonas had written on the scrap of paper, and they departed.

———

The primary gave two candidates for the state senate: Newell was again the Republican candidate and Seff Thompson, to the surprise of many, was the candidate of the Liberal Populists. And Floen had been successful in getting the nomination as representative in Washington DC. People wondered what had happened between Thompson and Jonas Olsen. It was pretty clear that they must have come to an understanding. Seff hadn't campaigned very actively, and the times he met the public he had made strong pronouncements about progressive action at the national and state levels but he had little to say about local issues. The Jonasville newspapers assured their readers that his political rebirth had been both as sincere and as thorough as anyone could desire, and that in his long alliance with Elihu Ward he had become dejected because of all the corruption in Normanville. Now he had set aside his personal as well as his *bisnis* interests and had decided to lead the fight to bring the disgraceful Normanville government to an end. And, Sofus Jensen wrote in *Nordlyset,* what else could you expect of such an honest and principled man—a tower of light in his church—than that he would follow the voice of his faith and his conscience. And in the *Herald,* Jepsen explained that Seff had been reluctant but that he was finally unable to resist the pressure from the party leaders as well as from the people. This was why he now was willing to sacrifice himself for the cause of good government. Personally, he was a quiet and modest man who would have preferred to live his life unnoticed by the public; but *vox populi, vox Dei,* wrote Jepsen. The voice of the people is the voice of God. When it speaks, we must heed it.

The seas of national politics were quite turbulent in the summer of 1912. Four years earlier, Taft had sailed into the White House on a wave of popularity created by Roosevelt, but as president he hadn't lived up to the expectations of the progressive wing of the Republican Party. And then the Republican National Convention had met in Chicago in June and had voted for a conservative party platform and renominated Taft. The liberal delegates, led by Roosevelt, marched out of the convention, held their own meeting, created the Progressive Party, and nominated Roosevelt as their candidate for president.

The turn in national politics signaled by the two conventions in Chicago also had consequences for local politics. In Garfield County it meant that the lines between the two political organizations were more sharply drawn. The dislike of Roosevelt and his followers on the one hand and the enthusiasm for him and his platform on the other were given powerful expression. The liberal side, in particular, campaigned aggressively and seemed to be gaining in popularity. Nevertheless, and not entirely without reason, those who were engrossed by the county-seat competition feared that the sharp divisions in national politics might have a disturbing effect on this very local issue. But Jonas was optimistic. The petition for a referendum had more than enough signatures. Indeed, the support in Arrowtown and its environs had been particularly encouraging, something that showed that Seff was keeping his side of the bargain. But Jonas knew that—just as in the previous campaign—many opponents had signed because they wanted to have a decision on the issue. So the campaign was run energetically and at full sail as if a kingdom and not a mere courthouse was at stake.

Ward received daily information from all parts of the county confirming that Jonas had reason for his optimism. There was little reason for celebration in Normanville. Seff wasn't the only local boss who had changed sides. And there could no longer be any doubt that Roosevelt was extremely popular and would take a large portion of the votes in the fall election. The liberal opposition made good use of this situation. They lectured the people that a vote for the Ward ticket was a vote against Roosevelt, progress, and clean politics. His desire to hold on to the county seat was equally suspicious, they said, and if he had his way, this would spell the end of democracy in Garfield County. The Liberal Populists in

Jonasville made good use of Roosevelt. He was the man, the savior of the nation. Hurrah! Hurrah! And remember, ladies and gentlemen, that Jonasville is the Roosevelt bastion in the county.

But Ward fought bravely for Normanville. He was up and about at all times, and his henchmen were all over the county to strengthen the farmers in their faith in the old political gods. Elihu had high expectations of little Tollefsen's Norwegian newspaper. It was distributed without charge to all Scandinavians in the county. After his last argument with Jonas, Tollefsen had become a warrior in the shining army of Normanville and he was busy working on an extra issue that would be distributed right before the referendum.

20.

August 27 was an unforgettable day in Jonasville. It was the day of the great mass meeting in the park. An enormous crowd—people from all over the county—came to town. A Norwegian orator from Minneapolis was featured as the main attraction. Seff Thompson and Floen were also scheduled to speak, in addition to one whose identity was kept secret.

Floen gave some words of welcome and introduced the speakers, first the man from Minneapolis, who thrilled his listeners with a lively account of the Progressive vision and the battle against the forces of reaction. Roosevelt was a Lincoln, a Washington, and a Jefferson all in one. His politics would be victorious because it was the politics of the future; his vision was of the people; his voice was as that of a watchman of Zion; his brilliant character was as a torch lighting a road through the dark wilderness, where for centuries the forces of reaction and prejudice had robbed and murdered and burned what the people had built. He concluded by congratulating Jonas and Jonasville, which now would be the proud county seat of the great Garfield County, and by poking a little fun at the "toothless political *bas* down the line," who couldn't understand that his days were over and that we were on a new avenue of progress, where he no longer had the strength to follow on his aging and rheumatic legs.

Thompson then attacked Ward with great wisdom and elegance. Seff had much experience with Elihu, he said, so he knew what he was talking about. He had doubts about turning his back on an old friend. But your conscience comes first, he told them, and when your conscience speaks, then a Christian has to bear witness, even against his best friends. And that's what he had come to do today. It was painful. His heart hurt so much he could hardly bear it, but he had no choice. His gray head throned proudly and handsomely on his still impressive figure. His white tie and his white shirt front were freshly ironed and starched. His sonorous voice and wide girth combined to lend conviction to his devious phrases. It was obvious that the county seat had to be in Jonasville. Jonasville hadn't only grown to be the largest and wealthiest town in the county but was also placed right in the center. He could stand before them as an impartial witness: they all knew that there hadn't been a close friendship between Arrowtown and Jonasville, nor, for that matter, were relations much better today. If he should allow himself to be dictated by self-interest, he would be against moving the county seat. However, above all self-interest there was one consideration that had to be honored: the public good. In Normanville they said it was all about one man's ambitions. This may be true. He himself certainly didn't think so well of Jonas Olsen, as they all knew, but he had to admit that he nevertheless admired the man who had been able to achieve what they all could see right in front of their eyes. And such things are not built without a certain amount of ambition, he said. Ambition was good when it served the public good. The danger they faced today, more than ever before, was the ambitious spirit of reaction that emanated from Normanville, a spirit that scorned and defied the will of the people and whose motto was: rule or ruin! What did they want? The spirit of Roosevelt—the spirit of progress, prosperity, and popular government—or did they want to be led by the nose by Ward's corrupt clique? That's the question!

Seff's speech was received with deafening applause. Floen had to wait five minutes before he could introduce the next speaker, "a man well-known in the county for the great work he has done for the church among the young, a man who served as evangelist among the early settlers before they had established congregations, a man who all his life had the best interests of the people as his guiding principle, in short— the honorable Napoleon Stomhoff." There was no spontaneous burst of applause at the mention of Napoleon's name. On the contrary, many were surprised when they heard who Floen had meant to characterize in such a fine manner. But there are always people who clap their hands, and even Stomhoff was not without supporters in such a large crowd.

Solemnly, almost ceremoniously, in his long black coat, he approached the lectern. He spoke in Norwegian about the early days and about what the pioneers had suffered and sacrificed. Wolves in sheeps' clothing had stolen the fruits of their labor: railroad companies, grain speculators, elevator companies, unscrupulous lawyers, corrupt journalists, and bloodsucking bankers. They had to struggle to avoid being eaten alive by these hyenas, Napoleon told them. Their struggle for the county seat was merely a chapter in their larger struggle for survival, the final battle between the old band of robbers and the awakening spirit of justice. To move the county seat meant to move the political and economic power into the hands of the farmers, where it should be. He continued for some time in this vein before he bowed and sat down. Most of those who understood what he had said thought he had spoken well. They could hear that he had become a fine politician.

The meeting had been a great success. Jonas was both pleased and proud. Many—very many—came up to congratulate him. It was as if they all felt that the battle had been won. Nor did Jonas himself doubt it. The whole affair, however, had made a rather unpleasant impression on two who were particularly close to him: Ragna and Jorshaug. When the pastor met Jonas right after the meeting was over, the latter smiled broadly and said: "Now I'm sure that Elihu is *dønʼfor!*"

"That may be," Jorshaug gently responded. He demonstrated no sign of enthusiasm. Jonas was surprised. Didn't the man *file* happy over getting the courthouse to Jonasville!

"But it's been a tough battle," he added. Jorshaug frowned but had no comment. After a while he said, "There is one thing I haven't been able to understand—this alliance between you and Seff and Napoleon." Jonas liked this. He laughed.

"Yes, you may not be alone in not getting it," he answered. "But politics is an intricate game and my power in the county is beginning to get recognition."

"Well, it certainly seems so," said the pastor. "But power is often a dangerous thing." His voice was mild and he smiled carefully. He was, after all, talking to his future father-in-law and the mightiest man in town. Even so, the way Jonas looked at him rattled him. He took his handkerchief and cleaned the dust off his glasses.

Further down the street, Jorshaug caught up with Ragna and Signe Marie, and he noticed that Ragna was unusually quiet. He said that the way things now looked it would be a great victory for Jonasville.

"Yes, isn't it wonderful!" Signe Marie exclaimed. Her mother smiled but had a troubled look.

"*Uff,* I don't like politics at all," she said. She was disgusted by the speeches of Seff and Napoleon, by the way Floen had introduced them, and by the whole farcical campaign. She hadn't been told anything but she could more or less guess what had been going on.

"Mercy me, without politics, we would have been bored to death out here in the sticks!" Signe Marie declared. "At least it gives some variation to our monotonous lives."

"Variation in itself may not always be for the good," said the pastor without looking up.

"I'm sorry, but I must agree," Ragna sighed.

"Sorry—sorry—sorry!" Signe Marie taunted her mother and shrugged her shoulders with evident impatience. "Should a new idea happen among us every fourth or fifth year or so, a tiny little idea, that neither Abrahamsen, nor Mrs. Fundeland, nor Lew Sharp has pondered from all sides at least a hundred times—well then we must have this sorry and sorry. Sorry—how I hate that word!"

"Signe Marie, you should be ashamed of yourself!" her mother scolded her.

"Sorry!" her daughter replied and laughed. "Sorry! But, to speak more seriously, we are only human. Do people have a right to demand that we should be perfect?"

"No," Jorshaug responded, "from a human point of view we have no such right. Nevertheless, we must all do our best to aim at human perfection—if indeed there is such a thing. We may not be able to achieve it, regardless of how much we may try, but should we lose sight of the great ideals, then life would become unbearable." Ragna agreed. My oh my, thought her daughter. Why must even the lightest remark be the occasion of a sermon?

"I suppose," she continued, "you would prefer that Ward kept his courthouse and everything else. You don't even want so little a change into our lives as a courthouse."

"That's quite another matter," said the pastor.

"I had never expected Napoleon to be such an orator," Signe Marie kept on. "He's really brilliant."

"*Uff,* how you talk!" Her mother interrupted her. "Napoleon is a rascal. There isn't a drop of honest blood in him. I fear that this courthouse campaign will lead to no good."

"Mercy me, what do we care about the people involved. We must hold on to our purpose. Napoleon is only a tool, perhaps even a tool in a hand larger than ours? Surely we know that unjust individuals may sometimes be used to further a just cause."

Neither Ragna nor Jorshaug said anything. They had come to the corner of Main and Lincoln, where the two women took off to the north. The pastor excused himself; his pastoral duties wouldn't allow him to come with them for supper, as Ragna invited him to do. He walked on home. He needed to be alone with his thoughts.

Ragna had also invited the Trulsens to supper. They were in town for the mass meeting and she had met Mrs. Trulsen in the park after it was over. It had pleased her that the Trulsens had begun to attend services in Jorshaug's church. Jonas was also pleased. The Trulsens have regretted their ways, he thought, and he congratulated himself that all now seemed to be going his way. He was strengthened in his faith when he met the Trulsens that evening. Mrs. Trulsen said that they had talked of leaving Vellesen's congregation and becoming members of the Synod congregation in town. Ole hadn't liked the way Vellesen had proselytized in Jonasville. He had warned him, he said, but it was no longer possible to reason with Vellesen. Before departure, they agreed that Jonas should write them in as members in Jorshaug's congregation without further delay. So it turned out to be a really blessed day.

When the Trulsens had left, Jonas strolled into town and to the hotel. He was eager to find out what people were saying about the mass meeting and the referendum. But he didn't get to hear much because Napoleon wanted a word with him and they went into an alcove called the ladies' parlor, where they would be undisturbed. Napoleon merely wanted to remind him that he and Thompson had kept their side of the bargain. The battle would be held in three days and there could no longer be any doubt of the outcome. So he would like to have the thousand dollars right away if that would be convenient. But it wasn't. This was something they could discuss after the referendum, Jonas said. Stomhoff didn't quite see it the same way, and they argued for quite some time. No way would Jonas give him the money now. But in three days? Yes, in three days they could talk it over, said Jonas. But then he had an idea. If Napoleon would do him a small favor before the referendum, he would give him an extra $50 right away. Well, said Stomhoff, what was it?

"In Tollefsen's print shop in Normanville there is a large extra edition of *Nordstjernen* that is to be distributed all over the county tomorrow.

Use your own methods, but make sure that edition doesn't get anywhere tomorrow. You'll know how . . ." He held out a brand new fifty-dollar bill and Napoleon grabbed it.

"All right, Mr. Olsen!" he said. "Is there anything else?"

No, that was all.

21.

The day after the mass meeting, an extra edition of *Nordlyset* attracted attention far and wide. Headlines across the front page introduced a full report of the meeting, with selected passages from the marvelous speeches and portraits of the prominent participants. In his editorial the editor extracted the relevant lessons of all that had been said. In particular he stressed the importance of the support given by Thompson and Napoleon Stomhoff, who had done their best to oppose Jonasville but who now recognized the error of their ways and had come over to the right side. So Ward's only remaining support were the businessmen in Normanville and the courthouse gang. His campaign had lost its last claim to respectability. Sofus Jensen had really exceeded himself. And people read and people said to each other: if only a tiny fraction of this is true, there is more than enough reason to move the county seat.

Ward long tried to disregard the personal attacks. But he realized that his cause wasn't as strong as he had thought. Indeed, he would lose his dominance in county politics if he wasn't able to get his machine going again at the last minute. He tried with new promises of favors to the small-town bosses who had always been able to deliver the goods at the slightest nod from Normanville. But now they reported that people had gone crazy. Rooseveltian progressivism in conjunction with what remained of the earlier populist opposition had attracted all dissatisfaction, and neither promises nor threats seemed to have an effect on popular opinion. The bad news he received from all townships at first made him angry and then discouraged. But he decided that whatever happened to him personally should not have an effect on his dynasty. So at this point he called on Miles Standish.

Ward's only son and heir—his daughter had died four years earlier—was twenty-one years of age. He was tall and handsome and had made a stronger impression as a member of the Harvard football team than as a student. He had spent most of his youth at schools in the East and he knew little about his father's business and other interests. He had come home to take a position in the bank and to begin to learn the business. People said that he was a sensible boy, a pleasant fellow, but not all that smart.

This was the first time Ward had talked *bisnes* with Miles Standish. And he told him that the time when all responsibility would be on his shoulders might not be far away. You could never know what might happen, and he no longer felt as strong as in his younger days. His business was considerable and would grow if it was tended well. He had been a conservative and careful man—in business as in all other matters. Nothing else would do. This was good *bisnes,* but it was also good politics and good religion. And it was above all good social science, especially for those called to responsibility for economic and political values.

So-called progressive politics was a lottery, even for those it was supposed to benefit. They all knew what they had, but no one knew what they would get if those troublemakers gained power. And since their theories were untried and since those who spoke most loudly of liberalism as a rule had nothing, it would be a folly to join them. Should there be any profit, you could be sure that the agitators themselves would run off with all of it.

Agitation for new social and political ideas was especially dangerous here in Garfield County, where there were so many foreigners and relatively few native Americans. The foreigners were hardly civilized and were easily led by the nose by any smart aleck of their own nationality.[36] As, for instance, this Jonas Olsen in Johnsville, who was trying to take the county seat from Normanville! These immigrants could fight no-holds-barred among themselves, even about religion, but should some idiot among them begin to question the respect due to American tradition and authority, then they became totally unreliable.

He admitted that he was fighting with this Norwegian for his very life. It wasn't a personal battle but a war for the right of the American to be master in his own home. We can have no foreign rule in America. This wasn't for himself. It was for the race. The new generation would have to take it up with renewed strength and intelligence. It was at this point in Elihu's monologue that Miles Standish astonished his father by remarking:

"I really can't see the point. Wouldn't it make more sense to assume that this struggle is hurting rather than helping our country? If it were up to me, I'd rather try to work with these people and let them understand that we regard them as our equals and that they have the same right to promote their cause as we do."

The old man leapt to his feet like a lion. So it had come to this, his own flesh and blood telling him that his life's work had been wasted. His own son telling him that the blood of one of the oldest and most respected families in the land was of no more value than that of the social outcasts of an unknown and worthless little country. Ward realized where his son's ideas had their origin. The universities had degenerated. They no longer showed respect for tradition. Any bastard of a Jew or a Swede was regarded as the equal of a Miles Standish Ward, whose forefathers had come on the Mayflower! You could no longer trust the so-called professors at these institutions. They concerned themselves with "modern thought" and this nonsense about equality, fraternity, and human rights, all of it imported from Europe.

Father and son had a long and stormy session. The father first took up his usual weapon—the sledgehammer—that he had used with success throughout his long life. But it was of little help here. Miles Standish at least proved to be a Ward in not being easily scared. And even though it hurt to discover that the young man was of a different mind than his father, Elihu was nevertheless a little proud that his son had the courage and the will to go against him. For the first time he realized that for all the international heresy he had been exposed to, he wasn't weak. And that was at least one point in his favor. But Ward was inflexible and uncompromising, and father and son parted with harsh words on both sides.

It had been several years since Miles Standish had spent a summer at home, and he had become increasingly worried about how his father had aged and how his work and his political conflicts were threatening to shorten his life. He had told him so, but apparently with no effect.

Three days before the referendum, Signe Marie was on her way to Stockdale in the new car. A daughter of Winthrop was a student at Vassar and had invited some friends to a farewell party. Jorshaug had promised to come but other duties had interfered, so she was alone. About halfway there, her motor stopped and refused to start again. Bollemo had inspected the car before she left and said it was in full order. But now the contraption had placed her out in the middle of the prairie and it refused to move.

She hardly had time to despair before she saw a roadster coming at full speed down the road. It stopped, and a tall young man stepped out and asked her what was the matter. Well, she didn't really know, but something must be wrong since she couldn't get it to go an inch. She noticed that the stranger looked at her with interest, which she didn't mind at all. He was well dressed and no less well mannered. Quite handsome too. He made an effort to find out what was wrong and stood bent over the engine a long time before he shook his head and said that nothing could be done except to get it towed to Stockdale and hand it over to a mechanic. But he needed a strong rope and so offered to drive to the nearest farm about three-quarters of a mile farther down the road and get one there. He went, but returned saying that since they didn't have anything strong enough he had telephoned the garage in Stockdale and asked them to come and collect the car. It would be safe here, he said. She was hesitant about accepting his offer of a lift to Stockdale but she entered the roadster and sat down beside him. And then he asked her forgiveness for not having introduced himself.

"My name is Miles Standish Ward," he informed her. She was shocked, to say the least, and she would have leapt out of the car if it hadn't already picked up speed. She looked at him and he was unaware of the lightning in her eyes. Then she looked down and blushed. "And yours?" he asked as he turned toward her.

"I—I am Signe Marie Olsen!" She lifted her chin and stared right ahead.

"Olsen from Johnsville?" Surprised.

"Yes!" Coldly.

"Now, this is interesting!"

"So, you think so, do you?" Still very coldly. "It hasn't always been with interest that the Wards have met the Olsens."

"No, perhaps not," he admitted. "But that doesn't make it less interesting." He had driven off at great speed but now he had slowed down so much that the car hardly moved forward. "What a great day!" he exclaimed.

"Certainly! And the weather is a safe topic." She couldn't repress a smile and had a sudden desire to study him more closely. But she wouldn't turn around to face him; that would be tantamount to bowing to a Ward. And between a Ward and an Olsen there couldn't even be a cease-fire—not to speak of peace. But she nevertheless stole an occasional glance at him. So he was about her age. His eyes: dark brown. His hair: the same, parted in the middle. His nose: medium-sized, well formed. His face: full, regular features, a nice and friendly smile. A thick handlebar moustache. He spoke easily and naturally and his laughter was sincere. All in all, a quite handsome and affable young man.

Neither of them said anything for a while. She noticed that he was looking straight ahead and was apparently in deep thought. Well, a Ward should have quite a lot to ponder when he met an Olsen . . . and to be ashamed of as well . . . And she reasoned further: When he speaks to me I won't say anything. I'll ignore him . . .

"Johnsville is quite a charming and pleasant little town," he suddenly said. She had decided not to respond but his remark invited a sarcastic reply, and that was just what she wanted to be—sarcastic. He deserved it.

"It's natural that you appreciate the advantages of our town when you come from the present county seat," she said sharply. He laughed. But she couldn't decide whether it was because he enjoyed her wit or because he was making fun of her.

"That may be," he admitted genially, as he accelerated his car a little. "I'm afraid that I'm not a very good booster. To me, all small towns seem alike." And then the man from the garage drove past them and left them in a cloud of dust.

"It seems that people will have a good harvest," he said after a while, looking out on the fields.

"Oh, are you also thrilled by harvests and such like?" she responded. "That's a topic close to my heart. And swine and cattle too." Sharply again. She would show him what she was good for—the snob!

"Yes, isn't it sad that we men are such materialists," he said. "It's the way we are brought up. But it's good to have a good harvest since there are so many who depend on it." She decided that he was being sarcastic too. He was making fun of every word she said, so she would simply ignore him. Not a word more from her. Not the way he was behaving . . .

"But I really prefer city life," he began again after a few minutes. "Don't you?" Goodness, yes, she thought. How often she had wished that she lived in a big city rather than out here on the prairie. But she was certainly not going to admit that to him.

"No, our town is good enough for me. But I must admit that had I had my home in Normanville, then . . ." He laughed again.

"You seem to be a great local patriot," he said. "When I now and then come home to Normanville it seems that you're right in your evaluation. The years I've spent in the East must have spoiled me." Then she remembered that he had mostly been away from home since he was a boy, that he had traveled a lot and had been at well-known universities and colleges, and she was suddenly in awe of his learning and experience. Oh, if she could only get out into the wide world! Didn't an Olsen have the same right to explore the world as a Ward! She looked briefly at him and saw that he now had a serious expression and seemed to be in thought. Then, quite unexpectedly, he turned toward her and said:

"I suppose you don't agree with me, Miss Olsen, but I must say that I'm sorry about the war our fathers have been fighting with each other for more than twenty years. It's such a waste—a pointless waste of energy on both sides."

"It hasn't been a waste of energy for Johnsville," she answered. "We'll get the county seat. But for Normanville . . ."

"You shouldn't be so intractable," he interrupted her, and laughed. "Tell me, have you planned to continue this war when you inherit the government of Johnsville?"

"I don't intend to inherit any government, but if I did, then . . ."

"Then there would never be peace and quiet in this county," he completed her sentence. "Then we should at least be happy that you don't intend to inherit any government. I'm a man of peace. We can surely make better use of our energy than to fight and persecute each other. There's so much to do, so many tasks waiting to be taken care of, and we often don't even see them because of our desire for power and possessions."

These were strange words in his mouth. This was how her mother and Jorshaug also spoke on occasion. But Signe Marie had never agreed with them. It had seemed so wishy-washy. And this was the son of Elihu Ward—the man who was responsible for all strife and who had done so much damage to her father! He had been polite to her, and she felt that she at the very least owed him a conciliatory response.

"Yes, I suppose there has been unnecessary bitterness on both sides," she said. He probably thought she was an aggressive and quarrelsome woman, and she didn't want him to have that impression. "And—and," she continued, "it may have been better if there had been less fighting and more understanding . . . I really don't know . . ."

But then their conversation turned to other topics. He told her some entertaining stories of life at Harvard, and then they spoke of this and that, things he had seen and done in the East. And all the while she sat there with only one thought in her head: I want to get out! I want to live!

When they came to Stockdale and she gave him her hand and thanked him for helping her and being so nice, he pressed it and said,

"This has been one of my most interesting experiences. May I have the pleasure of meeting you again?"

Signe Marie blushed when their eyes met. She felt less sure than she was used to when she said: "Perhaps we may meet again."

The rest of the day, she reproached herself for having blushed in front of the son of Elihu Ward. Think of all the young men who had blushed for her, and now she had blushed for Miles Standish! Mercy me . . .

22.

The news of the fire in Normanville came to Jonasville early in the morning two days before the referendum. On his way to the bank Jonas met Berge, who asked if he had heard the news? No, what was it?

"Tollefsen's print shop burned down last night at two o'clock," Berge informed him.

"Tollefsen's print shop? Burned down?" Jonas immediately thought of Napoleon. So that's how he had done it. Well, it wasn't any worse than what they had done to his own extra edition of the *Enterprize* five years ago.

"That was tough on poor Tollefsen," he said.

"And on Ward too," said Berge. "But the fire was limited to the print shop."

"Oh, the miserable shanty wasn't worth much. You know, it used to be his pigsty."

"Well then it had a tradition worthy of both Ward and Tollefsen," the druggist remarked. "But I wasn't thinking so much of the building as of what was in it, and in particular of the extra edition of *Nordstjernen* that was to be his last trump."

"An extra edition? That's news to me," said Jonas. "And it all burned?"

"Everything went up in flames—nothing is left."

"Well, well, justice finds strange ways. Too bad, too bad!" And they continued on their ways. Jonas paid a visit to Sofus Jensen. This was something for today's newspaper.

The fire was a serious setback for Ward. The extra edition had been, as Berge had put it, his last trump. People were deserting him in droves. The Irish were upset because Elihu had recently taken a few farms from some of their compatriots. And there were rumors that he had no sympathy for the foolish cause of Irish independence. The Germans were at best divided in two camps. The few native-born Americans were scattered all over the county and you couldn't count on them to vote as a block. Populism had made the Swedes politically unreliable, and most of them lived in the part of the county closest to Johnsville.

But the Norwegians were the largest nationality. They were often jealous of each other and fought among themselves about something they called Lutheranism, which they were all for but couldn't agree on exactly what it was. With this in mind, Ward had arranged to have a full history of twenty-five years of Norwegian Lutheranism in Garfield County in an extra edition of *Nordstjernen*. Jonas Olsen was the main character—an evil man who had always stood in the way of the ecclesiastical harmony that was desired by all others in the county. And now he was no longer content to be the pope. Indeed, he had set himself up as an autocratic czar and was trying to govern the people in secular affairs as he had in ecclesiastical matters. It was in many respects an excellent and well-written article that would surely have had an effect on many. But now it was all in ashes. Ward raged against his misfortune. Newell suggested that they could immediately print and distribute a flyer announcing that the Norwegian newspaper office had been burned down by the arsonists in Jonasville. He reminded Ward of the rumor that Jonas had set fire to Stunsrud's store in Minneapolis some twenty years ago. But Ward was reluctant. He had never believed in the rumor of the Minneapolis fire and was convinced that it was a creation of Napoleon. Moreover, everyone remembered what had happened to the extra edition of the *Johnsville Enterprize* five years earlier. If they now complained about the fire, they would only give the county something they could laugh about, said the old psychologist. When the latest issues of *Nordlys* and the *Garfield County Herald* arrived in Normanville later that afternoon, it became clear that Newell's plan wouldn't do at all.

Both papers had articles about the fire and described it as divine retribution for the sins of Ward and his henchmen. They had fought against truth and justice and now punishment had come upon them— as it always did. If only the people had been allowed to read the truth five years ago, as it had been laid out in the issue of the *Johnsville Enterprize* that Ward had stolen from the print shop and then publicly burned in his so-called park, then the county seat would already have been moved.

And both papers had a "Confession" by Napoleon Stomhoff, in which he declared that he had known Jonas Olsen all the years he had lived in Minneapolis and that he from the very first had been deeply impressed—as the *Herald* had it—by his upright character, his unsurpassed moral behavior, and his Christian unselfishness. It often happened, in the heat of battle, he had written, that one gives in to the temptation to say things about one's neighbor that may not be entirely in keeping with the truth. Thus many rumors had circulated about Jonas, and if he had ever done anything to make people believe in these rumors then he was now ready to pray to God and Jonas for forgiveness. This was the confession that Jonas had made Napoleon sign at their meeting in Stockdale three months ago.

———

Meanwhile, as most people in Jonasville were engaged in discussions of the fire, Ragna sat sewing in her living room, quite unaware of what had happened. At breakfast Jonas had for the tenth time defended his alliance with Seff and Napoleon, and both she and Jonas had used harsh words. As she was thinking it over again, Signe Marie came in with a book in her hand and sat down in the sofa. She began reading but suddenly laid the book aside and said: "I met a man yesterday who said that the fight between father and Ward is merely a waste of energy."

"Who would that be and where did you meet him?" her mother responded.

"On the road to Stockdale, but you wouldn't believe it if I told you who it was." And then she told what had happened and what the man had said.

"I assume that many think the same way. But your father after all has an excuse: he has had to carry on in self defense." Ragna felt obliged to say this to protect her daughter's respect for her father. "But who was this man?" she asked.

"Miles Standish Ward."

"Miles Standish . . . but that's impossible!"

"It almost seems so. Do you know him?"

"No. He has mostly lived in the East since he was old enough to go to school. Some of these Yankees don't think western schools are good enough for their children."

"He is tall and handsome and so interesting." Her mother looked closely at her and Signe Marie looked down. She was about to blush again.

"You must be careful when you are in the company of strange men," said Ragna.

"Careful . . . careful. That's what you always say! And I wasn't a bit careful. I let him know just what I thought."

"But wasn't that impolite? He may be a nice young man even though he has a bad father. People say that his mother was a good person." Neither said anything for a while.

"Tell me, have you met Jorshaug and talked with him recently?" her mother asked. No, she hadn't seen him alone for several days, Signe Marie said . . . not since the day after the public meeting when she had talked with him on the street.

Well, there was supposed to be a wedding! It had better be quite soon, preferably in early October. There was no reason for further delay. Signe Marie suddenly had something to think about. To be married! In a few weeks! And then—well then she would have to take farewell with life . . . Before her mother knew what had happened, her daughter embraced her.

"Oh, dearest mother!" she exclaimed. "Let me have another year! I can't do it now. Just one year, or even not till spring—June—I must get out . . ."

It felt so strange to have her at her bosom and Ragna had almost begun to reason with herself. But she stopped in time.

"No, no," she said firmly. "Impossible! And you'll find so much to live for in your new situation," she comforted her as she stroked her gently on her cheek. With a subdued sigh, which her mother took as resignation, Signe Marie got up and sat down again on the sofa with her book. But she wasn't reading. That afternoon she drove many miles across the prairie, and when Jorshaug came to visit at four she had still not yet come home.

At supper Jonas told them that Johan Utgard and Nyblom had gone to Johnson Township to speak with the farmers about the coming referendum. He had heard that people hadn't yet made up their minds over there. That was when Ragna said, "That's nice! Then I'm right again."

"Again?" said Jonas. "Can you remember a time when you weren't right?"

"You're right about that," she laughed. "But you know I have always said that you would find Utgard to be a fine man. The stories about him and Jørgine are pure nonsense. Jorshaug told me everything today. He had decided to get to the bottom of it . . ."

"That's what he said to me too . . . at least a year ago."

"Well, today he has visited with Utgard. Had you ever imagined that he and Hans Andreas were brothers?"

"Brothers? What rubbish is that? And why all this secrecy?"

"Hans Andreas spent time in Stillwater. Many years ago he was in a brawl in a Minneapolis saloon and became responsible for another's death. He didn't have to serve more than five years. Utgard came here just after his brother had been pardoned. The first year he was out, Hans Andreas worked in the sawmills, but he began drinking again and Johan got him to move here so he could keep an eye on him. In Norway, Jørgine had served in his parents' home and Hans Andreas had fallen in love with her. But his parents decided that she wasn't good enough for him. They met again here in Jonasville and after Alexander died they got married. Utgard encouraged them, hoping that she would be able to straighten him up. He was deeply in debt, but helped them as much as he could. So they were never without food. At times he also gave Jørgine some cash. But then she became aware of the gossip and kept her distance. After Hans Andreas died she wouldn't accept any help. So Utgard has decided to set up a fund for the education of those of her children who graduate from high school. The oldest of them, Alexander, is now sixteen and quite gifted. Johan would like him to become a lawyer. Jørgine has accepted this help for her children on the condition that Utgard makes his relationship with them public knowledge. He has promised to do so, and that is the whole story."

"*Gudnes,*" said Jonas. "It's a strange world we live in!"

"It wouldn't be so strange by far if only the people in it had a stronger sense of justice," Ragna said.

23.

The weather was beautiful on the day of the referendum. The sky was blue and the roads were dry. Jonas couldn't have wished for better. He was up early and satisfied with himself and the world. It was nine o'clock and he had already made a round of the town to make sure that everything was ready. He had met a few people who he had reason to believe didn't love him and wanted to make sure that they today would at least be loyal to their town. Severin Hansen and Moland were also up and about, visiting those people who Jonas for some reason didn't want to approach himself.

There weren't many laborers in Jonasville; perhaps a hundred or so in addition to the clerks who didn't own property or run a business. The railroad employed a crew of about sixteen men and Jonas made a point of paying them a visit. He wanted to demonstrate that he wasn't above visiting with the less fortunate even though he had become so powerful that he ran a whole town. He also wanted them to know he was working hard for a cause that was far more important for their prosperity than for his. He had even paid a visit to Ole Dampen and had a bottle for the crew boss, and when they both spoke with the railroad workers they were in full agreement: no one had so strong a stake in the question of the county seat as the railroad workers. It went so well that Jonas began to doubt the story he had heard that Ward had already bought the votes of the railroad workers. He had heard about it last night and now there was at least one person at each polling place who repeated and embellished the rumor. Jonas realized he had to be on top of everything. The slightest oversight could have fatal consequences.

He was busy that morning. Whatever the outcome, he would at least demonstrate that he had the town on his side. He stopped a group of ditchdiggers on the outskirts of town and told them about the importance of the referendum, noting that wages would surely increase to three dollars a day when the courthouse was built and that it was just as certain that prices would go down because of the large increase in sales. Down by Benvold's livery barn he found a half-dozen people standing around and conversing as if they had nothing better to do. Some were farmers who had left their homes on the prairie and built houses in town. Quite a few had done this recently, and some of them had been opposed to spending money on a new courthouse. They weren't much in favor of moving the county seat either, since that meant a new building that would again mean higher taxes. Experience had made them appreciate thrift. They reminded Jonas that the Jonasville newspapers had always claimed that the old courthouse was good enough. But would it be good enough if the county seat was moved? He didn't want to say too much about this now because it would of course be necessary to build a new courthouse if Jonasville became the new county seat. So he tried to avoid the issue. He thought it might be possible to get along with the old courthouse a while longer if it was fixed. That's the way he looked at it, but the decision wasn't his and people had so many views. But the question of building was not at all related to the question to be decided today. There was no reason to let one interfere with the other.

An impudent Irishman remarked that as far as he had understood it, the issue was whether Ward should continue to run the county or whether he should be forced to abdicate and let Jonas take his place on the throne. Jonas explained that this was a major misunderstanding. There were far more serious reasons for the conflict. He couldn't believe that there were still people who hadn't got the point. He wasn't interested in any kind of influence in the county government. This should have been obvious for all a long time ago. His one and only goal was a government by the people. Ward hadn't shown respect for our democratic institutions. And that was the only reason he was against him.

Over at the elevator Jonas met an American from around Stockdale, who said he was opposed to moving the county seat because Jonas and his party had used such dirty methods and attacked Ward as a person. But this was yet another misunderstanding. Jonas told him that he had the greatest respect for Elihu. People should learn the difference between person and principle.

So Jonas had been just about everywhere that morning. And he had done well. He was in good spirits as he came whistling into his store. And then he suddenly remembered that there were a few potential voters down on the South Flats that he hadn't yet met and talked to about their duties as citizens. And they might easily forget all about it. They might think that this was just another election day and not be aware that it was the most important day in the history of Jonasville. And it had been more than a week since he last had seen Lars in the Bend in town. Lars had a pretty good head on his shoulders, but he hadn't become very American. And Jonas suddenly realized that a single vote could decide the referendum. So Jonas again took his cap and set off for the South Flats, taking the Ford to save time. His first stop was for Livius, who was married to Dorte on the Porch.[37] But he wasn't home, and when Dorte began to inform him about the poor qualities of her neighbors, Jonas excused himself in the middle of her lecture and said that he was sorry he was so terribly busy today but that he would return some other day to listen to the rest of what she had to tell him. And then he saw Ole pottering about in his backyard and he called to him, asking if he would be making use of his right by popular sovereignty today.

"Do you mean if I'm going to *voda*?" said Ole. Yes, that's what he had meant. "Come in at the *storet* when you go to vote," said Jonas, "and get a *sempel* of our new *Exray* Coffee—the best on the market."

"*Mebbe* I will," said Ole. And then it was on to see Lars.

Lars hadn't been feeling so well lately. Jonas said he had come to talk about some work he needed done. The yard behind the store had to be cleared and there were a few other things as well. This was the first time that Jonas had come to see Lars in the eight years Lars had lived on the South Flats, and Lars suspected that this talk about work was merely an excuse. Jonas probably had other and more important affairs on his mind, and Lars got the idea that he might be able to negotiate a deal in his favor. He needed money for the doctor, medicines, and other things as well, now that he was so poorly.

Lars was far from being a candidate for the poorhouse. He had had the foresight to set aside a few hundred so that he would have a little to go on. A few years ago he had placed his savings with Johan Utgard. He was the only man in town he trusted. But since last spring he had begun to think that his money might not be safe even with him. So he had taken half of it back and placed it in a box that he had cemented into a corner in his basement. Not only would no one ever find it there, but it would be safe even if the house burned down. But no other living soul except Utgard knew about his savings. It had to be kept a secret. Otherwise he would have the assessor at his door and it would go to pay *kontytœxt*.

Lars didn't have a family. His first fifteen years in America he had worked in lumber camps and spent his money in saloons. Then he met Jørgine in Crookston and she was then both young and beautiful. So Lars had his one and only inspiration since he had left Norway. He decided to spend the rest of his life as a respectable husband to her and to stay sober. But Jørgine was reluctant. She didn't want a drunk for a husband. After a while she married Alexander, who drank more than a blind mare, which made Lars quite upset; he drank and he fought more than ever. But one night he happened to stagger into a *miten'hus*. At that point he couldn't care less about where he went. But the words of the preacher changed all that. When Lars went home from the meeting he had such a fear as he had never experienced, and the next morning he felt like a new person. Since then he had never set foot in a saloon.

But he was a wanderer by heart and it took several years before he settled down. When he eventually came back to Crookston he was told that Alexander and Jørgine had moved to Jonasville and that Alexander was the same sponge he had always been. So Lars made yet another important decision and moved to Jonasville himself. He was not getting any younger and he wanted a place he could call home. So when Alexander died and Jørgine was alone with all their children, Lars was yet again taken by strange feelings and asked her if Lars in the Bend now was good enough for her. But Jørgine—ever a strange woman— still didn't find such a union suitable, considering the life she had lived. No good could come of it. But before the end of the year she had married Hans Andreas. It was incomprehensible, and Lars pondered and brooded days on end. That was when he decided to ignore Jørgine.

"You are a sober and intelligent man, Lars," Jonas said. "And that's why I would like you to do this work for me." And since he was aware that relations between Lars and Jørgine were not of the best, he added: "You know, I often give Alexander occasional work, but he is only a child and, well, you know . . ."

But Lars began to think that Jørgine certainly needed the little money Alexander could take home. He spat out his plug of tobacco.

"No, I don't think I can help you," he said. "I don't really have the strength to do it."

Well, there wasn't much Jonas could do if he didn't want the job . . . Had he, by the way, heard about the referendum today? Yes, Lars had heard about it. Wasn't it about whether Jonas or Ward should run the county? It irritated Jonas to hear this misunderstanding repeated so many times. Didn't Lars read the newspapers? Today it would be decided whether the courthouse and the county officers should come to Jonasville. This was a matter of honor as well as of prosperity for the entire town. Lars of course knew all of this. He subscribed to *Nordlys*. But he had become contrary in his old age.

"Yes, I suppose it's a matter of great importance for me," he responded. "If I vote for it you'll perhaps give me permission to stand outside the fine building and admire it when you have built it. Or *mebbe* I'll have my law office there? Then I suppose I must vote yes."

"You're still quite a comedian, Lars," said Jonas. "But you will be voting today? This is your right and your responsibility. We live in a democracy. You're part of the government of the country, the state, and the county. You know that, don't you?"

"Oh," said Lars, pretending ignorance. "Is that the way it is? And I've always thought that I had nothing to say about it and that it was only you, this Ward fellow, and that Teddy Rosenfelt who were the government." So anyhow, he was going to vote, wasn't he? Well, if he actually was a member of the government he would of course want to vote; but he was feeling so poorly right now and didn't think he would be able to walk all the way downtown. By the way, he should have been to the doctor too, but he didn't even have the strength to get there. And, what was worse, he didn't have the money to pay him.

To get an end to all this, Jonas said that he would be happy to give Lars a lift to the polling place and then take him to the doctor. He would even make sure that the consultation with the doctor wouldn't cost him anything and that he got a ride home afterward.

After he had voted and after he had paid a visit to Hornemann (who told him that he was in good health), Lars was just about to enter the car—now to be driven by Bollemo—when Jørgine happened by with four of her children hanging on to her skirt. She stopped and stared. They hadn't exchanged words for a long time, but now she just had to make use of this unique opportunity to get him back for all his arrogance. She lifted her chin and said as sarcastically as she could:

"*Gudnes, grœcius,* what a fine man you have become!"

At first Lars wanted to respond in the same style, but as he looked at Jørgine he became aware of her ragged clothes, her old and worn-out shoes, her tired face, her bent-over figure, her neglected children—and his heart was suddenly filled with love and concern. Poor Jørgine! Poor children! And he walked up to her, completely ignoring her aggressive posture, and said in a voice that wasn't altogether steady: "If you would let me, I could lend you $50 . . . It may help a little . . ."

Jørgine was taken by surprise. She had never seen that much money at once in her whole life. She couldn't believe that Lars could have such a fortune in his possession. He was just being arrogant again and making fun of her just because her life had been difficult.

"Oh, you needn't stand there and make yourself proud," she said. "Is it my fault that Our Lord has blessed me with so many children?" He realized that she didn't believe that he had as much as $50 to give away. He had entirely forgotten that he had made the entire town believe he was poor.

"I have the money, Jørgine," he ensured her with all the seriousness he could muster. "And it is yours. I'll still have a little left over for myself." She stood there staring at him. This was beyond understanding.

"Are you serious?" she finally asked.

"Yes." She stood a while looking doubtfully at him. Then she dried off a tear with her sleeve, gave him her hand, and said:

"I must say that this is very kind of you, Lars. But I won't take any money from you or any other person, not in my present situation. But if you really . . ." She wasn't able to say any more. But they understood each other. Then he got into the car and drove up Lincoln Street just like a gentleman. And people stopped to look at him. They recognized Bollemo at the wheel and saw that it was Jonas Olsen's Ford, because it flew a little American flag in honor of the day. He has certainly moved up in society, they said.

24.

People began to assemble in the Jonasville park early in the evening. The results would be announced there as they came in from the townships. There was music by the Merchants' Band, and Severin Hansen, Moland, Karsten Floen, and Bollemo made up a quartet that sang election songs and other popular tunes. Sofus Jensen, the editor of *Nordlyset,* had the telephone at his ear, and his colleague, Jepsen of the *Garfield County Herald,* drove back and forth between the office and the park with the news from their correspondents.

The first report was from O'Brien Township. Only four had voted against the proposition to move the county seat. Hurrah! Hurrah! Hurrah! The next one was from Normanville. There, only four had voted for. The band played a funeral march. There were no more results for a while and the waiting crowd was entertained by the quartet.

Jonas sat in thought. He was touched by the loyalty demonstrated by the inhabitants of O'Brien Township. The members of the United Church congregation had been far more reasonable than he had expected. He was actually so moved for a moment that he almost reproached himself for on occasion having been too harsh in his judgment. But then he got the results from Johnson Township, one of the more doubtful ones. The proposition had been turned down by a majority of thirty-nine votes. A whisper went through the crowd and Jonas's hopes sank a little. He had after all hoped that this township, situated halfway between the two competing towns, would give a slight majority for Jonasville. The next report was from Grant Township, to the south. He didn't expect to win there, but because of the strong progressive movement among the farmers he had at least hoped that the majority for Normanville would be slight. So he was disappointed when they were told that Grant had rejected the proposition against a mere twelve votes.

"*Gudnes!*" he thought. "This is going right to the dogs." And then an inner voice reminded him of the loyalty of his old ecclesiastical adversaries in O'Brien Grove. Perhaps it would be a good thing to have all the Norwegians in America in one church. Hornemann was probably right when he said that we would be able to achieve so much more if we could only stand together. So Jonas made an important decision. If the referendum went his way, he would be a man of reconciliation. And it seemed to help. Just then Lincoln Township reported that the proposition had been carried with only nine opposing votes. Cheers! "The Star-spangled Banner." And then the results from Arrowtown: of the 400 votes cast, 375 were for the proposition. Seff had delivered the goods. More cheers! The quartet sang, "Say, Teddy, Oh Teddy!" Then they heard from Washington Township: a 153 vote majority for Jonasville. Then Stockdale: a majority of 300 for the proposition. Jubilation! Finally, at eleven o'clock, Floen, who had been reading the reports as they came to him, announced that Jonasville had almost 500 votes more than the majority of 55 percent required by law. They had won. For fifteen minutes there was so much cheering and hurrahing that nothing else could be heard. The band tried to play but were drowned out by the noise. When all voices were hoarse and Jonas had been carried around the park, the quartet presented a song written for the occasion by the captain of Scandinavie, Jonasville's only poet. The first and last stanzas of the lyrics were:

> Oh, Jonasville! Oh, Jonasville!
> The greatest town of all,
> We celebrate your fame today,
> We hasten to your call.
> Oh, Jonasville! Oh, Jonasville!
> Oh, Jonasville!

After midnight there was free beer in the saloons for all comers. Money was unnecessary that night in Jonasville.

Jonas was glad that Ragna was up waiting for him when he came home a little after twelve. It was almost more than he had hoped for, and even though she yawned and didn't demonstrate any great joy in the great victory, he nevertheless understood that it was a token of her recognition that she hadn't followed her "principles" and gone to bed at her usual time. Signe Marie had been in the park until all the reports had come in. She was now asleep on the sofa. She woke up and threw her arms around her father's neck and said it had been great. He was proud of Signe Marie . . . She understood him . . .

Pastor Jorshaug had an unexpected visit from his brother Lars that evening. He had accepted a position at the University of Chicago and only had time for a brief stay with his parents and brother before taking up his duties. So the next day, Jonas, Ragna, and Signe Marie were invited to dinner at the parsonage with the two brothers and their parents.

Lars Jorshaug Jr. was in many respects quite different from his brother even though they looked quite alike. Signe Marie noted that Lars was more lively and sociable. You could sense that he had been around in the world. He hadn't been in Garfield County since he graduated from the University of Minnesota, and no one knew much about him except that he was supposed to be a famous sociologist and that he had been married to a wealthy American woman and was divorced.

In Signe Marie's imagination, Lars had an aura of adventure. He was the only man she knew of in their neighborhood who had ventured out into the wide world and made himself a name among the Americans. He had written books and expressed radical views—views that were beyond her understanding but that she imagined were wonderful because they were different from those that were valid in Jonasville. So she had naturally been waiting all morning for the noontime dinner. She put on the most daring dress she had and turned a deaf ear to all her mother's admonitions that it wasn't at all appropriate for the occasion. Jorshaug seemed a little surprised when he greeted them at the door. She knew exactly why. He didn't approve of her bare neck and arms. But she had her independence . . .

The professor, however, was pleasantly surprised. To him, her dress expressed a mind of a different bent than that of Jonasville. It expressed a different desire, a protest against rigid, traditional views. So he assumed she was an interesting young woman and not just a beautiful one. They were placed next to each other at the table, and he was so engaged in conversation with her that he hardly had a word for the others. Several times Sivert, the pastor, had to repeat his questions to his brother. Ragna may have been the only one to notice that Sivert turned silent. Else Jorshaug was so happy to have both her sons with her that she hardly noticed anything else, and Jonas and the elder Lars were deeply involved in a discussion of county politics and patiently endured the interruptions of Signe Marie's youthful and merry laughter when her dinner partner said something apt or funny.

Just now they were talking about Venice, gondolas, and guitars. There was music everywhere—music and color, in nature as among the people . . . a natural freedom . . . carnival in Rome . . . an unrestrained people. In contrast he described a parade on Unter den Linden[38] . . . a demonstration of all that was Prussian . . . impressive, but rigid, lifeless . . . But all over Europe, people were liberating themselves from old traditions. In art, literature, and politics there was a search for new forms of expression. People were breaking away from old prejudices and were looking forward to a new age that beckoned a new and visionary generation like the breaking of a new day. And as Lars spoke—spoke without pause and in a language so rich in imagery that she listened to it as a strange, distant, and wonderful music—she laughed and smiled and welcomed it into her open and receptive mind. She was happy.

"But all this breaking up of the roots of tradition is surely a dangerous development," the pastor interrupted his brother. "People will lose their foothold in life."

"They will find a new foothold in the new age," Lars responded. "The old forms will have to surrender to the new. That is the law of evolution."

"There is another law," said the pastor. "The law of God. It will always stand above the law you speak of. Nothing can ever take its place in people's souls."

"Well, we will probably never be able to agree on that score," said Lars, "so we had both better move to more neutral waters."

"In gondolas with the music of guitars," said Signe Marie. She was in Venice and it was evening with a full moon.

After dinner Signe Marie played Grieg's "Foran Sydens Kloster" on the piano.[39] She felt she played it better now than before and that she understood it. Lars praised her performance and said that it was a pity she hadn't been able to get out and learn more than she could here. And then he told them about great musicians he had heard: Farrar, Melba, Kubelik, Paderewsky, Caruso, Scotti, Fremstad—well-known performers she had heard on the phonograph.[40] But this man had actually seen them perform in the limelight. He had followed them closely and observed how their deep-felt emotions had found expression, not only in their music but also in the most subtle nuances of their movements and their features.

"Oh, God! Had I only been able to get out into the world!" she whispered ever so quietly so that no one would hear her. He stood right behind her as she again faced the piano and fingered the sheet music nervously.

Then it occurred to Professor Jorshaug that he may have done this young woman a disservice by opening the door to a new world. She was, after all, destined to become a pastor's wife. His brother's wife. And then he thought, why my brother's? But he said:

"Well, that may be, but whether you are out or at home, the world is largely one of worry and regret. You must remember that!" The words were whispered in her ear but she felt every word to be the blow of a hammer. Partly in anger, but still smiling, she turned to him and said: "You have given me a beautiful dream and then, when I am in the middle of it, you take it away from me. That is not a nice thing to do!"

"You may be right," he answered. "But you will perhaps soon have another that is yet more beautiful."

What he actually may have meant was something she was still speculating on when she and her mother were walking home later that afternoon.

25.

When Jonas returned to the bank after the dinner at the parsonage there were several telegrams from out-of-town friends congratulating him on the referendum. One was from Lyman, the president of the H. & B., another from Johan Arndt Lomwiig. He owed much to these two for their support at the time of the founding of Jonasville and during the battle for the rights to section 13. Lomwiig had surprised all who knew him in Minneapolis in the 1880s by his rapid career rise in the railroad business. Three years ago he had become the head of the H. & B. Company's large land division. Lomwiig and Dagny Simonsen had made a nice couple. Jonas reflected on how she had come close to making an ass of him . . . Yes, she certainly had, but with God's help . . . And Ragna, in spite of all her "principles," had been great, yes she certainly had . . . And now he too had decided to become a man of reconciliation . . .

But here he sat philosophizing without looking at the other telegrams! There was even one from Normanville. It read: "Accept my heartiest congratulations on your splendid victory. But I'll be hanged if you have the county seat yet. Ward."

Jonas laughed. So like Elihu! He hadn't the slightest inkling of what Ward had up his sleeve. But he was quite sure that whatever it might be, there was nothing or no one that now could deny Jonasville the county seat. The people had spoken, and we live, thank God, in a democratic country. Within sixty days everything should be ready for the move, but the law gave them another thirty if they needed the extra time.

Then he walked out on the street where celebrations were going on everywhere. The Merchants' Band had played all day. Townsmen and farmers sang loudly as they walked arm in arm from saloon to saloon. Even the sober Johan Utgard had joined Severin Hansen, Bollemo, and Siversen in Berge's blind pig and he pretended to sing the baritone part to a new victory song by Captain Hermansen.

The town was like a child. Jonas didn't like drinking but he understood that people wanted to celebrate on such a great day. He ran into Nyblom, Flasmo, and other friends from the Grove in the hotel. Flasmo was drunk already and insisted on discussing church union. He had expected Jonas to anger and to begin to argue with him, so that he could catch him in a theological error. It was his notion of fun, but little fun came of it this time.

"I have arrived at the same conviction," said Jonas.

"You? What in the dickens . . ." This was quite a *sørpræs*!

"Well, I have speculated and thought about it for a long time and it seems to me that it would be best to try to come to an agreement. When the time comes, my vote will be for union." Iver had to think it over before he could be sure that Jonas was serious. "Well, then I should probably congratulate you." And then he turned to Nyblom and said: "We'll have to drink to this!"

Jonas never knew whether they did or not. He didn't like Flasmo's irresponsibility and he left them. The captain was serving at the bar between writing verses. A couple of drummers had just told him some interesting news from Normanville. Ward had suffered a stroke at noon and was partly paralyzed on his left side.

Ward's stroke was of course a topic at the Olsen supper table. Jonas had invited Nyblom, and the pastor and his parents were also present. He hadn't been able to find Flasmo. Jonas said something about the wrath of God. Old Jorshaug looked over at his son but didn't say anything. Ragna did.

"Oh, misfortune may come to us all. We have all deserved punishment." The pastor agreed.

"We most certainly have. In the eyes of God we are all equal." Jonas looked at him. What was all this about. Were they suggesting that he and Ward were equals? He was about to tell them something about this when he suddenly remembered his own doctrine concerning the role of good deeds . . .[41]

After a while, the pastor remarked that it would have been a good idea to close the saloons today. Many were getting pretty drunk, he said.

"Yes, people are happy," Jonas answered. "It was a great victory."

"It's a questionable happiness that finds such expression," said Jorshaug.

"It may even be a questionable victory if this is what it leads to," said Ragna.

Now they are at it again, Jonas thought. How could he be to blame that people were happy and took a glass or two in celebration? He turned to Jorshaug Senior.

"Well, what is your present view on church union, Lars?" Lars believed, as he had always believed, that if union could be achieved without giving up doctrine, then . . . And Jonas agreed. He had thought it over and decided to support the work for union too. The pastor and Ragna looked back and forth at each other and at Jonas. They weren't quite sure they could trust their own ears. Something had clearly happened to him. Then, just after supper, the telephone rang. There was a man at the hotel who needed to see Jonas immediately.

———✦———

It was none other than Napoleon Stomhoff who met Jonas half an hour later at the Scandinavie. He greeted him exuberantly and congratulated him on the referendum. It was unique, he said. We should be proud of a leader who worked so wisely for the commonweal. Jonas knew Napoleon too well to be affected by his flattery. Yes, he agreed, the referendum had gone quite well. And why did he want to see him? Well, could they perhaps talk about it in a more private place? And the two walked over to the bank.

"I'm sure you remember your promise," Napoleon said after they had sat down in Jonas's office. Jonas stared at him as though he knew nothing of any promise.

"What kind of promise?" he eventually asked. Stomhoff was so surprised that he didn't find words. What nonsense was this? He had been busy as a bee and worked like the devil to make the referendum go the way Jonas and Thompson desired, and now the man didn't even remember the "loan" he had promised him.

"Oh, *kom-off!*" he exclaimed. "You remember it very well. Would you just please sign the check. It should, as you know, be for one thousand." Jonas scratched his head as if he were trying to recall what had happened between them. Then he asked: "Do you mean the loan that you asked me about when we met in Stockdale?"

"Of course. What else should it be?"

"But don't you remember that you have already received that money?" Jonas smiled at him. Napoleon sat up in his chair. His face was red.

"Have I received them? What madness is this?"

"Take it easy! Take it easy!" Jonas warned him. "Don't you know a man named Tomlinson?"

"Tomlinson? What in the world does he have to do with it? And I don't know any Tomlinson . . . Well, yes, I once met a man with that name. He was employed by the Midland Farm Development Company."

"Really? But last year there were two Tomlinsons who both claimed to be associated with that company. I happened to meet them both— that is, Siversen met one of them . . ."

"I don't know what you are talking about. You must have started drinking." Stomhoff got up and towered over Jonas.

"Sit down," Jonas ordered him, and he obeyed. Jonas opened a drawer and took out a piece of paper, which he then gave him. It had evidently been placed there for this occasion.

"Sign the receipt!" he said. Stomhoff read what was on the paper:

> I, the undersigned Ludvig Napoleon Stomhoff, acknowledge having received from a certain Mr. Tomlinson $1,000 from Jonas Olsen as payment for services rendered.

"This is a base lie!" he cried. "I have never received any money from any Tomlinson!" Jonas chuckled. He took another piece of paper from the drawer.

"Well, that may be something you and Tomlinson will have to work out," he said. "Would you perhaps prefer to sign this one?" Stomhoff read it in fury.

> I, the undersigned Ludvig Napoleon Stomhoff, acknowledge that last summer I conspired with a person who used the name Tomlinson. I am guilty of fraudulently acquiring $1,000 as a cashier's check given on behalf of Jonas Olsen to the mentioned Mr. Tomlinson, who pretended to be a representative of the Midland Farm Development Company. I further declare that I was a party to the theft of a note for $1,200, signed by Nicolai

Nelsen to Jonas Olsen and placed in the safe in the latter's office
in the State Bank of Johnsville.

As Napoleon read this compromising document, Jonas took a third
piece of paper from the drawer and held it under Napoleon's nose. "Here
is the honored check!" he said. "The hour of reckoning has come, my boy!
Now I've finally caught you! But I'm not as bloodthirsty as you. I'm a
Christian and will be charitable. This is why I'm giving you the opportunity to sign the receipt instead of the declaration of guilt that you have
in your hand. And you know what you have to expect if you refuse to
sign. The penitentiary, my boy, where I should have sent you long ago!"

"But where is your evidence?" thundered Napoleon. "Where is your
evidence?"

Jonas calmly took a letter from the drawer and held it up between
them. Stomhoff got up and tried to snatch it out of his hand but was given
a powerful shove in his chest that made him fall back into his chair with
a cry of rage.

"Don't try to do anything foolish, my boy!" said Jonas. He was unruffled. "I'm not quite the man I used to be, but I can always handle a
little squirt like you." Again he held up the letter. The envelope was addressed to Nicolai Nelsen, Johnsville, and in the upper left-hand corner
read: "Return in five days to L. M. Stomhoff, Arrowtown, Minn." It was
in Napoleon's handwriting.

"Give me the pen," he said quickly. "I'll sign the receipt." He did,
and got up.

"Just one thing more," said Jonas, who also got up on his feet. "Within
a week you will be out of Garfield County."

"Will I? How would you know?"

"I know because if you don't get out I will hand the case over to the
Midland Farm Development Company. Understand?" Napoleon's answer was a look of hatred. He went toward the door. Jonas opened it for
him, gave him his hand, and said with a contented smile: "Thank you
very much for all your help!" He pushed him gently through the bank
and out into the street. Then he called Johan Utgard on the telephone.

26.

In September, Floen made good his promise to send Sigrid to Northwestern University. She had been anxious all summer that it would
come to nothing, since he so often talked about how expensive it would

be to have both his children at school. Last year Karsten had entered the University of Minnesota law school, and their father had said it was a drain on his pocketbook. Floen's congressional campaign had been quite expensive, so it was no joke. But Sigrid got off on schedule and was glad to leave Jonasville behind.

That was almost three weeks ago, and Signe Marie had had two detailed letters about everything Sigrid had seen and done in the big city. Chicago was perhaps not so remarkable, but for Sigrid it was like coming to a fairy-tale castle from a dugout on the prairie. The throbbing life, the fashionable people, the crowds in the streets, the confident behavior of city people, the well-regulated pace of the enormous traffic, the brightly lit business emporiums at night, Lincoln Park, the skyscrapers, the hotels, the boulevards, Lake Michigan, the ships, the concerts, the theaters, and the fun in the dorm—she had been impressed by it all. She had come to a strange new world and it was all so bewitching that she hadn't thought about her home in the prairie town except as something small, paltry, and boring.

Signe Marie was overwhelmed by Sigrid's letters. Her desire to get away flamed up again. Her greatest dream was the Chicago Conservatory of Music. But after many sighs and tears, she had finally given up all thought of postponing her wedding. Her mother insisted that it was too late to change anything. And then she had met Miles Standish Ward. Since then his words had reverberated in her inner ear. What he had said about their fathers had planted new ideas in her mind. She had begun to apply a new measuring stick to life around her. All that had seemed so important—the fighting and the competition between her father and Ward—now shrank in significance. She had tried to hold on to her former perspective—as she knew she should—but it now seemed so petty. The many new places she had become aware of—Boston, Harvard, New York, the East—loomed large in her consciousness. Professor Lars Jorshaug's lively conversation about Venice, Italy, carnivals, colors, and gondolas, and about the brave new mentality that was conquering the world, had made it even more difficult for her to continue along the well-trodden paths and to stay within the borders that had been drawn around her. Had he asked her, she felt that she would have followed him to the end of the world. But she had cried herself asleep after telling herself that her time for dreaming was over and that in less than a month she would enter the unchangeable world of a pastor's wife.

One day her mother said that Mrs. Fundeland had to begin work on her wedding gown. There was so much to be done in the remaining weeks . . . And then she had a third letter from Sigrid. She had heard Caruso! She had seen him on the stage with her own eyes and heard him sing for a large and well-dressed audience. Caruso! Signe Marie went up to her room and wouldn't come down to dinner. She was so unutterably tired of Jonasville and everything she associated with the little town. She had loved it; it was, after all, her father's creation and her family's home, the site of so many fond childhood memories: people she had regarded as kind and well-meaning even though they may not always have been inspired by justice and magnanimity; a landscape that appeared monotonous but that she had accepted as an inevitable presence; the farmers with their loads of wheat or on their way to church, slow in speech and movement but, as her father had so often remarked, reliable, steady, and solid—why had it all become so different? The town—her family's pride—now seemed a cemetery on a rainy day. The prairie was dull, naked, and ugly—a source of food. And the people, mercy me, their world had become so small. It was all about sowing and harvesting, one pig for slaughter and one for the market, some trade, some religiosity, some daily concern with matters that were none of their business, and some ecclesiastical squabbles on the side! How could she not have seen this before? She had to get away—get out into the wide world where there was light, space, and great visions!

It was as if she for the first time was sufficiently sober to survey the rugged road ahead. Her relationship with Jorshaug had intrigued her. It was so strange that this tall, quiet, and serious man, who had seen so much of the world and met so many women, admired and looked up to her. He was sturdy and solid, yet mild and gentle—so mature and restrained compared to the boys who spoke nonsense and danced with her . . . But now she realized what a barrier she had set up between herself and life by being engaged to him . . .

Such was her state of mind when she later that afternoon again confided her troubled thoughts to her mother. Even though the two hadn't been as close as Ragna had wished, Signe Marie nevertheless felt that she had to go to her mother when it really mattered. And now she told her about her new letter from Sigrid. She had heard Caruso. Chicago was wonderful. Mercy me—it would have been so wonderful to see it!

"But you know that isn't possible," Ragna said quietly. Her daughter interrupted her: "It must be possible! Others can do it, why can't I?"

"I think I can understand you," her mother said gently. She was thoughtful and there was an unexpected mildness in her voice. "But what can we do, my dear? There are several reasons why we cannot delay the wedding. First of all we must consider Jorshaug. He'll soon be thirty-seven. It would complicate your relationship to delay your marriage any further."

"But what if he agreed to wait until spring?" She was close to admitting what she really felt: that she had begun to fear the consequences of her decisions and was no longer sure that she wanted to be Jorshaug's wife. But she kept this to herself, well knowing how her mother would respond: duty, principles, honor, truth, decency, and all that.

"I don't think he would agree," Ragna answered. "And, as I have said, I don't believe it would be right to insist."

"But don't I have any rights?"

"Young people often assume far too many rights," said her mother seriously. "We live in an age of more and more rights and fewer and fewer duties. But sooner or later the time for duties will come. We cannot avoid our share. And they will seem all the more difficult if we have always avoided them. I believe this is not simply a law of life but of God."

"Oh, mercy me . . . Duties, duties, duties! Doesn't life consist of more than duties?"

"Certainly, much, much more, but the rest will follow only if we conscientiously take on our duties as we get to them. You have no right to expect to receive more from life than you give. If you get more from life than you have given it will always be at someone else's expense, and if your expectations have such a foundation, your life is based on injustice. Your smile will be paid by others' tears, your happiness by others' grief."

"We've heard all this before, mother. It's hardly news."

"It's life and goes much deeper than the daily news," Ragna responded, "and the truth is forever true, regardless of whether we are interested in it or not."

The doorbell rang. It was Jorshaug. He had kind words but—as so often lately—he was grave and pensive. He hadn't seemed happy since they had been in the parsonage on the occasion of his brother's visit. That evening he had—more than ever before—seen that he and Signe Marie hardly belonged in the same world, and he had begun to realize the price she would have to pay to submit her carefree and impulsive nature to the restraints of the life she was about to enter. At times he had reproached himself for allowing their relationship to lead to an engagement. He should have waited and considered the matter more carefully. Of one thing he was certain: she was the only woman who had fully conquered his heart and mind. Should it turn out to be God's will that he should relinquish her? Last night he had thought it over. Yesterday afternoon he had decided for the tenth time to visit the Olsens and do something about it. And again he had met with complications.

Lars in the Bend stood there with cap in hand when the pastor opened his door. He seemed strangely timid. Did he want to speak with him? Well, yes, he supposed so. Actually, about something quite important. He hesitated. He had, in a way, sort of made up his mind to marry. And he wondered if the pastor would be so kind as to let them do it in the church. It might seem surprising that he had taken such a great decision, being a poor man and all, but . . . His income wasn't the pastor's business, said Jorshaug. That was his concern, and he was after all reasonably able-bodied. But if he was going to marry, a woman was surely involved. Yes, Lars admitted as he fumbled with his cap, there was one. And did she have a name? Oh, certainly. He knew Jørgine, didn't he? And the pastor needn't worry about the decency of their relationship. No, of course not, said Jorshaug. When did they wish to have their wedding? Oh, as soon as possible, if the pastor wasn't too *bisi*.

And he had gone with Lars to the Flats and had done what was required and ascertained that they were as happy a couple as he had ever married. And Lars had said that Jørgine's troubles were over. So this was one of the reasons why Jorshaug hadn't gone to the Olsens' yesterday as he had planned.

27.

There was another reason why Jorshaug hadn't gone to the Olsens' yesterday. When he walked through the town after the ceremony in the Flats, he had checked his mail at the post office and found a typed letter, stamped on the train, that gave him new food for thought. The letter, signed "a friend," was a compilation of the stories about Signe Marie that had gone the rounds the last couple of years, with a few fabrications added by the writer. It was painful, he wrote, to have to warn the pastor, but his conscience gave him no peace. He was convinced that his words would be received in the same benevolent spirit in which they had been composed and that his intentions would not be misunderstood. The congregation was offended. It had even been said that people had come upon Signe Marie and the pastor in compromising situations. After the pastor had read the letter, he began to think of how the members of the Ladies Aid had recently been unnaturally restrained, but he hadn't paid much attention. Now he understood them better. He had no way of knowing that the letter was a deliberate mixture of truth and fiction. Nor did he suspect that the writer may not have had his best interest at heart.

Jorshaug knew that he was without fault—at least, that was his first reaction. And since Signe Marie was by nature frivolous and irresponsible, he was also sure that she hadn't deliberately erred, even though she may have behaved in ways that were not always in keeping with convention. Nevertheless, his clerical honor was at stake. He knew that there was no one who could be so easily hurt by the verdict of glib tongues as a clergyman in a small town. So Jorshaug soon saw that this could be dangerous for him. But his unselfish nature didn't long permit him to see Signe Marie's alleged transgressions only as they might affect his own position. Did he even have a right to expect of a young woman of her upbringing and character that she should bend to the demands made of him as a pastor?

After he had read the letter he felt as if he wanted to go off somewhere and hide from the greedily inquisitive eyes that had seen his humanity. He went straight home. The rest of the day and much of the night he reflected on his situation, and the next morning he saw that the decision he had made as many times as he had unmade it must be carried through. He must talk with Signe Marie. That was why he had come.

He sat down and appeared both distracted and lost in the realization that he saw neither beginning nor end to what had brought him there. He cleared his throat, said a few words about the weather, and cleared his throat again. Signe Marie found him comical. In spite of the things she had been through earlier in the day, she was tempted to laugh. But when she looked closer she understood that he had something on his mind. Ragna saw more than her daughter. She realized that a crisis was at hand. She left them alone, explaining that her maid had the afternoon off and that she had things that had to be done in the kitchen.

They sat a while in silence; she was on the sofa and he was on a chair at the far side of the room. Both had difficult confessions to make. Finally he got up and sat down at her side.

"How have you been these last few days?" he asked as he took her hand in his.

"Terrible!" The word slipped involuntarily past her lips. His hand was warm and firm, but his touch didn't affect her as before, and when he took her in his arms and kissed her it was almost as if she felt distaste. She freed herself and moved away. Her face was blushed and confused and she laughed a little to distract him. And he noticed nothing—nothing but the woman he loved and who loved him in return, and his only thought was that nothing would ever separate them. And how could he possibly talk to her about the nasty things he had come to discuss? No, that could wait. Nothing, he repeated to himself, nothing would ever part them. When she said that she felt terrible he assumed that she too had heard about the gossip. To console her he said: "I wouldn't pay too much attention to gossip. When your own conscience tells you that you have acted according to the strictest rules of decency . . ."

There was lightning in her eyes when she interrupted him: "Mercy me, haven't we had enough of all this talk of decency and propriety."

There was reproach in his voice when he said: "You can't mean what you are saying!"

"Oh yes, I do!"

"We must never disregard the rules of propriety. After godliness, propriety is . . ."

"Do you think I'm saying this because I wish to be improper?"

"How could you believe such a thing?"

"Oh, I don't know. It's so nauseating."

He sat with a surprised look on his face. She was so capricious . . . and so becoming . . . even when she behaved like a naughty child.

Then she changed her approach. She was again the smiling and impish Signe Marie that he had fallen in love with . . . Oh, he would carry her through life in his arms . . .

"You must find me horrible," she said, and placed her hand on his arm. He took it. "I'm like the weather in April."

"I haven't noticed. And as for the weather in April . . ."

"Oh, you needn't make up excuses for me. Would you say no to what I have been thinking of doing?"

"That depends on what it is. We should be careful with our promises."

"Yes, don't you think so too? It's so terribly risky."

"And what have you been thinking of doing?"

"You know how fond I am of music?"

"Yes, and . . ."

"Well, I thought that if I could have this winter, this school year, then I would try to develop my piano playing . . . attend the Chicago Conservatory. Would you let me do it?" She spoke hesitatingly, as if not quite sure of herself. He felt as if a cloud had settled before his eyes. So that's what she wanted. She wanted to get away from the town, from the people, from the restrictions and the rules of propriety, from him . . .

"But I thought . . ." He groped for words. Then he felt her soft hand on his forehead. It was warm and delicate. It was as if it could smooth his wrinkles.

"I know," she said gently. "You thought that we would be married in the fall. But I must get out of here . . . just this one winter, do you hear. You won't deny me this, will you?"

He got up and began to pace the floor. She could see that he was struggling with difficult thoughts and she followed him with anxious eyes. This was so unexpected. He had longed to get the wedding behind them so that they could begin their new life. He felt that this was how they could find each other. Their engagement had been a dream—at times an uneasy dream but nevertheless a sweet one. When he now reflected on their situation and asked himself if they had actually arrived at any deeper understanding of each other during the months of their engagement, he realized that he could not in truth say they had. And she had proved herself right in being inconstant—as the weather in April, she had said. And wasn't this new notion of hers—now, a few weeks before their wedding—a reflection of her inconstancy? Would this come to an end once they were married? Did a wedding change a woman? He didn't think so. But he couldn't give her up. She was his just the way she was. That was how he loved her . . .

Then he stopped in front of her. She sat still as a frightened child, not quite sure whether to expect punishment or forgiveness. "I'm afraid that I cannot deny you anything," he said. "And you don't actually have to ask my permission. You are your own master." In a second she had her arms around his neck.

"Mercy me, how wonderful you are!" she exclaimed. And then her sobs mingled with her laughter as she kissed him again and again in euphoric delight.

That same evening, two men sat over their whisky highballs in Big Christ's saloon in St. Paul. One was of medium height, broad shouldered and fat, and about forty. He was well dressed, and comported himself as one who had graduated from Broadway as well as Klondike and consequently had little more to learn about life. The other was also of medium height but thin and dressed in a long black coat.

"Cheers, Tomlinson!" the latter said as he lifted his glass with a smile. They touched glasses. Then the fat one said: "So the Tomlinson affair almost landed us in Stillwater?"

"*Gudnes,* yes!" the other answered.

"Well, you certainly won't get me to play Tomlinson again when you can't take better care of your *bisnes,*" the first continued.

"Well, anyhow, at least I got a fire going in the engagement between Jonas's daughter and her pastor," said the man in the long black coat. "By the way, I'm temporarily short of cash. Would you happen to have a spare ten-dollar bill in your pocket?" asked Ludwig Napoleon Stomhoff.

28.

One week later Signe Marie was in Chicago. It had been easy once she had Jorshaug's permission. Jonas had come to the conclusion that his daughter was right when she said that she had to see more of the world. He had of course provided for her upbringing and education with the best Jonasville had to offer, and he couldn't forget the professor from Minneapolis who had said that she was well-informed and intelligent. A pastor's wife held a very demanding position in life and some knowledge of the world would be a necessary addition to her education. It had been more difficult for Ragna to see eye to eye with her daughter. She couldn't rid herself of the thought that this step would have greater consequences than either Jonas or Jorshaug could realize. But since she saw no alternative, she finally gave in. Now she tried to comfort herself with the thought that Signe Marie, who was so musically talented, would make much of this opportunity to learn more.

Her departure caused quite a stir in Jonasville. But the town soon had something else to think about. Jonas and his inner circle had decided to move the county archives and all office furnishings and equipment from Normanville to Jonasville as soon as possible after the required

waiting period of sixty days. In the meantime they made preparations for the transition and for a celebration to which the entire county would be invited. All this was done by a committee chaired, of course, by Jonas. After a twenty-year struggle he could now look forward to the event that would cap his life's achievements. He had long impressed those who knew him with his practical abilities, intelligence, and resourcefulness but they had never seen him so engaged as with these preparations. The congressional campaign kept Floen, Jonas's right-hand man, very busy, and this too made Jonas's role all the more important.

The first of November was the date for the transfer of the county seat. Jonas was in his office at the bank on the morning of October 28. He had just been smiling to himself at the thought of Ward's empty threat when a clearly agitated Nyblom rushed in crying out in Swedish that those devils had come up with something. On the twenty-ninth, Judge Bracken would issue a court order against the transfer. County commissioners or other officers wouldn't be allowed to hand over as much as a sheet of paper or in any way assist in the removal of county property. Jonas sat paralyzed, staring at him.

The injunction would be issued at the request of Torfin Glombekken and Kristen Andersen in O'Brien Township, Nyblom continued. They had signed a statement that they hadn't been able to vote because the town clerk had failed to post the required notice within the date set by law. It should have been posted by August 22, ten days before the referendum, but Torfin and Kristen hadn't seen any such notice on any public billboard in the town at two in the afternoon on that day. And the two rascals claimed that because they had been busy on their farms, they were not aware of any referendum on September 1. The plans for an injunction had been laid in the greatest secrecy, but Nyblom had a paid agent in the enemy camp—Swanson, the bartender in McLaughlin's saloon in Normanville. Yesterday he had sent Flasmo to Normanville, where Swanson had informed him about the plot.

The town clerk in O'Brien Township, Norman Villers, was Kristen Andersen's son-in-law, and since Nyblom knew for a fact that notice of the referendum had been posted by two thirty that afternoon, it seemed quite obvious that the slight delay had been deliberate and that it had been done in collusion with Ward, to provide him with a pretext to have the referendum annulled should it prove to go against him. They weren't quite sure just what Ward wanted to achieve but they assumed that his intention was to try to delay the transfer of the county seat for another five years—the time required before a new referendum could be held.

Jonas was furious. But invectives wouldn't get them anywhere. They had to do something and do it fast. Jonas was the first to realize that the injunction must be served to all the county commissioners in order to be legally valid. With the exception of Rutherberger and Hansen, the latter a resident of O'Brien Township, they were all in Ward's camp. There were a few commissioners who belonged to the Liberal Populist Party but they lived in the southern part of the county and favored Normanville. Floen was out of town, so they consulted another lawyer, Lawrence, and decided to make it impossible to serve the injunction to Rutherberger and Hansen. This could only be done by removing them from Judge Bracken's jurisdiction and to some place where they wouldn't be found by the sheriff. But it would probably be difficult to get in touch with Rutherberger and Hansen, who for several days had been meeting with the other commissioners in Normanville, preparing for the transfer. Anything said on the telephone was soon known to all. Telegrams were easily confiscated. They had to make use of a messenger, who could get close to the two commissioners without raising suspicion.

Then Nyblom conceived a plan that was both daring and shrewd.

"I have the man," he said. It was so unexpected that Jonas was skeptical and asked who this might be.

"Torfin Glombekken, by gosh!"

"Torfin Glombekken? But he has contested the validity of the referendum. He has clearly sold his soul to Normanville."

"Of course, but that doesn't matter in the least." Nyblom was sure that Torfin could be bought for two or three hundred dollars. The only problem was that someone else could get hold of him and buy him back before he had completed his task. Jonas insisted that Flasmo go with him to make sure that he did what he was paid for. Then he wrote a letter to Commissioner Hansen. All that was required of Glombekken was to deliver the letter, keep his mouth shut, and get back to *Groven* as quickly as possible.

No one knows just how Nyblom persuaded Glombekken to take on the job, nor how much he paid him, but one hour later Glombekken was on the road to Normanville, driving his Ford at the speed of thirty-five miles an hour, with Flasmo beside him.

No sooner had Nyblom left then Jonas called a meeting of the committee and explained the situation. Before the meeting he had seen

Johan Utgard, who proposed that the committee reorganize itself as "The Johnsville Council of Public Welfare," with three members forming a direct action committee. What action? someone asked. It was impossible to say more about it, Utgard explained, but they would all have to take responsibility for whatever was found necessary. This was not a time for talk. If anyone was against direct action they should speak up now, so that they could be set under guard. This was *bisnes*. Jonas smiled. Johan was fearless and therefore strong in a critical situation. Jonas, Utgard, and Jacobsen were made members of the direct action committee, with the authority to do whatever the situation demanded. Their first official act was to have arrested a man who called himself Brindling, supposedly an insurance salesman from Minneapolis. Brindling had been in town for about a week and talked with everyone about insurance, but without selling any, to anyone's knowledge. The captain of the Hotel Scandinavie was the first to become suspicious, and when Brindling had his suitcase searched, they found letters that showed him to be a private investigator hired by Ward. The order for Brindling's arrest charged him with being "a vagrant and a public nuisance." That evening a telegram was sent to Ward: "Everything quiet. Nothing doing. Brindling."

In the meantime Glombekken and Flasmo had arrived in Normanville. At suppertime in the hotel, Torfin found an occasion to deliver his letter and Iver made sure that everything was properly done. Glombekken, however, showed no inclination to get in touch with his former friends and partners and seemed relieved to be on his way home again.

It turned out that neither Rutherberger nor Hansen had any knowledge of the injunction to be served the next day. The county commission had been there for several days planning the transfer and no one had indicated that there would be any obstacles. After having talked it over, the two spent the evening at McLaughlin's saloon with the other commissioners and the town marshal, Jim Flaherty. The others began to leave around eleven, so Flaherty was there alone with Rutherberger and Hansen. Hansen had been a big spender that night but had barely tasted anything himself. As the other commissioners walked unsteadily back to the hotel, they joked about what Hansen would say when the sheriff served him the injunction in the morning. They laughed at the skinflint who celebrated the victory of Jonasville by buying drinks for them. When Hansen and Rutherberger returned to the hotel at midnight, Flaherty staggered after them. He had been given orders to keep an eye on them until they were safely in bed. They said good night as they walked up the stairs to their rooms, but by then he had already fallen asleep in a chair in the lobby, as was his wont when he had night duty.

At seven the next morning Duffy came to the hotel to serve the injunction to the county commissioners. The three who belonged to the regular party were already at breakfast and told the sheriff that Hansen and Rutherberger had looked quite deeply into the bottle last night and had overslept.[42] So the sheriff sat down to wait. Half an hour passed and then another half hour. He began to get suspicious and had a talk with the clerk who stood yawning behind the counter. The clerk agreed to go and wake them up. It was eight o'clock and they had to be at the courthouse by nine. He walked slowly and with some difficulty up the stairs. A few minutes later he had more speed coming down. He couldn't understand it, but Hansen and Rutherberger weren't in their rooms. They hadn't even slept in their beds.

Duffy had no difficulty in understanding what had happened. They had obviously been informed and had disappeared during the night. What should now be done? Ward was still very ill and the doctor had forbidden him to accept any visitors except Newell. Miles Standish was at the Metropolitan National Bank in Chicago, learning about banking before he took over his father's business. So the old man was alone in his big house with a manservant and his housekeeper. Duffy went to Newell, and as he talked with him they got another telegram from Brindling in Jonasville: "They are here. Send sheriff immediately."

There was just enough time to get on the northbound morning train. An hour or so later the sheriff and his deputy were in Jonas's office. Newell had wanted to send a few more men but Duffy had answered that he wasn't afraid of those d—— Norwegians. He wanted to see Hansen and Rutherberger immediately, he said to Jonas. He spoke as one with authority.

"What's happened to Hansen and Rutherberger?" Jonas asked. "Have they done anything wrong?" Duffy laughed scornfully. It wouldn't do him any good to pretend ignorance, he said. Let's have them now, or else . . . Well, said Jonas, he knew nothing of their whereabouts but he would telephone the police and a few other places. If they were in town they would be sure to find them. Then he dialed a number. "All right! This is Olsen in the bank." He used Norwegian: "Send six men here immediately. Duffy, Hansen, Rutherberger." And then in

English: "You say you haven't seen them! I'm sorry. Good-bye." Then another number and again some talk in a language the two men of the law couldn't understand. No, no one had seen anything of Hansen or Rutherberger, he said to the sheriff. What did he want with them, by the way? Duffy admitted to having an injunction for them. But he wouldn't say more about it. It would be made public in due time.

They were still discussing the matter when six men led by Jacobsen and Utgard came in and surrounded the sheriff and his deputy. They were taken by surprise but Duffy tried to retain his authority. It wouldn't be the first time he had bluffed a handful of Norwegians. What did they think they were doing, he demanded. Didn't they have respect for the law?

"Certainly," said Jonas, smiling as he got on his feet. "The law is exactly what we have respect for. And because we hope that the law will continue to be respected in Garfield County, these men will accompany you and your deputy on a little excursion while the loyal citizens of the county make sure that law and justice are respected. And, please, don't cause us any trouble. You may both be hurt."

Utgard took Duffy firmly by the arm and Jacobsen held on to the deputy and they were both led out of the building. The others followed them. Two cars were waiting outside.

"I can't stop you," said Duffy, as Utgard shoved him into one of the cars, "but you are all witness to my protest."

"Sure, sure," said Jonas. Then he gave him a friendly pat on the shoulder and stuck a letter in his hand. The sheriff looked surprised at him and put it in his pocket. Jonas winked. Three of the men entered the car while the three others went with the deputy in the other. After a moment all Jonas could see of the cars was a great cloud of dust along the road to the west.

29.

Ragna had never felt so lonely and abandoned as during this period of unrest. She hardly saw Jonas. She didn't know the details of what was going on; he was grim and silent the few moments she saw him. And she didn't ask. She had tired of raising objections to so much of what he did. With a heavy heart she had noticed how tired and worn-out he had become. Their competition for power and wealth had been too much for Ward, and now she feared that Jonas too would collapse. Her only consolation was that he wasn't alone in this struggle but had the support of the entire town.

Ragna was also worried about Signe Marie. She missed her. The large house seemed empty and deserted. Her happy laughter no longer sounded from one end of their home to the other. She no longer heard her light and quick footsteps as she danced from room to room. Her place at the table was vacant and there was no one there to interrupt the silence of the few minutes she and Jonas sat together for their meals. Their few words were somber and there was no one there to make fun of them or to insist on another point of view.

Sometimes she sat in her daughter's room and contemplated one or another of her daughter's possessions. She would even fondle some of them. One piece that had attracted her attention was a small case with a string of pearls that she had given to Signe Marie as a birthday present many years ago, when she was still a little girl. They couldn't afford much at that time so it was an inexpensive trinket. But in her hand it brought back memories of long-gone times, and it was as if she wished herself back to the days when they lived in hope of a bright future, before their present affluence, the embodiment of their hopes and dreams.

Today—October 31—when she entered her daughter's room she was again overwhelmed by the same feelings. Again she began to touch the objects Signe Marie had left standing on her bureau. Then she happened to open one of the drawers and noticed a small box that she couldn't remember having seen before. She may have been spurred by curiosity or apprehension when she took the box and opened it. She made a little cry as she quickly closed it and put it back in place before sitting down on a chair. It was her daughter's engagement ring. So she wasn't wearing it in Chicago! Ragna was sure it had been left behind deliberately. As Ragna sat thinking, her eyes filled with tears. But she got up quickly and wiped them away as she told herself that she was becoming a sentimental fool.

She went down to the large and empty rooms downstairs. The mailman had delivered letters. One was from Signe Marie. Her hands trembled and her heart beat at a quicker rate as she opened it. The early letters from Chicago had been filled with impressions of a wonderful, new world. She had been everywhere with Sigrid. It was difficult to understand how they had time for it all. They had been to the top of the highest buildings and seen the tiny people move around in the streets far below, as ants around an anthill. They had been up 3,000 feet in an airship. They had been out at Fort Sheridan and had seen the soldiers drilling—generals and colonels in fine uniforms with golden braid and nice young men in khaki uniforms. They had seen the animals in Lincoln Park and had observed beer-drinking people in the German beer gardens. One Sunday they had gone by steamboat to Milwaukee. And could they guess who they had met on the boat? Miles Standish Ward. It had been like meeting an old friend from Jonasville. She was certain that he was very different from his father—so courteous and so helpful . . . She had written about their meeting three weeks ago.

The new letter told of further adventures. She and Sigrid had been to the theater and had seen Edward Sothern and Julia Marlowe in *Romeo and Juliet*.[43] They had been wonderful. Sigrid had been accompanied by a student at Northwestern and Signe Marie had gone with—well, yes, Miles Standish. He was great and they had had a great evening. And, she added, they had been invited to visit a niece of Roxberg in Normanville. They lived in Evanston. She was married to an American, Mr. Walker. They had had a wonderful time and played bridge. Miles Standish had also been there and Mr. Walker had been great. And—not to forget—Professor Lars Jorshaug had also been there and he too had been great—and so interesting. In Chicago, people said he was famous.

Ragna sat down to write in reply. Her main point was that Signe Marie for God's sake mustn't forget that she was engaged and that this status gave her certain duties and responsibilities.

—————

Meanwhile in Normanville, a sick man sat in his bed and pondered a letter. His doctor had just given him the good news that he was improving. Nevertheless, Ward was still so weak that they had to be very careful. He was told only a fraction of what happened. The court order had been his idea, but the doctor had strictly forbidden them to let him know that they hadn't been able to serve it and that the sheriff and his deputy had disappeared without a trace.

The mysterious disappearance of Duffy had caused much confusion in Normanville. At first even the bosses didn't know what to do. Eventually, Newell sent a telegram to the governor that the sheriff had been kidnapped and that there was mob rule in Garfield County. It was absolutely necessary, he explained, that the governor send the National Guard to restore law and order. But the governor hadn't been particularly upset by the telegram. He was well-informed about the long battle between the two towns for the county seat. The entire Midwest knew about it and about the men behind it. Moreover, the recent referendum had decided the matter in favor of Jonasville by a significant margin. So the governor answered that a deputy would come on the afternoon train to evaluate the situation.

But Ward was ignorant of all this. The doctor had said that he couldn't see any business correspondence, only family letters. But it turned out that even such correspondence could set Elihu's mind on fire. When Newell came to visit and to ensure him that all was well, he found him in a rage and with a letter in his hand.

"It's that idiot Miles Standish again!" he exclaimed. He gave the letter to Newell whose surprise was evident as he read it. Without a word he returned it to Ward, who crushed it in his yellow and withered hand and threw it on the floor with a grimace of contempt. Then he asked for pencil and paper and wrote a telegram with his unsteady hand, ordering Newell to have it sent immediately.

Later that afternoon when the governor's deputy was informed about what had been going on, he smiled and shook his head. It was obviously against the law to abduct the sheriff, he said. But it wouldn't do to attack an entire town. You simply couldn't arrest a thousand men. He also suggested that the legal basis for the injunction could be questioned. If the other party should succeed in having the injunction annulled—and he believed they would—the two plaintiffs could be found guilty of perjury. He also assumed that those who had aided and abetted them would find themselves in a problematic situation. The main point, however, was that they didn't, in his judgment, have a case for dismissing the referendum. But he would present a full report to the governor and should it happen that the sheriff didn't turn up, then he was quite sure that the necessary forces would be sent in to set him free. The governor's agent was both polite and diplomatic, but Newell, Bracken, and the county attorney all felt that the battle had been lost.

In the evening, Newell received yet a telegram from Jonasville: "Nothing doing. Everything quiet. Brindling." Consequently, all he did was to add four more men to the night watch. Then he and the rest of Normanville went to bed.

———•+•———

At ten that evening, Jonasville was a town of women and children. With the exception of a security committee of twelve, the entire male population had disappeared. Horses, lumber wagons, *buggyer*, trucks, and

other cars—anything and everything that could be used for transportation—had disappeared along with the men. People from the sur-
rounding farms joined the great caravan a little south of the town, and
at the agreed time it began to move.

A vanguard led by Jonas and Johan Utgard entered Normanville
exactly at midnight. The members of the night watch were taken outside
the city hall, tied up, and placed in the county jail, against the tears and
protests of the sheriff's wife. Eight men were sent to guard the jail and
the sheriff's home. Meanwhile, the main occupation force were stream-
ing into the town and heading for the courthouse as quietly as possible.
The doors were opened and—as directed by Nyblom, Hansen, and
Rutherberger—they took all furniture and equipment out to the waiting wagons and trucks. They broke a hole in the masonry of the vault
where the county archives were kept. In less than two hours everything
in the courthouse that could be removed was on its way to Jonasville.

Then they started on the house itself. The old ramshackle building
was loaded on heavy duty wagons, of which they had a plentiful supply.
It wasn't large for a courthouse but it was still quite a job to make it ready
for transportation. It was done by five thirty, and the nocturnal train
began to move out of town on the road to Jonasville.

McLaughlin, the saloonkeeper, woke up just before they started, and
from his window he could see the lights around the courthouse farther
down the street. He tried to phone Newell but was unable to get any
response from the telephone exchange. He realized that the line must
have been cut and he ran as fast as he could on his old gout-ridden legs
to warn the lawyer. Newell's first thought was the telegraph office—the
governor—the National Guard. But the telegraph operator was nowhere to be found. He was already bound and trussed in a ditch near
Roxberg's elevator. Messengers were sent to round up as many men as
they could, and fifteen minutes later a hundred men were on their way
to the courthouse square. They arrived just as the courthouse was beginning its journey to Jonasville. Jonas and Utgard stood waiting for
Newell and his followers, with several hundred of their men ready to
come to their assistance. Jonas was sure of his victory and he held out
his hand to Newell.

"We are sort of moving," he said. "I'm sorry we couldn't show Ward
the respect of doing it in daylight. Please give him my greetings. He is,
by gosh, the only grown-up man you have in this hick town."

Newell didn't answer him. He and the others merely stood there
looking at the remains of the greatness of Normanville. After a while he

said, "The battle is over boys. We have lost! Let's go home and go to bed."
And then he led his silent flock back into town.

In the main street Newell was taken aback by an unexpected spectacle: a man coming toward them with a wheelchair. In the chair was an emaciated figure. As they came closer, his assumption was confirmed: it was Elihu Ward. He had been more restless than usual all night, he said when Newell stopped and greeted him. So he had gotten out of bed and had seen the bright light down by the courthouse. He couldn't get anyone on the telephone and so he had ordered his servant to dress him and take him out in the wheelchair.

"You are up early for a sick man," said Newell, "but you are nevertheless too late. We have had a moving day in Garfield County." And then he gave him Jonas's message. "He felt sorry for you and said you were the only grown-up man in this hick town."

"Is that what he said?" Ward exclaimed.

"Yes, those were his very words." Elihu laughed.

"That, by gosh, is a greeting I can appreciate," he said, "both because what he said is true and because the man who said it is the only worthy adversary I have met since I came to Garfield County." And then he seemed to be lost in thought. Then he turned to Newell: "Do you remember the telegram we sent yesterday."

"Of course."

"I was wrong. Would you please send another as soon as possible?"

"With pleasure."

"Tell him I have changed my mind. His decision is all right."

<hr />

A week later Jonas is reading about the sensational moving of the courthouse in *Decorah-Posten*.[44] Ragna is at her knitting. Then she gets up and serves their afternoon coffee.

"It was crazy as it was and even worse the way they have written it up," he says as he tastes the coffee. But he laughs and enjoys it. She hasn't seen him in such a good mood in a long time. It is just as if he were young again. And then she too laughs, even though there hasn't been all that much to laugh about recently. As he drinks his coffee he continues to read in *Decorah-Posten*. Then he exclaims:

"I'll be darned! They write that I attacked Duffy and kicked him on his leg! It's awful how these newspapers make it up!" But he continues to laugh and seems to find the account great entertainment.

"But you haven't told me what you actually did with Duffy," Ragna says. "How did it come about that he was the only Ward candidate to be reelected."

A self-satisfied smile spreads over his face as he answers: "Well, you see, we had thought out the whole Duffy business in advance. We sent a telegram signed by Brindling to Normanville early on the twenty-ninth that Hansen and Rutherberger were here and . . ."

"But Brindling was in the jail?"

"Exactly! That's why we could do it. And it was funny how Newell and Duffy swallowed the bait."

"Now, that is another thing I can't really understand."

"*Velsør*, this can happen now and then—even to those who are pretty smart. They may figure it all to the smallest detail. It will *vork'out* so and so. But then fate sort of interferes and throws them off. It may be an idiotic little thing of no consequence. The point is that it is something that they haven't really *æpprehenda*. So they'll stand there with their calculations and sort of try to make it *korresponde* with this new element. And it is the last minute and they'll have to *hørry'op* and then you can *bette* ten-to-one that they'll fall into the trap. It is a sort of *dest'ny* that there is a *klogg* in the machinery. I've done it myself so I know how it can go. You may for instance want something so strongly that when you see the slightest *chans'* to *æchive* it you'll go right ahead and *luser fa'kultien* to *ris'ne*.[45] But we realized that we couldn't *rønne* too great a *resk* with Duffy. Lyman had telegraphed us that Normanville had asked for the National Guard. But *de'point* was that the sheriff could have created a major brouhaha afterward. He knew that he would be *defita i 'leksjen*.[46] We *seisa op situationen og ægria* that Duffy was liable to take *revench*.[47] He is both capable and ruthless and would be able to *mæka det hot* for us with what is left of Ward's party. It was Utgard who *figra* it out . . ."

"I wouldn't have thought that Utgard, who is such a man of principle, would have got himself mixed up in this political *figureringen*."

"Do you think that he sort of would have been too *'onest*? *Velsør*, Johan is no fool. As I said, we *deseida* that it would be better to have Duffy as our friend than as our enemy when he *disæpira* with this *injunktsjen* in his pocket. That's why I had Bollemo hit off a few words on his typewriter and I placed the piece of paper in Duffy's fist before they hauled him out of town. The same day we had a telegram from Siversen, who was sort of set to keep an eye on him, that it was *okei*. Duffy had *konsenta* to my proposal."

"And your proposal was . . ."

"Just that if he would be *resonabel* and *kipa* himself away until the courthouse had been *mova,* we would *ta'kær* of him. We didn't have many days before the election but Nyblom and Jacobsen *æt'vonst* began to *trœv'le* around to tell our people to vote for Duffy."

"But Jonas . . ." says Ragna. She is evidently not entirely convinced.

"Oh, *never'jumein'*!" he interrupts her. "Politics in Garfield County is no Sunday school. This hasn't been a war with *pop'guns.*" Then he sits down again with his newspaper. After a while: "Look here! They've even got the story of Floen's and Seff Thompson's *'leksjen.* The people down in Decorah are pretty good at picking up the news, aren't they."

Then he sits a while with his nose in the newspaper. Finally he puts it down and takes a look at the recent issue of *Kirketidende.* "It's strange," he says, "how the United Church is constantly taking over the views of the Synod."

Ragna agrees. "I read recently in *Lutheraneren,*" she says, "that they are having a new meeting in Crookston and that people from all the Lutheran synods have been invited."

Jonas thinks about it and says, "I think we should both go to that meeting in Crookston." Ragna smiles.

"You are getting to be quite conciliatory in your old age," she says as she gets up and gives him a kiss before pouring him another cup of coffee.

As Jonas is about to go back into town again, a telegram arrives for Ragna. It is from Chicago. She opens it with nervous fingers.

"Mercy!" she exclaims after reading it. Then she reads it to Jonas:

> Miles Standish and I were married this morning. Will be home
> in Normanville after six weeks' travel in the East and the South.
> Have Ward's blessings. Look for letter. Signe Marie

"Goodness! This is quite something!" Jonas says. Ragna has sunk into a chair.

"I have feared that this would happen," she says. She is quite dejected.

"Well, there isn't much we can do about it," says Jonas. He thinks about it and tries to make himself used to the new situation. "And as far as I've heard the boy is quite a decent young man."

"But she has been unfaithful to Jorshaug."

"Well, yes, it may not have been strictly according to the rules," he admits. "But he can surely find himself another wife."

"I don't think that is the point at all. And I don't understand what she means by Ward's blessings either."

"*Velsøri*," Jonas replies thoughtfully. "These Wards are pretty smart. They know a good thing when they see it. And this will add up to about half a million altogether."

But over in the parsonage a sad man sits reading a letter for the third time . . .

THE END

Notes

Translator's Introduction

1. See Orm Øverland, *The Western Home: A Literary History of Norwegian America* (Northfield, Minnesota, and Champaign, Illinois, 1996).

2. These figures are from Odd S. Lovoll, *The Promise of America: A History of the Norwegian-American People* (Minneapolis, Minnesota, 1984).

3. An English translation of the published version of this talk, "Our Cultural Stage," is in Odd S. Lovoll, ed., *Cultural Pluralism versus Assimilation: The Views of Waldemar Ager* (Northfield, Minnesota, 1977), 38–45. Wist's analysis of the essential difference between the identities of the first- and second-generation immigrants is an early expression of the views in Vladimir C. Nahirny and Joshua A. Fishman's 1965 article "American Immigrant Groups: Ethnic Identification and the Problem of Generations," reprinted in Werner Sollors, *Theories of Ethnicity: A Classical Reader* (New York, 1996), 266–81.

4. Biographical sources on Wist are Øverland, *The Western Home*; Wist, ed., *Norsk-Amerikanernes Festskrift 1914* (Decorah, Iowa, 1914); and Jan-Erik Imbsen, "Johannes B. Wist: Norwegian-American Leader" (unpublished MA thesis, University of Oslo, 1977).

5. Oivind M. Hovde and Martha E. Henzler, compilers, *Norwegian-American Newspapers in Luther College Library* (Decorah, Iowa, 1975); Wist, *Norsk-Amerikanernes Festskrift*.

6. Odd S. Lovoll, "*Decorah-Posten*: The Story of an Immigrant Newspaper," *Norwegian-American Studies* 27 (1977): 96.

7. Odd S. Lovoll, "*Decorah-Posten*," 77. If no other source is specifically mentioned, information below on *Decorah-Posten* is from this article.

8. As was common in nineteenth-century newspapers, the installments of serialized books were often printed in book-page-sized columns and arranged so that they could easily be cut out and saved for later book binding. Newspapers would also save the plates for some of their serialized books for later book publication, either for distribution as a bonus to their subscribers or for regular sale.

9. Letter to Ditlef G. Ristad, December 7, 1921. Wist has received a poem

from Ristad that he likes very much but he wonders whether a point in the poem "is made so clearly that the *general* reader will get your meaning—whether it, in other words, may not be a little too *intellectual—highbrow.*" (Archives of the Norwegian-American Historical Association, St. Olaf College. My translation. Wist underlined the words in italics.)

10. "Paa Prairien," *Decorah-Posten,* November 16, 1897.

11. "Blade av en nybyggersaga" (Pages of a pioneer saga), *Symra* 8 (1912): 19–49, and "Da Bjørnson kom til La Crosse" (When Bjornson came to La Crosse), *Symra* 9 (1913): 55–68. References below are to the respective volumes of the journal. Titles and quotations are my translations.

12. Johannes B. Wist, review of Ludvig Lima, ed., *Norsk-amerikanske digte i udvalg* (1903) in *Decorah-Posten,* January 5, 1904.

13. Words such as "deadbeat," "hypocrit" (hypocrite), "charget," "patronisere" (charged and patronize), and "satisfaktion," and a reference to a freethinker a character speaks of as "Vingerisol" (Robert Ingersoll), would have made little sense to readers in Norway.

14. See Eva Lund Haugen and Einar Haugen, eds., *Land of the Free: Bjørnstjerne Bjørnson's America Letters, 1880–1881* (Northfield, Minnesota, 1978).

15. One year earlier, on October 28, 1919, a few days before the first installment of what became his trilogy, Arnljot had a "Mellemmad" column in which he discussed the isolation of Norwegian Americans from the political and social life of the country as a function of Anglo-American rejection of immigrants as foreigners. This may be the first instance of a nonsatirical and nonhumorous style in his column.

16. One such editorial, with the title "Amerikaniseringen" (Americanization) is from April 9, 1920.

17. In this column, dated October 21, his character Bonifacius reports on an altercation between a Norwegian and an Irish American. After the latter has suggested that the former may not have understood him, the Norwegian American exclaims, "Vil du insølt mæ in my egen Hous'? Føst seie du, æ' e' kræsi, aa saa klæme du, at æ' ijtnaa understænd. Trur du mæbe, at æ' ijt kain Languagen?" (First you say I am crazy and then you claim that I don't understand. Do you maybe think that I don't know the language?) The English words such as "kræsi," "klæme," and "mæbe" may not be obvious to a non-Norwegian reader, since they are spelled to approximate Norwegian-American pronunciation.

18. Fredrik Voss Mohn Papers, Norwegian-American Historical Association, St. Olaf College. It may be assumed that although Wist wrote in Norwegian, Wist was well-informed about the Anglophone literary culture and intellectual life of his country, and that he was fully aware that he was echoing the view of Norris on naturalism as a form of romanticism.

19. Peer O. Strømme was a popular novelist, poet, and journalist—one of the few American-born writers who preferred to use the Norwegian language. Emil Lauritz Mengshoel, a socialist editor and journalist, had published his second novel, *Mené Tekel,* in 1919 and had seen it reviewed in Wist's *Decorah-Posten* on January 16, 1920. Carl Hansen became editor of *Minneapolis Tidende,*

and L. H. Lund was a journalist who published a volume of humorous sketches, *Vesterlandiana,* in 1916. See Øverland, *The Western Home.*

20. Italicized words are as in the original. Prestgard uses Wettergren's nickname, "Blaasaren," which in the translated text of the novel is given as "Butch." The "great" writer is Lars A. Stenholt, a popular writer who was despised by those who were concerned that he lowered the cultural status of their group.

21. Prolific Norwegian-American writers such as Ole A. Buslett, Dorthea Dahl, and Simon Johnsen came to the United States as children with their parents and had no formal education in Norwegian, the language in which they wrote. Writers such as Knut M. O. Teigen and Peer O. Strømme were born in Wisconsin, but in a settlement where Norwegian was the dominant language. Dahl, Teigen, and Strømme probably wrote more naturally in English than they did in Norwegian. Unavoidably, Anglicisms as well as errors in grammar and idiom would occasionally sneak into their otherwise quite flexible Norwegian writing. All writers, Wist included, would of course pepper their language with deliberate code-switching. Their books were, after all, American. Occasionally a book allegedly in Norwegian, but with such poor style and grammar that it made for painful reading, would enter into print.

22. The initiative for such archival preservation was taken in 1925, with the creation of the Norwegian-American Historical Association and its archives at St. Olaf College in Northfield, Minnesota.

23. The best work by Wist's fellow writers, Ole E. Rølvaag and Waldemar Ager, was published in English translation in the late 1920s and early 1930s, some years after Wist's death.

24. Drude Krog Janson, *A Saloonkeeper's Daughter,* translated by Gerald Thorson, edited with an Introduction by Orm Øverland (Baltimore, 2002).

25. In the Scandinavian countries the established Lutheran churches were (and still are) government institutions.

26. Historian Jon Gjerde has noted that immigrants typically had a "complementary identity" and observed that "faithfulness to an ethnic subgroup within a 'complementary identity' theoretically fostered a magnified loyalty to the United States" (*The Minds of the West: Ethnocultural Evolution in the Rural Middle West, 1830–1917* [Chapel Hill, North Carolina, 1997], 8, 60).

A Note on the Text and Translation

1. The chapter is a satire on the pretensions of the cultural life of the immigrant society. Jonas, because of his new standing as a clerk in a grocery store, has been invited to take part in a meeting to discuss the founding of a literary society. Among the participants are Lanberg and Lomwiig, and a Swedish intellectual and socialist named Mr. Newmanover. The meeting gradually disintegrates, and Jonas leaves when it turns into a night of poker and whiskey.

2. Some of these words and their English equivalents are: *ævnju* = avenue; *bordinghuset* = the boardinghouse; *campagnen* = the campaign; *caucussen, caucuserne* = the caucus, the caucuses; *county, countyet* = county, the county; *countysiten, countysædet* = the county seat; *courthuset, korthuset* = the courthouse;

delegat, delegater = delegate, delegates; *legislatur, legislaturen, legislaturses-sionen* = legislature, the legislature, the session of the legislature; *marshallen* = the marshal; *mortgagen* = the mortgage; *nominationen* = the nomination; *noten* = the note; *prærie, prærien* = prairie, the prairie; *saloon, salooner, saloonkeeper* = saloon, saloons, saloonkeeper; *settlement, settlementet, settler, settlerne* = settlement, the settlement, settler, the settlers; *Yankie, Yankien* = Yankee, the Yankee.

3. I remember my mother using the phrase *nosørri*. She had probably picked it up from her parents and older siblings, who were returned immigrants.

4. For instance, Glombekken is given a dialect from western Norway while his wife speaks a dialect that suggests an eastern Norway origin, and Iver Flasmo speaks in a dialect from Trøndelag, the same region from which the author hailed.

5. Solveig Zempel's unpublished University of Minnesota dissertation is a scholarly study of Wist's language.

I. Scenes from the Life of a Newcomer

1. The Red River Valley—the land on both sides of the Red River that separates North Dakota and Minnesota. Norwegian immigrants were the dominant ethnic group.

2. Dekora, Jova—Decorah, Iowa, the town where the author, Johannes B. Wist, lived and edited the newspaper *Decorah-Posten*, in which Wist's trilogy was serialized before its publication as a book. Decorah was the administrative center for one of the three main Lutheran synods among the Norwegian Americans, the Norwegian Synod.

3. The conflict between Norwegians and Swedes—Between 1814 and 1905 Norway was in a union with Sweden: the king of Sweden was also king of Norway. Foreign policy and defense were controlled by Sweden. The increasing political pressure for the greater influence of the *Storting*, or parliament, in the second half of the nineteenth century led to a political struggle between liberals (*Venstre*, or "the left") and conservatives (*Høire*, or "the right") but was also perceived as a nationalist conflict with Sweden. In 1884, members of a conservative government, supportive of the king, were impeached, and a liberal government took office.

4. Swedish immigration agent—The two languages, Swedish and Norwegian, are very close, and a Swede and a Norwegian would have had little difficulty understanding each other. The dialogue of Swedish characters is usually in Swedish in the original.

5. the courthouse—was built 1856–1857 on the corner of Fourth Street and Eighth Avenue South and was in use until 1895, when the courthouse section of a new courthouse and city hall was opened on the block defined by Fourth and Fifth Streets and Third and Fourth Avenues.

6. *regjeringsbygningsforvalter*—"manager of public buildings."

7. *Well sørri, in dis' her' kontri'e er vi alle læborers, ju 'no ... No læbor is simpelt in Amerika, og all offic'holdera tek sin tørn med at kline op.*—"Well sir, in this

here country we are all laborers, you know . . . No labor is simple (i.e., lowly) in America, and all the officeholders take their turn in cleaning up."

8. *Amerika er en demokratisk kontry, ju 'no! 'Onest arbe' er det, som kounter*— "America is a democratic country, you know. Honest work is what counts."

9. *Jeg har getta saa jused te' aa speak English, at jeg forgetter mig right 'long naar jeg juser Norsk*—"I have gotten so used to speaking English that I forget myself right along when I use Norwegian."

10. *hæng af languagen* to *kætche on te' de' most komment English*—"get enough hang of the language to catch on to the most common English."

11. *streetkarsen*—The streetcars of Minneapolis were at this time drawn by mules or horses. The first electric line was opened in 1889.

12. Stockholm-Olson—This saloon was at 1209 Washington Avenue South.

13. *lawn og porch paa fronten og tow'r i roffen*—"and porch on the front and tower in the roof."

14. the higher *commonskolen* in Norway—There is, of course, no such thing as a higher common school, and this is merely one of the many instances of the pretenses and illusions that are satirized by Wist.

15. *fer te be prest in dis' her' kontry'e*—"for to be a minister in this here country."

16. Norwegian will be a dead language—Norwegian was the dominant language in Norwegian Lutheran churches in the United States till the mid 1920s. Other Protestant churches, such as the Baptists and the Methodists, also had congregations that used Norwegian.

17. a conservative—In the 1880s the Norwegian Conservative Party supported a strong monarchy and the union with Sweden.

18. Kristiania—now Oslo, the Norwegian capital.

19. This is not as in Europe—In letters home, immigrants often explained that they had to work much harder than in Norway and they also frequently commented on the lack of class distinctions in the United States.

20. Butch—He actually called the bartender "Blaasar'n," literally "the blower." In many dialects this is a nickname that suggests a person who is both brash and strong, or macho, as he may have been called in more recent times. This bartender is probably modeled on a man named Wettergren, "whose sobriquet was 'Blaasaren,'" according to Carl Hansen, "the most prominent of the Cedar avenue Norwegian saloonkeepers . . . He was a big fellow with heavy black whiskers, wide-open, slightly squinting eyes, and a booming voice. In connection with the saloon he ran the Victoria Hotel . . ." (149).

21. Captain Opheim—K. L. Opheim; his rank of captain was in the Norwegian Rifle Club. Normanna Hall—located at the intersection of Twelfth Avenue South and Third Street. It was dedicated May 17, 1889, so this is an anachronism.

22. John Dobbelju—John W. Arctander immigrated in 1870 to Chicago, where he worked as an editor, and came to Minneapolis in 1874 and began to practice as a lawyer, specializing in criminal law. He was active in the immigrant society, in particular in the temperance movement and in the Methodist and the Lutheran churches, and he was highly regarded as a public speaker.

23. Sven Oftedal—(1844–1911) immigrated in 1873 on being called as professor of theology at Augsburg Seminary, an institution of the Conference, one of the three main Lutheran Synods among Norwegian Americans. He founded the weekly Minneapolis newspaper *Folkebladet* and was editor from 1877 to 1881. (Melchior) Falk Gjertsen—(1847–1913) Norwegian-American pastor, editor, and author who immigrated in 1864. Nina Draxten, *The Testing of M. Falk Gjertsen* (1988).

24. Bazaar—In his *My Minneapolis,* Carl G. O. Hansen writes about a large bazaar held in 1884 for the benefit of the Liberal Party in Norway: "Here, for the first time, I saw men whom I later in life came to know quite well but then only looked at, all the while keeping at a respectful distance, such as the attorneys Andreas Ueland and Jno. [John] W. Arctander. One night Prof. [Rasmus B.] Anderson gave his entire lecture, 'Fedrearven'" (59). Andreas (Andrew) Ueland—Norwegian-American lawyer and judge. His autobiography *Recollections of an Immigrant* was published in New York in 1929. Ole Gabriel Ueland—(1799–1870) member of the Norwegian parliament, one of the leaders of the opposition and a spokesman for the farmer's point of view. Lars M. Rand—(1857–1913) immigrated in 1874 and was a Minneapolis politician for the Democratic Party. He began as a member of the city council and then became alderman (1890–1910) for the Cedar-Riverside area, the sixth ward. He has been characterized as "a machine politician to his fingertips" who "personified the urban boss whose flexible ethical standards appalled clean government advocates but who, nonetheless, rendered indispensable help to foreign-born constituents at a time when the American welfare state was only a vague dream." Carl H. Chrislock, *From Fjord to Freeway: 100 Years, Augsburg College* (1969). syttendemai—the Seventeenth of May is the Norwegian constitution day (1814).

25. *Major* Ames—Albert A. Ames was mayor of Minneapolis (Democrat) 1876, 1883–1884, 1887–1888. Carl G. O. Hansen writes in *My Minneapolis,* "My memory goes back to the days, or rather years, when Dr. A. A. Ames, an advocate of a 'wide-open town,' seemed invincible in the mayoralty contests" (377).

26. Scandia Bank—was organized in 1883; Anthony Kelly, president, A. C. Haugan, vice president. Haugan was also active in local politics and was city treasurer 1893–1897 (Republican). Kristian Kortgaard—active in local politics, city treasurer 1891–1893 (Democrat). Louis Ness—Minneapolis police 1883–1899; captain from 1886.

27. John Stavlo—Minneapolis police 1886–1899. John E. Kvittum—Minneapolis police 1885–1899.

28. It's the *Eirisa* who *rønner police forcen*—"It's the Irish who run the police force."

29. *Ju' ban'*—You be[en]; a conventional way of indicating a Swedish or Norwegian immigrant English. In the original, Olson's dialogue is in Swedish.

30. Kongsvinger—in southeastern Norway, not far from the Swedish border, the main town in Jonas's home district.

31. *slip*—"sleep."

32. Americans—While Americans of British heritage usually referred to

naturalized Americans from other countries as "foreigners," the latter talked of the former as "Americans."

33. folk high school—*folkehøyskole,* a Scandinavian school based on the ideas of the Danish theologian and poet N. F. S. Grundtvig (1783–1872).

34. *100 Timer i Engelsk*—(100 lessons in English) by O. M. Peterson, was first published in Chicago in 1872. Harmonia Hall—was at First Avenue North and First Street. Jørgen Jensen—immigrated in 1873 and became an editor of several Norwegian-American newspapers, among them *Budstikken* from 1887. Hardanger fiddle—a traditional Norwegian violin-like instrument.

35. Ole Pedersen Vangsnes—Norwegian-American pastor who served in Minneapolis 1878–1899. The Church of Our Savior (Vor Frelsers Kirke) was established in 1869 and had their first church on the corner of Washington and Tenth avenues in 1871. A new church was built on the corner of Seventh Street and Fourteenth Avenue South in 1882. The Norwegian Synod was the more conservative of the three main Lutheran synods among the Norwegian Americans. Conference—The Conference for the Norwegian-Danish Evangelical Lutheran Church in America. In 1890 this church body and two other church groupings formed the United Norwegian Lutheran Church.

36. John Øfstie—his general store was established by 1877. Øfstie, like the author, was from Trøndelag, an area consisting of two counties near the city of Trondheim. The flattering portrait below may have been intended as a compliment to a friend.

37. Tom Lowry's rickety cart—the streetcar. Thomas Lowry, a young lawyer from Illinois, and Colonel W. S. King (with a consortium of investors from New York) organized a streetcar company in 1875. By 1877, Lowry controlled the company. In 1889 the mules and horses were retired and electricity was introduced. See Alfred Söderström, *Minneapolis Minnen,* 207–8.

38. So this country was really theirs—This kind of argument, based on early discovery and other exploits, was common with all European immigrant groups in this period. Such stories may be called "home-making myths." See Orm Øverland, *Immigrant Minds, American Identities: Making the United States Home, 1870–1930* (2000).

39. *dæmonitioner*—the clerk is trying to say "denominations." The pun (demon-itions) may be the author's critical comment on how other churches were perceived by orthodox Lutherans.

40. Skaal—now spelled "skål" in Norwegian and "skoal" in English, literally means "bowl" and is the common Scandinavian word for a toast. It is used much the same way as "cheers" in English.

41. Soria Moria—a legendary castle in Norwegian folktales. In Norwegian usage it often has the meaning of an illusion of greatness of wealth. The implications are rather obvious when it is used as the name of a bank, later in the novel. *Kubbe*-chair *(kubbestol)*—a chair cut out of one log. Troll's tail—some trolls have tails. Wist may have been thinking of *hulder,* a female being that lives inside the mountains, as do the trolls. What he actually wrote was *rumpe-troll; rumpe* meaning tail, but the literal meaning of this word is tadpole.

42. Stillwater—the Minnesota State Penitentiary was in Stillwater.

61. Swan J. Turnblad—Publisher of *Svenska Amerikanska Posten* from 1887. His home in Minneapolis now houses the American Swedish Institute. "Kuriko"—patent medicines and contraptions like electric belts were staples of immigrant press advertising. *Feltraabet*—("The Battle Cry") Minneapolis religious weekly newspaper, appearing first as *Familievennen* in 1885 and, from 1886–1889, as *Feltraabet*, a name probably suggested by the Salvation Army magazine, *The War Cry*. Halvard Askeland—later served as president of Sons of Norway, the largest secular Norwegian-American organization.

62. *Suerkru*—"sewer crew."

63. Pontoppidan Kingo Johnson—His first two names are the names of well-known Danish seventeenth-century theologians, both bishops, the former best known for his commentary to Luther's *Catechism*, the latter for his hymns. Up to 1814, Norway was a part of the Danish monarchy. Finnmark—the most northern county in Norway. "Terje Vigen"—a long narrative poem by Henrik Ibsen.

64. Dr. K. Hoegh—Knut Hoegh was born in northern Norway in 1841 and emigrated after completing his medical degree at the University in Christiania. He first pacticed in La Crosse, Wisconsin, and in 1887 came to Minneapolis, where he played a prominent role in the cultural life of the immigrant society. He died in 1925. O. J. Breda—was appointed professor of classical and Scandinavian languages at the University of Minnesota in 1883. He retired in 1899, when he returned to Norway. Søren Listoe—a Danish-American, was editor and publisher of several newspapers in Minneapolis in the 1880s and 1890s. He was active in state politics for the Republican Party and was appointed U.S. consul in Düsseldorf (1892) and in Rotterdam (1897). He held the rank of colonel. He had literary interests, and his translations to Danish include Albion W. Tourgee's *A Fool's Errand*, serialized in *Decorah-Posten* before its publication in book form in Copenhagen. Hans Mattson—(1832–1893) Swedish-American politician (Minnesota Secretary of State 1887–1891), civil servant, newspaper publisher, and diplomat. His autobiography *Reminiscences: The Story of an Immigrant* was published in St. Paul in 1892. Hans Gerhard Stub—Norwegian-American theologian, born in Wisconsin in 1849; professor at Luther Seminary from 1878.

65. Searlie—Olaf O. Searle had a ticket agency and land office in St. Paul.

66. Pastor Skogsberg's church—*Svenska kristna missionsföreningen i Minneapolis* was established in 1874 and Pastor Erik August Skogsbergh, then in Chicago, was called to serve the congregation in 1884. A church was built in 1879 on the corner of Fourth Street and Eighth Avenue South, and a new one, Svenska Missions-Tabernaklet, which could seat 3,000, was completed on the corner of Eighth Avenue South and Seventh Street in 1887.

67. *Køttet*—"cut."

II. The Home on the Prairie

1. *Groven*—The Norwegian definite article is a suffix (-en for a masculine noun). So *Groven* consists of the English word "grove" with the Norwegian suffix indicating the definite form: the Grove.

2. Trondheim, Stjørdal—towns in Trøndelag, the author's home area in Norway.

3. Searlie in St. Paul—the agent from whom they had bought their quarter section.

4. *chinchbuggen*—the chinch bug is a small insect that has been destructive to wheat and corn in the West. Lawyers and politicians, Jim suggests, have an equally destructive effect.

5. four saloons—the names reveal that two are run by Norwegians, one by an Irishman, and one by a Swede. When not otherwise identified, the owners of businesses in this paragraph have Norwegian names.

6. a Southern Yankee—Immigrants referred to all Americans of English stock as Yankees.

7. Hamar, Gjøvik—Hamar and Gjøvik are towns north of Oslo (formerly Kristiania), on either side of the lake, Mjøsa.

8. *biter* everything I have *rønna op ægænst* even in America!—"beats everything I have run up against even in America."

9. their Canaan—their Promised Land.

10. rods—a rod is sixteen and one-half feet.

11. dinnertime—dinner was a midday meal.

12. Conference—The Conference for the Norwegian-Danish Evangelical Lutheran Church in America; at the time, one of the two larger Lutheran synods among the Norwegian Americans. The other, of which Jonas had become a member in Minneapolis, was the Norwegian Evangelical Lutheran Church of America, called the Norwegian Synod or simply the Synod.

13. Småland—a region in southern Sweden. *Gudnaa's*—God knows.

14. Calvinism—this exchange between Jonas and Pastor Vellesen refers to the major theological conflict among Norwegian Lutherans in the United States in the 1880s, the so-called election controversy, in which the issue was salvation by the individual's faith versus salvation by God's grace, freely given and freely withheld. The latter position involved belief in predestination, and opponents claimed it was inseparable from Calvinist doctrine. The Synod leadership, inspired by the German-American Missouri Synod and its prominent theologian C. F. W. Walther, held to the latter position and the conflict led to a split in the Synod. Those who broke out were called the anti-Missourians. When Vellesen says that the Norwegian Synod is stuck in the Missouri swamps, this is a reference to their close association with the Missouri Synod.

15. Hauge Synod—named for a Norwegian lay preacher, Hans Nielsen Hauge (1771–1824), the Hauge Synod was more low-church than the Norwegian Synod and the Conference. They were more liberal in their use of lay preachers than the Conference and the pastors did not use the cassock and ruff then in use in the other Lutheran churches. All three synods eventually merged in 1917. Ingvald Eisteinsen (1843–1901), a pastor in the Hauge Synod, immigrated in 1872 and served a congregation in Minneapolis from 1884 to 1894. The true-life Eisteinsen could neither have baptized nor confirmed Ragna.

16. *präkare*—"preacher" (in Swedish).

17. *svitharter*—"sweethearts."

18. Missourians—i.e., the Norwegian Synod.

19. *brækket*—"broke."

20. *kørtena'n*—"the curtains."

21. *lus*—"lose."

22. *loiert*—"lawyer."

23. Northwest—at this time the Northwest was what is now known as the Upper Midwest. *Farmeralliancen*—The Farmers' Alliance movement spread through the South and the Midwest in the 1880s. By 1890 it was in many areas superseded by the People's Party or Populist Party.

24. ambulatory—although rural schools had ceased to be ambulatory by this time in Norway, the older system, in which the farmers in a school district would share the expenses by having the school and the teacher move from farm to farm for specified periods at a time, was well known among the immigrants. This system was often adopted for parochial schools in the pioneer settlements, before public or common schools were established. The so-called Norwegian Synod tried to enforce their policy of keeping the children in their congregations in parochial schools but soon had to give in to the demand among the majority of the immigrants for public-school education in English for their children. Parochial summer schools, however, where Norwegian and religion were taught, lived on into the 1920s.

25. Schmidt or Missouri—see note 13 and note 17 for Book II. Even the saloonkeeper is well versed in the theological controversies of the period. Indeed, there are many stories of inflamed theological debates among Norwegian Americans in the saloons of the Midwest in the 1880s. Friedrich August Schmidt was from Germany but became a pastor and professor of theology in the Norwegian Synod, where he became a leader of the faction that left the Synod because of disagreement on the issue of predestination.

26. *gopheren* and *blackbirden*—typically, the immigrant would resort to English names of animals and other things that were unfamiliar from the old country. There is very little code-switching in Ragna's speech compared to Jonas's. Her word for coyote is *prærieulven*, the prairie wolf.

27. Knute Nelson—(1844–1922) immigrated at the age of four with his unwed mother; was a soldier and prisoner of war in the Civil War; and became admitted to the Wisconsin bar in 1867. He was a representative in the Wisconsin state legislature from 1868 to 1869, and then moved to Alexandria, Minnesota. From 1872 he was regularly elected to county and state offices on the Republican ticket, culminating with the governorship in 1892. Still governor, he became a U.S. senator in 1895, an office he held until his death.

28. *jompe* the claims . . . *prove op* a claim—"jump claims" and "prove claims." One of the features in a series of laws (culminating with the Homestead Act of 1862) designed to help people secure farmland for their own use was that of preemption, the legal confirmation of the rights of squatters on public lands. To jump a claim was to seize the land of a squatter who had failed to comply with formal requirements; for instance, the payment of a registration fee. To prove a claim was to fulfill legal requirements for securing land by preemption, such as a certain degree of improvement or development and a set residency term. In

the text, Ward acquired land by paying people to fulfill the requirements on his behalf. This was an illegal but common practice.

29. *bønk* and *tamfuleri*—"bunk and tomfoolery."

30. Plymouth Rocks—a breed of chicken.

31. Targe G. Mandt—was from Telemark and had developed his skills in the smithy on his father's farm in Dane county, Wisconsin. Wagons from his factory in Stoughton were widely in use all over the Midwest.

32. *kros raaden*—"the crossroads."

33. *Minneapolis Tidende*—The "Minneapolis Times" began as a successor to *Grand Forks Tidende* in 1887 and had both a daily *(Minneapolis Daglig Tidende)* and a weekly edition. The daily was discontinued in 1932, and the weekly was bought by and merged with *Decorah-Posten* (Decorah, Iowa) in 1935.

34. Crookston—in Polk county in northwestern Minnesota, not far from the Red River and North Dakota.

35. *kjita* themselves to the *lekjen*—"cheated ... election."

36. Cleveland—Grover Cleveland, a Democrat, became president in 1884 and again in 1892. A Republican, Benjamin Harrison, was president at the time of these events.

37. The United Church was established in 1890 in the wake of a doctrinal controversy in the Norwegian Synod. Those who left the Synod called themselves the Anti-Missourian Brotherhood, and in 1890 they joined with two smaller groups, the Norwegian Augustana Synod and the Norwegian Danish Conference, to form the United Norwegian Lutheran Church.

38. "sanctification" and "justification"—These theological concepts, *helliggjørelse* and *rettfærdiggjørelse* in the original, are straight from Bishop Erik Pontoppidan's *Sandhed til Gudfrygtighed (Truth unto Godliness)*, first published in 1737, an explanation of Luther's *Small Catechism*. Pontoppidan's book was at the time the most influential book on Lutheran doctrine in Norway and among Norwegian immigrants in the United States. It remained the most-used textbook in Norwegian elementary schools for more than 150 years. Napoleon's error may have been that he was confused about the correct sequence in the process of the soul's salvation. Sivert knew, from Pontoppidan, that justification would have to precede sanctification. As the following doctrinal discussion among the men suggests, the uproar caused by Sivert's disclosure was more immediately related to the current disagreements about doctrine among Norwegian-American Lutherans. The concept of "justification of the world" and the question of the individual's personal faith as a prerequisite for justification were central issues in these doctrinal disputes, beginning in the late 1860s, and they were very much at the forefront when the Norwegian Synod broke apart in the late 1880s, and the United Church was formed soon after. The group that broke away from the Norwegian Synod and that eventually became part of the United Church was called anti-Missourian, because the Synod majority was influenced by the German-American Missouri Synod. The standard history of Norwegian-Lutheran churches in the United States is E. Clifford Nelson and Eugene L. Fevold's *The Lutheran Church among Norwegian-Americans*, 2 vols. (Minneapolis, 1960).

39. Koren, Larsen, Preus—Ulrik Vilhelm Koren (1826–1910), Peter Laur(entius) Larsen (1833–1915), and Herman A. Preus (1825–1894) immigrated

in the 1850s and were central figures in the Norwegian Synod. Synergism and unionism—synergism is the doctrine that the individual by his or her own free will must cooperate with divine grace in order to achieve salvation, and unionism refers to the name of the new church formed in 1890, the United Church.

40. Formula of Concord—The Book of Concord, collecting the doctrinal standards of the Lutheran Church, was published in German in 1580 and in Latin in 1584; it has remained the standard of orthodox Lutheran theology. One of its documents is "The Formula of Concord" of 1577.

41. almost every man—Only men had a voice in church matters.

42. called him to order—the Norwegian used on this occasion shows how the immigrants have been assimilated and how the assimilation affects their language. They follow, or try to follow, American rules of order and since they do not know of corresponding Norwegian terms, they use a direct, literal translation, "kaldte ham til Orden," which does not really make sense in Norwegian. They may have known about standard American rules of order through the little book, *Parlamentariske Regler* (Rules of order; Chicago: C. Rasmussens Forlag, 1880).

43. *Kirketidende*—The "Church Times," the journal of the Norwegian Synod.

44. *totalist*—Jonas of course means a teetotalist, one who abstains totally from all intoxicating drink.

45. *blein'pig*—blind pig; that is, a place used for the illegal sale of liquor.

46. Solør—a region in southeastern Norway adjoining the border with Sweden.

47. *hønte skonk*—"hunt skunk."

48. novels by James Fenimore Cooper—Several of Cooper's novels had been published in Norwegian translation in Chicago by the John Anderson Publishing Company, the publisher of *Skandinaven*, which was the largest American newspaper in the Norwegian language.

49. Delmonico—Lomwiig is being facetious in using the name of a famous New York restaurant for a rude establishment in the frontier town Normanville.

50. Pastor Juul—Ole Juul (1838–1903) was pastor in the Norwegian Synod and served in Our Savior's Church in Chicago from 1876 to 1893.

51. *unter uns gesagt*—(German) literally, "said between us"; i.e., confidentially spoken.

52. David Rytterskjold—The second name of the Nyblom baby is satirically pretentious, suggestive of Swedish nobility.

III. Jonasville

1. Cutter—a light sleigh drawn by one or two horses.

2. Winneshiek County—Decorah is in this Iowa county.

3. Willmar—The Norwegian Synod had a seminary in Willmar from 1883 to 1919.

4. the seminary in Hamline—Luther Seminary (the Norwegian Synod) in the Hamline area of St. Paul.

5. Johan Sverdrup—(1816–1892) The first leader of the Liberal Party (*Venstre*), which was the first political party in Norway.

6. be on first names—What he actually suggests is that they not use the polite, plural second-person form of the personal pronoun when addressing each other—a mode of address that no longer exists in English.

7. Gustavus Adolphus College—a Lutheran college in St. Peter, Minnesota, founded by Swedish immigrants.

8. the Ladies Seminary—the Lutheran Ladies Seminary in Red Wing, Minnesota, was founded by the Norwegian Synod in 1894; it closed in 1920. To Signe Marie it was probably more of a straitjacket than Jonasville.

9. Professor Kildahl—John Nathan Kildahl was president of St. Olaf College from 1899 to 1914. *Lutheraneren*—("The Lutheran") the largest church periodical; originally an organ of the United Church, and then beginning in 1917 an organ of the Norwegian Lutheran Church of America.

10. church unity—This is at the end of 1909 and a union among the three main Norwegian Lutheran synods was finally achieved in 1917.

11. Jørgine—a now-rare feminine form of the male name Jørgen. In the original text she is called "Jørgine paa Skjæret" (Jørgine on the Skerry, or Skerry Jørgine).

12. Ignatius Donnelly (1831–1901)—He was active in Minnesota politics, especially in liberal, third-party movements, and he was the Populist Party's candidate for president at the time of his death. His best-known book is the novel *Cæsar's Column: A Story of the Twentieth Century* (1891), about the violent end of American capitalist society and the establishment of an agrarian utopia in Africa.

13. Joseph Wheelock—editor of the *Pioneer Press*.

14. "The Great Cryptogram"—In *The Great Cryptogram* (1888) and *The Cipher in the Plays and on the Tombstone* (1899) Donnelly sought to prove that Francis Bacon was the author of the plays attributed to Shakespeare.

15. Lew Sharp—at times his name is Leiv Sharp. This is not an inconsistency, merely a vacillation between his given Norwegian name, Leiv, and an Americanized form.

16. V. Koren—Ulrik Vilhelm Koren (1826–1910) immigrated with his wife Elisabeth in 1853 and was a prominent clergyman in the Norwegian Synod, where he was president from 1894 to 1910. Today his wife may be better known than he is, because of her diary available in English translation: *The Diary of Elisabeth Koren 1853–1855* (Northfield, Minnesota, 1955).

17. master shoemaker Hoff—In Norwegian and other Germanic languages it has been customary to use the name of a person's profession as a title, such as in carpenter Nilsen or teacher Andersen. Since the word *hoff* means "court," his name in the original text is the occasion for some punning, and Dr. Hornemann calls him *hoffskomagermesteren*, or "master shoemaker to the court."

18. sixteen-to-one—The Sherman Silver Purchase Act of 1890 had committed the government to buy 4.5 million ounces of silver every month. Payment,

in gold, was to be at the ratio of one ounce of gold to sixteen ounces of silver. Cleveland took the initiative to have the act repealed in 1893.

19. Stillwater—The Minnesota state penitentiary was in Stillwater.

20. 1905—the year Norway became an independent monarchy, after severing the union with Sweden and electing a Danish prince to be king of Norway.

21. wishing they were back in Norway—Wist is here parodying the sentimental views of Norwegian visitors who could not imagine that the immigrants preferred to live in the country of their choice.

22. *Nordlys*—The name means "the northern lights." *Nordly* was, as Wist knew, the name of the first Norwegian-American newspaper in 1847 in Wisconsin.

23. Hauge Synod—See note 14 to Book II.

24. the Seventeenth of May—the day Norwegians celebrate their constitution and independence.

25. If you asked young people of Norwegian descent—These two paragraphs reflect immigrant reactions to American nativism in the early years of the twentieth century.

26. the Americanization of foreigners—The so-called Americanization movement swept the country between 1915 and 1918. It was a response to the First World War and the fear that the large immigrant population would not be loyal if or when the United States entered the war. The Americanization movement would thus have been fresh in the minds of both the writer and his readers, but would not have been among the experiences of Jonas Olsen at this point in his life. The snide remark about "a few well-intentioned ladies in Boston" may simply be intended as a comment on the view that American was synonymous with the culture and attitudes of Anglo–New England, or it may be a reference to the fact that one of the most prominent organizers of the national, indeed federal, Americanization movement was a woman: Frances Kellor. See John Higham, *Strangers in the Land: Patterns of American Nativism, 1860–1925* (2nd edition, 1963) and Edward George Hartman, *The Movement to Americanize the Immigrant* (1948). A useful sourcebook is Philip Davis, ed., *Immigration and Americanization: Selected Readings* (1920).

27. the parochial summer school—Among the Norwegian-American Lutheran Synods, the Norwegian Synod was alone in trying to establish a parochial school system. Most Norwegian immigrants favored the public school system. As a compromise, the Synod organized a system of summer schools, popularly called both *norskskolen* (the Norwegian school) and *religionsskolen* (the religion school), since classes and texts were in Norwegian and teaching the Lutheran catechism had a central place.

28. a bill . . . to limit the freedom of private and parochial schools—Such extreme anti-immigrant measures and attacks on the use of languages other than English were more common in the years after 1914 than at the time of the fictional happenings of the novel, a few years earlier. Beginning in 1889 with the so-called Bennett Law in Wisconsin, however, there were some attempts to make languages of instruction other than English illegal in public schools.

29. socialism—The fear of socialism was particularly strong in the United States after the Russian Revolution in 1917, coinciding with the end of the First World War.

30. Ibsen, Bjørnson, *Peer Gynt,* Grieg—Henrik Ibsen (1828–1906) and Bjørnstjerne Bjørnson (1832–1910) were the two most prominent Norwegian writers of their time. *Peer Gynt* (1867), a poetic drama, is one of Ibsen's main works. Edvard Grieg (1843–1907) remains the best-known Norwegian composer.

31. They would read them—Wist is being ironic. He was convinced that the Norwegian language would disappear with the immigrant generation, and that newspapers such as the one he edited and in which this novel first appeared would consequently be of no interest to later generations.

32. synergists—See note 38 for Book II.

33. Kristiansand—a city in the south of Norway.

34. rods—a rod is sixteen and one-half feet.

35. *disapira*—disappeared.

36. nationality—Today the common term is "ethnic group," a much later term.

37. His first stop was for Livius—note that Jonas is only concerned with men: women did not yet have the right to vote.

38. Unter den Linden—a main street in the center of Berlin. This negative view of German culture is strongly influenced by the climate of opinion during the First World War and is not representative of views in the United States in the prewar years.

39. Grieg's "Foran Sydens Kloster"—"Before a Southern Convent," a song by Edvard Grieg (opus 20) set to a poem by Bjørnstjerne Bjørnson. There are piano arrangements of many of Grieg's songs.

40. Farrar, Melba, Kubelik, Paderewsky, Caruso, Scotti, Fremstad—These are all well-known performers of the time.

41. good deeds—As a Lutheran, Jonas believed, or at least proclaimed, that salvation was by faith, not by good deeds. Thus, even being ethically superior to Ward would not make him more worthy of salvation.

42. the regular party—that is the regular Republican Party, not including those who had followed Roosevelt.

43. Sothern and Marlowe—Edward H. Sothern (1859–1933) was an actor especially popular for his roles in Shakespeare productions and in romantic comedies. From 1904 he appeared regularly with Julia Marlowe (1866–1950) and they became the leading Shakespearean couple of their time. They married in 1911.

44. is reading—The sudden shift to the present tense is not carried through consistently. After some sentences there is an unmotivated shift back to the past tense that has been used throughout the trilogy. Wist wrote under great pressure and had no time for revision. I have assumed that his shift to the present for the concluding pages was deliberate and that the inconsistency was not intended. Consequently, I have chosen to use the present throughout the last

section. There is more code-switching in the conclusion than in the earlier parts of Book III.

45. *luser fa'kultien* to *ris'ne*—"lose your faculty to reason."

46. *defita i 'leksjen*—"defeated in the election."

47. *seisa op situationen og ægria* that Duffy was liable to take *revench*—"we sized up the situation and agreed . . . revenge."

Bibliography

These books have been useful sources of information on the biographical, historical, and literary contexts of Wist's trilogy.

Atwater, Isaac, ed. *History of the City of Minneapolis, Minnesota.* Two volumes. New York: Munsell, 1893.

Hansen, Carl G. O. *My Minneapolis: A Chronicle of What Has Been Learned and Observed about the Norwegians in Minneapolis through One Hundred Years.* Minneapolis: self-published, 1956.

Hovde, Oivind M., and Martha E. Henzler. *Norwegian-American Newspapers in Luther College Library.* Decorah, Iowa: Luther College Press, 1975.

Imbsen, Jan-Erik. *Johannes B. Wist: Norwegian-American Leader.* Unpublished MA thesis. University of Oslo, 1977.

Lovoll, Odd S. *The Promise of America: A History of the Norwegian-American People.* Minneapolis: University of Minnesota Press, 1984.

Nelson, E. Clifford, and Eugene L. Fevold. *The Lutheran Church among Norwegian-Americans: A History of the Evangelical Lutheran Church.* Two volumes. Minneapolis: Augsburg Publishing House, 1960.

Norlie, Olaf Morgan. *History of the Norwegian People in America.* Minneapolis, 1925.

———. *Norsk lutherske prester i Amerika 1843–1915.* Minneapolis: Augsburg Publishing House, 1915.

———. *School Calendar, 1824–1924: A Who's Who among Teachers in the Norwegian Lutheran Synods of America.* Minneapolis, 1924.

Øverland, Orm. *The Western Home: A Literary History of Norwegian America.* Northfield, Minnesota, and Champaign, Illinois: Norwegian-American Historical Association, 1996.

Söderström, Alfred. *Minneapolis minnen: Kulturhistorisk axplockning från qvarnstaden vid Mississippi.* Minneapolis, 1899.

Ulvestad, Martin. *Nordmændene i Amerika: Deres historie og rekord.* Volume 1: Minneapolis, 1907; Volume 2: Tacoma, Washington, 1913.

Wist, Johannes B., ed. *Norsk-Amerikanernes Festskrift 1914.* Decorah, Iowa, 1914.

Zempel, Solveig, and Pauline Tweet. *Language Use in the Novels of Johannes B. Wist: A Study of Bilingualism in Literature.* Unpublished dissertation. University of Minnesota, 1980.

JOHANNES B. WIST (1864–1923) immigrated to the United States from Norway in 1884 and was editor of *Decorah-Posten,* the most successful and long-lived Norwegian-American newspaper. The trilogy *The Rise of Jonas Olsen* was his first extended fiction and was serialized in his newspaper from 1919 to 1922.

———

ORM ØVERLAND is professor of American literature at the University of Bergen. He is the author of *The Western Home: A Literary History of Norwegian America* and *Immigrant Minds, American Identities: Making the United States Home, 1870–1930,* and he is editor of *English Only: Redefining "American" in American Studies.*

———

TODD W. NICHOL is King Olav V Professor of Scandinavian American Studies at St. Olaf College and editor for the Norwegian-American Historical Association.